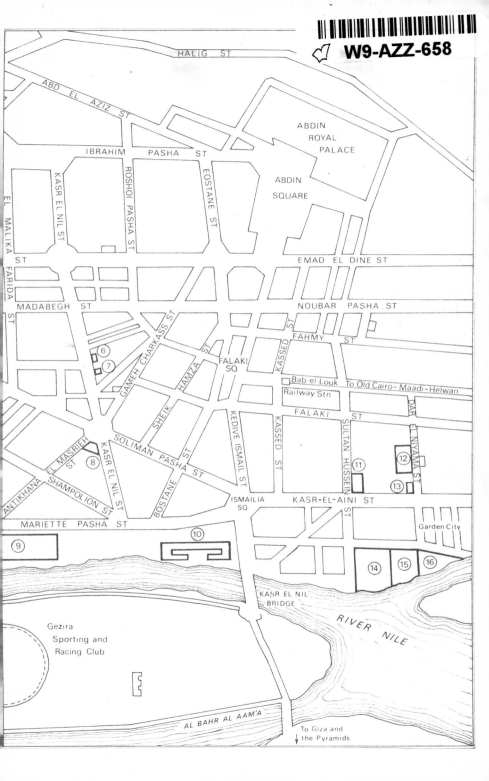

HALIG ST

ABD EL AZIZ ST

ABDIN ROYAL PALACE

IBRAHIM PASHA ST

ABDIN SQUARE

KASR EL NIL ST

ROSHOI PASHA ST

EOSTANE ST

EL MALIKA FARIDA ST

EMAD EL DINE ST

MADABEGH ST

NOUBAR PASHA ST

GAMEH CHARKASS ST

FAHMY ST

KASSED

⑥

⑦

HAMZA ST

FALAKI SQ

Bab-el-Louk
Railway Stn

To Old Cairo - Maadi - Helwan

SHEIK

FALAKI

DAR

KEDIVE ISMAIL ST

KASSED ST

SULTAN HUSSEIN ST

NIYAMA ST

SOLIMAN PASHA ST

EL MASRIEH ST

⑧

KASR EL NIL ST

⑪

⑫

⑬

ANTIKHANA

SHAMPOLION ST

BOSTANE ST

ISMAILIA SQ

KASR-EL-AINI ST

Garden City

MARIETTE PASHA ST

⑨

⑩

⑭

⑮

⑯

KASR EL NIL BRIDGE

Gezira
Sporting and
Racing Club

RIVER NILE

AL BAHR AL AAM'A

To Giza and
the Pyramids

NOEL BARBER

A Woman of Cairo

By the same author

NOEL BARBER

A Woman of Cairo

HODDER AND STOUGHTON
LONDON   SYDNEY   AUCKLAND   TORONTO

British Library Cataloguing in Publication Data

Barber, Noel
  A woman of Cairo.
  I. Title
  823'.914[F]   PR6052.A623

ISBN 0 340 34650 7

For the one and only Eve
with love from
Noel
to
Eve Raphael

ACKNOWLEDGMENTS

Though this is a novel, a few real characters flit through its pages, and their activities, as told by me, are based on truth, given the poetic licence of dialogue.

King Farouk did receive the education I have described, including almost daily shopping sprees to Kingston after he had been refused entry to Eton. He was a fairy-tale prince of high promise who in the end did become a compulsive eater, womaniser and gambler. He did give a man a hundred lashes for insulting him, then a reward of £1,000. Men and women did disappear mysteriously while he was king.

In the same way Gamal Abdel Nasser, the postman's son, did live through the schooldays I have described; as a boy he was hit on the head during a riot. Sadat did narrowly escape prison during the war when plotting to help Rommel in the desert to overthrow the British in Egypt. He did later go to jail. Even the description in the book of Mark Holt's visit to see Farouk and his collection of erotica is based on fact; a party of us were taken to the Kubbah Palace to see it after Farouk's abdication.

Against this factual background I have introduced my fictional family and these, I need hardly say, bear no resemblance to any persons living or dead.

I lived in and out of Cairo for several years as a foreign correspondent based in the Middle East, during which time I met Nasser several times, and Sadat, and on one occasion Farouk. I was a member of the Gezira Club, which features so often in this book, and in those balmy days of long ago when the Egyptians hated Britain but still loved the British, an Egyptian friend did me the honour of toasting me as 'an honorary Cairene'.

May I end by thanking my two colleagues Anthony Davis and Alan Wykes for all the invaluable help they have given me in researching this book. And my grateful thanks go too to Pippa Esdaile, who has typed her way through revision after revision of the novel as it grew and changed.

N.B. *London and Cairo, 1983–4*

THE CHANGING FACE OF CAIRO

The endpaper plan of Cairo shows the city as it was in the time covered by this book – until the revolution in 1952. Since then almost all the street names have been altered, and many other changes have taken place. A third bridge now connects Cairo with Gezira Island; a huge new hotel stands on the site of the old British Cathedral. The British Embassy's gardens, like those of the Holts', now don't reach down to the Nile, for Nasser decided to build a motorway along the bank of the river so that those evening strolls no longer lead to the peaceful waters of the river but to the lines of cars tearing along one of Cairo's busiest streets.

N.B.

CONTENTS

PART ONE

1919–1937

I

Life seemed so wonderful to all of us in those happy days in Cairo.

We lived in what I suppose you might call luxury, in our white house, with its lawns leading to the Nile at the end of our grounds, while the broad avenues of the city itself were lined with shops, hotels with dance bands, the Gezira Club with its polo and golf and swimming.

We were so *happy* – that is the word that springs to mind as we grew up – Serena, the most beautiful of them all, the daughter of an Egyptian Copt; Greg, my brother, who married her; Teddy Pollock, the self-confessed playboy – all friends who would dance the nights away after desert rides to the Step Pyramid at Sakkara or midnight swims at the Mena House. Then there was Aly, Serena's brother, and his friends – Gamal Nasser, the earnest young student, and Anwar Sadat, the eager debater . . .

Were so many of us blind because we didn't see the other side of life – the thousands of beggars, the heaps of refuse, the indescribable poverty? Our parents hardly seemed to notice. My father, the Egyptian Adviser, loved everything about the country, as did Serena's father, Sirry Pasha. Yet did they never realise the debauchery into which King Farouk eventually sank, or never comprehend the sinister motives of his ADC, General Osman Sadik?

I wonder sometimes whether the splendour of Egypt blinded us to the real facts of life, in much the same way as the servile smile of an Arab anxious to sell a scarab to a British Tommy masked a hatred of the foreign oppressor. But then Cairo was a city of intrigue which cast a spell over all of us. Beautiful and brown, selfish yet tolerant, it beguiled us, and the soft breezes from the Nile lulled us into a sense of false security.

I remember once, when I was very young, my father holding me as we watched the trams overflowing with passengers and I was even more fascinated by the shining tram-lines glinting in the sun. I asked Father where they led.

'Like everything else in Cairo,' he said. 'Round and round in circles, to everywhere and nowhere.'

When I look back, life seems first to have come into focus one hot Cairo afternoon in 1919 when Serena was barely a year old and I was ten.

I was too young really to understand why, earlier in the day, our tranquil life had been unaccountably replaced by worried parental frowns, anxious clucking by Mother, grunts of exasperation by Father, furtive looks from the servants. At the age of ten I felt that my father should explain the sudden tensions, the occasional noisy reports that sounded like cars backfiring.

'Father, you told me the other day that Egypt is a Protectorate,' I had asked. 'Why are the Egyptians so cross with us if we are protecting them?'

'Perhaps they don't want to be protected,' he said, adding cryptically, 'The pot's boiling over.'

'Don't leave the grounds on *any* account,' Mother interrupted, and made me promise.

'He couldn't go out anyway,' Father pointed out. 'Martial law's been proclaimed. And that means they'll shoot on sight.'

'Can't I even go to Garden City?' I exclaimed. On the other side of the road there was a playground in the area known by that name, a beautiful section with many fine buildings, including embassies. It wasn't as beautiful as our grounds, but it had one advantage: we could play with other children, under supervision. 'But as I don't have to look after Greg?' I asked; for my younger brother was in the Anglo-American Hospital having his tonsils out.

'He'll be back in a couple of days,' promised my father. '*Then* we'll go to the Garden playground, Mark.'

Holt House, as our house was known, was huge, as befitted the home of the Egyptian Adviser. Long and low, the recep-

4

tion rooms lay on either side of the Long Gallery which ran from one end of the house to the other. One side gave on to the short drive from the Garden City entrance, the other, with equally wide handsome double doors halfway along the gallery, faced on to the lawns and the Nile beyond.

The house had been built when Turkish influence on Egyptian architecture was still pronounced, and this accounted for the space of the grounds, the lofty rooms, and above all our favourite room for playing when children.

This was the Turkish music room, an appendage to the main rectangular building, built by a Turkish architect. It was not only soundproof but had a stage, and at the rear, high up and with no stairs visible, a gallery with a metal lattice screen where in the old days the ladies of the harem, using the back stairs, could climb up and watch, unseen, as the men below listened to the music.

It was the perfect place for hide and seek, but today there was no one to hide and no one to seek. I was bored. Suddenly there were more sharp noises and I ran out into the garden. Coming towards us was Madame Sirry, who lived in the next house to ours and which was almost as large. A wicket gate separated our two properties. She strode through the gate together with the year-old Serena and a nanny.

'Could we come in until the din's stopped?' I heard her ask my parents. 'My husband is at the Abdin Palace and took Aly with him – he likes to play in the guardroom with the soldiers while his father has an audience with the sultan.'

Aly was the five-year-old son of Madame Sirry, who, French by birth, had married Sirry Pasha, a rich Copt, and a close friend and adviser to the sultan, Fuad. My father called Sirry 'a member of the palace clique', and I knew that Father often discussed Anglo-Egyptian problems with him.

'Of course,' cried Father as my mother walked across the large green lawns. 'I have to go soon, but you'll stay for lunch, eh?'

Serena, the Sirry baby, was in her pram, and the nanny, a young Egyptian girl named Fathia, from the Sirry's estate in the Nile Delta, was rolling her eyes with fear.

'Don't be silly,' said Madame Sirry, not unkindly to the

nanny. 'You'll be safe in this garden. You watch over Serena, understand?' The girl nodded dumbly. I heard Madame Sirry whisper to Mother, 'I came because the servants have panicked. They don't want to be involved, in case Egyptians are ordered to attack the British. So stupid!'

'Of course you must stay for lunch,' Mother soothed her, while Father continued to prepare to leave for the High Commissioner's office. Mother and Madame Sirry – with me, of course – joined Father in the study, and Mother asked in her vague sort of way, 'Oh dear! They *do* enjoy making a fuss! What's it about this time?'

My father loved explaining things and he had great patience, especially with my mother. 'Zaglul is the leader of Egypt's National Party,' he began. 'I've always found him good mannered, but he *is* a fervent nationalist, and all this nonsense started after the war, when President Wilson made his fourteen-point declaration of self-determination.' He went on, 'Zaglul says it applies to Egypt just like any other country. I agree in principle, but only when the moment is ripe. But what did the Foreign Office mandarins do? They arrested Zaglul and booted him off to Malta. That will only cause more trouble.'

Father was right. Student demonstrators had already started rampaging through the streets, smashing up tram-cars in Cairo, with women students often leading the attacks, bringing the city to a standstill. Already eight British soldiers had been killed by mobs.

When Father left, my mother suggested to Madame Sirry that the two of them go into the sitting room for coffee, adding to me, 'You go and play in the garden. And keep an eye on Serena.'

'But Fathia's there.'

'Maybe she's more frightened than you are, Mark,' Madame Sirry smiled at me. 'I trust you. You'll be Serena's protector.'

'And don't tread on the flowers!' Mother loved her garden with the passion of someone who had turned three acres of dusty ground into a place of rare beauty – all in the twelve years the Holts had lived in Cairo. She had installed a pump to draw water from the Nile, and now the walls of our house were covered with bougainvillaea and other exotic creepers. The beds blossomed with cannas, fuchsias or hibiscus, edged with petunias surrounding green lawns stretching to the trees with glimpses of the river between the heliotrope of jacaranda, the white silky frangipani and the scarlet flame trees.

Above all, it was a happy garden. Even the lazy hum of dragonflies seemed to have a contented sound to them. There was no formality about the flowers, no horrible Turkish crescents or circular rose beds. Mother had really made the plants look as though they grew wild – wild but with great thought and care. She even had her own flower room, in which she changed all the flowers in the house daily; she had told me once that in a way it was her sanctuary; she was happiest of all when the gardener arrived with an arm full of flowers and laid them out on the marble table for her to arrange.

'Why don't you play in the cathedral tree?' Mother said to me now. 'That'll keep the sun off Serena.'

I was going to the tree anyway, for after the music room it was our favourite place to play. It was a giant, gnarled banyan tree at the end of the grounds near the river. No one knew how old it was, but it must have been very ancient, for its branches had turned and twisted downwards, like the hanging tentacles of some evil, prehistoric animal, almost alive. Over the decades the branches had reached the ground and taken root. By now they were huge, and formed a circle of pillars so that, under a canopy of leaves, my brother Greg and I could run in and out of what we had christened the cathedral tree.

At times, though, our imagination would be replaced by twinges of fear, and then the tree was no longer a cathedral but a prison in which I would be locked away for ever behind 'pillars' which had become bars, and I would become a prisoner for life, like the gangs of manacled men I sometimes saw in town, trudging hopelessly within a stone's throw of the smart shops and busy streets they would never see again.

Today, however, it was a cathedral tree, and I beckoned the nanny to wheel Serena towards the hiding place, inside the banyan's grotesque roots. Even though a baby, Serena was already beautiful, but still (with all the wisdom of a ten-year-old) I felt it a bit thick turning me into an assistant nanny.

I had just pulled the pram through the entrance when the garden seemed to erupt in a terrifying orgy of shouts and threats. Dozens of figures, who had obviously smashed open the Garden City gates, came racing into our grounds, shouting, 'Down with the British!' 'Egypt for Egyptians!' and even, 'Kill the British!'

I almost screamed myself, but peering through the roots I swallowed hard instead, the muscles in my throat suddenly hurting. My arms seemed stiff with fright and though I clasped the handle of the baby's pram I couldn't at first unlock my fingers.

I caught one glimpse of Fathia's eyes, white with terror, before she bolted for the wicket gate and the Sirry residence. And I was left, threatened by the howling mob, with Mother inside the house, but with Serena and I unseen. I heard more screams, picked out the word 'Traitor!' presumably directed at the nanny who had vanished, but none of the rioters realised from where she had come. Serena was still sleeping on her back, clutching a bottle in two tiny hands.

Never before had I seen hooligans trampling all over Mother's precious gardens. Yet I had often in my brief youth seen the contrasts in the daily face of Cairo. Once, looking at the plate-glass window of Cirucel's department store, I saw the reflection of a small alley that jutted off the main street. Suddenly – as though I had photographed it – I saw an Egyptian in a galabiya and the glint of his knife as he stabbed an English soldier in khaki shorts who had been haggling with a street trader at the opening of the alley. I screamed, but even before I could tug at my mother's skirts the street had emptied and my mother, irritated and hot, was dragging me away. Cairo was always like that – the rich and the beggar boys, the serene sun next to the sinister shadows, as close to each other as the neatly swept pavements in the shopping street and the stinking piles of refuse and excrement. But a mob ruining Mother's garden – that was different!

I was shaking with fear, hardly able to hold the handle of the pram. And I was terrified that Serena might suddenly yell and reveal our hiding place. Not that it mattered really; my prayer for silence was instinctive, for the mob was shrieking, trampling all over Mother's cannas, kicking and uprooting plants; they would never hear us behind our screen of branches. But where was Mother? And Madame Sirry?

There was nothing I could do. And when I saw some of the men wielding chisels and knives I was convinced we would all be killed at any moment. The noise brought out all our servants – a dozen of them, ranging from washerwomen to gardeners. Some came from the kitchen, the gardeners from the other end of the house, standing at first in bewildered groups as they watched the first rioters advance menacingly. I could see, through the bars of the cathedral tree, the puzzled looks turn to fear as first one then the rest ran back to the safety of the house, just as the Sirrys' nanny had done. Then Mother and Madame Sirry emerged from the french windows – and *they* didn't shrink back – not at first. I heard Mother exclaim something; Madame Sirry also shouted in rough, angry Arabic. But then, as the crowd moved towards the french windows, one of them threw a brick, or stone.

Others followed, picking up anything they could; it passed through my mind that they didn't want to harm Mother so much as to frighten her, for the crowd jeered, pulled up plants and small shrubs by the roots and hurled them in a hail of filth at the women. At last Mother and Madame Sirry retreated into the house. The mob hesitated, and then Serena, suddenly awake, started screaming her head off. I didn't know what to do. Heart thumping – not realising that no one could hear anything, with all the noise – I picked her up as I had seen nannies do, and put her over my shoulder.

Mother had deserted us! That was my only thought. But as I peered between the thick root-branches I saw Mother's face from an upstairs window. She knew where we were! She was making signs at me. They would have meant nothing to the rioters in the garden, even had they seen her, but to me they were wonderfully clear. First she gave me a blown kiss, then a thumbs up, and then – this I could plainly understand – she was holding one hand to her mouth, the other to her ear. She had telephoned for help!

At that moment I heard an even more sinister noise. Someone was creeping round the back of the grounds. I stood there shivering despite the heat, suddenly cold with terror. I couldn't see the man, for he was creeping through the grove of citrus trees that stood on their own near the river. I waited for someone to hurl a weapon at me. And then a face materialised directly in front of me. I couldn't see who it was because sudden tears blurred my vision. Then I made out a pair of eyes, the whites showing in a coal-black moon face, and my tears turned to a cry of relief.

'Oh, Zola!' I put my arms round his chest. 'We're all right now.' In many ways Zola, our head butler, was my best friend, a shining, black Nubian whose name had been so difficult to pronounce when my father engaged him twelve years ago that he had christened him 'Zola' after his favourite author.

'No, Master Mark,' he whispered, safe for a moment in the cathedral tree. 'I tell Lady Holt I come to get you. We escape quick – before they murder us.'

'I'm not going to leave my mother!' It was not bravado but fear that made me want to stay near her.

'Lady Holt, she all right. She got a gun.'

'Mother has a gun?'

'Come on – be quick. Your mother tell me to take you to the felucca. We escape by the river.'

Our felucca was little more than a rowboat, though every boat was called a felucca in Cairo. We always kept it moored on the Nile below our grounds.

'But why should they want to hurt us?' I whispered. 'Are they drunk?'

'Hash,' muttered Zola. 'They're filled with hash. Come on, Master Mark. We escape. They're Lady Holt's orders.'

I needed no further urging. I was afraid. I knew how dangerous Egyptians – especially anti-British Egyptians – could be when they smoked hash.

We quickly made our way towards the river. Then, at the top of the iron rail leading down to the water's edge, I stopped. On the far side of the river I could see the sugar cane and vegetables stretching out to the great pyramid of Cheops twelve miles away. I was hesitating because I wasn't sure what to do with the baby. I was still carrying the screaming Serena, and there was no way I could climb down the iron steps while she was in my arms.

'I carry Miss Sirry,' declared Zola. 'Lady Holt give me some money. She tell me we should keep half each in case we are separated.' Handing over two 100-piastre notes, he said, 'Give me the baby, and you go down first, Master Mark.' Zola's face was creased with fear, the need for urgency. 'When you in the boat, I hand over baby.'

'You won't leave us, will you, Zola?'

'Never fear, Master Mark.'

But he did – accidentally. As soon as I had floundered on to the bare planks of the felucca I started readying the mooring line for a quick take-off. I saw the heavy bulk of Zola above me and began thinking, incongruously, how funny he looked with his galabiya tucked up round his knees. It was the first time I had ever seen his legs.

Panting, Zola leaned forward, grabbing the iron railing with one hand while I took Serena.

'I've got her.' I, too, was panting. 'Here, hold the mooring rope.' But Zola – or was it me? – let it slip, and the rope went into the water with a splash.

I leaned out to grasp it, and had almost reached it when I had to pull myself back to steady the felucca, which was in danger of capsizing.

'Zola!' I cried, for this was a disaster. A small boy alone in a boat with a baby – on the Nile! I had visions of Serena falling out and drowning. 'Zola!' I cried again. 'Help me!'

'Master Mark,' yelled Zola, caution forgotten. 'Give me your hand.'

I tried, but I had only one hand to spare. Serena was in my arms. If I leaned over too much both of us would certainly topple out.

'I can't reach,' I said despairingly, while the baby, perhaps sensing danger, redoubled her yells.

Slowly, but not slowly enough, the boat started to drift

away from the steep bank. Now Zola was almost wailing.

'I can't swim,' he cried.

My last sight was of Zola standing there, clutching his head, as our boat slowly drifted away. I sat down – standing up rocked the boat – wondering what to do. There was nothing I *could* do. The baby now began to whimper, screwing up its eyes against the hot sunlight. I was as brown as a berry myself, and had no fear of sunburn, so I took off my shirt and draped it over the seat to form a kind of canopy, shielding Serena's face from the shimmering waves of heat.

Whenever a boat approached I stood up, balancing carefully, shouted and waved. Nobody noticed. And there was no way I could control the felucca. Her single sail was far too heavy for me to manipulate, though I was able to handle the tiller. I realised that if I could steer us *across* the river we would hit either Gezira Island or Roda Island just to the south. And Roda was separated from Garden City by only a narrow channel. If I hit Roda someone would push or row us across for much less than the 100-piastre note that Zola had given me.

Time and again we all but touched the canal bank, as we drifted between Roda and the mainland. We were off Old Cairo – part of the city we were never allowed to visit, and which Father had once described as 'a hotbed of depravity'. It *looked* horrible. The clean waterfront in our area, with its small boats, houseboats, even yachts, had given way to a river-bank which looked like a rubbish dump, much of the trash floating in the shallows. The buildings had changed too, as though to match the depravity of its inhabitants; squalid houses of peeling paint with small square windows out of which men and women peered furtively.

Suddenly, without warning, our felucca bumped into the bank. A stunted half-dead tree hung sadly over the water and I tied the mooring rope to it.

The boat safe, I climbed out with Serena in my arms – in itself a difficult manoeuvre. Twenty yards along a filthy alley two men approached. In Arabic I asked them if they could help. One swore at me, the other spat on the rutted dirt ground and pointed to the boat – and then they both ran towards it.

'That's my father's boat!' I yelled, running back towards them. 'Don't you dare touch it.'

'We're taking *all* British boats,' one of them sneered as both men jumped into the felucca and started to pull away from the bank.

I could feel the stinging tears of anger. I was helpless and alone, with a crying baby and not the faintest idea where I was.

In Old Cairo, according to my mother, beggars and gritty dust ruled the tawdry shops and the alleys of the bazaar, and even from the river-bank I caught a whiff of mixed spices – fish perhaps, the scent of sandalwood, pepper, onions, kebabs cooking.

I was so thirsty that I could hardly wait for a drink. And it occurred to me that Serena might be crying because she, too, needed water. I walked towards an open square, fingering the note in the pocket of my flannel shorts.

The entire square was filled with patches of dusty, once-green grass, several statues of men on huge horses, and at the far end an arcade with a long row of balconies above. Even though I had never been to Old Cairo before, the row of balconies reminded me of the Anglo-American Hospital where I had spent two days when *my* tonsils had been removed. Near me several men and women sat crosslegged eating monkey nuts and dried melon seeds, and then I heard, even before I saw, the brass castanets which every seller of drinks used to announce his presence. I ran towards him.

'Can I have a drink?' I asked. 'And for the baby, too.'

The drink salesman carried everything on his back, using a kind of harness. A jug with a long spout contained a sherbet drink. It was strapped to his shoulder, kept cool by a lump of ice. From the other side of the belt he carried a supply of glasses in a neat case.

'What about payment?' He eyed my scruffy form suspiciously.

'Have you any change?' I flashed a 100-piastre note.

'Where did you get that?' He was even more suspicious at the size of the note. 'Did you steal it?'

'My mother gave it to me,' I said; I was almost in tears.

'Well –' he started, still looking at me doubtfully, though he finally served me. I imagine that he needed every sale.

I gulped down three glasses of sherbet, but some instinct warned me (perhaps remembering when Greg was a baby?) that too much wouldn't be good for Serena. Anyway, she couldn't drink from a glass. The seller gave me an extra cardboard cup and I helped to quench her thirst by dipping my finger into the sherbet and letting her suck it. She gurgled with delight, and immediately stopped crying.

Hoping to find my way, I wandered into a narrow side-street of small traders, some shops little more than holes in an alleyway selling sweetmeats and honeycombs, and another sherbet seller. Not far away, a tiny shop was filled with dozens of birds in cages – all trilling happily, singing, they thought, to each other. 'Do birds sing love songs?' I had once asked Father. But I knew now that the birds were singing to themselves for each cage was lined with mirrors.

The street was alive with noises and strange faces and differing clothes – white turbans, red fezzes, black veils, arrogant sheiks, their faces carved like Red Indians; everyone jostled with one another for the right of way, the crowds hedged in not only by the narrowness of the streets but by the barrows filled with mangoes, their gold fruit brightened by nests of scarlet paper to keep each one from being bruised.

I knew – instinct again – that it would be unwise to mention the word 'British'. My Arabic was so fluent, I spoke it so normally, and I looked so filthy and brown that nobody yet had taken any notice of me.

I trudged on, hoping that by a miracle I might be making for home. At the corner I saw a man selling water-melon and bought three slices. Then, as so often happens in Cairo, a turn of the corner transformed the scene from the busy street to a foetid alley whose tall unpainted buildings blotted out the sun. Half a dozen ragged children were rummaging in a pile of stinking refuse, the flies congregating like currants round their eyes and mouths. Everywhere there was the smell of unwashed bodies. And venturing out from the rickety houses I saw two rats – more courageous than the hidden ones – heading towards the pile of refuse.

Near them was a boy with no legs – he looked my age, no older – who was squatting on a home-made cart made out of an old box and pram wheels. He looked at me wordlessly – perhaps he thought it was pointless for him to beg from one so young – but I felt the tears and gave him ten milliemes – a piastre. His face lit up with pure joy as he started to propel himself forward, using his hands to push his way along the filthy ground.

Three of the boys from the refuse dump had seen what had happened. With a yell of triumph they charged towards the cripple and grabbed the coin. He screamed, but without any hope of getting it back. All I could do was to give him one slice of the water-melon. I stayed with him while he ate it and Serena sucked the rest of the melon.

In some roundabout way we returned to the square, utterly lost, yet I couldn't get the picture of the little beggar boy out of my mind. In the far corner of the square, near the ornamental arcade, the tall slim finger of a minaret pierced the skyline, and I could hear the ritualistic chant of a muezzin calling the faithful to prayer – as much a part of our Cairo lives as the dozens of mosques and minarets themselves. For me, though, the doleful music seemed to emphasise the plight of the cripple. I sat down suddenly and could no longer hold back my tears.

An old man sitting on his haunches, watching us, smiled through toothless gums and mumbled, 'What's the trouble?'

'I'm lost,' I said, the tears stopping. 'Can you tell me how to get to Garden City?'

'You speak good Arabic.' His wizened face crumpled into another smile. 'But you are English, yes?'

'My father is Sir Geoffrey Holt, the Egyptian Adviser.'

'You must hide!' cried the old man urgently. 'Listen.' As he spoke, I heard shooting – sporadic rifle shots; two or three volleys cracked through the air. 'This is *thaura, thaura!*' he cried.

'A revolution?' I asked. 'I thought it was just a riot.' New fears began to bite into me.

'Where are your parents?' he said. 'Or have they already been killed?'

'My mother has a gun,' I cried, as though that settled everything.

'Then go to her,' the old man said. 'Quickly! *Inshallah!*'

'God be with you, too,' I repeated automatically. 'But I don't know where to go.' I was almost in tears again.

'You must know your address?'

I shook my head. I was aching, physically as well as mentally, to tell the old man where I lived, to share a secret, as though sharing would enable me to diminish my fear, but I didn't dare. The rioters might follow me, I thought, wondering if I had made a mistake in telling the old man that Mother had a gun. They would follow me, then kill her to get the gun.

And I was greatly worried about Zola. He was my friend, and I knew that in all family crises the Nubian was always blamed. I wanted to return home and tell Mother how brave Zola had been to organise our escape, but I was afraid she wouldn't believe me. I had read stories of Nubians who had received fifty lashes for being five minutes late for work. Poor Zola! He had failed in his duty. I was sure that's what my mother would believe. No, for the moment I had to hide.

Serena had fallen asleep, lying on the bare grass behind the statue of a man on a huge horse. I used my shirt as a pillow for her, and I was about to ask the toothless old man for help when an open truckload of British soldiers swerved round the corner.

I stood up and cried, 'Hooray!' They seemed to be on their way to some other place, for their rifles were held casually. I started to shout when suddenly, almost with the precision that follows a whistle blown as a signal, a huge wave of howling men and women surged out from an arcade at the back of the square. Some were armed with staves, some with axes, others with knives. They raced across the open square, a tide of frenzied human beings, towards the truckload of soldiers.

I crouched half-hidden behind the statue, each one of the horses' hooves as large as Serena's head. As I watched a terrible thing happened. The mob seemed to engulf the truck.

Men grabbed the driver through the cab window. Before any of the British soldiers had time to take up their guns and fire over the heads of the people – that, I knew, was the traditional warning – hundreds of men and women started rocking the truck. Some of the soldiers spilled out on to the ground. The crowd attacked them mercilessly, beating and kicking their heads. Soon, like a monstrous beetle trying to find its legs, the truck itself overturned completely.

I was too young in those days to appreciate what I realised later – the irony of the muezzin praying for peace and good-will and the 'faithful' Moslems drowning his chant as they screamed to kill.

I saw one man with a hatchet split open the face of a soldier just a few yards from us. Then he started to chop off the soldier's arms and legs. Others with knives butchered his colleagues. Two other soldiers were attacked with knives, while others lay either unconscious or dead, I couldn't tell which.

Some of the luckier soldiers managed to get back to the truck. One or two of them, having retrieved their rifles, started running across the square, shooting at anyone. I was too afraid to run towards the nearest in case he shot at me.

The men who had been hacked to death lay still in the sunlit square – what was left of them. Serena was too young to understand the sight, the men being cut up like sides of beef, when the worst moment of all arrived. A group of kids in dirty galabiyas grabbed pieces of the dead men's flesh, tearing it off if necessary, and ran round the square screaming, 'English meat for sale!'

One came right towards us, but didn't realise who we were and dropped the bloody piece of flesh at our feet. Serena, who was now at the crawling stage, was so excited that she crept towards it. A few inches before she would have touched it I pulled her away. She screamed with annoyance and fell over. As she did so she cut her face near the mouth on a small piece of jagged stone. I wiped the blood away with my handkerchief.

The truck which had been overturned now blazed with all the fury and excitement of a Guy Fawkes bonfire. I could feel the heat, smell the burning of oil or petrol, hear the screams of someone nearby. Around the burning truck a group of youngsters danced with excitement. Suddenly I heard the crack of a single rifle shot. A youngster in white threw up his arms, as though part of a dance, then pitched forward on to the truck, and in a moment the flames were racing greedily up his white clothes. Then fusillades of shots rang out – seemingly from all sides – and the scene in the square became even more macabre.

Two more Egyptian bodies lay spreadeagled near us, while others lay face down in the dirty water of the gutters edging the patches of lawn; still others were draped with a curious dancing grace over objects where they had happened to fall. As the rioters senselessly began to fire on one another, a young girl with half a leg torn off crawled screaming to the middle of the square. A woman, doubled up for safety, ran to rescue the child, reached her, and took her in her arms. There was another burst of shooting and two armed Egyptians who stood near spun round, dropped to the ground, and fired rifles. The mother and baby, caught in the cross-fire, were shot too.

Vaguely I remember the stench of the dead and dying. I remember that I tried to shout in a hoarse voice that wouldn't carry, 'Run while you still have time!' It was like trying to make myself heard against the rush of a tidal wave. I would have run myself, but the burden of Serena was too heavy and, apart from that, my legs felt as though they would double up beneath the rest of my body. I do remember clearly stooping to pull up the grey stockings beneath my flannel shorts. I had lost a garter from one leg.

I don't think I could have stood much more. I felt I was going to faint – the heat, perhaps – and sat there bewildered and forlorn, lost guardian of a baby girl surrounded by madmen, afraid to ask for help in case friends wouldn't recognise me. I was convinced that if the Egyptian rioters realised who I was they would cut us up too. In a curious way I was more frightened for Serena than for myself, perhaps because I was imagining myself watching her being butchered. Again I wiped a tiny trickle of blood from her face.

At that moment the senseless, sporadic firing was replaced by a more sinister, yet welcome sound – the crackle of machine-gun fire. Cautiously I looked round the edge of the huge stone horse. In the corner of the square where the British soldiers had been murdered another vehicle had swung round, braking savagely. I knew enough about the British army to recognise a Whippet armoured car which had a Maxim machine-gun poking out of a hole in the turret behind the driver's cab.

A burst of fire rattled across the square. As swiftly as the crowd had gathered it melted into the arcades. The truck advanced again, firing at any who lingered in the centre of the square, bent not only on restoring order but on revenge. Three figures which had run away must have ventured back, shaking fists, hurling abuse. I saw the machine-gun swivel almost laconically, as though in slow motion, fire a few shots, and the screams of rage and defiance turned into cries of death.

Soon I felt it was safe to leave our hiding place. I picked up Serena and gave her the last of the melon to suck. She couldn't really hold it for long and, leaning forward, let it fall to the ground. I stood up, knees wobbling, and waved furiously. 'I'm British!' I croaked. 'I'm British!'

A young officer ran over. 'What the devil are you doing here? Who are you? Where are your parents?'

I must have been so frightened and mixed up, so exhausted, that for a moment I couldn't speak, but at last I managed to find my tongue. 'I don't know where we are. We escaped in a boat –' Now the words rushed out in a torrent.

'Take it slowly,' said the officer and shouted to the sergeant, then picked up Serena.

At that moment he saw a lump of flesh which the kids had dropped and made to kick it off the grass, not realising what it was.

'Don't kick that!' I screamed. 'It's part of a soldier.'

'Christ almighty! Sergeant! Put these kids into the truck until we find out where to take them.'

The sergeant lifted us into the truck to drive us home but almost before we started I had fallen asleep, overtaken by a physical tiredness like that of an animal released of a heavy load.

When we reached Holt House it was to a hero's welcome. Mother, of course, was in tears, having long since feared the worst. I cried out before anything else that Zola had tried to save us and that it was my fault we had drifted away. 'Of course,' said Mother. Everyone was so happy that nobody blamed anyone. Indeed, Madame Sirry overflowed with tears and hugged me.

'I'm so proud of you, Mark,' she said. 'You're the protector!' And when Serena whimpered because of the cut on her cheek, Madame Sirry wiped it, then whispered to me, 'Go on, Mark, she trusts you, kiss the pain away.' Slightly embarrassed I did so, little knowing for how long the phrase 'kiss the pain away' would last, or that the tiny scar from that cut would never disappear until it turned into a dimple.

That was virtually the end of what my father always called 'the mad March riots'. More than a hundred Egyptians were killed and more than a score of Britons died, some murdered with frenzied savagery. But as bad as the deaths of men was the virtual strangulation of Egypt's tottering economy which followed.

My father was almost in tears.

'I love the Egyptians,' he said, 'but when they scent independence they're their own worst enemies. Independence takes time, patience. You can't rush it. As it is, the violence has wrecked the economy. It'll take at least six months before the railways are running normally again. A lot of the rolling stock has been smashed – and that means there's no way this year's onion crop can be saved. Without that thousands will simply not have enough food to eat. The Delta cotton crop will be ruined because there's no way of getting diesel oil to many of the estates that depend on pumped irrigation.'

Sirry Pasha, who was talking to my father, ventured, 'If the British hadn't kicked out Zaglul –?'

'I agree with you,' Father admitted gloomily. 'But the Egyptian passion for violence, for killing the goose that lays the golden eggs – that's a different matter.'

Apart from the wave of anti-British hate there was another factor: the end of the Great War was followed by mass starvation. War's end brought cotton back to the world market. Food crops were neglected, often by venal Egyptian landlords who were the first to ignore long-term problems and instead amassed vast fortunes out of cotton while the fellahîn went hungry. By 1919 five million peasants were living on the brink of starvation. In Cairo itself more than a million were without food.

Though I didn't know it at the time, this was an epoch-making moment in the history of Egypt, like the day a dam bursts. And though I remember how terrified I was, the moments of terror through which I actually lived came, with the passing years, to be fused with the events of which I later read, particularly the reason behind the explosion of national indignity, in which men, women and children raced through the streets, through the gardens, without any thought of the guns which faced them.

All that was a long time ago, that hot day when history was being written, while Serena and I were separated from our parents as we fled the mob. I know that to Serena the experience meant nothing, but to me, at the age of ten? I was young enough to take the adventure in my stride, yet old enough for the scars never to be forgotten.

2

I suppose that over the next fifteen years or so the close relationship between my father and Sirry Pasha – and consequently between our two families – was cemented because in many ways Father was more Egyptian than an Egyptian, while Sirry was more English than the English.

Sirry Pasha – no one ever called him by his Christian name of Victor – had been educated at Harrow and Oxford, whereas my father had insisted on sending Greg and me to the 'English School' in Heliopolis, the Cairo suburb, where in fact all nationalities studied. 'The best way to become a cosmopolitan,' he said – until I went later to Oxford and read Law in order to become a barrister, the vocation I myself had chosen and loved.

The friendship between the Sirrys and the Holts was founded on ties of diplomacy – each of their respective governments used each other as sounding boards – but their friendship went deeper than that, even though they were so different. Sirry Pasha, with his white hair and handsome face, *looked* a diplomat, the confidant of royalty. But Father was bustling, with a thatch of unruly grey hair like a mass of curly iron shavings. He was reputed to be 'difficult'; an eccentric. Sometimes at night he would go wandering round Cairo dressed in a galabiya. He spoke with a curious relish about 'women', though I soon discovered that it was all talk, his own fantasy world, which meant nothing. More serious in the view of some senior Whitehall officials were suggestions that he was a heavy drinker. The rumours arose when it became known that Father always began the day at 7 a.m. with champagne. Every morning Zola served the same breakfast in Father's Chinese study – a bottle of champagne, coffee and scrambled eggs, followed by toast and marmalade.

The study where Father worked radiated a warmth and cosiness of its own. The red silk walls showed off the Chinese mirror paintings to perfection, and the room abounded with shelves and tables and niches for his treasures. In many ways it was the hub of the whole building, though the house itself played a major part in my father's work and Egyptian visitors liked to enjoy a taste of British ostentation, when our Nubian staff would be arrayed in their 'Sunday best' galabiyas of navy blue edged with gold braid – the 'house uniform'.

Zola was an institution, the only man allowed to serve Father with his morning champagne. He had attended the family for twelve years since the day when, on a trip to the Sudan, Father had asked him to handle the transport and stores. From that moment Zola had stayed with the family, the ultimate in major-domos: watchful, happy, above all faithful, resisting the blandishments of rival households who offered him much more money to join their service. Like almost all Nubians, Zola was tall, handsome and black, of Semitic stock with a Negro strain. They had converted to Christianity in the sixth century, though by the fourteenth most had become Moslems. Zola came from the desert of northern Sudan where sometimes it only rained for literally a few minutes a year. Nubians made the finest butlers, waiters and chauffeurs in Egypt. Most, like Zola, were married but left their wives in their villages, visiting them just once a year.

If Father was eccentric, Mother could only be called an extrovert. She loved life, wore extravagant dresses, never missed a ball, a party, a dinner, and was in great demand because of her never-failing good humour. Father rarely accompanied her on these evening visits, so that it became accepted practice for hostesses to invite Father as well as Mother, but also to invite a spare man, knowing Father would decline, except to visit close friends like the Sirrys.

In many ways Mother, for all her openness, had a complex character. In the nicest sense of the word, she was a trifle 'dotty'. One friend described her perfectly as having a 'Billie Burke' vagueness. It was true, but delightful rather than irritating. Her life was punctuated with exclamations or questions: 'Where did I put that?' or even, 'Now, why am I going out this afternoon?' If she was given a diary she invariably mislaid it.

She was also very tall, just over six feet. I was a little taller still, but Father and Greg were an inch or two shorter – thus disproving the adage that a son is always taller than his mother. Her early inferiority about her height had been stifled at an early age – to her satisfaction anyway – after a dress designer told her that flouncy dresses made one look less tall. She believed it, and every dress she wore from then on had flounces of chiffon or taffeta; for years she had been known affectionately as 'Chiffon'. Even Father called her that.

She looked her best in the evening, always wearing a long dress for dinner, for she had a special eye – or was it an ear? – for taffeta, which was then much in vogue in Cairo, so that her every entrance was heralded by the whisper of her dress.

If we came of an old family – my father was the third baronet – so did Sirry Pasha, whose great-grandfather served the Khedive Ismail, and whose business acumen was a reflection of the booming nineteenth-century history of Egypt. For the Copts – the ancient race of Christian Egyptians – were, like Sirry, often more astute and quicker to see and seize sudden opportunities than many of their Moslem brethren.

It was grandfather Sirry who backed the son of Robert Stephenson when he built the railway from Alexandria to Cairo in 1852, transforming production in the Nile Delta. It was Sirry who also helped a young man who had run away from England, and reached Cairo in search of a fortune. The man was washing dishes in the seedy 'British Hotel' when old Sirry spotted his energy and helped him. In the end the Englishman took over the British Hotel and rechristened it with his own name, Sam Shepheard, turning Shepheard's into the most famous hotel in the Middle East – with Sirry owning ten per cent of the shares.

A few years later Sirry was included in a party of thirty-two ladies and gentlemen who made the first 'package tour' up the Nile by steamer; a venture so successful that the organiser, Mr Thomas Cook, opened a branch office in Ibrahim Pasha Street near Shepheard's.

Almost at the same time old Sirry took a gamble. 'It was the only gamble the old man ever took,' the present Sirry Pasha once told me. 'He said that every man had the right to make a fool of himself once in his lifetime, and he regarded the money as thrown away.' The gamble was to take some shares in a ten-year project to build the hundred-mile-long Suez Canal which was started in 1859. Progress was slow, dividends non-existent; it didn't really matter, because two years later, in 1861, the Sirry family tripled their immense fortune in another venture, almost without realising what was happening. For no one could imagine that the great new country of America would be torn by civil war – or that the strife in that distant land would have lasting economic repercussions in Egypt. Overnight, supplies of American cotton, mostly exported to Europe, vanished in gunsmoke. In a panic, European cotton-brokers turned to Egypt.

The Sirry family farmed large areas in the Delta. The price of cotton rose to astronomical heights. Exports from Egypt shot up within two years from $16 million in 1862 to $56 million, a lot of money in those days. The commercial role of cotton changed the economy of Egypt for ever, because once they tried it Europeans discovered that Egyptian cotton was more silky than American – the 'line' was longer – and that it could be mercerised more easily.

By then Cairo had become a treasure house of the East and a pleasure house for the West. Britain and France in particular swept the Cairenes off their feet in a golden flood. Bankers, explorers, engineers, merchants, tourists – there was no stopping them. Cairo in the latter half of the nineteenth century was an Eastern version of a Western gold rush. Of the 300,000 people living in the capital in 1872, 75,000 were foreigners, of which the British and French retained their predominance. The French considered themselves the social arbiters; they ran the social life of the city, the opera, concerts, famous dressmaking houses – in a word, culture. Theirs was the diplomatic language, always used in the mixed courts. Britain brought the railway, the telegraph, politics, commerce, and finally the building boom, when the British discovered a way to enlarge Cairo.

Until then the natural boundaries of the city had seemed to limit any hopes of expansion, even though the population was beginning to explode. Cairo could not spread to the east where the medieval Arab city, with the Citadel, its minarets and the tomb of the Mamelukes, was bounded by the waterless Mukattam Hills. No man could ever build on their white, rocky slopes. To the west the Nile barred all thoughts of expansion – until British engineers explained to Khedive Ismail that over the centuries the Nile had been moving slowly westward, leaving behind an unsightly, scarred, evil-smelling brackish countryside. That, said the engineers, could be reclaimed and used as building land.

'I will build a new Paris on the Nile,' the Khedive is reputed to have said. The Khedive then offered free land to those who promised to construct 'buildings of major importance' within eighteen months. Old man Sirry took thirty plots of land and built some of the finest palaces, embassies and villas in the 'new Cairo' – including our own beautiful house. I like to imagine, when I think of Sirry Pasha's vast wealth, that his forebears enjoyed good taste – and that he shared some of it with us, even though he was still our landlord.

The despotic spendthrift Ismail lost all his money. During the last eleven years of his reign, before he was deposed by the Turkish government, he borrowed £68 million from European bankers. Finally he even had to sell his shares in the now-completed Suez Canal. Old man Sirry kept his shares, now worth a fortune.

The present Sirry Pasha was only five years old when in 1882, after Ismail had been deposed, a nationalist uprising threatened the security of Egypt – which meant a threat to the Suez Canal, by now Britain's lifeline to the untold riches of her Indian colony. British warships bombarded Alexandria. British troops moved in to 'protect' Egypt from itself.

'And from that date,' said my father with a sigh, 'the British can be said to have begun their "provisional" occupation of Egypt.'

Fuad, the British-backed sultan who became king in 1922, had four daughters but only one son, who was the eldest child. This was Farouk, born in 1920. And so by the time the boy was eight or nine Fuad looked around for boys suitable to play with his heir. One unwilling playmate was Aly Sirry, Serena's older brother, after Fuad had suggested him to Sirry Pasha. This arrangement was not ideal, for Aly was six years older than Farouk – a big difference at that age, especially with a chubby, bossy youngster already precocious enough to warn servants who annoyed him, 'Wait until I'm the ruler of this country.'

Aly hated the job of 'playmate'. For though he had a charm of his own he was a rebel, and from his early years disliked royalty in principle. So Aly persuaded the young prince that Gregory Holt had suitable credentials – as indeed he had – to join the small circle of royal chums. Greg didn't like the idea any more than Aly, but at least he and Aly were companions of the same age.

It was Greg who told us all about Farouk's early days. Sometimes they would play at the Abdin, a 'town house', set in a mere twenty-five acres in the heart of Cairo, but mostly they preferred the Kubbah Palace at Heliopolis.

'The Abdin's rather like Buckingham Palace,' Father explained to us. 'It has five hundred rooms, so it's an office as much as a home.' Kubbah was a glorified country estate on the edge of the city. The walls surrounding the seventy acres stretched for six miles, and within those walls enchanting gardens surrounded the white stone palace with its five hundred rooms. And for the boys there was everything from a pool or lake for swimming to a football pitch. Though when the young prince took to the lake for a dip an escort of swimmers remained by his side; and when he played football servants dashed ahead to pick up the ball and place it at the prince's feet.

'All the games are rigged,' complained Greg. 'And he's such a baby that if he doesn't win he just stops playing.' The servants took good care that he always *did* win. When his tutors organised a paper-chase in the palace grounds, servants dipped the paper into Farouk's favourite eau de Cologne so that he could pick up its scent.

'It's ridiculous,' snorted Greg, continuing to grumble. 'And the grooms won't even let *me* ride a horse when Farouk is riding because they say I'm too much of a dare-devil.'

Nobody ever noticed that Greg was a trifle shorter than Mother because he was growing into such a superb athlete. It seemed to make no difference whatever he played, from tennis to polo; yet with it all he had no affectation. He never showed off. He just loved life – so long as it revolved around sport.

'Don't worry,' Mother soothed. '*You* know you are a good horseman. Why should you bother trying to impress a spoiled prince?'

'I'm angry because I'm better,' said Greg, refusing to be mollified. He already showed brilliant promise as a rider.

Of course the boys didn't go to the Kubbah Palace every day. There were lessons. Fuad was a tyrant of a father. He made Farouk rise at six every morning and spend the first hour of the day doing exercises before he could eat or drink. Sometimes lessons lasted until seven in the evening, depending on which tutor was in attendance. A French instructor taught gym, a Mr Hathaway from London gave lessons in maths and English, an Italian taught him fencing. Others taught him Arabic and the study of the Koran.

Farouk's worst agonies, however, were caused by his father's fanatical insistence that the boy crash-diet every time he showed signs of putting on weight. Young Farouk loved food and *did* tend to become chubby. His tutors were ordered to make certain that the young prince ate no food nor drank any water during lesson-times. The result was a desperate desire by young Farouk to grab any food he could without being discovered. Between lessons he would sprint into his mother's section of the palace, the *haremlek*, make for the kitchens, gulp down a bottle of fizzy lemonade, then loot the larder for cream buns which he would cram into his mouth at double speed during the few minutes before the next hour of tuition began.

To Greg and Aly, Farouk seemed to have a split personality, a baffling mixture of good and evil. One moment he would be loving, the next cruel. One day Greg found Farouk crying his heart out because his favourite pet rabbit had died. Yet two days later, when a frightened cat scratched Farouk slightly, the young boy dashed its brains out against a wall.

On the morning of his eleventh birthday Farouk was given his own car – an Austin Seven – which he was allowed to drive round and round the seventy acres of grounds. Driving was to become one of the few lasting pleasures of his life.

Farouk, Greg and Aly had one other 'friend' who was slightly older. This was a young Italian, Antonio Pulli, nephew of a palace electrician, who one day mended Farouk's electric train.

'Pulli is my greatest friend now,' Farouk had told Greg. And from then on they all played in the servants' hall at Kubbah, safe in the knowledge that Fuad wouldn't see them.

Pulli *did* become Farouk's closest friend – and later one of the most influential of his advisers.

Sometimes, when Farouk's sisters held a party, the boys would be invited, to stand and gawk restlessly. And on those occasions Serena would also be a guest. And so, in a curious way, all our lives were intertwined with the destiny of Farouk – my father's, of course, with old Fuad at first, then Greg and Serena, until finally I, too, became involved.

Of course there were downs as well as ups in the process of growing up, and it is sometimes difficult to look back and remember the turning points, especially during the times when I was away from home at Oxford or reading for the bar, while Greg and Serena, 'the boy and girl next door', were playing tennis together, he teaching her to dance – sometimes at the royal palace – or she watching while Greg raced off on his first gallops at the Gezira, on the way to becoming one of the finest polo players in the country.

Before that, while I was still at school, she had learned vaguely about the drama of the 1919 riots, but no details, only that I had been called her 'protector' – that was all. And so she did look to me to protect her when in trouble. Almost from the moment she could talk she would come to me when she fell or scratched a finger, to ask, 'Kiss the pain away, please, Uncle.'

Uncle, indeed! Of course there were reasons, even for that. She treated me as a grown-up, even then, whereas it was she and Greg who were growing up together. At one stage the difference in our ages was more pronounced because of a sartorial difference that separated the boys from the men – literally. Greg was still in shorts and school uniform. I was wearing long flannel bags, and I had even been measured at Collacott's for my first blue suit.

I acquired my title of Uncle when a distant relation of Chiffon's spent a few nights at Holt House on the way to take up an appointment in India. They had a small daughter, and she identified both the Holt boys with different words, 'Greg' or 'Uncle Mark'. I did nothing to dissuade anyone, for secretly I was very proud of my status as a grown-up. So

for a short time I became an uncle to Serena, first as a title,
later as a teasing term of affection.

I was still a serious 'Uncle Mark', though, when she was
ten and was rushed to hospital with, of all things, the dreaded
disease of typhoid. I was in London and knew nothing until
I received a cable from home: IF POSSIBLE PLEASE RETURN
URGENTLY AS SERENA VERY ILL WITH TYPHOID AND IS ASKING
FOR YOU STOP DOCTOR PHILLIPS SAYS YOUR PRESENCE COULD
HELP HER RECOVER FATHER.

Typhoid! I had read in the *Times* that there was an outbreak
in Upper Egypt, but the Sirrys! People like them and the
Holts didn't catch typhoid: we boiled water, we were careful
with milk. Typhoid killed thousands of people annually, but
not *us*, or our friends. I could feel the iciness that encased my
entire body as I reread the impersonal cable. Typhoid meant
death.

It never occurred to me to regard Serena as anything but a
member of our family. She was. It never entered my head to
ask why I was so affected. I was as grief-stricken as if the
same thing had happened to Greg. All I knew was that if
Serena had to die I must reach her first – to give her comfort
as her 'protector'.

Fortunately there was a new, quick way to reach
Alexandria. The British Airways flying boat service had just
been opened up to the East and called at Alex, and I arrived
there three days later, fearing the worst for every waking
minute of the flight – three days of my life lost beyond
recall – wondering if she would be alive when I reached
Cairo. I had cabled Father, and a message from him was
waiting for me at Alex with the news that Serena was in the
isolation ward of the Anglo-American Hospital and was 'as
well as can be expected'. The car took me straight to the
hospital.

I pushed open the entrance doors and walked to the reception desk where I asked for the number of Miss Sirry's
room.

'It's forty-six,' the receptionist replied. 'But you can't go
in, sir. Only look through the window in the door, and
there's a way you can talk through a grill.'

'Miss,' I flared, exploding with the frustration of fear and exhaustion, 'I've flown all the way to see this little girl. And I'm *going* to see her if I have to kick the door in.'

I ran up the stone steps to the first floor, taking them two at a time, and made my way to room forty-six. A nurse in a stiff blue dress with a white coif ran towards me shouting, 'You can't go in the isolation ward, sir!'

I took no notice.

There was only one bed in the room. Another nurse sat by the bed. She waved me away. I ignored her.

At first I didn't recognise the waif-like bundle of skin and bones that lay, wet with sweat, like a limp doll on the soaked sheet. She looked as though she was on the point of exhaustion, though reason told me that if she had really been on the point of death her parents would have been there. But the agony of that first sight of her! Her closed eyes were sunk into black circles. Her skin was blotched with red spots. She breathed as though by an effort in a despairing, moaning apology for sleep.

'You shouldn't be in here,' the agitated nurse whispered. 'But since you *are*, you can only stay a couple of minutes.'

I stood at the foot of her bed and watched. And then as I studied the heavy breathing, the moaning figure, she suddenly stopped moving. There was no warning. I caught my breath in despair. For one awful moment I was sure she was dead.

Instead, a wonderful thing happened. Slowly those large green eyes, sunken now in their sockets, opened. She saw me and the tears broke into a flood of relief as I fought to hold back my own tears. Then she smiled, a crooked, painful smile, and croaked, 'Darling Uncle, I knew you'd come.'

'Of course I came,' I said, the words choking. 'I'm your protector.'

She smiled, the movement of her lips accentuating, as it always did, the dimple at the corner of her mouth, the only legacy of the cut she'd received during the 1919 riots. By now it was growing into a bewitching trademark, as special to Serena's face as her green eyes and blonde hair – a rare combination, which Sirry Pasha had once explained discreetly by 'the entrance into our family' of a blonde Circassian slave in the days when the Circassians were the most beautiful and sought-after girls of the Ottoman empire and its vassal state, Egypt. There was more than a touch of the Circassian in the looks – and the character – of Serena.

'Can I have a drink of water?' she whispered.

'Of course.' I held out the glass and she sipped from it, grasping the glass with pitifully thin matchstick arms, and as I wiped the sweat from her forehead she took a second sip, then licked her wetted lips gratefully and asked, 'Kiss the pain away?'

Of course I did. Unthinkingly. The nurse looked at me horrified. I hardly noticed her, for within a few moments the bundle of skin and bone had fallen into an exhausted sleep on the sweat-soaked pillows.

A week later she had overcome the crisis, and was out of danger.

'It's a bloody miracle,' cried Dr Phillips, who was not given to strong language. 'I would have bet a pound to a piastre that the girl would be gone in less than a week. She'll pull through now. Must have been the sight of you.'

Twelve days later I felt feverish. Two days after that the first red spots appeared on my face, a sort of rash. Almost at the same moment I started having violent attacks of diarrhoea.

At least I knew the symptoms and had caught the disease in good time. Dr Phillips was round with an ambulance in half an hour and whisked me into isolation.

'With any luck we've caught it in time,' he said. 'But I don't understand why you got it. The nurses make a fuss, but in fact it isn't really contagious, if you don't drink from infected water, or –' Puzzled, he let the words trail off.

'It was the miracle,' I laughed.

'Meaning what?'

'She asked me to kiss her.'

'And you did?'

I nodded.

'After she'd just had a drink? On wet lips? You bloody fool, Mark, but I'm proud of you. That kiss gave her the will to live. Thank God we caught *you* in time. You'll be all right.'

Three weeks later Serena left hospital. Two weeks after that I was back in Holt House.

In the years of our growing up very little seemed to alter, perhaps because those close to us were sheltered from abrupt change by proximity. You don't notice grey hairs or stooped shoulders so much except after a long absence. And by 1934, when I was twenty-five, I had passed my bar finals in London, eaten my dinners at the Temple facing the Thames, been called to the bar and 'set up shop', as my father called it, as an advocate in Egypt.

In Cairo, with its multiracial, polyglot population, legal protocol was more lax than in London, and under the all-embracing term 'advocate' I was not only called upon to plead in court but under the Egyptian code of practice could deal with problems without employing a solicitor.

I took on any work offered to me, but soon found myself specialising in taxation and property – two never-ending problems in the labyrinth of Egyptian business. I didn't have many clients at first.

'Don't let that worry you,' advised Father, who had no inhibitions in suggesting to friends needing legal advice that they should consult me. I loved the work and was sometimes so immersed in its problems that I forgot to return home for dinner.

Greg was completely different. At twenty he was among the best five polo players in Egypt, utterly fearless, charming, good company, handsome and dashing; everything a young man should be, I sometimes thought, a trifle wistfully. And he knew what he wanted, though his ambition was rather different from mine.

One morning he knocked on the study door asking for help. 'Father,' he began, 'I'd like to play polo as a sort of full-time job.'

Father was having his breakfast, the scrambled eggs kept warm because he possessed a special hollow plate two inches thick. You could fill the space between top and bottom of the plate with boiling water through a small corked hole in the rim. He loved his special plate, and now he looked up with a smile.

'Have a glass of champagne,' he said. Then: 'How much would it cost?'

Greg had already worked that out. Polo was *the* game. The Gezira Club boasted three pitches – as well as its racecourse, tennis courts and swimming pools – and yet it cost Greg only £60 a month to keep six ponies in a mews (built by the British and very similar to an English cobbled mews) in Zamalek, an exclusive suburb in the northern half of Gezira Island.

He was playing polo almost daily. He turned out for the Punchers three times a week, but was also 'borrowed' regularly for regimental games if their star players were on duty. Three regiments – the 11th and 8th Hussars and the Royal Horse Artillery – were always competing for the King's Cup or the Regimental Cup or some other trophy.

'I'll stake you,' agreed Father. 'In the hope that you'll end up being the finest polo player in Cairo. Is that fair?'

'Wonderful!' cried Greg. 'And you don't mind if – well, I don't have to go to an office?'

'The world is full of brilliant men who succeed without earning money,' declared Father. 'Look at Douglas Jardine. Test captain against the Australians last year. Educated at Winchester, got his blue at Oxford. Jardine couldn't play as an amateur if he didn't have private means. I think that's a damned good idea of yours.'

But, as Greg told me later, Father did add, 'There's one thing. What about Mark? I'm not going to have him being jealous when he learns that while he's working I'm paying you money for doing nothing.'

'Doing nothing!' Greg spluttered. 'Polo doing *nothing*!'

'You know what I mean,' Father added hastily. 'It looks like fun – the idle rich image. Still, I'll help. You've both got your allowances from the family trust, but in addition, now I know how much extra you'll need to play, I'll match what it costs with help to Mark.'

Which he did. He was always scrupulously fair – one of the major reasons why for so long we had remained such a united family.

34

So now he paid the rent of my chambers overlooking the Ezbekieh Gardens, the salary of Salem my clerk, and of a secretary. 'There'll be no favourites in our house,' Father used to say.

Though our two families were very close, Aly Sirry was in many ways the odd man out. He didn't like socialising – and for the son of one of the richest men in Cairo that was enough to damn him, however unfairly, for Cairo revolved round parties. Nor did he like the British – and that was embarrassing to the rich Cairenes who supped regularly at elegant British dinners.

Sirry Pasha, who had entertained high hopes for Aly, was hurt and disappointed that his handsome son seemed morose, a loner. How different he was from Greg, who was the same age! Greg met all kinds of people, but never became involved with politics. Perhaps his attitude was a sign of a shallow mind; perhaps Aly·was deeper; there were rumours that he was thinking of joining the Wafd Party – the Arabic word for 'delegation', for the Wafd was a political party of many colours, bound together largely by a fervent desire to undo the British shackles. But though I was sorry for Sirry Pasha I didn't have any strong feelings one way or the other for Aly: he was the one who was missing out.

No one in the world ever had such a wonderful youth as those of us who lived in Cairo in those days. In the thirties we all laboured under the happy delusion that our life in Cairo would never end – and though a scowling Aly would sometimes shout, 'This is Egyptian soil and one day you British will be kicked out,' everyone laughed at him.

It wasn't only the Britishers who considered themselves lucky. Rich Egyptians, Moslems and Copts, Jews, Greeks, Italians – every race of the Middle East melting pot – had become an integral part of Cairo. And every one who became rich was able to enjoy the good life.

In many ways pleasures were cheap – which meant that pocket money went a long way when buying coffee at Groppi's, or other cafés serving the sticky sweets and pastries for which Cairo was renowned, or even, by now, milk-shakes (taking care that the milk was 'safe'). Cinemas showed the latest American movies and it cost virtually nothing to go to a matinée at the Metro or the Miami, or at the two cinemas which showed French films.

Life was made easier by dozens of innovations. The age of the taxi had arrived in the twenties, and by 1935 four thousand of them plied the streets of the capital, many filled with rich Egyptians who enjoyed the status symbol of wearing Western-style clothes. Tailors were still reasonable, but you could buy suits from many of the big department stores that had sprung up – Hanau, Sednawi or Cirucel, many of them French directed, and also offering such new-fangled feminine attire as cami-knickers. Rich women like Madame Sirry dressed in the latest Paris fashions, but off-the-peg clothes were enjoying a tremendous boom – even though the Egyptians demanded special materials, known as 'Oriental cloth', which had a sheen to it. The rich used special soaps (the favourite was made in Nablus and had a distinctive scent) and proprietors made certain that Nablus soap appeared in the cloakrooms of any newly opened French café, German brasserie or Greek taverna.

To us Cairo was as much a village as the West End of London was to the British – more so; for London was a city of many different villages, such as St James's, Mayfair or Chelsea. But in Cairo there was really only one village, hugging the Nile and Gezira Island, and behind it the Kasr el Nil, Cairo's Bond Street, crossed by Soliman Pasha Street, the Oxford Street of the Egyptian capital.

And as an added bonus it was – like any other village – filled with intrigue and gossip, for everyone knew the intimate details of the latest scandals that rocked the lives of our friends – or enemies.

Serena regarded herself as one of 'us'. Hers was the ideal happy youth, carefree and above all filled with the sense of excitement that any rich parents would have wished their children to enjoy, yet which somehow eluded the youngsters in Europe.

Certainly it was her inner happiness that shone through into her face, so that, even when young, there was far more to her than the stereotyped beauty of a model or film star. She had all those attributes: a flawless complexion, fair hair hanging over the back of a long graceful neck, a generous mouth with a quick smile giving more than a hint of mischief; and above all green eyes, dauntless, always looking one straight in the face. She was tall too, with – as all of us noticed – beautiful legs and ankles.

As there was no good school for girls in Cairo, Madame Sirry was educating her privately rather than sending her to Paris. Serena studied diligently, but she had two great learning loves. The first was books. She always seemed to have a book under her arm – no 'penny dreadfuls' picked up at Shepheard's bookshop, but classics borrowed from her father's library. 'But I also love good modern novels,' she laughed when I picked up *Cakes and Ale*, which she was reading. 'I devour them. I can't put them down until I've reached the last page.'

Her second love was one which had become a passion. It was painting. Serena's teacher was a Frenchman called Baptise, who in his day had been one of *Les Fauves*, who included Braque, Matisse, Vlaminck and others whose violent colours horrified one critic in 1905 so much that he dubbed them 'the wild beasts'. But Baptise was more than a painter; he had a genius for teaching others. Before long Serena was making remarkable progress.

Still, she *was* young, though for years it had been 'understood' that she and Greg would eventually marry, and perhaps that had added to her maturity. I don't quite know how these 'understandings' grew until one day I asked both Father and Serena, the first deliberately, the second by chance.

Greg had been playing tennis during the late afternoon, so on an impulse I asked Serena if she would like to try out a new innovation in the life of Cairo – one which had caused a sensation. It was a *thé dansant* and was held at Shepheard's every afternoon between four and six.

It was a wonderful discovery, for we both loved going out, though I rarely danced with Serena; and even on this late afternoon I whispered to her as we fox-trotted, 'The old ladies having tea round the floor are looking disapprovingly at me. They probably think I'm a baby snatcher.'

'Why do you always think you're so old?' It wasn't the first time she had asked me that question. It seemed to worry her.

'The cares of my profession,' I laughed.

It was absurd, the way my pulse quickened when I held her in my arms – ridiculous because she couldn't have been more than fifteen or sixteen on that day. Yet while I felt like a baby snatcher she seemed to span the ten-year difference between us with every step she took.

She left the club breathless with excitement, and as I walked her home across the garden from the Sirry house where I had parked my car she said, a little unsteadily, 'That was wonderful – let's do it again. But better not tell our papas. Mine's a bit stuffy!' Then she turned her face up to mine and kissed me, only this time it wasn't just a peck from a self-styled 'uncle'. With a quick whisper – 'You're wonderful!' – she ran off to her home.

More than ever before in my life I was suddenly assailed by doubts. Not just by one kiss, but by the way in which our deep emotions had almost unconsciously led up to the kiss. Was Serena really in love with her 'uncle'? And did I really love her? I had the feeling that we were in love, yet powerless to act against the decisions of others. That kiss had warned me that perhaps I was to blame for having acquiesced to arrangements made by others. Shouldn't I have had the courage earlier to confront our parents? I know everything had been agreed between both families – and happily agreed to by son and daughter – but instinct warned me that this kind of arrangement was a sure formula for married bliss to end in tragedy. And if ever that did happen whose fault would it be? Partly mine? Still, she *was* only a teenager.

That evening at dinner I asked Father, 'It's always assumed that Greg and Serena will be married when they're a bit older. How did you arrange it?'

'I don't remember. Do you, Chiffon? It's a long time ago.'

'We didn't *arrange* anything,' said Chiffon vaguely. 'You make it sound so awful. Arranged, indeed! Oh dear.' She groped for words. 'That's all right for Egyptians –' Realising what she had said, she added hastily, 'I mean the fellahîn.'

'I know,' I laughed. 'I was only curious.'

'I suppose really,' Father had been thinking, 'we encouraged it. Yes, that's a nicer word. Perhaps Sirry Pasha and I always dreamed of uniting our two families in marriage – we often used to talk about it before you were born. And Greg and Serena *are* beautifully matched.'

'But someone must have told them both,' I persisted. 'Made it clear what was – well, expected of them later in life.'

Chiffon protested, 'What are you driving at, Mark? Don't you approve?'

Before I could reply – that in fact I wasn't *driving* at anything – Father interrupted. 'Chiffon was right about Egyptians. Of course no one forced Serena to promise to marry Greg, but Egyptians *do* arrange marriages on the highest level. And though Sirry Pasha is enlightened he does often stick to the old ways. He did say to me that he was glad Greg and Serena liked each other, and that he was going to ask Serena what she thought about Greg as a possible husband when she was older. It wasn't an order, you understand: not the way he would run the lives of the fellahîn in the Delta. But Egyptians like to arrange things – and especially with their children. They feel – and who knows? They might be right – that marriage is too much of a gamble to be left to the young.'

'I wonder what Serena said,' I asked.

'I know what she thought. She was all for it.'

It was my turn to look astonished.

'You knew?'

'Of course. Greg came to me, and I'll never forget the words he used, it made me laugh so. He said, "Father, Serena has asked me to marry her." Apparently she had told Greg of her father's ideas, and Greg thought it was wonderful, and told me, "It'll be great if we don't rush. She's a real stunner, and it's a wonderful way to keep it all in the family." '

That was the night Sirry and Father came to what they called 'the arrangement'.

'Sirry told me it was the happiest day of his life,' Father went on. 'And we celebrated with a magnum of champagne. And after that it just seemed to be accepted by everyone.'

'There *was* one other way to unite the families,' I said dryly.

'Eh?' asked my father.

'Yes.' I felt suddenly annoyed. 'What about me? I could have cemented the family, couldn't I, if I had made a special arrangement to marry Serena?'

'You!' My father's mouth fell open with surprise. 'But you're – well, there's nearly ten years between you. You're almost old enough to be her –' He groped for the word.

'Her uncle?'

'She *does* call you that sometimes,' cried Chiffon.

'But you're a serious type,' said Father. 'Greg's a playboy. A sportsman.'

'Does that make him a better husband?'

'No, no, of course not. But your work! You're married to the law.'

'I do intend to get married one day.'

'Of course you do,' said Chiffon, while Father added, 'Well anyway, Sirry Pasha has brought up his daughter to be a good Egyptian. She would never do anything her father disapproved of.'

'Of course not,' I agreed. 'I was only wondering how it all came about.'

Actually, I knew of course without being told. It was just one of those things.

In many ways Greg was more in the limelight than I was because he was the sportsman personified. We rarely quarrelled and I was never envious of him, but Father had no daughter to flatter him and to show off, and so perhaps he became inordinately proud of Greg's sporting achievements. He treated his youngest son with almost comical pride, as if nothing that Greg wanted or asked for was too good for him – a new cricket bat, a new tennis racquet, and finally the polo ponies he needed. At five feet eleven, with broad shoulders and a slim waist, a well-placed head and a modesty that went with any success, he was liked by all of us – and in return liked everyone.

I wouldn't for a moment suggest that Father exercised a serious preference for Greg over me. Far from it. Just that he treated me much more as an equal. I was the one he turned to for a game of chess, the one who read 'good' books (because, as it happened, I genuinely liked them). And Father was delighted when I got a first at Oxford. But if I was the one whose scholastic experience could be shown off Greg was the one whose brilliance in sport was exhibited almost daily at the Gezira Club, and about whom people talked. So it was easy for me to understand why the proposed wedding arrangements had been planted in the minds of two pairs of doting parents.

Serena explained it in her own very Egyptian way, with logic, and with a strong sense of filial duty. We all sometimes tended to forget that she was not British or French, but that behind those steady green eyes there was a brain moulded by centuries of Egyptian thinking.

'There were two reasons,' she said. 'The first was that as a dutiful daughter I was taught to obey my father who had chosen, subject to my approval, a suitable husband. My father is wise and loves me and since I was expected to marry that led to the second reason: why not agree to marry someone like Greg? I knew him – we had grown up together – and he is what you British call a "gentleman". At least I knew he would be fun, he'd make a good husband, and it would make my father happy.'

'But haven't you forgotten one emotion – Love?'

'But I do love Greg!'

'Of course you do. But it's a kind of taken-for-granted love. It lacks –'

'Passion?' Was she being ironic?

'It wasn't the word I was going to choose.'

'You see, Mark, Egyptian women aren't *meant* to be passionate. Happy, yes, if we're lucky. But for centuries men have regarded women as objects for *their* pleasure. Even Victorian wives regarded sex as disgusting. Egyptian men don't *want* their wives aroused sexually. That's why there's still so much circumcision in Egypt.'

'Honestly, Serena, you talk as though you're back in the Middle Ages –'

'But history in Egypt *is* still part of our everyday life –'

'Maybe, but you can't tell me that with those smouldering eyes of yours you don't feel – well, more than looking forward to a life of – just *acceptance*.'

'I'm not. I am happy as I am – I've had a wonderful childhood, and parents I love. Greg is every woman's idea of a modern Prince Charming. What more can a girl ask for?'

'Me!' I said laughingly.

'Ah!' The laughter left her eyes. 'That wasn't part of the "arrangement".'

3

Holt House was splendid. So was the Sirry mansion. So were the beautiful gardens. But in the hot season a breath of air, a whispered breeze, was more precious than a cold drink. And when the khamseen, the desert wind, blew, life in Cairo became almost unbearable. The hot sand swirling round the city gummed the eyes, reddening them with conjunctivitis; men in the streets covered their faces, looking like grey spectres, while the khamseen whistled through every crack. I once saw the sand literally blowing into the house through the front-door keyhole.

Luckily from time to time we could escape the heat, thanks to Sirry Pasha, whose ancestors had acquired an estate of two thousand acres. It was a beautiful spot called Ghezireh-en-Nasrani, the Island of Christians, a few miles north of Cairo, where the Nile divides into two, forming the vast triangular country known as the Delta, stretching from the city to the sea.

You could reach Nasrani by rail, by road or – by far the most romantic – by boat along the great river itself. And this we regularly did – in style, for Sirry Pasha had nursed an ambition to build a special pleasure-boat of his own since the days when he was studying at Oxford.

He had fallen in love with one of the Salter Brothers' sixty-foot pleasure-steamers that were built in Salter's own boat yard at Oxford, and on which I myself, when studying there, had taken the traditional trip along the Thames through Wallingford, Reading, Henley and Windsor to Kingston. Sirry Pasha had promptly had it copied in Alexandria, and named it *Kismet*.

In a strange way so many of our early memories centred on the trips on the *Kismet*, and Nasrani. It had always been a house of excitement since the first visit I could remember, when I was very small and we had arrived after dark. Servants with lanterns guided us from the landing stage along a couple of hundred yards of tree-lined pathway, the lights bobbing like fireflies until we reached the compound with its fruit gardens, and then the warm lights of the house itself.

Now, the weekend after Serena had made that enigmatic remark, 'That wasn't part of the arrangement,' both families were sailing again to Nasrani on the *Kismet*, with its saloons of plush mahogany and brass, and forward of the central funnel a striped awning beneath which drinks were served in frosted glasses.

Both house and boat were fundamental parts of Sirry Pasha's life, and I knew that in his heart he hated being a member of the 'palace clique'. It was a job he had never wanted but which had been thrust upon him: to resign would have been an unpardonable offence. Yet he was so rich that he could have spent the rest of his days pleasurably immersed in his history books.

'All week I look forward to these three hours on the *Kismet*,' he told me. He was drinking lime juice, Father champagne, while I sipped a scotch. 'The unhurried pleasure! Did you ever read Rupert Brooke's Grantchester reverie on the church clock standing still at ten to three? It might have been written on one of Salter's steamers.'

Of course the Delta wasn't all as calm as Rupert Brooke's Thames. The water traffic was ceaseless, for the Delta is criss-crossed by canals and river tributaries, reflecting the pale pastel shades of the flat countryside, the only vivid flashes of colour coming from the birds – flamingoes, pelicans or kingfishers – and the sails of small feluccas or perhaps a waterside mosque.

One day we were barely half an hour away from Nasrani when a great commotion thrashed in the water ahead of us, and Serena and I leaned over the rail to watch.

The river widened where an inlet had been cut in the bank to feed one of the hundreds of canals that irrigated the Delta area. A dozen or so feluccas were formed in a circle, with fellahîn standing in their prows beating the water with paddles of tightly woven palm-leaves. At the same time they skilfully manipulated their boats, drawing inwards towards each other. In this diminishing circle the fish were trapped, though they tried to escape by leaping in silvered arcs high into the air. Overhead, hordes of voracious sea-birds waited, eager to snatch them. With perfect timing the fishermen jumped over the sides of their feluccas, nets ready to scoop up the quarry they had so cunningly concentrated in so small a space. Within a few minutes their boats were piled with squirming, gasping fish.

'Poor things!' Serena said, and there was real sadness in her voice. 'There's no escape for them. They dodge the paddles only to be seized by the birds. Then they get netted and in the end finish up in the Cairo fish market. There's a terrible – what's the word? –'

'Inevitability?'

'That's it.'

We reached Nasrani just before dusk. It was a beautiful house, which by now we knew as well as our own. Surrounded by fruit – oranges, lemons, peaches, nectarines, melons – and by palms, it was built of pink-washed limestone in two storeys, with square windows and shutters to be closed against the khamseen. The house and fruit gardens made a compound surrounded by a wall with a gate, giving on to a courtyard and a well in the centre into which you could drop a stone that struck the water not with a plop but with an eerie sound like a faint cry. 'A water sprite, my boy,' Sirry Pasha had told me when I was very young, 'who objects to having stones dropped on its head.'

The main entrance was a splendid archway leading directly to what the locals always called the 'guest chamber' where

servants were always ready with welcoming coffee, cigarettes, or something stronger.

The room was filled with low couches, brightly coloured
cushions and, when the generator wasn't working and the
electricity faded away, the servants lit palm-oil lanterns of
coloured glass, especially round the *dekka*, a long, low bench
running along the two walls. The bench itself was made of
sun-dried mud and draped with colourful shawls and long, flat
bolsters of fustian, the rough material, half-cotton, half-flax,
which takes its name from the Cairo suburb where it is made.

It was a room of brass tables, with intricately patterned
wrought-iron legs, Persian and Isnik prayer-rugs scattered
over the palm-leaf matting that covered the floor, and mysterious niches in which books and ornamental Egyptian drinking
vessels were displayed, and where occasionally a lizard darted
across the wall.

It was very 'Egyptian', and Madame Sirry more than
once apologised for what she called 'all this bric-a-brac,
like junk we used to pick up at the Paris Flea Market'. But
Sirry felt that a country-house in Egypt should look like
one, not be a poor imitation of Western furniture, and I
think he was right. It did indeed look like a home, certainly
more homely than the Sirrys' town house, where Madame
Sirry had installed masses of French furniture, most of it
pretentious and uncomfortable, the sort of chairs you felt
you had to perch on.

The next day was cooler. Father and Sirry Pasha were
engrossed in a game of chess. Greg and Aly had – as
usual – gone shooting in the scrub beyond the estate.

Serena had gone painting – and I stayed in one of the
smaller sitting rooms for most of the morning, wrestling
with a brief I had to study before my return to Cairo. Through
the square window facing on to the cotton plantation I could
see Serena. Suddenly she packed up her folding-easel and
paints and prepared to walk the quarter-mile back to the
house. I put down my brief and walked out to meet her.

'Any good?' I asked when I reached her.

'Awful!' She shook her head angrily. 'I wiped all the paint
off with turps so that I could use the canvas again. Baptise

will probably be pleased. I think he likes me to do some bad paintings when I paint without him.'

On our way back to the house, walking through the estate, we watched the fellahîn at work, supervised by the *ghuffrah*, one of the overseers responsible to both Sirry Pasha and the local sheik who collected the taxes. Serena waved to a woman in white who was making her way towards the house.

'Fathia!' she cried.

The woman salaamed, after which Serena embraced her and I shook hands, for Fathia was someone very special. She had been wet nurse to both Serena and Aly, and her two children had stayed on the estate ever since. 'My daughter is nineteen now,' Fathia said proudly. It seemed centuries ago since the riots started and she had run away in the garden and we had hidden in the cathedral tree.

'I see you're still wearing the gold earring which Mama gave you to celebrate my first tooth.'

When Fathia walked on and Serena and I were making our way slowly along the path leading to the 'fruit courtyard' I said, 'We always seem to be getting the past and the present mixed up. Ever since that horrible day. Even before.'

'Before the riots?'

'Yes. It was seeing Fathia just now that made me remember watching Fathia feeding you – just as though it was yesterday. I must have been nine, I suppose. She opened up her blouse from beneath and there was one of her huge breasts – and you were so hungry you could hardly wait. I was fascinated.'

'You ought to be ashamed of yourself!' She was laughing. 'Good job your mother didn't see you. Or my mother.'

'I took good care not to be found out.'

'So you were involved in my life from the very beginning. While I was being fed, then as my protector – that's the word Mama uses – and after that the typhoid. And then –'

As so often happened, we were both thinking of the same incident.

'I mean when I was thirteen,' she said, almost shyly. 'I was so frightened.'

I nodded. 'And I was all of an experienced twenty-two.'

★

It *was* so long ago – and yet, looking back now to those few moments of tenderness, I knew that they, in their own manner, had drawn us as closely together as on the day of the riots.

That had been at Nasrani, too. She had come into the living room where I was alone, and she looked as though she was going to faint, a slip of a girl as white as a sheet. She had been crying, I could see that, and she whispered urgently, '*Please* help me, Mark. Follow me into the pavilion. *Now!* We can be alone there.'

I hadn't the faintest idea why she was so upset, but I knew this was no moment for the sort of casual joke Greg might have made.

The pavilion, as it was called, was a summer-house in a glade beyond the orchards.

'What's the trouble?' I asked.

Without warning she burst into loud, uncontrollable sobs, and flung herself into my arms.

'Serena!' I let her head rest on my shoulder as the sobs racked her. 'What is it? What's the matter?'

'Oh Mark!' She lifted tear-stained eyes to mine. 'I'm going to die. I know it. I'm ill – and you're the only one I can talk to.'

'What on earth do you mean? You're not going to die. Why should you suddenly think so? Has your mother sent for the doctor?'

'No, no.' She looked almost frightened. 'I'm so ashamed. I've caught some terrible illness – I've read about venereal disease – I've told nobody.'

'But what is this illness? You can't catch VD, as you call it, unless –'

'I thought I'd get better – and then, when I was cured it all started up again. And I came to you. I always think of you first when I need help.'

'But what's the *matter* – what are the symptoms?'

'I thought I'd been cured,' she repeated. 'And then it all started again. Today after a month. I'm bleeding to death. And if it's VD Mama will never forgive me. I managed to pinch some hand towels which I threw away but –'

47

It had never entered my head that her mother hadn't warned her.

Holding her shoulders so that she faced me, I took out a handkerchief, wiped the tears from her face, and said gravely, 'Darling Serena. Don't worry. I know just what's the matter. You're not going to die. You might have a bit of a tummy ache, but you're not even ill.'

'I'm bleeding!' she cried.

'It's perfectly natural, what's happened to you. It happens to every girl. It means that you've grown up. It's called –' I was doubtful if she knew the word, but I couldn't think of any other way of explaining it – 'it's called menstruation. Once a month all women bleed a little. Didn't anybody tell you – prepare you? Your mother?'

She shook her head miserably, and I couldn't help saying savagely, 'It's a disgrace, not telling your own daughter.' Not for the first time I wondered whether Madame Sirry was more occupied with her social life than with her children.

'But why? What's it all about?'

I tried to reassure her, knowing that she always believed anything I told her. I explained as simply as I could how all women had to live with the monthly cycle of 'the curse', as many called it; and how it would stop when she was going to have a baby. She knew so little that I had even to tell her that she could go to the chemist's and buy some special pads.

While I felt all too suited to my role of Serena's uncle Greg continued in his role of dashing husband-to-be. He was not only the good-looking sportsman, he was a born winner. When he swam at the Gezira pool, always challenging anyone to beat him, even Serena had once said, 'My future husband really does have a magnificent figure,' and the girl she was talking to said, 'I'll have him if you get bored. He positively *glows* with health.' He did, shaking his head with its crinkly hair – like my father's – after a swim, the blue eyes always laughing.

He treated Serena with good-humoured affection, perhaps one of the secrets of their obvious happiness, the ability to laugh as well as be serious. And Greg was never jealous. That was remarkable, really, the way in which, back in Cairo, he allowed a beautiful girl to dance all night with other men while he was attending one of his innumerable bachelor 'polo dinners'. He never betrayed the slightest suspicion when someone took her out. A young American I vaguely knew called Jim Stevenson – who seemed quite pleasant – often escorted her, and I asked Greg once if he wasn't worried.

'Stevenson? If I can't trust her with him *before* we're married,' Greg laughed, 'it's a poor bloody look-out for the future.'

Everyone, of course, knew that Serena was 'Greg's girl', and that, I suppose, made it impossible for our friends to try and split them up or – to use our word of those days – to 'poach'. On the other hand, Serena, without realising what she was doing, unwittingly tempted them by instinctively regarding any man to whom she was talking with such rapt attention that he became fascinated by her. That was the Egyptian in her, that a woman's 'duty' was always to please a man.

I noticed that rapt attention a few days later when Greg reached the finals of the Gezira Club tennis tournament.

Greg had an instinct for tennis, as with all ball games; he played a serve and volley game, advancing to attack his opponent with the dedication of a man who *had* to win.

It was a beautiful warm evening, the stands behind the show court surrounded by the heliotrope of jacaranda trees, and Greg, as he was changing ends in the third and final set, gave Serena a 'thumbs up' sign, as though to promise her success.

The struggle, in fact, lasted nearly two hours. Both players were fairly equal, but Greg possessed one advantage. He *refused* to be beaten. He ran back to retrieve the deepest lob; he ran forward to scoop up the gentlest drop-shot; he lunged sideways for the almost impossible volley. In the end he won by 6–3, 4–6, 6–4.

'What a player!' cried Serena as the crowd gathered and clapped for the presentation of the President's Cup. 'No

wonder all my girlfriends are filled with hero-worship for
him.'

'And you?' I asked.

'Of course. He's our local hero. And he's so dashing.'

Smiling, she added, 'I'm so proud of him when he wins.
And he's so modest with it all.'

One of our old friends, Teddy Pollock, had been watching
the match with us. As Serena waved goodbye and, a possessive arm tucked into Greg's, made for the car, Teddy and I
decided to go for a drink. Odd, I thought; I felt rather irritated
by her display of hero-worship. And yet, why not?

Teddy Pollock had, like Stevenson, squired Serena several
times. As we drove towards Ibrahim Pasha Street he sighed
and said, 'There, but for the grace of God – or rather, the
grace of Greg – go I! Yes, to the altar if she were free. I don't
know why the hell the two of them don't get married, and
put all the competition out of our misery.'

Teddy was a playboy. He had made it official, actually
putting 'playboy' under 'occupation' on his passport, and he
was doing everything he could to live up to the title. He
attended every party, every dance, every race meeting, even
every yacht race when the season moved to Alexandria.
Yet he was utterly unspoiled, a charming man, with lively,
good-humoured eyes.

'You'd really like to marry Serena?' We were at
Shepheard's, on the balcony facing Ibrahim Pasha Street, a
perfect place for pre-dinner drinks, the street below overflowing with hawkers touting everything from camel saddles and
leather bags to 'priceless' scarabs and blue beads to guard
against the evil eye.

'Like a shot,' he replied frankly. 'She's perfect. Those green
eyes!'

I agreed. To me, her eyes, with their long lashes, always
held a laugh in them – a laugh mingled with tenderness.

Teddy was more poetic. He sighed, 'It makes you catch
your breath just to look into them. Even so, I'm glad I *can't*
marry her. Wouldn't work, old man.'

'Wouldn't work?' I must have looked astonished.

Teddy gave his slow smile. 'Beneath that beautiful exterior there beats a warm and generous heart –'

'Well, then . . .'

'And round that warm and generous heart, a tiny slice of ancient Egypt. The girl knows what is expected of her from life.'

'You mean Greg?'

'I suppose so. It's something they've grown up with. Mind you, with those two marriage *will* work.'

'Ah! So it's your fault?'

'Absolutely, old boy. I'm the culprit. Because if I ever do get married – which God forbid – it will be because I've fallen hopelessly in love, become insanely jealous. That's how I *could* have felt about Serena if Greg hadn't been around.'

'But they're in love.'

'Are you sure?'

'Well, as you just said they're an ideal couple.'

'Honestly, Mark,' he said, calling for a second round of drinks, 'you *are* a bit naive. You don't have to be hopelessly in love to be happily married.'

'You bloody cynic.' I used the words I had said to Serena.

'Not at all. Think about it. Ask yourself one question: which does Greg love most – *really* love most – his Serena or his polo?'

'You can't compare the two. It's like asking a kid which he loves most, his mother or his bicycle?'

'You're right. But I'm right too – you'll see. And don't get me wrong: Serena's in love in her own way. She'll make Greg a wonderful wife. But I have a feeling that she'll always keep a tiny fragment of her Egyptian heart – say ten per cent – in reserve.'

'And this mysterious other ten per cent? Any idea who that'll belong to?'

'For some secret love.' He gave me what I can only describe as an odd look as he lit up a Celtique. 'You'll have to think about that too.'

As he blew out smoke over my head, I said almost defensively, harshly, 'Why the hell do you smoke those filthy cigarettes? They taste like shit.'

French cigarettes had always been popular in Egypt, and Teddy blew out another long stream of smoke before smiling slowly.

'Life is full of shit,' he sighed.

What an odd remark of Teddy's! And how he had, by a look, by the cadence of his voice, underlined it! In those years before Greg and Serena married I had never thought of myself as more than – well, I suppose I *was* Serena's best friend: but even if I hadn't yet fallen in love with anyone I had a generous assortment of girlfriends.

Was Teddy insinuating that secretly I was in love with Serena? Absurd! I stayed on for another drink after Teddy had gone, mulling over his last remark – 'Think about that too.'

Why? I had never felt even the remotest twinge of envy or jealousy. Our relationship was close because we were so often thrown on each other's resources. Serena and I both shared a passion for good books, whereas Greg liked the latest Edgar Wallace. I enjoyed her love for painting because – without being an expert – I loved good pictures, whereas Greg turned to *Punch* for the latest cartoons. But we never met in secret, certainly not with desire. And anyway Greg was always dashing around, here, there and everywhere, and Serena used our house almost as her own, always had done. After all, we were 'the kids next door'. She came in unbidden if she saw me walking in the grounds. It had happened like that all our lives. Often we talked, first in the garden, later inside with the family, perhaps over our drinks if the evening chilled, while Greg was still propping up the bar at the Gezira Club with the rest of his polo team or his foursome at tennis.

It was also true that Serena used to tease me in private about what she called 'your secret love-life'. Cairo thrived on gossip; no sheets in a strange bedroom could remain unruffled without someone finding out – and telling. So when we walked in the garden Serena often gave me a sisterly hug and said, 'Go on – tell.'

'Tell what?' I would say, knowing perfectly well.

'You *know*. Sally Porter. Isn't she the latest one? Everyone knows you went to bed with her the night before last. It's true, isn't it? Come on – what was she like?'

And I would tell her.

Dusk was falling over Shepheard's balcony, but I ordered a fourth drink, thinking, why *were* we so drawn together, she so much younger, Greg so much more fun? Perhaps because we also shared another common gift – an uncanny unsought-for ability to read each other's minds. From time to time, all other thoughts blank, people talking across a crowded room, her eyes would meet mine and I would know her mind exactly. Can you read people in their faces if you know them intimately? Her half-smile, her green eyes, would confirm our shared thoughts, even from a distance.

I was also the only man (at least I presume I was) who realised that sweet seventeen-year-old Serena and Greg had sneaked into bed together long before they married. I was dancing with Mother – all flounces and exuberance – at the club that night, when I saw Greg and Serena, each dancing with other partners, exchange glances which told me in a flash they were lovers. The look between the two of them – especially the look in Serena's eyes – was as plain as if she had shouted the news aloud. At that moment she caught my eyes and smiled conspiratorially. From then on I was privy to a secret which had never needed words. That *was* the only time I experienced a sudden pang of jealousy, for I could visualise them in bed naked. It was almost like a moment of physical pain, as quickly ended as the look between us.

You might imagine that all we thought of in those days was having fun. But there was another side to life. My work, which I loved, led me to other faces of Egypt. Often I came into contact with venal politicians, or the fellahîn, starving under rapacious landlords. Murder, poverty, rape – and politics.

Between our years of growing up, Egyptian demands for independence, minor skirmishes, assassinations, reprisals – all pushed history along like the Nile itself: sometimes hardly noticed, at other times lashing it like floods. The strange adventures which Serena and I had shared just after the Great War had now been relegated in memory to a curious dream. But I remembered Aly, little more than a boy, proudly waving a flag when in 1922 Egypt was granted independence (with a few strings attached, such as British control of the army). Still, it *was* independence. The Khedive, who had become a sultan in 1914, now became a king – King Fuad, a despot whose new constitution gave him power to elect two-fifths of the senate, to dissolve parliament, to order elections – and to seize – in fact, to steal – land from down-trodden peasants or rich landlords to make him the richest man in Egypt; until he lost it all.

Fuad was not so lucky in his son, the young Prince Farouk. He jeered at the young boy's pale hairless skin, and once told Sirry Pasha, 'I have been given an effeminate son as the future king of Egypt. It is a curse upon me, a disgrace to our manhood.' One of the family doctors told Sirry privately that unless Fuad was very careful his attitude might cause eventual impotence in Farouk.

Two years later, the British head of the Egyptian army, Sir Lee Stack, was assassinated. Once again the British, fearful of losing control of the Canal, clamped down. Egyptian independence was 'down-graded', existing only in name, a sort of grace-and-favour throne, the court and the cabinet dangled like puppets by Whitehall.

Inevitably, over the years, as old sores were reopened, the cries of *'Istiklal el Tam!'* grew more vociferous, sometimes shouted in English outside British dwellings, 'Unconditional Independence!'

By the turn of 1935 a series of more serious demonstrations started, jamming the streets. More and more demonstrators, often students, flooded Cairo, and in November 1935, with passions inflamed by Ramadan, the obligatory month of Moslem fasting during daylight, I began to realise that there might be serious trouble.

I was not afraid. Neither was my father. What worried me

was a purely selfish problem. Teddy Pollock had invited me to a 'desert party' – an all-night affair, with an assortment of girls. We planned to start with dancing and continue with supper at the Step Pyramid at Sakkara, ending with breakfast in Teddy's flat. But the Nile Delta was in full flood.

'Will it be safe?' I asked. 'I wouldn't want your harem to get any underclothes wet.' The question was facetious, but with a grain of truth behind it, for during the autumn the Nile, vying with the Amazon as the longest river in the world, flooded dangerously after the monsoons hit against the mountains of Ethiopia, causing torrents of water to race across half a continent before spilling out on the coast of Africa. Long before that the Nile in the Delta had risen by up to seventeen feet, engulfing vast areas of land.

'You know darned well the Step Pyramid is above flood level,' said Pollock, smiling. 'You've been there often enough – and at night.'

I did know, of course. I don't really know why I asked the question; maybe because I wanted to ask another one, much more important.

'And what about the political situation? Will that be safe? Father says the students are heading for a showdown.'

'*Maalish*. Don't worry.' Teddy's voice was as laconic as his slow smile. 'Do you really think I'm going to let a bunch of hash-smoking students interfere with our fun?'

4

On a Monday morning in November 1935, Sirry Pasha phoned to invite me round for a quick evening drink. 'No other guests,' he said. Idly, I wondered what he wanted. It was unusual for Sirry to ask me round alone.

By chance his whole family was assembled when I arrived. Madame Sirry, as she was always called because of her French birth, was as elegant as usual. She must have been astonishingly beautiful when young, and it was easy to see how Serena was becoming the image of her mother; but Madame Sirry also possessed that chic which seems to come as second nature to so many French. Even when dressed in an old pullover and skirt she managed to look the most elegant woman in a room. Aly was there, his usual sulky self, and when Sirry mentioned that Teddy Pollock had told him several of us were going to hold a midnight picnic at the Sakkara Step Pyramid the following evening Aly interrupted. 'Better get home early before the riots. You must have read what that doddering old fool Samuel Hoare, the British Foreign Secretary, said on Saturday night.'

I could sympathise with Aly for being angry at the hamfisted way the British had acted. In London on the Saturday – that would be 9 November – Sir Samuel Hoare had made a speech at the Lord Mayor's Banquet in the Guildhall, in which he had told Egypt more or less bluntly that Britain did not think the time was yet ripe for Egyptian independence.

'I must say' – even Sirry Pasha was upset – 'that it's there in black and white. We've got a transcript of the speech. Let me read this bit to you.'

He adjusted his glasses. Was this the reason, I wondered, that he had asked me to call? Clearing his throat, Sirry Pasha read out the Foreign Secretary's words:

' "The allegations that we oppose the return in Egypt of a constitutional regime suited to the special requirements are untrue. With our traditions we could not do such a thing. However, we have advised against the re-enactment of the constitutions of 1923 and 1930, since the one was proved unworkable and the other was universally unpopular. History and geography have linked our fortunes. As friends and associates we must deal frankly with each other." '

'It's disgraceful.' I apologised for the sickly, oily words used to mask Britain's belief that Egypt was incapable of governing itself.

'It's our bloody country!' Aly almost shouted.

'Mind your language!' said Sirry sternly as Aly stalked

from the room. However outraged Sirry might feel, he was a great stickler for good manners.

'I do understand Aly's feelings,' he sighed. 'But he's so – so *vulgar*. I don't know what's come over him.'

'Nothing to worry about,' I said cheerfully.

'*Il est jeune*,' added Madame Sirry.

I almost retorted that you don't have to be *jeune* to be jejune, but I kept my mouth shut, because all Egyptians did feel very strongly that their independence had too many strings attached to it – such as the continued presence of British troops – yet the British felt equally strongly about the importance of guarding their lifeline to India – the Suez Canal – which could only be achieved by keeping British troops on Egyptian soil. And how much more vital the Canal was now, with the gloomy international situation: Hitler repudiating the military clauses of the Versailles Treaty, taking over the Saar, while even in poor Czechoslovakia the hated Nazis had somehow been elected the country's strongest party.

'And that,' I was really thinking aloud, 'inevitably means a German-Czech pact of mutual assistance soon, polite words for an eventual German merger, in itself a polite term for a takeover.'

'Oh, I know,' Sirry sighed again. The butler in his long green galabiya offered me another whisky. 'And France –?' He shrugged his shoulders.

'Monsieur Hoare is going to meet Monsieur Laval. Could they do anything?' asked Madame Sirry.

'One's as bad as the other,' I said.

'But if only,' said Sirry, 'the British would put more trust in the Egyptians. I know that with Mussolini on the rampage in Africa the Canal is vital, but our own army – surely we could guard it?'

It wasn't for me to say that the British felt they could on no account trust the Egyptian army. It wasn't a question of doubting their bravery. It was their corruption which made them untrustworthy. Everyone knew the story of the 'paper battalion' which existed only on paper, with highly placed officials collecting pay and rations for non-existent soldiers.

'But don't let's talk politics,' I said, adding with a laugh, 'Let's leave that to Aly and his friends. And Hoare.'

'Agreed! Especially as I've a favour to ask that has nothing to do with politics. Refuse immediately if it's inconvenient. It's not important enough to make a fuss about.'

'Anything I can do . . .' I murmured politely – and meant it.

'You remember Theo Davidson who dined with us the other evening? The American businessman who spends a lot of time in Paris running his import-export business?'

'Of course.' I remembered Davidson well, a tall angular man with a lantern jaw which signalled determination – and perhaps intolerance. My first thought, when we were introduced, had been that he could easily be cast as a fiery pastor threatening his flock with the damnation of hell if they didn't heed·his words. And I wasn't far wrong, excepting for the choice of religion, for he turned out to be a fervent Catholic who instinctively proselytised. Not too blatant to be offensive, but persistent enough to be boring. I didn't like him very much.

As Sirry Pasha started to ask me for the 'favour' I remembered that at our dinner Davidson had mentioned a daughter, saying, 'She's a wonderful girl, and a devout Catholic, like all our family.'

Davidson might have built up a highly successful business, but his daughter sounded a penance.

'Well –' Sirry hesitated. 'Davidson is a widower, and he has a daughter of twenty-one or twenty-two – about the same age as Aly – and the poor thing hasn't seen anything of Egypt apart from museums. So, when Teddy told me about your midnight picnic – well, I thought that if you don't have a partner you might give the girl the sort of treat she would never get on her own. Davidson and his daughter are returning to Paris in a matter of days.'

'It's not a question of partners,' I said. 'In fact I'm going with Greg to meet Teddy and some girls he's managed to rope in. I've only the vaguest idea who they are.'

'I wouldn't have worried you – I'm sorry now to have brought the matter up – but Teddy Pollock told me they're a girl short – and when I heard you were going –'

'What my husband means, *cher ami*,' said Madame Sirry sweetly, 'is that you're a young and handsome escort, and this poor *jeune fille* – a pretty girl, too – is all alone in beautiful Cairo.'

'If I can help –'

'The trouble is,' confessed Sirry, 'is that Serena was dying to go, and of course I said she was too young –'

'She's very envious,' said Madame Sirry, 'because she knows about your moonlight expedition, and that Greg is going. And two girls from *les pêcheurs* . . .' This was Madame Sirry's French way of describing the 'fishing fleet', the term used for British girls coming to Cairo to find husbands.

I had to admit that for a young girl visiting Egypt for perhaps the only time in her life we were offering her a party she would never forget.

'Oh yes, I know all about it,' Madame Sirry smiled. 'Trust Teddy to do everything in style. I get all the gossip from Serena.'

It *was* going to be a good party, starting with dinner and dancing at the Gezira, then by car to the pyramids, where we would get some horses and ride out to the romantic Step Pyramid at Sakkara. Teddy was sending servants ahead to provide the food and erect a *sewan*, an Egyptian tent consisting of hundreds of brightly coloured squares of quilted cloth sewn together, then hung in traditional desert fashion over a framework of poles. After supper, we'd ride back, change at the Mena House, with perhaps a swim there, then home to bed.

'Sounds exhausting,' said Sirry. 'When?'

'When what?'

'Bed!'

'Oh!' I laughed. 'When we can't keep awake any longer. I'll take her along – if you promise she really is pretty.'

'I promise you,' said Madame Sirry. *'Une belle plante.'*

'Called?'

'Parmi,' said Sirry. 'Has been ever since she was a baby.'

'What an odd name.'

'Apparently,' Madame Sirry explained, 'Americans are always using a regrettable phrase I often hear – "Pardon me". And as a baby she couldn't pronounce it properly, and kept saying "Parmi" until it became her nickname.'

Which was how 'Pardon me' came to be invited to Sakkara.

When I reached Shepheard's I was about to phone through to the girl's room when I saw Theo Davidson in the lobby.

'Parmi won't be down for ten minutes. Let me buy you a drink,' he said.

We sat at the bar and I had the uncomfortable feeling that he wanted to sound me out.

'Parmi isn't used to the high life you people go for in Cairo,' he said. 'My God! Mr Sirry's house! That's something, isn't it? Beats Hollywood every day. I'm a hard-nosed businessman who makes a good living, but I don't mind telling you I prefer simplicity to all this luxury. Once in a while, but –'

'You don't have to worry about your daughter,' I said.

'I hope not. She's only twenty-one, she's the only daughter I've got and – well, she's a devout Roman Catholic. She doesn't drink. Maybe you could give her the odd glass of white wine, but I expect you to keep an eye on her. Will you?'

'It's Ramadan,' I said lightly.

He looked puzzled. 'That some kind of drink?'

I said nothing. Better let him think it was an Arab version of lemonade.

'Apart from anything else,' I added, 'the party – eight of us – will include a married couple of British diplomats – not exactly chaperones, but still –' I shrugged my shoulders.

'Diplomats?' He sounded relieved.

'And you know that the picnic is in a specially erected tent – only one big place for supper? With servants going ahead to prepare the food and so on?'

'You've taken a load off my mind, Mark,' he said. 'I don't want to be a spoilsport, and I won't deny that our Parmi has spent most of her time in museums. She likes that kind of thing. Then Mr Sirry suggested the party. It's very kind of

60

you to take pity on a young lady you've never met. I'm sure she'll enjoy herself.'

At that moment Miss Davidson walked into the bar, and I nearly fell off my stool. Dull and dreary she might be, but beauty and brains don't always go together, and this girl was stunningly pretty, with large and beautiful blue eyes set wide apart, below a thatch of unruly blonde hair and the general impression of bouncing good health that one always associates with California, oranges, sunshine, open air. Madame Sirry had been as good as her word. And there was something else. It's hard to explain after a first impression, but though Parmi was very quiet, modest and well-mannered, I could sense a touch of suppressed mischief lurking behind that innocent face. She had a pretty little nose, and a mouth that looked as though she was trying desperately to hide a smile of excitement. With her thick mop of tousled blonde hair, she had a *gamine*, zany look, as though she would without warning suck her thumb and cast down her eyes.

'It's very kind of you to include me in your party, Mr Holt,' she said demurely.

'Call me Mark,' I smiled. 'You'll have to before the end of the evening, so we might as well start now.'

'Have a good time, you young people,' smiled her father. 'What time you hope to be home?' He turned to me.

Parmi looked at me for an answer. I watched her father's face carefully because I didn't see why I shouldn't tease him. 'I'll deliver her safe and sound around seven or eight tomorrow morning,' I said brightly.

'Tomorrow *morning*!' He almost exploded. 'She's never been out *that* late, even at the college ball. What are you going to *do* all night?'

'You see, Mr Davidson' – I spoke apologetically – 'it's what we call a desert party, and it's not *my* party. And at this time of the year the dawn over the Nile – well, that's the climax of the whole thing. After dancing at Gezira we're going to Mena House and then it's an hour's ride across the desert to the Step Pyramid. You've got your riding things?' I asked Parmi.

She pointed mutely to a small overnight bag.

'We'll have our tent, servants, supper by moonlight. Then, all in this large tent, there'll be lots of cushions and those of us who feel sleepy – well, they can rest.' I added quickly, 'In the big tent, all together. The servants will be on hand, so no – what do you call it in America? – no hanky-panky. Then we'll all ride back, have a swim at dawn at the Mena House – we've booked one bedroom for the girls to change in, another for the men – and back to Teddy Pollock's flat near Garden City for breakfast.'

'Seems a wild way to hold a party,' Theo Davidson said, stifling his doubts about his daughter. 'Well, honey, I trust you, and you, Mark.'

'Of course you can trust me,' said Parmi. 'You know me better than that.'

I didn't have to wait long for the next surprise. We were soon on our way, and she looked excited as I steered the car past parked vehicles in the drive of Shepheard's, turned left along the swollen river, then right across the Bulac Bridge.

At this moment, sinking back in the seat with a happy smile, she asked, 'Do they serve champagne at your parties?'

'White wine, you mean?' I teased.

'I hate it,' she said. 'Every time I can get out of the house I go for champagne.'

'I think we might manage some – just for you,' I said gravely.

Still quite innocently, she put a hand in my free hand, squeezed it, and said, 'I'll never be able to thank you. All these museums – do you know I haven't eaten one single meal outside of the hotel because Pa says the food is contaminated?'

'Nonsense!' I cried.

Guests had to be signed in at the Gezira, and as I led Parmi through the main entrance, flanked by two separate terraces, I pointed out the terrace on the left. 'It's reserved for ladies only,' I said. 'In case you don't like men.'

'Does anyone ever use it?' She looked astonished.

The guest book was kept on a table to the left of the main entrance lounge, and after I had signed her in I said, 'The others will be waiting, but I just want to show you something.'

It was an unwritten rule that guests visiting Gezira on buffet nights for the first time were always taken to see the 'set pieces' on the dining room tables before hungry diners ruined the visual culinary masterpieces.

Parmi was amazed by the display. There was everything from asparagus to pheasants which had, after cooking, been reconstructed – even to the main feathers – so that the unfortunate birds looked as though they had just been shot in the stubble of an English field. An ox-tongue protruded from the mouth of an 'oxhead' made of pâté. A centre-piece represented a felucca, even the sail constructed of cake, the rigging of spun sugar. Everything had to be eaten – either by the members and their guests or, at the end of the evening, by the Nubian servants, for it was a rule that the Gezira Club never offered yesterday's food.

'And none of it contaminated?' Parmi smiled.

'Not a bit of it. But just in case, let's go to our table and have a quick dose of medicine.'

'Meaning champagne?'

'I see you've picked up the local jargon.'

The evening really got off to a good start after one interlude that I wouldn't have missed for all the champagne in Cairo. Almost at the door of the room where everyone met for drinks, Parmi asked to go to the 'powder room'. I showed her where it was, pointed where I would be and said, 'I'll go in ahead to make sure of the table.'

Greg and Teddy were already drinking.

'I hear you've been landed with a blind date,' said Teddy.

I shrugged. 'My good turn for the evening.'

Greg leaned over to me. 'You know that old man Sirry tried to get me to look after the wallflower? But I got out of it – said Serena wouldn't like it.'

'Never mind,' said Teddy. 'We'll take it in turns to look after you.'

At that moment an apparition stood framed in the doorway. There was an almost audible gasp.

'Your blind date?' asked Greg teasingly.

'My blind date,' I said, and as I went to the door to lead

Parmi in, I whispered urgently, 'Just for fun, kiss me gently, just to make those bastards jealous.'

Parmi, as I was soon to discover, did nothing by halves.

'There you are, darling,' she cried and, putting her arms around my neck, stood on tiptoe and kissed me.

The long and short of it is that Parmi was the success of the evening. She was totally uninhibited, an amusing angel with come-hither eyes. All the men vied with each other to attract her attention. She loved the food, she loved the champagne (but didn't get drunk). At the buffet supper she loved everything.

'This I like!' she said as she tasted her first *kofta*, the minced-meat patties so soft you could eat them with a fork. 'Beats burgers out of this world.'

Because the open dining terrace was surrounded by the polo fields and golf course, you had the impression that you were dining in the heart of the country, instead of being a stone's throw from the dust of Cairo.

The others had arrived and I introduced Parmi – Miss Davidson – to the young diplomatic couple, Mr and Mrs Jones; then the two friends of Greg and Teddy, Angela Gray and Dodie Summers, the 'fishing fleet' girls, good sorts, straight from Roedean and pictures in *Tatler,* both agreeable, well-mannered, reasonably pretty, both looking for husbands but willing to play around while waiting, both – or was this my imagination? – a little crestfallen at the stunning competition I had brought along.

'Ah, I see the champagne's already flowing,' I said as the steward handed us glasses.

'Do you tango?' Greg asked Parmi.

'Or fox-trot?' asked Teddy with that slow smile of his. 'Greg's a terrible dancer. Feet like an elephant's. Wouldn't trust him an inch.'

'Patience!' I cried. 'I'm going to dance with Miss Davidson before I let either of you rogues touch her.'

As we danced I said, 'Your father is very strict – and very religious.'

'He *is* strict,' she sighed. 'I guess I've had religion drilled into me since I could first listen, and I *am* religious. It's second

64

nature now. I like going to Mass regularly and I feel empty
if I miss it. I believe in confession, no abortion, no divorce
and so on. I think our faith makes for happier lives. But even
so, you can be a true believer and still have a lot of fun. It's
one thing to remain faithful to a husband, but a single girl –'
She smiled. 'Well, the Pope didn't say that every unmarried
girl is perfect. Though in the end we all have to pay for our
sins.'

We left the Gezira about one o'clock, setting off in three cars
for Giza and the pyramids where we planned to change into
clothes more suitable for riding across the desert.

'Tell me, Mark,' Parmi asked, 'do you always live at this
pace – dancing, riding, supper in the desert then, according
to your promise, a swim before breakfast?'

'Me? Once every couple of months maybe. I have to work
for a living. Teddy? All the time. When we get back to his
flat, ask to see his passport.'

'For why?'

'You know how you have to fill in your occupation in a
passport?'

She nodded.

'His might amuse you. Under "occupation" he's written
the word "playboy". And it's true. It's an honest description
of a man who works just as hard as I do – at playing. He's a
first-class tennis player – like my brother Greg. He plays
excellent polo – though Greg is better. He's driven racing
cars at Brooklands, and can beat anyone at backgammon or
bridge. He's so darned busy playing that he just doesn't have
time to work for a living – in the sense that I work.'

'You like your work?' By now we were driving towards
Mena House.

'Love it. I don't do much in the way of court work – you
know, appearing in front of a judge and saving some poor
character from murder. But I'm involved in a hell of a lot of
litigation. I enjoy pitting my brains – or knowledge, if you
prefer –'

'And Greg?'

'He's only got one dream. To join the army.'

'Should be easy.'

'He's choosy. Greg's idea of getting a commission is not so much to fight – unless there's a war, of course, that's different – but to play polo. So he's been trying to get into one of the crack cavalry regiments. And that *is* difficult.'

'I wish him luck.'

'He'll do all right.' I looked at her. 'Are you enjoying yourself?'

'Just great. Pa would have a fit if he knew what a lot of wild boys and girls you were.'

'We're not wild,' I protested. 'This is in a way a special party for Teddy. God knows what excuse he's got, but I don't do this all the time.'

Then for a moment she didn't look so zany as usual, but said something that surprised me.

'Back home people think differently. I know you all work as hard as you play, but I'm sure when I return to America and tell them about this wonderful night – the American boys'll all think you're decadent.'

'Don't worry.' I swerved past a cart drawn by a camel and loaded with melons. 'We can take care of ourselves.'

'It's just like a western movie.' Parmi reined in her horse, and slapped its wet skin affectionately. We had just caught sight for the first time of the Sakkara Step Pyramid outlined by the moon.

'Or more like Rudolph Valentino in *The Sheik*,' said Greg, who had trotted to her side.

'It's so breathlessly beautiful. I never thought it would be like this.'

Parmi was not the only one to gasp with astonishment at the beauty of Egypt, though we – our family, our friends – tended to take it for granted. But visitors like Parmi had to adjust. Most had seen life through English eyes – apple orchards and hopfields and Cotswold cottages – so that the first sight of Egypt's brown beauty, the still Nile, the sheer size of the country's relics left them in a state of shock.

'The pyramids by moonlight.' Teddy Pollock looked ahead. 'Just like a travel poster. Only this one is real.'

'I *have* been to the Sphinx and the pyramids at Giza.'

'Nouveau riche!' cried Teddy. 'Sakkara was built around 3,000 BC, give or take the odd century. That makes it three dynasties older than Cheops. It's smaller, of course. After all, Cheops covers thirteen acres. Yes, thirteen. Did you know that when Napoleon, who had a mathematical brain, first saw the pyramids he worked out that the cubic content of Cheops would be enough to build a ten-foot high wall round the whole of France?'

The Step Pyramid was surrounded by hundreds of smaller tombs like a stone orchard, while dotted in-between were groves of date-palms, the clusters of dates in the moonlight like swarms of bees against the palm-fronds.

'It is smaller, you're right,' agreed Parmi. 'But it's also a different shape.'

'Teddy'll tell you all about it,' said Greg. 'He's been there with so many beautiful girls he's learned the description by heart.'

'You embarrass me,' said a pleased Teddy. 'But if you *insist*. The Step Pyramid was designed by a man with a wonderful name – Imhotep, who was the grand vizier to King Zoser, second king of the third dynasty. In those days they hadn't learned how to construct tombs like the Cheops. When they built the tombs in those days, they consisted of mastabas – no, it's not a rude word.' Teddy chuckled. 'A mastabas is a large stone rectangle. And when Zoser complained that he wanted a more imposing memorial Imhotep had the bright idea of sticking six mastabas in diminishing size, one on top of each other. So it became the Step Pyramid.'

'But why here, in the midst of nowhere?' asked Parmi.

'It used to be *somewhere*.' Teddy gave his slow smile. 'This used to be Memphis, at one time the capital of Egypt. Today it may be nothing more than ruins and mounds of mud, but in its day Memphis was one of the greatest cities of the ancient world.'

'Someone once said that the soil after the floods is the colour of a plum pudding. Do you have plum puddings in America?' asked Greg.

Parmi nodded.

'The ancient Egyptians called the rich soil *Khemi* – which translated literally means "Land of Egypt",' Teddy went on. 'But here's something to tell your friends back home. The word came through Arabic, and the definite article – the word "the" – in Arabic is *al*. And when one was added to the other, a new word was born for the Western world – alchemy. It's nice to think of the Nile's annual floods and its rich soil as being part of a mystical, magical process.'

'Well, this is what you wanted to see,' I said to Parmi. 'And the Nile is over there. You know, the Egyptians have a saying, "If you don't live by the Nile, you might as well not live in Egypt." '

We had been riding for over an hour along the route to Sakkara, which never looked more enticing than in the late autumn because of the way in which the annual Nile floods changed the face of the barren desert, turning it, for a brief spell, into an entirely different landscape.

The ground surrounding the area on which the pyramids had been sited was magical, the magic depending on the time of year. Now, when the Nile had overflowed, hundreds of square miles of low-lying land were flooded. The water never actually reached the Sakkara Step Pyramid, but between the river and the desert dyke roads helped the more astute fellahîn to reach their flooded plots of land. 'Oh look!' cried Parmi as she saw a flat narrow-boat, the peasants working by moonlight, tying the leading buffalo by its nose to the stern to guide the other farm animals to or from the safety of their villages.

'Soon the floods will stop,' I explained, 'and leave mud, and the peasants will start to sow. It's probably among the most fertile soil in the world.' Sometimes in the distance we could glimpse a paddy field, sometimes the dark outline of the low bushes of cotton, forcing their way upwards through water until finally they would become covered with the white cotton blossoms.

'Look at that!' To Parmi everything was new, and though it was the middle of the night she pointed to a grove of date-palms with their plumage. A blindfolded camel turned a water-wheel – as camels, oxen or cows had done since the days when the Bible was being lived.

The servants had erected our *sewan*, or tent, a hundred yards from the Step Pyramid. It was not very large, but it was beautiful. The men and women who sewed the brightly coloured patches of cloth were inordinately proud of their skills. So were the tent erectors. As a routine precaution the front entrance to a *sewan* in the desert was often discreetly hidden from any possible passers-by by a *mushrabia* screen outside. This particular one (quite unnecessary in the dead of night) was an intricately carved example of Egyptian home-made wooden trellis screens.

The entire ground beneath the *sewan* had been covered with mats, hired for the evening with the tent, and at one end Teddy's Nubian valet-cum-butler had covered a trestle-table with a white cloth, polished the glasses and put the champagne in buckets of ice. Three other servants in white galabiyas handed drinks round and prepared food.

'I know it sounds silly,' Parmi whispered to me after the servant had offered her a plate of foie gras with a slice of *baladi*, freshly baked village bread. 'But I'm sure I've seen that man before.'

'He's Hassan, one of the servants at Sirry Pasha's,' I said. 'Madame Sirry's had you to tea, hasn't she? He probably served you then.'

'You mean he's switched jobs?'

'No, no. People are always borrowing each other's servants in Cairo. The Nubians check with each other. The fact that Hassan is here means it's pretty certain Sirry Pasha is dining out. It's ideal for men like Teddy Pollock. He doesn't need a lot of servants for his bachelor flat – or rather two flats.'

'Why does he need two apartments?'

'I'll tell you one day.'

5

Nothing happened at the midnight picnic. It would have been difficult, anyway, and in fact most of us slept for three or four hours, on cushions – but each one in full view of the others. Nor did anything happen at the Mena House where we all had a wonderful swim and saw the sun come up before I drove Parmi, nestling close to me in the open Chrysler, back to Teddy's flat. She was half-asleep, not really tired, and said sleepily, 'I like you, Mark. I do like you – and though I'm not promiscuous, well, not very – this desert air –'

'Remember, I promised your father.'

'Promises!' She sighed sleepily. 'I wish I was staying longer.'

'Me, too. Here we are. Almost at Teddy's flat – sorry, I suppose you'd call it an apartment. Hungry?'

'Ravenous.'

We arrived near Garden City, not far from Teddy's home, around seven in the morning without any idea of the pandemonium that Aly had warned me about, of the crowds surging and swirling like dervishes in Falaki Street, near the Parliament building and Foreign Ministry – and barely a couple of blocks from our house on the river.

Teddy, Angela Gray and Ian and Peggy Jones had already arrived by the time we reached Falaki Street, but the crowd, mainly youngsters, was so disorderly that I left the car round the corner from Teddy's flat, in a side-street.

'They're all right so far – just,' I warned Parmi. 'But when an Egyptian crowd gets really annoyed – especially when they're hungry at Ramadan – the first things they smash up are expensive motor-cars. Better take care.'

'Easier to walk, you mean. Safer.' She was suddenly wide

awake. 'Do we have to go to Teddy's place? You're not scared?'

'God, no. But I'm hungry. I'm not going to be robbed of a free breakfast. Or your company!'

We pushed our way round the corner, with me forcing a passage through with my elbow when necessary and shouting in Arabic, 'Make way for a lady!'

'What's all the fuss about?' Parmi asked me as she grabbed my hand and I yelled, 'Make way! Make way!'

'It's that old windbag Sam Hoare,' I shouted. 'Means nothing to Americans. He's the British Foreign Minister. Made a damned stupid anti-Egyptian speech in London on Saturday night.'

'But it's now Wednesday morning?'

'I know. But it takes time for news to get to Egypt – especially during Ramadan. That's the strict Moslem fasting festival. It lasts for thirty days, during the ninth month of the Moslem lunar calendar. Like Lent, but ten times stricter. Between sunrise and sunset no one can take food or drink. You can't smoke, you can't even lick a stamp. It makes for very short tempers.' I added with a laugh, 'Unless you're pregnant. Then you're absolved.'

We finally reached the front door of Teddy's apartment, a block halfway along a narrow road branching off from Falaki Street. It was the top floor, with a roof-garden – a perfect vantage point from which to watch if there were any trouble.

After banging the front door of the block behind us we took the elevator and I explained to Parmi how all day Monday university students and secondary school pupils had been streaming through the Cairo streets waving banners proclaiming, 'Down with the British!' On that very morning, the Wednesday, several Egyptian secondary schools had gone on strike and were gathering in Falaki Street to be sure of hearing speeches by Egyptian leaders later in the day. Tens of thousands joined in. Soon the policemen's clubs were out and swinging savagely. One British officer with the security forces arrived in an open car and was severely wounded by a hail of stones. The police opened fire, shooting one student in the head and killing him instantly. Another student was shot and critically injured.

Throughout the morning every student seemed to be converging on Falaki Street, where in an immense, brightly coloured *sewan* Nahas Pasha, the leader of the Wafd Party, was ready to make his speech.

Teddy bolted the door after we had arrived.

'Greg and Dodie Summers haven't come yet,' he said. 'My guess is they were smart and went straight home. It's going to be a hell of a day.'

'First of all,' begged Parmi after she had been given some coffee, 'will *someone* explain what this is all about? What's this Waffle Party – did I get the name right?'

'Wafd, my dear.' Teddy spelled it out. 'And anyone who can explain the machinations of the Wafd Party in under twenty-four hours is a miracle man.'

'Let me try,' I said. 'It's an all-inclusive party. That is how my father explained it to me. Pashas and the fellahîn have equal rights. What's really extraordinary is that the pashas accept this. There are rabble-rousers, student demonstrators, but intellectuals too. It doesn't matter who you are, members of the Wafd are united by the strongest bond of all – the longing for independence.' I added wryly, 'Especially from the British.'

'And they're led by this Nahas Pasha?' asked Parmi. 'Is he a good guy?'

'Great. Honest, and a wonderful orator with a simple touch. Once, when he saw a boy beating a donkey, he told him sternly, "Animals cannot talk but they understand. Human beings can talk but they often do *not* understand."'

I tried to explain as briefly as I could Nahas Pasha's role in Egyptian politics. The Wafd, as I told her, didn't want a Communist-type ranter as leader but neither did they want capitalism. 'Nahas is the ideal middleman. He has a swaggering, jovial manner; he consumes huge quantities of his favourite drink, *zabadi*, or curdled milk; he walks everywhere or takes the underground from Heliopolis where he lives; he has a squint in one eye and dresses sloppily. But he is a magical orator.'

'*You* may sound reassuring,' said Parmi, 'but does my pa know? If I'm going to stay awhile is there any chance of phoning him?'

'Of course.' And to Teddy's valet I cried, '*Irziz!*' – the slang 'in' word for a telephone.

He led us to the phone in the hall, and I was easily able to reach Davidson. 'Parmi's waiting to talk to you,' I said. 'Don't worry. We're all perfectly safe in Teddy's flat, and just about to have breakfast. Here she is.'

'Pa, I've had a wonderful time,' cried Parmi, 'but everyone says it's safer to stay here until the trouble dies down.' There was silence as she listened to her father. 'Well, it's a sideshow I didn't expect to see,' she laughed. 'Honestly, Pa, it's safe. Mark says so, and so does Teddy.'

Davidson must have been reassured because she soon hung up, and we went to the roof-garden. Like everything which Teddy did, he had furnished it immaculately. It had white chairs and tables, umbrellas, and a canopy of bougainvillaea. But best of all it provided a spectacular view, as though half Cairo were spread out like a map before us. I pointed out to Parmi the wide Kasr el Nil Bridge and to the east the dozens of minarets, pointing upwards like manicured fingers, grouped together with the grim outlines of the Citadel as a backdrop.

Directly below us, the shouting, gesticulating throngs jammed Falaki Street, with the Justice and Finance Ministries on one side and the imposing façade of Parliament House straight ahead.

In their predominantly white clothes the crowd seemed to surge forward, not as individuals but as one relentless wave forcing its way like the white crest of floodwater, pouring through narrow streets after a dam has burst. Every now and again the police rushed in. Skirmishes erupted, heads cracked, splashes of scarlet dyed the white wave and the cries of the injured mingled with the anger of the rioters.

There was nothing we could do, so we made our way down the circular staircase, where a late breakfast had been prepared.

We weren't left hungry for long. There was not only coffee and rolls, but tart-tasting jam made from Cape gooseberries, salty white cheese and omelettes served with crisply fried fingers of aubergine, long and dry and hot, looking just like chips.

'We call them B and B,' I explained. 'That could be bed and breakfast, but B and B also stands for *bald* – that's eggs – and *bitingan* – that's egg-plant or aubergine.'

'Talking of B and B,' said Teddy after the second cup of coffee, 'we've got a longish wait before the big show gets into its stride. We're virtually prisoners here. Anybody want a snooze?'

The Jones couple gratefully accepted the use of the spare room, which had a double bed, while Teddy announced, 'Angela and I are going to examine my collection of photos. I've run out of etchings.'

That would leave us alone – and I knew how to be alone – if she agreed. I had the feeling that (unless she fell asleep!) the unusual excitement of the desert evening, even the drama in the streets below, might encourage her to partake in a once-and-for-all adventure in Cairo, something she would always remember. I wasn't thinking so much of 'taking advantage' of her – as of her taking advantage of me.

'Everybody seems to want to rest,' I asked her innocently. 'Do you feel like – well –'

She knew what I meant, but she looked round the room doubtfully – the servants, the Jones separated only by a door, Teddy and his collection of photos.

With a meaningful look at Teddy – and *he* knew what we wanted, even if Angela didn't – I said with an affected, casual air, 'I think Parmi and I'll push off. Try to make it to Shepheard's just in case – well, her father . . .' I mumbled.

'But he understands, I've explained,' cried Parmi. Did she look crestfallen at this abrupt ending to the 'adventure'?

Without replying, I whispered to Teddy, 'Angela doesn't know about –?' I inclined my head in the direction of the corridor. He shook a 'no'.

'Don't worry,' I said.

'Isn't that the way out?' she asked as I led her to the opposite end of the long narrow corridor.

Was she hesitating? Or making a tacit acceptance to a

proposition? It was hard to tell. She had made it clear that she was a fervent Catholic yet, I was thinking, differing religions take little account of sinning. It's being caught that matters! And I had the feeling that if this kind of adventure had happened in New York she might have had reservations; but here in Cairo, on the last days of a holiday, how could she resist the glamour, the desert ride, the dawn swim . . .

'Excuse me if I go first,' said Teddy, leaving Angela for a moment. At the far end of the corridor one wall was painted as a mural of birds. 'Came from Bali,' said Teddy. 'Beautiful, isn't it?' Parmi looked puzzled, for the mural – which looked like a wallpaper – covered every inch of the wall.

Except for a couple of almost invisible cracks and a tiny flap, at first unnoticed.

Carefully Teddy twisted the flap which was barely more than two inches square. It revealed a small black hole. He inserted a key. Most of the wall – the centre part inside the cracks – swung open to reveal a hidden door.

'Follow me.' I led her through the door.

'A secret room!' Parmi almost whispered.

I shook my head, while Teddy said in a loud voice, 'Sorry you had to push off,' and closed the door behind us. I added, 'Not a secret room, nothing so common. This is an entirely separate flat – sorry, apartment. It's got nothing to do with the Falaki Street flat except that Teddy owns both and joined them up. He finds it convenient from time to time to have a secret way from one flat in one street to the next in the next street. This one doesn't even have the same door, or the same street when you want to leave. This apartment block entrance is in Kasr-el-Aini Street.'

I led the way into the living room and bedroom. Facing the bed was a light on the wall, with a red bulb.

'That's just in case Teddy's in trouble,' I explained. 'Don't worry, nothing's going to happen. But if Teddy had to get out, or use this flat, he'd switch on the light which would flash red – time to warn anyone to beat a hasty retreat through the other front door.'

It was very neat, but Parmi hardly heard what I was saying.

'He's a genius! Do you mean that he keeps this apartment – just like that – all the time? In case?'

'I told you,' I smiled, 'Teddy's a *professional* playboy.'

'And now we're alone!' There was laughter in her eyes as she added, 'It looks suspiciously – what's the word? – *convenient* for Teddy – and friends like you.'

'It's Teddy's flat – and there's the front door,' I smiled.

'But is there a key to unlock it?' We were both laughing, in a giggly mood.

'I'm not in the business of luring innocent girls into secret flats,' I protested. 'Of course you can leave if you want to. Only you *did* say something about being left alone – and I thought this would amuse you.'

'It does,' she said softly, 'and I feel very, very happy.'

I couldn't believe the difference in Parmi when we were in bed. The zany humour vanished. She was gentle, but in a way deliberate; perhaps hungry for love – or sex would describe it better. And then finally, with a last frenzied movement, she gave a long sigh of satisfaction. 'Ah! That's it.'

Maybe two minutes passed in silence. I don't know: you can't measure time at moments like this. But suddenly, without warning, passion spent, she stroked my face and whispered, 'You're a man, Mark. A real man. You made it last. No one's ever done it like that to me before. Do you know it's three months since any man even *touched* me. All this feeling locked inside me: I hate the thought that in two days we'll be on our way home. What a pity we didn't meet the first day I arrived.'

'How do you think I feel?' I asked.

'Open up the champagne,' she said. 'And then' – again the curious, rather pleasant touch of shyness – 'who knows what'll happen?'

But we never made love again that day. Instead, as we lay naked on the bed sipping cold Mumms, the red light suddenly flashed on the opposite wall.

'Christ almighty!' I leapt out of bed, heard Parmi cry, 'Don't blaspheme!' as I panicked, spilling champagne everywhere. 'It must be something desperate, otherwise – here, darling, never mind your clothes, nobody knows who you are. But if Teddy allows anyone to come into this flat it must be to beat a hasty retreat. I don't know what the hell he's playing at.'

Naked, I started to push her into the bathroom.

'No!' I had second thoughts. 'Better go into the kitchen.' Opening a wardrobe I found a Sulka dressing-gown of Teddy's which was hanging with other spare clothes. I handed it to her, together with what was left of the champagne, almost as I heard the lock turning at the end of the corridor. Parmi, blonde hair awry, after one wide-eyed stare, darted into the kitchen.

I had just pulled the door to when I heard Teddy's voice in the hall. He knocked and came in just as I wrapped a towel round my waist.

'Got rid of the evidence?'

'What the bloody –?' I started, but he shut me up with his first words.

'You know me better than to let you down. It's a friend of ours – and he's in deep trouble. Aly Sirry, and he's hurt.'

I must have looked stupefied. 'What the hell's he doing here?'

'The police banged him over the head, together with a friend of his. They're both covered in blood. They came into the Falaki Street flat to see if I could help them, but the police started to chase them. Must have spotted them going in.'

'But why?'

'He was marching with the anti-British rioters. His friend is one of the leaders of the student demonstration – or says he is. It's all part of their cause.'

'Bloody cause my bloody foot,' I said angrily. 'What the hell is a capitalist bastard like Aly doing, playing at revolutions?'

'He means it. I've got to get him to the bathroom, clean him up. The police will be in the other flat at any moment. Where's your girl?'

'In the kitchen. With the champagne.'

'Great girl!' Teddy gave his special slow smile. 'Gets her priorities right. You going into the kitchen too?'

That had been the general idea, but at that moment Aly pushed his way into the bedroom followed by another man, or rather a youth. The youngster was in a hell of a mess. His forehead seemed to have been split wide open and blood was pouring into his eyes and nose. Aly was trying to sop it up with a handkerchief as it dribbled into his mouth, and both Aly's jacket and the man's shirt seemed soaked in blood. Aly, too, had a cut along his forehead, but it didn't seem to bleed as much.

'Here's the bathroom,' I cried, thinking inconsequentially of Teddy's carpet. 'You'll find towels inside.'

It was typical of Aly that he didn't bother to apologise or explain. Looking at my towel-draped body, he just said in his usual sulky tone, 'You seem to have been enjoying yourself.'

'It's not a crime,' I snapped back. 'You seem to have been enjoying yourself too.'

'Nothing really,' he muttered. 'A bit of blood on each of us.'

'I'll go back to my flat and keep the police away from this one,' said Teddy. 'But for Christ's sake get out of here pronto.'

'Don't worry. We've no wish to outstay our welcome.'

I had hardly noticed the other man until he returned from the bathroom. He was tall, with a prominent nose, olive-skinned, and with the same truculent 'The world owes me a living' attitude as Aly. Again there was no question of apologies or belated thanks. But he certainly had a nasty gash across his head, and it did occur to me that it was Ramadan, and nobody could even take a sip of water until sunset. I caught myself wondering whether illness absolved a man from the Moslem oath. He must be feeling weak.

Aly finally introduced the youngster to me. 'This is a friend of our family's, Mark Holt. My friend, Gamal. He's on strike from school and those bloody palace police deliberately cracked his skull.'

'When you leave here you can get out into Garden City. Nobody'll ever be able to trace you.'

'Thank you,' said Gamal. 'And now I think I'll borrow another towel.'

'He's very young,' I said to Aly when the youngster was back in the bathroom. 'Only a kid.'

'He's brilliant. I've known him for over a year. He's a born orator. Pure magic whenever he opens his mouth. You should have heard the speech he gave: made Nahas Pasha look like a beginner. He may be young, but he's got molten fire in his veins.'

'What did you say his full name was?'

'I didn't. But it's Gamal Abdel Nasser.'

6

I would never have given Aly's slight injury another thought had I not been surprised to read the following morning about it in *Al Guihad* and several other Cairo newspapers. My first reaction was that Sirry Pasha would be horrified; my second that he would be furious.

The newspaper story was brief. It read: 'Among those injured in the police battle was a student, Gamal Abdel Nasser, who will bear the crescent-shaped scar on his forehead for life, and Mr Aly Sirry, son of the well-known palace official, Sirry Pasha, whose wound was superficial. It is understood that Mr Sirry and his friend were later seen by police entering the flat of Mr Teddy Pollock, a friend of Mr Sirry's.'

From Serena later I heard how such detailed news had been 'leaked'. Apparently, after escaping from the second flat, Nasser had still been bleeding profusely so Aly took him to the nearest hospital. They had to sign their names to be admitted and receive treatment; and then an eager journalist tracked down the story.

I remember thinking that at least the item had not appeared in the *Egyptian Gazette*, the English language newspaper. People like Sirry set great store by the *Gazette*; for many diplomats it was required daily reading. But it was not until the next day that I discovered that it had *almost* been printed in the *Gazette*, and had only been suppressed on special instructions by the editor. It was a puzzling aside to the main events, and I only knew about it by chance when I ran into Donald Childs, a legal colleague, and he told me it had been suppressed because he knew the Sirrys were friends of ours.

'Suppressed?' I asked. 'By the palace?' The palace were the toughest censors in the Middle East.

'No. That's what's so odd. By the Americans.'

'You're joking! The *Gazette* might take heed if the British Embassy asks a favour – or if the palace orders it. But the Americans!'

'It's true. You know Bill Bennett, the assistant editor?' I nodded. I had run into Childs in Adly Pasha Street, so we went into the nearby Turf Club for a couple of gimlets. Childs was as puzzled as I was.

'What the hell's it got to do with the Americans?' I asked.

Childs felt the same and explained: 'Bennett told me he was pissed off when the request came through and flatly refused to delete the paragraph. Half an hour later – according to Bennett – the editor-in-chief phoned through and ordered the piece to be spiked.' He used the Fleet Street term for 'killing' a story.

'The American Embassy?'

'Not exactly.' Childs ordered a second round of gimlets. 'Do you know an American called Jim Stevenson?'

I realised – or thought I realised – what must have happened. 'Of course. This chap Stevenson knows the Sirry family. Including Aly – and Aly's sister Serena. There was probably nothing sinister in what happened. Just trying to do Sirry a good turn.'

'I'm not so sure. There's more to it than that.' Childs didn't expand on what he meant, and soon he was on his way to his next appointment. I had to wait a little while before learning that he was right – and before I discovered exactly what role Stevenson *had* played.

Two days later Sirry Pasha sent Serena into our garden to ask whether Greg and I could spare her father a few minutes shortly after breakfast.

80

'Aly's for it!' said Serena almost cheerfully, as we walked through the wicket gate separating our properties. 'Hobnobbing with the proletariat!'

'Where *is* Aly?' I asked as we walked into the house.

'Just getting up. Father told him to come and see him before breakfast. I rather fancy Aly's swallowing a quick cup of coffee.'

Over our long family friendship Sirry had, for as long as any of us could remember, always been quiet and gentle, but now, as he invited us into the dining room, he was spluttering with rage.

'What am I to say to my friends – or at the Abdin Palace – anywhere?' He pointed a finger at the front page of *Al Guihad*. 'How can a son of mine do a thing like this to his own father?' Then, more quietly, he added, 'Good of you to come. I wanted to catch you early – especially you, Mark, you might have left for your chambers. Have some coffee.' He rang a tinkling silver bell and some freshly made coffee arrived. 'American blend,' he said almost absently.

I poured out cups for us both.

'My own son,' he said bitterly. 'In an anti-government demonstration. Fighting the police. With some' – he almost burst a blood-vessel – 'whippersnapper student, the son of a postman.'

Greg was silent. I muttered a few words of condolence, but Sirry was torn between rage and tears. 'The only thing that makes life worth living is to have children of whom you are proud. But Aly – a *revolutionary*.' He spat out the word with disgust. 'How can any boy do this to any father? Tell me, Mark – what happened?'

'Nothing,' I replied cautiously. 'Nothing that I know of.'

'And you, Greg? You were there, weren't you, when the police came to Pollock's flat searching for them?'

'No, I wasn't.' Greg shook his head, relieved to be able to tell the truth. 'I never went to the flat that morning. One of the girls and I took a look at the crowded streets as we approached Falaki Street, and we went straight home.'

'And you?' He turned to me again.

'I never saw them in Teddy Pollock's flat,' I said truthfully – if only just.

'Yet you *were* in Teddy's flat – no?'

'We all were – except Greg. We planned to have breakfast there.'

'But though you were there, you never saw Aly there?'

'No. I told you.'

'If you say so, of course I believe you,' said Sirry Pasha with a certain coldness. 'But there are one or two things I don't understand. You say Aly was not there with you, yet Teddy Pollock tells me Aly did come to his flat. And that the police were there.' Sirry studied the tablecloth, averting my eyes.

I groaned. Pollock was a careless idiot. But I *hadn't* met Aly in Pollock's flat – and it was not for me to say that Pollock had two adjoining flats, one of them secret.

'I'm glad that you're *not* doubting my word,' I said equally coldly, 'because, however great the provocation, I'm not in the habit of having my word ever doubted. As it happens, I was *not* there. Greg *never* got there. Miss Davidson – you remember her, after all you asked me to look after her – she and I both decided it was too risky to remain. She knew her father would be worried about her, so we decided to get out.' It was none of Sirry Pasha's business how we escaped through the crowds.

'I see,' said Sirry heavily. At that moment Aly entered, dressed in a white cotton Egyptian nightgown edged with gold braid, not unlike a galabiya. I could see from his anxious glances that he was wondering how much – if anything – we had admitted.

'Good morning, Aly,' I said with a cheerfulness none of us felt. 'I was horrified to read in the papers all about you. Hadn't the faintest idea of the fun we'd missed by leaving before you arrived.'

I could sense the lessening tension. That would warn Aly not to involve me – or, indirectly, Parmi. Now Aly would be able to forget all about the existence of the second flat. As it was, Sirry exploded with fury against his son.

'What the devil do you mean by getting our good name

into the newspapers with those – those damned anar-
chists?'

'Father! Don't be so unfair. I just happened to be there. Just
as Mark and Greg might have been.'

'But they weren't, were they? You say you just *happened*
to be there! What about the newspaper article? Let me read it
to you. It's this man Nasser telling a reporter. Listen!' He
quoted, reading carefully: ' "I eluded the police thanks to my
good friend who was also injured." Well – were *you* the good
friend who went with him to hospital? Or did you just *happen*
to be there – as you put it?'

'Nasser *is* a friend of mine,' Aly admitted. 'If I did help to
save him from arrest, I'm proud of it. He's a wonderful man.'

'He's a precocious schoolboy,' snorted Sirry, 'who wants
his arse tanned. He's nothing but a bloody agitator. And
you!'

'I don't like the word "agitator". That's unfair,' cried Aly.

'What are you then?' asked Sirry scornfully. 'Dreamers?'

'Dreamers!' Aly almost choked on the word. 'No, we are
not dreamers. You, Father, are the dreamer – dreaming of
that fat comfortable life of the few which you think will go
on for ever.'

'And what are you going to do about it – you and your
schoolboy friend? Are you going to help?'

'Yes, we are.' Aly was trembling with flashes of almost
incoherent rage. 'We are going to create a new Egypt – for
Egyptians, not for' – with a look at me – 'for foreigners.'

Poor old Sirry gave a look of resignation and finally almost
whispered, 'Aly, listen to me.'

'No, Father, I won't. It's better not to talk. We no longer
speak the same language. I admire men like Nasser. And I
don't admire the damned politicians who keep the starving
fellahîn down while the bloated capitalists grow rich on the
proceeds.'

'Get out!' roared Sirry Pasha. 'And don't forget you're a
member of a bloated capitalist family. With enough money
to stay in bed in the mornings. *And* trim your nightgown
with gold braid. Did you tell your friend Nasser that? Or
does he think you're a poor, struggling postman, like his

father? When I think of the love and pride I've lavished on you, the hopes I had for you! You make me sick.'

'It's not only crooked politicians,' Aly muttered. 'You know why we started these demonstrations. It's the British. Why don't they get out of our country once and for all? It's *our* country, or it's supposed to be. Nasser says –'

'Nasser says,' Sirry repeated. 'Nasser says please tell the British to go home so that our school can run the country!' Turning to Greg and me, he added with a tired smile, 'You two had better go before Aly and Nasser take the Suez Canal away from you.'

Aly banged his way out of the room, followed more quietly by Greg, but though Sirry had suggested that I should leave too he begged me, 'Stay on for a moment, Mark. I'm worried about Aly.' I could see that. He wore his worry like his clothes, part of getting dressed for the day. 'If you can help me to – to tame him, anything you can do . . .' he asked me sadly.

'Of course. But he's headstrong. There's not much I *can* do.'

'The trouble is that I agree with some of what Aly says,' he admitted. 'Too many Egyptian politicians *are* corrupt. Did I ever tell you how Fuad robbed me? Yes, just robbed me. Legally, of course.'

I shook my head.

'Fuad sent for me,' Sirry Pasha recalled, 'and asked me how much I wanted for a few hundred acres of cotton land which we owned behind Nasrani. I quoted the market price of £500 an acre. Fuad said it was excessive and sent a government valuer – in Fuad's service, of course – who said the land was worth only £40 an acre. Fuad showed the figures to me, but then said that as I was an old friend he would give me £50 an acre. I had to let him have the land. A friend of mine who *did* resist a forced sale suddenly discovered that government surveyors had ordered irrigation channels serving his land to be diverted.'

He hesitated, as though recalling a painful memory, then added, 'So you see, life with Aly isn't made any easier by the knowledge that part of what he says is justified.'

I left the Sirrys shortly afterwards. I had no desire to listen any longer to family bitterness, and I felt sorry for Sirry Pasha and the way in which his dreams were being shattered – the dreams which every father has for a son.

'Well, at least his dreams for Serena will come true,' I said to Greg later. 'Especially when she marries you. And she's made of sterner stuff than Aly.'

Greg laughed. 'I've no worries about that. Serena will make me a super wife, and we'll have lots of kids and stick up for the bloody capitalists till the cows come home.'

'I wonder if Sirry *does* realise that Aly is – well, partly right,' I said.

'What on earth do you mean? It sounds like treason.'

'No, I'm serious. Put yourself in the shoes of an Egyptian. I know how vital the Canal is – and don't get me wrong, I'd fight for our rights until the concession to control the Canal for ninety-nine years runs out' – as it would in 1968 – 'but there are a hell of a lot of highly intelligent Egyptians who don't like seeing a bunch of foreigners ordering them around, telling them how to run their own country.'

'They can't bloody well run it themselves, that's the problem,' said Greg cheerfully. 'Ask them to build a brick shit-house and they just dig a hole with a roof over it. Aly's right in one way – I grant him that – but every Egyptian politician is on the make. They couldn't run a kindergarten without pinching the toddlers' lunch money. All the more reason for us to remain.'

Even Serena, who wasn't really interested in Egyptian politics, asked me, 'Who's right – Papa or Aly?'

'Depends on your point of view.' I put on my best judicial air, then added, laughing, 'Both, I suppose. But why do you ask?'

'A couple of weeks ago someone gave me a book by Lord Cromer, *Modern Egypt*. Written before you were born. He gave a wonderful picture of the benevolent British in Egypt. But then an Egyptian writer told me he was a terror.'

'I believe he was. Behaved rather kingly – a despot. But

don't worry about politics. Egypt would still be a quiet, living museum if that Frenchman de Lesseps hadn't built the Canal. *That's* what changed Egypt's destiny. But politics – forget them.'

'I was just curious, that's all. Seeing how happy some people are while others are so miserable.'

'That's the same the world over, from Singapore to San Francisco,' I said easily.

We were strolling in the garden, a few days after the desert party, and suddenly, as she so often did, she changed the subject and her mouth dimpled into a laugh as she asked me point-blank, 'How was she – your dizzy blonde? Good?'

'Good?'

'Yes. In bed, silly.'

It seems that Teddy, a noted gossip, had leaked a few details of the confrontation with Aly, and Greg presumably had told Serena. And there's nothing to be done about beautiful young girls like Serena probing in a curiously proprietorial way, except to treat them with jocularity.

'Not bad,' I answered with assumed nonchalance, and knowing that Parmi had left Cairo and so my reply wouldn't get back to her. 'I've known better. Not that bad.'

Serena walked round the gravel path that encircled the huge lawns and which we were forced to use when the gardeners had been over-enthusiastic with the water-pump, flooding the grass into a soggy quagmire.

The next moment she was walking by my side, and I suddenly realised how quickly she was growing up. And how dazzlingly beautiful she was, with that fair hair, that dauntless face, and the way her body had filled out. The days of the leggy schoolgirl had disappeared. And though Serena pretended to be a schoolgirl with me – all part of our game – she wasn't a girl any longer. She was, I felt sure, stirred by emotions and longings common to all men and women in the painful years of growing up, and I wondered how long it would be before she and Greg got married.

At that moment Zola walked solemnly round the gravel path, disdaining to soil his shoes on the soggy grass, hardly seeming to move in his green galabiya.

Still struggling from time to time to use words he didn't know, he announced gravely, 'Sir Geoffrey presents his complimentaries, sir, and would you join him in his study for a glass of champagne?'

'Oh shit!' Serena almost stamped her foot. 'Just as I was going to ask something interesting about sex.'

'Language!' I reproved her. 'A minute ago it was damn, now it's shit. Where *do* you pick up these words?'

'From Greg.'

7

The riots had not only shocked the Egyptian education authorities into closing their schools for a month; it finally seeped through to the British government – often woefully out of touch with local aspirations – that what had happened in Falaki Street was so significant that it merited more than a few soothing platitudes.

And so, despite many misgivings among the diehards in Whitehall, Britain agreed to take a momentous step, one that would fulfil the greatest dream of every Egyptian; it agreed to negotiate a treaty of full independence for Egypt.

Cairo went mad with joy on the day the news was announced. Three million people jammed the streets – two million of them crowding into the capital by every train, ancient bus, bicycle, felucca, even camel and donkey that could be used as transport. For infants there were makeshift creaking roundabouts made of wood and turned by hand. For the older children picnics in the green of Cairo's squares. Hookahs were passed round as they watched the rope-players, fire-eaters, glass-eaters, even live snake-eaters and other sideshows; the Ghawazi girls (girl dancers) and girls from the cheap brothels near Clot Bey and the fish market did a brisk business; while so, for that matter, did male prostitutes dressed as Ghawazi.

Among the most excited had been Aly Sirry. 'I know Father thinks Nasser is a stupid hothead,' he said to Serena (who relayed the conversation to me), 'but a lot of the success in forcing Britain to give in belongs to Gamal. I held a party in his honour when school reopened.'

According to Aly, Nasser had returned to school a local hero; except to the headmaster who refused to admit him back because of his fight with the police. The other fifth-form students immediately decided to strike. They lugged all their desks out into the school courtyard and threatened to burn them until the headmaster relented.

'But even better,' said Aly to me later, proud to be involved with his new 'friend', 'is that Gamal studied like hell during the month away from school and was one of the few who passed his exams last spring.'

'When the Treaty of Independence is signed later this year there'll be nothing left for your friend to do,' I teased Aly. 'And you too, for that matter. No time or place for agitators.'

'I think Nasser will try to join the army,' said Aly. 'But we haven't signed the Treaty yet, you know.'

My father was convinced that the actual signing of the historic document would be a formality later in the year.

'Though there's a lot of spade work to be done,' he admitted between sips of champagne at his study desk. 'And I've been given the job of doing most of the digging. Might have to go to Paris for a conference with the FO – they don't like coming to Egypt. Scared of snakes. Or maybe they like French girls. Why not? Fun, eh?' With a metaphorical dig in the ribs, and probably never having been to bed with a 'French' girl in his life, he added, 'No one in the world like 'em, m'boy. Up to every trick devised by man.'

Sighing as he returned to 'business', he said, 'As to the Treaty – when it comes off you'll be witnessing the biggest event in the history of Egypt since the Arab invasion. No troops will be allowed anywhere in the country, except along the narrow Canal Zone. Must safeguard our rights there. Fair enough. You mark my words, Mark, it'll be a new era for Egypt.' Then, switching again, he added, 'Might be fun if I have to go to Paris, eh? You like to come along? I can promise you – nothing in the world like it.'

There was no harm in saying I would love to, and no harm in pretending to agree with him that he was a great expert on French women. He had such a grasp of Anglo-Egyptian affairs that he was virtually irreplaceable, yet once he forgot the hard facts of his life's work he revelled in an imaginary life in which he was convinced he had been the lover of every exotic type of woman under the sun. He was a kind, good, and, I'm sure, faithful husband, but he had for so long enjoyed pretending that he had now come to believe his fantasies. Chiffon took it all in her stride, fluttering eyelids as she said, with no trace of worry or annoyance, 'Oh dear, there's your father on the rampage again.'

Greg and I had discussed his secret passions many times. We wondered if he had suffered some traumatic experience when young, because he really did have a split personality – on the one hand a highly knowledgeable expert, on the other an incorrigible sex fantasist. But he never strayed from the spoken word. Once at a royal reception he pointed out a very pretty girl, known to be 'fast', and my father actually whispered to me, 'I'm told she never wears knickers. I've a damn good mind to sit next to her and slip my hand up her dress. That'd teach her a lesson, eh?'

Poor Father! He would have run non-stop from Cairo to Alex rather than dare fondle a woman, however discreetly.

Any thoughts of a trip to Paris – however imaginative they might have been – were immediately forgotten by a sudden event which none could have foreseen, but which sent the Foreign Office – and my father – rushing to teleprinters in case any tactical changes might be necessary in the planning of the Treaty.

For on 28 April 1936 King Fuad died, at the age of sixty-eight, and the teenage Farouk succeeded him. He inherited not only a kingdom and untold riches but a legacy of hate. The whole country took the death of Fuad to be a joyous augury for the start of a new and enlightened royal reign by a dashing and handsome 'Prince

Charming' – the first monarch to rule a truly free Egypt.

Fuad had been a ruthless despot who built a vast fortune, mainly by a polite form of confiscation among other land-owners. Between 1917 and his death he had acquired a seventh of all the arable land in Egypt. Fuad had also ensured a ready market for his goods. Officials and police simply stopped all other fruit and vegetable trucks on the roads leading to big cities until the royal produce had been sold. At one time Fuad was the richest man in Egypt. He had a fortune of £30 million in Egypt and half as much again in Swiss and other European banks.

'I'm not sorry to see the old rascal go,' said Sirry Pasha soon after Fuad died. 'The new boy will be rich all right – and I hope will distribute some of his wealth.'

Farouk was sixteen and had been in England for seven months when Fuad died. The old king had hoped to send his son to Italy for his later education, but the British were adamant that he must acquire a British background – obviously at Eton. Unfortunately, the headmaster took one look at the young prince's entrance exam papers and flatly refused to enter the boy. Instead Farouk was sent to the Royal Military College at Woolwich. He failed the exams there. The examiner was perplexed at the way this young man sat stolidly regarding his pencil without writing a word on the blank paper. In fact, Farouk was behaving as he always did when he took his 'exams' at the Kubbah Palace. He was waiting for a tutor to approach him and supply the answers. Finally, Farouk bypassed the exams by enrolling as a Gentleman Cadet.

He had a mission of twenty men, including tutors and servants, who tended to his comforts in a grey, eighteen-roomed mansion on Kingston Hill, in gardens filled with rhododendrons and roses. It was called Kenry House. Fuad's first choice as head of mission had been the bombastic General Aziz el Masri, but Farouk's English nanny braved Fuad's wrath and stood up to the old despot. 'I told him,' she said to Father, ' "Majesty, you can't send a man with manners like that as head of the mission. He would never be invited a second time to Buckingham Palace." '

'You're right,' my father had agreed. 'And apart from that, Masri is openly anti-British. He hates us and loves the Germans. *Not* a good idea.'

The nanny's views prevailed, and one of Fuad's court chamberlains was despatched to London in Masri's place.

Farouk thoroughly enjoyed the months at Woolwich. He only attended lessons three times a week, cycling across to Kingston whenever he could and spending hours shopping, mostly at Bentall's, his favourite department store.

The news of Fuad's death reached Farouk when he was out practising jumps in Richmond Park. He was a bad rider who fell off frequently. Sir Louis Greig, then Deputy Ranger of Richmond Park, broke the news and waited for some sign of grief from the new king.

'I'll just do three more rounds of jumps,' said Farouk. 'Then I'll be with you.'

Sir Louis grabbed the reins and said angrily, 'Sir, you'll do nothing of the sort. Get down off that horse.'

Sheepishly Farouk dismounted. Fortunately he didn't overhear Sir Louis mutter to an aide, 'We can't have two kings of Egypt dying on the same day.'

When Farouk landed on Egyptian soil the country went wild with joy at the promise of a new era. No one had ever seen such rejoicing as for a day the fellahîn left their water buffalo, their cotton and clover fields, their orange and mango groves, simply to celebrate. Half a million people lined the streets of the capital as Farouk drove to the Abdin Palace. Women and girls strewed his path with tens of thousands of hibiscus and jacaranda blossoms. When he had passed by, thousands of peasants bent their tired backs and kissed the ground – before the first boy-king to mount the throne since Tutankhamen ruled his vast empire 3,300 years ago. And for those who could not reach Cairo there was an innovation: Farouk was the first king of Egypt whose words reached the corners of every village – by radio. And in Arabic.

'I start my new life with a good heart and a strong will,' he told them. 'With you as a witness, I promise to devote my life and my being to your good, to bend all my efforts to create your happiness. I declare it my duty to work with you for the good of our beloved Egypt, for I believe that the glory of the king comes from the glory of his people. With all the will I possess, I shall seek to reform the country. Allah is my strength.'

Afterwards Sirry Pasha said – and he was not the only one – 'My God, I believe the boy means it. And if he has the strength and doesn't fall by the wayside he may lead Egypt into a new era.'

'He's certainly very handsome,' Serena commented.

Fuad was hardly cold in his grave before the Egyptian politicians started jostling for power. In fact there wasn't much 'jostling'; Nahas Pasha, leader of the Wafd, could see that Britain would find it much safer to negotiate with a non-Communist government, and that this would help to ensure the ultimate signing of the Treaty. He was able to persuade his followers of this, so that less than two weeks after the death of Fuad Nahas Pasha formed an all-Wafdist cabinet.

'And that changes a few things,' explained my father. 'Nahas will do everything to get the Treaty of Independence signed. Anything. And he's got young Farouk behind him. My bet is that Farouk's so relieved he doesn't have to deal with a bunch of Communists he'll be delighted to have Nahas as Prime Minister.'

'Could do worse,' I agreed. 'At least he's open to any good suggestions.'

'Gracious me, we *do* live in stirring times,' my father almost chortled. 'We'll have to see if Sirry's going to keep his palace job under the new regime. Funny boy, Farouk. Very good-looking, but not all there, I'm told. Don't forget we're dining with the Sirrys next week. We'll find out then.'

'It's not a big do, I hope.'

'No. There were going to be eight, including Serena and Aly, but Aly's begged off, and Madame Sirry doesn't want to disappoint Serena. It's one of her first grown-up parties.'

'Is Greg coming?'

'No. But there's an American. Name of Stevenson.' Perfectly naturally, but with an almost lofty tone, my father asked, 'Do we know him?'

'I've met him occasionally. Seems a fairly decent type. Wonder why he's been invited.'

The dinner, in fact, was rather dull. It was curious, but though everyone loved Sirry Pasha – he was one of the rare men against whom there had never been a whisper of corruption – his parties were always hard going. Too formal, too 'important'. Perhaps it was Madame Sirry's influence. The French in Egypt fancied themselves as society leaders of the capital, and it showed.

Not that everyone didn't behave perfectly, including Jim Stevenson, who was polite to the ladies and asked intelligent questions of the men. For a man who seemed to have no definite job – and no need to work for a living – he had a remarkable insight into Cairo's affairs. It was he who asked the vital question about life under Farouk after Sirry had rambled on for nearly half an hour without ever really telling us anything new – at a time when everyone who mixed in diplomatic or palace circles was dying to know how the new ruler was behaving, and if it was true that he already had several mistresses.

'How do you get on, Pasha, with General Sadik? Have anything to do with the new ADC?' asked Stevenson suddenly.

There was a moment of stunned silence. My father burst out, 'What an extraordinary question!' The fact that Farouk, barely three weeks after the death of Fuad, had appointed a new personal ADC was a closely guarded secret. Probably only three or four men in the British Embassy knew.

'How on earth did *you* know that?' Sirry Pasha looked at Stevenson with astonishment, while Chiffon asked faintly, 'Who are we talking about?'

'*Il est un cochon!*' Madame Sirry gave vent to a furious outburst – it was quite out of character for her to speak so violently.

'I quite agree,' said Stevenson. I too had heard the rumours, including one going round the High Court that Sadik was used as a kind of procurer to appease Farouk's insatiable appetite for women.

'I do not like him very much,' said Sirry Pasha carefully. 'But fortunately our paths won't be crossing very often.'

'How did you know about Sadik?' asked my father.

'I don't really,' confessed Stevenson easily. 'I just seem to have heard the news around.'

'Watch your step when Farouk sets eyes on you,' I turned to Serena. 'I mean it. I'm told that when Farouk sees a girl he likes he signals one of his acolytes to arrange the time and place – and fee if necessary. And that's it.'

'Disgusting!' cried Father.

'How much?' teased Serena. 'The fee. Is it millions and millions?'

'Mark is right,' said Stevenson. It always amazed me how casually the Americans slipped on to Christian-name terms. 'Watch your step when Farouk's around.'

The conversation, understandably, often turned to the old and hated king, and Stevenson was able to produce some startling statistics when, after dinner, the men took coffee and port in the dining room. The Americans, he said, had produced a shattering analysis of the state of Egypt towards the end of Fuad's reign. Farouk was regent of sixteen million inhabitants, but only two million could read and write. Hardly any of the villages had drinking water. Few had a doctor.

'There are three thousand doctors in Egypt,' added Stevenson, 'but none of them ever leaves the cities. That's why disease is rampant and why Egypt has the highest infant mortality rate in the world. Farouk will have to do *something*. One in four children die in the first days of their lives. And as for those who do live' – he shrugged helplessly – 'there's hook-worm, tunnel-worm, and one in two, at least, suffer from eye diseases. You've only got to walk through the streets of Cairo to count the number of blind people.'

'Where did you get these statistics, Stevenson?' my father asked clipping one of his best Havana cigars.

'I read about them in the survey I mentioned.' Stevenson was always vague when pinned down. 'I was checking some Middle East statistics last time I was in Washington, and someone handed them to me; he knew I was interested in Egypt. Why do you ask, sir?'

'Because I happen to have seen the report,' said Father crisply, 'and it's top secret.'

'Well,' said Sirry Pasha hastily, 'this is the country Farouk has inherited. Still,' he added, 'the Kubbah Palace gave him a remarkable start in life.'

'I hope he manages to get away from his palace and visit the countryside,' said my father.

'I wonder.' Sirry Pasha sounded doubtful. 'An ironic fact emerged the other day when I had to check on the royal garages. Farouk is mad about driving, as you know. We discovered that he inherited or owns over a hundred cars, ten of them Rolls-Royces. Yet, though it's only a twelve-mile drive to Giza, he's never visited the pyramids.'

Sirry Pasha and Father settled down to a game of chess, but before we joined the ladies I buttonholed Stevenson in the cloakroom. I was still thinking about the incident at the *Egyptian Gazette*.

'What's all this I hear about the Americans trying to control the British Press?' I asked jokingly.

I must give Stevenson credit for laughing openly without a split second's hesitation. If that laugh was not spontaneous it was a masterly piece of impromptu acting.

'Oh, you mean the *Gazette* and Aly? He's a real sucker, that boy, always looking for trouble. As to the *Gazette*, nothing to it,' he added in his easy, almost lackadaisical way. 'I like Aly, in spite of his faults. But I like all the Sirry family. I was just trying to help.'

'Good of you.' The irony was wasted. 'I wouldn't have the nerve to go round to a newspaper editor and ask him to kill a story –'

'Not for a friend?'

'Not for anyone.'

'Nothing to it,' he repeated cheerfully. 'After all, I do a bit of freelance journalism, I know most of the boys – including Bill Bennett. I just asked him to do me a favour, that's all.'

I wondered. According to Childs when we met in the Turf

Club, Bennett had been 'pissed off' because pressure had been brought to bear over his head after he had refused to comply with Stevenson's request. It didn't quite tally with the story Stevenson told.

On a sudden impulse I asked, 'Tell me – are you some sort of spy?'

'A spy? You ought to know that a *real* spy never admits to being one.'

'Well, let's put it another way. Do you work for the US government?'

'You *are* persistent,' Stevenson laughed. 'No wonder you're such a good lawyer. Yes, I do work for the United States government. Yes, I don't go around telling everyone. That satisfy you?'

'For the time being.'

8

My father had long since been in the habit of leaving notes outside our bedrooms if he wanted to see one of us – Mother included – the following morning. His usual method was to pin a piece of paper to the outside of the door, so that I could take it if I arrived later than the note; otherwise the servant would bring it in with the early morning tea. A few days later, my father asked if I could go and see him.

He hadn't mentioned any time, and as I was leaving for chambers immediately after breakfast I knocked and walked into his study at eight o'clock.

'Ah m'boy, just in time for a glass of champagne.'

'But it's eight in the morning!' I said without thinking.

My father ran a hand through his curly grey thatch of hair and looked at me with genuine astonishment. 'What on earth has that got to do with it?'

'Sorry. I just thought –'

'Champagne can be drunk – in moderation, mind you – at any time of the day or night. Have you ever? Well, don't tell your mother, but I can tell you, m'boy, champagne tastes better than ever if drunk from a lady's slipper.'

'You wanted to see me?' I interrupted.

'Did I? Oh! I thought you just popped in for a drink. Now then – what *did* I want?' He riffled through some papers on his ancient Chinese desk and said, 'Ah yes! Of course. Egypt's new man, Farouk. He's only sixteen, no experience of the job, so the FO wants me to fill them in on the chap and other problems before they get down to the final draft of the Treaty. And, m'boy, they've summoned me to meet the mandarins in Paris.'

He rolled the word round his tongue.

'So I said to myself, Paris, eh? Let's make a holiday of it. I've already told your mother she's coming with me. She can go to dress shows and so on while we study a different kind of form. Under bright lights.'

'We?'

'Of course. We have to make it a family holiday. Orders from Whitehall.' And quite forgetting that I was all of twenty-seven, he added seriously, 'A trip to Paris should be part of every man's education. And I don't mean at the Louvre. I'd like to take you and Greg to Paris and pick up a few hints from French girls before you settle down. About time we had a holiday together.'

'That's wonderful!' I cried. 'Thanks, Father. It sounds great.'

It did, for we were approaching the hot season when legal business would be slack, with many offices transferred for the summer to Alexandria. I was earning good money in my law practice, and lived at home for nothing; but even so, a holiday with Father was like winning the Calcutta Sweep, for once away from home he insisted on travelling in the utmost luxury – *en prince*, as he called it.

He would never dream of venturing abroad – and by now 'going abroad' meant leaving Egypt – without Zola. On board any ship taking him either to Marseilles for France, or Genoa, if he wished to travel via Italy, he demanded the largest and most luxurious cabins. On a wagon-lit it was single berths only; in hotels, a view, a large sitting room, a car and a chauffeur. Life at home was luxurious enough, but from youth our lives had been detonated by our holidays, for which we had always been given extravagant supplementary pocket money.

'Sounds great!' I repeated. 'When do we start?'

Before we left for France I had to keep a promise, to give, with others, a talk on the judicial systems of the world to students at the law school of Fuad University. It was a fine university, crammed with several hundred students.

Among the lawyers due to speak I waved to an old adversary, Fatah Azzam, one of the toughest prosecutors in Egypt. He always looked vaguely scruffy, ash on the lapels of his crumpled suit, but he was shrewd and never missed a trick in court.

'Good to see you, Holt.' He shook hands. 'But what a waste of time – this rabble! They'll never make lawyers, let alone good advocates.'

'You're right.' Donald Childs, my colleague, had joined us. 'In fact, studying has become a status symbol, and among the middle-classes half the students never really actually study seriously at all. They – or perhaps their parents – just like to boast that they're reading law.'

At the end of the last lecture one student came up to me at the desk and said, 'Excuse me, I didn't have time to thank you.'

Puzzled, I answered, 'There's nothing to thank me for. My talks were very informal. If you've enjoyed them –'

The young man was dark-skinned, bushy-browed, with a prominent nose, and looked vaguely familiar. I noticed that he had a deep crescent-shaped scar on his forehead.

'You don't remember me?' The question was almost belligerent, as though it were impossible that I should forget him, and I was about to murmur a soothing, 'So many students –' when I *did* remember where we had met, and who he was.

'Of course.' I held out a hand. 'Nasser, isn't that the name?

I do remember. The time you and Aly escaped from the police in Teddy's flat. I was rather underdressed!' I laughed, adding more seriously, 'I didn't know you were planning to become a lawyer.'

'I don't think I do want to be a lawyer,' Nasser muttered. 'I'm just picking up a few hints while –'

'So that you can say you went to law school?' I was thinking of what Childs had said, and added rather sharply, 'You may find it boring listening to lectures, but I also find it boring having to come and talk to people who attend university and then say openly that they're not really interested. After all, I'm not a university professor, I give talks for nothing – to try and help students.' My voice must have betrayed my annoyance.

'I'm sorry, I didn't mean it that way,' said Nasser. 'There are other difficulties.'

I realised that he was wrestling with some problem and needed a sounding board. 'Let's have a coffee,' I said on impulse. 'No, not in the canteen; round the corner there's a quiet café in Ahmed Pasha Street. A lot of university dons use it.' Nasser followed me across the street to the Ahmed café where we sat down and I ordered two Turkish coffees.

'Masbut?' I asked. Nasser nodded that he too liked his coffee normally sweetened.

'It's not that I don't *like* law,' he immediately explained. 'I can't tell really – not yet. But if I study, I'll have to live at home.'

His eyes looked into mine with intensity, and he added, 'I can't bear the thought of doing that, because I can't stand my stepmother.'

So that was it. He went on to explain how his father, Abdel–Nasser Hussein, had married again, and the new wife hated her stepson. 'Now it's got so bad, my father is so angry, that sometimes we hardly talk to each other for weeks – a father and his son. What kind of a life is that for me?'

'What's the alternative?' I asked.

'I tried to get a commission in the army. I applied for admittance to the Royal Military Academy.'

'Wasn't that aiming a bit high?' I remembered that Nasser's

father was a postman, and the academy was Cairo's equivalent of Sandhurst in Britain.

'Yes,' answered Nasser, almost savagely. 'They asked me if I knew any pashas or beys. They turned me down because I had no family connections, the right sort of background. But I plan to try again. I've got an appointment in a few days with someone in the War Office. I'm hoping. After all, now that Egypt has been promised independence, we'll need a much larger army.'

I wondered. And wondered, too, when, if ever, I should see Nasser again, but it's extraordinary how, in real life, you meet a man, as I had done in Teddy's flat when Nasser was injured, never expecting to see him again, and then months later you suddenly meet, and then seem to go on meeting. Why should two people miss each other all those months, then meet twice in a week?

For that is what happened a few days after my encounter with Nasser at the law school. On the eve of our departure for France, I bumped into him again – at the Sirry house next-door. Greg had already made his way through the wicket gate to collect Serena for dinner. I popped in just to say goodbye. As I reached the french windows leading from the Sirry garden I heard several people talking inside the house and almost didn't come in. Then Aly saw me, opened the windows wider and shouted, 'There's a friend of yours here, Mark. Come to say Hullo.'

There was Nasser, talking to Aly and Greg. Then I saw Jim Stevenson.

'The "Friends of the Opera" are giving a big ball while you're both away,' explained Serena, coming forward to greet me. 'Mummy's on the committee. So Jim has promised to take me. With Greg's permission.' She whispered to me, 'It was either Jim or Aly – and Aly's so stuffy, always spouting politics.'

I rarely had the chance to study Stevenson at close quarters. Unfairly, and for no reason I could offer, I didn't warm to him. Perhaps there was a certain antipathy between us because we were an outgoing group of friends and his reserve jarred.

Only it was more than reserve: it bordered on secrecy. I always felt suspicious of him. His easy manners, his apparent dislike of work, his fondness for squiring pretty girls, all seemed out of harmony with his cold, pale blue eyes. Though Stevenson seemed unconcerned, his eyes were not. They were never still, and roved continually, as if judging the merits of others present. Or was I imagining it? And was I – stupidly and with no authority for presumption – vaguely jealous because he took Serena out for dinner and dances?

'Have you heard Gamal's news?' asked Aly, interrupting my thoughts.

I shook my head.

'He's leaving law school.'

'I rather gathered he might,' I said dryly.

'Since I saw you,' said Nasser, 'I managed to get another interview with the Under-Secretary of State for War. He's agreed to let me report to an examination board in a month or two. He'll let me know the date within forty-eight hours.'

'Congratulations,' I said, adding, 'with any luck you won't have to live at home.'

'The smallest army tent in the largest desert in the world would be good enough for me,' said Nasser fervently.

'Best of luck to you,' I said as Nasser held out his hand, shaking mine with an almost formal gesture, as though investing it with a hidden meaning, like a Masonic signal. I felt that he was silently thinking, 'At least here's one Englishman with whom I'd like to remain friends.' But perhaps that too was my imagination.

'That friend of Aly's is going to be very disappointed if he doesn't pass into the army,' I said to Serena as Nasser joined Aly in the other corner of the room. 'He *should* be accepted. I think he's damn good officer material.'

'You make it sound like a length of cloth,' laughed Serena. 'He's a bit of a firebrand.'

'The army'll soon cut him down to size.'

Aly and Nasser were in deep conversation. I caught snatches, Aly telling Nasser, 'I can't promise anything – my father was so furious about what happened. But he might be able to pull some rank for you. Leave it to me.'

At that moment Madame Sirry and her husband walked into the room. After perfunctory introductions – Sirry Pasha treating young Nasser with courtesy – Madame Sirry came to talk to me. I was struck again, as I always was, by her beauty – and her style. Father had once said of her, 'She's at her best in a sequinned ball gown standing at the top of the curved bedroom stairs, surveying the guests below.'

And she *did* have a regal air – but often, as at this moment, I thought how much more fun Mother was, a little 'dotty' perhaps, oddly dressed for one so tall, but always exuberant and alive.

'I do hope you have a good time in Paris, Mark,' Madame Sirry said, in French. 'Don't let your father lead you astray – or will it be the other way round?'

'We'll all look after each other.'

'Well, Greg won't need watching.' I wondered whether she meant what she was saying, or whether she was issuing a veiled warning, a tip-off for Greg to be a good boy. 'After all,' she added, but this time without a smile, 'he's in love with the girl he's going to marry. He's going to find Paris very boring.'

'I'm sure he will,' I agreed dutifully. And doubtfully, though I hope the doubt didn't show on my face. I couldn't see Greg spending each evening at the Opera or studying at the *Institut* on the Left Bank.

Sirry Pasha interrupted. 'That *is* young Stevenson, isn't it?' I nodded.

'I thought so,' he added, 'but all Americans look the same to me.'

'Oh come!' said Madame Sirry almost sharply. 'That's a very foolish remark to make.'

'Yes, it is,' admitted Sirry Pasha. 'Sorry, dear. But what I really meant was that the Americans *we* meet – in the government or the diplomatic corps – all look as though they're stamped from the same mould. So are the British – in *their* mould. People in government seem to get rid of their faces. Faceless, that's what they are. Deliberately, perhaps?'

'Including my father?'

'Definitely not,' Sirry laughed. 'There's no mould for him.

He's the exception that proves the rule.'

'But Jim Stevenson' – I stole a glance at him as he stood looking by the french windows – 'does he fit into the American government mould?'

'Does he not?' Sirry looked surprised. 'I rather thought he was the typical foreign service diplomat. Some undefined job. I don't really know what.'

Before the final details of the Paris trip were arranged Father explained to me the role he would have to play. I was intrigued because, since my first successes at the bar, he had taken to talking things over with me, at times almost as though probing for legal advice. I think he felt isolated at times. Greg was not interested in politics. 'And Chiffon doesn't know what on earth I do at my desk all day,' he laughed.

When Father had first broached the plans for the Paris trip he had merely said that the Foreign Office wanted him to fill in the background about the young Farouk.

'But it's more than that.' Father gave a chuckle. 'I'm being sent officially on an unofficial holiday.'

'You mean – in secrecy.'

'If you like to put it that way – though my actual presence in Paris can't be kept secret. But it's supposed to be a fortuitous coincidence. Sir Johnson McCarthy of the Cairo desk in London sent me a message in code.' Father handed the decoded flimsy over the desk, pouring some champagne as I read:

> You know all the Egyptian political leaders personally and Nahas Pasha in particular. They admire and trust you. Of course the ambassador will be in the spotlight and all British decisions will publicly come from him, but we feel that any secret bargaining will be better left in your hands, and if anything goes amiss it will be better that the government is not officially involved. This suggestion has been taken after consultation with the ambassador.

'Interesting.' I handed back the sheet of paper. 'There must be a bit of hard bargaining ahead if the government doesn't want to know officially what's going on.'

'Exactly. Britain *is* prepared to concede a great deal – and so they should. After all, it *is* Egypt's country. But there'll be a price to pay. First, a firm commitment by Egypt that we keep a zone in which to station British troops on the Canal.'

'And –'

'There is another problem the FO wants to sort out. With Hitler getting increasingly belligerent in Europe, and Mussolini throwing his weight about in Africa, Whitehall believes it's possible that in the event of war with Germany we might have to fight Egypt. It's not likely –'

'But it's impossible!'

'Let's hope you're right. I'm inclined to think that in the long run Germany may prove more dangerous than Italy. Look what's already happened in Germany in the last eighteen months. Jews outlawed – monstrous! The vulgar new German flag, the Swastika. Germany has got the Saar back, she's repudiated the military clauses of the Versailles Treaty, and this year she's occupied the demilitarised Rhineland zone. Not bad for a one-time corporal to have achieved.'

'But Italy –?'

'I know the Italians *look* more menacing. But that, m'boy, is because we see the Italian aggression from nearer home – here. We could make a stand against Italian aggression, but the French have no guts. What about last year's Hoare-Laval pact? Hoare was bad enough – a brainless idiot – signing the pact on Abyssinia, but as for Laval! Well, you only have to look at him, Mark.' Father almost spluttered. 'He's a third-rate gangster. France is going through a crisis of appeasement. We are too, but not as badly as them.'

'I still think you're too pessimistic. Any thought of war is so horrible.'

'You don't believe it's possible, and it'll be my job to persuade Nahas Pasha, too, that the whole thing is ridiculous. That way they'll give in to the clause the FO wants to insert.'

'Which is?'

'That in the unlikely event of war in North Africa Egypt will make available to Britain the use of their ports, airfields and lines of communication and administration, including the right to martial law and an effective censorship.'

'Will the Egyptians stand for all that?'

'Hope so, though not if it's an official proposition, with all the attendant publicity. But if I tell Nahas Pasha that it's absurd nonsense he'll be inclined to agree and use that agreement to fight for something else he wants – and which we don't mind if he gets.'

I could feel as we talked the sense of challenge that was exciting Father. The Egyptians were not easy to deal with. They distrusted all British officials – except Father. And they actually *enjoyed* secrecy in negotiation. If Father could work quietly behind the scenes to help bring off a deal that would make the Egyptians agree – yes, it was certainly a challenge.

What we would always think of in our memories as 'The Paris Holiday' centred on a large suite at the Ritz. At first my father had quite a lot of work to do; and in fact at times I was dragged in to help. It was mostly legal or translation work – after all, I was so fluent that I never really knew whether I was speaking English, Arabic or French – but I also helped with the collating of documents. I was not, of course, involved in any of the many public sessions, but it was soon easy to discern a fundamental difference in the approach between the two sides negotiating the Treaty. With Nahas Pasha now Prime Minister under Farouk, he realised that his political future depended on the prospect of '*his* Treaty' being signed. On the other hand, the British were deeply worried about the prospect of German aggression, and so they insisted above everything else on adequate protection of the Canal – by Britons.

'You can see this in the constitution of the two delegations,' said my father. 'All the Egyptians are politicians, while most of the British are either soldiers or technical specialists. So, while Nahas is dreaming of a political treaty, Whitehall regards the whole thing more as a technical exercise in defence.'

My father felt strongly that when Egypt did become independent the Treaty should be a real one. 'But independence has many shades of meaning,' he sighed, and poured out some champagne in the small Ritz bar off the rue Cambon, which he preferred to the more grandiloquent one behind the place Vendôme. 'What I'm fighting against is the military minds which are agreeing to end what was really the colonisation of Egypt, without giving them *real* independence. There'll never be friendship in Egypt if we give them a Treaty promising independence but insisting that we have the right to station British troops on Egyptian soil.'

'But the Egyptians will agree?'

'They'll have to. They've little choice. And we can all argue that the Canal Zone isn't *really* Egypt since the Canal is leased to the British. But look at this.' He handed me a clipping from a Cairo newspaper, commenting on Britain's 'right' to station troops in the Canal Zone. The first paragraph read: 'The occupation of Egypt is supposed to end with the departure of British troops when the Treaty is signed. Now we see that the Treaty is merely a change of label.'

Mother, of course, had hardly time to notice where Father was, or what was happening in the corridors of power. She was in her element, going the rounds of the fashion houses, buying outrageous clothes, or shoes from Mancini in the place Vendôme, for she was very proud of her small feet.

'I don't really like Chanel,' she confided. 'Too severe. But I adore Scap.'

'Who's he?' asked Father.

'*She!* Schiaparelli,' said Mother witheringly, adding, 'and you didn't even notice my new dress.' I had seen it. Indeed, I had been startled by it, one I can only describe inadequately as the ultimate in frou-frou, made of white material apparently hanging down in layers from every part of the dress. 'After all, it is a warm day,' cried Mother defensively. 'Don't you like it, Geoffrey?'

'It's you to a "T", Chiffon,' Father agreed absently. 'How much did it cost?'

'I don't know, silly. All these francs – I can never work them out. Anyway, it was ready-made and I told them to send the bill to you. Today I'm going for another fitting.'

'In taffeta?' Father teased. He loved Mother, but was quite

oblivious to the fact that her height made some of her dresses unsuitable. All he could see was the twinkle and laughter in her face above the outrageous clothes she affected.

Happily, Chiffon was convinced that she dressed in the height of fashion. After breakfast in our suite that morning, she said to me casually, 'Doing anything special this morning, Mark?'

Falling into the trap, I shook my head.

'Be sweet, darling, and come with me. Just for once. Going to a dress show is so much more exciting if you can share your enjoyment with someone. And your father never comes with me.'

I looked to Father for help – but all he said was, 'Why not, if you want to? I won't be needing you today.'

'Just this once,' I agreed doubtfully.

'You're an angel.'

Never again! Mother had a fitting for a dress already chosen, then sat down to watch the parade of the mannequins. The clothes were mostly for young girls, but Mother saw one dress, clapped her hands and cried, 'That's for me! Tell the *vendeuse* I want it finished before we leave Paris.'

The *vendeuse* herself was determined not to take advantage of a tall, angular middle-aged lady just for the sake of making a quick profit, but nothing could stop Mother from ordering it. The *vendeuse*, with supreme tact, suggested, 'It's a beautiful dress, Madame, but I wouldn't like you to order it without seeing the others.'

'I don't want to see anything else,' cried Mother impatiently. 'You can measure me right away. And I want it before I leave.'

'I wonder –'

'Are you a saleswoman or not?' asked Mother crossly.

'Of course, Madame.' The *vendeuse* looked tactful but resigned. 'I'll have you measured for the dress right away.'

'Wait for me, darling,' Mother said gaily. 'I won't be a moment.'

I thought I caught a smile of amusement in the girl's eye while Mother was in the fitting room, and suddenly realised that she thought I was a young gigolo-type lover keeping the elderly client amused, and served.

The impression wasn't lessened when Mother, so pleased and touched by my attendance, cried as she emerged from the fitting room, 'Let's go, darling. I'm so glad you approved, and you've been so sweet, I'm going to take you to Charvet and buy you a pair of silk pyjamas.'

The pace of Father's talks slackened after a week, during which time Greg expended all his energy on secret visits to places he never divulged.

'But where do you go?' I asked him after breakfast one day. 'How do you fill the time?'

Greg was never secretive, but somehow we never seemed to have much to tell each other. Different characters, I suppose.

'I wander round the Left Bank galleries and antique shops,' he said.

'I *am* surprised,' I couldn't help telling him.

'I wanted to buy a painting as a present for Serena,' he said. 'I know she's mad on art, so I thought it'd please her. And then, I've been made a temporary member of the Racing Club. I've met several tennis players who've taken me to unknown bistros. Great fun.'

'Don't become another playboy like Teddy Pollock,' I laughed.

'Me, a playboy!' Greg was genuinely shocked. 'I work as hard as anyone – at sport. Train every day. It's a full-time job winning at polo or tennis or cricket. I'd probably earn more than you if I became a pro.'

Eventually we knew that Father would ask us to go to the Folies Bergère, to him the height of decadence. Sure enough, he did, telling Mother that he was taking us, but that it would be unseemly for her to go. She arranged instead to meet some friends of hers, probably with a sigh of relief. Father made no secret of *his* relief. He probably felt that he couldn't really enjoy watching the bare-breasted girls in their huge head-dresses if Mother was watching too.

'Makes you excited, just looking at them,' he whispered gleefully when we were comfortably seated in the first row of the stalls. I might have felt the same way had I known one or two of them, but I found the girls rather impersonal, though Greg insisted, 'All of them in the Folies are on the game if you're rich enough – and good-looking.'

'But how do you meet them?' I asked. 'They look so remote – so unavailable.'

It wasn't a problem which worried Father because he was delighted just to watch – and imagine – and after supper I took him straight to bed at the Ritz.

Not Greg, though. He wanted to meet one of the girls and he told me later how he managed it. He walked round to the stage entrance with an entire handcart filled with roses in their narrow shopkeepers' tin green vases. He had bought the lot – flowers, handcart and all. And when the first of the identical long-legged girls opened the stage door he offered her the flowers, saying he had bought them just for her. She was so impressed – also with a handsome Englishman's rare command of French – that she went with him to Maxim's for supper, then to bed.

'Hope you didn't get a dose of clap,' I said at breakfast, feeling vaguely guilty on his behalf at the thought of Serena waiting patiently at home.

'Can't spend all your youth in a monastery,' said Greg. 'Better to get it out of your system before marriage. And my God! That girl! You'll have to try her, Mark.' Adding slyly, 'Want an introduction?'

But I didn't need any introducing because, though I had virtually forgotten her, I already had a girl in Paris. Well, I hadn't forgotten, but actually during the first week we were so busy I never gave the girl a second thought; I was so fascinated, observing the kind of a future that was being plotted for Egypt, and how statesmen went about forming it, that I had no time to think about girls.

By the end of the second week, though, the public forum had given way to the secret committee meetings with their leaks, innuendos and drearily phrased official communiques. This was partly the reason why, without having made any particular plans, I strolled down the faubourg St Honoré, past the Elysée Palace, turned left opposite the restaurant

La Crémaillère, along the avenue Matignon and up to the Rond-Point past the beautiful fountains – looking as ethereal as girls in nightgowns – when suddenly a bus whizzed past and there, standing on the open-back platform was a dizzy blonde, hair blowing in the breeze.

'Parmi!' I cried, but she had gone – Parmi, who spent months of each year with her father in Paris. Back at the hotel I consulted the *Bottin* and there was Theo Davidson's number and the address of his flat in the rue du Bac on the Left Bank. I telephoned immediately.

She was in. 'I've tracked you down,' I cried. 'Any chance of meeting? Dinner? Lunch?'

I could hear the suppressed laughter. 'Wonderful, Mark! Of course. Anything you say. Why not come round for a drink and we'll plan our next few days? Pa is away in Limoges, trying to arrange a big deal with Havilland China. He won't be back for four days. Come right round.' And with her typical puckish humour, she added, 'I've got the most beautiful kitchen.'

I didn't understand. 'You're offering to cook dinner?'

'No. But I remember you're a bit kinky, you like girls in kitchens.'

We only went out for dinner once, to the Coupole on the boulevard du Montparnasse that first night, more of a pilgrimage really than in search of gastronomic delights. I must have gone there first when very young, for the space and the height, the careful jigsaw pattern of the shining wooden *banquettes*, to say nothing of the impression (no doubt untrue) of half-starved artists, has remained with me for ever.

'I'm going to start with oysters, a dozen Claires' – Parmi hadn't lost her sense of fun – 'just in case I need the strength.'

I started instead with one of my favourite hors d'oeuvres, *céleri rémoulade*, unobtainable in Cairo. This we followed with two huge plates of *blanquette de veau*.

And when the waiter in his striped shirt offered us a choice of sweets, Parmi looked at him with those wide open blue eyes, twisted her blonde hair, and said innocently, 'We're both so tired we've got to go to bed straight away.'

For the rest of the time we strolled round the Left Bank or

made love. It was an interlude of delight, and though at first I had wondered if her religious fervour might prevent her enjoying herself to the full – to say nothing of me – she acted throughout without any inhibitions.

And she made no demands. She never hinted at any permanent arrangement; that we might fall in love.

Once I caught her off-guard, so to speak. We were having coffee at the Deux Magots when she said that she wanted to buy something, would be back in five minutes, and would I wait.

As she left I caught a glimpse of her entering the squat, square church of St-Germain-des-Prés. She had said she wanted to *buy* something. Discreetly, I followed her into the church. Parmi was on her knees, praying devoutly, murmuring words aloud, oblivious to the world outside. Then she got up, went to a small altar and lit two candles.

I should have left well alone, for I reached the café before she did, but instead I asked casually, 'Get what you wanted? What did you buy, darling?'

'Some candles.' I realised that she could not lie about religion, and so wisely didn't ask her where they were, since she carried no parcel.

But how wonderful it was to see her again! And exhausting – it must have been, for on our way back by sea to Alex, walking round the deck, Chiffon said to me, 'Oh dear, Mark, I'm worried about you, all that work. You're not sleeping well?'

'It was Paris, Mother. I never can get used to sleeping in strange beds.'

'I shall write to the Ritz about it. Or your father's secretary will when we get home.'

Long before we reached Alex the tiredness had been washed away by the sea air and two undisturbed nights of sleep. But it was Greg who asked me, 'Where the hell did you vanish to on the last few days?'

'Never mind me,' I retorted. 'What have *you* been up to?'

'Couldn't manage more than two nights in the week,' Greg grumbled. 'Spent a bloody fortune on the first two evenings, but then ran out of money. You know the drill – they make you wait half the night so they can chalk up the profits on their share of the drinks, and then when it's over they want you to go home by taxi twenty minutes later.'

'You're in a bad way,' I sympathised. 'Why don't you and Serena get married? Save you a fortune.'

'Plenty of time. I adore Serena – who doesn't? – but why eat porridge all your life when you can enjoy wild oats for a few more years?'

'Bit unfair on Serena.'

'I don't think so.' He ran his hands through his crisp, curly hair. 'Egyptian women understand that a man has to live before he – well, vegetates into marriage.'

'What a recipe for a happy married life!' I said, really horrified.

'Oh, don't get me wrong,' said Greg. 'We'll have a wonderful life together. But marriage is – well, a *state*. Carpet slippers and female questions if you're late back from the club. Know what I mean?'

'Actually, I was thinking of Serena.'

'Don't worry. The minute she insists, I'll obey. But give it a few more months, eh? And by the way, you didn't answer *my* question. What have you been up to?'

'I happen to be a bachelor,' I pointed out.

'Yes, but what have you been up to?' he repeated.

'I have friends in Paris,' I said loftily. 'I like to look them up, and mine cost me nothing. Just a few bottles of champagne, with a girl to bring me breakfast in bed.'

'Christ! How did you find her?'

'Don't blaspheme!' Unconsciously I echoed Parmi, before adding, 'You know her. Remember Parmi? The dizzy blonde?'

'Of course. She lives in Paris. You lucky sod! And you mean to say you kept her all to yourself? You're a sly one.'

'I didn't want to make Father jealous,' I said modestly.

9

My chambers were just off Ibrahim Pasha Street, their old-fashioned windows overlooking the pretty, well-watered Ezbekieh Gardens with their welcome patch of green and ancient bandstand in the middle, where in the old days bands of British troops played in the gardens after dinner. The Scottish pipers were so popular that Egyptians started pipe bands of their own, and there are still several shopkeepers in Cairo who do nothing but sell or repair bagpipes.

My chambers, too, were old-fashioned, very British in their furnishings: the solid, old, polished partners' desk, the mahogany filing-cabinets, the burnished stainless steel deed boxes, fireproof, and housed in an ornate casing of stainless steel tubing, moulded into curlicues, and resting on shelves so that you could draw out each metal deed box separately. In itself my deed box stand was a handsome piece of shining furniture envied by all my colleagues. Like everything else, it had been shipped out from London after my time at the Temple, where I had eaten my dinners. It was a relic of my youth, not a relic of my achievements, a reminder of happy memories, of my tiny chambers in the Temple, between Fleet Street and the Embankment, with the lawns spreading down to the river, the uniformed attendants saluting in an atmosphere of dignity, where no voice was raised. Life had passed by in a whisper then, a far cry from the strident outpourings of the Egyptian courts where every race – Arab as well as European – was convinced that the more impassioned the plea the more certain a man would be to win his case.

The office was not quite so comfortable on this particular day – because the July temperatures had soared into the eighties, and I had no air-conditioning. In fact I was thinking of leaving early when my clerk, Mohamed Salem, knocked on

the door. Salem had been clerk to my predecessor; and he
had a face the colour of polished walnut. His coal-black eyes
lit up with pleasure whenever he scented business, for as in
England legal clerks were a coterie to themselves, though in
Cairo they had far more opportunities, due to a fundamental
difference between the legal systems in England and Egypt.
In England a client had first to consult a solicitor who would
then, if he thought it necessary, suggest a barrister to plead
or to give counsel's opinion. In Egypt the title of barrister
did not exist. I could do the work of both a lawyer and a
barrister. Though I had read for the bar in London to further
my knowledge, I was regularly consulted on all kinds of legal
problems.

This was what happened now. Salem handed me a strip of
pasteboard which read: 'Mr Basile Theocrates, Theatrical
Representative.'

'Should I see him?' I asked Salem. 'Any idea what it's
about?'

'Yes, *sir*! This gentleman is the agent for Samia, the singer.
And she's here too. Very beautiful.'

'All right.' I was intrigued, for Samia must have been the
only woman in North Africa famous enough in a man's world
to be known to everyone by just a single name. Samia: it was
a beautiful name, conjuring up many visions, yet I had never
seen her, nor had ninety-nine out of a hundred people who
worshipped her as fervently as Americans worship a Hollywood star. For though she was a famous Egyptian singer
Samia's fame was due to the radio. Every Friday she sang on
the Egyptian radio – and people switched on in every house,
palace even, every tent, every shop, every village square from
the Persian Gulf to the Atlantic coast. Still young, she was a
sensation, and my father – more Arabic than many of his
Arab neighbours – would never miss her performance,
though mercifully my mother insisted that he had his own
radio set in the Chinese study.

What also intrigued me was that she had started her career
as a poor peasant girl who had ridden her donkey from village
to village giving impromptu concerts, asking for a collection
of a few milliemes after the show. Suddenly she had been

'discovered' by the radio. After that there was no stopping her. She gave concerts at dozens of theatres, including Santy, the biggest open-air theatre in Cairo, and the Ramses Theatre. Eventually she received an invitation from one young man who loved music – and girls. The sixteen-year-old Farouk, slim and handsome, invited her to sing at the Abdin Palace.

'Show Miss Samia and Mr Theocrates in,' I said to Salem.

Theocrates proved to be a typical second-rate, oily Greek entrepreneur, all expansive hands, cheap eau de Cologne and subservient smile. I wondered how much he was managing to take from Samia.

The famous singer was very different. I wasn't sure what I had expected, though I knew that most people in show business tended to be 'difficult', overbearing, self-important. Instead I received a pleasant surprise. She had no airs and graces, and as I indicated to her the most comfortable of my two old leather armchairs I could see that she not only had a happy smile but was far more beautiful than I had imagined. She had what I can only call a gentle brown skin, soft and pliant in a perfectly formed oval face; a small nose, and very dark hair hanging loosely over her shoulders. But as important as the beauty was her openness of character. I had read that she was twenty-three, and she was surprisingly articulate considering her modest start in life. I had the feeling that she retained a peasant simplicity together with her more worldly outlook, as though she enjoyed the trappings of success, but missed the innocence of her early struggles. But perhaps I was imagining things. Certainly she clapped her hands with genuine delight when I spoke to her in Arabic.

'That makes it so much easier,' she smiled. 'I was expecting that Mr Theocrates would have to interpret. I tried so hard to speak your language, but I never succeeded.'

'Well, we've got the language problem settled, so if there is anything I can do to help you.' I paused and asked, 'By the way, what made you choose me – especially as you didn't know I spoke Arabic?'

'An American friend of mine,' she answered simply. 'He just told me that if you ever had a problem, British lawyers are the most honest.'

'Highly complimentary,' I laughed. She was the kind of girl with whom you laughed easily. 'Do I know him?'

'He knows you,' she replied. 'And admires you, as you've guessed. It's a Mr Jim Stevenson.'

Stevenson! How flattering. And how unexpected.

'Of course I know him,' I said. 'Now, Miss Samia, what can I do for you?'

She smiled. She looked so happy, as though success would be in her grasp for years to come, that I was totally unprepared for the shock of her next words.

'No, Basile,' she stopped the Greek talking. 'Let me handle this, please. I need some advice from Mr Holt. You see, I have to make a very important decision. I have been told that I will only be able to sing for another year. After that – phut! My voice will have gone and I will have to find another way to make a living.'

I was horrified. Perhaps it was the nonchalant way she announced such terrible news that staggered me. But that was her way of treating misfortune.

'I have my life,' she smiled. 'Only my voice is going, the rest of me is healthy, *hamdu li'llah!*'

'Yes, God be praised,' I echoed. 'But are you – have you been to a doctor?'

'I have. They all say the same thing. Perhaps it is too much singing, but I have a minor illness and my voice is on the way out.'

'May I ask – the illness?'

'It's a very long name,' she hesitated. 'I'm suffering from hypo-thyroid glandular trouble.'

'It means nothing to me, but surely a good doctor –?' I left the sentence unfinished.

'She has been to the best –' interrupted Theocrates.

'Basile,' she said, 'you have been very clever in finding the address of this charming Mr Holt, but will you leave us now? I would like to explain the details of the advice I need. You understand?'

'Of course,' he mumbled, but not liking it. 'I will pay a visit to you later, sir, to find out what decisions you are making about Miss Samia.'

'Of course.' I led the way to the mahogany panelled door – another of the keepsakes I had brought all the way from the Temple.

'Basile takes ten per cent of everything,' she explained almost humorously after he had left. 'After all, he did get me my first broadcast, so I owe everything to him. But when it comes to major decisions I am the best salesman. Now, Mr Holt, here is my problem. I will speak plainly. I hope I will not shock you.'

I watched her sitting opposite my big desk. She looked so young – well, I thought, in one way she has the bloom of youth, but in another there were the faintest traces that the bloom might not last much longer.

I tried a little small talk. 'What a strain it must be, not only getting to the top but staying there.' Clients often take some time to unwind, to confess.

'It is. And you can only do it – what is the proverb? – by burning the candle at both ends. I like that. If you work hard, you might as well play hard. So I won't shock you?'

'Nothing shocks me, Miss Samia. If I can help you, of course I will try. But I don't quite see how –'

She hesitated for a moment.

'His Majesty admires my voice very much,' she said slowly, adding with a wry smile, 'and now he wishes to admire my body – in private.'

She was so attractive that I caught myself thinking, How lucky to be a king and be able to command.

With a slight, amused sigh, she said, as if reading my thoughts, 'I see you envy him.'

'Madam,' I said, 'who wouldn't? But how can I help you?'

'Arabs always take a long time to get to the point.' She had a touch of laughter in her voice.

'Well – as I said, Madam –' I offered.

'Call me Samia. It's the only name I've got.'

'Samia, then. Now – to business.'

'It is not as simple as it sounds,' she confessed. 'But basically I would like you to check on the deeds relating to the transfer to me of a nightclub in a building in the Kasr el Nil. It's not far from Groppi's at the corner of Soliman Pasha,' she explained.

'And the building belongs to . . .?'

'The king is giving it to me as a present.'

Her plan was simple. After the king had begged and begged her to become his mistress, she learned about her voice, without telling Farouk, and finally agreed to go to bed with him – but on one condition. He would set her up in a nightclub where she could be assured of a reasonable income for the rest of her life.

'The place – the building, everything – would be *mine*, you understand. The king would give me the deeds of the building as a present, and enough money to restart the nightclub, which is awful at the moment. That's all I ask. But it has to be *mine*, so that I could open a butcher's shop if I wanted to. Absolutely mine for ever so that nobody can ever take my livelihood away from me.'

I could appreciate her point of view – a peasant attitude to the acquisition of land and property.

'Well, Mr Holt,' she went on, 'the king has agreed to everything. I've even inspected the premises, but I'm unhappy about one or two items in the title-deeds. I've seen too many people given land and then have it taken away.'

'You're right to be careful. But with HM?'

'The king agreed, then handed the entire problem over to his personal ADC, General Sadik.'

'Oh, him.' I was thinking of Madame Sirry's, *'Il est un cochon.'*

'You feel as I do?'

'I hardly know him, but from what I've heard about him I wouldn't trust him an inch.'

'Neither would I. All I want is to be sure that the deeds which General Sadik's solicitors have given me don't have any loopholes in them – that I can do anything I want with the building, spend the money on the proposed nightclub just as I want to, just as the king has promised I can. It must be mine, you agree?'

'Of course.'

I put the documents she gave me in my drawer, promising

to read them as soon as possible, and as Samia prepared to leave, I looked at my watch. Half past twelve. On impulse, walking round the desk I asked her, 'Have you time for a drink? A glass of champagne?'

'Do you always spend your profits so quickly?' she laughed.

'Not often. But I thought –'

'I'd love to. Where?'

'A surprise. To meet your greatest fan.'

'Fans? Oh no. That's work – having to put on what I call my fan face!'

'This one is different. Trust me. After all, you should; I'm your advocate.'

I opened the door of the Chrysler and we set off the short distance along Soliman Pasha Street, crossed Ismalia Square, and at the corner of Kasr-el-Aini Street turned right and made for the compound of our house, next-door to the embassy.

'What is it?' she asked. 'It's beautiful. And the entrance!'

'Wait till you see the gardens on the other side. They lead right down to the Nile.'

She looked at me, puzzled.

'Don't worry.' I braked outside the porticoed front door. 'It's home.'

'All of it?' she laughed. 'And this fan of mine? Is he one of the Nubians?'

'White as snow,' I laughed, leading her along the panelled Long Gallery with its old masters in heavy frames. We reached Father's study.

'See that electric bulb painted red over the door?' I pointed to it. 'When that's on, nobody is allowed even to knock. But when it's off – like now –' I knocked.

'Come in, come in, whoever you are,' cried Father, and it was typical of him that before he even greeted me or my visitor he said, 'Pretty girl, m'boy. Is this a formal presentation? To introduce your intended?'

'Father! You'll embarrass this young lady.'

'Great believer in first sights,' he grunted. 'Here, my child' – pointing to the bottle on the desk – 'have a drink. Best time of the day for champagne. But of course you're a

Moslem. Don't drink, eh?'

'But I do!' Samia laughed – and her voice had all the melodious timbre of a singer.

'Like your voice,' said my father. 'Pretty girl and a pretty voice. Good on you, Miss – Miss what?'

'Take a deep breath, Father.'

'You *are* getting married,' he said, suspiciously.

'It's your favourite singer. That's why I asked her to pass by for a moment and meet you.'

'Not Samia? It can't be!'

He jumped out of his chair, took both of Samia's hands in his, looked at her fingers, then kissed her hands almost fervently. 'Well, well, delighted to meet you at last.' Peering over his half-moon spectacles he grumbled, 'No one has a right to have a beautiful face and a divine voice. Melba was a horror to look at. And nobody *knows* your face. This Moslem fetish for not being photographed! With a girl like you, it's criminal. You should be on posters pasted on every wall.'

He poured out a second glass of champagne, adding, 'I have all your records. Play 'em over and over again, but only in this room. My wife hasn't got a musical ear.'

He rambled on, as excited as he always was when involved in anything Egyptian. 'Well, I never!' he said.

'Samia must be going.' I interrupted a long discussion in Arabic (in which he did most of the talking). 'I promised her that I'd only keep her a couple of minutes – to see you. And I want to show Samia the garden before I drive her back to Zamalek.'

'I understand. Come again. Next time without this young feller here. I'll take you on a tour of the Cairo you've never seen.'

'Is that a promise?' It was a polite goodbye remark, but my father seized on it.

'Yes, it is. Shall we make the date firm?'

'Father,' I said gently. 'Samia must be going.'

She shook hands, English-style, but as we made for the door my father planted a kiss firmly on her cheek and whispered to her in Arabic.

As we walked into the garden, she was laughing.

'What did he say that was so funny?' I asked.

'What a man! He whispered that he would like to meet me again, but alone. And you know what he said: "I may be getting on, but I can still –" '

'I'm sorry. I had an idea that he would say something like that.'

'Are you like him?' she asked. 'Propositioning strange women?'

'They do say I take after him, but I never make advances to lady clients. Very unethical. I could be disbarred if I did that sort of thing.'

'But when you've sorted out my legal affairs?' she said flippantly, but before I could respond there was a laughing voice and a 'Hullo' from the Sirry gardens and Serena came through the wicket gate.

'Sorry.' She smiled. 'I didn't know you had a friend with you.'

Knowing Serena, she was perfectly aware that I hadn't been alone.

She stopped, waiting for me to say 'Come on in', and I, in a way, was delighted to introduce them.

We all walked together in the garden for a few minutes before Serena left us and Samia announced that she too must go.

As we drove back to Samia's flat in Zamalek, she made an astonishing remark.

'You didn't tell me your neighbour's daughter was in love with you.'

'Serena? She's going to marry my brother.'

'She may be getting married to someone else,' said Samia. 'But she's mad about you.'

'I'm afraid it just shows how wrong you can be. Serena is nine years younger than me, four years younger than my brother. He's more her age, more fun.'

'Then forget what I said.' Samia pointed out the block of flats. 'I was probably wrong. I thought I caught a look in her eyes.'

Two days later I was walking in the garden when I saw Serena painting, her easel propped up in the soft grass.

'Quite a girl, your singer,' she looked up, speaking carefully. 'Attractive.'

'What do you mean, "*my* singer"?' I teased. 'I've only met her once. She came to see me at my chambers for advice, and I thought it would please Father if she came to the house.'

'She's got her eye on you,' Serena said, almost crossly.

'Come off it. I've never met her before. I don't know what on earth you're talking about.'

'You come off it, Mark,' she said. 'Remember me? I'm a woman.' She dabbed on some Chinese white.

And then, curiously, she added, 'I caught a look in her eyes.'

10

I was not sure what loopholes, if any, I expected to find in the deeds of Samia's proposed property, but I certainly found them – by the dozen.

The deed of sale had presumably been drawn up by General Sadik's lawyers, on his instructions. The premises of the nightclub comprised the central section of the 'three-part' building in Kasr el Nil, with communal walls to the two outside properties. Samia's building was, so to speak, sandwiched between the other two. It quickly became apparent that Sadik, banking on the 'peasant mentality' of a girl who was delighted with her impending good fortune, had expected her to sign the deed automatically, perhaps overawed by the palace connections.

But Samia was no simple peasant. She had clung to success by the shrewd manipulation of her talents, and was instinctively suspicious of the deed. So was I. When my staff made legal routine searches about adjoining property, the picture became even blacker.

There was only one course of action – telephone General Sadik's solicitors and arrange for a conference.

Three days later, much to my astonishment, an Egyptian voice insisted on being put through to me by Salem, after my clerk had popped his head round the corner of the door and whispered importantly, 'I understand it's a very big fish, sir. Won't take no for an answer.'

The man on the phone wasted no time when Salem switched the call through. 'General Sadik at the Abdin Palace will speak to Mr Holt.'

'And Mr Holt will speak to General Sadik,' I said coldly.

Sadik's voice was smooth enough; but a note of menace underlay it. 'I understand you've been investigating the deeds of the premises which the singer, Samia, is to receive from HM as a present?'

'I have, General.'

'With what object, Mr Holt?'

'The object of assuring my client that all is well, General.'

A tiny pause, an intake of breath. 'You have no need to worry, Mr Holt. I can assure you everything is in order.'

'No doubt, General. But *quod erat demonstrandum*. I am pursuing routine enquiries with that end.'

The note of menace returned. 'I suggest that in view of the delicate nature of the transaction it would be unwise to pursue the matter any further.'

'Unwise? Some might see in that word, General, the suggestion of a threat.'

'No, no, Mr Holt. Let that word be – as you lawyers say – stricken from the record. Let us say that perhaps in view of the *delicate* nature of the transaction it might be more circumspect – yes, that's it, *circumspect* – not to peer too closely.'

'General,' I said. 'I am completely unconcerned about the nature of the transaction, delicate or otherwise. I am acting for a client who has asked me to investigate a draft deed of gift. In my opinion, which is what I am being paid for, several clauses in that draft deed – I will put it circumspectly, General – need clarifying. I can attend you at your office, with your solicitors present, at any time that doesn't clash with my appearance in court.'

He edged away from my challenge. 'No. I'll come and see you at *your* office.'

We met three days later. I had seen Sadik at several functions, had even been introduced to him briefly on one occasion, but I had never actually spent time alone with him, been able to study him.

I recognised the type: in court he would be a contentious litigant, a devious witness. His built-in servility was hidden behind a parapet of arrogance. He was in his fifties, I imagined, well-tailored, but his grey suit didn't quite disguise his girth. He was powerfully perfumed. His silk handkerchief was embroidered with two-inch initials sticking out of his pocket. Four of his manicured fingers bore rings – all of them set with oversized gems cut as scarabs. His black hair was pomaded to disguise its thinness and I almost expected to see runnels of sweat glistening between the carefully stretched strands; but his skin was dry, like that of a dead snake. His eyes, set too closely to his aquiline nose, didn't smile.

Sadik, I knew, had risen from nothing – a junior officer, he had finally insinuated himself into the Abdin Palace. He was the royal pimp, got up as the king's ADC, and he knew all the techniques of enticing women into the company of the sixteen-year-old Farouk.

'General,' I said, 'in no circumstances would I have my client sign the deed in its draft form.'

The scarabs glittered under the lamp as he tapped his fingers on my desk. 'But surely, Mr Holt, the point of a draft is that it is subject to approval by both parties?'

'Indeed, General. And I would never recommend approval of, for instance, clause 10b.'

He pretended not to know the clause I was referring to.

'Clause 10b? Enlighten me, Mr Holt.' Heavy lids hooded the eyes for a moment.

'That clause, General, strictly limits the amount of noise to be made on the premises after eleven o'clock at night.'

'Reasonable, I'd have thought. Presumably the neighbours have some rights.'

'They have indeed, General. One neighbour runs a fashion boutique; on the other side is an office. I have spoken to both tenants and both assure me that they close their premises at five-thirty each evening and are quite indifferent to any noise that occurs after that. And since the purpose of the gift is to enable Miss Samia to run a nightclub – an enterprise that can scarcely take place without noise – it seems strange that a stipulation limiting it should have been inserted in the deed by the' – I paused to give emphasis to the next word – 'by the *new* landlords.'

Sadik chose to ignore my emphasis. 'No doubt a slight adjustment to the clause would satisfy all parties, Mr Holt.' He was giving way on a small point to secure an advantage.

'No doubt, General. But it is not only clause 10b that is worrying me.'

'Then what *is* worrying you, Mr Holt? I'd be glad if you would come to the point. Neither my time nor my patience are unlimited.'

'You have come here at your own request, General, no doubt for good reasons of your own. A more orthodox course would have been to confer with your solicitors.'

'Well?' he blustered angrily, and sharper, 'Get on with it, man.'

I undid the pink tape that tied the documents on my desk. 'As you know, General, there are three properties joined together, Miss Samia's being in the middle –'

'Of course I know.'

'– and our surveyors say that the two outer properties are in a poor state of repair; particularly the outer walls, which before long will cost a great deal of money to make safe. Though this would appear to be of no concern to my client – the middle section of the property is in an excellent state of repair – an extraordinary clause in the deed obliges my client to share the cost of repairs, scaffolding, maintenance and so on, with the other parties. Such expenditure could ruin her business.'

Sadik gestured with a dismissive hand. 'I know nothing of this.'

'Does His Majesty?'

'Of course not. You can hardly be so naive, Mr Holt, as to suppose HM concerns himself with trivialities of this nature.'

'Indeed not, General. Stupid of me.' I went on as if genuinely puzzled. 'My understanding of the affair is that His Majesty wishes to make my client financially independent for the rest of her life. The way some clauses in the deed are phrased could after a few years leave her penniless.'

Sadik rose. He was too clever to reveal his weakness by anger. 'Enough. I'll have a word with my solicitors. They'll find out the owners and put a stop to all this nonsense.'

I smiled coldly. 'There's one other thing,' I said. 'Do sit down, General. A moment now will save you a great deal of trouble. I understand that the entire block of property is owned by a firm called Managos Investments. This concern is in turn owned by Papazian and Company in Alexandria.' I paused to let that sink in. 'I'm sure you know what I'm going to say, General. Among your many interests you have a controlling share in a firm called Sakkapoulos and Company in Kenissa el Guildida Street – and they own Papazian.'

Sadik sat down again.

'So?'

'So, General, your controlling interest in Sakkapoulos makes you effectively the owner of the building in question. Your business interests are no concern of mine; but those of my client are. It is my opinion that, without His Majesty's knowledge, you planned to take this peasant girl for a ride, believing her to be prepared to sign any impressive legal document without seeking advice.'

The cold eyes glinted. 'What you say, Mr Holt, is without doubt slanderous. Because you say it in the privacy of your office with no witnesses you think you can get away with it. But –'

'No, General. I am trying to prevent *you* getting away with what you thought was a nicely parcelled-up little scheme. I've prepared a new deed which I suggest you take to your lawyers now. In the meantime I'll not tell the whole truth to Samia.'

He took the document I held out to him without a word,

turned and walked out. Even after he had gone I could smell Sadik's cloying scent and walked to open the windows.

Three days later the deed – *my* deed – arrived with a polite note from the owner's solicitors agreeing to all my changes.

Before I next met Samia I had two intriguing conversations, both by chance.

At home one evening I was preparing to go out for dinner at Shepheard's roof-garden, and popped into Mother's sitting room to 'pay my respects' (Father's phrase for not forgetting our manners). She was having a drink with Dr Phillips, the family doctor who had brought both Greg and myself into the world.

I kissed Mother, then shook hands with the doctor. 'Nothing wrong?'

'No, no,' he said. 'One of the girls in the kitchen wasn't well, so I promised I'd look in.'

It was one of Father's rules that whoever worked in our house – from Zola or the gardeners to the humblest kitchen maid – were always treated by Dr Phillips. As my father would often put it, 'Zola is a damned sight better butler than I could ever be. We both need each other – in good health.'

'Nothing to worry about?'

'Well,' sighed Mother, 'Zeinab has done it again. So *very* inconvenient.'

'Oh, that,' I laughed. 'I'm glad it's nothing serious.' Zeinab, who worked in the kitchens, already had two illegitimate children. 'We know the father?'

'You must be joking,' chortled Dr Phillips. 'A Nubian never tells.'

Dr Phillips always stayed for an extra drink and he sat down, talking about the latest news of Alexandria where he had just been staying.

As I was about to leave, I asked casually, 'Can you give me a bit of free knowledge, Dr Phillips?'

'You can pay for it with yet another drink.' He held out his glass with a laugh.

'It's a girl I met recently – a singer – and her voice is suddenly going. Terrible. I asked her why, and she said she's suffering from something called hypo-thyroid glands. Surely there must be *something* she can do?'

'I'd have thought so,' said Dr Phillips. 'There are some tablets which might –'

'She's a strange girl,' I interrupted. 'She told me she has an aversion to pills. She refuses to take any tablets. Says she can't keep them down. They make her sick.'

'Very stupid of her. There's no way of treating hypo-thyroid glands except by tablets. No injections. Does she drink a lot?'

I shook my head. 'Not that I know of.'

'Drugs?'

'I'm sure she doesn't.'

'Well, check on her arms – if you'll let her put them round you,' he joked. 'For needle marks. That could make it impossible for her to take proper medication. But it's the long-term effects she'll have to watch for if she doesn't take treatment.'

'Not only her voice?'

'That first,' he explained. 'Without treatment she'll develop a voice that gradually gets hoarser; she might put on weight – and then she'll tend to have bouts of depression.'

'Thanks, Doctor. I'll warn the lady.'

Later that same day, at Shepheard's where I was dining with some clients whom I hardly knew, I ran into Jim Stevenson and Greg.

Stevenson looked as relaxed as ever, and in many ways I almost envied him. He always appeared so – not dapper, that would be the wrong word – so neatly casual, as though he just happened to wear the one suit of clothes that was right for the occasion. And his casual air fitted perfectly with his modulated, modestly American Boston accent.

Greg happened to walk into the roof-top bar almost at the same moment as Stevenson, and I couldn't help contrasting the two men: Greg had the aggressive look of one who owned Shepheard's; Stevenson the assured look of one who didn't really care *who* owned it.

'What'll it be?' I asked them both, adding to Stevenson, 'I owe you a drink.'

'Me?' He looked genuinely puzzled.

'Sure. You gave my name to a very attractive lady: Samia. She asked me to help her.'

'I hope you were successful.'

'Hundred per cent. Thanks to your introduction.'

'Good. She's a sweet girl.'

'I didn't know you knew her.' I twiddled the ice in my scotch and soda, wondering, intrigued, what Stevenson would reply.

'Sweet girl,' he repeated.

There was nothing more I could say. It was as neat a brush-off as though he had said, 'Why don't you mind your own business?'

There was a pleasant and unexpected conclusion to the case. I had tied up Samia's fortune so securely that it would take an earthquake to wreck it.

'I shall never forget what you've done for me. Never,' she told me a few days after the contract had finally been signed. Then, getting out of my office chair she walked round the desk and kissed me. 'There! That's part of my thanks.'

'Really!' I pretended to be scandalised. 'I could be disbarred for professional misconduct.'

'It might be worth it.'

'I must admit that you kiss as beautifully as you sing. But no,' I protested. 'If my clerk came in and found you kissing me –'

'Then,' she said, almost shyly, 'perhaps another time. At your house? Then I could say hullo to your father.'

'But you're a client, Samia. It's absolutely forbidden. Even for such a beautiful client as you.'

My voice had suddenly gone husky. 'I'll tell you what, you can pay me now – fifty piastres – that's ten bob in English money – and my clerk will come in and make out an official receipt. Then our legal relationship will be ended. Closed.'

I clanged the bell on my desk with the palm of my hand.

Salem's eyes opened wide and he flashed his teeth as he studied the fifty-piastre note. I told him gravely, 'Please make out an official receipt. Keep the money in the petty cash until you next go to the bank.'

When he left the room, eyes still staring, Samia turned to me. 'You are clever,' she laughed.

Later that night, in her villa in Zamalek, just across the Bulac Bridge, she said to me, lying in my arms, 'You nearly didn't come with me, did you? Were you afraid?'

'A little, perhaps. You might have turned me out on the doorstep.'

'I wondered whether I should. Then I thought, why?'

'I'm glad you didn't.' I smiled, thinking how exciting a sudden adventure can be, and pleased too that, even in bed, she had been gentle, with none of the aggressiveness I associated with successful 'showbiz' women.

Leaning over her, letting her enjoy stroking me wherever her hands wandered over my naked body, I surreptitiously examined her arms.

'What the hell's this?' I said, suddenly harsh. I knew the tell-tale marks of a hypodermic needle.

'It's nothing. Please.'

'Tell me – is it cocaine?'

'Just occasionally – my white lover. Nothing to worry about. Sometimes I need to be pepped up. But I'm careful. I don't abuse it.'

'Samia, you're a fool!' I cried. 'You could die.'

'I won't. I may not sing, but I won't die.'

I leaned over the bed, hunched up. 'I've been to see my father's doctor. No' – I could sense the fear in her eyes – 'I didn't tell him your name. But he told me that your throat problem might be cured if you took some special medication pills.'

'I'll *never* take any pills. I tried once when I was singing, and I was sick during the performance. It was terrible. I've tried again, I promise, but I can't keep them down. Even though I know my voice will go nothing else will happen. So don't worry. Come and kiss me.'

I did. I hadn't the heart to repeat Dr Phillips' warnings. I couldn't even imagine – I didn't want to imagine – the picture he had painted for me of a puffy, deformed woman in place of this slender creature.

'Don't abuse it,' I begged her. 'You're so beautiful – and so gentle. And the cure – you *must* take medication.'

'I can't,' she said sadly.

It wasn't until I was driving home at half past three in the morning that I thought of the way men and women living on their nerves in show business so often needed the stimulus of drugs. And as for Samia's future, I found it hard, even after talking to Dr Phillips, to believe that a girl like Samia just couldn't take her pills and swallow them. But there *were* people who found it impossible. And what Samia had said bore the stamp of truth.

It had been a wonderful evening, and I had no premonition of the way my world was going to crumble about my ears until I reached home.

I stepped over the sleeping form of the guard outside and let myself in. The lights were on, and as I walked through the hall I noticed an envelope on the silver salver where letters were always left.

It was for me. Idly I turned it round. The writing was unknown to me. The stamp was French, the postmark Paris. Without thinking I ripped the envelope open. A single sheet of notepaper fluttered out, and one glance at the signature told me it came from Theo Davidson. Even then I had no idea what it contained. Until I read the cold, opening lines:

Dear Mark,

I learn that you have seduced my only daughter. I have to inform you that she is pregnant, and I expect you to meet me urgently to discuss what must be done.

11

For two days I didn't breathe a word to anyone. Once or twice I almost told Father – I knew he would be sympathetic – but my legal training cautioned me against making hasty announcements. Of course I would have to tell the family soon, but first I needed time to reflect, for the shock was shattering – the thought that a few moments of pleasure could change my entire life. On the other hand, and thinking practically, I knew I could do much worse than marry a fun-loving, attractive girl who at least would keep me amused and make me what is called 'a good wife'.

Looking back later on my two days in silence, I wondered if I were clinging to last-minute hopes that it was all a mistake, that I would receive a cable from Parmi, 'Ignore Pa's letter stop false alarm no problems.' Of course it was ridiculous – but mistakes *did* happen, didn't they? No, reason warned me. In this case they *didn't*.

On the third morning, waking early, I decided that before anything else I must phone Parmi, even though she wouldn't know if her father's letter had reached me. In 1937 you could never be sure when a letter from Europe to Egypt would arrive; it depended on the whims of thousands of ill-paid, uninterested civil servants. But I had to contact her. I would telephone Parmi first from my chambers, then return home and announce the news to the family.

It was a beautiful morning, and after a quick shower at six o'clock and a glass of iced mango juice I went for a walk, crossing the Kasr el Nil Bridge, making my way along the Giza Road, lined with its slightly perfumed eucalyptus trees, planted years ago to offer shade to men and beasts when the heat of the day pressed down on the city.

The Giza Road was already alive with people. The first

shops were opening, the first cups of coffee being served. The water or sherbet or sweetmeat sellers were preparing their wares, each one hoping to earn enough piastres to live until the next dusk. Kids in dirty striped pyjamas played with makeshift toys on the dusty pavement, while the road itself was crowded with every kind of vehicle; not only a few cars but supercilious-looking camels, disdainful of the cruelly laden donkeys. Everything was an excuse for noise – the drivers yelling instructions, advice, curses, beating the donkeys mercilessly as they tried to get to the market before their rivals.

Drivers of the camels, oxen or horses that pulled the typical flat carts loaded with vegetables had a better time of it. They knew every inch of the road, and so did their animals. It was as though man and beast had struck a bargain to do as little work as possible. Some of the drivers lolled back, chewing pieces of their load of sugar cane, while others sat upright, more alert, eyes staring. I could see them, even from a distance, with the look of someone who has been smoking hash.

Hash was not only an opiate to make men forget their poverty. Perhaps the rich took hash for different reasons? I saw one man, obviously not poor, in silken robes and with brightly coloured *bulga* on his feet, walking unsteadily. He was drugged, followed dutifully by two veiled women, their eyes darting, watching, each time their husband was in danger of falling. Four children followed, oblivious to the flies that were just waking up and making – as they always seemed to do – for the eyes.

I returned home, and after another shower, and a pretence at breakfast, I drove the Chrysler round to my chambers. Salem was already in his office.

Mlle de Clozet, my secretary, would not arrive for another hour, while Salem opened his eyes wide with surprise to see me so early. He knew that I had no cases or interviews planned for that day.

'Could you get me some coffee?' I asked. But then I thought of the rigmarole which such a simple request entailed – sending out, waiting interminably, then the inevitable appearance of a grubby individual with a brass tray suspended from three hanging chains like a single scale; the tiny cup of coffee, the usual glass of tepid water.

'Any chance you could make me some American, Salem? I want to telephone through to Paris and I didn't have time for a proper breakfast. I need some coffee badly.'

His teeth flashed, almost glistening in his nut-brown face. He didn't mind making coffee, though it was the secretary's job rather than that of a clerk. But what widened his smile was being privy to something intriguing. He returned with the coffee in a few minutes.

'God. I needed that.' Taking a sip of the bitter liquid I put the cup down carefully on my blotter – the leather-work on my partner's desk was too precious to ruin – and searched in my wallet. 'Here's the number.' I held it out to Salem. 'Find out what the delay is likely to be, will you?'

He examined the piece of paper I had given him and asked, 'You want me to make it a personal call?'

'Please. A Miss Davidson. Miss Parmi Davidson.' I spelt out the nickname. Salem's black, liquid eyes lit up with anticipation.

I was almost sorry to disappoint him – because I knew perfectly well that if Salem remained in the outer office when the call came through to my room he would listen in without compunction. Mlle de Clozet's presence would have prevented it, but with Salem alone in the other office – it was the chance of a lifetime. And then every clerk in the High Court area would know the precise details of my private life.

At the same time, I couldn't even obliquely suggest that Salem would ever stoop to listen in to a conversation. That would be an insult. Instead, I told him that I would use the phone in the outer office – *his* office – because for a long-distance call the line would be clearer than if I took it on the extension in my own room.

'When the call comes through,' I suggested, 'you can go for a coffee with your friends.'

With a resigned air he said that the delay would be about half an hour, and when the shrill bell finally rang he left. Slightly apprehensive I lifted the instrument off its hook. And then, the moment I heard Parmi's voice, all worries vanished. Distance annihilated apprehension. I had forgotten the effect her voice had on me, her sense of fun. It was just the same as the last time we had met – and though in trouble her voice still held in it a sense of suppressed laughter. Does that sound odd? After all, she *wasn't* laughing. But that was the quality that I heard. There was a kind of reassurance, the way she said, 'Gee, Mark, I'm sorry about all this – it's my fault as much as yours. But don't worry –'

'Is your father still furious?' I asked.

'I tell you, he's so damn mad he's dreaming of horsewhipping you – on the steps of your club. Isn't that what they do in London?'

I couldn't help laughing. 'So long as he doesn't whip you instead of me.'

'Mark, what can I say? I'm so sorry – it's such a mess. Do come and see me soon. Please.'

'I will, Parmi – just don't worry. I'll try and book a ticket today.' I had a sudden vision of her, that beautiful little-girl-lost face, her huge wondering eyes. I was just about to continue when she spoke again.

'You know, Mark, you might have a bit of a row with Pa. But there's no question of you having to marry me if you don't want to. I'm not going to be a burden –'

'Well, Parmi, you *are* supposed to be pregnant.' As a joke, I added, 'I don't see what you can do about it except drink lots of gin, jump off a wardrobe and hope for the best.'

'I've tried that,' she laughed. 'Doesn't work. But I could –'

I misunderstood what she was about to say. 'Oh dear! I didn't think Catholic girls condoned abortion. Not even in a Swiss clinic.'

'Not *that*!' Even on the phone I could sense her outrage.

'I thought of something else,' she rushed on. 'I know of a place just outside New York – a friend of mine went there – and you can have a baby there in a proper hospital and then' – a slight hesitation – 'it's adopted without your ever seeing it.'

This time the pause was longer. I had a curious sense of gratitude. Of course, what Parmi said was nonsense, but she *had* made the offer. It must have cost her an effort because above everything else she was a girl with a good heart, warm and giving. She just wasn't the kind of person who would dump a baby with foster parents. I gulped then, hoping that my tone of mock severity carried across the crackling line all the way from Cairo to Paris. I said firmly, 'One day my father is going to die.'

I heard a gasp, 'Don't ever say a thing like that!'

'And when he does, I'll be Sir Mark Holt. And when *I* die my son – our son – will be Sir whatever-we-call-it Holt. And if you think I'm going to allow an heir to an old title like ours to be called – well, Hank or Junior, maybe playing in the Bronx or whatever they call it –'

Even realising that I was proposing to her, even at a moment of crisis in our lives, her sense of fun was such that she couldn't help asking, with a giggle in her voice, 'But what if it's a girl?'

'Then we'll have to try again.'

'Mark, I don't know what to say.'

'Say nothing. I'll leave for Paris as soon as I can.'

'I'm so happy, I could –'

'I know what you're doing.'

'You do?'

'I'd take a bet on it. You're twisting that beautiful thick blonde hair of yours, holding it above your head like a little girl. Right?'

As I put down the phone I couldn't help wondering what Salem would have made of our conversation.

Knowing that to Parmi every day before we met would be miserable, I thought I might fly to Paris. Egypt's first airline – Misrairwork – which had been founded four years before, had now been reorganised under the shorter name of 'Misrair'. I phoned Bill Little of Thomas Cook's in Ibrahim Pasha Street, adjoining Shepheard's. I met him for a coffee on the hotel veranda, to ask his advice.

'I'd forget it,' he said bluntly. 'It's a hit-and-miss affair. Even now the company has only got four de Havilland 86 Expresses, a grandiose name for a plane that only carries fourteen passengers. And there's only one flight a week to Paris. If there's any problem –' He shrugged. 'Let me book you by boat from Alex to Marseilles, then a sleeper to Paris. There's quite a delay on cabin space, but I'll get you off in a few days.'

That was the best I could do. I returned to my chambers to collect my car and told Salem, 'I'm going home. You can get me there if you need me.'

I had decided that I might as well announce the news to the family as soon as I could.

Driving back slowly, I tried to arrange the turmoil in my thoughts. It wasn't *love* I had for Parmi, but did that matter? What had Teddy Pollock said to me on the veranda at Shepheard's? 'You don't have to be in love to be happily married.' Was that true? I suppose that a glowing, happy friendship might give one more peace of mind than the kind of relationship which Noel Coward had written about in *Private Lives* in 1930, and which had been played by the Cairo Amateur Theatre Group a couple of years previously – consisting of 'fighting, fun and fucking', as Teddy had summed it up.

That other evening when Teddy and I had had a drink at Shepheard's, he had been talking about Greg and Serena, and *they* seemed happy to be settling for 'love' of a quiet kind, not a passion that would tear them in two with tantrums of jealousy and anger. I had a sudden thought – just as I drove past the English Cathedral facing the Nile at the end of Malika Nazli Street. Greg's attitude to marriage I could easily understand. But would Serena settle for 'comfortable' love for ever? Or would she end up by missing something? She was as carefree as the rest, but she had hidden depths, deeper emotions beneath the surface she presented to all of us.

By the time I arrived back Zola was waiting to open the door, warned of my presence by the crunching of car tyres on gravel. I almost ran up the steps.

'Do you know where my mother is?' I asked.

'Lady Holt is in the small sitting room,' he announced, and I made my way there and said, 'Darling Mother, I've got some family news to give you. Very important. Can we go and see Father in the study? And rope Greg in. I want him to be there.'

'It sounds very mysterious – and very important.' Chiffon smiled vaguely, almost apprehensively as she got up from the sofa.

'Don't often see you in here,' were Father's first words of greeting as Mother stepped into the study. Eyes twinkling mischievously, he added, 'You came for a glass of champagne, eh, Chiffon?'

'You know I never drink in the mornings – and you should stop, too.'

'But you?' He looked at me.

'Thanks, Father. I'd love to.'

'And you, Greg?' Greg, who had joined us, nodded and Father rang for Zola. 'Looks as though we'll need some replenishments.' This in a way was a private chuckle, for Father had a small refrigerator hidden inside a lacquered Chinese chest standing against the wall opposite his desk. It held half a dozen bottles, but even though I could easily have opened the chest it was an understood thing that Zola always performed personally any ceremony involving champagne. He came in now, eyes shining, blue-black face wreathed in smiles.

'Well, why the Wafd?' Father often used the word for the Egyptian Nationalist Party – which also happened to be the word for 'delegation'.

There was no point in delaying the news – or at least the first part of it. Zola held out a glass on a silver salver for me, another for Greg.

'It's me, Mother,' I said ungrammatically. 'I'm going to get married.'

'Good Lord!' exclaimed Father. 'Whatever next?' – almost as though I had been caught out in a situation he had never envisaged.

'Oh dear,' fluttered Chiffon. 'Are you really?'

'Good show – at least I hope it is.' Greg held out his glass in a brotherly toast.

'It's not Samia?' Father asked, almost hopefully.

'No,' I laughed. 'It's not Samia.'

'That singing woman!' Mother's voice held a note of asperity. 'Thank goodness for that.' It was unintentionally ironic, the way she happily approved of Greg marrying an Egyptian 'lady', but was horrified that I might have married a famous Egyptian singer. 'Then who?' she asked, almost crossly. 'Don't keep us in suspense, Mark. It's bad manners.'

Before I had a chance to speak, Greg butted in, 'I know who it is. The girl from Paris.'

'You mean the Folies Bergère?' Father cried. 'The one with the long legs? Good gracious! A dancer in the family.'

'I'm right, aren't I?' Greg winked at me.

I nodded. 'But I'm sorry to disappoint you, Father. It's not the Folies girl. That one, well, she belonged – for a couple of nights, anyway – to Greg.'

'How vulgar of you boys,' Chiffon sighed.

'It's Miss Davidson,' I said. 'Greg guessed. Parmi Davidson, the daughter of the American businessman. You met Mr Davidson when he visited Cairo. He's a friend of the Sirrys. I met Parmi again when we all went to Paris for the conference.'

'What a lovely girl!' sighed Greg. 'She looks as though she eats men for breakfast.'

'Please, Greg! Do you have to be so vulgar?' said my mother sharply, adding doubtfully, 'An *American!*'

'And,' said Greg, with a sideways glance at me, 'now you know why poor Mark was so tired on the boat trip back from Marseilles.'

'You're going away, my dear?' Mother, as often happened, had only caught half Greg's remark, heard the words, 'boat trip' and misunderstood. 'I suppose we'll all have to go to Paris?'

'Suits me,' cried Father hopefully. 'Probably have to spend at least a week there, what with all the preparations and so on.'

'What a pity we can't make it a double wedding,' said Chiffon wistfully. 'You and Greg.'

'But Serena and I haven't even fixed the date,' Greg pointed out.

'So you're engaged, I suppose?' asked Father, turning back

to me. 'Good idea to take your time and have a long engagement.'

'Not for us,' I said shortly. They had to know sooner, rather than discover it later. 'I *don't* believe in long engagements. We're planning to get married right away.'

'But the clothes, the dresses, the bridesmaids!' Chiffon wailed. 'You can't rush the fashion houses of Paris.'

'It's not going to be a fashionable wedding,' I began guardedly, unable immediately to explain why. Instead I added, 'Parmi comes from a strong Catholic family. She is particularly devout, and so is her father. But I'm certainly not going to change *my* religion. And she can't change hers, even if she wanted to. So the easiest thing to do, I suppose, is for me to go to Paris – Bill Little is already trying to get me on a boat – and then marry quietly at the British Consulate or whatever you do.'

'But what an anticlimax!' cried Father. 'I'd been rather hoping –'

'If we do it my way,' I hurried on, 'we can sort out the religious problems later.' Then I waited for a long, long twenty seconds and added slowly, carefully, 'Not only for Parmi – but for the baby too.'

There! I'd said it!

There was a moment of stunned silence, broken by Greg who almost ceremoniously raised his glass again. 'To Parmi – our new daughter!' he toasted, adding, 'You sly old dog. I suppose it *was* in Paris?'

I nodded, and said to Father, 'Could I have another glass of champagne please? Medicinal.'

'And I never guessed. And you didn't give Parmi my advice,' said Greg.

'What advice?'

'If you can't be good, be careful. If you can't be careful, remember the date.'

I couldn't help laughing. It was a wonderful way of breaking the tension.

'I'm sure she's a lovely girl,' Mother said hesitantly, almost in tears as she twisted a corner of her tiny handkerchief. 'But I never thought that *you*, Mark – what are people going to say?'

I put an arm round her, suddenly realising that it must be an awful blow to any mother when a son and heir gets himself into a marriage tangle like this.

'I'm sorry, Mother,' I hugged her. 'Really I am. But Parmi is a sweet girl – and she'll be a wonderful addition to the family. All you have to do is tell everybody that I've suddenly fallen in love –'

'Better make it quick,' said Father. 'If I know my Cairo, all the women will be counting the months, working it out before the end of the week.'

'*Please!*' Mother was so angry she stamped her foot. 'You men seem to treat this sort of thing as a joke. I'm very sorry for that poor little girl and the way you took advantage of her. It's not a joke. I find it disgusting. That – that sort of thing – it's supposed to be *after* you're married. But this! We have to make the best of a bad job, but that doesn't mean that I approve of what's happened – or the way you regard it as a joke. It's immoral and disgusting.' And with that Chiffon flounced out of the room.

'It's amazing,' said Greg when he and I left the Chinese study together. 'She's living in another world. One in which "gentlemen" just *never* behave like that.'

'And women are always taken advantage of.'

'Of course.'

'I hope I haven't hurt her too much.'

'She'll get over it. It's the shock. When you produce a grandchild, she'll be all over you.'

12

Two days later – shortly before I left to catch the first available boat for Paris – Serena, whom I had been trying to avoid, almost bumped into me as I was driving slowly through the front gate in Garden City. I knew, of course, that Greg must have told Serena. 'Secrets are only fun if you share them,' he often said.

All the same, as I jumped out of the car I was a little nervous. What would her reaction be? Would she be angry, or hurt, or indifferent? True, it was none of her business – except that she was virtually 'family'.

She came walking towards me, dressed simply in a white pleated skirt and white cotton blouse edged with red cuffs and collar. How natural her expensive yet simple clothes looked on her tall, slim body! Not for the first time I silently congratulated Madame Sirry for the flair she had bestowed on her daughter.

She said nothing at first until, almost hesitantly, she smiled. 'I do hope you'll be happy.'

'You've heard the news, I see.' I too smiled. 'And I suppose Greg has filled you in with all the grisly details.'

'Well, Greg's not noted for keeping secrets. He used a funny phrase – a shotgun wedding.'

We had been standing there almost awkwardly, until suddenly, almost without thinking, I said, 'Let's drive to the Gezira for tea.'

'Love to,' she said simply. 'We could go across the Bulac Bridge. I was going painting, but I can give that a miss.'

Unlike the Kasr el Nil Bridge leading to Giza, which was always choked with traffic, the Bulac Bridge led only to the dead-end of Zamalek, filled with magnificent gardens and residential property, including several opulent palaces. The bridge was always quiet, and as we crossed over the busy river Serena touched my arm and said, 'Let's stop and look at the Nile. Just for a moment.'

Unlike the bridge, the Nile was never empty. Apart from houseboats lining the banks together with privately owned feluccas, it was a 'working river'. On this early evening there was a minor traffic jam on the waterway. Half a dozen *ghiassa*, Nile boats with huge sweeping lateen sails, made slow progress, the boatmen running from prow to stern to keep the craft from bumping into each other, pushing off those dangerously close with poles – and an unending stream of curses. One carried stone from up river, another a huge load of earthenware water jugs, mainly a load of *ballas*, the kind of jugs made in Upper Egypt which women carry on their heads. A native Cairene could even tell the area where the jugs had been made by the faint difference in colour.

'That load of *ballas* came from Kena,' Serena cried. 'Look. They have a greenish tint.'

A sudden flurry of wind blew across the bridge.

'Watch out!' she laughed, as without warning the gust blew up her pleated skirt. 'I don't want to be barred from Zamalek!' I laughed too, at that brief moment, as I saw those long, tanned legs, above exquisite ankles and her casual pair of French espadrilles.

Suddenly, with tears brushed hurriedly aside, she said sadly, 'I feel as if my best friend is going away for ever.'

'Nonsense!' I replied, almost too cheerfully. 'One day you'll become my sister-in-law. You're *family*. And as for parting – nothing can ever split our families.'

'I know. I'm being silly. Lend me your handkerchief, Mark. It's the shock, I suppose.'

'Smile, please!' I laughed, and helped her back into the car. Driving through Zamalek, I could see the grey-green leaves of the eucalyptus trees shiver slightly.

'Hope it's not going to be a khamseen.' I looked up, making conversation.

'Do you think your wife will like it here?' said Serena in a curious flat voice. It sounded odd to hear the phrase 'your wife'. I wondered if she had used the words deliberately.

'She'll have to,' I replied.

We drew up near the main entrance.

'Let's have tea by the pool,' I suggested. It was shady, and the splashing of bodies in the water made everything seem cooler.

'I'm glad I'm getting married for one reason' – I tried to keep the conversation light – 'It'll stop me from eyeing pretty girls like you.'

'It's never stopped any married man,' she retorted, the tears forgotten. 'Or you, for that matter. I know all about you and Angie Gray and Dodie Summers and Sally Porter . . .'

'All of them.' I returned her smile. 'But mostly you.'

'More than that singer girl?'

'Samia?'

She nodded. 'I thought you were smitten on her. I know that you – that you, well –'

'How did you know?'

'The eyes! Every Egyptian woman talks with her eyes. For centuries it's been the only way a veiled woman could show her feelings for a man. Habits like that are deeply ingrained.'

'No wonder I could read your thoughts when we so often thought the same things.'

'At last you realise!' she said. 'Just as I was talking to you with my eyes, so was Samia when she looked at me. She told me without words that she liked you – a kind of warning. But you like me more than you like her, don't you?'

'Yes,' I answered gravely. 'And I always will.'

'Sometimes I think there must be something wrong with us,' she said. 'When I imagine what you've done to all those girls – jumping into bed with them – everyone but me!'

I poured out another cup of Earl Grey. 'It's hard to explain, Serena,' I sighed, 'but, apart from the fact that you're virtually engaged to my brother, it's just because I *don't* value the friendship of the other girls that I've popped into bed with them. They didn't matter. You're different. You *do* matter.'

'I might have the same feelings and desires as other girls.'

'Of course. And don't think that I'm blind – that I haven't guessed about you and Greg.'

'It's a pity in a way – sometimes I imagine – you and I . . .'

She turned away, to look at the crowds laughing and enjoying themselves, when without warning she cried, waving, 'Look who's over there. Jim Stevenson.'

Slightly annoyed – but relieved too? – I turned, and I was surprised, not at the sight of Stevenson about to interrupt our tea, but at the man who was accompanying him. He was dressed in civilian clothes, but there was no mistaking General Osman Sadik.

'H'ya!' Stevenson brushed a couple of kisses on Serena's cheeks and, before introducing Sadik, said to me pleasantly, 'Good to see you, Mark. I believe congratulations are in order?'

'Everyone seems to know,' I muttered.

'That's Cairo for you,' said Stevenson with his agreeable smile. 'May I present General Sadik; Miss Serena Sirry, Mr Holt.'

'I know your father well.' Sadik bowed in Serena's direction, his lock of pomaded hair falling forward.

'We've already met,' I almost growled, not having the courage to refuse the hand he offered me.

'Of course,' said Stevenson. 'You acted for Samia, didn't you?'

'Samia, yes.' I looked perplexed. 'But' – carefully – 'what's that got to do with the general?' I knew, but why should Stevenson know?

Nothing could ever disturb Stevenson's easy manner. 'I think it was you who told me, General,' he said, 'that you had helped Samia – and met Mark in the process.'

'Mark knows everybody.' Serena was making conversation.

'My congratulations on your forthcoming marriage.' Sadik turned to me politely, almost formally. 'I don't think I've met the lady?'

'Not yet. I hope I shall bring my fiancée to meet you. At present she's in Paris.'

Stevenson turned to Serena. 'May we join you?' Without waiting he drew up two chairs and started to order a round of drinks. 'It's almost time for a drink.' To me he asked, 'You take scotch, don't you? And you, Serena?'

She shook her head.

Serena turned to Sadik. 'We don't often see Egyptian generals here.'

'I'm too busy as a rule. Affairs of the palace, you understand.' Sadik wore an important air. 'I *am* a member, though. One of the Egyptian quota.'

The word 'quota' was used deliberately. The Gezira Club was mixed, but only up to a point, for it was predominantly European and only a percentage of Egyptians was allowed to join. Understandably, it had always been a source of irritation to the Egyptians. In any event, there was a waiting list for new members as long as the Gezira racecourse.

'In a way I'm here on business,' explained Sadik confidenti-
ally. 'His Majesty, who is an honorary member, of course,
wishes to pay an unofficial visit to the club, perhaps for
dinner. And naturally I have to – what was the phrase you
used, Mr Stevenson?'

'Case the joint.' Stevenson gave me a lazy smile.

'And you are the – er – caser?' I asked, thinking, why
the hell should an American be advising the king's ADC?
Stevenson seemed to have a finger in every pie. Why had he
advised Samia to come to me for advice? And how did he
know about Sadik and Samia?

'General Sadik happened to mention that the king had
enquired about the club – so I offered.'

The extraordinary thing about Stevenson was that nothing
ever ruffled him. I had been quite openly sarcastic, but he
appeared not to notice; he was either remarkably
well-behaved – or a man trained for a job in which he would
never be permitted to lose his self-control.

'Do we know when His Majesty is coming?'

'On Thursday – unless he changes his mind,' said Sadik.
'And one of my jobs – apart from organising the secret
service, and so on – will be to ask the committee if they
would kindly ensure that if HM dines at the club the tables
nearest to his could be reserved for – shall we say, suitable
guests.'

I didn't say anything – but I was thinking, damn it, this is
a private club. The committee would never stand for reserving
tables for 'guests'. On the other hand, you did have to book
tables for dinner, otherwise you would never get one.

'You would do me a great favour,' continued Sadik
smoothly, 'if you, Miss Sirry, could be persuaded to come.
HM holds your father in the highest esteem. No, no, not to
dine with the king. At an adjacent table with people like those
with you now, your friends. You and your brother, Mr Holt.
Your father, Sir Geoffrey, is a tower of strength to His
Majesty.'

'If His Majesty decides to dine at our club, we won't be
involved? I mean, presented or that sort of thing?' I asked.

'Please don't worry. Nothing like that. You are friends

enjoying yourselves – and, shall we say, making a screen round HM – just in case someone has too much to drink – I'm sure you understand. Your friends and Miss Sirry will be sufficient guarantee of –' He let the sentence trail off.

I was still vaguely irritated, perhaps by the way Sadik presumed that because the king was all-powerful nobody would say 'No' to his planned presence at 'our' club. Because Farouk *was* all-powerful. He could close the place down overnight if he chose to.

The king could erase anything which displeased him from the cabinet agendas, approve the appointments of ministers, magistrates, civil servants, doctors and staffs of embassies. No member of the royal family could leave the country without his consent. Even the date when the police changed from summer to winter uniform had to be agreed by him. He was a despot from another age, who needed no reason to decide on any action he chose to take.

There was nothing I could do except stifle my annoyance.

13

The prospect of the king dining at the Gezira Club did not excite me unduly, for I had other things on my mind. In two days I was leaving for Paris – I would have been almost relieved had I been forced to sail earlier. I wasn't in the mood for a party, especially one graced – to use an unfortunate word – by the presence of royalty. For by 1937 Farouk's behaviour was growing more and more outrageous, particularly with women. I knew that you were expected to behave with more decorum in a club than in a restaurant, but still I had niggling doubts. The king made his own rules.

'I'm sure he'll behave,' said my father when he saw me in my black tie and asked where I was going. 'But I must say he's beginning to act very strangely. He drives like a madman.

After a recent crash he issued a decree forbidding any cars in Egypt to be painted red. If they're red, they've got to be resprayed. His are the only red cars allowed in the country, so they can be instantly recognised. If there's any trouble, the police can act discreetly before it's too late.'

An alarming number of reports were being received at the British Embassy. The king was making regular visits to dubious nightclubs where he would pick up belly dancers or other cabaret artistes.

Needing someone to arrange these assignations, the king had apparently found the perfect man in General Sadik, aided by the Italian Pulli, Farouk's boyhood friend who, since those early days, had continued to live in the palace as a general 'help' but with no clearly defined job. Sadik was the principal royal pimp, and in his visits to sleazy nightclubs his routine hardly varied. The king would be installed at the table nearest the cabaret act, and as soon as he had picked the girl he fancied – and they ranged from belly dancers to female contortionists – the king would leave, but Sadik would remain, and after the show the girl would be taken in a royal car 'for an audience' in the palace.

There the king would be awaiting the girl; inevitably he would be dressed in what he called his 'lounging clothes', in effect an Arab-style nightgown.

'The secret service says,' added my father, 'that Sadik gets a rake-off – in kind, not in money. When it's time for the girl to leave Sadik takes her to a flat of his not far from the Abdin. Poor girl!'

'And if she refuses?'

Father shrugged his shoulders. 'There's nothing the girl can do. You know how Cairo works. She could be sent to jail for prostitution – even if it's not true. Or Sadik could get the nightclub closed.'

'What a shit!' I said.

'Does Sirry Pasha know about this royal visit to Gezira?' asked Father. 'And that Serena's going?'

I shook my head. 'Not unless Serena's mentioned it. I haven't. It's Greg's job, not mine, if anyone wants to warn Sirry Pasha.'

'I hope it's all right,' Father sighed. 'Serena's a beautiful girl, and when Farouk sets eyes on a real stunner I'm told he can hardly wait to tear her clothes off.'

'We'll protect her,' I laughed.

In fact what we always called 'the king's party' turned out to be highly enjoyable. Everyone was teasing me that in a couple of days I was going to Paris to get married, and leaving all the beautiful girls behind.

'Your last night of freedom,' Greg gave a mock-sigh.

'You won't be far behind,' I retorted.

'It's all the lonely girls I'm most sorry for,' laughed Serena. 'Since Greg is virtually married –'

'And already married to polo . . .' murmured Teddy, with his slow drawl and equally slow wink.

'Exactly. And so the problem of looking after all the pretty girls in Cairo is going to fall on your shoulders, Teddy – and yours,' Serena smiled at Jim Stevenson.

'Not me. I'm too busy.'

'Doing what?'

'Learning the art of doing nothing.' Stevenson returned the smile.

'I've already patented that process,' Teddy complained. 'I'm a *professional* playboy. You're just an amateur.'

It was that kind of party: cheerful, extrovert, well-mannered, on a balmy evening, kissed by a warm breeze whispering through the feathery casuarina trees and the heliotrope haze of the jacarandas. As befitted the club habits, the music was subdued, its tempo little more than a polite rhythm.

'It's out of this world,' sighed Sally Porter, tapping a foot to 'The Touch of Your Lips'. 'I could dance all night.'

The king arrived about ten o'clock, entering very discreetly, surrounded by six friends, including the inevitable Sadik, who bowed slightly at us as he passed. I saw the king, who was wearing dark glasses and a scarlet fez, look searchingly at our table – and the girls.

For a moment he smiled fleetingly at Greg as he recognised his one-time 'playmate' of the Kubbah Palace; Greg inclined his head slightly – an instinctive gesture, I was sure, because already the king had a commanding presence, a charisma. Farouk didn't *order* his fellow guests around as they sat at his table, he just expected them to wait on his words. He had the aura that goes with kingship, no doubt about it.

'He's got something else,' whispered Teddy Pollock. 'Notice how he mentally undresses every girl he sees? He's a womaniser all right.'

'So long as he doesn't undress *me*,' whispered Serena.

'He already has done,' Greg laughed. 'But don't worry. Old King Fuad used to say that our new king is not very well endowed in that department.'

I watched curiously, but discreetly. The first thing Sadik did was to order half a dozen large jugs of fizzy pop; fruit juices with a froth on them, presumably poured from bottles into the jugs. To my astonishment the king poured out six large glasses, one after the other, and drank each glassful in a gulp. Then something else intrigued me. Each of the men ordered the same menu – but each time a portion of food was placed before a guest at the royal table, *four* portions were placed before the king. He ate the lot – more, he *wolfed* it all greedily, tearing a dozen or more pigeons apart with his fingers, almost savagely, and sucking the last scraps of scrawny meat off the tiny bones as though he were on the verge of starvation.

'What I find fascinating,' Greg whispered to me, 'is that all his chums hardly notice, as though this is his normal appetite.'

The king wiped his hands in a large silver bowl, dried them – and that, I thought, was that. Not at all. He signalled for more soda pop and then ate three large plates of chocolate ice-cream.

'It's unbelievable,' whispered Serena. 'Where does he put it all?'

'Hollow legs!' Greg whispered back.

The king was fairly slim, though there was more than a hint of fat in his neck, hands and wrists. We had been asked not to look too obviously in his direction, to respect his wish for privacy in a private club, especially as his guests behaved with composure and indifference, as though they never noticed the royal food being gulped down with such nauseating greed.

'Must be worms,' said Teddy.

It was Stevenson who said, more seriously, 'I'm told that the king suffers from a physiological defect. Not enough thyroid – or too much, I'm not sure which. I only heard this, but I'm told that this is what gives him his enormous appetite.'

Most of us only snatched discreet glances. In fact the men were indifferent; he was nothing in our lives.

'We move in different circles, thank God,' said Teddy.

Sally Porter, though, was fascinated. She had difficulty in taking her eyes off Farouk. She hadn't been long in Egypt, where she had joined an oil firm as an executive secretary; she was still gawking at the treasures of the country lying around her – the sun, the water, and now the brush with royalty at close quarters.

'Here I am, whisked from King's Lynn to King Farouk.' She had a very agreeable smile, but she was a little unused to the kind of life she had been thrust into in Cairo.

'I know a cat may look at a king,' I whispered to her, 'but looking and staring are different. Don't overdo it.'

After the coffee had been served I asked Serena for a dance on the small square of polished wood. As usual she was dressed simply, the simplicity disguising a highly expensive dress, so simple that only a Sally Porter would know that it cost twenty times as much as a similar copy from Cirucel, the department store in the Kasr el Nil.

Paul Jackson's band – an institution at the Gezira – was murmuring its way through 'These Foolish Things' and without thinking I pressed her a little closer to me. 'I love you in blue,' I said. 'Pale blue. It's ravishing.'

'Mama chose it.'

'Wise mother!'

'Sometimes I wish I could choose something myself. But she says that at nineteen –' She stopped suddenly then said impulsively, 'Oh, this music! I love this tune. Except that sometimes it makes me wonder if I'm foolish too.'

'You're too young to be foolish.'

'I can't believe that. You're getting married next week. Do

you realise this is my last dance with an unmarried Mark?'
She squeezed me back. 'I'll always think of you when Paul
Jackson plays this tune. Our tune.'

'Our tune,' I agreed. 'Your dimple – *our* dimple – looks
beautiful tonight.'

Suddenly the lights over the tiny dance floor were dimmed
and she drew closer and we danced cheek to cheek. It was
almost dark, and she whispered, her voice choking, 'Kiss me,
Mark – no, on the lips.'

I kissed her gently, her mouth barely open. 'Be careful, my
beautiful Serena,' I whispered.

'Mark, darling, thank you.' I could feel a tear on one cheek,
feel the anguish of a voice torn with emotion. 'I'll never say
this again, I promise you. I swear it. But Mark – I love you.
I've never really loved anyone else.'

Paul Jackson was crooning, 'These foolish things remind
me of you.'

'Everything reminds me of you,' she whispered, then broke
into French. *'La femme est faite pour l'homme. L'homme est fait
pour la vie.'*

'Don't cry, darling, please don't cry.'

'I won't. I mustn't. But if only I thought – you –'

'You know the answer.'

'I want to hear you tell me. Just this once in the world.'

'I've always loved you, too.' I squeezed her. 'Since you
were a girl. I never wanted to show it. You were always a
girl to me.'

'One day perhaps – or one night –'

The dimmed lights suddenly became a little brighter, breaking the spell of secrecy.

'Who knows? When we're both married couples, bored
with each other –' Then I gave a short laugh, hoping to
change her thoughts. 'What a fine thing for a lawyer to be
discussing – arranging to commit adultery in the years to
come! It's so unethical I could be disbarred.'

The light had given her the chance to smile. 'One day,' she
said softly. 'In the meantime – you leave for Paris the day
after tomorrow?'

I nodded. 'It won't make much difference, especially as

Chiffon has insisted that Parmi and I stay in the house until the baby's born. The east wing is completely self-contained, with its own kitchen. I wasn't sure about it at first – but now I think it's a good idea. At least it means that our two families will be able to walk from our garden to yours, just as we've always done. And, you know, Parmi's only twenty-two – much nearer your age than mine. You'll be good friends.'

'Parmi might not like me.'

'Of course she will.' I was scornful.

'You sound like Greg!' And as the music showed signs of ending, she whispered urgently, 'Stay here. Lingering, so we can dance the next one.'

'Okay.' People often did clap and remain on the floor at the end of a dance. 'Unless someone else comes to claim you.'

The band struck up another slow, haunting melody, 'The Way You Look Tonight'.

'I'll never forget these tunes. They'll always bring back memories. And this night. We dance so well together. Oh, Mark! I do hope marriage won't at least spoil our friendship.'

'Why should it?' I asked. 'Will your marriage to Greg change your feelings for me?'

She shook her head. 'Never!'

'That goes for me too. The only thing –' I hesitated.

She looked up at me, cheek touching mine as we danced slowly. 'What?'

'Nothing will change,' I said with a sigh, 'but how different the future might have been if only everything had gone differently from the time when I first looked after you – during the riots. That strange afternoon – in a curious way it's always haunted me.'

'Me, too. The memory of it, as Mama told it to me.'

At that moment, when we were both lost in dancing – and our thoughts – I felt a tap on my shoulder.

'There's no cutting in at this club,' I growled angrily before I saw who it was.

'My apologies.' It was Sadik. 'I'm not cutting in for myself. It's –'

'What's the trouble?'

'His Majesty asks if he may have the pleasure of meeting

Miss Sirry at the end of this dance. I will come to your table when the music stops.'

As Sadik gave a slight bow, and the music ended, I steered Serena to our table. 'Do you think I should go?' she whispered.

'You've no option. It's a royal command. Bloody man. Anyway, he won't bite you.'

Almost before Serena had sat down Sadik walked towards her. Out of the corner of my eyes I watched him as he approached.

'A repulsive pimp,' Greg whispered.

Serena left. And from that moment we had to look on as discreetly as possible, waiting and wondering. Serena, we could see, was placed next to the king and they were talking animatedly. There were gusts of laughter, nothing solemn, and Farouk was obviously enjoying himself. After half an hour I saw Farouk gesture to the floor, saw Serena nod and they danced. He was surprisingly light on his feet. He danced only once, then, as they returned to his table, he looked up at the moon and the bright starlit night, sighed, studied his watch and gestured to Sadik who was waiting to escort Serena back to her table. The king shook hands with her, covering one of hers with both of his, and smiled politely as Serena bobbed a mini-curtsy.

When she returned to us she said, 'His Majesty wants to say Hullo to you, Greg.' She added mischievously, 'After all, you were his playmate.'

Greg went over. I saw the two men laugh, and Farouk seemed to be telling him something that made Greg smile, before my brother rejoined us. 'He joked about our days at the Kubbah,' said Greg, 'playing football and so on. And then told me to tell you, Mark, that he had heard very good reports, from a certain lady, of your skill as a lawyer, and that you will be hearing from him. I told HM you were leaving in a couple of days to get married, so he asked Sadik to arrange for you to have an audience tomorrow.'

'Tomorrow? What the hell can a king be in such a rush about?' I wasn't as well acquainted with him then to know that he was impulsive, and always did things in a rush. Five minutes later a waiter handed me a note from Sadik asking me to present myself the following day at the Kubbah Palace. How extraordinary.

Out of the corner of my eye I saw Farouk prepare to leave. The men at his table stood up deferentially. The king took a last swig of fizzy lemonade, then whispered something to Sadik. The general looked towards our table.

As the entourage moved towards the doors Sadik stopped by us and whispered to Stevenson. I heard Stevenson whisper back, 'Her name is Sally Porter.'

Sally heard too, and turned pink.

Sadik bowed and said to everyone, 'His Majesty asks me to thank you for your discretion. He has enjoyed himself enormously, and regrets that he hasn't had time to meet all your friends. But,' he hesitated, 'if you, Miss Porter, would please follow me, His Majesty has told me he would like to meet you. He is waiting near the exit.'

'That means that you'll be on the list for future functions,' I whispered to Sally.

'With pleasure!' Sally cried, flustered and nervous. I couldn't help thinking of the different way in which Serena had behaved, whereas Sally, flushed with excitement, was probably already waiting to write to her mother in King's Lynn with the staggering news that she had been received 'at court' – even at the exit.

Sadik underlined the difference by offering, very politely, advice he would never have dared to offer to Serena. 'His Majesty, I'm sure, would not expect you to make a full curtsy. But still –'

The inference was clear: Remember how to behave.

Sally disappeared. For a few moments we forgot all about her, as Serena retailed the details of her audience.

'No,' she insisted, 'he didn't ask me to go to bed with him. He did say he hoped to see me again – soon.'

'Ah!'

'But he couldn't have been more charming. And he dances divinely. Better than you, you clodhopper.' She blew a kiss to Greg, who grinned cheerfully.

'It seemed a wonderful evening. He really looked as though

he enjoyed your company,' said Stevenson, putting into words exactly what I felt.

'But what did you talk about?'

'He said I was the most beautiful girl in the world, so I replied, "Sire, I am honoured at such a compliment from the most beautiful man in the world." After that we got on like a house on fire.'

'Ah!' Teddy shook his head. 'Flattery will get you everywhere.'

'Well, he *is* beautiful,' said Serena defensively. 'And he has the most beautiful manners too.'

At that moment someone asked, 'Whatever happened to Sally? Do you think he's taken her back to the Abdin Palace? We know what happens *there*.'

'He wouldn't have the nerve,' cried Dodie Summers, in the tone of voice which really meant, 'Why didn't he ask me? I'd have gone like a shot.'

I beckoned a club servant to see where Miss Porter was, if anyone had seen her go, if she had left with the king.

A member of the secretarial staff arrived and said, with an embarrassed air, that Miss Porter had left by taxi.

'Alone?' I asked.

'Yes,' he nodded. 'She seemed very upset. I'm afraid, sir, she was in tears.'

We only dragged the details out of the assistant secretary with difficulty. He had seen everything, even heard snatches of the conversation. He had been hovering behind the royal party at the edge of the ladies' private enclosure in the gardens near the club entrance. He noticed that one of the king's friends was standing very close to him carrying, of all things, an ice-bucket.

Unaware of what was about to happen, Sally approached the king, murmured something about 'What an honour –' and gave a deep curtsy. Farouk took one hand, which meant that she had to make the curtsy last. Uttering only two words at first, the king snapped to his friend, 'The ice!' And as poor Sally held her head down, the king picked up a couple of cubes and pushed them into her cleavage.

Sally gasped as the cold ice slid down inside her clothes.

The king took off his dark glasses, looked at her impassively, and the secretary heard him say to her slowly and clearly, 'You may be a pretty young lady, Miss Porter, but remember it is bad manners to stare.'

Then without another word he stalked off into his scarlet Rolls-Royce and roared away in a flurry of dust.

The next morning, intrigued but rushed, as this was my last day before leaving, I presented myself at the Kubbah Palace on the outskirts of the city, after the mile-long drive through the seventy-acre grounds. I was obviously expected, and immediately shown into an extraordinary room which might have come straight from the *salles privées* of Monte Carlo. There were full-sized roulette and chemin de fer gaming tables and a billiard table, and when I idly picked up some playing cards I was intrigued to realise that the backs all had erotic pictures either of nude women in 'available' positions, or even couples in sexual scenes. In one corner of the room was a keyboard hanging on the wall, with dozens of keys, and I was looking at it when the king walked in.

'I hope you didn't mind coming to the Kubbah,' he said. 'This is my home. Abdin is an office – and filled with spies. I wanted to talk to you privately. Nothing to worry about, just a bit of advice.' He noticed me looking at the collection of keys.

'They are keys to apartments all over Cairo. You'll notice that each key is labelled with a girl's name. I don't need to tell you any more, eh? Any time you want to borrow a key . . .'

I smiled politely, thinking, Why the hell am I here? What can the king possibly want?

'I call this my gaming room,' Farouk was saying. 'But first I want to thank you for the confidential way you handled Samia's affairs. I, too, want to become involved in a property arrangement, and I want it done with the same discretion. That's why I asked you to come. The property is for my own use abroad – but no one must ever know.'

'I understand, Majesty. It will be easy to arrange.'

'Well, just so you can get an idea of my taste in furniture

and décor and so on, let me show you my private quarters.'

'You won't be wanting a gaming room, sir?' I laughed.

'I think we can dispense with that. Wait, and I'll explain.'

He then took me on what I can only describe as a 'conducted tour' of his private quarters in the west wing of the four hundred rooms of the Kubbah. They included four bedrooms with sunken baths in green alabaster and enormous walk-in wardrobes – 'I've got a hundred suits and a thousand neckties,' he announced with almost naive pride.

But most fascinating was his collection of pornography. I had heard rumours about his 'taste' in pictures. Hundreds of erotic postcards lined the walls of both bedrooms and bathrooms. A collection of fifty or so drawings depicted every possible variation of sexual activity. I peered at the signature: F. Fabiano.

'I don't know him,' said Farouk. 'Sadik found them. But my best ones are colour slides. You need one of these viewers to look at them.'

'Fascinating, sir,' I murmured, and they were, though not calculated to stimulate anyone but a pervert. It was incredible that any man – let alone a king, who collected girls like other men collect butterflies or stamps – should go to such lengths to fill his rooms with such trash – not only the pictures, but a schoolboy collection of plastic nude statues, drinking mugs, even corkscrew handles in the form of nude women, and amber phalluses.

'However, to business.' Finally Farouk came to the point of my visit. It was very simple, and obviously he had chosen a 'neutral' advocate like me, knowing that no Egyptian or French lawyer could have resisted the temptation to share such a confidential secret.

The king wanted to acquire privately a large apartment in Washington or New York. In no way could it be connected with him, yet it had to be ready for him to move into at a moment's notice. 'And when I say nobody must know,' he added, 'I mean even the trusted members of my entourage – even General Sadik. You will in fact be the only single person aware of the identity of the owner.'

I resisted the temptation to ask, 'A bolthole, Majesty?' Was he scared of losing his throne? Or was he just instinctively hedging his bets against war or revolution, an uncertain future? In fact, I rather sympathised with him. It was a sign of intelligence I hadn't expected.

'It's very simple, Majesty,' I said. 'I will get a selection of photographs of properties in America. When you've approved a choice I will form a Swiss company that will acquire the property for you.'

'I already have arrangements with a Swiss company,' he interrupted.

'Better have another, a separate one,' I advised him. 'This company would deal with only this one property. I'll get a secret agreement with the company so that the company is owned by me. Then I'll give you, Majesty, a secret letter confirming for your eyes only that you own my Swiss company. That way your own Swiss lawyers, and mine, will never be able to connect the deal with you. If ever you want to take up residence in America, you'll have all the proof you need that the property is yours, sir.'

And it was as simple as that. Some months later, a Swiss company acquired the freehold of a four-bedroomed luxury apartment in New York in the famous Delamere Building on Park Avenue, near the corner of 56th Street.

But long, long before that I had left for Paris, to meet Parmi.

14

I was peering out of the window at the Gare de Lyon as, with a final sigh of steam and a squeal of brakes, the engine stopped against the station buffers. Parmi had promised to meet my train, but I had wondered what that moment would be like. After all, we hadn't *wanted* to get married. Would she be bitter, ready to make the best of a bad job, but feeling herself aggrieved? I hoped not.

I needn't have worried. She was standing, waving frantically and blowing kisses. It is curious how when you are
parted from anyone, even briefly, they look different when
you meet again. The immediate impact, perhaps. Reality
replacing blurred memory? Whatever it was, I almost gasped
at the vision of a girl showing all the other men and women
on the platform that she was only waiting to embrace me. As
I climbed down the steps and put down my only suitcase,
she kissed me a dozen times, pressed her body close to mine
and whispered, 'Goddamnit, I've wanted to see you again so
badly.'

She linked her arm through mine as we walked under
the high glass vaulted dome of the station to the exit and
whispered, 'We're going to be married soon, darling! So I
can say anything. Including the fact that I'm mad about you,
and I've been imagining you making love to me every night.'

Squeezing her, I said, 'If only we had a place to go to. But
you know what hotels are. My room at the Ritz will never
be ready at ten in the morning.'

'We're going home, to the same bed where we made our
baby.'

I looked horrified.

'I love it when you look scared. You change in a second
from the strong silent lawyer into a terrified little boy. Don't
worry. Pa's at the office. I dropped him off on the way to
the station. He'll return to the apartment around noon and
I'll go out. That way you two can sort things out. But before
that –'

'Aren't you scared – your father? I don't want him to catch
us.' My nervousness must have shown, for she said again,
'Don't *worry*. You worry too much.'

'All right, come on,' I said huskily and jumped into a cab.

I hardly noticed the stairs leading to the Davidsons' apartment in the rue du Bac on the Left Bank. The last time I had
climbed them to meet Parmi had been the day which changed
my life.

'Don't let's wait,' she whispered urgently, undoing her
skirt, pulling her blouse over her head, shaking her thick

blonde hair and taking off her panties all – so it seemed – in one flowing movement until she stood there, naked except for a tiny blue suspender belt holding up her stockings.

Later she made some American coffee and said, 'I feel so relaxed – for the moment.'

'I feel relaxed, too. Relaxed enough to remind you that I came here to marry my crazy girlfriend. We'd better discuss the details before you go.'

'I suppose so.' Her voice was suddenly small and worried.

'We can't wait a day longer than necessary. After all' – I kissed her with the gentleness of after-love – 'we've got to consider my parents as well as your father. They've accepted everything, but Mother's been very distressed. Cairo's not Paris, you know. You can't keep secrets in Cairo.'

'I know. I'm sorry, I never asked about your mother. Will she –?'

'She'll adore you,' I reassured Parmi. 'But not as a live-in girlfriend with an over-large tummy.' Then more seriously I added, 'I know we have different religions, but we could get married at the British Consulate.'

There was a moment of silence – I could feel the change in atmosphere.

'The Catholic religion is enormously important to me,' she said finally. 'But if you insist, I suppose – it might be a good idea, though, not to mention our plans to Pa right away.'

'You mean – because *he's* a Catholic?'

'Fervent,' she admitted. 'So why not let's get married secretly? At the consulate if you like. And maybe we can make some arrangement about a Catholic church service or blessing later.'

'Getting married *is* difficult,' I sighed.

'Don't worry. But if we get married at the consulate will Pa have to know?'

'He won't have to know – but he might find out. I believe there has to be some sort of public announcement: the equivalent of the banns. And with Father's name and diplomatic job the news would certainly get into the Paris *Daily Mail*.'

'Isn't there *any* way people can be married in secret?'

I shook my head. 'Does it mean so much to you – to be married in a Catholic church?'

She tried to explain. 'To a Catholic, and to me, it just wouldn't count. Without being married in a church we wouldn't be married in the sight of God.'

'Does it really matter? I mean, *we* know we'll be married – and there's only one God – and it'll be legal,' I added with a laugh.

'In one way I shouldn't mind. Getting married – any way – is the important step, and you've been so wonderful about it. But apart from Pa being livid I don't want to take any chances on the future – of us, our baby.'

'What on earth do you mean?'

'I know it sounds silly to you, but – the wrath of God. I want to make sure that God never punishes me for not taking my marriage vows in church.'

She had just poured me a second cup of coffee when suddenly she cried, 'Whoopee!' She twisted her hair, opened her eyes wider, giggled and clapped her hands, kissed me, and asked what sounded to me the most irrational question. 'Darling, do you ever get seasick?'

'Honestly, Parmi!' I was almost irritated, especially as I was already thinking of the prospect of meeting her father soon.

'But *do* you? It's important!'

'We're supposed to be planning to get married. But if it pleases you, no, I've never been seasick in my life.'

'Wonderful! That solves everything. I couldn't bear it if you were seasick just at the very moment you were putting the ring on my finger.'

It took perhaps half a minute before I realised the full implication of her suggestion.

'You're a genius.' I hugged her. 'What a brainwave! It solves everything. If we want to get married as the result of a shipboard romance the only way is to get the captain to marry us. We won't be denying you your religious beliefs because a marriage at sea, though binding, must be the same for all religions.'

She was silent for a moment, the usual frivolity in her voice absent as she said, 'I'm so deliriously happy. A wedding at sea! It's the most romantic idea in the world.'

'Romantic, practical, secret,' I laughed. 'And now, young lady, it's half past eleven. Better go. I'll meet you for lunch at Maxim's. One o'clock.' Lifting her skirt to give her an affectionate pat on her bottom, I said, 'No panties?'

'Too hot,' she said. 'And, darling, try to understand poor Pa. I was the apple of his eye in his garden of Eden, but I'm afraid he regards you as the serpent.'

After Parmi had left I had twenty minutes or so before Davidson was due to arrive, and I needed a few moments to compose my thoughts. I hoped we could be friends – friendly enough, anyway, to be compatible in-laws. But the reason I asked for a private meeting was to make one thing abundantly clear. I wasn't going through life with a father-in-law able to taunt me with seducing his virgin daughter.

In dozens of court cases I had seen how parents really knew nothing about their children, and I remembered vividly one particular case in which I had acted for a young man who had been stabbed by the father of a girl whom the man had seduced. The father defended the attack because, as he said in court, he was fighting to vindicate the honour of a daughter whose virginity had been despoiled.

He very nearly won the case, for a girl's virginity is highly prized in Egypt. But then I was able to bring witnesses and prove that the daughter had taken occasional lovers before she went to bed with the man who made her pregnant.

Parmi had told me that she had done just that, and I wasn't going to have Theo Davidson labouring under any delusions. If we wanted to live together harmoniously after a shotgun wedding I had to tell Davidson the truth.

Davidson arrived at midday. I could hardly remember what he looked like: tall and thin with a sour face and a thatch of blond hair, from which Parmi had obviously inherited hers.

He opened the door, and without a greeting suggested, 'Better come up to my study.' The room was a spacious, sloping-roofed attic in which he had a stack of filing-cabinets, a typewriter, a large desk, and along one side a long table with a marble top on which rested an assortment of books and papers. It was very business-like.

'Come in,' he said tersely. 'At least' – bitterly – 'you had the decency to come and see me.'

'What did you expect me to do?' I asked. 'Get married by proxy?'

'Is that your British idea of humour? You trying to get fresh? Just listen to me, young feller –'

'We'll listen to each other – but quietly.' I tried to speak calmly. 'This whole business is unfortunate. But basically it concerns Parmi and me. Remember that.'

'Oh! So the father doesn't count?'

I sighed. 'If you like to put it like that. It's *our* lives that matter.'

For a moment I thought he was going to lunge at me.

'You can make yourself count if you want to,' I added hastily. 'It's your choice. Parmi and I, as I told you, are going to get married. Whether or not my father-in-law and I are friends depends' – I took a deep breath – 'on how you behave, and if you try to understand.'

He actually grabbed a large ruler and looked as though he would break it.

'You've got a goddamn nerve – seducing my daughter and then telling me – hell! – how to behave. Thank God Parmi's mother isn't alive to hear your effrontery.'

'I didn't seduce your daughter.' I spoke quietly with an effort. 'We seduced each other.'

'I get you,' he snarled. 'So now it's Parmi's fault?'

'Yes. Her fault just as much as mine,' I said evenly.

'You bastard!' He was red with fury. 'You think a girl's to blame when a grown man seduces a virgin.'

'You might as well face the facts, Davidson. Parmi admitted before we went to bed that it wasn't the first time. She's had lovers before me.'

'I'll kill you if you ever say that again!' His voice was taut with fury. 'You bloody British bastards are all the same.'

'You can call me a bastard if it makes you happy, but nothing you can say changes the facts. I didn't seduce Parmi.'

His whole face seemed to change, to crumple.

'Listen, Mr Davidson,' I said. 'If we are going to be on speaking terms after Parmi and I are married it's essential you know the truth. Otherwise you'll spend your whole life patronising me. And I won't have that.'

'I still can't believe the things you say,' he said. 'My Parmi –'

I realised he was beginning to believe me. 'Mr Davidson,' I said. 'Parmi's no worse – and no better – than a million other girls. They all like to try it, you know, if they get the chance. You really thought that your demure little girl was untouched, eh? Do you remember that night in Shepheard's telling Parmi that as a special favour she could have a couple of glasses of white wine?'

He nodded.

'She started drinking when she was sixteen.'

Poor Davidson. He suddenly sat down.

'My baby,' he said over and over again. 'All this time – lying –'

'They're not lies,' I consoled him. 'It's consideration – the way all kids behave in order not to hurt their parents, especially those who expect too much.'

'*Why*, damn it all? Why did you have to tell me?'

'You know why. Because otherwise you'd have despised me for the rest of your life. Once you accept what's happened – and know it's true, but not the end of the world – it'll be better for both of us.'

After what seemed an age, Davidson got up from a stool on which he had been sitting and sighed, 'I'm going to have a coffee.' He walked off and from the kitchen shouted, 'Where the hell's the percolator?' Suddenly I felt myself going pink. It was probably in the bedroom. I tried to get there first, but he beat me to it.

When he came out he was carrying the percolator; but he also carried something else.

'She must have forgotten to put these back on after you'd finished.' He threw Parmi's panties on the floor. 'You know where the front door is.'

★

I couldn't tell what the future held for any relationship between Davidson and me, but certainly he can't have mentioned our row to Parmi because, when we met later for lunch, she was her usual sunny self and merely said, 'It seems as if Pa's accepted the inevitable.'

'I hope so.' I tried to be non-committal. 'But all the same,' I added, to help Parmi, 'I've managed to get two small cabins on the *Côte d'Or* sailing from Marseilles in three days. I realise that you're his only daughter and it must have been a hell of a blow to him, so perhaps he'd be happier if I didn't meet him again until after –'

'You were just going to say "wedding"! Isn't it exciting? But you're right. Only a couple of days before we leave for Marseilles.'

The *Côte d'Or* was a sturdy old ship which had plied between Marseilles and Alexandria since Greg and I were children – and probably before. And because Father always travelled *en prince*, with the faithful Zola in attendance, the Holts were well-known passengers, with my father being held in some awe – for all the French dearly love a lord – which of course he wasn't, but which the French always insisted on calling him.

Captain Marchand had been on the line as long as we had, and on the second day out to sea he came to greet me.

'*Bonjour, mon cher capitaine,*' I said and introduced Parmi.

'*Elle est belle!*' he cried. 'It only seems yesterday since you were in sailor suits, and now – *eh bien*, where did you find this jewel, Monsieur Holt? You must protect such a precious *objet* by marrying her before someone steals her.'

'You're sweet,' cried Parmi.

'You're absolutely right,' I agreed. 'And as you say, she's so precious that every moment of delay is dangerous.'

'*Bien sûr!*'

'So, Captain Marchand, we plan to get married as soon as possible.'

'Good advice, sir.'

He still didn't realise that our good-natured fun was the prelude to a more fundamental question.

166

Looking ridiculously young and beautiful, Parmi's eyes gazed straight into those of the captain and – inevitably – she twisted a lock of blonde hair and said, 'You are so sweet – and so helpful.'

'Helpful? I do not understand. How?'

'Captain Marchand,' I said firmly, 'Miss Davidson and I are engaged to be married. Both have our parents' approval. Both of us are of age. But Miss Davidson is a romantic. So she would like to be married here – at sea – by you, Captain.'

'Bless my soul!' he cried. *'C'est fantastique!* Of course, of course. I am honoured – if you are both certain. Romance, eh! She *is* romantic. What a treasure!'

'That's wonderful of you, Captain,' said Parmi and, standing on tiptoe, she reached up and kissed him.

'Bless my soul!' he repeated. 'I must get my best uniform pressed. Marriage at sea. Shall we say at four o'clock tomorrow on the forward deck?'

'Four o'clock tomorrow,' I agreed. 'Do you think someone could rustle up a few flowers – a small bouquet for the bride?'

'Everything shall be done with finesse,' he promised.

And so it was. Of course, within ten minutes of our conversation with the captain the news had spread throughout the ship. Every passenger was stealing glances at the romantic young couple – especially Parmi. When we entered the small mahogany-lined bar for a pre-lunch drink everyone stood up and clapped and cried, *'Bravo!'* and *'Bonne chance!'* The barman produced a bottle of Dom Perignon. 'With the captain's compliments,' he explained.

Captain Marchand was relishing the importance of the occasion, and admitted that he had never solemnised a marriage at sea, and was careful to point out that though it would be perfectly valid it would have to be registered when we arrived in Cairo. According to him, a marriage on board ship was valid if it was concluded in, as he put it, 'the form of law of the country to which the ship belongs'. The ceremony had to be performed on the high seas, and not in foreign waters, and the right to marry at sea, he explained, had been unquestioned since about 1815 when voyages took months, not weeks or days. And, of course, there was a kind of 'bonus'

which pleased Parmi. Though the service was interdenomi-
national, the fact that it was being performed by a Frenchman
made it virtually certain that a Catholic would marry us.

The wedding went off without a hitch on the bridge, with
the first mate as the main witness, and the captain demanding
a traditional kiss. Then he threw a champagne party for
all the first-class passengers and announced, 'Monsieur and
Madame Holt, it would have given me great pleasure to
bestow on you a handsome present, but *hélas* the cupboard
was bare. However' – with an impressive pause – 'during the
ceremony of marriage I took the liberty of arranging to
transfer all your luggage. With the compliments of the *Côte
d'Or* you are now installed in the bridal suite on the boat
deck. And' – raising his glass – 'it has the largest bed on the
ship.'

15

It was surprising how easily we settled down to married life
in Cairo. Father, of course, fell in love with Parmi, and she
paid him a courtesy call almost every day around eleven for
a glass of champagne. Mother, after a few days of wariness,
quickly realised that Parmi was not the 'difficult' kind. Soon
she was asking her daughter-in-law if she would like to help
in the flower room, her most private sanctum. A few days
later she suggested to Parmi, 'Why don't you call me Chiffon?
Everybody else does.'

Chiffon and Parmi, of course, had one important character-
istic in common: they were both scatter-brained. Everybody
adored Chiffon but, unlike Madame Sirry, who enjoyed being
leader of the cultural set, Chiffon's popularity rested firmly
on her great good humour, her love for a party – *any*
party – and her outrageous clothes. She spent Father's money
like water, and was never offended when he refused to ac-

company her on any of her various outings. When she was invited to the opera – Madame Sirry was on the committee and had had her own box for many years – Chiffon went more to be seen than to listen. And since Parmi's love of music was limited to the latest American records by Artie Shaw or Paul Whiteman she didn't like the opera either.

In fact, when Madame Sirry offered Chiffon seats in her box, Mother would wrinkle up her nose. On one occasion she even said to Parmi, 'There are three cocktail parties that night and I'm invited to them all. Why don't you come with me? And you, Mark, I know you like opera, why don't you go with the Sirrys?'

'You don't mind?' Parmi looked at me appealingly. 'Soon I'll be too fat to go out in public, but *three* parties in one evening!'

'You go, darling.'

I found in those first months that my life had changed dramatically for the better – *our* life, I should have said – for we had the best of both worlds: all the privacy we needed in the east wing of the Holt House, all the servants, cooks, laundry girls; yet we had the advantage of beautiful grounds and of a communal life when we preferred it.

It was true that Parmi didn't have a friend of her own in Cairo, but she was such an extrovert that our friends soon became hers as though they had known each other all our lives. Our circle of friends had always been closely knit and fun-loving. And since Parmi was safely married the fishing fleet girls liked her because she presented no threat; while the men enjoyed her company because she was attractive and fun to be with. She never had time to be homesick. When Chiffon, after some months, suggested that perhaps Theo Davidson would like to visit Cairo for a holiday, Parmi wrote with the invitation, but later, one day just after breakfast, told me:

'Pa asked me to thank your mother, but he's going to America on a three-month trip, and I'm rather glad really. I think everything'll be so much easier with Pa when the baby's born.'

'By the way,' I asked, 'what shall we call it?'

'It!' She threw a pillow at me. 'You make it sound like a

parcel! *Him* – or, if you insist – her. Anyway, what name do you have in mind?'

'Evelyn,' I replied promptly.

'Absolutely beastly! You're horrid. What on earth made you choose a name like that?'

'I don't like it either,' I said airily. 'But it's the same for either a boy or a girl. Makes it so simple. All right, we'll wait and see.'

'So long as it's a Catholic.'

'I promised you that,' I said. In fact we had already had a 'blessing'. In those days the Roman Catholic religion was still strictly applied in most churches, and normally a non-Catholic husband might have to undergo many formalities; some Catholic priests would even refuse to marry you in church. But Cairo – well, Cairo was more understanding, and we had no difficulty in finding a priest who came to our house and gave us the blessing that I knew would make Parmi happy.

'Strictly speaking I shouldn't,' he smiled, 'but I believe that God should be understanding and make exceptions. I think this is one of those occasions.'

'Thank you, Father,' said Parmi after praying on her knees. 'And thank you, Mark.'

Occasionally I wondered whether Parmi might prefer to live in a flat, away from the family, but was being too considerate to say so.

'Do you ever feel you'd be happier if we lived on our own?' I asked. We were strolling in the garden towards the river-bank. 'Just say the word and I'll soon find us a place.'

'No, sir! It's too comfortable here. And quite apart from the fact that Chiffon seems to like me and I love your father – the old reprobate! – it's just great having a gang of friends around. I often felt lonely in Paris. My pa was wrapped up in his work – I'd very few friends – but here it's all go. Teddy and I are going to have lunch at the Gezira, then he's taking me to see the Coptic churches in Old Cairo.'

Teddy Pollock turned out to be of enormous help for he loved to parade his knowledge of Cairo, which was encyclopaedic, and in Parmi he had a captive audience, for like ninety-nine out of a hundred Americans she had an insatiable curiosity. She was now *living* in Cairo – and she was determined to be treated as a true Cairene. Teddy was a better guide than I could ever have been.

Parmi was five months pregnant by now and Cairo's hot, smelly, noisy streets were no place for a long walk, but on this occasion Teddy laid on the adventure with typical panache. First he drove her to lunch along the beautiful tree-lined residential avenues of Zamalek. It was still a beautiful island, linked with its elegant bridges to Cairo, yet in the heat the trees had a bedraggled, woebegone air, as though tired of life.

'In a way they are just that,' Teddy explained to her. 'The Egyptians are totally indifferent to plants. Zamalek was created by the British, and the whole of Cairo used to be covered with trees. The trouble is, the Egyptians don't have any feeling for nature. Arabic dictionaries are even vague about botanical names.'

'We lunched at the side of the pool under the trees. Lovely,' Parmi eagerly recalled on their return, and sighed happily. 'And all those kids!'

'Kids?' Teddy didn't understand at first. 'Oh, the caddies.' It was a tradition at the Gezira that every lunchtime all the young caddies working on the club golf course assembled in the open air not far from the pool, where a teacher provided by the club gave them lessons with a blackboard in reading and writing.

After lunch Teddy drove to the edge of the old city, parked the car and hired a gharry with an old nag which he kept all afternoon. As I learned later, they walked through narrow streets, keeping the carriage waiting, browsing through holes in the wall grandiloquently called 'shops' or pavement-sellers offering everything from strings of beads to loofahs.

They had stopped at the great square outside Abdin Palace, flanked by tawny façades of old arcades, the lawns filled with scarlet and yellow cannas, and had sucked sliced mangoes and eaten roasted corn-cobs and then driven to the Street of the Tentmakers to watch women sewing the brightly coloured squares of cloth which would later be joined together to form huge tents.

Near the Sultan Hassan Mosque before reaching the Citadel Teddy had signalled the cabby to stop at a modest café bearing the name 'Hyksos'.

'We'll just have a cup of tea there in honour of this old nag.' Teddy patted the neck of the scrawny horse between the shafts.

'Don't worry, I'll explain,' Teddy had laughed. 'The Hyksos tribe of Asiatic nomads introduced the horse into Egypt. No, before your time! About 1700 BC. They rolled across Sinai, conquering Egypt's foot-soldiers with horses and chariots, forcing the Pharaohs to retreat to Thebes, as Luxor was then called.'

She had reached home just before sunset, with the palms across the river growing black against the sky.

'And you saw the Coptic ruins?' I asked.

'Yes. All that history – and in front of your eyes! Makes everything in America look so new.'

I had never been to the Coptic ruins and the remains of Babylon, once a Roman fortress guarding the head of the Delta, or to Sargia, where the Holy Family rested when escaping from Herod into Egypt.

'That's when the Christians settled in Egypt. You didn't tell me that the Greek word for Egypt is Copt.'

I had wondered, of course, what Serena's reaction would be to Parmi's arrival. After all, what had that moment at the Gezira Club meant to her – and me? Over the years the 'special relationship' had, almost without our knowing it, changed, crystallising in that moment on the dance floor into an ache of physical longing – at least on my part, and I was sure on hers too – a kind of feeling that our 'friendship' – for want of a better word – was incomplete. If she really felt like that, then I faced the prospect of Serena and Parmi hating each other.

But of course there was another possibility: Serena was young, and all my fears might be groundless. The scene at the Gezira might be less important to her now than it had been then. On the dance floor I had been unmarried; now I had a wife, and Serena's Egyptian sense of decorum – as well as her more youthful attitude to life – might have relegated those moments to a schoolgirl crush ended by events.

In a way I hoped so. Yet at the back of my mind I had a niggling feeling that it wouldn't be resolved as simply as that – for her as well as for me.

As it was, the friendship flowered better than I had expected – I would say cordial but not effusive – especially as the two girls were so different in character and outlook.

There was one particularly good reason for this: propinquity. Until now, Serena, who was now nineteen, had never had any close girlfriends, and when she wanted to meet Sally Porter or Angela or Dodie (or anyone else) it involved making arrangements, telephoning, planning where to meet. Suddenly, at a stroke, all that had changed. She had acquired a 'sister'. I heard Serena cry from one garden to another, 'Parmi! Like to go to the Plaza this afternoon?'

'What's on?'

'The latest Deanna Durbin movie, *One Hundred Men and a Girl*.'

'Great. What time?'

'Ten minutes?'

'Be with you.'

Another – and unexpected – incident brought the two girls together. Visiting the small room Serena used for painting, Parmi was intrigued, even astonished.

'But you're a professional!' She picked up some of the canvases.

'I'm not,' Serena laughed, 'but I'm trying hard, thanks to Baptise.'

'Who? Sounds like the name of a church.'

'He's been my teacher for years. You must meet him. He's very old, who's now become a close friend and helper. I've learned everything I know from him.' Suddenly she asked, 'Would you like me to paint you? I don't always succeed, but I'll try if you like.'

'I'd love you to. Let's fix a date, some time.'

The relationship was made easier because, though Parmi

was three years older than Serena, the age difference shrank as Serena was old for her age and Parmi young for twenty-two. Sometimes they went to Groppi's for tea. Often in the hot weather they went to the Gezira, though Parmi was too embarrassed to swim in the pool.

But the Gezira, with its huge open spaces, gave an impression of coolness even on the hottest day, simply because it was so large and so green, with its racecourse, golf club and three polo grounds.

Even when Greg was playing – which was three times a week at least – Serena only watched big matches to please him.

'I find it so boring,' she confessed to Parmi.

'Maybe it'd be less of a chore for you if I came along sometimes?'

'The weariness of a camel's journey is halved if two of them cross the desert together.'

'You sure say the oddest things! What the hell does that mean?'

'It's an old Arab proverb. But I *don't* mean,' Serena's voice tinkled with laughter, 'that you and I are both old camels!'

Only once did Parmi make a snide remark about Serena, and I don't think it was actuated by malice, but more because it was what she would call 'a good crack' at that particular moment.

It was on the night when Chiffon invited her to accompany her to the three parties and I decided to go to the opera.

'Sure you don't mind?' she had asked.

And when I said No, she added, 'Anyway, you'll be able to talk to Serena.'

'She might not be there.'

'She'll be there all right when she finds out you're going.'

Parmi, now firmly 'family', was automatically included on our regular visits to Nasrani in order to escape the heat. The movement of the boat trip in itself provided the next best thing to air-conditioning in the steamy atmosphere which left everyone gasping. And Nasrani was cooler than Cairo. There was water everywhere, an emptiness about the estate – even the fellahîn were not as closely packed as the men and women in the city.

'Gives us a chance to breathe.' Parmi drew in a lungful of air.

We didn't have much time to breathe deeply on the first day, though, because Nasrani was plunged into a modest drama involving the servants.

We were sitting in front of the archway when Serena, who had been talking in the kitchens, suddenly ran in crying, 'Where's Papa? I could kill that man!'

'In the fruit garden,' said Greg. 'What's the matter?'

'Never mind.' I had never seen Serena so angry. Running out through the archway to the well, where Sirry Pasha often sat on an old stone seat, I could hear her calling, 'Papa! Papa!'

At first Sirry Pasha couldn't be found. He must have gone for a walk, so Greg went to look for him.

'What's the trouble?' I asked Serena.

'Fathia's unmarried daughter is pregnant.'

I must have looked surprised at her anger over the predicament of an estate worker's daughter.

'You don't understand.' Her green eyes were smouldering with fury and her dimple had disappeared in the straight line of an angry mouth. 'It's *Fathia*! In Egypt a wet nurse like Fathia is held in the highest esteem. What happens to her – and her family – is a reflection on *our* family. Fathia helped to give us a good start in life. In Egypt there are hundreds, thousands, of nurses who feed the babies born to rich people, and everyone has always treated them with the highest respect since the days of the Pharaohs. You can't just brush history aside like that.'

Such an outburst! And a salutary reminder to me that, though Serena looked 'normal' when we all went dancing with the others, this green-eyed Egyptian, descended vaguely from a Circassian slave girl, didn't always view life as I did.

Greg came back with Sirry Pasha in a few minutes, and Sirry told me later what soon became common knowledge, because he asked me for legal advice. Sirry Pasha had stormed into the servants' quarters, confronted first Fathia – who was in tears 'at the disgrace I have brought on the Sirry Pasha's family' – and then cross-examined the daughter, a pretty girl called Hekmet, who worked in the kitchens. They quickly discovered who had seduced her. It was a man called Akif, one of the *ghuffrahs* or overseers. The name of course meant nothing to me.

'I'd like to kill that man.' Sirry Pasha was himself in a towering rage by the time he told me. 'That poor girl was a virgin. He's a slimy brute, a hook-nosed bastard. I never did trust him. I'm going to the cotton gin and find him and then kick him off the estate. If I ever see him on my land again, I'll have him flogged.'

Without thinking, I said, 'What about some financial reparation?'

'What do you mean?'

'Well, when a man gets a girl into the family way,' I said, without realising the irony of my own experience, 'he should be made to pay.'

'I don't suppose he could scratch a hundred piastres together.'

'You'd be surprised. Would you like me to threaten him with legal action? I'd squeeze something out of him and hand it over to the girl. My experience is that men are usually more frightened of threats involving a court case than of a good beating. Most men have something to hide. But after you've taken me to him best leave us alone. He'll be even more scared if he thinks you've handed the matter over to a trained advocate.'

'Very kind of you. Let's go after lunch.'

Just to make sure that I had the facts confirmed I thought I should have a quick word with Fathia, whom I had already met.

'I'll take you,' offered Madame Sirry. Like most French-women she was immediately practical where money trans-actions were concerned, and added, 'Fathia was my *nourrice*, the wet nurse when Serena and Aly were born. As you can imagine, she is *désolée*. She seeks retribution. And to the fellahîn retribution can only be counted in money.'

'I'm sure you know there's no Egyptian law that demands

maintenance of a putative father,' I explained. 'But I'll do my best.'

Fathia was brought before me.

'*Effendi*,' she began. 'It is my daughter, the daughter of my loins –'

'Madame Sirry has told me,' I said gravely. 'Hekmet is with child and you seek recompense from the culprit, Akif the *ghuffrah*. Am I right?'

'Four moons have waned,' Fathia said.

So an abortion was out of the question. 'And in five more moons,' I completed for her, 'your daughter will bring shame on your master's house. Am I again right?'

She nodded.

'What recompense do you seek that would be just?'

'Only the great can measure the atonement to be made to the humble,' she said with dignity – leaving the ball very much in my court.

After lunch we set off in a small ten-hundredweight truck, for the cotton fields were at the far end of the estate. Driving leisurely, we passed the vegetable gardens, the orchards, the olive groves, the plantations of sugar and dates and the pumps controlling the irrigation system. Then we came to the edge of the cotton plantation which seemed to stretch to the horizon – row after row of short bushes with the heads and bodies of the fellahîn moving through them.

'They're inspecting for boll-worm,' Sirry Pasha explained. 'It's the worst of all the pests, and there's very little you can do about it except puff arsenical dust over the bolls – the pods that hold the cotton seed and fibres. Otherwise rip out the bush and throw it away. Between March when we sow the seed and August when we harvest it you can lose a hundred acres to boll-worm; so I give a bonus to any of the fellahîn who spots the worm in time to save the cotton.'

For the moment Sirry Pasha had all but forgotten Akif. He never moved around the estate without an instinctive examination of all the ground over which he rode. 'And there,' he pointed to some other bushes, 'those plants have got Black Rust on the leaves. That means lack of attention to the drainage.'

Stretching out, he picked one of the pods from the nearest bush. 'Incredible to think that the flowers die on the same day they open, and leave this.' He stripped the outer leaves back from what looked not unlike a miniature cauliflower to reveal a tiny ball of lint, a sort of compressed dandelion clock.

'Now let's get to the ginning shed and find this man Akif.'

The ginning shed consisted of an extensive roof of thickly woven palm-leaves supported by slender, stripped palm-tree trunks. At one end was the loading bay where a dozen fellahîn were loading wire-bound bales on to a three-ton truck.

'Where's Akif?' asked Sirry Pasha.

'At the other end of the engine shed, sir,' someone shouted. The term 'engine shed' sounded out of place. A 'cotton gin' had been part of the world's language since the cotton pickers in America's deep south shortened 'cotton engine' to 'cotton gin'. In some parts of the Delta, though, the fellahîn still used the old word.

We walked towards the other end of the long building, alongside a Foden steam engine puffing contentedly away like an old man with a pipe. It was coupled by a continuous leather belt to a machine that clumped and banged and popped and clutched and seemed determined to destroy itself.

'Looks terrible,' admitted Sirry Pasha, 'but nobody's found a better way since Eli Whitney invented the gin at the end of the last century. And it's so damned simple.'

It was. A drum whirring round with pointed teeth tore the cotton fibre from the seed, after which revolving brushes collected the fibre and pushed it out, leaving the fluffy mass ready for baling at the other end. Then it went to the Lancashire mills to be pulled into ropes, twisted, then turned into thread.

We had reached the end of the gin. The door at the far end opened on to a large shed where tools and spare parts were stored. In one corner was a cubby-hole which, with great imagination, could be described as an office.

Sirry Pasha looked round for Akif, saw him in a corner and said without preamble, 'Ah! You deserve a good thrashing. Don't deny anything. I know all about you and Hekmet.

But here is Mr Holt, our advocate. He has advised me to leave the matter in his hands.

'I'll make a short inspection tour in this area. One of the fellahîn will fetch me when you're through.'

I can't say I liked the look of Akif. Not only did he have a hooked nose, but shifty eyes set too close together. What always baffled me was how pretty girls could so often seem to fall for such men. I decided to go straight into the attack.

'Sit down, Akif,' I said sternly, pointing to the rough Windsor chair behind the old-fashioned desk where presumably someone worked out accounts or time sheets.

He remained standing, saying, 'I am only a lowly worker, *Effendi*. It is only the wise and powerful who may sit.'

His yellowish eyes gleamed with cunning. He was as well aware as I that he who stands has an advantage over he who sits. As all judges know, elevation gives an illusion of power.

'Sit down!' I shouted. He cringed rather than sat, while both of us used the rather ornate Arabic employed for occasions such as court appearances.

'Great is the power of your house, *Effendi*,' he began.

'It is indeed,' I snapped. 'And I have learned that you have made great with child the daughter of Fathia.'

'Allah has willed that the daughters of the field are for man's pleasure,' he almost smirked. 'They draw a man to them with their wiles. But the greatness of your house lies in its justice as well as in its power. It is written in the Koran that justice for the unfortunate is of all things the most sacred.'

'Exactly,' I said. 'I am glad you understand so well. The unfortunate Hekmet will, then, in the justice that so concerns you, receive from your wages five piastres a month so that the child can be clothed and fed.'

He slid from the chair and almost knelt before me. 'But I am a poor man, *Effendi*,' he cried. 'I have many who depend on me for bread. Five piastres a month! It is impossible.'

I knew it was, of course. Like most *ghuffrah* who moved up from the mere fellahîn stage, they always seemed to inherit a round of responsibilites. Five piastres a month would simply mean that someone else would go short, or Akif would increase his petty fiddles, get caught and be fired – which would do nobody any good. All the same, honour had to be satisfied, face had to be saved.

'It is the will of Allah that you should pay,' I said, giving the impression, I hoped, that I was on very good terms with the Almighty. 'I will arrange with Sirry Pasha that you shall work an hour more each day' – I pointed to the Foden steam engine that drove the gin – 'cleaning the machine, for which you will get five piastres a month to be handed over to Hekmet.'

That hit home. The *ghuffrah* hates menial tasks that can be allotted to the fellahîn. It diminishes his status. He looked up at me. 'You are a hard man, *Effendi*.'

'But just,' I retorted. 'Now, go in peace.'

He tried to assume a certain dignity, but it was more of a scuttling movement as he hastened out of the office. I might not have secured a fortune for the poor Hekmet; but at least she would be better off than if Sirry Pasha had kicked her seducer off the estate.

16

Nearly every summer anyone who could find a good reason – or was rich enough – normally bolted from Cairo for the sea-breezes of Alexandria. Many court and diplomatic officials had their 'summer season' there. But this summer no one left. For in the summer of 1937 the king officially succeeded from the regency to the throne, and marked the occasion by touring the country, culminating in July with three huge balls, each for over a thousand guests, at the Abdin Palace.

The story of the royal parties had already captured the imagination of the Europeans, anyway. It read like a chapter out of *The Arabian Nights* and tourists flooded to Cairo to see the celebrations in a country which offered much more as well – including a standard of luxury disappearing in Europe. In Egypt there was something for everyone. All the girls in the world in the Clot Bey area, all the sport at the Gezira, all the dancing at the Semiramis and Shepheard's, all the gambling you wanted at the Paradiso, to say nothing of the pyramids and boat trips up the Nile to Luxor.

'It's crazy for foreigners to come to Egypt in the hot weather,' said Father. 'But the royal shindig isn't the only draw, you know.'

'What else?' I asked.

Father hesitated, searching for a simple explanation. 'A feeling among many people that the life they know may not last much longer. Fears of war. People are coming to Egypt – and other places too, of course – for one last fling in case they never get another chance. Many British politicians who ought to know are worried about Mussolini's adventures in Africa – and about this extraordinary fanatic Adolf Hitler.'

'But why Egypt? Why not – well, say the beaches of Greece or Portugal, or wherever?'

My father chuckled. 'I have a theory that the average Englishman – the *average*, mark you – likes to pretend that he's visiting a foreign country, but soon begins to feel lost if he doesn't hear English accents around. Egypt fits the bill perfectly. A sea voyage by way of introduction, plus the sinister atmosphere of what they call "the mysterious Orient" – and English spoken everywhere. In fact I saw a sign outside a small restaurant the other day. It read, "Baked Beans on Toast". In Egypt! Ye Gods.'

'Father's right. Probably half the tourists think Egypt is part of the British Empire,' Greg laughed.

English *was* almost a universal language, of course. Out of Egypt's foreign population of nearly quarter of a million, sixty thousand were officially British; though, since they included Cypriots, Maltese and Indians, there were in fact barely ten thousand 'pure' British. It was enough to give visitors a feeling of security, but not enough to destroy the illusion that they were in an exciting and slightly sinister foreign land.

The most extraordinary by-product of this 'invasion' was

the demand for black market tickets for any function in which they had a chance to see the king, when he made his public appearances. Forged tickets were everywhere.

'Social' Cairo was in a turmoil. Residents who hadn't booked early stood no chance of getting a dress fitted, their hair done on the day, a manicure or a corsage (very popular that season). Each of the three receptions included a buffet and dancing – a never-to-be-forgotten chance for the ladies to display their finery, and for the men to be bored.

'Though as far as I can see there'll be so many guests that nobody'll notice anybody else's dress,' I said.

'They'll notice mine!' promised Chiffon, and I didn't doubt that she was speaking the truth.

'And mine!' cried Serena, who was to be presented to the king on this, her first 'official' ball.

'They won't admire your *dress*,' cried Greg. 'Bet you a thousand piastres. They'll be too busy admiring *you*.'

I might have approached the evening with more enthusiasm had Parmi been able to go. Officially she wasn't expecting the baby until September or October, but we knew that in fact it was going to be born in August – a 'seventh month' baby. So there was no way she could go to the Abdin. And, too, she was feeling the heat badly, though I had installed air-conditioning in one small room in the east wing.

'Would you rather I didn't go?' I suggested.

'Of course not. You must go.'

I would have said No except that I knew the Egyptian secret police would check carefully on those who refused what was in effect a royal command – unless you had a really good excuse.

'If it's any consolation,' Father consoled Parmi, 'you're missing the most boring evening of anyone's life. It's different for Chiffon.' He always spoke of her outrageous clothes with a certain pride and love that was touching. 'She goes to be noticed, to shock. She actually enjoys this sort of thing. As far as I'm concerned, it's endless waiting, too much food, and in the end warm champagne.' Turning to Mother, he added, 'Don't forget to take your tiara out of the vault.'

'As though I would,' she retorted.

I can't say how Sirry Pasha and Madame Sirry regarded the evening, though palace receptions were routine to them, but Aly agreed to go, mainly because he knew the palace would take note of his refusal, if only to check on possible anti-monarchists – especially as Aly now had a police record for his involvement with Nasser.

Serena, however, was the one who could hardly contain her excitement. Day after day she ran into the garden to report to Parmi or anyone who would listen on the latest progress of her dress, what kind of hairstyle she should adopt (as though Madame Sirry hadn't already decided) and even detailing the intricacies of the curtsy.

One evening Madame Landau, for twenty years dressmaker to Madame Sirry, gave Serena her final lessons in curtsying.

'You see, it's much more elaborate than in England.' She showed how she curtsied and explained why.

'Now, Serena, as you bow and bend your knee, you drop your right arm almost to the ground in a sweeping gesture, like this.' She made the movement. 'Then upwards like this until it's almost over your head. It's not difficult really.'

'But why?' asked Parmi.

'It's an oriental throwback to the idea of putting ashes on your head as a gesture of humility,' explained Madame Sirry, while Madame Landau made Serena practise until she was perfect.

A few days later we were all asked round to the Sirry house again, this time to see a 'dress rehearsal'; in fact it was a last try-on of Serena's ball dress. There were still a lot of pins around, which Madame Landau was removing, sticking them into a pin-cushion strapped to her arm. Finally she took the last of the pins out of the dress, stood back and said with satisfaction, *'Eh voilà! C'est parfait. Je ne peut plus rien faire.'*

Serena was standing in front of a full-length mirror which had wings, so we could see her from several angles. Though I could not pretend to know the intricacies of haute couture without Madame Sirry's asides to the others, I could see enough to cry spontaneously, 'It's magical!'

'That's the tulle,' explained Madame Landau, pleased. 'It

always has the most ethereal effect – providing the girl is beautiful.'

The dress was in the most delicate shade of heliotrope – almost the colour of a jacaranda – the dress off the shoulder, the neckline edged with the same material. A satin belt held in the waist, and below were three layers of gathered tulle. She wore only one piece of jewellery – a single row of pearls – together with two gardenias in her long blonde hair, which had been done up, even for the rehearsal. I noticed matching heliotrope shoes peeping from underneath the dress.

'I'm glad you approve,' said Madame Sirry to Chiffon, adding a motherly warning to Serena, 'It's enough off the shoulder as it is. You won't want to exaggerate the décolleté with all that frou-frou.'

'And you like it?' Serena asked us all.

'Exquisite,' I said.

'Better remember what your mother said about that saucy neckline,' said Greg. 'Or you'll have HM panting after you.'

The journey to the palace was purgatory, and though I knew that if Parmi hadn't been pregnant she would have been excited at the splendour of the occasion, she didn't know how lucky she was to be able to miss it. Father, Greg and I wore white tie and tails, Chiffon an extravagant creation in blue and white that seemed to have flounces everywhere and must have almost suffocated her. We had plenty of room in the old family Rolls, which Father only used on what he called 'state occasions'. But in those days even the most expensive cars didn't have air-conditioning.

The Sirrys left immediately before us in their large Cadillac, and we followed them into what soon became an unending line of traffic, controlled by hundreds of police; very efficiently, in fact, but the jams built up because of the delays in identity checks at the gates of the palace grounds, and then the stops at the palace as car after car disgorged its passengers.

Father was an old hand at these occasions, and at the last moment Zola had carried in a hamper with some sandwiches and two bottles of champagne packed in ice.

'I really think you're exaggerating,' said Chiffon, patting

down some flounces. 'A hamper for a journey of less than a mile!'

'It's not a journey of less than a mile,' Father corrected her. 'It's a journey of two hours.'

'I'm with you, Father. Champagne helps a lot.' Greg held out his flute glass. 'Do you think two bottles'll be enough?'

Abdin was in the heart of the city, barely more than a few blocks from our house in Garden City. It lay in magnificent grounds, and once we had passed through the guards at the ornate entrance gates it took us nearly half an hour's crawl to reach the palace steps, the Sirrys just ahead of us. Sirry Pasha and Aly were resplendent in their obligatory court dress, more like a frock coat than tails, reaching to the knees, with green silk lapels – only worn at court – and three regulation gold buttons on either side of the jacket below the lapels. The jacket was always worn open, displaying a white silk waistcoat below a white tie. And of course the scarlet splash of a fez which was never removed until it was time for bed.

Two attendants sprang forward to help the passengers out. Madame Sirry emerged, then I caught a brief glimpse of Serena. How could she look so cool and calm in a torrid July heatwave? Greg blew her a kiss. She gave the merest hint of a wave – just a movement of the fingers of one hand – and walked up the imposing steps as the attendants opened our car door.

'Very impressive!' I murmured to Greg, and they were. Each was dressed in white trousers, highly embroidered monkey jackets, white gloves and red tarbooshes. Like most of the staff they were Nubians.

Men of the Egyptian royal guard, in full dress uniform and carrying lances, lined the broad staircase leading to the reception rooms. At the top of the stairs were several large rooms grouped around a central room. Each room, Father knew from experience, had its own buffet, giving a much more intimate atmosphere.

The tables were laid for eight, and the Holts – and to our delight the Sirrys – were seated in the 'Suez Canal Room', though at different tables.

Each of the various salons or supper rooms led into one

vast central room, the Byzantine Hall, acknowledged to be one of the most beautiful rooms in the Middle East – not vulgar, like so much of Abdin, but a perfect setting for a reception with its priceless mosaics and dozens of candelabra, all lit by candles, reminding me of an enchanted room from an old picture book I had always loved as a boy.

The king, I had been told, would have supper in the Diplomatic Room before moving into the Byzantine Hall where the favoured guests would be presented. And after that, dancing.

We sat down. A ceremonial (but to us hidden) fanfare of trumpets announced that supper was about to be served. Though this was a buffet there was a menu, with the royal crest and a bow of green ribbon, the national colours, attached to one corner. On the other side of the card was printed a list of cabaret turns, and I was delighted to see that Samia was to sing. But it was the menu that really excited my attention. How could *anyone* eat so much! Later I pocketed it as a souvenir. It read:

Consommé de volaille froid
Tronçon de saumon à la Vénitienne
Soup de mer à l'Orientale
Galantine de faisan d'Ecosse truffée
Agneau de lait à la Bergère
Chaud-froid de pigeons en belle-vue
Aiguillettes de veau à la mode
Poularde de Bresse Lamberty
Yalandji Dolmas
Pâté de gibier à la Mirabeau
Langue de Charolais à la gelée de Porto
Asperges en branches sauce divine
Dinde de Fayoum rôtie froide à la gelée d'or
Salade Gauloise
Baklawa Pyramidal
Charlotte aux fruits
Gâteaux Marguerite
Petits-fours variés
Glaces assorties

Petits pains au caviar
Friandises
Fruits

'Not bad for a scratch meal,' Greg laughed.

'But what on earth is "sauce divine" with asparagus?' asked Chiffon. 'How can anyone improve on hot butter or Hollandaise?'

We hardly had time to discuss it all before dozens of waiters in scarlet and gold appeared with stacks of golden plates and politely offered us two choices: we could make our own way to the nearest buffet and load our plates with food, or we could trust the waiter to pick out portions of any dishes we requested.

'I'm not going to ruin my dress for anyone,' Chiffon told a waiter. 'Just some galantine and salmon, please, then if I'm still hungry I'll ask for more.'

After supper, those guests who were not being presented sat down in the Byzantine Hall, where a throne had been placed in front of hundreds of narrow gilt chairs forming an auditorium. The room looked magnificent, every candle lit, every spare inch of available space filled with flowers.

Greg and I sat on a couple of chairs near the front. Father and Mother were in another room, waiting to pay their respects to the king. The diplomats were to be presented first, and it was all over very quickly. Farouk came in with a couple of aides, sat down and the diplomats filed in according to protocol. I saw Sirry receive a royal smile. Father also merited a smile of recognition, but I was in no position to assess the royal reaction when Chiffon, all blue and white, gave an English curtsy.

I had looked around for Serena, but couldn't see her. I wasn't worried, but I would have liked to give her something on the lines of a 'thumbs up' signal. However, all the young ladies had been shepherded into an adjoining room. Only when the procession of diplomats had ended did the girls prepare for their turn.

At precisely spaced intervals, a chamberlain in the hidden room nodded to the girl next in line, at which moment she walked the seemingly endless strip of carpet to the royal 'throne'.

Soon it was Serena's turn. She was so cool and collected she might have been strolling across the lawn at home. She stood erect, head and long straight neck above equally beautiful bare shoulders. 'She looks like a play on her name,' I thought. 'A serene Serena.'

She curtsied perfectly, prepared to move on as Farouk smiled, but then he leaned forward and whispered something. The next girl came along the line as Serena half-turned, so as not to place her back directly to the king. Then she was in the next room. The ordeal had taken barely half a minute.

'You were wonderful,' said Sirry Pasha. 'I'm very proud of you.' We all congratulated her and someone offered her a glass of champagne.

'He whispered to you,' said Greg. 'What did he say?'

'Oh, nothing special,' said Serena airily.

'He must have said *something*. That he liked your hair, perhaps?' asked Madame Sirry.

'Or your neckline,' Greg teased her.

Serena hesitated. 'Mama,' she said finally, 'you'll never believe this. Never. He just whispered one sentence that any ordinary boy could have whispered to any girl. I know I'd met him before, but still —'

'But what *did* he say?'

'He just whispered, "Hang around. I'll see you later when I get rid of the mob." '

Sirry Pasha said nothing. But I had never seen him look so angry.

When the dancing and cabaret turns had started, and after I had heard Samia sing, I told Mother I was going to go back home, if only to cheer up Parmi.

'I'll stay on,' said Chiffon. 'I'm going to dance.' Greg also wanted to stay and dance with Serena.

'The Sirry table is at the far end of the room.' Father pointed to it.

Mother was already on the floor, so I walked with Greg to say goodbye to the Sirrys.

'I could kiss you, you look so beautiful,' cried Greg to Serena.

'Not in public!' warned Madame Sirry.

'I caught sight of your mother,' said Sirry Pasha. 'She looked in great form.'

'Never misses a dance,' I laughed. 'But I'm going to slide out quietly. Poor Parmi is on her own. It's a bit mean of me to stay out late.'

I threaded my way back towards Father through the crowded tables, filled with chattering people.

'Ah!' cried Father. 'Look who's come to take pity on me, sitting here alone.'

It was Samia, who had sung three songs after dinner. Was it my imagination, or had she grown a little plumper since our last meeting? But Father was delighted to see her.

'You sang like an angel,' he told her.

'It was for you, Sir Geoffrey. My favourite fan.'

'After the king?' I teased.

'No,' she sighed, with mock-despair. 'I don't think he is interested in me any more. He says I'm putting on a little weight.'

A footman came, whispered to Father and handed him a note. 'It's Sirry Pasha,' he said. 'Excuse me, my dear. I gather that HM wants me to be presented to him in his private dining room.'

'I heard you had got married,' Samia said almost shyly after Father had kissed her hand and left. 'And that your wife is very beautiful.'

I smiled. 'Well, so are you. Tell me, Samia, how is the nightclub going?'

'Wonderful. Thanks to you, there's never been a hitch. I'm not singing very much these days. Only gala concerts – and the occasional royal command. Why haven't you been to see me? We're very respectable. It's called the Sphinx. Not very original, but –' She shrugged.

'I must come. I've heard all about it. Greg says it's wonderful.'

'Do!' Impulsively she laid a hand on mine and said, with a husky break in her voice, 'The champagne will be on me – or anything –'

'What are you thinking about?' I broke the silence.

'You.' She smiled. 'Just thinking of the past – that night – and how wonderful it was.'

'Better than the king!' I laughed, to ease the tension.

'As it happens, I never made love with the king.'

I must have looked astonished. 'But the nightclub – and tonight's singing?' As she poured out some champagne I asked, 'What on earth do you mean?'

'Just that.' With the trace of a secret smile she said, 'He's not a bad man really,' then added carefully, 'but – well – the evening was a flop. He's not – not very well *endowed*.'

'Samia!' Instinctively I looked around, afraid we had been heard.

'I wanted to make him happy,' she sighed. 'I owed it to him. But it was awful. I tried to excite him. I undressed myself – and then I undressed him. I helped him with' – a trace of the giggles again – 'with everything, but in the end I left having done nothing – but clutching the deeds of the nightclub. As far as my relations with our friend are concerned, I'm still pure.'

'Poor you,' I murmured.

'Shall I let you into a little secret? I haven't made love to any man since you and I spent the evening in my flat.'

I must have gaped.

'Don't worry, Mark, I'm not going to ask you if I can become your mistress. I wouldn't want to hurt your wife – or that other girl – what was her name? – who I thought was in love with you.'

'Serena?'

'Ah! So you know who I mean? No, don't worry. I don't like men that much, but you were the last who excited me.'

Almost embarrassed, I looked round for Father or Chiffon for help. Instead, interruption came from another quarter.

'Good evening, Mr Holt.' The greeting came from behind our gold cane chairs, but I knew that oily voice before I saw the man.

'Good evening, General Sadik,' I said. 'Of course, you know –'

'Of course.' Sadik sat down uninvited. 'The evening is

going well, I think. Are you enjoying it?'

I nodded.

'I'm only sorry that your wife couldn't come. It would have given me great pleasure to meet her.'

'She's expecting a baby,' I said shortly. 'So of course she had to refuse.'

'I understand. In the meantime, you have Samia to keep you company. An old friend, eh?'

What a wealth of suggestion he managed to squeeze into the word!

'Old *client*,' I corrected him firmly.

'Not old friend, too?'

'I don't understand, General.' I got up angrily.

'Why are you so distressed, Mr Holt? All men – and many married ones too, I fear – have their lady friends. But in court circles the surveillance of many ladies is almost a matter of routine.'

I felt a sudden shiver; not so much fear as anger. This man was telling me insolently that, as a 'matter of routine' Samia, while awaiting the king's pleasure, had been spied on; which probably meant that in some police file, or perhaps Sadik's personal dossier, would be my name. I don't know what I could have done – would have done – but luckily there was another interruption. As a raven-haired woman approached, Samia said, 'I must go, Mark. I'm late already. Give my respects to your father.' With a nod to Sadik she left, even before the woman joined us.

The general was not disturbed in the slightest. 'This is Lala, my wife. Mr Mark Holt,' he said, performing the introductions.

I took my first look at Sadik's wife. Even though it could never have entered my head that one day Serena and I would be ranged against her in a sordid and dangerous court case, I had an immediate sense of evil.

Her face was as smooth as glass. No mask could have been more expressionless. She must have paid dozens of visits to Dr Andropoulos, the most famous plastic surgeon in the Middle East, whose consulting rooms were in the Groppi building. Every scar, every wrinkle, had been smoothed away so that the scarlet lips looked as though they were set in a baby's face. Even round the eyes the crows' feet had been erased, as though by a rubber; only the black malevolent pupils moved.

She was as thin as a pole, but her hands were covered with brown spots. She looked what she was – a pathetic woman trying to beat age. While it carried authority, her voice grated, and held a touch of sarcasm or irony every time she spoke. She gave me the impression of a woman who hated everyone. A formidable enemy, I thought.

After a few pleasantries she said to her husband, 'You've sent Miss Sirry off to meet HM? Or have you hidden her away?'

At the 'Miss Sirry' I pricked up my ears. 'She's engaged to my brother, you know.'

'Yes, I do know,' she retorted, making even an agreement sound insolent. 'She's beautiful – almost more beautiful' – with a sideways look – 'than Samia.'

She knew. I could see it in those mocking black eyes.

'It's all arranged,' Sadik assured his wife, then explained to me, 'HM is charmed with Miss Sirry. He's having supper with a few close friends in the Gold Room. That's a private dining room used only by His Majesty when he's with close friends. I think an equerry has already escorted Miss Sirry there.'

Father returned to our table as Sadik and his wife left, and we both decided to go home early, telling Chiffon that Father would send the car back as soon as it had dropped us. It was only one o'clock, and as Zola opened the door, he said to me, 'Mrs Parmi' – that was Zola's way of identifying her – 'asked me to let her know when you arrived, then she'll come and join you, sir.'

'What did you think of the king?' Father asked me when we had a nightcap.

'He has his eye on Serena.'

'That apart. As a man? He behaved much better than I'd expected. Great dignity, despite the rumours I've heard.'

'He was on his best behaviour.'

'That's true,' he agreed. 'But his best behaviour was good.

It's bloody hard work handling a thousand people, being polite to people you don't know.'

Parmi arrived, kissed Father first (as she always did) and asked, 'Was it fun?' We sipped a final glass of champagne as I told her that Serena had been invited to a private supper party with the king.

'Not alone?'

'God, no! Old Sirry Pasha would throw a fit,' I laughed.

'Decidedly no,' added Father. 'Especially as, according to Sirry, the king's fallen in love with the daughter of a judge in Alex. Sirry says he wants to marry her.' Father stifled a yawn when Parmi suddenly said, 'Pa, a curious thing happened this evening.'

I looked up. So did Father, as Parmi put down her empty glass. 'That overseer – you used a funny name, was it a ghaffir? – on the Sirry estate in the Delta. He came here.'

Father looked puzzled. 'Here? I don't think I know who you mean.'

'I wouldn't have thought twice about it,' Parmi went on, 'but then I remembered who he was. On my very first visit to the Delta, months ago, he had just made one of the girls on the estate pregnant –'

I sat up with a jerk, suddenly wide-awake. Akif!

I rang for Zola. 'Hope I haven't kept you up,' I said.

'No, *sir*!'

'What's all this about a man coming to the house? What exactly happened?'

He explained – at tedious length. Akif had come first to see Aly. He then came to our house saying Aly had given him permission to see our 'historic' home. All lies, of course. He was so persistent that Parmi came to find out what was happening. The man had actually tried to look into some of the rooms, including the famous music room. Finally Zola had forced him to leave.

'And that's all there is to it.' It was Parmi's turn to yawn. 'Must be a crank.'

I wondered. After all, I had threatened the man with court action. And Egypt was a country of long memories, of vendettas, of revenge.

'Come to bed, darling.' Parmi linked an arm through mine. 'It won't be long now before I get this weight off my tummy.'

17

Within a few days Aly gave a party – as though to show his friends that his would be more lively than any of the royal parties. And the date had been carefully chosen to coincide with a weekend when the Sirrys would be at their estate in the Delta. 'And that,' as Aly had explained airily, 'gives me a chance to invite *my* friends – even if you don't like all of them.'

'Am I included?' I asked.

'A borderline case' – Aly could have a sense of humour when he wasn't being difficult – 'but I love Parmi, so you have to come.' This with mock-resignation.

The Sirry house had been built at about the same time as ours, and shared the peculiarity of having jutting wings. The Sirrys' consisted of a small ballroom, ours of course of the music room.

'Those old architects knew a thing or two,' I had explained to Parmi when she first arrived. 'Each annex is built at the far end of the other house, with those vast lawns separating them, so if we ever want to hold a symphony concert in our music room, and the Sirrys want to hire a dance band in their ballroom, neither could hear what was happening in the other house.'

I had half-persuaded Parmi not to attend the party and at first she agreed, only to compromise. 'I'll just pop in for a couple of minutes, if I don't look too grotesque.'

As we walked through the gate into the gardens of the Sirry house she was saying, 'I like Aly, and I think he's misunderstood.'

'He's all right,' I agreed. 'A bit of a hothead. He'll probably

194

grow out of it. After all, he has to think of his father's position at the palace. In England or America the problem of a radical son wouldn't stop the father holding a job, but here – one breath of scandal by any member of the family and poor Sirry would be for the chop.'

However politically motivated Aly may have been, he was also the only son of a famous father, so he managed to steer a course between different sets of acquaintances – simply because men like Teddy Pollock or girls like Dodie Summers were taken for granted as old Cairo friends. And he was adept at behaving correctly when he had to – though he was not always as polite to his father as to them.

We crossed the Sirry garden to be met by Aly at the doors of the ballroom at the far end. 'There's someone here who wants to meet you again, Mark,' he began. 'He didn't *meet* you, Parmi, but you were in the same flat when he arrived with me.'

'Oh, that! That's the past catching up with me.'

We walked inside. Someone offered me a vodka and mango juice, the 'in' drink of Cairo. Dodie and Angela Gray were talking to Teddy Pollock and Jim Stevenson. Teddy waved at us across the room, and only then I saw who wanted to meet me as Gamal Nasser came forward, hand outstretched. His six-foot frame had filled out and he was no longer a youngster, but despite his prominent nose and sombre face he looked warm and friendly as he smiled and shook hands.

Aly introduced him to 'Mrs Holt'. Though I imagine he had probably told Nasser about the naked girl in the kitchen of the secret flat Nasser never, by even a twitch of a private smile, gave any indication that Parmi was anything other than the quiet, pregnant American wife of a British advocate, anxious to meet local friends.

Nasser said to me, 'You see, I made it! I was accepted by the Royal Military Academy and now I'm a *Mulazim Tany*, a second lieutenant. Even though I may only earn twelve hundred piastres a month. But never mind. I feel as though I'm helping to build the Egypt of tomorrow.'

He spoke with fervour; but though it smacked of a political utterance it did not jar on me. It may have been the sort of platitude people make on platforms to enthusiastic audiences; but when Nasser smiled it was just a simple statement made by a man who believed passionately in what he was saying. Whatever faults he may have had, Nasser was certainly genuine.

'You're not in uniform?' I asked the question because another Egyptian officer was talking to Angela, and as Parmi went to join Serena and the rest Nasser, still with Aly next to us, beckoned to the other officer in uniform.

'We passed out of the academy together.' Nasser introduced us. 'Anwar, this is Mr Mark Holt, son of Sir Geoffrey Holt. Lieutenant Anwar el Sadat. We're both stationed together at Mankabad, a military dump on the edge of the desert in Upper Egypt.'

Sadat was young, but he had a striking face, large eyes that never blinked when he spoke, and thick lips. He seemed very affable and, even though he was barely out of his teens – he was almost a year younger than Nasser – his voice changed from gentle softness to an intense and almost crisp accent when he was roused – which seemed to happen every time he discussed what would happen to his country.

'The future of Egypt,' Sadat said, 'depends on the young officers like Gamal and me. Independent young officers, not the old fogies. They don't really care for the independence of Egypt. All they want is to become generals. I'm sure you understand, Mr Holt,' he added, his voice becoming crisper, 'that it's only natural for the young Egyptians to strive for independence.'

'Of course,' I agreed politely, adding with a touch of malice, 'We have the same problem in Scotland.'

'Scotland?' Both looked astonished. 'You mean Scotland in the UK?'

I nodded, enjoying the joke.

Parmi, who had returned to the main room with Serena, nudged me, 'I think I'll make my way home.' She turned to Nasser and Sadat, 'I hope you'll excuse me, but as you can see I'm not my normal self.'

'I'll take you home, then come back.'

'You'll do nothing of the sort.' It wasn't Parmi's voice, but

Serena's. 'You stay with Aly's guests,' she said, sharing a laugh with Parmi. 'Aly likes Mark to come to his parties because it gives his friends a touch of respectability.'

I tried to argue, but in vain.

'All right, but I won't be long,' I promised at last, knowing that Parmi's nurse would be there, together with the rest of the staff.

As the two women walked away I noticed another Egyptian whom I did not know. 'Who is that?' I asked Nasser.

'That's Adli Hakim. I'll introduce you.'

Then Nasser added, 'I hope you understand, Mr Holt, that though we young officers of the army – men like Anwar and myself – are hoping to build a better Egypt, it must be achieved by legal means. No bloodshed, no violence. Adli Hakim and his followers share our aspirations for independence, but some of them are – well, prone to violence.'

Sadat chimed in. 'We want all the help we can get,' he said, 'but we *don't* want the Moslem Brotherhood to govern Egypt.'

I needed no further warning. Obviously, Hakim was a member of the Brotherhood, the subtle but highly political organisation which went under the cover of promoting unity amongst the followers of Islam. That was the public image, but behind the apparently religious fervour was a highly organised and often violent group avid for independence – by any means. There had been more than one case of opponents to the Brotherhood who had quietly disappeared.

'Even though I don't trust them,' Sadat admitted, 'there's no reason why we shouldn't make *use* of them. They're highly organised.'

I didn't particularly like Adli Hakim either, but we shook hands; after all, he was Aly's guest. Nor did Hakim strike me as an important member of the Brotherhood. He was no 'evil genius', no sinister plotter. We made small talk for a while until I heard Hakim ask Aly, 'I'm stifled. I need a breath of fresh air. Would you like to go for a stroll in the garden?'

'I think I should attend to my other guests,' said Aly cheerfully, 'though I have to tell you that the Holt garden next-door is better than ours.' They were at the ballroom door by now and Aly said to Hakim, 'Come back soon, eh?'

'Who's Aly's friend?' asked Angela, who, along with Greg, had wandered up to me.

'He's called Hakim, a member of the Moslem Brotherhood,' I explained.

'Looks like a wet dish-rag.'

'The Brotherhood's a tough bunch,' I warned her. 'They have a secret initiation ceremony, then they have to grow a small wisp of fuzzy chin beard to show they're members.'

'But if they're advertising that they're in the Brotherhood,' Angela pointed out, 'why do they have to swear an oath of secrecy?'

'Ah! That bears out my theory,' Greg chipped in. 'There's no fun in having a secret unless you share it.'

I was thinking of strolling home across the garden, for this was not my kind of party and I had nothing in common with any of Aly's friends apart from the fact that I quite liked Nasser. But at that moment Jim Stevenson beckoned me.

'Anything wrong?' I asked as he steered me into a corner.

'I didn't realise that you knew Adli Hakim.' Stevenson's usual nonchalant drawl had been replaced by a more urgent tone.

'I don't. Only just met him.'

'What's he doing in the garden?'

'Why ask me?' I felt vaguely put out. It wasn't Stevenson's garden. 'Is it a crime to stroll round the garden on a warm night?'

'Frankly, yes. You don't know Hakim. He's a killer, a professional hit-man for the Moslem Brotherhood.'

Looking across from the Sirry garden towards our own, I could sense the tension increase in Stevenson's voice.

'Who's that in *your* garden?'

I could see nothing but a shadowy figure, the face unrecognisable.

'One of our servants?'

'Servants be buggered. Come on, Mark, wake up! Where's Parmi? Serena? Is your father in the house? Your mother?'

I nodded, words beyond me. Then suddenly a torrent of anger exploded in me. 'I think he's that bloody man Akif!'

'Who?'

'He was found in the house the other day. Said he'd been told he could look around.'

As we looked, Akif blended into the shadows, and was lost from sight. Hakim too had disappeared. Suddenly our two voices jumbled into a cross-talk of urgency.

'Don't shout!' cried Stevenson.

'You must be crazy. Sound the alarm.'

'No noise, damn it, Mark, you amateur! We need to approach *silently*. This is an assassination attempt. I'm sure it's Sir Geoffrey – I've been told that he's on a Moslem Brotherhood anti-British hate list – so you *must* get to your father. Hakim and his crowd are mad. If they think there's an alert they'll shoot or throw a grenade – and they won't give a damn about killing themselves.'

I raced outside on to the lawn.

'Come, Mark! Every second counts. Run as you've never run before. You make for your father's study, but be careful. Don't force your way in, or it could all be over.'

'And you?'

'Where will Parmi and Serena be?'

'In the east wing, over the music room.'

'I'll find the girls.'

As we reached the Holt House I couldn't have spoken a word if anyone had offered me a million piastres. Yet Stevenson wasn't even out of breath. All he said was, 'Quietly, for God's sake. Before you do anything, find out if you can hear anything through the back door to the study.'

A dozen thoughts flashed through my mind as I raced to the house. Why Father? He was the greatest friend Egypt had had since 'Boyle of Cairo'. He was the architect behind the 1936 Treaty of Independence. Politicians might assassinate each other regularly, but – why should anyone want to kill a man like my father?

Or was it yet another instance of that terrible scourge of Egypt? A crime of vengeance, one of hundreds each year, especially in the Delta villages, where men harboured grievances, real or imaginary, for years, even handed them on as 'inheritances', often to end in murder. Did Akif still nurse a sense of grievance because I had forced him to pay a girl *he* had wronged? And was he also a member of the Moslem Brotherhood, and had he been persuaded that vengeance would be magnified tenfold if my father were killed instead of me?

Head spinning, I had just reached the back door of my father's study before the background hum of the evening's first cicadas was split by the sound of a single shot.

'God almighty!' I cried. It sounded as though it came from the music room. It was followed instantly by a scream. No, it was more like a wail, a woman's cry, then a babble of voices, screams, cries, shouts. But my heart gave its first leap of hope, for it wasn't Chiffon who had screamed. Nor Parmi. I was thinking that if Father had heard the shot the accomplice might have fired to make him come out into the open.

The main entrance to my father's study was in the Long Gallery, so that visitors normally came through the 'front entrance' in Garden City, but Father did have a second door giving out on to the lawns at the other side of the house. This was only used when Father went for a garden walk, without having to traverse the Long Gallery, or if someone from the embassy wanted to see Father privately, though it was an absolute rule that nobody used the door unless specifically given permission to do so. It was never locked in the daytime, only at night when Zola made the rounds, jangling his heavy bunch of keys.

All these thoughts were gnawing into my brain as I ran, crouching, one thought tumbling over the next. Who had been hurt? One of the servants? Why had the sudden noise ceased? I could imagine frightened servants running away – but if they had done so, I would have seen them, heard more cries. Why were there no more shots? The sudden crack of one shot, the female scream, had been followed by a silence more sinister, more frightening than any noise.

I reached Father's study door, having to fight with all my reserve to obey Stevenson and not to burst in. I knew his advice made sense, but my father was in that room . . .

As I hesitated, I could make out a voice. It wasn't Father's. It was either Hakim or Akif. I couldn't tell which, and I still had to fight not to follow every instinct and burst open the door.

At the other end of the house another shot shattered the still evening air. It was strangely muted, and so were the screams that followed. The music room was supposed to be soundproof. Stevenson would be there. He must be. Suddenly I had great faith in him.

Almost unexpectedly the sound of my father's voice came from behind the door, angry, disjointed phrases. 'What the hell do you think – I demand –'

Instinct presented me with the chance of immediate action. I couldn't rush to the door, but the reaction in the study to the shooting had allowed my father to protest. Whoever the man was, his mind could not be centred entirely on Father. This was no reasoned argument – there was no time for that – it was my instinct, pure and simple. If I had wondered who had shot who, if Father wondered, then the terrorist must be wondering too.

I heard my father raise his voice once more, 'Damn you! I demand –' The other man shouted, 'You are in no position to demand.'

'– see my wife.'

As the other man answered, I gently turned the outside knob of the door, opened it a bare three inches to show a crack through which I could see the *other* door – the one leading from the study to the Long Gallery. It was closed, offered no sight of the men inside, but I might at least learn by listening.

It was the voice of Akif. I was sure of it.

'Come!' he cried angrily to my father, and I could almost imagine the wave of a threatening gun. 'The time has come. The second shot was a signal. We can go to Mr Hakim.'

'And if I refuse?'

'You will be shot – here. You don't believe me? Try it. You will be shot like a dog. And your wife later.' The voice was almost casual, the tone of a man driven by hate.

'Come,' he repeated. 'You go first. Move! And remember – the safety catch is off.'

I could see my father through the crack as he reached the

door, could see his hand turn the handle. It squeaked slightly, as it always had since I was a boy. Then Father was halfway through the door and Akif's hand – with the gun in it – appeared like a close-up of a photo. There was one second left to act. Two seconds at the most.

I never *planned* the way I would attack. There was no time for that. But blind instinct warned me that if I simply hurled myself at Akif hoping to wrest the gun free I would never reach him in time. He would fire the gun instinctively. I had to do better than that.

As I heard Akif shout 'Go!' I realised that Father was actually passing through the doorway into the gallery. Akif was not expecting my door to be open: his face would be turned the other way, towards Father's back. I didn't even need to charge. Of course he would catch sight of me – the sudden, sharp movement of the opening door – he would swivel round, raise his gun to shoot . . . but I wasn't going to present that kind of target.

I pushed open the door, and half a second before he caught sight of me hurled myself forward, diving the three or four feet for Akif's ankles and shins, in what I devoutly prayed would be the best – and most important – rugger tackle of my life.

I felt the man tumble on to the carpet, my arms pulling at his ankles. Akif shot wildly, and I could see his cold face with its funny wisp of beard filled with surprise. As he landed the gun fell, to end up by the corner of the desk. I gasped and tried to reach it, just as Akif did too, so that we were both scrabbling towards the gun while pulling furiously at each other. Suddenly Akif's face was blotted out – by Father. Only he didn't do anything expected; he never did! Through the haze of smoke, the pungent reek of cordite, the fear – I saw Father, knowing he was no match for Akif, simply jump on top of his face.

Not quite on it: the man had swivelled at the last moment. So Father then kicked him, and this time, as Father told me later, Akif gave a smothered cry of rage and started spitting out blood from split lips. More blood poured from his nose, though I couldn't see it at the time; but it was enough to give me the chance I had been waiting for.

As Akif moaned I got to my feet and kicked the gun away from him. 'No time to tie him up,' I gasped. 'They've got Mother. Maybe Parmi too. In the music room, I think.'

'We can't leave him here.' Father looked as though he would keel over.

With a savagery born of fury that my father and mother should be threatened like this – a savagery I didn't suspect I could ever have felt until then – I grabbed a heavy teak Balinese idol and, almost revelling in the sudden look of fear in Akif's eyes, I crashed it down on his head.

'Come on!' I gasped, grabbing the gun. Father was panting. Suddenly he looked at me, almost for the first time, and cried, 'You've been shot!'

I couldn't believe it. I had felt no pain. But now I saw a dull red stain spreading over my shirt along the right-hand side of my chest.

'It can't be serious,' I said. I wasn't being heroic, only afraid we wouldn't reach Mother in time. 'They're in the music room,' I repeated, perhaps to reassure myself that I had guessed right. 'Let's make as little noise as possible. You all right, Father?'

'I'll follow you,' was all he managed to say.

As we ran up the Long Gallery I was wondering if the noise of shots might have attracted attention in the Sirry house, but the two houses were a long way apart, and a party was going on; to them the only real noise could have come from the backfiring of motor-cars.

But then another thought struck me with such fear that I started to sweat. Where was Stevenson? Had one of the shots we heard hit him? Was he dead, or still alive?

'They're inside!' I pointed to the entrance to the music room. 'Don't go in. If you did – without Akif – Christ, he could kill you on the spot.'

'What are you going to do?' Father whispered back.

'The harem grill,' I said suddenly.

It was years since, as children, we had crept into the old Turkish gallery with its partition, so that the ladies of the harem could peer down through the metal grill from their private room and unseen watch the men below. It was approached through a secret door which faced flush with the corridor on the upper floor, and in the old days the Kisler Aga, or chief eunuch, would doubtless have placed himself firmly at the entrance to the ladies' gallery.

As everywhere in the old house there was a jungle of back stairs unknown to visitors, who walked up the grand staircase in the centre of the Long Gallery. But we had known the winding small staircases by heart, as perfect hiding places during parties or places for snatched kisses when playing postman's knock or collecting forfeits.

Tiptoeing up the back stairs I gently pushed open the harem door, crept in and, invisible to anyone in the room below, peered down.

On the stage where in the old days musicians used to play stood Hakim, holding a revolver, not a slim one like the one I had taken from Akif, but a Colt. In front of him stood three people, arms folded across their chest – obviously by order, for they were not moving. One was Parmi, another Mother, the third Stevenson.

The well of the room, where in the old days the audience would have listened to a concert, was crowded with the cowering servants. In the centre sprawled a wailing mother who cradled a baby that was screaming with pain. And there was Serena, tearing strips of cloth from her white dress to make improvised bandages. Zola approached the platform and I heard him tell Hakim, 'This baby is badly hurt. We need water.'

'Shut up,' snarled Hakim, and I wondered if he was getting worried. There was a limit to the time one man could hold a room filled with hostages without something snapping. He was holding the gun firmly, yet he looked quickly at his wrist-watch: he must have expected Akif to return with my father before now.

As I peered through the grill, Stevenson tried to break the deadlock.

'Well, Hakim,' he said, almost cheerfully, 'you don't seem to be doing very well, do you?'

'Shut up! Or I'll shut you up.'

'You're sure your buddy Akif hasn't done a bunk?'

'I said shut up!'

'He's your buddy, not mine.'

What happened next was horrifying. Without a second's warning, and with the chilling detachment of the professional killer, Hakim's right arm, with the gun in it, swung in an arc and the butt of the Colt slashed across the American's left cheek. As the weal spurted into blood Hakim, who had never taken his hand off the trigger, snarled, 'Be grateful you're still alive.'

Stevenson stumbled but kept to his feet. But his eyes – and ears – were on Parmi.

She gave one terrible scream – from pain, not fear – swayed, and clutched her stomach in agony. Stevenson, the left side of his face covered with blood, tried to hold her, to stop her falling. He couldn't.

Screaming, 'The baby! The baby!' she fell, first on to the stage then, rolling in pain, and before anybody could stop her, over the edge into the well of the room, perhaps two feet below. Serena rushed towards her, cradled her, and shouted, 'Air, air!'

Perhaps I saw this after, not before or during – I will never know – for in that split second of time I acted in the only manner I could. I had a gun, but there was no way I could shoot Hakim: I had never handled an automatic before in my life. Stevenson was mopping blood from his face which was almost torn open. Chiffon was screaming. So, almost at the moment I heard Parmi scream again and move her legs convulsively, I emptied the barrel of the automatic – five bullets – through the harem grill. To someone who had no idea there was anyone else in the room the effect must have been electrifying – a fusillade of shots from nowhere. A sense of an unknown terror flashed through the entire room.

I caught a glimpse of poor Mother as she fell backwards off the platform – luckily into the arms of Zola, who was able to break her fall. And as the startled Hakim's attention lapsed it gave Stevenson his one chance; which was all he needed.

Despite the agony of his wound, he sprang – the only word

I can use – as though he had some secret source of energy, and within a second had his hands round Hakim's neck. He must have known exactly which point to squeeze, for Hakim immediately dropped the gun, and fell to his knees.

Even before I started to race from the harem room I heard Stevenson shout, 'Serena! Take my car and get Parmi to the hospital. And you too, Mrs Holt. Get help.'

By the time I reached the main door of the music room I was able to take poor Parmi in my arms, crying, unable to stem my tears. She looked on the point of death. Her face and skin were white, the lips pallid, and her breathing irregular, a series of sighs. Her few muttered words were barely whispers.

'Will she be all right?'

'It's the baby,' said Serena. 'It looks as though it's started. Chiffon and I will take her to the car. You follow – as quickly as you can.'

She didn't say 'In case it's too late', but the unspoken fear was there.

I climbed on to the stage. Stevenson stood with one foot across Hakim's neck.

'Zola,' cried Stevenson. 'Get everyone out of this room, please. And take the other baby to the hospital. I'll follow you in a moment.'

'Sir, the baby is dead,' said Zola.

'What happened?' I asked as the servants trooped out of the room and I caught sight of Father.

'One woman – I don't know who it was – rushed to the stage to beg Hakim to let her go with her baby, who was ill. He threw them both – yes, threw them – off the stage.'

'I'll call the police.'

'No, not the police,' said Stevenson sharply. 'The army's the best. And the embassy. This is one time for your father to pull rank. But not for five minutes. I want to be out of the house before the army arrives.'

'I ought to go to the hospital – Parmi! Christ, if anything happens to her –'

'Give me that five minutes, then we'll go together.' With a wry smile that obviously hurt he said, 'You look as though a dab of iodine wouldn't do *you* any harm.'

'What about you? That face of yours –?'

'I'd hate to look in a mirror, but it's superficial.'

'I'd better get the army in.'

Again he shook his head. 'If the police or the army get hold of Hakim he'll spend the rest of his days in jail being looked after, all expenses paid. We – sorry, I – have special codes of punishment. Unofficial, you understand, but for a brute who pitches a baby on to the floor – don't worry.' He looked at me, seeming to have forgotten the pain in his cheek. Incredibly, his voice, mannerisms, had almost reverted to normal.

Aware of my wavering thoughts, he said, almost gently, 'Remember, Mark, this man came for one reason only – to kill your father. The fact that he almost killed you and has knocked me about – well, that's something else. But if we hand this man over to the police he'll live in some sort of semi–comfort.'

Hakim was beginning to come round, the liquid–black eyes glazed with fear.

As he stirred and moved Stevenson, in that same nonchalant way, without any trace of anger, pushed him over with his foot so that he lay on his stomach. Then he reached for Hakim's revolver, and without a word grabbed the Colt by the barrel, knelt down on Hakim's forearm and with one savage blow cracked the gun down on to the Egyptian's elbow. The man screamed. I could hear the bone crack, but Stevenson hit him once more to make sure – and it was an extraordinary sight to see the way in which all the stiffness, all the firmness, all the strength, seemed to dissolve into a dangling, useless limb.

One elbow seemed to erupt in blood before Stevenson half-rolled the body over and hit him again – this time on the other elbow. Hakim had passed out by then, but one thing was certain – he would never be able to use either of his arms again.

'Personally, I'd rather be dead than immobilised like this,' grunted Stevenson. 'But for his sake I'm delighted he'll live instead.'

'I'll telephone to get the army now,' I said hoarsely. 'God, I hope never to see that again.'

'Better check on the other bastard in your father's study,' Stevenson suggested. 'Then – the hospital.'

I had forgotten all about Akif. I dashed now to the study – but he had vanished. Somehow he must have recovered consciousness – I couldn't see how he could have done it – but he wasn't there, and I was too worried about Parmi to care.

'So that leaves Akif free to try again,' was all my father said. 'Go to Parmi, Mark. And give her our love.'

'Come on, Jim,' I cried. And we drove off in a mad rush, to the Anglo-American Hospital – and to Parmi, praying silently that we would not arrive too late.

18

'Don't worry about your wife,' said Dr Phillips introducing the gynaecologist. 'This is Dr Haseltine.'

We had reached the Anglo-American Hospital, and Haseltine wasted no words. 'She was almost at term when she fell. It's a great shock, and our first examination shows evidence of internal bleeding, of a ruptured placenta. That's the reason why the baby must be born by Caesarian section.'

I must have looked terrified, and blurted out, 'Is that dangerous?'

'It's routine,' he assured me. 'It's much safer for the child's sake. There's always a danger of complications after a bad fall so late in a pregnancy. A Caesarian bypasses any problems.'

The Anglo-American Hospital had a special VIP reception lounge and Stevenson and I agreed to meet there later, after he had his face stitched up. 'I'll go to the out-patients after I've seen Parmi,' I said. 'See you later in the VIP room.'

Parmi was in a private ward, looking like death. Dr Haseltine said, 'Just pop in for a few minutes, Mr Holt. She's already under sedation, then we're going to operate. Don't forget she's had a severe shock – the baby too.'

She was drowsy, but smiled with an effort. Although she was quiet I could still hear in my mind the fearful scream as she fell off the platform.

I knelt by the side of the bed to be closer to her. She lifted a hand to stroke my face and said sleepily, 'All that blood on your shirt, darling.'

'Never mind.' I kissed the hand. 'So long as *you* are all right.'

Suddenly, like a wave of apprehension, she moaned, and cried, 'I've got a succession of blinding headaches where I hit my head when I fell.'

There was nothing I could do. 'It's the fourth or fifth time.' She was almost in tears with the sudden gust of pain. Without warning another sudden fear twisted her face. 'If anything should happen to the baby –'

'Don't say things like that, please.'

'But if –'

'Nothing will' – anything to console her.

'If, Mark – *just if* – after all, things do happen to babies – you'll have it baptised for me, won't you, by a Catholic priest?'

'Don't worry so. Everything'll be fine. But of course I would. You and your "ifs".'

'Everyone's been wonderful. Chiffon helped me so much. Serena too. Promise not to forget to tell Pa, if –'

'I'll cable him as soon as the baby's born,' I said, but she was already asleep as I tiptoed out of the room.

In the corridor the first person I bumped into was Serena.

'How terrible it all is.' She kissed my cheek. 'Your mother's gone home. She says your father needs moral support. And you need *medical* support. Let me help you.'

'Jim Stevenson was much worse. He's already being treated.' In fact, my wound was not serious. The bullet – of which I had no recollection – had missed the bone, and all I had was a sore flesh wound through the right arm just below the shoulder. After it had been treated I returned to the VIP room where Serena was waiting for me. Soon Stevenson reappeared, his face heavily bandaged.

'Looks worse than it is,' he intoned, with his Bostonian accent. 'The doc put in six stitches. He guarantees that in weeks the scar will have gone. He'll replace the bandages with dressings and plaster over the stitches in a few days. How's Parmi?'

'On the operating table.' I must have sounded scared. I think sometimes people are more scared when friends or lovers are being operated on than when it's themselves.

'It's a question of waiting,' said Serena. I realised that she was beginning to cry. I had seen her tears before, but they had been the tears of love. I had never before seen tears of despair. 'All that death, the wounds –'

'Don't worry.' I squeezed her hand. 'Everyone's alive. A bit battered but still – alive.'

'It's not that,' she cried. 'Oh! I didn't mean that you don't matter – your pain, and poor Parmi. But it's something deeper that makes me so depressed. *Why*, Mark? All this killing and hating suddenly erupting in your quiet, peaceful garden – just when British and Egyptians were happy together, enjoying each other's company.'

There was no way to explain briefly. 'If you ask me to give you a simple answer, then all I can say is for the same reason they would have killed me in 1919. Hate.'

Serena left soon after that and I settled down for a long wait. The gynaecologist had told me to go home, promising to telephone – especially as the hospital was only ten minutes away across the Kasr el Nil Bridge – but I couldn't do that to Parmi – and the baby – and the worry about the knock on Parmi's head when she fell. I felt – I *hoped* – that when Parmi came round I would be the first person she would want to see. I had to stay.

'It could take a little while,' Dr Phillips warned me. 'But if you insist on staying you might as well be comfortable. Come with me. And you too, Mr Stevenson, if you'd like.'

I must have looked puzzled, for he added, 'We have a small canteen for doctors and surgeons. Sandwiches and coffee – *and* a bar, though' – he gave a laugh – 'I'm afraid all drinks have to be paid for, in cash.'

It was a small, clinically pale green room with half a dozen hard chairs, wooden tables. A couple of large scotch and sodas went down very well.

It was while we waited that I was able for the first time to prize open another corner or two of the secret life of Jim Stevenson.

'After all,' I began, 'you saved my father's life. You're not going to pretend it was just a lucky chance?'

'No, it wasn't,' he agreed. 'I knew that Hakim had met Aly once before and I received information that Aly had invited him to his party – though I think it's probably more true to say that Hakim invited himself. So I got myself invited too. I wanted to see how they all behaved together. But I didn't know about the other man. I've no doubt Akif's name is in the files, but he hadn't come into my orbit.'

'What made you suspicious?'

'When Hakim asked to stroll in the garden because he said he needed a breath of air. There was more air in the ballroom with its fans than in the garden. And the Hakim type of man isn't usually a garden-lover. Then suddenly there was the other man – unknown, but when you told me about Akif trying to look round the house, well – it didn't take much working out.'

'When you shouted to me, you yelled one word at me. "Amateur!" Does that make you a professional?'

'You said it, not me.' Stevenson gave me his lazy smile and ordered another round of drinks.

'I don't suppose I should ask questions –'

'Right.'

'But in a way you *did* make me your helper –'

'If you must know, I work for Washington. You know that there's the beginning of a vague movement among discontented army officers in Egypt – they call themselves the "Free Officers". Well, I believe in them – because the political and military cliques are rotten to the core. But of course it's not my job to yell my head off in support.'

'Not with the Moslem Brotherhood?'

'I am *not* in favour of killer squads – in any country. And though the Brotherhood includes many fanatics it's only fair to say that it has moderate members too. And I *am* in favour of men like your father in positions of influence. Even though –'

'You have reservations?'

'Well, the State Department doesn't approve of too much British power in the Middle East. It's better if it's shared out equally.' He added dryly, 'We are always told that if Britain ever gets a toe-hold in any country it usually ends up making it a colony.'

'That's ridiculous, and unfair.'

'That's what I'm told.' Stevenson refused to be rattled. 'And of course America is against colonies.'

'Like Hawaii? I seem to remember that used to be British once. Or the American Virgin Islands? You bought them from Denmark, didn't you, for a measly twenty-five million dollars – just to protect America when the war broke out in 1914. Come off it, Jim! What with Puerto Rico and the Philippines – ceded to America as a direct result of the Spanish-American war – you're just as bad as the British – only not quite so successful.'

Stevenson laughed but there was no malice, just an acceptance of life as he found it. 'It's a well-known axiom,' he said, 'that every country which has acquired other people's land always cries "That's different!" when others criticise it.'

'That's different,' I echoed.

Several times I telephoned to the girl at the reception desk to see if there was any news, but Parmi was still on the operating table. So in a way the 'cross-examination' of Stevenson helped to still my fears, to take my mind off the operation. This was the first time I had seen the sheer professionalism of Stevenson 'at work'. One thing, however, did puzzle me.

'It's your character,' I said. 'I can understand the speed of your reactions when Father's life was threatened – I understand because it's part of your job. The professional instead of the amateur' – my smile robbed the remark of any offence – 'but *afterwards*. The deliberate way you insisted on dealing with Hakim instead of handing him over.'

'You found that brutal? More brutal than killing the baby in the music room?'

'But the police – the courts –'

'I like to make the punishment fit the crime. The trouble is that usually it doesn't. It does if I'm around; but it's not a side of my character I usually allow others to see. You happened to be involved.'

Finally, Dr Phillips beckoned me with a smile, 'All over, Mark. You may come and see your wife.'

'She's all right?'

'Fine. Dopey – she won't recognise you – but –'

'And the baby –?'

'A little girl.'

'Wonderful!'

We had arrived at Parmi's room. Haseltine, the gynaecologist, was there with her. She lay on her back, her face as white as the sheet which covered her. I held her hand. It was wet, burning. Her forehead glistened with sweat, and her breathing was laboured.

'Don't worry,' the doctor assured me. 'She was very excited – more so than normal. She'll be absolutely all right.'

'She's so hot!'

'Come outside, Mr Holt. Your wife must have all the air she can. The fewer people who are in the room the better.'

As soon as we were outside, I said, 'And the baby?'

He hesitated. 'There are problems. Respiratory. We've put her in the intensive care unit because she's having difficulty breathing normally. We had great difficulty in getting the baby to breathe in the operating theatre. I don't want to alarm you, but I wouldn't be doing my duty –'

'My God!' I breathed.

His silence was more powerful than any words.

I saw Parmi for a few minutes in the middle of the night. She had come round, was very weak, but I could see the excitement in her face as she said, 'They won't let me see her yet. I'm too weak. But is she beautiful?'

'Just like you.' I kissed her gently.

'I'm so happy. So happy.' She drifted into sleep even as I tiptoed out of the room. The nurse told me that Parmi was still in a very nervous state and would be sedated. She virtually ordered me to go home. I did, and never stirred until seven the next morning when Dr Phillips telephoned. I sensed bad news from the tone of his voice.

'My wife?' I cried.

'Fine. Sleeping peacefully, Mark. But I wish I could say –'

The baby had died just after six o'clock that morning.

It was not until I was driving to the hospital that I was struck by a sudden terrible thought: during the few hours that our little daughter had lived, struggling for breath, I had completely forgotten my promise to have the baby baptised.

PART TWO

1938–1942

19

When Parmi first returned from hospital she was understandably depressed. She was polite, even in her way kind, but
remote. She seemed to turn inwards, and all her sense of fun
and her zany humour vanished in a haze of self-recrimination,
as though she had to pay for what had happened, for our
failure to make our daughter a Catholic and properly baptised.
As the days passed, her depression did not lift. She even began
to have increasing doubts about the validity of her marriage
to a Protestant.

Our marriage had been blessed by a Catholic priest, true,
but in a light moment, months before, I had said to some
friends, 'It presented no problem. You can get anybody to
do anything in Cairo if you pay enough.' Parmi saw the
half-truth behind the jest. I had, she believed, rigged the
blessing, a ceremony which was virtually unknown in the
Catholic world of the thirties. So, to her way of thinking,
she had not only conceived an illegitimate child, but her
unbaptised daughter could never go to heaven unless Parmi
could atone. She even insisted on sleeping apart. Did that
mean she had sworn an oath denying her bed to her husband?
Or was it simply a revulsion brought about by a tragic train
of events?

And how much had Parmi been influenced by her father?
Theo Davidson was not at all a pleasant man but he was a
powerful one. It would be very easy for him to exert influence
on her in the regular letters which he sent, but which I never
saw. I had the feeling more than once that Davidson was
manipulating Parmi in the hope of persuading her to leave
Cairo and return to America.

Later another factor complicated the whole matter. She
began to be plagued by blinding headaches, increasing lassi-

tude, moods of ever-deepening depression. And that, explained Dr Phillips, was due to the fact that she had also hit her head badly when she fell off the stage at the time of the pregnancy. But often she would feel better; sometimes the headaches would be intense. And of course to the emotionally disturbed Parmi this was further evidence of the way her God was punishing her.

Sometimes when I sat in the evening studying a brief I would steal a look at her. Her face had become drawn, empty. She gazed in the distance beyond the walls of the room. Even the wild blonde hair had become stringy – still neatly brushed, but no longer vibrant. When I spoke to her, trying to cheer her up, she seemed to jerk her mind from a thousand miles away.

Even worse was the look if I happened to touch her on the way to bed. We slept in separate rooms and once at her door, when I smiled and tucked my arm into hers, merely to try to make her smile, I caught for a split second a look of physical distaste in her eyes.

I asked Dr Phillips for advice and he offered to fly in a specialist from London. 'But I don't really advise it,' he sighed. 'The original post-natal depression has grown into a kind of religious mania.'

He shook his head. 'She's not really unusual, you know. I've known cases of acute post-natal depression that have been cured, even after years.'

As to the future – 'I wish with all my heart that we could go back and be like we were,' Parmi said one evening. 'But we never can. I have sinned. I have to pay for it.'

'And me? Do I have to pay too?'

'I'm afraid so. I'm dead inside – dead. Perhaps one day there'll be a resurrection.'

I wondered. There were certainly no immediate signs of a 'resurrection'. I did my best to help, but there was no way I *could*. What I found hardest to understand was the speed with which Parmi had moved from a woman of sweet innocence to a woman overwhelmed with remorse and guilt. Had she slowly grown more and more morose, hating me, I could have understood more easily.

Of course the double shock of the terrorist attack, then losing the baby, had been traumatic; and nobody expected Parmi to go out dancing the week she left hospital. But the speed with which she changed was almost terrifying; it was something you see when someone has a stroke and emerges in seconds as a physical wreck. Only Parmi's breakdown wasn't physical, it was mental. It wasn't even hate which transformed our relationship. It was worse – utter indifference.

We struggled along as best we could for what seemed like months – I lost count of time during that anguished period – until finally she decided to move out of our house to a small flat near Teddy Pollock's in Kassed Street in Garden City. She was near to us, but she preferred to live alone. Yet it was a curious relationship. She would come round sometimes when she was, as she put it, 'feeling on form' and help Chiffon with the flowers, even staying for lunch or dinner. Yet she seemed perfectly happy in her small apartment until suddenly she announced that she was going to stay with her father in New York – and act as his hostess and housekeeper.

Davidson had been over to see her twice. And he warned her – and me – that war in Europe was inevitable, and that Parmi should be taken to America.

'It'll be safe over there,' he declared. 'This time the United States is going to take good care that we'll never again have to send our doughboys across the Atlantic to rescue the British.'

When she finally left she asked that I did not journey to Alex to see her on board the ship. And when she had gone she left behind one chilling message which later I discovered to be taken from the Athanasian Creed in the Book of Common Prayer:

Whosoever will be saved: before all things it is necessary that he hold the Catholick Faith. Which Faith except every one do keep whole and undefiled: without doubt he shall perish everlastingly.

★

In a way I was relieved when she had gone. Chiffon said goodbye to Parmi with ill-concealed relief, and asked me, 'Couldn't you get divorced now?'

'Not a hope,' I replied gloomily. 'She'll never divorce me. I think she believes that's part of God's punishment.'

'But you're not a Catholic.'

That, apparently, made no difference. The divorce laws were not as lax in the thirties, especially for Catholics, as they are now, and though I had read reports about 'quickie' divorces, as they were called in America, when you could end a marriage without both parties being present, they were sometimes followed by charges of bigamy by one of the partners bent on revenge.

I had even been to see the Catholic priest who had blessed our marriage. He was gentle and understanding.

'The trouble,' he said, 'is that your wife is a sick woman. Excessive zeal is a kind of sickness, you know. Yes,' he smiled, 'even excessive religious zeal. Many of us are more understanding about marital problems than you may think, but your wife is plagued by her conviction that she has greatly sinned. It may be exaggerated, but the thought of her permitting divorce proceedings is out of the question.'

I had read about marriages being annulled.

'Marriages can be annulled, even if there are children, but Mr Holt, you as a Protestant cannot ask His Holiness to annul a Catholic marriage. And you must be aware that your wife, who *might* be able to ask for an annulment, would never agree to do so. She *wants* to suffer. She believes that is her way to redemption.'

In many ways it was Serena who helped more than anyone else to cheer me up when I was down. She was nineteen now and her wedding to Greg had been arranged for the autumn. She had blossomed from a lovely girl into a rare and beautiful woman. It was astonishing what a difference a year made. She had a maturity about her. I wondered if – impending marriage apart – her work with Baptise, the French artist, had helped to form her. Art alone, no. But Baptise had a remarkable talent not only as a painter, but even more as a teacher who put Serena on the right path, then allowed her talent to develop naturally even if still under supervision.

He – and Serena – almost always painted in the open air, from nature, and I rarely saw them at work except once, when the old man and Serena set up their easels in the Ezbekieh Gardens. Baptise, who looked the part of a painter, with his beret and his snowy white beard, had started out by drawing bold charcoal strokes on his flat, tightly stretched canvas. Serena, I could see through the window as I watched, was more hesitant until Baptise grabbed the stick of charcoal – so fragile it immediately broke – grabbed her right hand in his and forced her to draw boldly under his guidance.

Baptise loved slapping on colour, often with a thick impasto, smearing it on with a palette knife, yet the curious thing is that he was never able to 'tame' Serena. They painted the same subjects, used the same colours, yet somehow, in the exciting metamorphosis of art, he produced a bold exciting masculine painting and she a delicate feminine version, each of the two painters reflecting their own personalities.

'I'll never make a man of her,' Baptise sighed one day.

I remember that day in particular for, though from time to time I watched them through the windows of my chambers, I never went down to see them as they were painting. (I was too afraid of Baptise's wrath!) But at the end of the day's work Serena would come up to see me, the canvas still wet so it had to be handled carefully. Without my knowledge she and Baptise had each painted the Victorian building in which I had spent so much of my working time, with my windows in the centre, and in one of them the faint shadow of a man looking down on the gardens.

'I shall call it "Portrait of an advocate looking at the painter",' she smiled. 'It's for you, Mark.'

It was delightful, a soft gentle study in browns and greens, with the faint outline of myself showing through the glass of the window.

'I wonder what you were thinking of when you painted that,' I asked.

'You'll have to steal my diary to find that out,' she said. 'All my closest secrets are in it.'

The painting has been hanging in my chambers ever since. Every time I look at it I imagine the day I was peering out of the window, and I see the beautiful painter working below.

Though she was much concerned with painting, Serena also had what she jokingly called 'My Royal Life', for by now she had been invited several times to the Abdin Palace. Sirry Pasha saw to it that everything was above board. Sometimes Greg was invited too, sometimes she went to make up a party as a spare girl. But I had the feeling that General Sadik was easily able to find out when Greg was playing polo abroad or at Alex, that he could tell the king when he could invite Serena alone.

'There's no question of him trying to – well, make me,' she laughed. 'He's too busy with his bride-to-be.'

That was probably true, for we had all seen the announcements that the king was marrying the following January. It would be the most glittering start to 1938.

'You've no idea how impetuous he was when he courted her,' Serena told me. 'I heard the whole story from Papa.'

The future queen was Safinaz Zulficar, the sixteen-year-old daughter of the highly respected Judge Zulficar of Alexandria. She had joined Farouk's sister on a holiday where the king first met her. He had been fascinated but at first controlled himself. Not for long.

Sirry Pasha remembered the exact date – 21 August – when the king first decided to marry, because he was in the Abdin Palace when Farouk announced, 'I'm going to drive to Alexandria – right away.' He ordered an ADC, Omar Fathi, to accompany him. Affairs of state, appointments, arrangements – all were ignored.

'Well,' the king asked Sirry Pasha and Fathi, 'aren't you going to ask me why?'

The ADC replied, 'I never interfere with what Your Majesty does.'

'I'm going to the most important meeting of my life,' Farouk announced, and walked off.

The king roared up the Delta highway in his Alfa Romeo, paying scant attention to humans or animals who got in his way, and finally jammed on the brakes in front of the judge's home. Safinaz's parents were out, but almost abruptly Farouk blurted out a proposal of marriage. Safinaz didn't refuse what she called 'a great honour' – they had met many times with Farouk's sisters – but she did add, 'I must first ask my father.'

Unfortunately the judge was in Port Said, on the point of leaving for a two-week holiday in Lebanon.

'I can't wait two weeks!' cried Farouk, and asked to use the telephone, where he issued a string of instructions. What happened next was incredible. Judge Zulficar had just said his goodbyes on board the ship leaving for Beirut when uniformed police rushed on board and confronted him. There were no charges, no explanations. In front of all the passengers the judge was hustled off the vessel like a common criminal. It was not done out of petulance. Farouk just didn't think of the embarrassment to his future father-in-law.

That night, after having been driven to Alexandria, Zulficar was summoned to the Montazar Palace outside the city, where the king told him that he wanted to marry his daughter. Sirry Pasha never learned the details of what happened that night, but in the end the judge agreed to the marriage – he really had no option – though he suggested that they were both too young, and should first be engaged for a few years.

Farouk would have none of it. He told the judge, 'I want to be married within six months.' That night the wedding day was fixed for 12 January.

As soon as the government published the wedding date Farouk announced that Safinaz would immediately change her name to Farida, 'The Flawless One'.

The country rejoiced. Prince Charming was taking a radiantly beautiful bride in true fairy-tale fashion. And at first Farida was happy. Farouk showered her with presents, he was attentive, he showed her off proudly at dances and official receptions.

'So you see,' said Serena teasingly, 'I've missed my chance of being a queen, or even a royal mistress. And I'm not likely ever to be asked to spend the evening alone with him.'

'Thank God for that.'

'Or,' she said almost shyly, 'even alone with you, for that matter.'

'Whose fault is that?' I smiled, thinking that though from time to time she would walk into our garden she did seem careful not to be left alone with me. Had Sirry Pasha said something? Or had the recent tumultuous events – the assassination attempt on Father, the change in Parmi – warned her, perhaps, that if she wanted happiness with Greg she must put me out of her mind? As I had tried to put her out of mine.

At first I thought so – indeed, part of me hoped as much. But then, one evening, during a weekend at the Sirrys' estate on the Delta, a curious thing happened. Greg and Aly had gone shooting, the Sirrys were resting, and we were left alone on the veranda. It was very hot. I had a couple of long whisky and sodas and she was sipping a *karkade*, an infusion made from hibiscus flowers, when suddenly she laid a tanned hand on top of mine and sighed, 'It might have been so different.'

But it wasn't the words I noticed, it was her face. It was as though she had been mesmerised. The sensation only lasted for a second or two, but during those moments her face changed as though wearing a mask – or was it taking off a mask? The beauty had been replaced by a kind of hunger, as though, without daring to let me know, without saying a word, she had, at the careless touching of our skins, been seized by an overwhelming burst of desire she was unable to control. I had the feeling that for a few seconds she was caught off-guard, her feelings naked, and she wanted nothing more than to drag me into the nearest empty room and pull me against her – up against a wall if there was nowhere to lie down. It was an extraordinary sensation.

'Ah! Here come Greg and Aly.' I saw them outlined behind a man with a team of oxen yoked to a plough so primitive it might have been in use three thousand years ago. 'Looks as though they've got a good bag of birds.' I waved to their distant figures.

'Poor little birds,' she said sadly. 'Poor little Parmi. And poor little us.'

20

There had never been such a joyous three days within living memory. Cairo – no, all Egypt – went wild with excitement as 'the love story of the century' finally reached its climax, the day of the wedding.

Already Farouk had endeared himself to millions of his subjects. He had built model villages on the royal estates. He had given away hundreds of royal acres to peasants. He had opened schools and hospitals. And, unlike his father, he went regularly to Friday prayers.

It was a story of youth triumphant. Not only was Farouk a handsome and generous man giving Egypt the promise of a better way of life for his subjects, but his bride was a fairy-tale figure of breathless beauty. Millions of people lined the streets to catch a glimpse of Farida, who was dressed in a Paris gown of white, silvered lace, and with a train fifteen feet long. Through the state-carriage windows they could see her veil, first used by the Empress Eugenie and presented to the ruling family at the opening of the Suez Canal. On her head she wore a priceless diamond tiara, and round her throat an equally priceless diamond necklace.

When Farida reached the palace she did not meet Farouk. According to the Moslem religion she waited in an adjoining room, but Sirry Pasha, with other members of the court, saw the ceremony, with the king dressed in the black and gold uniform of a marshal of the Egyptian army. Farida's father first received an envelope containing half the royal dowry. Farouk and Judge Zulficar shook hands, pressing their right thumbs against each other, while the judge said, 'I betroth you to my daughter Farida.'

Looking every inch the handsome young king, Farouk, according to tradition, repeated three times, 'I accept her betrothal from thee, and take her under my care and bind myself to offer her my protection, and ye who are present bear witness.'

After the signing of the marriage contract, Farida made her entrance from the waiting room. A white flag was run up from the palace masthead. A hundred-and-one-gun salute started firing as the couple walked together along the corridor flanked by its reception rooms, the long hall jammed with heavy sofas and chairs, wall lamps and eighteenth-century French mirrors – an ugly part of the palace which Farouk scornfully called 'the hot box'.

Finally the bridal couple descended the wide staircase, and the guests went to the three large reception rooms filled with presents. 'Though they obviously didn't include them all,' Sirry Pasha said. 'Especially a Mercedes sports car sent by Hitler, and a stable of horses sent from Arabia.' Still, the gold and jewelled ornaments on show were worth more than a million pounds.

But it was not only a fairy-tale wedding for the few privileged who attended. It was above all a shared occasion. Mingling with the huge crowds, I cannot remember a day in which happiness – however fleeting – was shared by so many, in which even the poor and the lame were not forgotten. As all Egypt celebrated with a rare taste of meat from sacrificial bullocks – an agreeable change from camel flesh – Farouk ordered and paid for the erection of three huge *sewans*, open day and night to feed more than a hundred thousand of the city's poorest.

Fireworks lit the sky for three nights running, and the climax of the first evening arrived when, in a break with strict Moslem tradition, Farouk and his queen appeared on a palace balcony especially erected near the entrance to the palace gates so that all could see. Farida broke tradition in another way: no one had ever seen a scantier veil.

On the following Friday Farouk went to prayers. As he was about to enter the mosque, he exchanged his royal prayer-rug with that of a beggar, telling him, 'In the eyes of God all men are equal.'

★

No wonder that in Egypt everyone forgot the threats of war in distant Europe. It was a mood of euphoria that lasted almost through the rest of the year. True, the London newspapers had been filled with stories and photographs of men digging trenches in Hyde Park, air-raid wardens issuing gas masks, food stores being hoarded in secret government caches. As though to rub home the grim fears of war, the meetings between Chamberlain and Hitler were invested with a quality of hopelessness. The unprepossessing Chamberlain was no match for the bullying Hitler, yet he had to be seen to try hard, if vainly, to avert the inevitable.

Then suddenly at the end of September the crisis abated, and Chamberlain, after a final meeting with Hitler, was waving a piece of paper and crying, 'I believe it is peace in our time.' And peace – or would 'armistice' be a better word? I wondered – replaced fear and the British newspapers, now reaching Cairo in a couple of days, were filled with 'normal' news – the *Queen Mary*'s fastest-ever crossing of the Atlantic, the plans to build the *Queen Elizabeth*, the prospects for the winter football season – all barometers of peaceful pursuits, evidence to the average European that Hitler had been bluffing, and that Britain had called his bluff.

The European holiday resorts were overflowing. Even Greg had achieved his greatest ambition by being elected captain of the Punchers polo team when they were invited to play at an international tournament in Deauville. Everyone was determined that life should go on without further interruptions.

Mussolini presented a slightly different problem, because Italian belligerence affected Egypt more closely. Daladier, the French premier, had meekly acknowledged Italy's conquest of Abyssinia, while Italy annexed Libya – which meant that a formidable new enemy now faced Egypt's long western frontier.

A month or so before Greg and Serena were due to be married, our two families went to Nasrani for the weekend. Greg was on his way back from France, while Aly was spending a week at Alexandria with Nasser and Sadat, both of whom were on leave.

'You're very thick with your chums,' I said to Aly just before we left. 'What on earth can you find to talk about for a whole week?'

Aly explained with a certain show of importance, 'They're leaders of a group in the army trying to find new ways to improve life in Egypt. Eliminate corruption, particularly in the palace clique – that sort of thing.'

'But if they're army officers, where do you fit in as a civilian?'

'I'm the contact man with sympathisers outside the Egyptian forces.'

'Men like Hakim and Akif who tried to murder my father? Aren't you dealing with dangerous people? And you said you were against the palace clique. Isn't your father a member of just that clique?'

'That's different,' he said angrily.

'It always is.'

'You can jeer. But thousands of civilians are fed up with crooked politicians, and are looking to young army officers for a lead. Gamal has appointed me a liaison officer.'

In the end only the two Sirrys, the two Holts, Serena and myself set off before lunch in the *Kismet* at its usual dignified rate of knots. The captain – white-topped cap tucked under his left arm – joined us for a pre-lunch pink gin.

'We'll reach Nasrani at the usual time?' asked Sirry Pasha.

'Yes, sir. I've received notification of a wedding party that will be crossing by ferry before we reach Nasrani, but of course we have precedence – unless the ladies would like to see the ceremonial journey across the river to the bride's new home. It's very colourful.'

'I'd love to see it, Papa,' cried Serena.

Sirry Pasha nodded indulgently, giving instructions for an early lunch to be served.

We reached the ferry crossing soon after two o'clock, at a point where the river was about quarter of a mile wide. From its banks irrigation channels had been cut like veins to feed the parched Delta. We moored next to the ferry at a landing stage from which a sun-cracked road wound out of sight through a grove of acacias. On the opposite bank a similar landing stage gave on to a cluster of adobe houses with the minaret of a mosque rising from its centre.

'The bride's destination, I believe,' explained the captain.

The raucous cries of sea-birds overhead were interrupted by the faint music of the wedding party approaching. Though Sirry Pasha might be more English than the English, his handsome features revealed a response to a culture thousands of years older than anything Europe could offer.

'What you're hearing, Mark,' he said as we leaned over the gunwale, 'is an echo of what is probably the oldest music in the world. It may sound strange to you, but it says something to us of – well, human frailty perhaps, or even human bliss.'

'It sounds so romantic,' said Serena.

'The song's been written specially for the bridal couple,' explained Sirry Pasha. 'All about their characters – with a great deal of wit worked in. Moslems are great ones for gentle mockery.'

Along the road winding through the acacias the wedding group approached through little waves of heat and dust, as though walking on water until the mirage merged with reality in the shape of musicians with their strangely syncopated rhythm, while singers behind them chanted a dirge-like, unharmonised melody. The colours of the robes and fezzes shifted like a kaleidoscope in the brilliant sun. It was, Sirry Pasha said, a wedding of some substance – possibly the children of fairly rich landowners.

Behind the musicians came the bride on a caparisoned camel. She sat in regal splendour, protected from the sun by a gold and blue shawl stretched over a framework of palm-branches fixed to the saddle. Half-hidden within this canopy, the bride sat robed in white, with the gold and silver coins of her dowry stitched to her veil and the richly embroidered circlet that bound it to her head.

The wedding song had now been taken up by the crowd of friends, neighbours and hangers-on who had all been invited to the pre-nuptial congratulation ceremonies and gift-giving. The halt and the maimed from the bride's village joined in as best they could. All would be welcome at the wedding feast. When the bride reached the ferry the music stopped, as though swept into silence by an unseen maestro's baton.

Almost hidden by a group of women attendants – the equivalent of bridesmaids – the bride was then conducted on board the ferry. The canopy was re-erected amidships, and she sat down on small coloured cushions which the women had produced from inside their kaftans. Small, brilliantly coloured rugs were produced as though by magic and on these the bridesmaids sat cross-legged, while the men of the party presented the bride with vividly painted boxes containing gifts – clothes, utensils, anything the village thought would please her.

'And where,' I asked, 'is the groom?'

'At home – waiting,' said Sirry Pasha.

'It's all so beautiful,' Serena sighed. 'Beautiful and simple. I wish we could get married like that. A village wedding.' Then suddenly laughing as she watched, she looked at her father and said, 'I don't need any of *that*.'

'Need what?' The question came from Chiffon, who was looking on next to Serena.

The bridesmaids were now busy grinding antimony into dust with brass pestles and mortars.

'They'll make a lifetime's supply of kohl to darken her eyelids,' said Sirry. 'And *that's* a custom which goes back to the days of Salome.'

'So beautiful,' repeated Serena. 'Sometimes I wonder –'

'Wonder what?' asked her father.

But Sirry Pasha never received an answer, for at that moment a heron swooped down from a wild palm on the bank and distracted our attention by landing precisely on the bow of the *Kismet*, where it remained, still as a figurehead, for the rest of the journey.

I can't remember ever seeing Serena with such a faraway look in those green eyes. All through dinner she sat silent unless asked a question, and even then she had to be jerked from dreams back to reality.

'What on earth's got into you?' Madame Sirry asked quite sharply. 'You're sitting there like a dummy in a shop window.'

'I'm sorry, Mama. I've got a bit of a head. I feel stifled. Is it very hot tonight?'

I tried my best to cheer her up, but I knew what she was really thinking. She had been deeply impressed by the village wedding. But had she seen herself going to a new home on the ferry? To meet Greg? Or – someone else? Or maybe she was just bored. After all, my father was now in his early sixties, Chiffon had recently celebrated her fifty-eighth birthday, and the Sirrys were much the same age. Sirry Pasha in fact looked much older, aged by bitterness as he watched Aly's activities, though the word 'revolutionary' was never mentioned in his house. Still, it was Aly who had invited Hakim to the party that had so nearly resulted in my father's assassination.

Suddenly, as dinner ended, Serena cried, 'Papa! Can I go out for a breath of fresh air?'

'Walking around at this time of night? It's nearly ten o'clock. I can't go with you, I'm going to bed. I'm tired.'

'Mark, please?' She looked at me appealingly. 'Let's go for a drive. Can we borrow the open two-seater, Papa? You don't mind, Mama? I'm going mad cooped up here.'

'Well,' said Madame Sirry, 'it *is* stuffy. And so long as you have your protector with you.' She smiled at me.

'I'll go and get a shawl – in case a khamseen blows up. Meet you at the car, Mark.'

It was odd, the casual manner in which she took my acceptance for granted, and as she ran out of the room Father said to me, 'Hope you're not tired. But I must say Serena looked off-colour.'

'Don't be late,' said Chiffon.

'I won't.' I kissed her. 'Promise.'

As I reached the old roadster which was always kept at Nasrani Serena was just closing the back of the boot.

'What's that?' I asked.

'Tell you later,' she said as she jumped in the car.

Then, as I started the engine and prepared to turn left where

231

the Nile ran alongside the road in the direction of Umm Dinar – the main road to Alex – she laid a cool hand on mine at the wheel and said, a little unsteadily, 'The other way, Mark. Turn right.'

'To Sakkara? It's only a few miles down the road.'

'To Sakkara,' she repeated.

The name, the romantic nature of the place, the horse rides by night – this and the desert meeting the green of lush, Nile-watered fields, was so much a part of our youth that to many of us in that remote corner of yesterday the hopeful question 'To Sakkara?' was like a password, tantamount to an invitation. In the past, when we had asked a girl if she'd like to go to Sakkara by moonlight, she had known what to expect and we had known what to hope for; especially in respectable families where privacy for the young was considered suspicious.

'What's in the boot?' I asked.

'A bottle of champagne.' She curled happily on the bench seat of the car.

'Warm champagne?' I teased her.

'No. I pinched the champagne and all the ice in the fridge and put it in a sack.'

I smiled. There was nothing to say, though I had no intention of indulging in a night of adventure with the girl who was to marry my brother in a month. As usual she knew just what I was thinking. We both knew; the words were taken for granted.

'I agree with you,' she said, almost gravely. 'But you might at least thank me for getting out of dinner early. It was pretty dreary.'

'For a girl of nineteen your skills are highly developed. You *deserve* a glass of champagne.'

'As soon as possible. Ah! Here it is. It doesn't take long.'

There was a full moon. 'A Tallulah Bankhead moon made of cardboard,' she laughed – and it made Sakkara look even more beautiful than it always was: very green, every inch of watered land cultivated, the clusters of tall, straight date-palms like exclamation marks black against the stars.

The Rest House at Sakkara – a place where during the day

tourists came to enjoy their picnic lunches – stood on a desert platform at the edge of a large cluster of palms, overlooking thirsty green fields watered by the Nile floods, surrounded by the ghostly outlines of hundreds of minor tombs. It was the sort of heady night, the moon so strong and round that it might have been drawn with a pair of compasses. And beyond the green fields, where the water and the irrigation canals ended and the ground was brown, stood the Step Pyramid.

'It's the smell of the earth, freshly watered, that's so wonderful,' I said.

'You're right.' Serena took a deep breath. 'It's so beautiful we must toast the past. Where's the champagne?'

I took the bottle out of the boot. 'The ice must be melting. Did you think of glasses?'

'I forgot them. Don't worry. There must be some cups inside.'

There were, but she said, still laughing, 'They need washing, and I don't trust the water. Let me wash them in a bit of champagne. Safer. Here. Give me the bottle.'

I untwisted the wire and prised open the cork gently so it didn't pop and waste the bubbles. A few drops of liquid oozed out.

'Fine,' said Serena. 'I'll wash them.' She swished a little champagne round each cup, threw it out, looked around but couldn't find a cloth.

'Hold the cups,' she said. 'This'll do.' Without a word she pulled down her silk underskirt and started drying the cups, making sure she had cleaned off any ingrained dirt.

'It's the edges I don't trust,' she said, almost too lightly. 'All those filthy lips that must have touched them. Better to hold the cup in your left hand, then you'll drink from the side other people don't use.'

As I poured out the champagne I had the greatest difficulty in keeping my hand steady. It wasn't only the sudden urge of sexual excitement that stirred me, it was the casual way in which Serena had taken the piece of silk that had been next to her skin and without a thought had pressed it next to the inside of my cup. And now I was drinking champagne from it, champagne touched by her slip. Just like Father's pretence of drinking champagne from a slipper! All kinds of erotic pictures jostled in my imagination.

'Champagne not corked?' She was teasing, as usual reading my thoughts.

I shook my head, for a moment beyond speech, suddenly feeling a wave of self-pity at the thought that within a month Serena would be married – as though I, with a wife of sorts, had any right to feel miserable about the wedding of another woman.

We sat on the wooden steps of the Rest House and looked across at the black shadows against the bright moon.

'I wonder –?' she began, staring into her cup.

'What?'

'I don't know,' she sighed. 'Sometimes I wonder – Greg's wonderful, everyone loves him, but – marriage? I wonder sometimes whether I'm marrying the wrong man.'

'It's a bit late to think of changing your mind,' I said.

'It's never too late – until you're married.'

'All this wisdom coming from a girl of nineteen!' I deliberately kept my tone light. I didn't really want to listen to confessions.

'You don't understand. *You're* the problem.'

I felt another surge of excitement. Careful, I warned myself. I wasn't going to get entangled.

'You're scared!' she laughed.

'I'm not,' I said crossly.

Almost without knowing what she was doing, she suddenly twined her fingers in my hand, holding it differently, more tenderly, like an experiment.

'We always peer into each other's minds,' she said. 'I can see into your mind right now.'

'You don't know what I'm thinking,' I laughed. 'It's a fervent hope that Sirry Pasha won't be waiting for me at Nasrani with a shotgun.'

'You're not!' Her tone was suddenly almost fierce. 'You're not, you're not.' She put the cup down on the wooden floor, stood up next to me and suddenly started hitting me on the chest with her clenched fists.

'Hey! What's all this about?' I held her two narrow wrists.

'It's because we can never lie to each other. We *know* what we're thinking. We're both thinking at this very moment that we want nothing more now – *at this moment* – than to make love with each other.'

I let go of her wrists and pushed her away. 'You must never say that.'

'But it's true, isn't it?'

'What if it is?' I said gently. 'It isn't a crime to think. To be alone in the desert with a girl I've always – well, how could I think of anything else? It's true. You always do know my mind.'

'And mine? Can you read that?' There were tears in her eyes. 'You know that I want you now, at this moment, more than anything I've ever wanted.'

'I know, darling.' I stroked her ash-blonde hair and kissed her quietly, for by a trick of the moonlight her perfect features, with their high cheekbones, looked pale against the black shadows of the Rest House porch, and even the husky tone of her voice sounded lower, more exciting.

'But he *is* my brother,' I ended lamely.

'I'm not trying to get you to steal me away from him. You know that. I don't care if we *are* engaged. I'm not talking of marriage for us. I'm talking of something else. Just kiss me and I'll tell you.'

'It's crazy,' I muttered. 'Crazy – and it's bound to lead to trouble.'

I leaned forward and kissed her on the cheek.

'No, silly! I don't mean a mistletoe kiss.' Almost mocking-ly, she asked: 'What will you do if I kiss you?'

'The married kind of kiss?'

I too could be ironic, but she thought I was being serious and replied, 'No, the kiss of lovers – at the moment of wanting, before they've ever made love.' And gently holding the lapels of my thin jacket she pulled me towards her, not unwillingly, and said, 'Like this.' Then – no tiptoeing necessary to reach my face – she opened her lips slightly and touched the inside of my mouth with the tiniest tip of her tongue.

At the end of the kiss, she whispered, 'And there's something else. But first, now *you* kiss *me*!'

'You said "something else". What's "something else"?' I knew the answer before the end of the kiss answered for me.

'A present to each other. A gift that only we can give each other.' She held my face in her hands, and kissed me again with open lips until I thought I would be unable to control myself for another moment.

'I know the gift.' My voice sounded hoarse.

'Of course you do.' She smiled secretly, but a happier smile now, the tears wiped away, a smile born of triumph, the knowledge that she had only to say the word and I would give in.

'Just this once. As though just for tonight we're married,' she said almost shyly. 'Once and for ever. We owe lots of things to other people. But this we owe to each other, even if it never happens again.'

'It never must. It never will.' I knew that she had won – thinking, Thank God she has! 'Never, my beloved Serena. Oh God! I've dreamed of this so often. I've imagined it.'

'Me too. Come on.'

'I'll get the rug from the car.' I ran out and returned almost immediately. I knew that in the three or four rooms were some old divans where visitors sometimes rested in the mid-day sun.

'Come along.' She held out her hand to take mine. 'The place is empty. It's only used in the daytime anyway. It's deserted.'

'Are you sure it's safe?'

'Yes. But even if it wasn't I couldn't stop now. Don't worry. Can you turn on the light?' I found the switch by the door. There was only one miserable, dim, naked bulb, lighting a rectangular wooden room, the unswept floor dusted with sand which had blown through the crack under the door. There was a rough deal table, half a dozen wooden chairs – and the divan.

'Lock the door,' she whispered. 'No, leave the light on.'

There was no key, but a heavy bolt. I pushed it home and then, spreading the car rug across the divan, I carried her and laid her on it, then knelt by the side and leaned across and kissed her as I had never kissed any woman or been kissed in all my life.

It was all so sudden, so casual, so inevitable, that I had no time to feel guilty. I hardly knew what was happening, how it was happening, until without premeditation we were struggling and panting and kissing in each other's arms.

'My darling, darling Mark.' Her mouth was still wide from the open-mouth kisses which had almost suffocated us, like two lost souls about to drown, gasping for air, gasping for the last moment of life.

'We've waited so long for this.' Once again taking my face in her hands, she whispered, 'Don't ever feel guilty. You're like my long-lost lover. I've wanted you so badly, and now for one night you're mine. There's nobody else in the world alive tonight. Just the two of us.' She kissed me more gently this time, then sat up, pulled her white dress over her head, and took off her silk panties as I undressed.

Then, both naked, we were in each other's arms again, me squeezing against her breasts, stroking them for the first time in my life, beautiful, rounded, with the firmness of youth, as she, too, stroked me. She leaned over on top of me, breasts just touching me, long slim legs across mine, and before kissing whispered, 'Not yet. I know it's mean of me, but I just want this moment to last a little longer.'

In the end, though, it was she who suddenly gasped, 'Now!' And it was she who shifted her position slowly and guided me inside her – just in time, for her as well as for me. For she moved only once or twice, and then with a joined cry of rapture, every particle of our bodies seemed to fall into tranquillity at precisely the same moment, as though every muscle, every nerve, seemed spent and still, with me small inside her, swimming in the physical love we had poured on each other.

She turned slightly, and not knowing really what she was saying, kissed me quietly and murmured, 'Together! It's so beautiful I could cry with happiness.'

Leaning her head against my shoulder, her hair half in my eyes, she said softly, almost talking to herself, 'It's like the last link in a chain that had to be forged. It had to happen one day, just to complete the chain.'

I was stroking her long legs and her flat tummy again, damp with love and heat and us together, and I murmured, never quite sure how a girl of nineteen could be so knowing, 'I love your philosophy, darling!'

'But it's right! We've' – with a moment's hesitation – 'we've got the *wanting* out of our systems. From now on and for evermore, whenever we meet, we'll never again have to wonder what it would have been like if –'

Her hand stroked me, and as I felt myself stirring again she added, 'Don't you see what I mean? Whenever we meet, I'll know exactly what this secret bit of you, growing with excitement in my hand, looks like and feels like, and now you know the hot feeling of me. Look at me! Here in this horrible light! Don't you think I'm beautiful?'

I stroked her. 'Exquisite and desirable.'

She had stretched out on her back, strong blonde hair like a mane on the coverlet, small breasts with pink nipples upright and below her flat flanks, almost boyish, her secret hair, thick and a shade darker, and below that the longest legs in the world.

'There,' she said, repeating. 'Aren't I beautiful?'

'No words can describe it,' I said and lay on top of her and kissed her as though I would never stop.

The second time was more relaxed for both of us, and it was in its way even more loving, as though we had already come to terms with each other, no longer as strangers when undressed.

'It's because we know we love each other – in our own way, which has nothing to do with marriage,' she explained.

'Can I just look at you once again?' I said after it was over. 'Like taking a photo to remember.' And then I explored her again and kissed her for the first time just below her stomach.

'In a way,' she was thinking aloud, 'we've been in love all our lives. A different love.'

'Perhaps. Though you were so much younger.'

'Maybe I was. But one of the reasons I always felt so close to you was that you never laughed at children's love.'

We lay down for a little while, too happy to talk.

I knew that from this moment onwards my life would never be the same again. I would gain something, lose something. As I kissed her once more I should have been torn with remorse for betraying my brother – but I had gone too far for that, and in the way that one's life is supposed to flash by in the moment of drowning I felt as though I was drowning in her love, and in those moments I was thinking, How did it all start between us? I mean, *really* start? What has made us exchange the innocence of friendship for the guilt of love? She had started it, for there is a wide gulf between longing and doing, and Serena knew that even if I could not – or would not – jump across the divide, she would. In a way, ridiculous though it sounds, she was impelled by kindness as much as by passion. She didn't actually feel sorry for me, in the way one feels sorry for a shabby beggar, but rather a kind of sorrow that I had been so close to her in every way, yet until now I had been unable to share her ultimate gift to me.

She raised herself on one elbow, and asked suddenly, 'Do you miss Parmi?'

'You know the answer. No. One of the attractions of Parmi before the baby died and she changed was that our relationship was based on pleasure. *Only* pleasure, do you understand? Now, you are here alone with me, and I'm frightened because there's a world of difference between pleasure and love. Pleasure was simple.'

'But I don't please you?'

'Of course you do! More than anything in the world. But if pleasure is a simple emotion then love is pleasure and pain together.'

'Don't say that, Mark, don't *ever* say that. Even if at times there is pain, isn't it worth it?'

'I hope so. But what do we have to look forward to? What kind of future? Deceit? Lies?'

'No lies,' she said. 'Just silence. Kiss me again before we go.'

'You've already been very silent,' I said.

'Then kiss me. Kisses were invented for the moments when one is lost for words.'

We dressed in silence, part of the spell broken. I helped her to button up the back of her white dress, and we poured out the last drop of champagne into one cup and drank from it in turns.

As I was about to go towards the car the full force of what had happened to us hit me, and I stumbled on the Rest House steps as though hit physically. She sat down next to me.

'We can't just let it go like this,' I groaned.

Putting her arms round me, she kissed me gently and whispered, 'We have to.'

'But wh .' I asked desperately. 'Let's run away.'

'If only we could!' she cried.

'Why not? Let's bolt! I've got enough money. I'm madly, hopeless! in love with you, Serena. We can't just throw this away.'

'And you're supposed to be the sensible one,' she smiled sadly. 'What about your career?'

'To hell with my career!'

'And our parents?'

'Don't we owe something to ourselves?'

'We paid that debt to each other this evening.' She still had that small, sad voice. 'I'd give anything in the world to be your wife. But we're in Cairo, my darling. Imagine what would happen if we did run away. Our families – who believe in respect – torn apart. You a married man. We couldn't marry, me jilting your brother almost on the altar steps. Oh, my darling Mark, I love you so much, but if we did this we'd be giving up the love of our fathers for each other. I know that my father, whom I love, would never allow me in his house again. You're just as in love with your father. He'd despise you. We'd end up hating each other.'

'But we must do *something* to keep us together.'

'Let the future take care of itself,' she said. 'Just let us love each other in the way we always have done.'

'You'll get married, go on a three-month honeymoon and forget all about me.' Self-pity was beginning to take over.

'Never. I'll send you secret messages. In a code that nobody knows except us.'

Puzzled, I asked, 'I don't understand. How?'

'Wherever I am, whenever I'm thinking of you – you at Sakkara – I'll just send a postcard with one word on it.'

'The word?'

' "Hullo!" When that postcard arrives – just that one little word that means nothing to other people – *you* will know what it means.'

As we drove home, all she said was, 'It's terrible to say this, but even if, as we've promised, we never make love again, I'll always love you in my heart.' Out of the corner of my eye I saw her cross her fingers – and smile.

She fluffed out her hair and touched up her lips and then, with a gesture I knew so well, smoothed down the creases of her frock.

Five minutes later we had reached Nasrani.

'It's not even midnight,' I whispered as we tiptoed through the archway and into the silent, sleeping house.

'Less than two hours.' She gave a little sigh. 'And it has to last a lifetime.'

21

When in September 1939 war finally broke out, the world we had known in Cairo seemed to vanish overnight, and the months since Greg and Serena were married the previous November seemed to be telescoped into a different age. They had set off on their three-month honeymoon in America with the world at peace, and a stream of cheerful postcards arrived at both Holt House and the Sirrys', a dozen of them addressed to me, and bearing the simple word, 'Hullo!'

And when they returned it was with the announcement that Serena was expecting a baby, due in July, but which was actually born a month prematurely in June – 'Due to too much gallivanting around and travel,' said Dr Phillips primly.

It was a fine boy, christened Jonothan, and I could not help but wonder if perhaps he was my son.

'I'm glad he arrived early,' Greg confided later in the year. 'This way Serena's got over the birth, the baby's fine, and now that war finally has been declared I can join up without having to worry about her, especially now that she's settled in her own home.'

'Home' was a magnificent villa on the Nile in Zamalek, facing the British Cathedral on the opposite bank of the river. It was called the Villa Zelfa, named after a Turkish princess, and the Sirrys had given it to Greg and Serena as a wedding present.

Though the first months of war hardly touched Europe Cairo blossomed as never before. 'It is,' one young lieutenant happily told me as he gazed rapturously from the roof-top terrace of Shepheard's, 'the most glamorous war in history.'

To the thousands of British troops posted to Cairo it must have seemed like heaven-sent bliss, a bliss in which they had exchanged the jittery months of the phoney war for the heat of the sun and the stacked shops of a country at peace.

The city — brightly lit after the warm dusk — was dotted with nearly a score of open-air cinemas with prices as low as fivepence a seat. There was no blackout, no rationing. Restaurant menus ranged from prawns to steaks, from dry martinis to champagne; there was everything, in fact, that a man had missed in those dreary months in England. One newcomer could not believe that razor-blades were plentiful, and promptly bought a hundred, convinced the supplies could not last. Others hoarded cigarettes, unable to realise there would be just as many on sale the following day.

The difference between the miseries of wartime London and the glamour of Cairo was so marked that no one noticed the noisome smells of the city: the beggars, the blind in the street, the half-starved pariah dogs lolling, tongues open, in the sun, or howling piteously at night as they searched for scraps. People took the dirt of the city streets in their stride, grateful when the *sakkas* — the water carriers — sprinkled water from their goatskins to lay the dust.

Officers who were billeted out could choose flats, often in

the tall buildings overlooking the Gezira Club, where they were, as honorary members, able to swim or play polo, tennis or golf. Shepheard's, the Turf Club, the Gezira or Madame Badia's cabaret, with its belly-dancers, and Samia's Sphinx nightclub, were packed with officers carrying swagger canes or fly whisks and displaying one new and dashing item of footwear – suede 'desert boots', which they wore, with their clipped moustaches, as part of their uniform.

Cairo was a paradise limited only by a soldier's rank or finances. The Egyptian pound was virtually on a par with British sterling, with 97 piastres to the £. For twenty-five piastres – then five shillings – an officer could eat his way through a six-course dinner at Shepheard's. But in a different way the British Tommy was just as well-off as his officer. The sun was there for all. He could get a substantial meal with beer for five piastres – a shilling. There was free swimming at the barracks in Heliopolis, free cinemas every night; and above all, as a background to the sun, a bevy of beautiful girls of every nationality – not only Egyptian, but French or Italian, Greek or Syrian. The troops loved them, because the faces of the girls reflected the laughter of freedom, not of fear. For those who did not want to become 'involved' but still hungered for the forbidden delights of Cairo, there were the brothels of Clot Bey and the area to the north-east corner of the Ezbekieh Gardens. They were so busy that the girls sometimes had to operate in the alleys or under the arches behind the tawdry streets.

Though Egypt, as an 'independent' country, was not at war with the Axis Powers, she had broken off diplomatic relations with both Germany and Italy. And Britain had naturally invoked the clause in the 1936 Treaty which Father had helped to formulate, when he told Nahas Pasha in Paris that 'as a gesture' Egypt should allow Britain to station troops in Egypt 'in the unlikely event of a major war'.

Well, the unlikely had happened, and now Egypt was an armed camp, a British armed camp, for Britain maintained two headquarters in Cairo. The BTE (British Troops in Egypt) operated from the Semiramis Hotel on the Nile, while General Headquarters Middle East commandeered a huge block of flats in Garden City, not far from our house, and surrounded it with a barbed wire perimeter. BTE was part of the pre-war forces concerned mainly with guarding the Canal Zone, whereas GHQ(ME), commanded by General Wavell, was the headquarters of the army facing the Italians in Libya.

The Egyptians were divided. The army was filled with hatred; so were most members of the government. But the businessmen were torn, for trade was booming. The British soon employed thousands of civilian workers. The soldiers themselves had nothing to do with their pay except spend it, so if the shopkeepers nursed any hatred of the British, they hid it behind welcoming smiles.

I had found it difficult at first to decide whether or not to join up. The war seemed everywhere, yet remote. I could not realise it was real. Greg, however, was determined to become an officer.

'I've talked it over with Serena and she understands,' he declared, when we went one afternoon to play tennis at the Gezira. 'I'm going to join the 8th Hussars.'

We had just finished three sets and were towelling after our showers when Greg made his announcement. We were due to have a family dinner that evening at Greg and Serena's new home.

'I'm going to pick up Teddy at Shepheard's – probably have a drink there – and Chiffon's coming to the villa at half past eight with Father. You go on; we won't be long.'

Later, when I'd arrived at the villa, I climbed the marble steps to the beautifully proportioned entrance hall, perhaps thirty feet long with a double stairway at the far end leading to the upper storey. The ceiling of the entrance hall had been pierced so that the first floor was like a large gallery guarded by iron railings, over which you could look down on the hall. Two chandeliers hung from the ceiling far above, through the aperture, to light the ground floor hall.

'It's exquisite,' I told Serena.

'You wait till you've seen our bedroom. That's really something.' She led the way up to a high-ceilinged room painted in what I call 'Italian blue-green', that slightly faded blue which makes a perfect background for the painted scrolls which decorate so many beautiful rooms in Italy.

'You've never seen a fitted cupboard like this one,' she almost giggled. 'Go on – open it!'

Fitted cupboards lined one entire wall, and this double door looked like any other. Only it was not for clothes: the doors opened to reveal a many-sided mirror, with two more lining the inside. It was a practical arrangement for a girl who wanted to see her dress from every angle.

'Only I don't think the Princess Zelfa had that in mind!' said Serena. 'You realise that all the mirrors have been placed so that you can see yourself in bed from a dozen angles? And the bathroom's even sexier.'

She led on to a room in which only the taps and the old-fashioned gas geyser were not made of pink marble. Three steps led to the marble bath itself, with marble partitions at either end, one for the loo, the other for the bidet.

It was while I was admiring the bathroom that Serena slipped a hand in mine, and said gently, 'I often think how miserable I was in America. I'm so glad you got my postcards. I missed you dreadfully.'

'Me too. I've never been so miserable. But now at least we can see each other. And you've got the baby. You look happy.' I stroked the smooth pink marble almost lovingly.

'Looks don't always tell the truth.' She gave a half-sigh.

'What *do* you mean?'

'Nothing really,' she laughed shortly. 'Mustn't over-dramatise! All married couples have their ups and downs. The baby's a great consolation.'

I didn't know what to say. Suddenly she grasped my hand on the pink column, put an arm round my neck and held up her face to me.

'For old times' sake,' she said before I kissed her, all my heart expressed in the touch of our lips and tongues.

At that moment the bell rang.

'The first guests!' She pushed me away. 'I must talk to you, Mark, I *must*.'

'Any time you say.'

245

'I'll phone you at your chambers. Maybe we could meet at the Gezira while we watch Greg play polo?'

'For two chukkas? All of fifteen minutes?'

'I can tell you everything in five,' she said sharply, and swept out of the door.

For a moment I had been startled by the intensity of her voice, horrified even; but then, as dinner got under way, I began to wonder whether Serena had been exaggerating. We were only nine at table – the Sirrys, Father and Mother, Teddy Pollock, Jim Stevenson, and the host and hostess. As for signs of tension, there were none. Perhaps they had had a row earlier in the day, I thought, and she's the one who had been over-dramatic. For Greg was laughing cheerfully, making sure that everyone was having a good time, always bringing Serena into the conversation when necessary, always with a smile of love. 'Darling, what happened to the painting you did of Yosemite?' Or, 'You should have seen Serena in Saks Fifth Avenue. Come on, darling, admit you went a bit wild.' It was all said with a laugh, and they seemed as happy as newly-weds should be. Before the end of the evening I was reflecting that if there had been a lovers' quarrel it had already been patched up.

I was surprised when the following day Serena phoned me at my chambers, and – knowing that *all* clerks, let alone Salem, listened in – heard her ask, 'Greg's playing for the Hussars on Thursday. Any chance we can both go and watch?'

'Damn!' I consulted my diary. 'I'll be in court most of the day.'

'Oh dear!' There was real hurt in her voice.

'But I'll tell you what I could do,' I suggested carefully. 'Why don't you go round to your mother's after polo? I'll come in as soon as I get out of court, and we'll both hang on and meet Greg soon afterwards.'

That would be discreet enough to bore Salem! Polo players *never* went straight home after the last chukka. They had to see to the ponies, shower, discuss with the secretary times of future games, meet the teams for drinks – all part of the ceremonial of an afternoon's polo.

246

'Marvellous,' she said. 'See you at my mother's.' What we both left unsaid was that a walk through our grounds was just about the most private place in Cairo.

I arrived at the Sirry house at half past five – after polo had finished, but not before post-polo drinks at the club. Madame Sirry had gone next door to have tea with Chiffon, so Serena suggested, almost ironically, 'Let's go and walk in the Holt garden where we can be seen to behave properly. I know how cautious your legal training makes you.'

I laughed, but loved the idea, for it was quite like old times, Serena and I walking slowly round the long gravel path towards the citrus grove, the Nile peeping through the trees, and down by the bank the grotesque cathedral tree, long since relegated from a sinister playground to a showpiece for adult visitors on a summer's evening.

Still convinced that the 'lovers' tiff' had been healed, I said cheerfully as we walked towards the river, 'I must say Greg looked in great form at dinner.'

She nodded, kicking some dead weeds along the gravel path. 'He's changed astonishingly since marriage. It seems only yesterday that he was an overgrown schoolboy making feeble jokes. Now he behaves like a man. And he did tend to be selfish. Now he's kind and considerate.'

'To you?'

'Especially to me,' she said. 'But I chose the words carefully – kind and considerate.'

'Well –?'

She stopped suddenly and looked at me full in the face. 'But I want more than that.'

'Meaning what? You can't tell me Greg's no longer in love with you.'

'No, no. In his own way he *does* love me.'

'Well then –?'

Her large green eyes, locked into mine, never wavered, though her mouth started to tremble until she checked it.

'He's gone off me completely – in bed,' she said finally.

I felt such a sense of shock that I would have given anything to have taken Serena in my arms, covered her with kisses, let her cry on my shoulder if she'd wanted to. But we were in full view of two houses, a couple of dozen pairs of servants' eyes probably peeping at us from behind windows. I steered Serena back towards the house.

'But it's not possible,' I cried. 'Darling Serena – you and Greg off sex? He used to be nicknamed "the ram"!'

'I didn't say he's off sex,' she said sharply. 'I said he's off *me*.'

For a moment I could only stare at her, unbelieving.

'It's true, Mark. I know he adores me, and when we share our bed he kisses me, but even if I touch him – you know, help him, kiss him – nothing. Even with the mirrors the result's the same.' She paused, twisting the ends of her hair in her hands. 'Don't you think I feel a bitch? But you're the only one I can talk to. I must tell you about Greg. *Everything*, Mark. But don't let me down. I couldn't bear it if you went all prim and proper and –'

'I couldn't bear it either, and if it's true that you and Greg can't make love – or he doesn't want to, or whatever – well, it does ease my conscience over Sakkara.'

'Mine too – because I'm not really that kind of woman. That time at Sakkara, I never felt guilty about that. It was part of the pattern of our lives. But if we were tempted in the future –'

'Tell me about Greg,' I said gently. We were seated now on the veranda in full view of anyone who cared to look, and in a perfectly natural position to greet Greg when he arrived. Serena gave me a large scotch and soda and took a vodka and mango juice for herself.

Their sex life had been perfectly normal in America, she said, and it had been just as perfect when they first returned to Cairo and Serena was already pregnant.

'But then what changed it?' I asked.

The problem was very simple. Among the many friends they had met in America was a married couple whose husband had insisted on being present when his wife gave birth to their child. Greg, too, was determined to watch Serena's baby being born. He adored her, he wanted to share in her suffering by helping with his presence and when, back in Cairo, the baby was born Greg watched the birth, was the first to hold the little boy and hand it to Serena. He was crying with happiness.

Only one thing marred the beauty of that birth. When Serena was able to make love again Greg suddenly found himself impotent.

'But a man doesn't get like that overnight.' I must have looked astonished.

'Who said anything about impotence?'

'You did.'

'I didn't, darling. I even hear whispers that Greg pays fairly regular visits to your old friend Samia – at the Sphinx, where everything's laid on.'

'But *why*? You're so beautiful. And you say he loves you still?'

Serena was as baffled herself – and so desperate that finally she went to see a Dr Arch, an American who had started up as a psychoanalyst in Ibrahim Pasha Street. It didn't take him long to discover the root of the problem, after he learned that Greg had watched the birth of Jonothan.

'My dear, you're the most normal person in the world,' Dr Arch had told her. 'Women are having babies every hour of every day, and it's the greatest miracle this world offers. For a woman it's the supreme triumph of her life – if she wants the baby. But if you watch a birth – it can be gruesome.' He paused.

'I wonder what the average husband thinks when he sees his beautiful wife, shaved, then her vagina being stretched and stretched, and all the blood, the pain and screaming. The dirt of the placenta, the umbilical cord. I may be old-fashioned, but I don't think that's the picture a husband really wants to see of his wife.'

'But in America –' Serena started.

'Many men *do* gain great inspiration from this American idea. It brings many couples closer together. But in your husband's case – and this is not uncommon – what has happened is that he has a memory of you screaming, your vagina stretching, the baby half out – and now, every time he looks at your body, he doesn't see you as you are, he sees you as you were. And he may see it for a long time, I'm afraid. Even if he loves you, every time he tries to have intercourse that memory flashes into his mind and he can't get an erection. There's no way he can blot that out – not yet.'

Serena turned to me. 'As I was leaving Dr Arch, I happened to mention to him that Greg wanted to join up. "Encourage him," the doctor said. "If he sees some war action, his memory of the birth will diminish. And if he's separated from you for a while so much the better. He'll tend to remember you as you are now: a beautiful young lady." '

I was still considerably shocked but a second scotch was helping me when I heard Greg's voice as he came through the house to the veranda. 'Anybody there? Ah, there you are. Come on over to Holt House,' he said excitedly. 'I've been accepted. The Hussars.'

Walking through the wicket gate, Greg tucking an arm into Serena's, what I had learned only minutes ago seemed like a dream. Here we were, Greg unsuspecting, while I was thinking of the revelations Serena had just shared with me, revelations that undermined the whole of their marriage.

As we reached the house, Greg ran ahead across the lawns, shouting, 'Chiffon! Father!'

Mother appeared on the veranda, crying, 'What's the trouble?'

'No *trouble*.' Greg hugged her as Father appeared. 'I've been offered a commission in the 8th Hussars by Colonel Mackenzie. He said he was damned glad to have me on a short service commission. I'll have to do a month or two of square-bashing at OCTU – the Officers' Cadet Training Unit – but it's a doddle. He arranged for me to have my medical next week, then I'll be in uniform a week after that. I'm going round to Collacott' – the best military tailor in Cairo – 'to be measured.'

A week later Greg presented himself for his medical. He told me all about it later, when, in a broken voice, he asked me to come round to the Villa Zelfa. He took a triple whisky in one gulp before telling me.

The doctor took his pulse, his blood pressure, then called in another doctor and asked him, 'Just double-check this, will you?' He did. Greg could see the two men discussing him. He was then asked to take an ECG – an electrocardiogram – in a cubicle, where suction-tipped electric wires linked to a machine were stuck with a kind of gelatine to his wrists, ankles and chest. The doctor asked question after question, always probing.

'Do you ever feel sick? Have you ever been sick, apart from hangovers?'

'No, sir.'

'Any dizziness?'

The question gave Greg quite a turn. Only the previous week he had come off the tennis court, and had had a sudden attack of dizziness. It had occurred several times after violent exercise.

Unwillingly Greg admitted, 'It has happened, sir.'

'I'm sorry, young man,' the doctor said without preamble. 'I'm going to give you a chit to see your own doctor and a specialist right away. And' – drawing a deep breath – 'right away is important. I mean tomorrow, not the day after tomorrow.'

'What the hell's the problem?' asked Greg desperately.

'Don't get alarmed. You'll live to a ripe old age. I have no doubt of that – but only if you take care – and immediately.'

'For God's sake, Doctor – what *is* the matter with me?'

'You're suffering from something called atrial fibrillation.'

'What the hell's that?'

'Put very simply, your blood doesn't flow from your heart through your arteries with proper regularity. Sometimes it's normal, sometimes it speeds up, sometimes it slows down – and when it's *not* normal, when it isn't pumping through *and* you take violent exercise, then you get this dizziness. The condition isn't desperate, but it does need immediate treatment. Nothing drastic, just a course of the correct drugs.'

'And this – this drug cure. How long?'

'It's not only a cure that you need. It's a preventive for the future. You have to keep the fibrillation under control. You'll have to take your pills for quite a long time – some people take them for ever – just to keep the heart-beat steady.'

'And the army?' Greg asked, knowing the answer.

'I'm sorry, young man. That's out. Even if you feel a hundred per cent fit after a couple of months' treatment you'd never be accepted.'

For Greg it was a tragedy beyond any he could have envisaged, and the first thing he wanted to do was drown his sorrows.

'Come on,' he said to me, 'let's go to the Gezira and get stoned.'

We didn't stint ourselves that night when it came to ordering drinks, though I couldn't match Greg's intake. Nevertheless, I was totally unprepared when, without warning, I saw tears start trickling down Greg's cheeks.

'I know you'd set your heart on the army,' I said lamely, 'but the army's not everything.'

'It's not that,' he muttered. 'That's just the last straw. Yes, the last bloody straw.'

Then the verbal bomb exploded.

'It's Serena!' he said, and shouted angrily for more drinks.

I felt a queasy fear turning my stomach, but all I said was, 'Serena?'

He nodded. 'I've got to talk to someone,' he said desperately. 'You know I love Serena, but I can't . . .' He hesitated. 'Well, the fact is' – the words suddenly came with a rush – 'I can't do it any more. I try, God knows I try. I just can't.'

I sat in shocked silence followed by acute embarrassment as I listened to a desperate confession which he thought was a secret while I knew all about it.

'It's hopeless,' he went on. 'I feel such a shit. I know that Serena and I have never been passionately in love, but she's a great girl – best wife a chap could have – and it all went fine at first. Now – it's killing me – and her.'

I tried to be hopeful, choosing my words carefully. 'Maybe it's a passing thing,' I said. 'I hate to use the word "impotence" – it's always cropping up in legal cases – but Greg, it does pass.'

Almost savagely he said, 'I'm not bloody well impotent. I get a stand like a ram if I pick up a girl at the Sphinx. It's only Serena.'

'You thought of trying to find out why this has happened?' I asked guardedly. I couldn't let him know that I knew why, because Serena had told me in secret.

'Meaning what?'

'Well – one of those psychoanalyst blokes.'

'Never!' he snorted. 'What will he do? Show me how to perform? No bloody fear. But it's not only me I'm sorry for. I can go to the Sphinx. It's Serena. She enjoyed it with me. Now she's left high and dry.'

22

It was Teddy Pollock who first suggested it, after I had said almost casually that if there were ever conscription (though it was hardly likely to apply to Britons domiciled in Egypt) I wouldn't hesitate to do anything asked of me; on the other hand I didn't want to be dragged into a dreary job cooking potatoes or working on army accounts. Nor did I want to become what many of my army friends contemptuously called 'a legal wallah' – red tabs, a staff car, and with words speaking louder than actions.

'I agree with you, dear boy' – we were meeting at the Turf Club for lunch – 'but if you want a bit of derring-do stuff – rather fun actually – why not join my outfit?'

'You? Going into the forces?'

Teddy nodded. 'Signed up a month ago.'

'What as?'

'A spy, since you ask.'

'You, a spy! I don't believe it.'

'Well, that *is* a little exaggerated. I've become a DSO.'

'A what? Sounds like getting a medal just for enlisting.'

'No gongs given away in our group. I've been cleared for District Security Office, Egypt. Sort of undercover work, digging out the dirt on undesirables. With your fluent Arabic and French and your legal background, you'd be a cinch.'

I volunteered a few days later. Six weeks after that I left my practice and was gazetted as a major. I was fitted with a uniform at Collacott's and joined the Intelligence Corps, which was the cover for DSO. My office was in Garden City just outside the GHQ perimeter with its two main pillars, one grey, one red. In fact I could see the office from my bedroom window.

Together with Teddy Pollock and a dozen other officers in conspicuously new uniforms I was given a brief idea of my duties. DSO Egypt came under the umbrella of Security Intelligence (Middle East), and we had to use the contacts which someone like me would already have after years in which I had been involved with criminal courts. Positive vetting of suspects would play a major role – investigating anything from reports of radio transmitting to enemy propaganda or compromised personnel. I would build up a network of local agents. What intrigued me most was my DSO identity card, and the powers it gave me. It was a three-folded green card, bearing on the front page:

SECURITY
PERSONNEL

and underneath, AUTHORITY AND IDENTITY CARD, with a signed oval stamp half covering the words, 'Security Intelligence Middle East Valid till 31.12.44'. The card bore a printed number. Inside was the usual passport photo, my name, description – 'Major, Intelligence Office' – my unit, 'GHQ MEF', together with the usual particulars required on a passport, even down to 'Any peculiarities?' But the most intriguing information was on the third side of the card, printed in both English and Arabic:

The bearer of this card is engaged in Security Duties. He is authorised to be in any place in any dress at any time in the execution of his duty. All persons subject to military law are enjoined to give him every assistance in their power and all others are requested to give him all facilities for carrying out his duty.

The powers granted to me – if I behaved myself – seemed almost unlimited, but one fact above all others was impressed upon me – and could lead to instant transfer to the infantry for anyone disobeying the order.

'Remember you are here by courtesy of the government of Egypt,' explained the colonel who briefed us. 'You are working in a foreign country, which has its own police force. And though your duties include clandestine work of a highly secret nature they are strictly limited to the *gathering* of evidence. You have no powers to arrest. Under the provisions of the Anglo–Egyptian Treaty of 1936' – how I remembered that fateful summer in Paris! – 'the only person who can arrest anyone on Egyptian soil is an Egyptian. Disobey this cardinal rule and you will be shipped to the most uncomfortable desert outpost for the rest of the war.'

I knew this, of course. Too many Britons, with the comfortable passing years, and with so many Nubians or Egyptians as our servants, tended to regard Egypt as some kind of British Protectorate, however loosely defined. That was why, when I became involved in court cases, I often had to work in harness with an Egyptian advocate – very often speaking French, a relic of the Mixed courts when French was the only language permitted in Egyptian courts of law.

'If you get on to something hot,' added the colonel, 'phone me if I'm available – and if the problem is big enough. Otherwise phone straight through to the Cairo city police. They'll send an arresting officer around,' explained the colonel.

Three days later I received confirmation that all members of DSO could live in flats or, in cases like mine, at home. 'There's no need to wear uniform except on special occasions,' added the colonel. 'In fact it's better not to – because of the job you have to do.'

★

No one underestimated Greg's initial shock at failing his medical, 'but,' as Father observed philosophically, 'he's the sort of man who'll bounce back.'

Greg did, thanks largely to Serena, who refused to allow him any trace of self-pity, and laughed off his first thoughts of enlisting as a private in the infantry – he felt sure he would be able to fool the local medical board.

'The trouble with Greg,' sighed Serena on one occasion when, with various family members, we sat next to each other at lunch in her villa, 'is that he's an incurable romantic. The doctor's warned him that he'll have to take pills for at least a year, if not longer.'

'But what's he going to do?'

'Jim Stevenson and Greg are starting something.'

'Stevenson?'

'Why not?' she laughed. 'You are funny. Every time I mention his name you sound cross.'

'I'm not cross,' I answered crossly. 'But his name does seem to crop up with peculiar frequency. Almost as though he's a member of the family. How on earth can Stevenson help Greg?'

'They're in the process of forming a company together.'

I must have looked astonished. 'A company! But Greg's never done a stroke of work in his life. What sort of company?'

'It's called The Anglo-American Information Service.' There was more than a trace of amusement in Serena's eyes.

'Well, of course I'm delighted,' I said doubtfully. 'Though I'm slightly baffled about Greg's duties.'

'You'll have to ask Greg about that. He *says* that it'll definitely help the war effort. Exchanging information, or something like that. I'm not sure.'

'Well, Stevenson always seems to have plenty of information. And secrets.'

At that moment we all got up from the table and moved into the sitting room for coffee. There I saw a side of Greg I hadn't seen before. When Hekmet, the nanny from Nasrani, presented baby Jonothan to the guests, Greg picked him up, tickling him under the chin. He was only a few months old, gurgling and laughing and Greg said, 'Isn't he just like his father?'

He was – and Greg's obvious devotion to the baby was touching. I had never expected Greg to show affection for a baby so publicly. I had somehow envisaged him as a husband and father who dutifully saw his child for ten minutes before bed each evening, until it was time for him to ride a horse. And for me it was doubly touching, knowing the non-sexual relationship between his mother and father.

As we sipped coffee, I asked myself, What should I do about Serena? The immediate nature of my intelligence work was such that I was going to spend most of my time in Cairo.

'In fact,' Brigadier Monson, the commanding officer of my unit of DSO had told me, 'you've got two jobs to do. One will be to keep in touch with Farouk – I know you've met socially. The second problem is more difficult: we're having a great deal of trouble with German espionage agents. You will eliminate them.'

'I wouldn't know how to begin, sir.'

'Yes, you would,' said the brigadier sharply. 'You happen to have done a certain lady in Cairo a great service in the past. Oh yes, we know all about it. If you need to pick up some leads you'll spend the evening, the night if necessary, at the Sphinx. Miss Samia, who's quite attractive, I'm told, knows everything. She's your pot of gold.'

As we finished our coffee, Serena took up Jonothan and showed him to me, saying in a kind of baby talk, 'Here's your Uncle Mark to say Hullo to you.' And then, with a long, significant pause, added, 'Hullo!'

My eyes met hers, and I could feel my pulse racing.

'I've got to talk to you,' she said in a whisper. 'Can we meet – this evening?'

'Seven o'clock,' I said, stroking Jonothan's head as I did so. 'I'll be back from work by then. I'll be in our garden – at the end of the lawn.'

She nodded quickly, and turned away.

I shouldn't have done it. I shouldn't have given way to my emotions, for if I had gently said No, it would have *been* No. But I wanted to see her as much as she wanted to see me. And for her there was an added reason – I sensed she craved an hour or two of escape from her sham life with Greg.

I got there a few minutes before seven, to find Serena already waiting for me.

'It seems a long time since Sakkara, when we promised to make love only that once,' I said, as we walked together across the lawn towards the cathedral tree.

'We were both expecting then that Greg and I would have a normal marriage,' said Serena, putting her arm through mine. 'Well, it didn't work out. But I've kept my side of the marriage bargain. I've been a good Egyptian wife – even though it's been months since Greg even touched me.' With a sudden small laugh, she added, 'I'll bet if I touched you there'd be some reaction.'

We had reached the end of the lawn and were standing close together, just a few feet from the tree.

Very carefully, as though I were taking a mite out of her eye, I moved up next to her and, in case anyone saw us, took out a handkerchief to make the pretence look more real. My legs were pressing against hers, and she could feel the bulge.

She returned the pressure for a second, then as I moved away gasped, 'Oh God!' and I saw in her expression that same look of tension and desire that had been etched on her face that evening in Nasrani. Then it had passed, as others had interrupted us. This time she looked up at me, trembling, and whispered, 'Can't we – now – quickly?'

'Where? We'd be mad. Someone might see us.'

'In the cathedral tree? We hid there once before in our lives. *Please*, Mark, if you love me. Just for a minute. It'll only take a minute.'

'Your clothes?' I murmured, even then walking towards the hidden depths of the tree.

'Standing up,' she whispered. 'Just for a few moments. Just so I can feel you inside me.'

'Be quick,' I said. 'And don't worry, darling. No one saw us; we'll be safe here.' I wanted to help her, give her confidence, so that she would not spoil everything by being afraid. Not that it mattered. I don't think that if anyone had walked under the tree at that moment she would have been able to stop. She held up her pleated white skirt, then breathing hard tried to tear off her panties. She couldn't. 'Rip the bloody things,' she panted. 'Pull them off!' In the end she took them off herself and stood there, bare to the waist, her skirt tucked like a roll of cloth round her stomach, her legs apart, as I fumbled at my trousers.

'How beautiful!' She was almost moaning as she grabbed me, helping to guide me in. 'There! Inside me!' she cried as she leaned against one of the tree's root-branches, and I plunged into the heat of her, right in, moving gently to make it last.

And when it was all over she just said, in that small voice of hers, 'What fools we were not to chuck everything up for love. What fools!'

She was literally trembling as we emerged from the tree, and my legs felt like jelly, as though I had emptied myself to give to her all the love I had within me.

'I don't know about you' – I had to look unconcerned as though we had just walked through the trees – 'but I've got to sit down.'

At that very moment I heard my mother's voice – she was in the garden. 'Oh! There you are. Coming in for a drink?'

I nearly fainted. Chiffon must have been within a few yards of us. Without thinking, she added, 'I don't really *like* the cathedral tree. It's so – so secretive. I always imagine awful things happening there, like servant girls misbehaving because no one can see them through those branches, even in daylight. Don't you think?'

Women are always more self-possessed than men. In a perfectly normal voice, Serena cried, 'We were waiting for Greg at Mama's house. We'll go there now – see you there if you come over.'

The moment of danger past, Serena turned to me and said, 'I must see you again soon – secretly.'

'We mustn't,' I said, suddenly guilty. 'After all, Greg is my brother, and whatever's happened between you two – and us – we shouldn't have done this, acted as we did.'

'I know we shouldn't. But now that Egypt has done away with the eunuchs and the harem and has won some sort of emancipation for women I've every right to have a secret affair with the man I love, so long as I don't disgrace the family name. After all, Greg behaves worse than I've just done. He takes *any* girl, just for kicks. I only take one man – for love.'

'His brother.'

'Yes,' she said firmly. 'His brother.'

And so it started. Somehow in the weeks that followed we seemed to reach a more happy-go-lucky relationship. I don't know how; but it was one in which the times when we could meet alone were determined by opportunities, often infrequent. In a way it was better for both of us. We were never far apart, and even when we met at other people's parties the fact that we were together, perhaps dancing a couple of times in an evening, made me happy. Of course I wanted to see Serena every day of my life, but I couldn't; for the time being anyway, circumstances – and work – restricted our meetings.

Then there was Greg. In truth, I didn't see that much of him, as he had his own life centered on the Villa Zelfa. We didn't avoid each other, and I am sure that he never for a moment suspected that there was anything between Serena and me, so that when we did run into each other at the Turf Club or Shepheard's he was exactly as he had always been. And I, of course, was busier than I had been for years, as well as being subject to military discipline – such as it was in my rather special job.

Perhaps one of the reasons Greg and I didn't meet often in Cairo itself was because the true Cairenes like Teddy, Greg and I felt a vague irritation at the way 'our' beautiful city had been taken over by the military. Unfair, I know: but Shepheard's, the Gezira, every bar in town was packed with men in khaki, so jammed together you almost had to queue for a drink.

Soldiers seemed to be everywhere. The days of quiet midnight picnics at Sakkara had gone – and many of us wondered if they would ever return. Though everyone dressed for dinner at the Saturday dances things were not the same. The city was a madhouse, and in the first months of war seven drunken soldiers were killed when they fell trying to climb the Cheops Pyramid.

It was at Shepheard's that I heard the first details of the newly formed Anglo-American Information Service. Jim Stevenson asked me to meet him and Greg on the balcony facing Ibrahim Pasha Street.

'Thought it was about time Greg and I filled you in with news of our new venture,' he said.

Greg was in high spirits. 'Actually played two chukkas today,' he boasted. 'For God's sake don't tell Serena or she'll have a fit. She'd rush round to my specialist and report me. One chukka a week's my limit. But they were short this afternoon –'

'Take it easy,' I said. After all, I couldn't blame Greg for ignoring his doctor. As I looked at him, outwardly fit, smiling after his triumph of the afternoon, I had a sudden picture of Serena naked, those narrow flanks – almost boyish – above the long legs, and I felt terribly sorry for him. All that beauty, able to look at it, take it for granted – all those mirrors! – but unable to satisfy himself, or her.

Stevenson beckoned a waiter. The speed with which the man in his long white robe ignored everyone else clamouring for drinks on the crowded terrace told plainer than any words that he had been heavily tipped before we arrived. But then Stevenson was a master at arranging detail.

'What do *you* think of our business?' Greg asked.

'Don't know anything about it yet,' I lied.

'Not to worry,' said Stevenson easily as the drinks arrived. 'In actual fact, Greg's just the man we need.'

Probably true, I reflected, knowing Stevenson's sources of inside information from America. The name Gregory Holt, with its well-known connections to my father, would make a wonderful impression, and help to disguise the fact that the Anglo-American Information Service was actually run for the United States government, under a cloak of secrecy. And Greg could, quite innocently, open many doors for Stevenson, who was not above using friends to achieve US government goals. Stevenson's job would be to disseminate information which the US government wanted published, while Greg would use his name to plant that information. Even if Greg didn't have close connections with the Egyptian Press, our father's name was a byword in Cairo, and the first thing that Greg had done was to hold a magnificent Press party at the Villa Zelfa.

All this information came from a routine check with the British army authorities, always touchy about propaganda. I discovered that Intelligence had already analysed the work of the new company. Their report agreed that 'the operation' (as it was described) could conceivably print news that was slanted, but could hardly be blue-pencilled by the censors. The report quoted several instances of news items from the Information Service which had been allowed to pass the censor. One was a single paragraph – just what the vernacular newspapers loved to use as free 'fillers':

> General Aziz el Masri, who is known for his pro-Italian and pro-German sympathies, dined privately with HM King Farouk recently at the Abdin Palace.

That was the kind of item which had a telling effect, for in Cairo political readers of newspapers were experts at reading between the lines. After all, they had been subject to various kinds of censorship, official or otherwise, for years. This paragraph inferred that the king was pro-Axis, which was true, though had the news been printed as a bold unequivocal statement, 'The king prefers the Germans to the British', it would never have passed the censor. And of course the private dinner between the king and General Masri *had* taken place, though it had never been announced in the court circular.

It was Stevenson's job to know the secrets of Cairo. It was also part of his duties to undermine confidence in the king.

'Yes, I was rather pleased with that one,' he said in his indolent way when I taxed him with the news item. 'Don't ask me how I found out that it was true,' he added. 'A good reporter never reveals his sources. In fact,' he went on more seriously, 'Greg and I *are* doing an important job of work, but you must understand our priorities.'

'And what are they?'

262

'I'll explain over dinner,' said Greg. We each signed our chits for drinks, and Stevenson said, 'Which is on me. I've booked a table at Sofar's.'

Sofar's specialised in Lebanese food and I loved the small, unpretentious restaurant in Alfi Street, just a few steps from Shepheard's. It served a huge selection of *meze*, the spicy Middle East version of hors d'oeuvres.

Once there, we ordered some raki, diluting the small glasses of colourless liquid with water, turning it cloudy.

'So now,' I smiled, 'what about these plans of yours for dealing with our war?'

'Let's order first. As I said, dinner's on me.'

'The Anglo-American Information Service must be doing well.'

'It's not exactly in profit yet.' Stevenson gave his easy laugh. 'But it's not short of capital.'

We ordered a dozen different dishes, including tabouli, a kind of salad of cracked wheat, parsley and mint, to be scooped up with crisp cos lettuce leaves – never a fork or spoon – while the tahina or hummus was scooped up with flat pieces of Arab bread. And after that, kofta, flat patties of lamb, grilled on a skewer over charcoal and served piping hot on a bed of coriander leaves. It had been one of Parmi's favourite dishes.

Not until we were sipping our thick Turkish coffee did Stevenson try to explain.

'You've got to understand that all our thinking is based on a British victory – that's Roosevelt's assumption, despite the terrible defeats so far. The world can't afford to let Britain lose. And as far as we're concerned in Egypt Roosevelt also knows that Farouk is pro-German. We would eventually like to see Farouk go, to have a genuinely free and independent Egyptian government.'

'Well? What more do you have up your sleeve?'

'Let me try to explain. If the Germans are beaten then the British – who are clearly standing alone against half the world – will emerge as more powerful in the Middle East than in the last days of peace. Right?'

I nodded.

'But then,' he continued, 'Roosevelt doesn't want that either. He wants Britain to win – of course he does, he's trying to do all he can, short of war – but he's determined that after victory Britain won't be in complete control of the Middle East, and that includes Egypt. Yet the conservatives here – men like Serena's father – know that while Farouk remains a corrupt dictator the British will have every excuse to retain power in Egypt, to prevent full-scale revolution by the fellahîn. Ergo – discredit Farouk, kick out the avaricious Egyptian landowners, and slowly, given victory over Germany – we've got to assume *that*, of course – the young officers may be able, in Roosevelt's view, to take over Egypt in a bloodless coup.'

'And where does Greg come in?'

'I'm the front man,' Greg said. 'I'm a loyal Englishman, but I rather like the ideas of the anti-Farouk officers.'

'That's true,' agreed Stevenson. 'I'm a backroom boy. I've got the finest team of informers in Egypt – you know my work, Mark, so there's no point in being modest – and not one of them knows my name. The news reaches me through devious channels. And the one thing I don't want is to plant information that obviously comes from neutral America, which is trying to keep out of the war.' He added with a touch of sarcasm, 'So as to be in a stronger position than an exhausted England to win the peace – which is much more difficult than winning a war.'

'Enough about us.' Greg called for another round. 'What about your job, Mark? Anything secret about that? I mean, undercover sort of stuff?'

'In a way. But probably Jim knows everything about it.'

'Not *everything*,' he admitted, laughing. 'But you'd be surprised how much the Egyptian civilian employees at the army bases are prepared to talk for a little baksheesh.'

I wondered what either of them would have said had they known about my *real* secret. As it happened, Serena and I were meeting the following day, after she had phoned me to say that Greg would be attending a polo dinner at the Gezira.

In the event I was never able to keep that particular appointment. Almost at the last moment I was sent for to deal with what at first seemed to be a routine check on a few drunks, but which in the end led me along a tortuous trail leading, with help from Samia, to many old 'friends' – including General Sadik, Nasser, Sadat – and a pocketful of German spies.

23

At first the investigation which was to ruin my Thursday evening seemed purely routine. A *sol* – the equivalent of a warrant officer in the Egyptian army – was found wandering apparently drunk near the perimeter of GHQ. Rumours of German spies infiltrating into Cairo made the area highly sensitive, and the man was detained for questioning.

The offence wasn't serious. The *sol* wasn't inside the perimeter which the army regarded as British territory, but drunken soldiers always posed problems, and the simplest way to deal with this one would be to send him quietly back to his unit.

Only he wasn't drunk. He stood there smiling stupidly, then did something very odd. He sat down on the ground, almost gravely, stretched out flat on his back, mouth open, and immediately fell into a deep sleep, punctuated by snores.

I knew the symptoms well from a dozen court cases. The man was stoned on hashish. Even so, it would be best to return him to his unit, so I asked Sergeant Collis, who was on duty, to find out his identity. He was Warrant Officer Abbas Hatem of the Egyptian Camel Corps.

'Let's see what else we can find,' I suggested to the sergeant. 'Go through his pockets carefully.'

For a few moments the sergeant was silently busy. Then: 'Look at this, sir!' He produced a huge wad of notes. 'I've never seen so much money.'

'That's a hell of a lot, Sergeant, for a *sol* who earns about six hundred piastres a month.'

'There's over five thousand!' The sergeant had been counting the notes.

'Nearly twelve months' pay. No wonder he can afford to get stoned. Check everything else you can find, Sergeant.'

The pockets contained the usual assortment of objects found in searches, including an Anglo-Egyptian phrase book – which I took as a sign that the man was a cut above the normal Egyptian soldier. He had a clean handkerchief (also surprising, most handkerchiefs in Egypt never seeming to be washed), a penknife, some loose change and an old-fashioned metal propelling pencil.

Idly I twisted the pencil so that the lead would appear. None did. A refill was needed. I knew the pencil, a popular French one called Helix, in which a supply of thin lead was stored in the end opposite the point. It unscrewed easily, and I must admit that at first the pencil didn't strike me as having any significance; I simply decided to make it work.

When I unscrewed it, however, there were no lead refills. Instead the tiny space contained something white. A rolled-up piece of thin paper had been squeezed into the end of the pencil.

I prised open the paper. It was thin, tiny and dirty and contained an obvious message: 'Freedman Wed S'. I hadn't the faintest idea what 'S' stood for, and who was Freedman? The name jogged a vague chord. No one could expect an untrained DSO to know odd names like Freedman, but a legal training helped me to remember names that cropped up in the course of my work, or even when reading briefs. And if I couldn't actually remember a man's name I could at least remember that I *ought* to remember it. That was how I felt now.

'The *sol* will be out for a good three or four hours, Sergeant, probably even longer,' I said. 'Keep an eye on him.'

I phoned through to Records, which by now contained a massive file of virtually everyone in Egypt tainted with suspicion. An hour later GHQ came on the line.

'Records here, Major Holt. Found your man, sir. Freedman is in the pay of the Germans, very pro-German. He's also been in the drug traffic for years. He's been *wanted* for years. Supposed to live in Beirut, has a dozen different names, each one with a different passport. Arrived this week with an Egyptian passport, left the next day.'

Of course! Freedman had been involved in drug smuggling before the war, and had been caught some years ago using a false passport. I hadn't been involved, but I recalled that he'd got off on a technicality – which in Egyptian courts could mean a large bribe.

The connection between Hatem and Freedman seemed fairly obvious, though I hadn't the faintest idea what 'S' stood for.

Almost as I rang off Sergeant Collis produced another piece of paper saying, 'Well, sir, this is how our friend spent *some* of his money.'

It was a tattered bill for a bottle of champagne bought at the Sphinx nightclub.

I had had a mug-shot of Hatem developed while I waited for Records to come through, and now I told Collis, 'I'll just go down to the Sphinx and see if anyone remembers him.'

'Some people have all the luck,' he sighed.

I smiled. I was thinking of the time when the redoubtable Samia could fill the famous Santy Theatre in Cairo whenever she chose to sing. And that was hardly more than a year ago.

I had seen her several times, for she seemed to know everything that was going on in Cairo. The Sphinx had changed drastically from the decorous nightclub Samia had opened, and someone – the king, who was a regular visitor, perhaps? – had persuaded her to import a few pretty girls and open a private bar – with bedrooms – behind the main bar facing the street. It was all done discreetly, but, almost without realising it, Samia woke up one day to realise that the successful singer with the innocent voice had become the madame of a high-class brothel – and was coining a fortune.

Nothing of this showed to anyone strolling along the Kasr el Nil. Outside was a pavement terrace with basketwork chairs, inside an impeccable bar, for the secret of the Sphinx lay in its discretion. Any man with a jealous wife could be seen sitting on the terrace or entering the Sphinx without arousing suspicion. It was popular, to say the least. Piped music churned out Arab dirges, brass tables dotted the airy room and lazy fans turned above. A Nubian with a coloured waistcoat, baggy trousers and red fez dispensed thick coffee from *ibriks*, tiny copper jugs with long handles. Willowy girls in yashmaks, their flimsy clothes in fact quite decorous, took orders for drinks, including the 'house speciality', a Suffering Sphinx. In short, a respectable, decorous bar with enough local colour to please any tourist.

At the far end of the bar was a small door which looked as though it might lead to an office. It was deliberately inconspicuous, for not everyone wished to be seen going into the room behind. And no one was allowed to pass through the door without a nod from Samia.

Then you entered a different world. It had one long straight bar running the length of the room, staffed by a dozen beautiful girls of different races and colours, but all dressed in white Grecian-style dresses.

There was only one peculiarity. The first girl in the line wore a short Grecian white skirt: but nothing above the waist. The second girl had a Grecian-style top, but no skirt. And so on, along the line. Every half-hour, with a great deal of giggling and remarks of encouragement from the clients, the girls changed tops for skirts or skirts for tops.

'So this way,' Greg had laughed to me once, 'you can size up all aspects of any girl you fancy. And they're all available – together with replacements.'

Samia herself had changed since we first met. She was still beautiful, with a figure that seemed to slink between the tables, as in a throaty voice she welcomed favoured customers. But the tell-tale trademarks of the drug addict were beginning to show – sleeves covering arms, her increased use of dark glasses. She was still the most exciting woman in the Sphinx, but for how long? I wondered.

Samia and I sat down at the table in the first bar and she clicked her fingers for champagne. I looked around. Half the people hadn't the faintest idea that a brothel was hidden behind the unobtrusive door. Samia too was surveying the clientele, and suddenly her face changed, and she waved to the front door and cried, 'General Sadik! Welcome!' It was her way of warning me.

I already knew that Sadik was a regular visitor to the second bar at the Sphinx. He came towards us, shook hands – I couldn't refuse – smiled and made some commonplace remark before saying, 'And how is the beautiful Mrs Gregory Holt?'

'Fine, as far as I know,' I replied shortly.

'Only last week His Majesty was saying to me that he hadn't seen the young couple recently, and he must arrange to invite them.'

'Sounds wonderful, General. I'll tell my brother when next I see him.' I had to make an effort to be polite, for Sadik could be a dangerous enemy.

'See you later, General,' I said as he moved from the table.

'I hope not!' He laughed and looked meaningfully towards the small door. 'Sorry, I didn't mean to be rude, you understand. I am always pressed for time when HM is in Cairo.'

I was glad when Sadik passed through to the second chamber, for then I knew he would be occupied for an hour or so – which meant that he couldn't spy on me.

'Come into my office,' said Samia shortly, and I followed her into her private room, closing the door to blot out the Arab music. It was a normal office except for two large one-way mirrors through which she could keep an eye on the girls in both bars.

'I wondered if you knew this man – and who he met. He was at the Sphinx the other night.' I showed her the photo of the *sol*.

Samia studied it, her beautiful hands resting on the table. 'Of course,' she said. 'It's a warrant officer called Hatem. He comes here regularly. He's a big spender for an NCO. Works with a man called Freedman – ah! I see the name means something to you. Ostensibly they're in the drug smuggling business, but my guess is it's a cover.'

'For what?'

'Espionage. Besides, you don't pay smugglers in British five-pound notes. Cairo's flooded with them. I'm told they're all printed in Germany.'

'But *how* is smuggling a cover for espionage?'

'I'll simplify it.' Samia poured out more champagne. 'You asked about the letter 'S'. It stands for Sadik.'

'Sadik – a spy!'

She shook her head. 'No. Though, of course, like the king he's pro-German. But not a spy. Freedman *uses* him. Sadik's in the hashish trade up to his neck. Uses camels. And he's untouchable.'

I knew that camels were used extensively for smuggling hash. It was very simple. For years fifty thousand camels were imported into Egypt annually for slaughter to provide meat for the fellahîn. Half the trade came from the east or from southern Sudan. Recently the police had discovered slabs of hashish, made up into the usual flat cakes, hidden under the luxurious camelhair which grows thickest near the hump. Smugglers had in effect half scalped the hair from the hump, glued slabs of hashish to the camel's skin, then glued the hair back, covering each slab.

That was one way. Even more popular – and safer – was to force the camels destined for slaughter to swallow metal capsules containing hash. A camel is a ruminant and chews the cud, so smugglers packed the hash into containers fifteen centimetres long and four centimetres in diameter – just large enough to stop them from passing from the first stomach, the rumen, into the second, from which they could be evacuated; but just too heavy to prevent them from being regurgitated. Some camels which had been slaughtered on police instructions contained up to twenty-five capsules.

'Are you telling me that Freedman smuggles German messages into Cairo by camel? It's not possible. You can't just pick one camel out of fifty thousand and find a message in its belly!'

'You can, if the camel's marked. And if Hatem is told – as I believe he is – to keep a particular camel back from the slaughterhouse. He then has the camel killed, though I don't know who he hands the vital canister over to.'

'It's incredible.'

'My dear Mark, camels have been used for centuries to smuggle. Why not messages instead of hash? I don't know the contents, of course, but my bet is that they contain information that's difficult to pass on by word of mouth. Plans, radio schedules and so on.'

'How do you know all this?'

She laughed. 'It's my job to know everything. And remember: I'm very pro-British – thanks largely to you. But I'm also a good actress. So if I pretend to be pro-German – and if I'm in the hub of things –'

The information was so startling that I decided not to tell the Egyptian police anything about Hatem. I'd release him without any report so that he could make his own excuses. Much better to keep a watch on Hatem until we could find out the date of the next meeting with Freedman.

'I'll let you know,' Samia promised. 'Hatem has one special girl upstairs who pretends to be German. She'll get anything out of him – not directly, but by wheedling, arranging to meet him outside, finding out his movements.'

'And a woman –' I laughed.

'Women can find out anything.' She laughed too. 'Did you know about Aly Sirry, and his friendship with Sadat?'

'I knew they'd met. In fact Sadat was at the Sirry house the day the Moslem Brotherhood tried to assassinate my father.'

'That was a bad business. Such a nice man. I think your father rather fancied me.'

'I'm sure he did – and still would,' I agreed.

'And did you know that young Sadat is helping with a plan for General Masri to defect to the Italians?'

I whistled. That *was* big news.

'Are you sure? Sadat?'

'Absolutely. Masri is still seething with rage because of what the British did to him.'

I had never met Masri, though I knew he was a tough little firebrand, always ready to scream abuse at the British. He had been trained by German instructors in the Turkish army and become Chief of Staff. Britain had long suspected him of having secret contacts with the Axis, but though searches of his quarters had led to the discovery of thousands of forged English five-pound notes nobody had at first been able to pin enough on him to justify a British demand to an Egyptian government for his dismissal as Chief of Staff.

Until, that is, documents and letters between Italy and Egypt, the leakage of secret plans, proved beyond doubt that Masri was guilty of collaboration. He was then demoted from his post, although he kept his rank.

'He still commands a lot of support in the army,' said Samia. 'I'll tell you more when we meet again, when I can speak more freely.'

Towards the end of the first week of September I went with my family to Nasrani, more of an oasis of peace than ever in these times of war, even though the Sirrys went less and less, for the estate seemed to have changed, been overtaken by the effects of war. There was a shortage of labour; half the fellahîn were drifting to the towns in search of easy work. The *Kismet* was in dry dock, for the captain had volunteered for the merchant navy; while travelling by road had become a jungle of military traffic.

Sirry Pasha, however, encouraged, I didn't doubt, by Serena, asked us all to spend the weekend at Nasrani to celebrate my thirty-first birthday on 9 September.

'It'll actually be a Monday,' said Sirry Pasha, 'and I suppose you'll have to return from weekend leave before then, but we'll celebrate on Sunday.'

I drove up on the Saturday, taking Serena's mother and father in my car, while Greg took Serena, Jonothan and Aly in his car. Father had an official-looking Rover with a sticker on the windscreen and was driven by the chauffeur.

It was a beautiful weekend, filled with people, so there was no prospect of Serena and I being left alone. Even so, it didn't seem to matter. Because of the others, the wish to sneak off alone was absent; and as for even thinking about making love in the family house with Jonothan there, to say nothing of my own brother – well, it never did occur to either of us.

Everyone was in a good mood. Serena looked radiant, and I felt terrific, and found myself wondering whether there was not something odd about my character, in that I could sit and laugh on the sofa with my secret lover, with her husband sitting next to us, laughing too? Why was it that I had no feeling of guilt, yet the moment after we made physical love I always felt guilty? Serena, too. When roused, she behaved like a tigress. But sitting now, playing with Jonothan, she could have been any normal woman looking after her family without a care in the world.

During the afternoon Greg and Aly, as they so often did, went shooting for snipe, and Serena and I and Jonothan – with Hekmet keeping an eye on him – spent a wonderful, peaceful afternoon, basking in the autumn sun and playing on the lawn in front of the house. Not a uniform in sight!

Jonothan was fourteen months old now, crawling every-where with an insatiable curiosity, sometimes trying to stand up for a few tentative steps, falling down, not with tears, but with a quizzical glance at Serena that reminded me of a questioning look I sometimes saw in Greg's eyes – or was it Father's? Jonothan seemed to burst with the joy of life, blue eyes behind curly hair, always smiling, with a generous streak in his nature which made him keep on finding things to give to his mother – a flower, a stone, crawling to Serena and offering them to her with a grin. When I think of Jonothan it is always of a smiling baby with a flower in his hand. I don't think I ever saw him whimper.

'He really adores you.' I held out an odd-shaped small stone, but he shook his head vigorously and found another one which he presented to his mother.

'Jonothan is my only link with sanity,' she said. 'Without him, I think I'd die. Especially with Greg the way he is – all smiles in public, yet nothing but frustration when we're alone.'

'You're lucky to have Jonothan.' I hesitated, for this was a subject we never discussed. 'You may be pleased to know that I love him too.'

Almost as though he understood, Jonothan suddenly plucked out a flower, crawled the distance between us and offered it to me.

'Thank you.' I took the flower gravely and then, as he often did with Greg and Serena, he pulled himself up, holding on to my knees. Once on my lap, he held out clutching hands and offered a pair of rosy lips to kiss me – making a smack just before he actually touched my face.

'He hasn't got his timing right,' Serena laughed out loud, and watching her Jonothan laughed too. So did I.

'I'm so happy, doesn't it sound ridiculous?' Serena wiped the tears of laughter away. 'Just to be with you – and Jonothan –'

'You look happy,' I smiled. 'Not – well, frustrated.'

'Mark! What do you think? I'm Egyptian. How do you think the ladies of the harem used to get rid of their frustrations when the sultan had three hundred wives?'

'Honestly,' I laughed. 'Not in front of the children. You ought to be ashamed of yourself.'

'Children?' she asked in an odd tone, then laughed. 'Ashamed? I may have to be "ashamed", as you call it, for a couple of weeks.'

'Riddles!'

'Mark, I didn't tell you at first and – no, it's not disastrous, but I'm going away for two weeks.'

I must have looked utterly dejected at the abruptness of her news, for she laughed again, and explained, 'It's not the end of the world. But Mama and Papa have borrowed a villa with a private beach at Alex for a couple of weeks, and they asked me – begged me – to go along with them.'

'Must you?' I felt selfish, but I couldn't prevent the question springing to my lips.

'We forget sometimes that they're growing old. Greg doesn't mind. He'll stay in Cairo, and Hekmet will be there with Jonothan. And I need a break – not from you, you know that – but from life at the Villa Zelfa. It's exhausting, like playing a part twenty-four hours a day.'

'I'll miss you so much.' I suddenly felt empty inside. 'But of course I understand.'

'It's only two weeks.'

'This war's overrated.' Father carefully cut the end of his Havana and passed the clipper over to Sirry Pasha. 'These troops doing nothing in Africa – while all these people are being killed in Europe. France gone, Belgium, Europe. And no adequate defence by us. It looks as though British troops were sent to the wrong country.'

Late that night I said goodbye to the family, for I had to be on duty early on the Monday morning. I gave Serena's hand an extra squeeze as I kissed her, and the others, thanking them for a wonderful birthday party and a happy break.

'Cheers,' Greg cried as he waved me off.

That was 8 September, the day before my birthday. Five days later, on Friday, 13 September 1940, a boiling hot day, the Italians invaded Egypt.

All through that long, hot summer we had read the catastrophic list of German victories – the agony of Warsaw, the brutal bombing of Rotterdam, country after country toppling, one string of Allied defeats after another; the debacle at Dunkirk – out of which we had at least salvaged a little pride in defeat; then the peaceful handing over of Paris to the Germans, a capitulation out of which no one salvaged anything but shame.

With half Europe overrun, an emboldened Mussolini increased his list of conquests. Libya was already Italian. In July they invaded Sudan. In August they took British Somaliland. And then on the hot Friday in September they invaded Egypt at Sollum, a township linked to Alexandria by the coast road and the railway. One by one the lights on the Mediterranean coast went out as the Italians, released from fear of any French attack in North Africa, swarmed to the borders of Egypt and beyond.

I didn't know at first what was happening, for I had spent two days trying to sort out the fate of seven young British conscripts who had been arrested after a brawl in the Gold Cock, a sleazy bordello just behind St Mark's Church, near Clot Bey Street. It was much favoured by other ranks. Normally 'drunk and disorderly' offences or a brawl were dealt with by the military police. However, this was not an ordinary fight. During the struggle an Egyptian had been killed – knifed.

The conscripts were unshaven, huddled in their miserable cell which was more like a cage in a zoo than a room for human beings: the lack of freedom, the smell of excrement and Lysol – and fear.

They had sobered up with astonishing rapidity at the mention of the word 'murder'. I could see the fear in their dulled and bloodshot eyes as they protested their innocence. I reassured them – for I doubted very much whether the soldiers had killed anyone. If a man had died accidentally in a bar-room brawl I would have kept an open mind. But in my experience soldiers (commandos apart) didn't carry flick-knives. Egyptians did – in common with a dozen other Mediterranean nations to whom a knife was as much a part of a man's dress as a handkerchief. The military police assured me that no weapons had been found on the premises. The whole thing smelt. Someone was setting up the British.

In fact there was no need to worry, for I was talking to the men when an MP sergeant strode to the cell doors, not noticing me, and shouted, 'Double up! A-ten-shun! Come on, you shower of lucky people – you don't know how lucky you are, courtesy of His Majesty and Mr Churchill. Come on – 'op to it!'

'What's happened?' I asked when he saw me.

'Dunno sir, but there's a big flap on. All units on standby. So this shower – begging your pardon, sir – will be rejoining their units at the double.'

Less than an hour later I heard what the 'flap' was: the Italians' invasion of Egypt. I rushed back to GHQ, for though most people joked about the Italian army those of us in Intelligence knew that all our brave talk about British defences in Egypt – the planes and tanks, the garrisons in Kenya, the promised Free French help from Syria, the crack regiments in the Western Desert – all masked a stark truth: this was the start of Mussolini's drive to the Suez Canal, and the Italian forces now pouring across the frontier into Sollum outnumbered the British by ten to one, in men and machines.

It would be unfair to say there was panic in Cairo, but the unease and fear showed in the faint traces of smoke in Garden City as people with secrets to hide burned the evidence. There was no panic in the British Embassy, to my knowledge, but if you worked for, say, the Free French, it was safer to get rid of any incriminating evidence, for most people thought it would only be a matter of time before the Italians rolled across the coast road to Alex then came south through the Delta.

At first the roads of Cairo were blocked with frightened people until the army took swift action, stopping *all* civilian traffic on *all* main roads. It was simply halted, without exception, and left free for military vehicles. Civilian traffic on the railways also ceased at a stroke. All transport routes were thus left free. It provided a startling and simple solution on how to avoid the chaos that had clogged the roads of France earlier that summer.

My first thought was for Serena, stranded in Alexandria, and as soon as I could I went to see Father.

'It's indecent,' cried Chiffon, 'the Italians strutting around Egypt!'

My father held up a hand – politely, never aggressively – and said, 'They've not got very far yet.'

He picked up the telephone. He was one of those men who never became flustered, and also seemed to know exactly the right person to contact in any emergency. He spoke quietly, replaced the old-fashioned brass instrument on its hook, and said, 'It seems that the first reports of invasion are exaggerated. It is true that the Italians have crossed the frontier from Libya and reached Sollum; but it's only an unimportant settlement near Capuzzo and Bardia.'

'Surely if the Italians advance, it'll be along the coast road or the railway through Sidi Barrani and Mersa Matruh. It's the direct route to Alexandria, only three hundred miles away.'

I switched on the radio – on the off-chance that there might be some hard news. Surprisingly, the invasion of Egypt was admitted. I had thought it might be censored, but I soon began to feel certain that it had been published to give Egyptian critics a chance to attack British rule.

Sure enough the news was followed by a report that Ismari Sidqi, an ex-premier, had said bitterly, 'The Italian offensive is not an aggression against Egypt, but against another belligerent on the territory of a third and occupied power.'

'Hot stuff,' my father almost chortled. 'There's going to

be a big upsurge in pro-Italian and pro-German sympathies, you mark my words. The Egyptians like to back a winner – and they're fed up with being reoccupied by us, anyway.'

There was little more news – except a sudden bulletin on the radio announcing the 'details' (of which there were none) of two Italian air-raids on Alex.

My mother read my thoughts – that Serena was in Alex. 'Don't you think we should tell Greg what's happened? He might be worried.' Greg was at the Gezira, playing tennis. He was now allowed to play doubles.

'I'll phone him. He won't have left yet,' I suggested.

In his calm unruffled way my father picked up the jade paper-knife from his Chinese desk and said mildly, 'No one was injured in the raid. All the bombs were dropped outside the city. And as for any danger to Serena, well' – with a wintry smile – 'I hardly think the Italians will reach Alex before Greg arrives.'

'But I should at least tell him?'

'I wouldn't,' said my father. 'If you do, he'll probably race up in that huge car of his and rescue a damsel who isn't in any sort of distress.'

'I suppose you're right,' I agreed. 'There can't be that much danger to Alex. I'll go to the Villa Zelfa and leave a message for him.'

But Greg never started that game of tennis at the Gezira Club, for when he arrived to play with a group of army friends he was told that all leave had been cancelled. The officers had returned to their units, and it was the match secretary at the club who told Greg of the Italian invasion.

Greg's first thought after rushing back to the Villa Zelfa was to telephone Serena. He made the connection almost at the moment I arrived at his house, so I only heard snatches of a one-sided conversation, Greg shouting because the line was bad.

'But why can't you come home? No, *here, home*' – he repeated the words as though she hadn't been able to under-stand or hear them. 'Take the train then!' Several seconds of silence followed as I watched him pressing one finger to an ear in order to catch her words. 'Why not? It's not possible?'

Cupping one hand over the phone, he turned to me. 'All the sodding railway traffic is cancelled except for the military.'

I nodded. I had already checked on possible ways of getting Serena back to Cairo quickly. Not that there was yet any need to panic. The nearest Italians were still hundreds of miles away.

Greg pulled out a cigarette from his round tin of fifty, lit it and shouted into the line, 'All right. No problem. I'll drive up and fetch you.'

I shook my head vigorously. Looking at me, he cried into the phone, 'Hang on!' And to me, 'Why not?'

'The Cairo–Alex road's been closed to civilian traffic.'

'Jesus!' cried a furious Greg. 'They can't do that!'

Sometimes when faced with angry men – as often happened in my work – I found myself almost instinctively talking in the mild unruffled tones of my father, almost using soothing words like a syrup to stop a bad cough. 'They can, you know,' I said. 'After all, like it or not, Egypt *has* been invaded.'

'Balls!' he snorted. 'A few bloody Chianti-swilling Italians – and all this fuss!' He gave an all-embracing sweep of his arms, as though the Italians were personally preventing him from using his road, his railway. Not for the first time I wondered whether his sudden bursts of anger had anything to do with his sex problems.

'My car!' I tapped his chest to interrupt him. 'I can go. You could come with me.'

'What do you mean? Damnation. We've been cut off.' He banged the receiver on its hook angrily, and repeated, 'What do you mean?'

'My pass allows me to go anywhere. Everyone in DSO has one.'

I explained why.

'Can I borrow your car?'

I grinned. 'Come off it, Greg. You know I can't do that. Apart from anything else, I have one pass, which I carry, and a sticker that's sealed to the windscreen and stamped.'

'So what, then?'

'I can take you – and drive you to Alex, then drive you

and Serena back – late tonight or tomorrow. I don't see any problem.'

'With you decked out in uniform?' He sounded almost jealous of my rank.

'Don't be such a bloody fool,' I laughed. 'You know that in my job they prefer me to be a civilian whenever possible. I keep my ID card in here.' I tapped my inside breast pocket. 'Makes me a sort of plain-clothes copper,' I laughed. 'I can go pretty well where I like and no questions asked.'

'Let's go,' said Greg.

I had been warned to expect long convoys of heavy military traffic, but I knew that most vehicles would be travelling northwards to Alex – like us – so all I would have to do was hold the horn down hard and overtake for the 120-mile trip. We might meet a little local traffic – donkeys, carts, the occasional camel – but that would be all. Nothing going fast.

'Except us!' said Greg. 'Can I drive? I could cut half an hour off the time you'd do.'

There was no malice in his words; it was a common joke that I wasn't a fast driver, whereas Greg drove like a crazy fool in his desire to get from A to B before anyone else. To be fair, it wasn't a question of getting to a destination any earlier but more a tangible expression of the thrill of living life to the full. And Greg was a very good driver – just as he had been a crack polo player. He did everything well because his reactions were superb, timed to a split second. He could turn a car or a polo pony round before others had even started to swerve. I wasn't the least bit afraid to let him take the wheel.

'I'll have to pretend that I'm not feeling very well if you get stopped for speeding,' I warned him.

'Okay. But I'll bet you a fiver I can do the trip in two hours.'

'You're on.' We set off along the Giza Road, with its double line of eucalyptus trees, then just before reaching the pyramids turned right, and then on to the straight desert road, a strip of black shining macadam, with its edges of sand for animals or overtaking, hardly a bend, only shimmering heat, mirages on the first leg to the Rest House at the Wadi Natrun.

The military traffic was lighter than I had expected. I wondered if the flap had been exaggerated, some pompous general giving an order that was totally unnecessary – at this stage, anyway.

'You're going to lose your fiver!' Greg pointed to the Chrysler's speedometer, hovering between eighty and ninety, leaving a cloud of dust behind the car.

A few miles south of the Wadi Natrun we had to slow a little for a convoy of some fifty heavy trucks and armoured personnel carriers, but virtually nothing opposed us, so Greg just drove along the other side of the road on the sand, waved on for the most part by military traffic police on their Harley Davidson motor-cycles.

At the Rest House in the wadi we stopped for a drink – a couple of warm but welcome beers – and Greg announced that he was making a note of the time 'wasted' and would deduct it from the overall time taken. 'I mean to win, you know!' he cried. 'Come on. Half a glass of this weasel pee is enough.'

Shortly after the Wadi Natrun there is a rise – one of the rare inclines, and it is here that the desert road also makes an equally rare turn – barely discernible, so modest that it presents no danger, though many a tipsy soldier driving at night has ploughed straight on and ended in a dune.

As we made the slight turn and faced the incline, with a few straggling palms marking the oasis ahead, I saw a cloud of dust. On the other side of the hill a car was approaching at great speed – just as we were speeding to meet it.

At that moment a string of camels sauntered casually into the road leading from the oasis. There still seemed nothing to worry about. But then the other car came into view. Because it was at the exact top of the incline it seemed to leap into the air ahead of us like a prancing horse. Trying to swerve to miss the camels, it careered towards us with a screech of brakes and the screams of animals. Then it came on, hurtling along broadside, out of control. I shrieked to Greg, 'Pull her to the right!' But it was too late.

24

How long I lay unconscious I don't know. I had been thrown clear of the car on impact, and somehow I managed to get up. Stumbling, I felt my way through misty eyes by grabbing lumps of metal, vision blurred, hardly realising I was holding a car door, a driving mirror, a fender, anything I could clutch to keep upright. Still teetering on my feet, I began waving frantically at the first vehicles of the convoy we had passed earlier, and which had now caught up with us. Greg I saw was sprawled unconscious in the smashed Chrysler. I hardly noticed the other car at first. Barely able to stand, I tried desperately to tug at the wheel which was pressed against him, pinning the tops of his legs. But it was hopeless to try to disentangle the twisted metal, for the entire front of the car had been crushed.

As the convoy reached us, grinding clumsy gears into neutral, I heard a whistle blow and saw a motor-cycle roar up. I almost keeled over as a man left his machine on the side, rushed over with a pair of strong supporting arms, and in a rich Yorkshire accent muttered, 'Ba gum, laad. It's made a reet bloody mess!'

The road ahead was strewn with tangled metal. I vaguely realised that one of the camels had been killed, a fact which didn't register at first because two others were unconcernedly ruminating. My eyes were out of focus but I stared intently to look more closely. There seemed to be two cars in front of the Chrysler.

I must have passed out again. I woke – perhaps a few seconds later, for the scene was unchanged – to find the burning taste of brandy being forced between my lips. As I spluttered and coughed another man arrived.

'Sergeant-Major Durrant,' he announced. 'You all right?'

'My brother,' I managed to gasp out. 'Is he alive?'

'Don't worry,' he soothed me. 'They're trying to get to him now. What happened? And – can you understand? Can you identify yourself?'

'Inside pocket. Official pass.' I had to force the words out. 'Please – my father – contact him, Sir Geoffrey Holt in Cairo.'

'Will do.' He examined my papers briefly. 'Now lie back, Major. We'll get your brother out.'

'Is he all right?' I asked the question almost without feeling. There is nothing like danger to kill emotion.

I saw the doubt flicker quickly, swiftly masked by professional detachment. 'He's alive, sir – but not in good shape. We've got an ambulance at the rear of the convoy. It's coming now.'

I was suddenly aware of searing pains and aches, though miraculously no bones seemed to have been broken. I had a blinding headache that hit me right behind the eyes, and when I wiped what I thought was sweat from my forehead the back of my hand was stained red.

'Nothing serious, Major,' Durrant said. 'Superficial. Here, let me wipe it away.'

I was puzzling over the wreckage straddling the road. 'I didn't know there were two other cars,' I said. My brain was fuddled, I knew, but I could clearly see one car to the left, the other twenty yards away to the right.

'No, sir, just one car. It must have been doing a hundred. It's one of them new-fangled French things, front-wheel drive, they don't have a real chassis.'

'I don't understand.'

'It hit your car broadside on. Because there isn't a chassis to take the shock the other car was sliced in two as clean as a knife through butter. The front seats are over there, the back –' He gestured to the other side of the road.

'My God! How terrible.' I had to fight not to vomit. 'I never saw anything like it. The' – I hesitated – 'the pas–sengers?'

'Four of them, sir. All killed. Two bodies still in the front seats, two children in the back. The driver's a bloody murderer, begging your pardon, sir. We've left the bodies there till the military police finish their inspection.'

'My God.' I began to feel hot salt tears gushing down my bloodstained face.

I could still see the two pieces of the car, the bodies entombed in the metal graves. On the other side of the road, by the sandy track, was another gruesome sight. Two of the camels were still standing quietly, but nobody was going to waste the carcass of the third one. From nowhere half a dozen men had arrived and were already busily engaged in cutting up the body for meat before the vultures arrived. The sight was too much. This time, and without warning, before I could even turn my head, I was violently sick all over myself.

At that moment the ambulance clattered to a halt, a young doctor in horn-rimmed spectacles rushed over, and I thanked God that he spared me any indulgent preliminaries. I heard the sergeant mutter to him, and caught the words, 'A major in DSO.'

'Delayed shock,' said the doctor. 'I'll give him a shot to keep him down for a bit. Get him into the ambulance while I help to free the other man.'

I hardly realised that he had torn open the sleeve of my shirt and swabbed the flesh before I felt the prick of the needle. The effect was almost instant drowsiness but now, even though I was hardly hurt, fear and imagination took over and I remember feeling that I was about to die. I was convinced that these were the last few seconds of my life; and I was not thinking of Greg, I was not thinking of the people in the other car, I was not thinking of the other driver who had behaved so murderously. I just cried from the heart, 'Serena, darling, I'll always love you.'

The second time I opened my eyes I could just make out a sparsely furnished, whitewashed room, the walls pierced only by two small windows and a single naked electric bulb. I was in one of a dozen iron bedsteads ranged round the room. I felt rather than knew the rough sheets; no pillows, no blankets.

In the next bed to mine lay a man on his back with both

legs held up, in an inclined position, the feet higher than the rest of his body. I was in some kind of cottage hospital, and at first I couldn't tell whether or not the man next to me was Greg, for I stared fascinated at an entirely different kind of macabre picture. Half a dozen shadowy figures in what looked at first sight like the flowing robes of ghosts were standing up against a wall, each one with his galabiya lifted so that his penis hung over a chamberpot.

An Egyptian nurse was trying to cajole the old men, 'Come along now. Try harder! This is your last chance before I put you to bed.'

Dimly I realised that this must be one of the old people's homes which had been built in dozens of settlements in the Delta, doing wonderful work for old and infirm men, cripples, beggars, human derelicts left on the refuse dump after their useful life had ended. It was obviously a primitive place.

One old man pointed to the still figure of the man in the bed next to mine and announced in a quavering voice words that sent a chill through my aching bones, 'That's the man who murdered four Egyptians. Two of them babies. He's British.'

I closed my eyes, trying to blot out their words, the sound as they piddled into stone jars, the spitting and throat-clearing. Suddenly the commotion stopped and another nurse shooed the old men out of the room. There were new voices, respectful, hushed, as a nurse led a visitor towards my bed. I opened my eyes. And there stood my father.

'Thank God you've come,' I cried. 'How did you get here so quickly?'

'This was a time for me to pull rank. I've arranged for a private ambulance to get Greg to the Anglo-American Hospital.'

I knew the place well, the tall grey building on Gezira Island.

'I'll be fit enough to travel with you. How's Greg? What are his –' I hesitated.

He leaned over the bed and stroked my bruised face, trying to comfort me, to pour his warmth into me, to prepare me for the worst. 'Greg's alive, but he's pretty bad. I don't know any details yet, as I've only just arrived. I suppose Greg was driving?' I didn't have to answer. He already knew that Greg's legs had been jammed by the steering wheel. He sighed, and took a deep breath. 'Both thighs were broken by the steering wheel. But the doctors can do wonders.' He was on the verge of tears. 'They pull the bones straight, give them a chance to mend. A long job.' He sighed again.

'And Mother?'

'I don't think she realises how serious it is.' He smiled faintly. 'I tried to soften the blow – just said that Greg had broken his legs. I think she feels he'll be out and about in a few weeks. Sometimes it helps that Chiffon is a little – shall we say, vague?'

'Poor Greg. Anything – well, any other injuries? His head?'

'A mild concussion, though the local doctor had to stitch his head up. And his left arm's broken. Both feet, too, as far as we can make out.'

One awful thought kept recurring in my mind, one I couldn't drive out, one I didn't dare ask: Would Greg ever be able to walk again?

The same thought must have occurred to Father, although all he said was, 'We can only hope and pray.'

The ambulance from the Anglo-American Hospital had arrived. The attendants, neat and official in white overalls, came in with a rolled-up stretcher. Greg was still unconscious, of course; put to sleep, I was told later. As I watched, the two men placed the stretcher in position while nurses carefully held his legs.

'It's a private ambulance,' my father explained. 'So it will only take one stretcher and one passenger as well as the orderlies. The doctor should travel with Greg. Do you think you could come with me in my car? Are you up to it?'

'Sure.'

I felt better once I had escaped the claustrophobic atmosphere of the old people's home with its line of men and their chamberpots and the cheerful nurse crying, 'Come on now! Try harder!' And the sight of Greg in the next bed – invisible

286

to me except for a misshapen lump under the sheet.

'Oh, Father!' I stumbled towards the car, leaning on the shoulder of an Arab member of the staff. 'What a bloody mess!'

'It'll be all right, I hope.' He made sure I was comfortable in the car. 'When we get settled in you can tell me quietly what happened. There's bound to be an enquiry – a military one.' He paused. 'Why weren't you driving?' It was a leading question, directed by a trained mind demanding the truth.

I lied instantly.

'We had to get to Serena quickly. I wasn't feeling too well, so it seemed sensible for me to let Greg drive. But of course the road was closed to private cars, so I had to go along with him.'

'But it wasn't official, was it?'

This time I told the truth instantly.

'I explained that to my CO. I do have the right to travel anywhere and take any action I think necessary. But I did cover myself and tell the brigadier the truth – that I wanted to get my sister-in-law out of Alex.'

'Greg drives like a madman,' said my father suddenly.

Knowing the importance of establishing a 'fact' from the very first moment – especially if you have to rearrange what facts there are to suit yourself – and knowing too that all the witnesses in the other car were dead, I said, 'We weren't exactly dawdling – Greg never does – but he certainly wasn't going too fast.'

The only other people who might conceivably be called as witnesses to any military enquiry or civil case were the two elderly camel-drivers and, I vaguely remembered, a couple of kids. And I knew without any enquiry that they would be furious with only one person – the man who had driven his car into one of their camels and killed it.

I asked Father, 'Does Serena know?'

He nodded as the car sped along, past convoys going north, leaving us with an almost free right-hand side of the black road. 'I got one of Wavell's staff to telephone to GHQ. Apparently some general who has to drive to Cairo is giving her a lift.'

He drove carefully past a couple of overladen donkeys plodding wearily ahead. 'I left messages for Serena to make straight for the hospital. They'll be keeping a bed for you too.'

'I don't want a bed. I'm all right.'

'Better have a check-up. It's not every day that a man gets hurled out of a speeding car.'

'Still, don't you think I ought to go and see Mother first?'

'Perhaps – if you feel up to it.'

I did spend the night in hospital. Father insisted, as did the army. So did the civilian doctor. He said they would put me in some semi-surgical bed – I couldn't understand exactly what – but which would enable me to lie flat and rest my bones more than would be possible in my own bed with its friendly hollows. I might not have slept as well as I did, had not the doctor given me a pill, but I woke the following morning with a ravenous appetite.

The first person I went to see was Greg, after a nurse had told me he was awake. He was a few doors away in the same corridor, and a nurse took me there, still in my pyjamas and dressing-gown.

Why, I don't know, but I had assumed that Greg would be alone in the room when I arrived. Not so. Two elderly French specialists – *professeurs*, they liked to be called – were conferring gravely, and who else should be there but Serena.

'They wouldn't let me come to see you,' she whispered. 'You talk to Greg. I'm going to have a word with the specialists.'

'This is a bloody poor show.' Greg was obviously in pain but felt for my hand with his good right arm. 'I knew I should have let you drive.'

'We'll soon have you up and about – not to worry.' I tried to be cheerful, but half of my mind was listening to Serena, her voice showing animosity towards the doctors.

'May take a bit longer than you think.' Greg wheezed with the effort of talking.

'Don't say anything. You'll need all your strength.'

288

'It was that bloody camel.' He tried to grin. 'What's Serena on about?'

'I dunno.'

She and the two French specialists seemed to be arguing, and once or twice Serena's voice was raised in anger. She wasn't shouting, but her usually soft voice was strident.

'*On ne discute pas les choses comme ça avec les femmes,*' I heard one doctor say.

'Well, I'm a *femme*,' cried Serena furiously, 'and I *am* going to discuss my husband's future, whether you like it or not. I forbid you, is that clear? *I forbid you.*'

'I can do nothing if you take that attitude.' The doctor shrugged his shoulders angrily. '*C'est votre décision.*'

The other one added, in a voice suddenly sinister, '*Mais êtes-vous sûre que c'est pour le mieux?*'

Serena put her hand to her mouth, biting a knuckle, then almost in tears whispered, 'That was a wicked and cruel thing to say to me.'

'Life is cruel, madame,' retorted the doctor. 'Good-day to you.'

As the doctors stalked out of the room a trim English nurse came in and said pertly, 'Can you leave us for a few minutes, please? Just one or two things I have to do.'

'What was all that about?' I asked as Serena and I sat on a small bench at the end of the corridor. 'I've never seen you so angry.'

'Those French butchers wanted to amputate – both legs.' She was white with anger and fear, and almost in tears.

'Amputate!' It was a dreaded word, final in its awful implications, but this was the first time I had faced the possibility. 'Both of them?' I found myself whispering.

She nodded miserably. I had thought, with the incoherence of the accident and all the other problems involved, that Greg might have to walk with a limp, maybe a stick, but – *amputation*.

'It can't be necessary. Oh, Serena, poor you.' I put my arms around her. 'And poor Greg. He must be given a chance. Surely his bones will mend?'

'That's what I said to the specialists.'

'You refused?'

She nodded. 'I had to. But then the French doctor said that awful thing – telling me that he hoped I was doing the best thing for everyone. Isn't – isn't any chance better than none?'

'Of course it is. Those bloody French love playing with knives. Father has already arranged to see an English bone specialist. He's supposed to be the best in Europe – and he's only here as a surgeon who's been sent to the Middle East.'

Dr Collins was a large man with a jolly smile and the kind of embracing warmth that would make any patient feel that they were the only person in the world who mattered to him. He had wispy grey hair, spectacles and had, so my father told us, specialised in bone surgery in Harley Street all his life until volunteering for war work.

'We'll take a good look at this young man,' he promised Serena, 'and if there's anything to be done we'll do it. I've saved a great many legs in my life, don't you worry.' Dr Collins later allowed us into the room while he made a preliminary examination of Greg. 'I've found that most patients like to have their pals or wives around – unless there's a lot of blood, eh?'

He felt the bones gently and carefully, but most of all he studied the X-rays, as though reading the possible destiny of a man by examining a few indistinct pieces of film. He wasn't satisfied with them, and sent for a portable X-ray machine which was soon wheeled into the bedroom. Dr Collins then re-photographed Greg's legs, his arms, feet but most of all his thighs.

We waited for the results of the new X-rays in an adjoining room, and before long Dr Collins came in with the sheaf of large pictures and said briskly, 'Now, let's have a look at these together, shall we?'

'I'm not sure I can understand them,' said Serena.

'Quite easy, really.' He was one of those men who actually enjoyed sharing information, in direct contrast to the French obsession with medical secrecy. 'Just like reading a different language, my dear, nothing to worry about. I'll explain everything.'

He showed the first photographs on a wall against a light.

'That's the left thigh. You see. There – and there – the breaks.' He pointed them out.

'The problem is simple,' he went on. 'And it's no consolation for me to tell you that this is an almost classic injury when two cars crash head-on at speed. From what I can tell' – he peered at me over his spectacles – 'you're the luckiest man in the world to be alive.'

He traced the details of the X-ray pictures with a pencil. 'Here' – he pointed to the solid white patches on the shadowy grey of the legs. 'There are five fractures on the left thigh between the knee and the hip – there. And here' – he pointed to the grey patches between the fragments of bone which showed white. 'Here are the four gaps where the fractures have separated. The same with the other leg – there are four fractures. It's the direct result of pressure on the steering wheel. The thigh bones had to break under the shock. Altogether it's broken your husband's thighs in nine places. To say nothing of the other injuries.'

As I sat listening I shivered for a moment at the unreality of it all. There was the avuncular Dr Collins pouring out his sympathy to his patient's wife, unknowing that the girl in front of his surgery desk was my lover. And what was poor Serena thinking? In her own way she loved Greg. Did she feel pity more than love?

What would happen now? I couldn't prevent my thoughts. What if Greg didn't fully recover? Would Serena feel differently towards me? I shouldn't ask questions like this, but nobody on earth can prevent such thoughts. They were chased away by a mental picture – Greg, Serena and Jonothan, all playing at home. With Greg in a wheelchair.

'What do you think, Doctor?' I had never heard Serena's voice sound so small, so frightened.

He hesitated a long time. It passed through my mind that he was deciding how strong Serena was. How much should he tell, how much withhold? But it might not have been that, for very deliberately he studied the large gloomy X-ray plates again, then once more, until finally he looked at Serena and said, 'Personally I am against amputation. At least until we've tried everything else.'

'Thank God!' cried Serena impulsively.

'And,' I asked quickly, 'what does "everything else" mean?'

'Both legs have been drastically shortened following the impact. Shortened by the break, of course. There are huge gaps – here.' He pointed to the grey area. 'The impact not only broke the bones, it pushed them out of place. So what we have to try and do is pull the broken fragments of bone back into their original positions. And then hope they will knit and grow together again.'

'And that means?' I asked.

'It's a tedious but quite normal treatment, once you've been able to straighten the bones – that's where I come in,' said Dr Collins. 'If that part of it is successful, then I'll have to put both legs into traction.'

In frightening detail he explained what he would do. Through each shin bone just below the knee he planned to drill two holes across the leg, then insert pins in each shin bone crossways, so that the ends would stick out at each side of each leg. Cords would be fastened to each side of the pin in each bone, and the other end would be attached to weights that would hang over the end of the bed.

'That's oversimplifying it, you understand,' he explained, 'but with luck it should be possible – with the steady weights pulling the leg through the shin bones – to keep them straight, lengthen them both so gradually that, in a healthy man, the bones should have a fair chance of knitting together.'

'What about my husband's heart condition?'

'Don't worry about that. The months of enforced rest should help tranquillise the fibrillation.'

'But straightening the legs?'

'That's my job,' he repeated gently. 'And I'm delighted to be here in Egypt at this moment – more by good luck than anything else – to try and help you. I'll have to put him to sleep for three or four hours while I manipulate the bones.'

'And then?'

'Then comes the real test of a man's character. Once I've put him in traction he won't be able to do anything. He'll be on his back, with the cords pulling at his legs so that it will be impossible for him to move even slightly from the thighs down. Obviously he won't be able to turn on his side. A nurse will just be able to squeeze a bedpan below him once a day, and even that will have to be expertly done.'

'For how long?' asked Serena.

'A minimum of five months.'

'Oh no!' Serena almost wailed. 'Poor Greg. He's so active, Doctor, so full of life.'

'He's alive,' said Collins gently. 'For most people that's the most precious thing to cling to. For the others – that's what I meant when I talked about a test of character.'

'And at the end of five months?' My voice sounded hollow, empty.

'Well, Major Holt, I wouldn't be honest if I didn't tell you both that it's a fifty-fifty chance of the bones mending. I'll put it no higher than that.'

'Greg's a fighter,' I cried. 'He's the sort of man who has the will to get better – the –'

'And that's half the battle,' interrupted the doctor. 'I've seen some remarkable recoveries from bodies smashed almost beyond recognition, but only because the will was stronger than the desire to give in.'

'He *has* got that.'

'It'll be up to you – and your families – to help him, stop him when he suffers from bouts of – well, depression.'

When he had gone, I said to Serena, 'You're the one who's got to fight Greg's battle for him.' As I dropped her at the Villa Zelfa, I asked, 'What's going to become of us?'

'I don't know. Though I do know that yesterday an extraordinary thing happened.'

'Yesterday?' I was puzzled.

'Yes, yesterday. The doctor in the convoy who rescued you came to see how Greg was. I met him in the corridor and Dr Collins, who was in a rush, introduced us in passing, just as "Mrs Holt". The convoy doctor asked me, "Serena Holt?" And when I nodded he told me of the last words you uttered as you passed out on the side of the road. And then he added, "I'm so glad your husband wasn't hurt. It's wonderful to see two people so much in love."'

25

It was after the second or third month in hospital that Greg, lying flat in his bed, developed a desperate sex urge. There was little anyone could do about it, of course, but Serena told me that one afternoon, thinking he was asleep after lunch, she opened the door of his room quietly so as not to risk waking him. But he *was* awake, with his right hand under the sheet, and from the movement she knew instantly what he was doing.

He was so excited that, far from stopping, he whispered, 'Close the door!' He spoke urgently, giving orders. 'Sit there. No, *there*, where I can see you. Please, darling, take off your panties and open your legs – just so that I can see everything.'

'No!' she cried. 'Somebody might come in.'

'Christ! Think of me! Be quick!'

Unwillingly she did as he asked, sitting back in the low armchair facing him, her skirt halfway up her thighs.

He had just stopped moving when the sister came in. Swiftly Serena was able to give the appearance of sitting normally, but her heart was pounding, she had difficulty in breathing normally and she felt slightly sick.

'You shouldn't, Greg,' she said when the sister had gone. 'It's beastly. And it's bad for you.'

'You mean I'll end up in a loony bin? Isn't that what all fathers tell their sons?'

'I didn't mean that, darling. But it's –'

'Sordid?'

She was silent, miserable.

'Any other suggestions?' he asked sarcastically.

'Don't be angry, darling. I understand, but' – she hesitated – 'at home, alone, it was one thing. Here –'

'You don't understand. I'm stuck in this bloody bed. I'm damned lucky not to have broken my right arm. At least I can use *that*. All I asked you to do was help me, excite me. What's so sordid about that?'

'The nurses, Greg. They're always coming in and out. And they never knock.'

'So what?' He was almost shouting now. 'What the hell do I care if a bloody nurse comes in?'

'But if one sees us. You might think of *me*.'

'Think of you! That's a good one. What about thinking of me?'

'That's unfair.'

'Is it? What have *you* been doing today while I've been lying on my back?'

'Greg, darling, I've been waiting at home. Painting with Baptise.'

'That decrepit old pansy.'

'He's not, as it happens. He's just a very old man who helps me to paint.' Very quietly she added, 'And helps me to pass the time between visits to my husband. When you're not with me, I'm very lonely.'

'I'm lonely too!' Serena had never seen Greg so angry. 'And if I want the next best thing to a bit of fun do your duty and help me.'

'It's *not* my duty.' It was Serena's turn to be really angry. 'And if you need any help when you're playing with yourself why don't you get one of the girls from the Sphinx to come and see you?'

'Don't worry,' Greg shouted furiously. 'I'll do just that. At least they're willing.'

'Don't forget to sign the chit,' Serena retorted and walked out of the room.

The phrase 'sign the chit' was well-known in Cairo. In those days you signed for nearly everything; and it was common knowledge that in some of the better-known houses of pleasure young bachelors short of money towards the end of the month could sign a chit and pay on the first day of the next month.

When Serena told me about the row between Greg and

her she said, crying, 'I felt awful. It was so disgusting. What makes me feel worse is the fact that before the accident, when Greg was having trouble, I *did* do what I could to help him.'

I must have looked annoyed – I had a picture of Serena, with all those bedroom mirrors, trying to 'encourage' Greg – because she said, 'Don't be angry, please. Greg's your brother, and it *was* my duty to try and help him.'

In fact, before long Greg carried out his threat, and from time to time some very pretty girls, attired more modestly than they would have been at the Sphinx, started to arrive during the siesta time to 'pay their respects' to the patient. No one at first realised who they were, but I was certain that not one of them had a stitch of clothing under their demure and modest dresses.

Some of them were ideally suited to Greg's need, particularly those who specialised in 'encouraging' the more elderly clients. There was one beautiful Indian girl, known as Jasmine, who with a Siamese girl at the Sphinx had invented a new name for passive lovemaking – one destined to go into the English language, though not in every dictionary. It was called 'relief massage'.

According to reports from Jim Stevenson, who had tried it, it was performed so expertly by girls like Jasmine, and with so many extra tricks, that, in his words, 'Frankly, it's better than the real thing. Because when you're dealing with girls like Jasmine *they* decide when you reach a climax.'

I remember that when Stevenson told me I said that I hadn't known he patronised the Sphinx, to which he retorted, 'Where do you think I get my information?'

The visits to Greg could not be kept secret for long. Sooner or later some visitor who haunted Samia's club recognised girls like Jasmine, and then everyone in Cairo knew, except apparently Chiffon. The Anglo-American Hospital had elastic visiting hours – especially for patients with VIP status – and one day Chiffon arrived at Greg's room just as Jasmine, dressed in a beautiful sari, was about to leave and Greg was half-asleep.

'Such a charming girl,' Chiffon told us that evening at dinner. 'I don't know if she's at the embassy, but her visit had a very restful effect on Greg. Usually he's so edgy these days, poor dear, but this afternoon he looked positively contented.'

This was a rare, quiet evening at home for my mother, for Chiffon was having the time of her life. 'War suits me,' she confided. She seemed to go out dancing almost every night, and was inundated with invitations to cocktail parties given by elderly staff officers anxious to find any middle-aged ladies. They soon discovered that Chiffon was always *fun*. By now even the pretence of inviting Father, knowing he would refuse, had been abandoned. He had announced that he would attend no public parties except those given by old friends; so Chiffon was in her element. For though Cairo had always had many *young* bachelors, now there were dozens of senior officers delighted to enjoy her company.

Yet it was Father who asked me one day into his study, almost absently offered me a glass of champagne, and said abruptly, 'What's all this I hear about Greg's Indian girlfriend? Is it true that she comes from the Sphinx?'

'Greg's on his back. He doesn't have a girlfriend. How could he?'

'Is she from the Sphinx?'

I sipped my champagne and nodded. No use trying to fool Father. 'Greg's going through a bad time,' I said as carefully as I could.

'Does Serena know?' he asked.

'Yes,' I replied flatly. 'She was bound to find out. Some of the other girls from the Sphinx have been to see him too. One French girl –'

'French, eh?' His interest suddenly switched. 'Pretty?'

'Saucy rather than pretty.'

'What's she called?'

'I think her name's Suzanne. But she's always known as Crêpes Suzette.'

'You seem to know a lot about these girls.'

'I go to the Sphinx regularly,' I said, without telling him the real reason.

'You do! I *am* surprised.'

'I do work in Intelligence,' I laughed.

'Ah! That's different. Mata Hari stuff, eh? Would you take me to the Sphinx one evening?' he asked suddenly. 'In the course of duty, I mean.'

'All right,' I said rashly, but without making a definite date. 'Why not?' I explained the peculiarities of female attire in the second bar.

'Doesn't leave much to the imagination,' he chuckled. 'I'll keep you to your promise! Meanwhile I'll go and have a word with Greg. He must stop this nonsense.'

'No, no!' I was horrified. 'Let Greg think it's his secret. Don't on any account give him the impression that you're angry with him, or even upset.'

'But still – poor Serena. And what's going to become of Jonothan?'

'Father, you sound as if you're expecting the marriage to split up. Nobody's going to get divorced, you know.'

'But Serena?'

'Yes, Serena,' I echoed. 'She has great courage, she's the one who's really suffering.'

She was. She had come to terms with the facts, but her pride had been deeply wounded. She visited the hospital almost daily to see Greg, and the question of the girls was never again mentioned. She and Greg were on 'friendly' terms, and I wonder if Greg ever realised that everyone in Cairo knew what he was doing.

'If I didn't have you and Jonothan,' she admitted on one of our rare meetings alone, 'I think I'd have killed myself. If only' – she suddenly looked wistful, forlorn – 'if only we had a place where we could meet regularly alone. To make love of course, but more than that, to be together. Just alone.'

'Shall I try and find us a flat?' I asked. 'It's difficult, with officers in every spare flat in Zamalek. But –'

'Oh, Mark! If only you could. Wouldn't it be wonderful?'

In the end we did find a flat – but in the most extraordinary circumstances. It was Teddy Pollock who, of all people, was able to arrange everything, after he had made an astonishing confession.

'Confidential, old boy,' he drawled. 'One spy to another.

But Angela Gray and I were married in Beirut shortly before I joined up. I had to keep it dark when I enlisted because Angela's working as a statistician for the Egyptian government. It's not exactly secret, but some of the documents must be confidential, and if either the Egyptians or the British found out we were married there'd be all hell to pay.'

'I don't see why.'

'Come off it, Mark. A husband and wife swapping secret information between two countries which don't trust each other – and probably in bed each night, going over the day's work! I'd be sent off to the loneliest desert outpost in Egypt – and the Egyptians would ship Angie back home as an undesirable alien.'

'Why tell me?' It seemed a natural question – and very unwise of Teddy to share a secret like this.

'I trust you,' he said simply, 'because I need you. I need someone I can trust to come and see me fairly often in my apartment. You can imagine that the gyppos are keeping an eye on me since I joined up. Nothing serious, just checking. If you pop in for a drink regularly it'll give me just the right touch of respectability. And' – he hesitated – 'you don't look that happy, Mark. Well, you've had a rough time, I know – so if there's another girl, or –' He let the words tail off.

'All of us in your flat?' I didn't understand.

'Angie doesn't live with me, for God's sake. She lives in my secret flat. The one where you met Nasser. You of all people ought to know about that.'

Then I understood. For Teddy and Angela it was a perfect cover. They lived in different streets, yet all they had to do was unlock the door and spend each night together.

'But you see, the reason I told you is that I know the Egyptians must tail Angie from time to time. There's nothing they can pin on her, of course, but until we got married she shared a flat, like most girls working in Cairo – for the fun of having company as much as to save money. Now suddenly she lives on her own. Nothing wrong about that, but the gyppos are *always* suspicious. And she can't really invite the other girls – Dodie Summers and Sally Porter and that crowd. The first thing they'd want to know is why she had decided to live alone – and with who.'

'Whereas if I come round – the son of –'

'Exactly! Cosmetic, old boy. And if you by any chance have a girlfriend, she could visit Angie and the two of you could swap around without a soul ever guessing the truth.'

What a wonderful solution to our problem! But dared I entrust our precious secret to anyone? I wanted to badly. I hated the furtive meetings we occasionally arranged. I told Serena, and she never hesitated.

'But that's wonderful!' she cried.

I still had vague worries over being found out. Over the 'cosiness' of settling down, so to speak, in a flat.

'Honestly, Mark.' She was becoming almost angry. 'You do split hairs. Look at it objectively. I was asked by my father and agreed to marry in the Egyptian tradition a nice young man chosen for me. I married him and then, poor dear, it wasn't his fault, the cheerful sportsman turned into a cripple. Then you married a dizzy blonde and *she* turned into a religious fanatic. Yes, Parmi *is* a fanatic. It's wicked to chain a man for life just because he behaved honourably. Especially in the name of religion. Now we've a chance to make some happiness for ourselves, and I'm not going to settle for an occasional jig-a-jig in the back of a passion-wagon.'

I couldn't help laughing – at her Egyptian word for lovemaking and her American word for an opulent roadster.

'What about the danger of discovery?' I asked.

'I don't think there is any,' she said. 'I know you're afraid that after a few drinks at a party Teddy might let something slip. Well, I don't think he will.'

'We'd be in terrible trouble –'

'We would, that's true. But think of the difference. We might be the centre of a scandal that would rock Cairo, but that's all.'

'I might lose my law practice.'

'That's gone for the duration of the war anyway. They couldn't sack you from the army just for having an affair. But think of what Teddy and Angie stand to lose if *they're* discovered. He's secretly married, he's lied to the army authorities. And as for Angie – well, the newly-weds wouldn't even be allowed to live in the same country till after the war. Of course we must take the risk.'

So I told Teddy.

'I feel a real bastard,' I confessed. 'With my own brother. But honestly, despite outward appearances, their marriage isn't all it seems to be. On the surface, fine, but – well, I won't burden you with our private family secrets.' I sighed. 'What a load of shit life is.'

'Remember what I told you that evening at Shepheard's? Almost the exact words. And warning you about Serena keeping ten per cent back. And she was keeping it back for you. I told you. What you tell me now doesn't come as any great surprise.'

And so started a strange quartet. Two or three times a week I went to see Teddy for drinks. The old *bouab* – the doorman, often an informer, rather like a French concierge who tips off the police – had known me for years, and would smile an acknowledgment when I arrived. Around the same time Serena would go to Angie's flat for drinks.

It was all perfectly normal, providing we didn't arrive until after six, when Teddy's valet normally left, unless Teddy was giving a dinner party, when he would engage extra help.

It was strange how the foolproof alibi, the locked doors, the separate street entrances, all helped to stifle my feeling of guilt, to give us an appearance of normalcy we would never have been able to achieve had we been furtively hiding in sleazy hotels. Instead, the snatched evenings were among the most enchanting of our lives. In a way it was the nearest thing to having a 'home' of our own, for though Angie returned early each morning to her adjacent flat – before Teddy's manservant arrived – she never used our bed, so that it was 'ours' – *our* sheets, *our* stock of drinks, *our* boxes of biscuits.

And even though our time was always limited, there was still enough for us to indulge in the luxury of not hurrying; not even hurrying to make love, for sometimes we would deliberately wait, sitting, kissing on the sofa like a newly married couple, stroking legs, slowly reaching my hand above her skirt, feeling the soft skin where the top of her stocking ended and the warm flesh began.

Sometimes as I touched her leg she would seize my hand and push it further up to the join and then after all the playing at love we would suddenly need to end the make-believe, and make love on the sofa, the urge was so desperate.

At other times I would arrive and, as Angela went off into Teddy's flat and I moved through the secret door, we would embrace silently and, still with no words spoken, all the miracle of instant love achieved by thought alone, we would make love, then dress, and spend the rest of the short evening in the perfection that comes only to lovers when satiated – that different world from the one when so-called 'love' is followed by boredom.

Of course I went to see Greg regularly; not every day, for Mother was there, and Father popped in twice a week; and so did all his old friends. But one thing was lacking, because of the nature of Greg's broken bones: accurate progress reports. By now – early in 1941 – he was not in pain. The weights pulling at his legs through the pins in his shins had been so carefully graduated that Greg really didn't know they were there – and of course he could not see them. The traction, as it was called, had been perfectly arranged by Dr Collins.

'My only fear is that someone will bang against the end of the bed and tear the pins out of my legs,' Greg said one day when Chiffon and I went to see him. 'Otherwise I haven't even had any bedsores. I'm just bored as hell, that's all.'

I tried several times to pump Dr Collins, but though kindly and honest he refused to commit himself even to me, though I did say that, as Greg's brother, I felt I merited any forecasts, good or bad.

'My dear Major Holt,' he explained. 'There's no reason why I shouldn't tell you everything I know – but there's nothing to tell. We take X-rays regularly, but they don't really tell *all* the truth. Some of the bones seem to be knitting well, but others –' He shrugged his shoulders. 'I'm not in a position to make *any* firm forecasts. As I said when we put your brother into traction, it's a fifty-fifty chance. Another six weeks and I'll be able to give you a more detailed report.'

None of this was known to Greg. It was better that way, for though at times he suffered from moods of depression on the whole he regarded no news as good news.

Life was made easier because, despite the war, he – and most of us, for that matter – wanted for nothing. Though Greg could not be moved off his back he had arranged for a refrigerator to be installed in his room, with a table next to it along one wall, loaded with bottles, as well-stocked as any bar, with drinks that had to be kept cold – fruit juices, champagne and so on – on ice. Life in Cairo was summed up in one sentence when Sirry Pasha visited Greg while I was there, though he didn't realise the significance.

'Here's a bottle to cheer you up,' he said to his son-in-law. 'Personally I prefer Krug, but there's a temporary shortage, so I hope you don't mind accepting Dom Perignon.'

It was astonishing, the abundant supplies in the midst of war. When one very rich pasha married his daughter off the entire garden was covered with priceless carpets, and one table thirty feet long was filled with nothing but bowls of caviar.

'Have some more porridge, old boy,' I heard an exultant young subaltern say.

What made life in Cairo even more incongruous was the topsy turvy nature of the war after Mussolini's sudden invasion of Egypt. When the enemy took Sollum on that hot Sunday in September many people thought it would be only a matter of time before they reached Alexandria, especially when three days later, after Italian forces had marched across the sea-fringed desert, they took Sidi Barrani against little organised resistance.

Places like Sollum and Sidi Barrani were mere dots on the map, clusters of mud huts, watering holes on the long single-track railway and coastal road leading from Libya to Alex. Yet, when translated into British newspapers, each one was a defeat – yet another loss to illustrate the global nature of the conflict, extending the dangers to Britain from Europe to a new continent.

Unaccountably, the Italian forces decided to 'rest' at Sidi Barrani, while the British used the time to reinforce Mersa

Matruh, a few miles east of Sidi Barrani, which became our northern headquarters. The British troops might have preferred Cairo or Alex but they enjoyed one bonus – the most beautiful beaches in all North Africa. It was to this beach at Mersa Matruh, as spotlessly white as snow, that Cleopatra took Antony to bathe in a sea that seemed to reflect all the tints of the rainbow.

Then, early in December, a mechanised detachment of British, Dominion and Free French troops set out from Mersa Matruh and took back Sidi Barrani. By mid-December they had retaken Sollum: Egypt was safe again. In one glorious week our forces recovered four hundred square miles and took thirty thousand prisoners, for the loss of a hundred Allied soldiers killed and seven hundred wounded. Before long our troops moved westwards to Cyrenaica, holding it lightly except for the town of Tobruk, which had a harbour we could use.

It was shortly after we had routed the Italians that I ran into Aly.

'Was it you who said that your friend Nasser was in El Alamein?' I asked. I was, in fact, carefully bringing the conversation round to Sadat without mentioning his name first. I had been intrigued about Aly's relationship with the man after Samia had told me of their meetings.

'And Nasser's friend in the army?' I pretended I had forgotten his name. 'Chap with a dark moustache who's always smoking a pipe.'

'Oh, you mean Sadat. He's around. I think he's stationed in Cairo.'

'I saw him once or twice,' I said carefully, but lying. 'He was with General Masri.'

I could almost swear that Aly's sallow cheeks were touched with pink.

'What do you know about Masri?' He seemed astonished.

'Not a lot,' I admitted. 'But enough to know that as you're a friend of Sadat's, and he's a friend of Masri's, the less you see of Sadat the better.'

That evening Teddy and Angela, Serena and myself went to

304

Groppi's for dinner and dancing. There was no reason for gossip in an occasional encounter, and this was a special evening to celebrate an exciting achievement by Serena. Behind her back, Baptise had quietly arranged for her to have a one-woman show.

She had been painting steadily, and over the years had accumulated dozens of canvases. Her personality was so strong that she had subtly outgrown the influence of her teacher, benefiting from his technique but then drawing away from the vivid colours of Baptise's *fauve* influence to become mellower, gentler. And she had discarded Baptise's own technique of using a pallet knife regularly to achieve an almost solid impasto. Instead she painted thinly – diluting the paint with a lot of turps – until she achieved an almost ethereal look in some of her canvases, particularly portraits. What impressed me when Baptise explained the subtleties was that she in no way produced a photographic likeness, yet the subject was immediately identifiable.

'She is the true artist, monsieur,' said Baptise. 'She sees what is not to be seen, only what the eye sees beyond the eye. Is it not so?'

It was true. Many of her paintings had a haunting, even sad effect, as though she were looking for something she could almost grasp, but never quite hold.

The Gallery Laffont, in the Kasr el Nil, was holding a private viewing, by invitation only, the following evening; as on all social occasions in Cairo, a black-tie affair.

'I'm dreading it, I'll be so embarrassed tomorrow,' said Serena. 'Suppose nobody comes? I mean, only three or four. I'll feel such a fool.'

'They'll turn up,' I reassured her.

'Especially as the invitation mentions that champagne will be served at the private viewing,' said Teddy.

In fact, the show was almost a sell-out, and quite apart from the quality of the paintings other factors certainly helped. Serena still signed her paintings 'Serena Sirry' and M Laffont, the French owner of the gallery, had been quick to capitalise on such a famous family name. He had lavished money on publicity, so that everyone who mattered in Cairo

305

society had received invitations, and there were posters every-where. And the prices were high. 'People like to buy expens-ive paintings, not cheap ones,' explained Baptise.

Even at the first evening a large sprinkling of red dots signified firm sales, including one in particular which I had reserved for myself the day before the private opening, when the paintings were being hung. It was a self-portrait of Serena, looking just as I knew and loved her, gentle, wistful, a little sad, as though life were too good to be true and too good to last. That was to be mine, and I insisted on paying the proper price for it. At the show itself I bought a second, smaller canvas, an enchanting portrait of Jonothan. Somehow Serena had captured the essence of the baby.

'And he looks every inch a Holt,' said Chiffon, who was dressed in a long, flowing creation in ice-blue so startling that even Father murmured, 'It's a little hard on the eyes, m'dear.'

'It's the height of fashion,' snorted Chiffon. 'I had it copied from *Les Modes*. Really, Geoffrey, sometimes I think you have no taste.'

Madame Sirry was delighted with the success. As a well-known patron of the arts she basked in reflected glory.

'It's very good indeed,' she said to Father. 'To be honest, I would have preferred my daughter to become a musician, but painting is next best.'

Sirry Pasha gave his approval but with at first a touch of reserve. Figurative art had for long been frowned upon by good Moslems, and as for portraits of living people – they were only just being accepted.

'I'm not a Moslem myself, of course,' he explained to me. 'But I hope my Moslem friends don't take offence.'

There was no need for him to worry, for the show received an unexpected seal of approval. Without any warning, King Farouk arrived.

I had not seen him for some time, and I was aghast. The legends about Farouk's gargantuan appetite – and the way in which his face and figure had changed – had gained wider and more regular circulation, but still I was horrified at the change. Not too long ago, he was not only handsome but almost girlish, as though he never needed to shave, and Sirry

Pasha had told me that once when he and the king went for a swim in the Abdin pool Farouk didn't have a hair on his chest.

It was very different now. The heavy jowls always looked as though they needed a shave. His hair was growing in tufts on the back of his fingers. Another of Sirry Pasha's tales was that Farouk's bathroom was now cluttered with reducing machines and that the twenty-one-year-old monarch pedalled furiously from time to time on his bathroom bicycle. 'But it's pathetic,' Sirry had added. 'For as soon as he's dressed he eats a couple of dozen eggs, a dozen bags of potato chips, and half a gallon of fizzy lemonade.'

This was the king who had entered the art gallery, so gross and bloated that a shiver of disgust ran through me. He was followed by the inevitable General Sadik. The king held up a hand and murmured affably, 'Please! This is a private visit. Just behave as though I am not here.'

With that he walked round the room to study the paintings and the chatter started up again. Suddenly the king turned to Serena and after enquiring about Greg's health he studied one painting with extra care, and said, 'Mrs Holt, I congratulate you. You are a credit to your illustrious father and to the name of Sirry. I would like to buy this portrait. General Sadik will arrange the details.'

He pointed to the very self-portrait of Serena that I had bought. 'You have captured the beauty of your face,' he added. 'And something else besides.'

'I'm sorry, Your Majesty.' Serena looked embarrassed. 'That red dot on the frame means it's already been sold.'

The king leaned forward, smiled pleasantly, and peeled the tiny red dot off the frame.

'Now, it *hasn't* been sold!' He laughed.

'But sir,' she said awkwardly. 'It *has* been sold – and paid for. Any other painting that pleases Your Majesty – I would be honoured to present it to you as a token –'

'I want this one.' He spoke now like a king, not like a visitor to the gallery. 'I will double what the buyer has paid for it.'

'I don't think, Your Majesty –'

'Well – treble it! Four times as much, five if the wretched man insists; I wish to own it. Who has bought it?'

'I am the wretched man, sir,' I said, hoping my anger wouldn't show.

'Ah! Major Holt. Well?'

'Well, sir?'

'It is the king's wish.' He waved a podgy beckoning hand imperiously. 'Ah, there you are, Sirry Pasha. Perhaps you would explain something of royal protocol to – to Major Holt, whose knowledge of Egypt does not apparently run to the customs of the Egyptian royal family.' He looked at me coldly. 'When the king wants something – I shall expect it to be delivered tomorrow.' He stalked out of the gallery.

Only one or two people near the king had even the faintest inkling of what had happened, but Serena was in tears.

'I won't let him have it, I won't!' she cried. 'A true king would never behave like that.'

'*He* does,' said Sirry Pasha sadly. 'I don't know what to say. I'm all for standing out against such disgraceful conduct, but the king is a law to himself. And it's you I'm thinking of, Mark. You know the king, you know what he could do.'

'I'm in the army now.' I was still seething. 'He couldn't touch me.'

'That may be true,' Sirry Pasha agreed. 'But he could take it out on your mother and father. He could even force me, your landlord, but an Egyptian subject, to sell him Holt House, and have your family evicted. He forced that course with another British official who stood up to him. He's a spoiled brat, and I hate the idea of submitting to blackmail. But a royal command –' He sighed, then added, 'You heard what happened the other night. He offered an attractive married woman a lift home. Her husband, an officer, was on duty, but she still politely refused. "It's an order, madame, as well as an invitation," growled Farouk. In the end she had no other course than to accept.

'He was driving his black Cadillac convertible – as a change from his black Citroen – and after they had been travelling for a few minutes he pulled into a shady corner and began to plead for the ultimate favour. A traffic policeman, hearing the lady's cries of distress and not recognising the black car, raced to the rescue. Farouk pulled out his revolver, fired into the air, and as the wife, in a torn dress, managed to escape and the policeman recognised the king, he roared off into the night, with a laughing, "Officer! Return this lady to her husband with the king's compliments."

'He told me once,' Sirry Pasha concluded, 'that he preferred well-known married women; it added zest to the conquest.'

'I wish I'd never painted the wretched portrait!' Serena was still in tears. 'Let's get out of here.'

In the end, neither the king or I got the painting. A few days later, in an extraordinary sequel to the angry scene, General Sadik visited the Villa Zelfa on behalf of the king who, he said, would forgo his 'rights' to the portrait if I would do the same. The king, Sadik told Serena, realised how upset Mrs Holt had been by the incident, and wished it to remain the property of the artist. The only stipulation was that the portrait should be hung in the Villa Zelfa.

When Sadik arrived there were several guests at the villa, drinking cocktails before dinner, and were stunned witnesses to the general's news. He then went on: 'His Majesty has been inundated with official receptions. He is exhausted. He asks me to tell you that he is free on Friday' – that was the Moslem Sabbath – 'and would be delighted if you could invite him and a young lady to a quiet supper at your home.'

'I realise that His Majesty has exchanged one royal command for another,' said Serena icily. 'So I presume I have no option. Shall we say nine o'clock on Friday? And, of course, the original purchaser of the painting' – with a smile to me – 'must also have the opportunity to see it.'

Farouk had already visited the Villa Zelfa when Greg and Serena gave a 'welcome back' party after their honeymoon, and the king had said then how charming he found it, and how he hoped to be invited there from time to time for quiet evenings.

After Sadik had gone Serena said to me, 'I can't ever remember being so angry. When I think of the power which that bladder of lard wields, and the way he abuses it – well, I sympathise with men like Aly's friends who want to kick him off the throne.' She smiled. 'You will come to the dinner, yes?'

I wondered if Farouk's gluttony was inherited. The royal family had always been huge eaters – though on nothing like the same scale as Farouk – but in Egypt obesity was often confused with virility.

'Maybe it's a disguise for *lack* of virility,' I suggested to Dr Phillips, who was among those invited for dinner that evening.

'That's too simple an excuse.' He shook his head. 'I've always believed the poor man's so depressed because he's sexually frustrated that food has become a substitute. It's a true story that he was underdeveloped when a boy – his testicles and so on were not as strong as they should have been. This is not a mysterious disease, you know. Many men are not as well endowed as they wish.'

'But how has it affected the king?'

'There'll be a word to describe it one day. And a name for the disease. His trouble may be caused by two glands, the pituitary gland in the brain and the adrenal glands near the top of the kidneys. The pituitary may be producing too much cortisone, which automatically causes fat, and the other, too much androgen, a sex hormone, which has caused him to start sprouting hair.'

'It's horrible,' said Serena, 'to see such beauty turned into such a beast.'

'And don't forget,' said Dr Phillips, 'that his early life might have upset those glands. His father Fuad was a bully, who jeered at him for being effeminate. That kind of father can put mental signposts to a young boy which can change his life. Old Fuad never treated Farouk like a man – never gave him a chance to become one.'

But it was Stevenson, who had seen the original incident at the gallery, who had the last word to Serena. 'You have done more to fight injustice than you realise. You have publicly rebuked the king, even if he is too thick-skinned to realise it. And,' he said, with his lazy wink, 'what a news item for our Information Service!'

That Friday was the start of several intimate dinners given for Farouk at the Villa Zelfa.

It had been Stevenson's idea. It was no secret to any of us that his activities for Washington included gathering derogatory information about the king, especially his open infidelity to the beautiful Queen Farida. It was only one part of his job, but one for which he used the Anglo-American Information Service as a convenient cover. Nor was this branch of his activities undertaken with the thought that it would produce quick dividends.

'If we can pick up dirt about Farouk and his cronies during the next ten years or so,' said Stevenson cheerfully, 'the dividends will be huge. Anything detrimental. Sex orgies. You know – the same kind of stuff that sells newspapers.' It was said in a bantering way, but with a serious overtone.

It was the perfect psychological moment for Stevenson to approach Serena for help. She was still consumed with hatred for the king following the incident of the portrait. Stevenson asked if she would consent to hold occasional dinner parties for the king at her home. After all, Farouk had asked to be invited.

At first the idea horrified her.

'You have nothing to worry about – if you and Mark trust me,' he said. 'I give you my word that until Greg recovers and can be host either Mark or I – if you'll have me – will be one of the guests.'

'And what about Farida?'

'She doesn't come into the picture. The king is already bored with her. It's open gossip that he has a dozen mistresses – he doesn't even pretend to hide it. That's the whole purpose of our operation. He will be delighted to have you as hostess in a private villa, with his current girlfriend invited. It's the perfect place for us to overhear gossip.'

At first I thought the idea abhorrent too and said so. I hated the idea of Serena being involved; though she had no delusions about Stevenson's role in Cairo. It had been impossible for the Sirrys to ignore what Stevenson had done during the attempted assassination of Father.

'I still think it's ridiculous,' I said. 'And anyway, if I do help I'll have to clear everything with my commanding officer.'

To my surprise, my CO was delighted and did everything to encourage me, which was why I finally agreed to the idea. By now, indeed since the king's marriage in 1938, his debauchery was increasing almost nightly. Soon he brought different girls to every dinner, often asking Serena's permission to retire for a private talk with the lady of his choice in the Villa Zelfa's study, a rose-coloured silk-lined room with a leather-lined soundproof door where presumably Princess Zelfa's husband had escaped to seclusion in days gone by.

'So long as he never tries anything on Serena,' I said to Stevenson one evening.

'He'll never be left alone with her. Not even in the study, if we're in the next room. And anyway, Greg should be out of hospital soon.'

'I suppose so.'

'That'll require quite a period of readjustment,' said Stevenson. 'Not only for Greg and Serena but – for others.'

'Others? Who?' I was always suspicious of 'subtle' remarks by Stevenson.

'The girls at the Sphinx,' he said innocently. 'Who else did you think I might mean?'

It was during this period when we were 'playing' at being spies that the real spy story on which I had been working burst wide open. For two weeks I had to go underground, and it all started with one laconic message for which I had been waiting. It read, 'Come' – Samia's shorthand for 'Come to the Sphinx urgently.'

26

The Sphinx was crowded. The girls in their yashmaks and flimsy robes served drinks. Bill, the barman, shook White

Ladies or stirred dry martinis, and the Nubian in his multi-coloured finery poured out cups of thick coffee from his minute brass-handled pots. Background music consisted of records of Arab songs which Samia had made famous and through which she now relived the atmosphere of the past in order to promote the atmosphere of the present. Under the ceiling a thin haze of cigarette smoke eddied with the lazy, shaking movement of the revolving fans.

The minute Samia saw me walk through the front door she slid over to the only empty table, which bore a card marked 'Reserved', and clicked her fingers to one of the girls. She didn't have to give any orders.

'We'll talk in my office,' she said as I sat down and sipped the inevitable champagne. 'But put on a front for a few minutes, then go into the inner bar. The balloon's going up. Freedman didn't come this time, but he did go to the frontier at Qantara.'

What was Freedman, the German spy, doing at Qantara, a staging post near the Suez Canal?

'Abbas Hatem has been back here – spending a lot. You remember him? General Masri has been around too. And so has someone else – your brother-in-law, Aly Sirry.'

'Quite a bunch,' I murmured. 'But why the panic?'

'Because the "bunch" – to use your word – are planning big things. There.' She finished her glass of champagne. 'You go into the second bar' – with a twinkle in her eye – 'as though you're a naughty boy.'

As I got up I asked casually, 'Is the Indian girl – Jasmine – still working here?'

'No,' Samia, who knew every rumour in Cairo, just said with a shake of her head. 'She left for India – in rather a hurry.'

The inner room – the *real* Sphinx – always had the boisterous atmosphere of a changing room after a tough rugger match, the girls giggling, though always with an eye to business. Halfway along the wall facing the bar was a small door leading to Samia's office with its two-way mirrors. Once we were squeezed into her room, I began, 'What's going on at Qantara?'

'Fifty camels sent by Freedman for slaughter in Egypt are passing through Qantara on Thursday next. A dozen or so will be branded with the Greek letter delta.' With her fingers she drew in the air the triangle which formed the letter delta, and which had given its name to the most fertile triangle of land in the world, the Delta stretching from Cairo to the north where it lapped the Mediterranean.

'And you're sure the camels are sent by Freedman?'

'Absolutely.' She lit a cigarette; she had always been a heavy smoker but recently she had affected a long ivory holder. 'But this is what makes this consignment so significant: Freedman isn't smuggling any hash on this trip.'

'How did you find this out?' I asked.

'Men like Abbas Hatem are always getting stoned,' she sighed. 'Then they tell all. He's definitely working for the Germans, and of course he's mad about the girl he thinks is a German at the Sphinx. He's even asked her if she'd like to be one of his couriers.'

'I hope she does. What's her name?'

'Anna. She's really Polish. Her mother and father were killed in Warsaw. Hatem's waiting for a message from Freedman — radio schedules. I don't know where their radio set is. All I do know is that he's loaded with cash — more dud fivers. You don't know the trouble I'm having trying to get rid of them.'

'Samia!' I pleaded, for she liked to digress. 'Stick to the point.'

'One thing Anna did worm out of Hatem — in bed, of course — is that they're planning for a big Egyptian fish to defect to the Germans. My guess is that the details will be in the camel together with the radio schedules.'

'If only we can find out without letting Hatem *know* we know.' I was thinking aloud.

'But the details, apparently, are all in one camel,' Samia went on. 'Yet a dozen are being marked with a delta, Hatem says. You can't slaughter a dozen just to find the right one. It'd give the game away to Hatem and Freedman immediately.'

Samia took another puff at her cigarette and asked, 'Do

314

you think the big fish is Masri? I'm told that he and Sadat have been meeting regularly.'

'I'm sure it is,' I agreed. 'But I'm surprised about Sadat.'

'And Aly Sirry has seen Sadat too.'

'Oh no,' I groaned. 'I told Aly to keep away from him.'

'You can't stop people meeting,' said Samia.

'How is Aly involved?'

'Curious. He recently bought a second-hand pick-up truck. You know, the sort they use for work in the desert.'

'What the hell would Aly want with a pick-up truck?'

'He didn't buy it for himself. He sold it.'

'How did you find out about this?'

'Since the outbreak of war anyone who sells any vehicle has to report the sale. It's just routine red tape to be filed away, but one of my informants who I pay in kind at the Sphinx thought it interesting that Aly Sirry sold the truck just two weeks after acquiring it.'

'Who to?'

'I'm almost sure it's Sadat.'

'Wouldn't be surprised. Thanks, Samia. You're a darling.' I gave her a quick kiss.

'Hope you find the right camel – though I don't see how you're going to.'

But I had a plan. Previously I had had a talk with an elderly, grey-haired officer called Captain Gregson, who would have looked more at home lecturing at Oxford than wandering about in khaki in Cairo.

Gregson was one of a team experimenting in dozens of ways to improve new techniques in the armed forces; some doctors were attempting new cures for burns, other experts were trying to discover how to tamper with radio techniques in the hope of misleading the enemy with false broadcasts, while men like Gregson were experimenting with mine detectors for use in the western desert.

'It's perfectly simple.' He showed me his metal contraption, which had a large ring attached to a metal box and a long handle, with a flex attached to earphones. 'Very sensitive. Here, let me try it out on you.' He ran the ring over my body, and when it touched my trousers, where I had a metal penknife in my pocket, the contraption gave a resounding bleep.

'Would it detect metal in the stomach of a camel?'

He looked puzzled until I explained how camels were used for smuggling hash in metal containers. 'Do they really do that to the poor camels?' he asked. 'How beastly men are.' He was convinced that by turning on the power to full strength he could succeed.

I had reported all the circumstantial evidence to my commanding officer, who gave me a free hand until we found the capsule — if we found it.

'But for God's sake make sure you cover up your tracks,' said the CO. 'Half the value of the operation will be lost if the Germans realise we know what's happening.'

I laid my plans carefully. I arranged to buy a camel which was taken just south of Port Said to the Qantara Frontier, Customs and Quarantine Station — to give it its full name. Hatem wouldn't be there, of course; as a warrant officer in the Egyptian army he would have no excuse to supervise the dozens of apparently innocuous camel caravans. His job would come later.

We found the dozen delta-marked camels with the others and placed them in a compound as if to await the virtually automatic passage through the customs. Once they were in the compound, my man branded the 'spare' camel with the same small blue triangle, and Captain Gregson went to work on the others with his metal detector.

At first I thought we were going to fail. Over and over again we couldn't raise a bleep.

'I hadn't reckoned with the thickness of the camel's flesh,' Gregson admitted. 'With a mine, it's just underneath a sprinkling of sand.'

The man who had branded the spare beast pointed out the exact spot where the rumen — the smaller stomach — led to the larger one. Capsules were always made large enough not to pass through the rumen, but they tended to lie at its bottom.

That was the extra information we needed. The eventual

bleep was so faint that even with earphones I could hardly hear it, but Captain Gregson cried, 'We've done it! This camel's got something inside it.'

The Qantara customs post had its own small abattoir where camels were slaughtered for random checks, and when the camel was cut open there was the capsule.

I let others wash the filth, then open the capsule and photograph the contents, after which it was resealed and forced down the throat of the reluctant replacement camel.

All this had taken only a few minutes, for speed was imperative. There were always plenty of civilians ready to report unusual delays.

The rest of the camels went through customs, sedately and superciliously, unaware that they were soon to be slaughtered.

The contents of the capsule were considered to be of such potential value that I was rushed from Qantara to GHQ with the photographer to attend a full dress conference. Even allowing for the laconic official language, the results were startling. The contents contained two alternative plans for General Masri to defect to the Germans. The vital part of the memorandum read:

> The third Saturday of month X has been designated for the operational flight of General M.

'Masri, of course,' commented Brigadier Monson.

'I like their subtle way of saying "defect",' I commented.

'This is really interesting,' the brigadier went on. 'Listen to this: "An Italian aircraft with RAF markings will land at dawn on the Saturday at the airstrip near Gabel Rozza on the Siwa Road west of the Qattara Depression. The general and one companion will proceed to the rendezvous in the pick-up truck already provided by S. The aircraft will proceed to Beirut."

'Still under Vichy France,' the brigadier pointed out. Then, reading aloud, he continued: ' "Overall responsibility for arranging the schedule will be arranged by S." '

'Who's he?' one of the other officers asked.

'Must be Lieutenant Sadat,' replied another aide. 'We know he's been seeing Masri, and when we learned this we arranged for the Egyptians to have him transferred to Mersa Matruh.'

'Has he gone?' asked Monson.

'Any day now, sir. He managed to delay the transfer by pleading sick leave. We're having him watched.'

'Not good enough.' Monson had a decisive way of speaking. Nodding to one of the other officers he said curtly, 'There's only one place for a really sick officer, and that's in hospital. Under supervision. Arrange for a doctor to examine this man.'

An unwilling Sadat went into a military hospital that afternoon.

Then came the instructions for General Masri. And they *were* instructions. There was no, 'It would be appreciated if the general . . .' or that kind of politeness. They were military orders:

General M will proceed immediately on arrival at Beirut to the radio station and start broadcasting anti-British propaganda to the Egyptian army. All scripts have been personally supervised by Dr Goebbels in Berlin. General M will later tour North Africa to make personal appearances and continue broadcasts.

In all, there were three minutely written pages of instructions, each one dealing with a different subject. The second contained an alternative plan in case the general failed to keep his rendezvous. Arrangements had been made with a young Egyptian officer, Squadron Leader Hussein Sabry, to steal a plane from an Egyptian air force base near Benni on the Fayyum Road, south of Cairo, where many of the personnel were bitterly anti-British.

The memo added:

This is not, repeat not, to be used except in extreme emergency, for the fact that an aircraft can be stolen from under the noses of the RAF will cause an immediate tightening of security, and we do not wish this to happen.

'That's as maybe,' growled Brigadier Monson. 'We have quite a few so-called dissidents in the Egyptian air force, well and truly paid to give us all the help we need.'

The third page was obviously meant for a German spy – with the codename 'Cheops'. It contained a detailed list of radio transmission times and wavelength changes. I told the brigadier I'd be asking Samia to find out more about this 'Cheops' – or at least about any clandestine radio reports.

'Is she to be trusted?'

'She told me where to find these, sir.' I tapped my copy of the documents.

'Carry on, Major,' he said, and at this point I stepped out of the picture and various departments went into action, so I only heard what happened next in fragments from different sources over the following few days.

First – now that we realised how Aly had been implicated in providing the truck for Sadat – an army mechanic tampered with the engine just enough to allow it to run a few miles out of Cairo before it would stall, and so make it impossible for the driver to keep the rendezvous with the Italian plane on the Siwa Road. What I didn't know was that, with Sadat in hospital, Aly had volunteered to drive the truck. British agents, suitably hidden, waited and watched as the Italian plane flew low over the rendezvous point, saw no truck, no recognition signals, and so turned back.

Aly was interviewed at length but was not arrested. However, a senior DSO officer went to see Sirry Pasha and told him what had happened. Sirry never really recovered from the shame of Aly's actions, but luckily, since my participation in the case was behind the scenes, he did not know of my involvement.

Masri then made his second attempt to defect. When everything was ready for Squadron Leader Sabry to steal the plane near Benni, an RAF engineer was sent to 'vet' the escape plane. British Intelligence had several pro-British Egyptian civilian employees pretending to be 'disaffected' at every Egyptian airfield, and the engineer did nothing that would

give cause for suspicion. He merely 'rearranged' the oil indi-
cator.

On the following Monday, with Sadat still in hospital in
Cairo, Sabry and Masri taxied to the runway. Just as they
were airborne the plane ran out of oil. Sabry assumed he had
switched on the oil, but the supply had been accidentally
switched off, and Sabry had to make a forced landing in a
tree near Benni. Both men were arrested, charged with high
treason, and later interned.

Sadat was also arrested – but though everyone knew he was
implicated he was able to deny all knowledge of the plot since
at the time he had been under supervision. He was released, and
was able to enjoy at least one more year of freedom.

For more than two weeks I had been underground, working
on what came to be known as the Masri case, and during that
time I was able to phone Serena only once, a guarded 'Hullo'
from Qantara. But she was able to give me one piece of news.

'I'm so glad you phoned,' she said, 'because tomorrow's
the big day for Greg. After almost six months he's going to
stand up.'

I was not present during the time of Greg's triumph, so I
only heard what happened from the people who were there.

Dr Collins had warned us all that even when the bones
knitted the legs themselves would be as wobbly as jelly. Greg
would need crutches for weeks, probably a metal stick after
that, with callipers fitted round his legs to give extra support.

He had been measured for these while lying in hospital.
The metal rods of the callipers were attached at the top
to strong leather trusses just below his crotch. There were
supporting straps at the knees and the bottom tips of the steel
rods were bent at right angles to slot into holes which had
been bored into the heels of two pairs of Greg's shoes.

Finally the ropes and weights were removed, and the pins
through Greg's legs pulled out under a local anaesthetic. Then
Dr Collins, his strong arms lending support, encouraged
Greg to make the first tentative move.

'Now, try to sit up,' said Dr Collins, as Serena told the
story. 'Because of the callipers you can't bend your legs very

much, so turn over on your stomach and slide off the bed like this.'

'I can't!' Greg was panic-stricken.

'Let me give you a hand.' Dr Collins tried to roll Greg over.

'No, no,' cried Greg. 'You could break them.' According to Serena he was sweating with fear.

'They won't break,' said Dr Collins. 'Don't be afraid.'

Still Greg hesitated. It was totally out of character.

'Come on, Mr Holt.' Dr Collins was growing a trifle exasperated, but trying to help, to understand Greg's fears. 'Why don't you put one arm on your wife's shoulders?'

'No, no! Leave me alone.' He brushed Serena away. 'I'll do it myself.'

It took a long time, but finally Greg did turn over, and as he slid off the bed attendants handed him the two crutches. Suddenly, as though by a miracle, a wobbly, frightened Greg was on his feet again. The fear was still there, and he found it almost impossible at first to take even one step forward, but he stood up.

'There! It wasn't so bad, was it?' asked Dr Collins.

'It was bloody awful!' cried Greg, but more cheerfully. 'I need a stiff drink. Serena, give me a double scotch, will you?'

After a look of doubt, she poured out a minute measure.

'Oh, come off it, darling,' he cried.

'Your wife is right,' Dr Collins advised. 'I wouldn't drink if I were you. Too much false confidence could be dangerous.'

'Come on, Doc! This is a celebration! Thanks to you I've got my legs again. Don't be a spoil sport.'

'Well, have your drink in bed,' suggested the doctor.

'No. I want to stand up, for a toast. Even if I *am* on crutches.'

Dr Collins was not too pleased. When later Greg had gone back to bed and was sleeping he turned to Serena and warned her gravely, 'It's still too early to say that *everything* will be a hundred per cent cured, but all the signs are that he'll make a complete recovery. On the other hand, if Mr Holt overdoes the drinking – if he stays out of bed too much for a few weeks – you know what I'm trying to say. His bones are getting tougher every day, but they need to be stronger still: that's why the callipers are there. You understand?'

'But I can't stop him from having a drink. He's very – difficult.'

'I know. And I realise that he's a grown man. But if I had him in my military hospital, there wouldn't be a drop of drink for miles around.'

It was ironic that when Greg started to walk again I was away on duty. And once again I was absent on a job when disaster struck. And so, once again, I had to hear the terrible story from Serena and friends.

No one will ever know what happened that afternoon when Greg fell down. He refused all attempts to wring an explanation out of him; all that any of us can do is piece together the fragmentary evidence as best we can. It seems that Greg had got out of bed carefully enough, helped by a nurse, and was now getting used to his crutches. But after the fall all he would growl was, 'Isn't it bloody simple! I fell out of bed.'

But had he fallen out of bed? Or had he stumbled while mixing drinks at his 'bar'? That was the obvious conclusion, because there were two glasses, a half-empty bottle of scotch, which Serena knew had been full when she had brought it to him earlier in the day.

All that anybody really knew was that Greg was found unconscious on the floor of his hospital ward. One of his callipers had been loosened – that he must have done himself – and the leg, stripped of all support, was grotesquely mis-shapen. The patient months of suffering which Greg had so stoically endured had been smashed in a drunken moment.

The hospital immediately rang up Serena, and it was from her that we learned what little there was to tell. Dr Collins came round as soon as he could.

'All that time, all that brave effort wasted,' Dr Collins told Serena, trying but failing to hide his bitterness.

'Does that mean' – she hesitated at the awful word – 'amputation?'

The doctor shook his head. 'No, my dear, he has been

spared that. But he will be in a wheelchair for the rest of his life. He'll eventually be able to walk a few steps with a crutch, enough to get from the bedroom to the toilet, or into a car, or perhaps to the dining room table. But that's the limit. If he takes more than a few steps, his legs will just give way beneath him. They'll crumple up. And then bones will start to break in other places. I'm sorry, my dear, especially as you've been such a wonderful and patient wife, but he will never be able to walk properly again.'

27

It was another three months before Greg was able to leave hospital – in a wheelchair. And during those months the fighting in the Middle East underwent dramatic changes in which the exultant voices of the victorious were drowned in a chorus of crushing defeats.

It had seemed so easy the previous autumn, especially when, after recapturing Sollum, Allied troops had achieved an almost impossible victory by the middle of February, 1941. In two months they had destroyed an Italian army of more than nine divisions, taking 130,000 prisoners and destroying 400 tanks and 1,300 guns at a cost of 500 Allied killed, 1,373 wounded and 55 missing.

When Brigadier Monson sent me for three days to Dehra Dun, I could hardly believe my eyes – not only at the mountain of enemy guns and tanks, often abandoned in perfect condition by Italians who also left behind stacks of clean sheets, silk pyjamas, *real* beds, beautiful blue cavalry cloaks, wine and Grappa and thousands of cases of Pellegrino water. And for the pampered officers of Graziani's army there was a convoy of plush motor caravans filled with attractive young women whose sole task was to pleasure the officers.

Back in Cairo the British basked in glory. At the Sphinx

Samia was even offering free drinks to officers of the 11th Hussars, distinguished by their cherry-coloured slacks, inevitably known as 'the cherry pickers', for these were members of the famous 7th Armoured Division which had spearheaded the fighting, and had also earned the nickname of 'The Desert Rats'. Cairo shopkeepers were coining money, their dislike of British occupation replaced by avarice as they sold anything from camel saddles to erotic postcards, especially to the free-spending Australians singing 'Waltzing Matilda' as they careered through Cairo, half a dozen sharing an ancient horse-drawn carriage.

After the blitz in Britain – the battering of cities like Coventry and London and Plymouth – we needed a morale-booster. We got it in North Africa, with British troops in command as far west as Benghazi. Cairo was safe.

But by the spring of 1941, hardly two months later, everything had changed dramatically. In the last week in March Brigadier Monson asked me to report to his office. I lunched first with a couple of fellow DSOs at Shepheard's. I remember the date particularly – it was 27 March – and I had just eaten a huge steak when I read in the *Egyptian Gazette*, 'The meat ration in Britain has from today been reduced to six ounces per person per week.'

'I want you to go to Alex and make your way by slow stages to Mersa Matruh,' said Monson without preamble.

'How long, sir?' I never asked reasons from the 'Brig'; he liked to explain things in his own way.

'A week or so. I just want you to drive around the various camps and listen to all the rumours. I particularly want you to report to me on the readiness of the troops for sudden fighting.' He hesitated. 'You know how it is after a string of victories.'

'Ready for sudden fighting?'

He nodded. 'There's been a bad botch in security. Not our fault; I refuse to accept any blame. But still – ever heard of General Rommel – Erwin Rommel?'

'Vaguely. Didn't he lead the panzer division that routed the French on some river – the Meuse?'

'That's your man. And he's a hell of a different proposition from Graziani, and old "Electric Whiskers" ' – he used the nickname for the Italian General Berganzoli, who had surrendered unconditionally.

'And I take it Rommel's coming here?'

'He's leading a crack new panzer division called the Afrika Korps. But you've got one thing wrong.'

'Sir?'

'Rommel's not *coming* here. He's already here – in Tripoli. With all his armour in position, and spoiling for a fight.'

'But he can't be here, Brig!' I burst out, using the name by which we all knew him but used only in times of great enthusiasm – or great stress.

'That's where Intelligence has buggered us up,' said Monson bitterly. 'Not DSO. General Wavell was horrified when he heard.'

'But how can a German motorised division land in North Africa without us knowing a thing about it?'

It was, as Monson explained, due to the British government. In the months before Italy entered the war Whitehall wanted to appease the Italians, and in the words of the official document which Monson now read out to me, 'HM Government wishes to do nothing that might impair the existing relations with Italy.'

'That directive was not rescinded until Italy entered the war,' explained Monson. 'And, of course, it applied to all the Italian empire in Africa. We weren't allowed to plant a single agent in Italy or North Africa until Mussolini declared war. There was no way on earth we could infiltrate men into the field for months. So Rommel chose the time, the place, and the first thing any of us knew about it was after the German troops had landed.'

According to Monson, Wavell believed that Rommel would be unable to mount any attack before May, though he did concede that it was possible the Germans might attack in April. In the event I had only just reached El Alamein by car when on 31 March Rommel launched his attack.

My orders had been to proceed slowly, and so when I remembered that Lt Nasser had been posted to El Alamein I thought I would look him up and see what his reactions were to our splendid victories.

He was enthusiastic enough. 'But I don't like the way your men strut about,' he said. 'As though they own our country. I will give them credit, though, as fighters. Maybe they don't think that *we're* to be trusted.'

'What do you mean by that?'

'Your Prime Minister, Mr Churchill, has ordered all Egyptians out of the war zones. It's an insult.'

It wasn't the moment to tell him that Churchill obviously didn't want the Egyptians around if we became involved in any heavy fighting because of their anti-British attitude.

'Any ideas where you're going to be posted?' I asked.

'Back to Cairo, I hope. At least I'll be able to meet my friends without British officers spying on us.'

'The Free Officers?' I remembered the name he had used to describe them.

'Don't laugh, Major. It's only a dream for the moment, but dreams have a habit of coming true. We've already laid the groundwork. I tell you this, Major Holt, because it's true, and I like you. You helped me. And I like your father, I respect him.'

'And Sadat?' I laughed. 'You know he just escaped going to jail by the tassel of his fez.'

'I heard about that. He's a bit wild, but a true Egyptian. I heard about his part in the Masri affair.'

'Tell him to be careful,' I warned Nasser seriously. 'Or the next time he *will* go to jail.'

'Sadat can take care of himself. He's the sort of man who'll end up in jail – or as President of the new Egyptian Republic.' It was Nasser's turn to laugh. 'I wonder which one.'

'Maybe both.' I laughed back. 'Come and see me in Cairo. I mean it. At home. We'll have a quiet meal together.'

At that moment two things happened. A signal from 'Brig' ordered me back to GHQ, adding, 'Expect you report tomorrow a.m.' At the same time the sirens started wailing, while the Tannoy warned, 'News has just reached us that enemy troops are attacking Benghazi.'

We were hardly in the firing line – yet. But the warning was clear, and I had time only for a cursory farewell to Nasser.

All I learned on that first Monday evening before I drove back to Cairo was that Rommel had broken through British defences at the village of Mersa Drega near El Agheila, and that the British had withdrawn, abandoning fifty armoured cars and thirty light tanks. Rommel was racing ahead in three separate mechanised columns: one on the road to Benghazi, two across the desert to Derna and the port of Tobruk.

During the next few days Cairo bordered on panic. Gone were the high spirits and the free drinks. Benghazi fell to Rommel. The 2nd Armoured Division, which had just arrived from Britain, had been decimated as a fighting force. The 3rd Indian Motor Brigade was overrun in its first action. The 9th Australian Division was trapped in Tobruk. Rommel raced ahead, taking Bardia, Sollum, Cappazo.

It was small comfort that while the Germans advanced on land the British navy won a notable victory in the battle of Mapatan in the Aegean Sea, sinking a battleship and five cruisers, with 3,000 Italians killed. But though it was heartening news, as far as Egypt was concerned, we were back where we started.

'Worse,' muttered Teddy gloomily. 'Old "Electric Whiskers" was one thing, but now we're up against the Germans – and look what they did to France.'

During all these despairing defeats I had been seeing Serena at the secret flat but – and this was not because our love was waning – we seemed to be going through a patch when our meetings became less frequent. For one thing it was now virtually certain that Sirry Pasha's beloved Nasrani would be requisitioned as a military base, and sometimes Serena had to go there with her father, to remove all sorts of personal property. For another, the rehabilitation of Greg seemed to be consuming more and more of Serena's time. On top of that I was promoted to colonel – presumably as a reward for my part in the Masri affair. And also, I was sure, because of my occasional dinners with Farouk; Brigadier Monson set great store on my 'friendships' in royal circles. As a colonel, I joined the 'Brig's' 'kitchen cabinet', where all secret information was assessed by Intelligence. The group consisted of only five officers and it, too, was time-consuming, especially in moments of crisis.

This was what happened when we learned that, on orders from Whitehall, nearly fifty thousand of our troops were to be transferred from North Africa to fight a lost cause in Greece. I remember when Brigadier Monson told us the shattering news. Benghazi had just fallen. Rommel was just – only just – on Egyptian soil. To divert crack British troops at this juncture seemed madness.

One colonel asked, 'Sir, which troops will be sent?'

'As far as I know,' said Monson, 'the 6th and 7th Australian Divisions, the New Zealand Division, the Polish Brigade Group, and what's left of the 2nd Armoured Division.'

'But that's almost everything,' someone said. 'Why, sir? Can you tell us that?'

'It's not for me to make guesses,' said Monson, unable to keep the bitterness out of his voice. 'Maybe the British government feels that, for political reasons, we must send help to the Greeks now that the Germans have invaded Greece.'

Though the news was highly confidential, the British Embassy had to be informed, which of course meant that Father knew. He was not only horrified but so depressed that he cried to me, 'Why, Mark? Just tell me that. *Why?* Do you think Churchill is to be trusted? And what about the reaction in Australia? It's just like Gallipoli all over again! Churchill didn't exactly cover himself with glory on *that* occasion.'

With rumours of withdrawal, an air of gloom seemed to invade every souk, every alley in Cairo. Sirry Pasha told us that Farouk was now openly boasting that the Germans were bound to win the war, adding, 'And I'll be delighted if they do kick the British out.' Poor Sirry freely admitted to my father that he had now been relegated to less important palace duties.

'I'm little more than a glorified flunkey,' he said. 'Something Aly did displeased Farouk, and he takes it out on me.'

Sirry Pasha still had no inkling that I had been concerned with the Masri case – and consequentially the involvement of Aly and Sadat. Even though the two men had been exonerated the slur had stuck, a black mark against the Sirry family. Was Serena a black mark too, I wondered?

Sirry had become old for his years. By 1941 he was sixty-three, and showing his age. His once sprightly step had become a slow, measured tread – only one degree above a shuffle – and he had stopped his regular walks, and used his car whenever he had to leave home. I think in a way he felt that, though he was reconciled to the virtual loss of Aly as a son, he missed the Serena he had loved even more. For Greg had once been so close to the Sirry family that marriage to Serena hardly made any difference to their relations. But after the accident, the months of suffering, the demands on Serena, even the rumours reaching Sirry Pasha about the girls from the Sphinx – all this had meant profound changes. Both families were on edge, the happy-go-lucky days of wandering through the gardens or weekends at Nasrani seemed as remote as childish dreams. The war was partly to blame with its daily dose of bad news. 'Gloom is as catching as flu,' said Sirry Pasha with a rare smile.

Even Madame Sirry had changed.

'I know it makes no difference to *our* friendship,' she said to Chiffon. 'But oh! How *could* the British be so beastly, killing all those Frenchmen at Oran?' She had never forgotten the British naval attack on Oran in which nearly a thousand French were killed when the *Dunkerque* was badly damaged.

'But think of that wonderful man de Gaulle,' said Chiffon, who loved the small contingent of Free French in Cairo, a city which we sometimes forgot had been stamped with French influence since the times of Napoleon. 'I adore their officers, so charming, and such good dancers. And de Gaulle!'

'An upstart!' snorted Madame Sirry. She was not exactly anti-British, but many of the French disliked the British in Cairo with their supercilious empire-building attitude, and in a way some French – especially those in France, I was sure – rather hoped the British would lose, if only to put them in their place. As one Frenchman told an Egyptian friend of mine who repeated it to me, 'The French people will never forget the humiliation of losing the war, but they'll never forgive the British if they don't lose it too.'

It was Serena, though, who suffered most for, since Greg's fall in hospital, he had grown impossible. I could, and did, feel deeply for him, for the despairing future in a wheelchair which he now knew lay ahead of him; but my heart really bled for Serena who had to put up with his tantrums and a new indulgence: waves of self-pity. Sometimes he would burst into tears, and if Serena didn't console him the pity would turn to unaccountable rages. And all this at a time when she was worried at the way in which her father was being virtually demoted by Farouk, while the king was letting it be known, through Sadik, that all would be forgiven if only Serena would . . . we didn't need to spell it out. As if that were not enough, there was Aly, growing more and more difficult. And just when she needed me most (or so I flattered myself) I was often unable to meet her, for work at DSO – secret by its very nature – increased week by week as the tide of war turned against us.

So it was that for one whole month I was sent to the Canal Zone, planting secret agents and organising hidden stocks of explosives in readiness to blow up the Canal should the Germans reach Suez. I arrived back from that assignment two days before Greg was due to leave hospital, and Serena and I spent the last night together in the secret flat.

It was a night filled with love and tenderness, for we both realised that this was the end of an era. With Greg back home, a permanent invalid, when if ever could we meet? Those evenings in the flat, bought at the expense of Greg's months in hospital, had been the nearest thing to perfection we knew. As we lay there, she in my arms, I was almost afraid to fall asleep lest I should miss one minute of her warmness enfolding me. I had started by counting the weeks we expected to be able to meet like this. I had reduced them to counting the hours, then the minutes, and now the seconds were ticking by, signalling the end of our happiness.

'Don't be sad, my beautiful Mark.' She turned over in bed and pressed herself to me. 'Just wait a little while, and we'll find a way.'

'I don't see how.' I refused to look on the bright side.

'You said that once before.' She was stroking me now, rousing me, in the middle of the night.

'Did I?' I turned over so that I was on top of her.

'Yes, you did.' She made way for me. 'There. Isn't it beautiful just lying, you inside me? Before we heard about this flat you hated the idea of sneaking off to cheap hotels. And then out of the blue – ah yes? Right in! It's so marvellous when you move slowly.'

We both moved gently, right to the end, and I can hardly remember our climax, it was as though we both came at the same moment, hardly moving, and I fell asleep on top of her, my mouth kissing one of her breasts. And that was how I woke.

It wasn't until I had made some coffee, early the next morning that she confessed, 'We'll have to find a way, but it *is* going to be a full-time job looking after Greg at home. And it's worse because he's so different, so bad-tempered. Sometimes I think he really hates me. And his arms, from using them to propel his chair, are like bands of steel. As though he's making up for the loss of his legs. He gripped my wrist the other day – I don't think he really knew what he was doing – and I swear one more squeeze and he'd have probably broken it.'

Chiffon was as upset as Serena by Greg's behaviour, though she didn't realise the actual fear that worried Serena; Mother just couldn't believe that her son, however cruelly mutilated, could strike terror into any woman, let alone Serena. But she could read the signs.

'He must take hold of himself,' Chiffon declared almost tearfully. 'My heart breaks for the poor boy.'

'And Serena. In a different way, she's also suffering.'

'How can you say that? *She* can walk. While poor Greg –'

'I know, Mother. I didn't mean that kind of suffering. But Greg's so changed. Frankly, he treats Serena abominably.'

Throughout the summer and into the autumn of 1941 the battle for North Africa swayed back and forth, though Rommel never quite reached Alexandria. Wavell was quietly succeeded by General Auchinleck as C-in-C Middle East, yet there was an unreality of the desert war in Cairo, even after the disastrous defeats in Greece. When, in May 1941, Captain Robert Crisp reached Cairo, surviving the German victory in Crete, he found himself playing cricket for the Gezira Club against an England XI, and hit the page one headlines in the *Egyptian Gazette* after he had taken Wally Hammond's wicket, to the applause of hundreds of troops watching lazily from under the shade of jacaranda trees. The truth was that 'our war' had taken a back seat in the newspapers because of the invasion of Russia in which, during the first stage that summer, more than three million Germans attacked along a front of more than a thousand miles. It was cataclysmic. By November the Germans were fifty miles from Moscow.

No wonder that the formation of the Eighth Army passed almost unnoticed, even when this new, integrated battle force raised the siege of Tobruk, and took Benghazi; for almost in the same week there was another stunning twist to the war that made us forget North Africa. Just before Christmas the Japanese navy and air force attacked Pearl Harbour without warning, with 350 bombers, torpedo planes and Zero fighters from six Japanese carriers. It was early on a peaceful Sunday morning, and the Americans were totally unprepared. Five battleships were destroyed, three more put out of action and ten other warships sunk or seriously damaged. Nearly 200 American aircraft were destroyed and 2,403 Americans were killed. Within hours Japanese forces were attacking Hong Kong, Singapore and the Philippines.

It was one of the greatest military disasters in history, yet it had its positive side, for as Brigadier Monson put it, 'Now at last America is in the war. We may have a lot of trouble ahead, but the combined force of America and the Empire are unbeatable. The Japanese must have been mad.'

During the long months of 1941, with Greg back home, Sirry Pasha had done everything he could to help. He had built a lift to the first floor in the Villa Zelfa, while the front steps in the garden outside the entrance had been cut down the middle; one half remained as they had always been, marble steps, but the other half had been rebuilt as a sloping ramp.

The hospital had found a male nurse, of whom Greg approved, and he had been given a room in the Villa Zelfa so that he could attend to Greg, lifting him in and out of his bath and performing other chores. Greg had told Serena that he wanted a bedroom and bathroom of his own. Thankfully, Serena had agreed.

I don't know how much Serena and he quarrelled after Greg moved into the Villa Zelfa, because in public he took the greatest care to try to conceal his crippled legs, often by the most ingenious arrangements. Though he couldn't climb stairs or walk more than a few feet, he could sit normally. So when entertaining he had worked out a plan. For drinks he would be seated normally, his dangling legs completely covered by a thin blanket, before the first guests arrived, so they saw nothing amiss. Just before dinner, at every party, he would invariably suggest amiably to Serena that the guests should go and look at the latest plant in his garden, or the improvements in the study – or whatever he thought of. Everybody always agreed – knowing perfectly well that in those few minutes the male nurse would arrive in the drawing room with a wheelchair, rush across the corridor into the dining room, and seat Greg at the top of the table looking perfectly normal, often crying cheerfully, 'Where's everyone? Come on! I'm getting peckish.'

'But the moment the guests have gone,' Serena said to me on one of our rare meetings, 'he complains about everything. The other night he tried to slap my face but I dodged. Just because I heard he'd been to the Sphinx. In a wheelchair!'

That was the night I said, 'Why don't you leave him? Not for me – not yet, not officially – but because of Greg. Cruelty is a perfectly valid reason for divorce. And darling, however much you try, he'll never be the happy-go-lucky man you married. I'm really worried for you. I think he's consumed with envy and jealousy because you're young and beautiful and he's –' I shrugged my shoulders. 'My fear is that one day when you can't reach one of us – he'll – well, something inside him will snap, and he'll attack you.'

'From a wheelchair? No, Mark, he might want to, but he'd never actually do that.'

I suggested to Serena that I should have a word with Greg, but she actually paled at the suggestion.

'No, darling. *Please*.'

'Greg would take criticism from me. He'd understand.'

'How little you know your own brother,' she said sadly. 'Of course he'd listen and understand.'

'Well, then –'

'To your face. But once you'd gone he'd take it out on me. He would, my love. Without mercy. He'd accuse me of going to you behind his back. He'd probably accuse me of sleeping with you.'

'Deny it.'

'I'm not a good liar. And anyway, he'd be livid. And then he might really attack me physically. No, darling, never talk to Greg about himself – or me. Promise.'

I promised.

28

By December 1941 the government had given formal notice to Sirry Pasha that Nasrani was to be requisitioned by the army during the first week in February, so Sirry Pasha tried to arrange a last weekend party for Saturday, 31 January, before the military moved in. It was one of those plans which seemed destined to go awry.

Greg didn't want to go, understandably, because he found a car journey uncomfortable. Aly wasn't to be found – perhaps he was consorting with his army friends as 'liaison officer'. Father expected to go, but was suddenly summoned to an embassy meeting to discuss the increasingly anti-British outbursts by Farouk, and what action should be taken on a diplomatic level. Chiffon would go, and I was secretly delighted with the turn of events, for a weekend without Greg and Aly meant that I would be able to spend more time with

Serena alone. Who knows, I thought, we might drive the few miles to Sakkara.

I arranged with Brigadier Monson for weekend leave and planned to drive to Nasrani on the Saturday, returning on Tuesday. Then I received the unexpected signal, 'Come'; and I knew what that meant: Samia wanted to see me urgently that Saturday evening. With Rommel poised on our doorstep, spy mania in Cairo had become an obsession and there was no way I could get out of the meeting. Apart from any feelings of 'duty' I knew that if by chance it was ever discovered that I had ignored a call from the best informer in Cairo in order to spend the weekend in the country, I would never operate as a DSO again.

However, as transport always presented a problem I was able to offer to drive the Sirrys with Serena, Jonothan and Chiffon to Nasrani on the Saturday afternoon in my de Soto, which I had bought after the crash. With its official pass stuck firmly to the windscreen, we could avoid all routine checks. I deposited the family, then returned to Cairo, promising to drive back to Nasrani on the Sunday morning and spend the day and two nights there. So at least we could salvage some time together at the start of 1942.

Back at Holt House, Zola opened the front door for me and said, 'Sir Geoffrey is on the veranda, Major – no, *sir*, sorry, Colonel!' He beamed at his skill in remembering ranks.

'A pity you couldn't spend the weekend at Nasrani,' said Father as I walked through to join him.

'You too.'

'Embassy. I hate going there. A lot of waffling. That's a new word I've just learned. But there's even talk of diplomatic reaction to Farouk. And you?'

'I've got a job to do at the Sphinx tonight. Orders.'

'Interesting?'

'Yes.' I nodded, and on the spur of the moment added casually, 'Care to come along? Just for a drink.'

'Really? You mean it? I wouldn't be in the way of your duties?'

'Not at all.'

'The inside bar?'

'Of course. But Father – just to see what it's like. I don't want to have you *and* Chiffon on my conscience.'

'You have my word! You know, my boy,' he beamed and opened another bottle of champagne, 'it's wonderful for a father and son to have such a relationship. Shall I put on my Egyptian clothes?'

'Better be on the safe side,' I nodded. 'Never know who we might run into.'

As he dashed upstairs to don the galabiya which he often wore at night he was like a schoolboy being taken out for a treat. I had made the suggestion on impulse – after an earlier promise, it is true – and at first I wondered whether I had done the right thing. But still, why not let him fill in a gap he had created in his fantasy world?

'Will the French girl – Crêpes Suzette – be there?' he asked when he came down.

'I imagine so.'

In many ways I will always remember that evening for the sheer happiness and excitement I was able to bestow on Father as a sort of gift; an unknown experience which he had imagined a thousand times in his life, but had never lived.

And the Sphinx! I knew I was on safe ground there – so long as I kept an eye on him.

At first as I pushed open the front door, accompanied by a man in a blue galabiya, Samia didn't recognise Father. But then she suddenly realised who he was and ushered us both to her own table, always reserved. 'How pleasant to see you, Sir –' she said, then stopped. Nobody used surnames in places like the Sphinx. 'And what brings you here?'

'Your music, my dear.' Father, gallant as ever, knew that they were playing one of Samia's old tunes. 'And you.' And I must say that on this evening she looked ravishing, in a kind of dissolute, tempting way.

'And nothing else?' asked Samia, almost archly.

'Well, a peep, eh? You know, my dear, I've never been to a place like this in my life.' As though it was a major confession, he added, 'Not even in Paris. I just want to experience a visit before it's too late.'

'You have chosen the best place in the world,' Samia smiled

at him. 'Though I must say,' she went on with a laugh, 'it's the first time I've ever heard of a son taking his father to a place like this.'

'I wanted to make my visit look more casual,' I said with mock-innocence.

'A good idea,' she said, almost laughing. 'Now, Mark, I want to talk to you in the office, but what I've got to tell you can be said in a couple of minutes. Why don't you take your "friend" into the inside bar, introduce him to one of the girls –'

'Crêpes Suzette?' asked Father eagerly.

'You can have her for all night,' laughed Samia.

'No, no. Just for a drink.'

'Meanwhile,' Samia suggested to me, 'you two can talk to each other in the bar for a few minutes, then come through. The girls will look after – our friend – I'm sure.'

I led the way from one room through the double doors to the next, from one world to another. My father followed me, closing the doors carefully one at a time, and took one look. A girl with beautiful bare breasts gave him an Egyptian, *'Ahlan Wa Sahlan, Pasha!'* He replied gravely to the welcome in the time-honoured fashion, *'Ahlan Biki!'*

He looked around. Most men had girls sitting at their tables, while some girls were on men's laps – a sign they had been booked, and were expected to go upstairs, or at least that the men would pay for the girls' time.

'What a splendid place,' he whispered. 'I'm so glad you invited me. Which is Crêpes Suzette?'

I had whispered instructions for Suzette to serve the 'unknown Egyptian', and she now came forward, bare-breasted and naked except for a short pleated Grecian skirt above her knees.

'I am, m'sieu,' she said.

She shook her peroxided blonde hair and giggled.

At that moment the half-hour struck on a chiming grandfather clock in the corner. As always, it was a signal for outbursts of laughter and boisterous humour by the males, for this was 'changing time'.

'Back in a moment,' Crêpes Suzette laughed, and vanished

behind the long white counter with all the other girls, to reappear almost immediately with a white blouse covering her breasts, but no skirt.

'Well,' cried Father, looking at her. 'I'd never have guessed! Black and white. Your – er – natural hair must be *very* dark, my dear.'

Crêpes Suzette whispered as she stood next to Father, almost leaning over him, 'It is very strong, m'sieu. Feel how strong it is.'

My father put a hand out towards her head.

'*Non, m'sieu! Ici!*'

'Now, Crêpes Suzette,' I said sternly. 'Behave! My father just came here for a drink, not to do anything.'

'*Oh, le pauvre! Ce n'est pas gentil!*'

'Don't give way, Father. I'm going to have a word with Samia. Back in a couple of minutes, then we'll make tracks for home.'

But I had barely begun discussing with Samia the latest information about the German spy codenamed Cheops – or the secret transmitter – when, through the two-way mirror in her office, she noticed a new – and unwelcome – visitor.

'My God, Mark! It's your brother Greg!'

'Jesus! And my father inside! Can you get him out – quickly?'

In her line of business Samia had learned the art of quick thinking, speedier action. 'I'll go to the front bar and hold Greg back for a bit,' she said. 'You get Crêpes Suzette to take your father upstairs to one of the bedrooms, and tell her to stay upstairs with him until Greg leaves.'

Fortunately Greg, with his wheelchair, took a fair time to manipulate the entrance.

'Does he go upstairs?' I asked Samia.

She shook her head. 'There's no way he can get there. But he often comes into the inside bar for drinks. Everyone knows him – and admires him, the girls tell me. Leave it to me.'

Through the mirror I could see that Greg had now passed the front door. Samia had walked into the outer office and grabbed his hand and was insisting on offering him a glass of champagne in the first bar. I dashed into the inner bar and said to Father urgently, 'There's a panic. Somebody coming in you mustn't see.

'Who?'

'Christ, Father! It's top secret,' I said. 'You must get out. No, not through the outer bar: the man's there, about to come in. Suzette, take my father up to the best bedroom. Now listen carefully, Father. You and Suzette will have to stay in that bedroom until the other man goes. Even if you have to stay all night.'

'All night!' He looked nonplussed.

'Don't worry, it won't be as bad as all that. Samia will come and see you and arrange everything. Come on now, upstairs. I'll disappear into Samia's office – I don't want to be seen either. When the coast is clear Samia will send a car to take you back.'

'In a bedroom with Crêpes Suzette – all night!'

'Well, not all night!' I took him to the foot of the stairs leading to the bedrooms. And then, because I loved Father, and he was having the time of his life, I added, 'Go quickly! And if anything *does* happen while you are forced to wait, nobody'll ever know.'

'But –'

'You *must* go quickly.' I was halfway up the stairs with him by now, and desperately anxious to hide myself. 'Just go.'

I ran down the stairs, looked back, and my last view of Father was when he reached a turn in the steps, turned and then – of all things, but with his own special brand of humour – gave me a quick Churchillian 'V for victory'.

I had planned to drive early to Nasrani the next morning and I was already up when Zola knocked on my bedroom door at seven and asked me, 'Sir Geoffrey wonders whether you'd care to join him for breakfast, sir.'

I had to go, to find out what had happened.

'I didn't arrive back until five o'clock,' he beamed. 'And I can't remember ever feeling so hungry!' He was wolfing his scrambled eggs, piping hot on his special double plate. 'I'm ravenous.'

I hesitated before saying jokingly, 'Sleep well?'

'Mark, my boy, I can't lie to you. I was fascinated. Do you know, in the end, when most people had gone home, we had a sort of feast in my room? Yes, some cold food, iced champagne, and *four* girls. In their pretty little white dresses – or half-dresses. All trying to force me to – well, enjoy myself, if you understand what I'm trying to tell you.'

'It's our very own secret,' I said.

Curiously, after breakfast, as I prepared to set off for Nasrani, I felt a strange pleasure, as if I had bestowed some precious gift to a friend. What had happened, I had contrived. But I had no sense of guilt, only the knowledge that I had gladdened the heart of this old friend, and I forgot that he was my father. I forgot, too, that his wife was my mother, for the whole experience had been delightfully innocent. And I knew it would never happen again.

29

I returned to Nasrani in time for lunch, and though we tried to be cheerful the knowledge that we had no idea when we would see the house again made us feel as though we were meeting a dying relative for the last time.

Further, the war looked like lasting for years, for it was global now, a line of killing with no end, like a death-ray along the equator. And when the war *did* end the world would be changed, we knew. Once a government gets its hand on land it never seems to relinquish its hold.

Arriving at the Delta lushness of Nasrani after the desert drive was like arriving 'home', for the estate had for so long been intertwined with our lives; and as though to mock our depression that Sunday afternoon it seemed to flaunt its delights to provide us with everlasting memories. I can't remember ever seeing so many pigeons before, even though the Delta has pigeons in, on and around even the humblest shack with special white dovecots built for the wealthier residents. When we drove round the estate in the battered old car, taking Jonothan on Serena's knee, a flock of pigeons, with an alarming sound of beating wings, almost darkened the sky.

We were making for the groves of date-palms beyond the brightly coloured beanfields and a large field of roses which Sirry Pasha grew to sell for attar.

Sirry Pasha grew nearly five hundred acres of date-palms, standing in lines like soldiers, the cultivated palms only forty or fifty feet high compared with the tall, wild trees. As he had explained to me when I was a boy, 'Every date-palm has a tax on it, and if they grow too tall they don't bear as much fruit. So we keep them pruned.' A carefully trimmed cultivated palm not only produced up to seven hundredweight of dates a year, but leaves to make baskets, beds and fans, as well as roofs for houses.

'What will your father do without Nasrani?' I asked Serena as we jumped out of the car for Jonothan to play in a field of clover.

'I can't bear to think about it,' said Serena. 'It'll break his heart. Nasrani is Papa's real life. Mine, too, I think. And what about these poor people, our friends as well as workers?'

All around us the fellahîn, young and old, were tending their own tiny patches of crops. The small children loosened the rich soil round beds of potato plants, tomatoes, cucumbers, melons, pineapples, using pronged sticks. The older ones were busy with narrow spades and forks.

'I suppose the real problem,' I said carefully, 'is that the war is getting closer to Cairo every day. And the army's got to prepare to defend the capital.'

'I understand that. But after all, this is productive land. I'd have thought Papa could have been more useful to the war effort by managing the estate and providing food than seeing that the king's hundred cars are properly polished.'

She stopped, looking in vain for a four-leafed clover, then got into the car. I lifted up Jonothan who was already toddling and saying his first words. He held out some clover crying,

'Mama!' then presented me with some saying, 'Papa!'

'Not quite,' I laughed. He called everyone Papa.

'Adopted!' She laughed back. Jonothan clapped his hands with glee, without knowing what we were talking about, but sensing our happiness.

Only when we were driving along did she say, 'What's so terrible is that all our lives seem to be crumbling around us.'

'The *world* is crumbling around us.'

'I know. But I can only see the world as we are affected. What will happen if the Germans win the war?'

'I wish I knew. I think Greg would be allowed to go free. After all, he's married to an Egyptian, and no danger to anyone.'

'And you?'

'I suppose a prisoner-of-war camp – unless I could escape. But' – with a short laugh – 'there'll be nowhere left to escape to.'

'America?'

'It's a long swim.'

'Oh darling, it's all my fault really, talking like this. I'm sorry. It may never happen. I just had a sudden fit of the blues. All I know is that, even though I don't see you as often these days, all my heart is yours. If only you weren't married, I'd take the plunge and get a divorce. But Parmi' – with a note of bitterness – 'won't she *ever* be kind to you?'

I hesitated before replying as casually as I could, 'I doubt it. By the way, I had a letter from her yesterday.'

'A letter! And you never told me.' She was too astonished even to be irritated. 'I think you might –'

'Don't worry.' I took one hand off the wheel and squeezed hers. 'I haven't read it myself. It arrived last night when I was working.' I had a sudden vision of 'working' with Father at the Sphinx. 'As you and I are married in all but name, I thought you should have the doubtful honour of tearing open the envelope and reading it aloud to me.'

'Do you really want me to open it?' she asked, pleased at the compliment.

'Of course. I just told you. You and I shouldn't have any secrets. Besides, I don't give a damn what's in the letter – unless they're divorce papers.'

'It won't be that,' she said bitterly. 'Not with Parmi's ogre of a father. But I'll bet she's not sleeping alone at night. It's the hypocrisy that sickens me.' She thrust the envelope into her bag. 'I'll wait until we get home.'

As I drank a scotch and soda after dinner, and we were alone on the veranda, she at last tore open the letter. Her voice was expressionless as she read out:

' "Dear Mark, It's a long time since I wrote to you, but that does not mean that I don't often think of you with friendship, and worry now that we are all in the war. Are you in the forces? And Greg? I can just see him in a dashing officer's uniform. Please write and let me have news. And of your family. I read about the terrible shortages in Britain. Even though we're now in the war, America is a rich country and if you have any problems foodwise in Cairo (or wherever you are) I will send supplies to you. I am the honorary secretary of a Catholic welfare organisation that sends Bundles to Britain, and I guess I could easily send a Bundle to Cairo. It seems so sad that our joint lives, which started with so many laughs, should have ended the way they did. And I have long since realised that I had no right to blame you. But something snapped in a way I was powerless to stop." '

Angrily Serena said, 'A fine Christian she turned out to be.'

'I told you not to bother to read it,' I said easily. 'It's like getting a letter from someone you don't know.'

'Not this bit.' She read on, subtly scornful, not so subtly angry. 'Listen to this: "When the war is over I would like us to meet again. Time heals many wounds." ' Mimicking, she repeated, ' "Time heals many wounds." I like that! I'll bet her boyfriend has let her down. She wants to come back to you.'

'Not a chance,' I laughed. 'Come on. We're going for a drive.'

'At this time of night?'

'Yes. I want to talk to you.' To the others I called, 'We're going to have a look at Sakkara in the moonlight. Come on,

Serena.' I gave no one a moment for discussion.

Sakkara was unchanged. This time we had no drinks with us; it wasn't a seduction.

'This is where it all started.' I kissed her gently, but tried to speak without passion because I knew I had to force a traumatic change on Serena.

'You don't think that in a way it all started in 1919 – and then when we caught typhoid together? And *all* our lives?'

'It *has* been all our life. But this is where we first made love – and that changed everything. We sealed our love here. Love, tenderness, joy, even guilt and remorse.'

'What are you trying to tell me?' she asked.

As we sat on the wooden steps of the Rest House, the date-palms black against a moonlit sky, I said, 'I promised you that there was no way I would go back to Parmi – if she ever wanted me. But I'm going to make a proviso.' To rob the words of any offence, I added, 'It's my legal training – covering myself.'

'And it is?'

I took a deep breath, hesitating longer than I realised.

'Well?' she asked. 'What is the important proviso?'

'Divorce Greg,' I said abruptly.

'Divorce? I wouldn't dare. Our families!'

'You'll have to.' I sat opposite her now, turning, holding both her hands in mind so that we faced each other, no thought of drinks, or lovemaking.

'Listen to me, darling,' I said. 'I will stay with you all my life, but you must make the first move.'

'But surely –'

'*Listen!* I'm deadly serious. You must divorce Greg. It's the only way. Then once you're free I'll come and live with you openly after a suitable interval. No nonsense. We'll move into the same house. We'll be married – in the sight of God if no one else.'

'And our parents?'

'Yes, I know, at first they'll be shattered. And then they'll accept it.'

'They won't,' she whispered. 'They'll never forgive us.'

'They will. Remember, Serena, I'm a lawyer. I've acted for

clients with marital problems since I left the Temple. In nine cases out of ten stubborn parents finish with tears of reconciliation. Legally, apart from anything else, you should divorce now.'

'Why *now*?'

'Well – the longer you put up with cruelty, the more the defence will suggest that if you could live with a man for so long he can't be such a beast.'

'It's such a terrible step – and Greg?'

'I shouldn't say this, but the way Greg's behaved – yes, I know the provocation, but I honestly believe it's dangerous for you to share the same house.'

'It would be so different if I were a girl alone – and if we lived in Australia or wherever. It would be so easy. We could just pretend. Nobody would ever know,' she said sadly.

'I don't *want* to pretend! I want to be proud of our love. I want everyone to see how happy we are. I want everyone to *know* that we would be married if only my bitch of a wife would free us. But if Greg, an invalid, was still your husband – and you left an invalid, a cripple, and had an affair with his brother – ah! That's different. People would despise us both. But if you divorce Greg, even in his state, if everyone agrees that it would be dangerous to live with him – then we could live together openly.'

'Why now?'

'I hate to sound mercenary, but from my point of view as a barrister the war excuses everything. Including unprofessional conduct because I'm not practising. I'm a soldier. The war will give Cairo time to get used to our love affair before I go back to the bar. It'll not only be accepted by then, it'll be forgotten.'

At first she said nothing, afraid, but then she told me something that horrified me.

'I know you're right,' she admitted. 'You're only putting into words what I've been thinking about for a long time. Especially last week.'

'Did he beat you?'

'Not quite.' I could sense the sad smile in the moonlight, rather than see it.

'But last week?'

'It was the final insult. I didn't mind him trying to slap me
– he *is* having a rotten time, after all – but last week –'

'Well – *what?*'

'He's got it into his head that Farouk and I have been
lovers.'

I burst out laughing. 'He must be mad! That man!'

'I laughed too, it was such an absurd idea. Although God
knows Farouk has tried hard enough. But then Greg took the
lift downstairs, armed with a pair of garden shears –'

'To attack you? Was he drunk?'

'I suppose so.'

I still didn't understand.

'It wasn't me he wanted to attack. It was my portrait. The
one the king tried to buy. *Your* painting. Our painting. He
slashed it, over and over again. He cut it to ribbons.' Suddenly
she burst into tears. 'I'll never forgive him for that. And
he kept shouting, screaming, "That's what I think of your
friend. Show him *that* when you next entertain him, you
whore."'

She was still crying, but less violently now, and as I leaned
over and kissed her I said, 'Let *me* tell Greg. He could be
violent. Let me break the news to him.'

'Never. That's something I must do. I'm not a coward.
And I'm not one of those wives who leaves a note on the
mantelpiece when she walks out on her husband.'

'I'm afraid.'

'Don't worry. I'll warn Hekmet. I'll tell her to expect
trouble, that Greg may have a violent reaction if he's drunk.'
The daughter of Serena's wet-nurse had worked in the Villa
Zelfa since it was opened.

That night, after we got back to Nasrani and the house
was in darkness, I whispered, 'I'll put on a dressing-gown
and come to your room,' and she nodded happily. Now
that she had agreed to the divorce I think we both felt that
a great fear had been removed, one that had been there,
often unspoken, since Greg returned home from hospital.
Perhaps that was why we now both slept so blissfully in
each other's arms.

The last thing I remember asking her was, 'When do you plan –?'

'As soon as we get home. We drive back on Tuesday, so Wednesday morning.' With a touch of happy humour she added, 'I'll make a note in my diary, the one you'll never see. "Wednesday, 4 Feb, decided to divorce Greg and go to live with Mark for ever." '

4 February! Little did we know what a vital day it would be – not only for us but for King Farouk and Nasser and all Egypt.

30

I awoke on Wednesday with an awful feeling of bad news in the offing. At first I couldn't pinpoint it, just as when I was a child I would sometimes wake up knowing I had done something wrong and would face an unpleasant day. Of course! As Zola brought me my morning tea and a copy of the *Egyptian Gazette*, I remembered. Serena's confrontation with Greg: I wouldn't be there, but I dreaded the prospect.

Sipping my tea I glanced at the *Gazette*. In the Pacific the Japanese had occupied Manila and invaded Burma. There were some atrocity stories following the fall of Hong Kong. Singapore seemed on the point of surrendering, as did Rangoon. In the Crimea the German offensive against the Russian armies continued without respite. What an utterly depressing day!

Throwing the newspaper on the floor I showered then dressed quickly and made my way to GHQ, where I asked if I could see Brigadier Monson. 'Only for three minutes,' I told the sergeant. Normally I never met the brigadier except at our conferences or when laying plans for a 'special job'. Monson preferred to leave each of us to pursue without interference any chosen line of enquiries, having first given him the broad outline. However, for some reason on this morning we had been told to keep in touch with GHQ and advise of any unexpected departures. And I had decided to ask for an extra day off. I wanted to go to the Villa Zelfa in spite of Serena's pleas not to interfere – because, frankly, I was frightened for her.

Normally the 'Brig' would nod his assent, knowing the long hours we often worked. This time, he studied his yellow army-issue pencil, twirled it round, then looked up and said, 'Sorry, Mark. I'm afraid it's no go. Tomorrow any good?'

I shook my head. 'May I tell you the problem?'

'It won't help,' he said dryly.

Briefly I explained what was about to happen.

'I'll tell you why I've got to keep you on tap,' he said. 'There might be gunfire in Cairo before the day's out. Including the Abdin Palace. No, I'm not exaggerating. And you'd be required for special duties – you especially. I can't say more than that.'

'The *king*, sir?'

He thought for a moment before saying, 'Yes, the king. Can't say more. Sorry about your sister-in-law. When did you want to see her? This morning? Well, tell you what. Return home, and stay there unless your sister-in-law sends an SOS. Give me her phone number, so that I can contact you if you go there.' He scribbled down the number of the Villa Zelfa. 'After all, everything's within a five-minute radius. If the balloon goes up I'll get you either at home or at her place. But no going out for a drink – not even in your garden. I might want you urgently.'

'Thank you, sir.' I was dying to know what 'balloon' might go up, but Monson wasn't the kind of man who invited questions. Besides, he might not know the details himself. I phoned Serena and whispered, 'I'm staying at home in case you need to phone me.' Then I rang off. There was always the danger of someone listening in on an extension.

The shrill stammer of the phone came around half past ten. It was Hekmet, the servant. She screamed out just one word, *'Nakba!'*

'Disaster?' I echoed. 'What's the trouble?'

I could hear vague sounds of screams, shouts, a cry of pain, all filtering through the telephone, which had obviously been left dangling off its hook. I raced for the front door, jumped into the de Soto, crashed in the gears and tore across the Kasr el Nil Bridge, klaxoning furiously, dodging carts, donkeys, scraping one handcart but not stopping for a moment. I thought of nothing, saw nothing, until I screeched to a halt at the villa and raced across the slippery marble hall to the sounds of anger and fear upstairs.

At the far end of the hall was the marble staircase – perhaps twenty broad steps – leading to the first floor. It wasn't really a landing in the normal sense, and originally had been a huge first floor, with the staircase leading to a room used in the old days as the Turkish equivalent of the harem where ladies entertained. Princess Zelfa had changed that by cutting a large oval well in the ceiling so that she could peer down at the entrance hall below. The well – for want of a better word – was perhaps twenty feet long, ten feet across at its widest point, surrounded by a railing, except where it met the top of the staircase.

This first-floor room was so spacious that even as I raced up the stairway I realised there was more than enough room for Greg to career round, aiming his wheelchair wherever he wanted.

I reached the top of the stairs to be greeted by an astonishing scene. Halfway along the oval well was Greg, purple with rage. Serena was at the other side, ready to run in the opposite direction if he moved towards her. He did now, screaming, 'You bloody whore! You dare to divorce a Holt!'

One sound of his voice told me he had been drinking. I ran towards him and tried to grab the wheelchair, but he slipped out of my grasp. Serena was now at the other end of the well, farthest from the stairs. Hekmet was closest, and when Greg raced away from me she tried to hit him with a broom handle. Greg wrenched the broom from her and hit her across the back with such force that the handle broke. She fell to her knees screaming.

I realised immediately what I had to do. Because of the terrifying way he manipulated his wheelchair, making sudden switches of direction no one dared approach him. But there was no way he could get down the stairs; he could only reach the ground floor by the specially installed lift at the back of the room, so if only we could reach the stairs we would be safe – with time enough to get out of danger, even perhaps to immobilise the lift.

I shouted to Serena as soon as she saw me, 'Make for the stairs! I'll try and keep him occupied.'

Only Greg was too quick. When he had first spied me at the top of the stairs he had tried to run me down, propelling himself forward with those incredibly strong arms of his. But when he saw Serena make for the stairs he twisted round to block her only hope of escape. She ran back, so that she was leaning over the rail at the far end of the well, ready to run in either direction. Hekmet just lay moaning in a corner.

'For Christ's sake, Greg,' I gasped, trying to approach him from behind. I had vague thoughts that I might be able to tip up his wheelchair so that Serena could slip past him to the safety of the hall below. The plan nearly succeeded, as with a bellow of rage Greg suddenly decided to back his chair up against me. I was hit full in the stomach, almost winded by the unexpected move, but as I fell I managed to shout to Serena, 'The stairs! Now!'

Hekmet managed to escape, but like lightning Greg shot his wheelchair forward again, blocking the top of the stairs as Serena ran back to the opposite end of the well.

'Keep out of this,' he shouted.

'Leave Serena alone!' I could only gasp back. To my astonishment, at that moment he *laughed*.

'You're drunk!' I cried, trying to taunt him to attack me and give Serena a chance.

'You'd be drunk if your wife spent all her time in bed with a fucking Egyptian.'

Rising painfully to my feet, I said firmly, 'You damn fool. Leave her alone.'

'Just get out of my house.'

Without warning, as though forgetting me, Greg pushed off towards the other end of the well, hoping to grab Serena.

Once more there was a chance.

'Make for the staircase,' I shouted again to Serena.

Immediately Greg spun his wheels round and started to race straight towards the main stairs. It seemed incredible that he could travel so swiftly, switch direction so deftly, all from the power of his arms.

Serena had almost reached the stairway – the only gap in the railings – when she slipped. I felt rather than saw Greg's shadow above the fallen figure, as Serena tried to scrabble her way to safety. I too stumbled, but on the broom handle with which Hekmet had tried to fend Greg off. As I righted myself, I picked up the broom handle and hurled it across the open space.

It hit Greg on the back of his head. He seemed impervious to pain, just stunned with rage, but in that split second Serena was able to make the stairs, almost falling down them, but grabbing the banister rail just in time.

'You bastard!' Greg screamed, his arms twisting the wheels round and careering the chair towards me. He almost skidded round the edge of the railings as I tried to run. But I couldn't get round the corner of the railings in time, and in a moment I was trapped.

'For Christ's sake, stop it!' I tried to force out the plea, but as I felt the dizziness, the lack of breath, I somehow struck out a foot and kicked at Greg's paralysed legs.

It was instinctive, but now it was Greg who screamed – from anger or pain, I didn't know which – and with barely a second to spare I pulled away from him. Greg stopped only a moment to gather himself, then swivelled round and turned on me, all pain forgotten.

As he rushed me again, I sidestepped. He managed to grab an arm but again I kicked myself free. It was a struggle between his arms and my legs, for I couldn't grip him anywhere – he was too elusive, too quick on the turn.

Then it happened. I pretended to try and escape down the stairs, but as he cut off my escape I switched direction. For once he didn't move quickly enough. He chased my back, so that I never saw the actual moment he lost his balance.

Turning round, I caught sight of Greg's terrified face, saw the frenzied scrabbling of his fingers as the wheelchair teetered on the edge of the stairway.

351

It was too late. His screams mingled with the crash of tearing steel, just as it had done on the road to Alex. As I looked over the railing, Greg was thrown clear of the wheelchair, but it seemed to follow his body, to chase it, tumbling over and over until the smashed hunk of metal skidded halfway along the floor, to leave Greg lying at the foot of the stairs.

I can't remember who reached him first. I can't really remember anything. Servants, terrified by the screaming and fighting, slowly crept from their hideaways. Serena ran into the hall, presumably from the kitchens where she had been trying to get help. It was a signal for the others to emerge. I almost fell down the stairs in my eagerness to reach Greg before she did, to hide from her the ugliness of his crumpled, bleeding body.

I knew before I reached the hallway that he must be dead.

Serena was sobbing, crying, 'It was all my fault.'

'No, it wasn't,' I said. 'Don't look. We've got to do something.'

My training had long since made me view sudden death dispassionately; but not this time. This was my brother, Greg, the 'sporting hero' dogged by bad luck all his life – an unsuspected heart problem, a car crash, a cripple, even impotency. Poor old Greg: no wonder he took refuge in the bottle. Despite the savage fight I had to hold back tears as I bent over the crumpled heap of bones. I needed only one look to see that he had broken his neck.

'Shouldn't we carry him somewhere – another room – or –' Serena sounded almost hysterical.

'Leave him here for the moment,' I said gently. 'I'll call the doctor. Why don't you go and sit down in the drawing room? Get some coffee. I'll come and fetch you after I've made a couple of phone calls.'

Face drawn and white, she said, 'I will. But Mark, though I said it was my fault it wasn't. He *had* been drinking. He even had a big glass of neat vodka before breakfast.'

'Don't worry,' I reassured her. 'I could tell that the moment I set eyes on him. Go on now; I'll look after everything here.'

I did have cause to worry, in fact, because I felt the doctor should see the body before it was moved. Also, the family had to be told – and yet, hanging over me like a threat, was the expected call from Brigadier Monson. But as I made for the telephone I was thinking of something else: if the brigadier hadn't let me come here Serena might not have been alive at this moment.

I telephoned Dr Phillips and told him what had happened. Next I telephoned Father, told him that Greg had fallen accidentally – and fatally – down the stairs and asked if he had the courage to tell Chiffon.

'I'll tell her.' I could hear the anguish in his voice.

Sitting down with Serena in the drawing room I tried to comfort her, but I had to warn her too – 'I'm expecting to be called away at any moment. In fact I shouldn't be here, but Hekmet called –'

'I know. Thank God you came. I hope she's all right.'

'Only, Serena, I may *have* to go. There's a big flap expected in Cairo. It was terrible, darling – but take some consolation, if you can, that it was over so quickly.' I hesitated, almost praying that the phone would ring, summoning me back to GHQ. 'There's nothing we can do now except wait for the doctor. And my parents.'

I called to one of the servants to bring some brandy, and after we had taken a stiff gulp each we perhaps felt a little better. I would have liked to have gone into the garden, to have talked to Serena quietly, away from the anguished faces of the servants, but I did not dare stray from the telephone. For there was something I had to say.

Finally, after the second drink, I said to Serena, 'What happened was merciful for Greg.' I paused, to let my words sink in. 'Apart from us there's Chiffon and Father. How much better for them that this should have happened instead of Greg ending up a drunk. And he would have got worse. To all the world it was an accident. No one will ever know that this morning you asked him for a divorce – or what really happened. It's ironic that by letting our families keep their illusions, by hiding the truth, our paths will be made easier.'

The telephone rang before she could utter another word. I knew it was GHQ.

'Must you go?' she begged me. 'I'm so frightened – and alone.'

'Don't make it harder.' I put my arms round her, then walked quickly over to the phone. It was the call I'd expected.

'Yes, Sergeant,' I said into the receiver, 'I'll be right over.' Putting it back on the hook, I said, 'Bear up, my beloved. And don't think ever again of the past. Look to the future. It's our only hope.'

31

Within five minutes of my arrival at GHQ Brigadier Monson summoned his five closest aides for a working lunch of sandwiches and army coffee sent by the NAAFI. Around me sat five officers anxious for news of the mysterious flap – well, four officers, for frankly at this moment I was past caring. I had to be there, but only to go through the motions until I was able to get a proper grip on myself.

One of the others eyed me curiously. I must have looked a sight. There was blood on my hands which I wiped away with my handkerchief. My tie was undone, but I hardly noticed. Before my unfocusing eyes swam the picture of Greg at the foot of the stairway, and the anguished face of Serena, half fainting with terror. My body felt as though it were held together with elastic bands, with about as much co-ordination as a rag doll's. I ached from head to toe after a physical assault of such ferocious intensity that I was lucky to be alive, and my head was splitting.

As we waited for the 'Brig' to arrive, one of the officers muttered to me, 'You look bloody awful, Mark. Been on the tiles?'

I was still wondering what to say when Monson strode in. Nothing escaped his eyes. He took one look at me and said,

'I see your presence was necessary.'

'Very much so, sir.' I told him and the others that my brother had been killed in an accident, and left it at that.

'I'm sorry about that, Holt. I can see why you look all in. Wish I could release you. But you've been earmarked for a special role. I'll get you off-duty as soon as I can, but I know you'll understand that I wouldn't keep you here if I could avoid it.'

'I'll be all right, sir,' I said.

'Good.' He knew that work would be good for me. 'I wouldn't want you all to miss this, but I didn't want to start any rumours too soon. What I have to say is for your ears only.' He paused, not deliberately – or was it? Nonetheless it added drama to the moment when he announced, quietly, 'Gentlemen, plans have already been prepared to attack the Abdin Palace at twenty-one hundred hours and force His Majesty to abdicate. The ambassador has given the king until nine this evening to form a Wafd government, or else – well, if there's any trouble, British tanks will go in.'

With a buzz of excitement bordering on incredulity we all waited for details. I was not alone in having felt for some time that some crisis involving the king might blow up. Egypt was filled with pro-Axis sympathisers. Students even paraded with banners 'Long Live Rommel' and 'We are the soldiers of Rommel'. I knew that Farouk, now twenty-two, wanted to appoint the violently pro-German Ali Maher as his new premier. The British ambassador, Sir Miles Lampson, had warned the king that only the Wafd Party under Nahas Pasha could control the internal bitterness in Egypt. And Farouk hated Nahas Pasha.

But a palace coup!

'In fact,' 'Brig' told us over that memorable sandwich lunch, 'the ambassador warned the king that unless he does instruct Nahas Pasha to form a cabinet Farouk must expect the consequences.'

Farouk, it seemed, had flatly rejected the ultimatum, but when he began to realise that Lampson wasn't bluffing he did try to form a coalition under Nahas Pasha in the hope that this would satisfy the British. It might have, but it didn't satisfy Nahas, who insisted on choosing a cabinet consisting entirely of Wafdists.

'There's no doubt that Nahas Pasha is the only man who could control the pro-Fascists,' said Monson. 'And help Egypt by helping Britain. Of course, to the king he presents as great a menace as we do.'

The brigadier then outlined in some detail what had been planned. Somehow, inevitably in Cairo, instinct had already warned the people that a crisis was in the offing. More and more students were marching round Abdin Square with even more banners: 'Down with the British!' and 'Long Live the King!'

With Farouk convinced that the British would never dare attack the palace it was imperative for us not to present a show of force until the actual moment of confrontation. So a convoy of armoured vehicles would set off as a decoy towards the pyramids, and presumably for Alexandria. They were to take good care to advertise their presence, passing close by Abdin Square for all to see, but skirting it. Meanwhile we would be waiting.

At the very last moment – half an hour before the deadline of 9 p.m. – a battalion of men armed with Sten guns would surround the palace. Four tanks had been earmarked to move into Abdin Square. The ambassador, when he arrived at the palace, would be accompanied by a platoon of officers with drawn revolvers.

'It's absolutely imperative that Intelligence is kept fully in the picture,' explained Monson. 'The embassy has agreed that we shall supply two of the officers accompanying the ambassador.' He named one other officer of his kitchen cabinet and then turned to me, 'You, Colonel Holt, will go too, because you know both the ambassador and the king, and you speak fluent Arabic. And because the king knows you – in case he needs assistance. The plan, if the king abdicates, is to get him out by the back door.'

'Do you think he will abdicate, sir?' I asked.

'Dunno. But Lampson hates Farouk so much that he'll probably be disappointed if he doesn't.' He looked at us, then at his watch, and said, 'Right, let's go to work then.'

At 7.30 p.m. we duly met to take up our positions. The sense of impending drama was so intense that I actually found myself, almost without realising it, downing a neat triple scotch in one gulp. Though it might seem callous to say so, Greg's death, and the horrors that had attended it, seemed part of another world.

'Right!' We set off in our khaki-camouflaged armoured cars, behind the squadron of four American-made Stuart Mark III tanks. They waited in a back street, then noisily moved into position facing the gates and railings of the palace grounds. We waited in the armoured cars for the moment when the ambassador arrived.

At exactly 9 p.m. the ambassador's yellow Phantom III Rolls came sedately to the front of the palace gates, preceded by an armoured car. From the sidelines I could see everything. The armoured car stopped, as though waiting for someone to open the gates.

The hesitation was short-lived. If anyone gave an order I never saw or heard it. The gates were closed, of course. The armoured car revved up, then lurched forward. There was a grinding sound of metal as it smashed through the gates. The six members of the 'bodyguard' were still in our cars and we were soon following the Rolls along the path to the front doors of the palace itself. We jumped out and ran ahead, revolvers drawn.

The astonished guards made no attempt at resistance and were quickly disarmed.

As Lampson reached the top of the broad stairway leading to the king's study on the first floor, a chamberlain in frock-coat barred his way and I heard him beg Lampson, almost in tears, 'Not this way, Sir Miles! Not with soldiers.'

Lampson – six feet six inches tall and weighing twenty stones – didn't even bother to respond, but strode straight into the king's study, a sombre room lined with leather-bound books, mahogany everywhere, and a few priceless knick-knacks dotted on empty sections of the polished shelving. Yet this critical moment, which would decide for years the future of Egypt, turned out to be a total anticlimax.

Farouk was sitting behind his huge desk.

'I have come for Your Majesty's reply.' Lampson glared at the king. Even normally the ambassador had a belligerent look, but his appearance was even worse on this evening because of a painful sty on his right eye.

Farouk looked around. I saw a faint smile of amusement as he recognised me, and then Lampson was reading from a prepared text, accusing the king of breaking the 1936 Treaty by encouraging politicians to hold power while he knew they were working against the British and openly supporting the Germans.

'You have also flouted democratic ideals,' said Lampson, 'by refusing to appoint a government which has popular support. By these and other acts Your Majesty has jeopardised the security of Egypt, and are unfit to rule.'

Farouk said nothing. I am sure he found it hard to believe that Lampson would dare to force the issue, convinced that it would lead to open rebellion in the streets. Perhaps Lampson saw the hesitation, for instead of presenting the abdication form politely, he scornfully threw it on the desk.

The abdication had, by a curious coincidence, been drawn up by Sir Walter Monckton, who had worded a similar document for King Edward the Eighth, and who happened to be in Cairo.

Farouk picked up the form with disgust, and then made an astonishing remark – astonishing, considering the circumstances. 'Isn't it rather a dirty piece of paper?'

Almost at the same moment he picked up the pen to sign the document which would end his reign, then suddenly changed his mind, as though tired of being treated like a flunkey by Lampson. He threw the pen down and said coldly, 'I shall send for Nahas Pasha and ask him to form a government – of his own choice. The audience is ended.'

Lampson looked flabbergasted, and I couldn't help but admire Farouk's composure, as the king turned his back on us and walked out of the room without a backward glance. Lampson, his face puce with anger, had no choice but to stalk down the stairway, and we followed.

Considering that he was only twenty-two the king had

behaved with far more dignity than I would have believed possible. And he was still in office – if only just.

I personally have always felt that Lampson was not the best diplomat to have in Cairo during those troubled times when the Germans threatened the country. He could be bluff and genial when it suited him, but in his later years he was not only overweight but ponderous, and easy to lampoon in the vernacular press, which hated him. I felt as Sirry Pasha did – that it would have been almost as easy to force the king's hand politely instead of slapping his face in public. And that scene on that historic day – or rather, the way it was conducted by Lampson – was never forgotten, never forgiven by Egypt. It was a turning point.

I think Nasser summed it up a few days later when we met in Cairo. He had now been promoted to captain and posted to Cairo as an instructor, where he had an unrivalled opportunity to sift out sympathetic officers.

'I know *you* understand the Arab mind, and what has to be done in war,' he said. 'But the way your fat man Lampson handled it was not right or proper. Wasn't it your essayist Thomas Carlyle who said that manners maketh the man? You can't get away with spitting in the face of a head of state.' Sarcastically, he added, 'Even if he *is* only an Arab he's still a king.'

Within a few days of the Abdin Palace confrontation Nasser officially decided on the name 'Free Officers' and no would-be revolutionary could have been given a more compelling urge to join Nasser's movement. 'Lampson gave us the chance on a silver platter,' he said. 'If – no, not if, *when* – the Free Officers take over Egypt, we will have to offer a special prayer of thanks to your ambassador. For everyone in Egypt knows how he insulted our king – and that means Egypt – and it's provided just the spark we needed. Who knows,' he added with a rare smile, 'one day we might even get our Canal back – thanks to Lampson, who gave us life because he was vindictive.'

32

The months skidded by to the summer of 1942. By July Rommel was at El Alamein, an easy two-hour drive to Alexandria. A forward patrol of the Afrika Korps tanks had reached Burg el Arab, even closer, a few miles from Alex. The demolition gangs were ready to blow up military installations in the port while the British fleet had gone, seeking more safety on the high seas than in Alexandria, with its threat of bombs aimed at sitting targets.

Globally, the picture had never looked more depressing. If Alex went Malta would surely be lost, and with it the last vestiges of our sea power in the Mediterranean. And with the Germans in control of the Suez Canal, India would be threatened on both flanks – from Japan in the east, from Germans and Italians in the west.

Once again, Cairo started to panic. Only with the greatest difficulty could the military police keep the roads free from the choking chaos of refugees. British families were evacuated when possible, often to South Africa. From our house in Garden City I could see columns of smoke from the next building like sinister smoke-signals: the British Embassy officials were again burning confidential papers.

Then suddenly there was a lull. What we didn't know was that Rommel's troops were so exhausted after their incredibly swift offensive that they could not fight another hour, though they could have reached Alex in two days. If the respite didn't give the British enough time to reinforce their positions it did at least give us all the chance to breathe. The imminent fall of Alexandria didn't materialise. As swiftly as the panic had started, Cairo again began to breathe more freely. The shops reopened, the advertisers paraded their wares in the columns of the *Gazette*. Alex had been saved!

And how could you take war seriously when you were pampered with luxury – food, servants, Taittinger champagne – anything? For Sirry Pasha's birthday I had no trouble in buying fifty of the finest Partagas Havana cigars from Amar, the tobacconist in the Kasr el Nil. The price of a 'celebration dinner' at the Waterloo Club, the exclusive meeting place for warrant officers and sergeants, was reduced by 5d. And after dinner you could go to see Humphrey Bogart in *All Through the Night* at the Metropole, or Ann Sothern in *Lady Be Good* – if you queued.

The *Egyptian Gazette* announced that Dr Levy-Lenz, 'the finest specialist in plastic surgery', had returned to Cairo from abroad 'and is now receiving patients at his clinic in Groppi's building'. The department store Orosdi-Bak in Abdel Aziz Street (which liked to describe itself as 'the Selfridges of Egypt') announced a complete new range of 'foreign-made' fabrics, furniture and clothes. In all those bewildering memories of the lush life behind a hedge of bayonets I can remember only one slight discordant note.

'Look at this!' cried Serena, laughing. 'Now the war's really hitting us.'

'This' was an advertisement inserted by the Nile Cold Storage in Soliman Pasha Street, which read, 'We regret that we cannot supply any more Rose's Lime Juice until the war is over.'

The tragedy of Greg's death was still fresh in our memories that summer, yet for Father and Chiffon the loss was harder to bear than for Serena or myself. We of course knew the facts; they did not. It never entered the heads of either set of parents that the terrifying morning of hate had been anything other than an accident. So though all four were shocked and distressed, they were spared the final indignity – the truth. And they were also able to seek some solace in the knowledge that death had at least spared Greg from a life of misery in a wheelchair.

During these months Serena and I met alone only occasionally – sometimes at the secret flat, sometimes at the Villa Zelfa, which Serena insisted on keeping on. Her parents thought it was morbid, and so it was, but there was a reason behind the decision. All the servants slept out of the house with the exception of Hekmet, who had become Jonothan's nanny. And when I wanted to pay a discreet visit to Serena – usually late at night – she would arrange for Hekmet and the baby to have what she called a 'treat' – a night spent being fussed over by Grandmama. We had to do this because we couldn't use the secret flat for several weeks, as Teddy was sent to Alexandria and I couldn't afford to be seen going to his place when it was empty. There were spies everywhere.

Even then there were times we couldn't see each other for days – or rather nights – on end. Fortunately both of us in our different ways were able to help wipe out the trauma of Greg's death. I did it by working hard. Serena had her own way of blotting out what she called 'black moments' – by painting. She was painting more and more now, and becoming better with every canvas she filled. There was talk about a second one-woman show by Monsieur Laffont who owned the gallery which had first shown her work and was convinced it would be another sell-out.

Sometimes she and Jonothan, with Hekmet, stayed at Holt House with us. Yet on those nights a curious streak of perversity prevented her from making love. We were fast approaching the time when we would announce to all the world – and especially our parents – that we were going to live together. It was only a matter of weeks now, not months, before Serena, as she put it with a wry laugh, 'moves into my lover's house and becomes – well, not a kept woman, but you know what I mean. And since I love you, and am going to stay with you all my life, I'd like to start on – I know it's the wrong word, but a fresh start, a clean start.'

'I don't consider there's anything dirty about our love,' I reproached her.

'Of course not, darling. Not *us*. The rest of Cairo. Even Jonothan and Hekmet, asleep in the next room to mine at Holt House. I want Jonothan to grow up thinking of you as his father.' She sighed. 'Feelings are so difficult to explain. Don't you understand?'

I didn't, but I tried. Now that months had passed since

Greg's death all I wanted was for us to live together, openly.

'We will,' she promised. 'I want it more than you – well, as much!' She kissed me. 'But waiting is – what did the poet say? – such sweet sorrow. And meantime, if you're feeling – what's the word the poet didn't say? – if you're feeling randy, there's always the Villa Zelfa.'

'I still think that house is morbid.'

'It's available,' she laughed. 'Even if we don't need the mirrors.'

Sirry Pasha had his own worries. The loss of Nasrani was a blow from which I doubted he would ever recover. I wasn't thinking of the financial loss, though the crops in the Delta could easily yield up to £50 an acre, which meant a forfeited income of nearly £100,000 a year. But deeper than that was the loss of his past, his heritage, the only place he had truly loved; and though the requisition orders had been accompanied by promises to return the property once the war was over I knew that an army rarely if ever derequisitions property. Politicians change, and tear up agreements. Nasrani had gone for ever.

'Worst of all,' said Sirry Pasha gloomily, 'for the very first time since the days of my grandfather I have to send the servants out shopping for fruit and vegetables and meat and fish.'

I was aware that Farouk – and Sadik as well – knew all about this, but had refused to lift a finger, though the king could have prevented the requisition without any difficulty. I had also heard that Sadik actually encouraged the king to approve the order.

The confrontation at the Abdin Palace, even though he had carried it off with dignity, had changed Farouk profoundly. His behaviour became more and more outrageous.

At times he drove his Citroen round and round Cairo's Opera Square, especially if there was a concert that night. He had fitted a special electric horn which simulated the screams of a dying dog. The screams were so loud they could be clearly heard in the auditorium of the Opera House.

In a flat to which he had been invited at Zamalek one

evening, he walked out on the balcony overlooking the river after ordering an astonished servant to collect all the caps belonging to British officers. When he had enough, he took out his revolver and threw the caps one by one into the air, shooting at the spinning targets. 'Much more fun than clay pigeon shooting,' he laughed to the horrified hostess who had dashed out to see what the shooting was about.

Yet at other times he would be full of what he called 'the fun and games that I used to enjoy in England'. On one occasion four junior RAF officers out for a spree one night were driving to the Sphinx when their car broke down. A black Citroen braked and the portly man who was driving asked if he could help.

'We're going to the Sphinx,' said one.

According to Samia, who told me the story, the driver said, 'So am I. Jump in and I'll give you a lift.' During the drive the man asked the RAF officers what they thought of Egypt – and especially Farouk.

'Do you want it in prose or poetry?' asked one laughingly.

'Sing it,' cried the driver, and the four joined in a ditty that was being sung in every military camp from the shores of the Mediterranean to the Sudan. The music was easy to remember because the words had been set to the Egyptian national anthem:

> King Farouk, King Farouk,
> He's a dirty old crook
> As he walks down the street
> In his fifty-shilling suit.
> Queen Farida's very gay
> 'Cos she's in the family way.

When the car drew up in Kasr el Nil the officers tumbled out with thanks as the portly man parked his car. They arrived at the bar before him, and were looking over the girls when the man came in, sat alone, and whispered to one girl who brought the RAF officers a magnum of champagne; pointing to the benefactor who raised his glass in a toast the half-naked waitress murmured, 'With His Majesty's compliments.'

Yet at other times he seemed mad. He drove more recklessly than ever before. He picked up girls almost every
night, sometimes with disastrous results when people didn't
recognise his car. One evening Farouk was attacked by brig-
ands on the Giza Road. Two women passengers were shot,
and as one of the robbers was about to kill Farouk the leader
said, 'Let the fat pig go. He's not worth a bullet.'

The entire police force of Cairo was mobilised, and the
men were tracked down within the hour. All except the
ringleader were immediately shot, on Farouk's personal
orders. The ringleader was sentenced to a hundred lashes for
calling his monarch a fat pig, after which Farouk gave the
bleeding, half-conscious man £1,000 for saving his life.

Sirry Pasha, who knew a great deal about the recurring
scandals revolving round what he called the king's women,
had begged Serena to leave Cairo. He had, he told her, the
chance to rent a furnished villa at Aswan that was
beautiful – and safe.

'Don't you agree with me?' Sirry asked me over lunch.
'We know what the king did when he demanded the painting
of Serena. And those dinners!'

'They're over,' said Serena shortly. 'After Greg's death I
had every excuse to demand privacy.'

'But he makes his own laws,' said Madame Sirry, and even
she, turning to me, asked, 'Don't you agree it's dangerous?'

'I do,' I nodded, for Sirry was right. If the king insisted on
inviting Serena to the Abdin Palace too frequently she might
find it difficult to extricate herself from trouble – especially
with Sadik around. And if she continued to refuse, the king
could easily make more trouble for the Sirry family. But
though Sirry Pasha and his wife were right to be concerned
I dreaded the prospect of Serena living in Aswan while I was
still in Cairo. *If* I stayed in Cairo. For that was another thing.
I hoped that my knowledge of the area, and my languages,
would keep me in the city, but all of us lived under the
constant fear of being posted far away. This was the army,
with all its bumbling red tape, and even if the 'Brig' fought
for me there was always the danger that my specialised

knowledge would be ignored and I could be posted anywhere. With that possibility hanging over us both, every moment we had together was doubly precious.

Somewhat lamely I now added to Madame Sirry, 'I don't think the king would stoop so low.'

'Thanks a lot!' laughed Serena, deliberately misunderstanding.

'He'd do anything, the *cochon*,' said Madame Sirry, while Sirry Pasha merely grunted, 'I hope you're right.'

If only Sirry Pasha had insisted! If only I hadn't been so selfish!

Three weeks later I had to go to Alex for a few days and when I returned I phoned Serena, hoping to hear that Teddy was back and we could use the flat. It was still empty. Teddy had been sent to the Canal Zone and wouldn't be around for a few more weeks.

'Then let's dine at Shepheard's,' I suggested. 'I'm dying to see you.' But that was out too.

'It's Mama's birthday – 10 July – and I promised to have dinner at home. But you come along.'

'Not tonight,' I said. 'I'm exhausted. What I really want is to go to bed right away – in your arms, in the flat, and sleep until six tomorrow morning. I just couldn't keep awake and indulge in small-talk. I'll probably dine in the mess, and see you tomorrow.'

'But I can't wait till tomorrow.' I could sense the smile of happiness in her voice. 'You're not the only person in this duo who needs the other.'

'You mean you're – randy?' I asked. She had loved the word since she had 'discovered' it.

'What do you think? Six whole days without you!'

'I'll come,' I said.

'No, I've got a better idea. I'll leave dinner early and go straight home to the Villa Zelfa. You've got your key. Hekmet and Jonothan are going to spend the night with Mama anyway. We'll take a chance.' Whispering, she added, 'I can't wait to put my arms round you. Ring the bell, so that I don't get frightened if I'm home first and hear sudden noises. I hope to be there by half past ten. If I'm late and there's no reply let yourself in and wait for me.'

Everything went wrong. I was called from dinner in the mess to deal with some inane enquiry, merely because I happened to be there and the duty officer was busy, so I didn't reach the villa until after midnight.

I rang the bell. No answer, which puzzled me: Serena wasn't a heavy sleeper, and it wasn't like her to arrive home so late, but I thought that perhaps she had decided to stay the night with her parents and had been unable to contact me after I left the mess. On the other hand, the most likely reason was the simplest. She had fallen into a heavy sleep and hadn't heard me ring.

I inserted my key in the front door, and, always mindful of security, pushed the door open quietly – and froze.

Sitting on a chair at the foot of the broad stairway, at the far end of the marble hallway, was a man in uniform, a gun resting on his lap.

'Leave as quietly as you entered,' said General Osman Sadik quietly. 'Get out before you get hurt. Go on!' He waved the pistol menacingly.

'What the hell are you doing here?' I advanced a couple of steps, my first fears replaced by anger.

'I said, *get out!*' He stood up, gun in hand, pointing it straight at me. I was still just inside the door, but now I advanced another step.

'Where is she?' I asked.

'Enjoying herself with the king. And thank your lucky stars for that soundproof door.' He jerked his gun in the direction of the door. 'But one step more and you won't ever know what happened.' At first I was sure that he meant it, especially when, with a sneer, he added, 'You're out of your depth here.'

But, although I didn't doubt that shooting me would have been a pleasure for him, I realised that perhaps he couldn't afford to, unless he had a cast-iron reason, for the king was in the next room, and if Serena rushed out and found me dead she would start such a scandal that Farouk's rocky throne could topple. Lampson, the ambassador, would be only too delighted to reinstigate abdication proceedings. On the other hand, if the king discovered that I knew about this particular visit to Serena, I would be in serious trouble.

I didn't for a moment think the king was raping Serena. She would be furious inside the study, but even if she had to dodge round tables and chairs, even if he grabbed and tore her dress, there was no way in which such a gross man could easily harm her. True, the door was soundproof, but not against screams of terror. Probably she was treating him as a child and telling him to go home to his palace – in effect, if not in those words. All the same, Farouk's unwelcome attentions made my blood boil.

I wondered if I could grab Sadik's gun. The only way was to goad Sadik into making a mistake. I didn't know what I would do then – but I had to do something.

'You never made it with Samia, did you?' I began. 'I did.'

'Shut up!' he hissed. 'And what about the lady in the next room? I suppose you think –?'

Sadik *couldn't* know about Serena and me – not really. Certainly not about the secret flat, though his men might have watched the occasional visits I made to the Villa Zelfa. But now there was one thing that he did know: that I had my own key, not usually given to casual visitors.

At that moment the study door opened. I heard a man's voice inside, speaking in Arabic. I recognised it immediately – Farouk's.

Serena stood there, framed in the doorway. I noticed that she was wearing a blue silk dress – one of my favourites. Then she put her hand to her mouth. Her eyes were rooted in fear. Sadik's own eyes switched to Serena. As he looked at her, I banged into him and as he crashed down I knocked the gun from his fingers. I heard Farouk shout in annoyance from inside the study. I didn't doubt that I had been right – the king had been begging rather than forcing. But one look of fear from Serena made me realise instantly the real danger. What if the king came out and saw me? I would compromise him immediately. I sensed rather than saw the panic in Serena's eyes as, with little more than an inclination of the head, she motioned towards the two huge walk-in cupboards on either side of the front door, and mouthed the one word, 'Hide!'

But what good would that do? Sadik was still there to tell Farouk of my presence. I don't know quite what happened next, but as I broke free Sadik, still on all fours, scrambled towards the gun which had slid away on the marble floor towards the study door.

For a split second I took in every detail of the tableau as though it were a stage set, filled with actors not ourselves. Serena stood with her back to the study, her whole body tense at the danger of Farouk entering. I could hear the lumbering movement of an obese man trying to struggle out of a low chair. There was another cry of anger from Farouk – words I didn't catch. Sadik had reached the gun, and his right arm was stretched towards it. At that moment Serena ran forward and stamped on Sadik's hand with her shoe. As he screamed with rage the king shouted again. Then, almost in slow motion, I saw an astonishing thing: quite deliberately Serena tore at the top of her blue silk dress, baring one shoulder, then ripped savagely at her bra until one of her breasts was bared. Then and only then did she scream and bend down to pick up the gun.

I heard the king shout, 'What's going on?'

Serena had the gun in her hand and as Sadik moved towards her she aimed it at him, and pulled the trigger.

For a moment I gasped with disbelief. Then once more Serena screamed and, as I darted towards one of the built-in cupboards she had indicated, I had one last glimpse of her – eyes staring, dress torn, left breast bared, gun smoking, and Sadik on the ground, blood dripping from his nose and mouth. Once in the cupboard I couldn't see a thing, only listen. Where was the king? Then I realised the reason for the delay, as I heard the lumbering footsteps of Farouk at last coming into the hallway.

The only thing I didn't know was whether or not Sadik was dead. He had looked dead. But as Serena screamed again – and *that* I knew was simulated fear, a scream on purpose – I heard her cry, 'Your Majesty, help me – he tried to tear my clothes off. He threatened me with a gun.'

I heard Sadik groan, then the gasp of pain as he summoned up one last effort to warn the king, but could only manage one word: 'Holt!' Thank God he didn't have the energy to cry my full name! Farouk obviously thought that Sadik had been calling '*Mrs* Holt' for I heard him shout, 'I know who she is, Sadik. What's *happened* here?'

I could still only listen, sweating. But no further sound came from Sadik.

Instead it was Serena, crying, 'He pointed the gun at me! After he tore my dress he dropped it to the floor, and I was so frightened – for you too – that I – I grabbed it and pulled the trigger.'

'You little fool!' shouted Farouk. 'Here. Help me.'

I heard his heavy breathing, as though he were turning over his aide. I hadn't the faintest idea of Sadik's condition until I heard a breathless Farouk almost groan again with anger, 'My God! You've killed him!'

'It was self-defence.' I could hear the break in her voice. I would have given anything to rush out and help her, but I knew that for once I had to stand still. I heard a lot of conversation I couldn't make out – almost as though the king were whispering. I was thinking desperately – not that there was anything I could do. Though I hated to admit it to myself, this was one time in her life when Serena must play the game out alone.

The muttering ceased, and the words were more audible.

'Nothing of this must ever leak out.' I could tell from Farouk's voice that he had recovered some of his composure. 'One word and I'll have the entire Sirry family sent to Upper Egypt. Understand?'

'I may have killed him, but if you –'

'Shut up!' I could smell tobacco: the king must have lit a cigarette. 'You and I are the only two people in the world who know. *I'm* not going to talk. Neither are you. Now' – in the words of one used to giving commands – 'I'm leaving. I've got the Citroen. You will leave ten minutes after I do. Understand? That's an order.'

I heard Serena cry out, as though distraught, 'But where shall I go?'

'How the hell do I know? Go to the Sphinx if you like. Or your parents, I suppose. Just leave this place in ten minutes. Give me your front-door key. In an hour someone will come and collect Sadik. Poor fool – I liked him, and I told him not to mess around with my women.'

'Your woman!' she said scornfully.

Ignoring the remark, he added, 'And this carpet – and the floor. There's some blood. Everything will be cleared up. And *you* don't come near the Villa Zelfa for at least a month.'

'My clothes?'

'Buy some new ones,' he retorted. 'Meanwhile Pulli and my Italians will arrange everything.' He was referring to the three Italians who all but ruled the life of the king, with Pulli, a general factotum, second only in hidden power to Sadik.

I heard the king's ponderous footsteps as he came towards me. They stopped outside the cupboard where I was hiding, hardly daring to breathe. Farouk must have been within six inches of me, separated only by the slatted door.

'You're a fool, Serena,' I heard him sigh. 'But you are beautiful. Maybe that will save you.' Unbelievably I heard the sound of his kissing her cheek as he asked, 'But remember. One word – and you'll never see Cairo again. Not as long as I'm king of Egypt.'

The door banged. Almost collapsing from the tension, I emerged from my hiding place. The body of Sadik lay on a priceless rug at the foot of the stairway, almost at the same spot where Greg had died. Serena stood, her face white, and almost fell into my arms, weeping.

'My God!' she was crying, 'the place is cursed. What have I done? What's going to become of us?'

'Nothing,' I promised, though without much conviction. 'Don't look down,' I said as her eyes were drawn to the body. 'Nothing if we get out of here quickly. Farouk can't afford another scandal, not on this level.'

'But I killed a man!'

'Please – come *now*! Every second is precious. If the king's men find you or me here –'

'I must explain how it all happened –'

'Later. Don't waste time now.'

'Where shall I go?'

'To Holt House. You can stay the night. If you go to your parents' house and your mother wakes and she sees you with your dress torn – well.' I tried to smile. 'You look as though someone's tried to rape you.'

'I can't stay the night at your place.'

'You can. I'll make sure it's prim and proper. We've just got to be careful. And nobody must see you in this state.'

Serena was not normally the kind of woman to panic, but I had never seen her so close to it. After all, she had killed a man – however great the provocation. And with the king involved. For a moment I thought she was going to run out of the house half-naked.

'I must get out of here,' she cried, making for the door.

'Wait a second. I'll get you something to wear,' I said. In the cupboard where I had hidden only a few moments previously were half a dozen light coats, the sort worn in Cairo after the sun had gone down.

'Here, take this.' I grabbed the first one. When I touched her shoulder to put on the coat I could feel the goose-pimples. 'This way.' I held her arm as I made for the side door leading to the street where I had parked the car.

Though the road was deserted she followed me in a daze, speechless with fear, looking around as though we might be followed. Only when she was huddled in the de Soto did she begin to relax. I started the motor, felt the soft purr and slid the car into gear.

'It's all right now, darling.' I held her hand as we slid quietly towards the Bulac Bridge.

'Will I be charged with murder?' She must have known that she wouldn't, but she needed assurance.

'Of course not! Who's going to charge you? The king? While trying to rape you? Remember: you were provoked. I was the only witness who knew what was happening, and by God if Sadik had told the king I'd probably have ended up at the bottom of the Nile with a large stone tied to one leg.'

She was still shivering when we reached Holt House. The old

guard was, as usual, fast asleep on his trestle bed. We crept into the Long Gallery, then to the small sitting room facing the veranda, and I poured out a couple of drinks – a large scotch for me, a neat vodka for Serena.

'Now.' I sat next to her on the sofa and put an arm round her shoulder. 'Tell me what happened, why you were there,' I asked gently.

More relaxed after the drink, she explained. 'I got home from dinner about half past ten, as I planned, and I had hardly arrived when the bell rang. I thought it must be you at that time of night – you'd promised to ring so I wouldn't be frightened – and I ran to open the door. My God, I was terrified! There stood the king. Behind him was Sadik. Without thinking – instinct, I suppose – I .curtsied, and he just said, "Good evening. May I come in?" What could I say? He waddled into the hall with Sadik behind. That bloody man – even as Sadik closed the front door he was smirking. You know that smile of his.'

'Couldn't you keep them out?'

'I said to the king that it was late – I suggested that perhaps another time – but Mark, he *is* my king.'

'But he's a monster!' I cried.

'I didn't think he'd play any tricks,' Serena said flatly.

'But what did you talk about? Did he try anything?'

'Not a bit. He told me he loved me, that he always had, and when I asked about his wife, his marriage, he waved his hand and said that if I wouldn't become his mistress, if there was no other way, he would divorce the queen so that he could marry me.' She looked down at her glass.

'I couldn't laugh at him. You must understand, darling, he *is* our king, and he's such a pathetic creature really, in between the moments of horror. I had to say how honoured I was and tell him that I had to be sacred to the memory of Greg, and there was a nasty moment when he asked, "And to the memory of your brother-in-law?" But I passed it off. But I was terrified, especially knowing that Sadik was sitting outside in the hall. I *do* despise Farouk, but I had to be polite. Just remember how polite you used to be when we dined with HM at the villa.'

'I know what you mean.' I poured out another scotch, though Serena shook her head. 'Of course I don't blame you.'

To get rid of Farouk she had half promised to dine with him at the Abdin Palace. 'You see,' she added, 'I was terrified that at any moment you might arrive and ring the doorbell. It must have rung, but neither of us heard it in the study. But even though the door to the study is fairly soundproof I *did* hear a noise. I made an excuse to leave the room. The king was sitting down in a deep leather sofa. Thank God he was. It takes him quite a while to get up unaided. It gave me just enough time to see what was happening between you and Sadik, to warn you, before he could come out into the hallway. But then I saw Sadik trying to get up off the floor. You looked stunned –'

'I was – especially when I saw you deliberately rip your dress.'

'I tore it instinctively – so that I could blame Sadik. I saw the gun on the ground and I grabbed it. I suppose at first I only meant to threaten him. Honestly, Mark, I couldn't tell you exactly what happened – I was certain Sadik was going to kill you. I remember whispering to you to hide in the cloakroom cupboard – I *think* I did –'

'You did.'

'And . . .' Her voice broke off. 'I still can't believe that on my way home I was dreaming of the moment when you would put your arms round me – and now, only two hours later, Sadik is dead – and I killed him!'

'Don't think like that. You might have killed Sadik, but Sadik, by doing Farouk's dirty work on Nasrani, killed the soul of your father. Is that too far-fetched? I believe Sadik deserved to die.'

For the first time she relaxed. 'Thank you,' she whispered.

'Enough for one night.' I kissed her. 'It's three in the morning. Take a sleeping pill. And if you sleep late I'll have time to concoct a good story for my parents. Tomorrow you can move in with your father and mother – for a few weeks.'

'A few weeks! Oh, Mark, what a terrible night! How much can happen in a couple of hours. If you had been delayed a day – if I had suggested you stay at our house – if, if, if.'

'Don't cry, beloved.' I tried to console her. 'It *has* been a terrible night. But –'

'There are no buts. I had planned the greatest surprise of all for you.'

'The greatest?'

'I was going to say that we've waited long enough, to suggest that you tell your parents tomorrow that we start to live as a married couple. *That's* what I was going to tell you at the Villa Zelfa. That and –' She hesitated.

'And –'

'It doesn't matter now. I'll tell you when we do live together. But for the moment we can't – mustn't even be seen together, apart from family meetings.'

I knew she was right. She must do nothing, absolutely nothing, that would cause the king to link our names.

'It's only a postponement.' I stroked her ash-blonde hair, damp and almost lank with fear. 'But I think you're right. Whatever else happens we don't want any gossip – about anything. But in another three months it'll all have blown over and I'll officially welcome you as a "non-legal" bride to Holt House. Can you wait as long as that?'

'If I have to,' she whispered.

33

At first there were no problems. The king's men had obviously spirited Sadik's body out of the villa, together with any incriminating evidence, such as the bloodstained rugs. He was buried, hurriedly, with full military honours. According to all the newspapers he had died of 'a sudden heart attack'.

Serena moved into her parents' house next to ours, and advertisements soon announced that the Villa Zelfa was for sale. She told everyone that she couldn't stand the loneliness any longer, or the memory of Greg's tragic death. It was a perfectly plausible explanation.

Then the rumours started to circulate, first in the various souks, later in the higher echelons of Cairo's trade guilds, finally reaching the Gezira Club. They were not connected with Serena – not at first – but the noise of the shooting, the banging of doors, the sudden spurt of a car engine – the king had a habit of roaring away noisily – caused a few neighbours or their servants to draw aside their curtains. The villa stood in its own grounds, but noise carries, and they *heard*, even if they saw nothing – and enquired. Two hours after the first disturbances the noise started all over again. A group of men arrived at the villa, and at the sounds of their van curtains were drawn apart once more. Several people saw a sack being dumped in the back of the van, together with a couple of carpets.

All in all, and despite the suspicions that the sack might have contained a body, there was no real substance to the rumours, although Teddy, back from Alex and, knowing nothing of what had really happened, said to me flippantly, 'Glad to see Serena's alive and well.'

'Why shouldn't she be?'

'I'm only joking, but I heard a terrible rumour in Alex that she'd been murdered. You know, living alone, intruders. Someone said they'd seen a body in a sack being carried out of Serena's villa.'

I tried to laugh it all off, but I felt sick with apprehension.

'You all right, old boy?' added Teddy curiously.

'Sure. Drank too much last night.'

As the days passed, it became clear that any events which had given rise to rumours were based on all kinds of false trails. None involved Serena, even though it was her house, for it was also quickly confirmed that she had spent the night with her mother-in-law after dining with the family. So most people imagined that robbers had entered her house, knowing she would be absent, in order to steal valuables. The sack probably contained the family silver. And someone had actually seen two priceless carpets being stolen. It was a story Serena didn't confirm, or deny.

However, several other questions demanded answers, questions from one person in particular: Sadik's widow, a woman I think I detested even more than I had Sadik himself. With her face-lifts, her mask-like features and vitriolic tongue, she was both implacable and vengeful. Some of the details of what happened later came through DSO channels.

Mrs Sadik could not stand up against the king openly. For one thing he had, soon after her husband's death, sent for her and doubled the pension to which a general would normally have been entitled. The newspapers reported that the king had told her, 'It is a small gesture compared to the loss of one of my dearest friends.' But the gift made Mrs Sadik suspicious. Why had she not been allowed to see her dead husband's body? I did not know what Farouk or his aides told her as an excuse: perhaps that the general had been away on a secret mission, and that the coffin had already been nailed down by the time she could be told of his death.

Whatever the official version, Mrs Sadik might *think* that her husband's memory had been insulted by such a hasty funeral, but that was between her and the king. The rumours about the Villa Zelfa were separate, and at first had nothing to do with Mrs Sadik. Then slowly the rumours began to change. I couldn't at first understand it, for I didn't have the faintest knowledge then of what Mrs Sadik was really doing.

Until one day I received the first of several shattering shocks.

Sirry Pasha asked me round to the Turf Club for lunch. When I arrived he shook hands with a smile, then sat down heavily. He looked tired and depressed.

'I know how friendly you and Serena have been,' he began as we tackled a shrimp cocktail. 'Perhaps I shouldn't ask you this question, but –'

I went cold, and felt myself blushing at the prospect of being confronted by the end of the question. But I was wrong.

'I know it's not true,' he added quickly, watching my apprehension, 'but has Serena been having an affair with the king?'

I burst out laughing, creasing my face into relief. 'Good

Lord!' I cried. 'Whatever made you think that? Never, never, Sirry Pasha.'

'The dinners?'

'Don't we all have to do as we're told when the king commands?'

'I suppose so,' he said doubtfully.

'What made you ask?'

'The stories that are going around the souk. I heard that they're inspired by that woman Mrs Sadik. She's spreading it around that Sadik was with the king at the Villa Zelfa the night that her husband died so suddenly.'

'I can't believe it,' I lied. 'She *has* entertained the king, but Stevenson and I promised that she would never do so unless one of us was present. I'm sure that promise has been kept.'

'I'm glad to hear you say so.' Sirry Pasha sounded relieved. 'So often in Cairo rumours get sparked off, filling the air with smoke. And sometimes there's no smoke without fire.'

'There is this time.' Whatever else happened, I had to make sure that Sirry Pasha had peace of mind – if only to prepare him for the shock of telling him within three months that his beloved daughter and I were going to live together publicly. In the thirties that wasn't done, not in palace circles.

Events now moved swiftly. An item, vaguely worded, suddenly appeared in one of the Cairo newspapers:

His Majesty King Farouk, who has often dined privately at the Villa Zelfa with Mrs Serena Holt, an intimate friend, is reported to have ceased visiting the lady following the recent rumours which forced Mrs Holt to sell her villa at Zamalek.

Serena, white-faced, showed me the clipping. 'Can I sue?' she demanded.

'And risk a court action?' I replied. 'With you standing up in the witness box telling deliberate lies?'

'But it's a lie about the king!'

'I know that. But the other rumours. In Mrs Sadik you're

up against a vindictive woman. I arranged to have her tailed by a DSO man. She's been going round questioning all your neighbours' servants, the night watchmen, anyone she can find in your area.'

'If only I'd never opened the door to him that night,' said Serena bitterly.

'Serena should never have started inviting Farouk to those dinners,' echoed Father only a few hours later.

He too had read the paragraph. I could do nothing but say, 'Ridiculous!' when he asked me virtually the same questions which Sirry Pasha had asked. The interesting thing – at the time – was that no one suggested the possibility of foul play where Sadik was concerned.

The next shock was even more shattering. It came from Jim Stevenson. Now that America was in the war, he had joined an outfit called the OSS, the Office of Strategic Services. I hadn't seen much of him since he had become an ally. There were hundreds of Americans in Cairo now, and Stevenson seemed to melt into the busy scene. I suppose, really, that we were all so busy that the days of parties or meeting for drinks had disappeared with the passing years. But he did say that he would like to meet me as soon as possible, so we arranged to have drinks at the Gezira. It was always cool there just before sundown, sitting by the pool, though there were too many unknown officers around for my liking.

Stevenson wasted no time.

'You know what Sadik's widow is saying?' His usually disarming smile had vanished and he looked positively glum. 'That the king had Sadik murdered because Sadik knew too much about Farouk and Serena. It's absurd, I know, but the rumours are all over town. People are talking about nothing else.'

'There never would have been any rumours if you hadn't organised your bloody dinner parties for the king,' I burst out angrily.

'That's unfair and you know it. Your reports to DSO have been invaluable.'

'How do you know?' I couldn't keep the sullen anger out of my voice.

'America's in the war, remember? We're pardners, as they say in the movies. It's what we call the Exchange of Information Act. We're pooling resources. Though I've got the advantage over you. Ours is a civilian agency so the red tape is cut to a minimum. In the British army red tabs and red tape go together. So my reports on Cairo have probably never reached Brigadier Monson.'

'Well, there's nothing we can do about the talk,' I said flatly.

'The trouble is' – he was choosing his words carefully – 'it's not what you or Sirry Pasha decide to do, it's what Farouk decides.'

'Farouk?' I must have looked astonished. 'He can't do anything.'

'Why not?'

'Well –' I had to be careful. 'He's above rumours, above scandal, and if he's implicated, as this Sadik woman implies . . .'

'Come on, Mark. Something fishy's going on. A body in a sack? A widow prevented from seeing the corpse of her husband? A convenient heart attack in private, with the cause of death certified by the king's own doctor? Sadik didn't die of a heart attack. I believe he was shot.'

'Shot?' I felt as though I had stepped into an ice-cold shower. What did Stevenson know, this mysterious man who seemed to poke his nose into every cranny of our lives?

'What makes you say that?'

'Let's say it's an informed guess.'

'How did you –?'

'Our secret services should have *some* secrets, Mark. One day – when you least expect it – I'll tell you. That's a promise: don't forget it. In the meantime, I really came to warn you.'

'Well – I'm not implicated,' I lied uneasily.

'Of course not.' Was Stevenson telling the truth, or was *he* lying easily? 'But before very long you may get a summons – via your commanding officer, of course – to make an unofficial visit to the Abdin Palace. To meet with Farouk.'

My heart sank, a hundred thoughts racing through my mind. All concentrated on one question: did Farouk know?

'Not to worry!' It was as though Stevenson, with his easy-going smile, had read my fears. 'The American Minister, Alexander Kirk, has told me to tip you off. The king is furious. Not with you, but he wants everything hushed up, the scandal squashed. And every shred of gossip seems to lead to Serena and her involvement with Farouk.'

'What's Kirk got to do with this?' I said angrily. I had met the American, a decent enough chap, but I couldn't help asking, 'This is an *Egyptian* problem. Why do the Americans have to be brought into this? How the king solves his internal squabbles –'

'Keep your cool,' said Stevenson. 'You know as well as I do that Farouk likes Mr Kirk. It's been part of my job to make sure that they *do* like each other – while he's king,' he added wryly. 'But seriously, don't get sore, Mark. I'm just tipping you off that something big's going to happen. And all I know is that the king sent for the American Minister to ask his advice. That's all there is to it.'

'But an American offering advice! It's preposterous.'

'More preposterous than the king asking to see you?'

'Why doesn't Farouk ask to see Serena?'

'You know darned well the king could never meet her while the rumours are flying around. There'd be a new crop of tales about her before she left the palace. And as far as I can gather Farouk thinks you're the best person to act as a go-between. He knows how fond you are of Serena; I suppose he's always known it since the incident with the portrait. He also knows you're a friend of Egypt – even though you were in the palace when the British smashed open the palace gates with their tanks. But you – well, you give the impression of being guileless. A very useful attribute in a spy. As the old Arab proverb says, "A good man's face is like an open picture book." '

Serena and I met at the secret flat three days later – nervously, for I felt sure she would be followed day and night. Still, with the double entrance, the different street doors, it was safe. It was what I *told* her that destroyed her evening.

I couldn't disguise my fears, and nor could she. We spent a miserable evening trying to guess what Farouk could do, if anything, and why I might shortly be dragged into the affair.

'I'm worried for you, darling,' she said. 'But I can't believe that he suspects about us.'

'No. At least, I hope not.' I was thinking, What a bloody fool Stevenson was to talk about my face being an open book. 'No, it's impossible.'

In fact, neither of us could have guessed what Farouk did decide to do to protect his image. Or rather, what he ordered Serena to do.

When the command came through to Brigadier Monson that I was to present myself at the Abdin Palace he gave *his* orders: 'You go in the most impressive military car we can find, with a military driver and an escort in the front seat. I don't know what this is all about – I've heard rumours, of course, about your sister-in-law, but it can't be about her. Anyway, the more that DSO keeps in touch with HM the more we can learn. So report straight back to me – in person.'

I reached the Abdin Palace five minutes before the appointed time. The guards at the front entrance didn't give my car the usual perfunctory search which everyone normally had to undergo. They had obviously been told to pass me through. A flunkey opened my car door, and I walked up the splendid staircase, where another flunkey, this time with a silver chain round his neck, led the way to Farouk's private study where, only a few months ago, I had been witness to Lampson's attempt to force him to abdicate.

The room was unchanged, lined with books which I was sure the king never read. Farouk sat at a large desk, behind which was a portrait of his father, the old king Fuad. Farouk had put on weight, even in the few months since our last meeting, and he looked jowly and unhealthy. But his fat face was smiling underneath his scarlet fez. He wore a frock coat with 'palace trimmings' of dark green silk lapels.

'Colonel Holt.' He seemed quite affable. 'It is a pleasure to see you. A much happier occasion than our last meeting when that man Lampson behaved so abominably.'

382

I kept a discreet silence. Lampson *was* my ambassador, even if not my friend.

'At the same time,' he continued, 'I have some news which I know will upset you. I have asked you to come, because I am told that Mrs Holt is in trouble, and I want to help her.'

Still I waited in silence.

'Our dinners together at the Villa Zelfa have always been most agreeable. But now the rumours –'

'Your Majesty,' I spoke for the first time, 'is surely above rumour, sir.'

The king looked at me gloomily for a moment, fidgeting with a paper-knife.

'Of course. But Colonel, you know the way of the world – and of women. Mrs Holt is a close friend, a valued friend, and she has on occasion invited me to the villa when' – he coughed with what I took to be a clumsy effort at discretion – 'there were no other guests.'

'I understand Your Majesty,' I said carefully. 'Many ladies are attracted to Your Majesty, and naturally they are flattered to receive your friendship.'

Farouk nodded. 'General Sadik, as you know, died of a sudden heart attack. He wasn't in Cairo; he was away on a special mission. Not that it matters. Mrs Holt had asked me to visit her alone.'

More lies! I raged inwardly. We both knew that Serena had dined with her family. For a moment I thought of saying that I had thought she was with her parents, but then I thought, No, too stupid. Let's see what he has to say.

'However, as you know,' Farouk continued smoothly, 'rumour breeds rumour. And General Sadik's widow has a vituperative tongue. Especially as General Sadik kept a diary of his appointments. And now I'm told that Mrs Sadik has the diary.'

So *that* was the problem! That was why the rumours were so persistent, why Mrs Sadik was pursuing them so vindictively. I wondered what the critical entry had revealed.

'But Your Majesty, can't you – er –' I was about to say 'steal the diary' but then thought the word too ugly. 'Can't the offending pages be destroyed – by accident?'

'They're hidden,' said Farouk. 'We went through her house with a toothcomb while she was at the funeral. I've no idea where they are. And I can't put too much pressure on the wretched woman; the scandal would only spread. Somehow she's got her knife into your sister-in-law. She thinks she had something to do with the general's death.'

Intuition, gossip, whatever it was, that last remark was chilling.

'If there's anything I can do to help, Your Majesty?' I said innocently.

'There is.' Farouk pushed the point of his paper-knife into the thick pad of his blotter, almost as though he were stabbing Mrs Sadik. 'I have decided that it would be better for all concerned if for a little while Mrs Holt left Egypt.'

My mouth dropped open, but as I started to form a question he said coldly, 'Please refrain from interrupting me when I am speaking.'

'My apologies, sir,' I mumbled.

'Everything has been arranged with the American Minister. She will go to the United States.'

'America!' I cried. 'So far away. The *danger*, sir!'

'Minimal. Mr Kirk assures me that the Americans regularly fly some new and powerful aircraft called Liberators between our country and the United States. Mrs Holt will fly south to a point in West Africa, then to the Azores, then on to New York.'

My heart sank. I faltered, 'But where do I come in, Your Majesty?'

'This operation has to be done with discretion. I don't want to be involved with Sirry Pasha. The man is an irritating bore. My name – my decision – has to be absolutely secret.'

'But sir, couldn't she stay in South Africa?'

'No!' His voice was suddenly harsh. 'Out of *all* Africa, that's my decision. I like you, Holt, and if you hadn't been in the army, I'd have suggested you go along.' I must have looked surprised, for he added ironically, 'Yes, I know all about you two. Sadik told me several weeks before he died. He knew everything.'

Not everything, I thought bitterly.

'You will tell Mrs Holt this evening. You know Mr Stevenson, of course. I've asked Mr Kirk to arrange for Stevenson to accompany Mrs Holt on the flight, though he will return to Cairo immediately.'

'But what shall I tell Serena? How can I tell Sirry Pasha? It'll break his heart.' I didn't dare to add 'and mine too'.

'Better one heart broken than have a bit more of my throne chipped away,' Farouk said coldly. 'If you like, tell her father that Mr Stevenson wants to marry her and take her to New York. Tell her anything you choose.'

With that he dismissed me – by pretending to study some papers.

As I saluted and walked to the big double doors of his study Farouk looked up and added: 'I appreciate that you are feeling bad about this. I give you my word that when the war is over I will personally arrange for you to be released immediately from a German POW camp and given a passage to America. That's a promise.'

Back home, I walked round and round the garden, stunned, bewildered and seething with fury. I couldn't believe it, I couldn't accept that during the agonising moments at the Abdin Palace I had been present at the modern equivalent of the medieval Star Chamber. How could it be possible for one gross and cruel man to wield such power?

All kinds of mad thoughts rushed through my mind. Could I appeal to the ambassador? To Monson? Of course not. This was strictly an Egyptian affair, and on such a high level that no foreigner would dare to interfere.

I toyed with the idea of going to see Sirry Pasha and begging him to intervene, but dismissed the thought. He was powerless – even worse, in semi-disgrace.

If only we hadn't been at war, I thought over and over again. If only I hadn't played at being a hero and volunteered. I would have closed my chambers the next day and started a new life in America with Serena and Jonothan. But there *was* a war, and I *was* an officer in His Majesty's service, and I *was* chained to a country from which she was shortly to be banished.

And of course there was one other factor, and this we could

never discuss with anyone: Serena had shot and killed a high-ranking Egyptian officer. There was no way she could refuse to obey the royal dictum. If the truth ever came out – rumour crystallising into fact – or if Serena demanded to remain in Cairo and face trial, pleading self-defence – then her fate would be far worse than banishment: it would be death. For Farouk would never allow her to be brought to court. He would have no compunction in arranging for men like Pulli to stage a fatal 'accident' in which Serena was the victim.

In fact, during the last hours together, this was the line of reasoning I took with Serena, in order to give her hope; and hope too to both sets of parents – all suffering from shock beyond belief.

'I know it's terrible, my darling,' I said. 'But honestly, I'm surprised that the king *didn't* arrange for you to be killed in an "unavoidable accident". No, I'm not being macabre. He'd stop at nothing to protect his throne. Even before this happened, I thought of persuading you to leave Egypt for your own safety.'

'I wouldn't have gone,' she smiled through her tears.

'You would if I had begged you to. Somewhere like Kenya, so that I might have been able to visit you on a long leave. If only I had insisted!'

Even now I can't bring myself to write in detail of those three days before the parting, days and nights filled with heartache and tears. Chiffon refused all parties, she was so upset. Father stayed in his study, so grumpy no one dared approach him. Madame Sirry took to her bed, really ill.

Of course, we did all realise that this was not the end of the world. It was the circumstances that made it so awful: as though Serena had been sentenced to life imprisonment. Yet it wasn't as bad as that, I knew. She would only be separated from us until the end of the war. Then, even if she couldn't return, I could go to see her. But the war! When would it ever end, this global conflict, in which every military disaster meant more years needed to reach eventual victory?

Poor Sirry Pasha had made no attempt to hide his tears. But one evening he turned to me and said, 'The war won't last for ever, Mark. And when it's over – and if we have any money left – I'm going to offer all the Holts and all the Sirrys a trip to New York. Let's pray that we won't have to wait too long.'

On an impulse – perhaps feeling the need to share the hidden reason for my grief – I said to him, quietly, 'You know that I'm in love with Serena. I always have been.'

'Yes, I know,' he said gently. 'I could see it shining from both your hearts. We made a terrible mistake, your father and I, trying to decide other people's lives for them. It seemed such a good idea at the time. My heart bleeds for you, Mark. And for her.'

Serena refused point-blank to let me see her off at the airfield.

'I won't have any tears, my beloved,' she said. 'And if you came, I'd make an exhibition of myself. I love you with all my heart, and I'm going to treat my flight to America like a wartime parting in reverse. Think of all the poor soldiers in Britain leaving their wives for years to fight here. Well, instead of the soldiers going off it's me who's leaving you.'

PART THREE

1942–1952

34

I had been told that, with a stop-over in the Canary Islands, it would take Serena two days to reach New York. As I walked across to the Sirry house I was thinking that at that very moment she must be flying over the blue ocean, puffs of white clouds above. I was wondering what she was thinking, as perhaps she was wondering about me. At least that is what I imagined, as though reading a story, for at times I still couldn't believe that everything had happened so suddenly; that I wouldn't wake up, rub the sleep out of my eyes and think thankfully, God. What a horrible nightmare.

But I mustn't wallow in self-pity, I thought. This wasn't a life sentence, keeping us apart for ever. To me the real horror of the events lay not so much in the separation but in the despicable role Farouk had played in the affair. And when I felt at my angriest I took some consolation from the thought that after all Serena, whatever the provocation, *had* killed a man.

Sirry Pasha knew that something fearful must have happened to cause Serena's sudden departure, but he couldn't possibly connect it with General Sadik's fatal heart attack. He knew, though, how I felt about Serena, and said once again, 'It's not the end of the world, Mark. Just a wartime situation in reverse.'

He still wore a cloak of worry, and when he asked me to help myself to a drink I smiled as I said, 'I'll be all right.'

'In fact, I wasn't thinking of Serena,' he surprised me.

'I thought you looked – well, depressed.'

'To be honest, I was thinking of Aly,' he confessed. 'I'm getting more and more worried about him. Nothing serious, but he spends such a lot of time away from home.'

'He *is* young.'

'I know. But I wonder? I have a feeling it's woman trouble.'

Knowing what a fool Aly had made of himself over Sadat, I thought if that were all Sirry had to be worried about he was lucky. I laughed and said, 'Well, that's for the young too.'

'I'm not really worried, Mark, but he let something slip the other day – a casual remark about a flat. I only hope he's not got involved with some bird' – he relished the slang word from his old Oxford days – 'and set her up with somewhere to live.'

'He wouldn't be the only one.' I was remembering the happy times spent in Teddy's secret flat.

Sirry smiled at me with real affection. 'By the way, Serena told me she'd left a parcel for you. I've no idea what's in it.' He got out of the chair, not as easily as he used to. 'Old bones creaking a bit,' he admitted.

'I wonder what's in it.' I took the parcel, knowing in my heart – and from the feel of several slim books – that it must contain Serena's diaries. How carefully she had guarded the secrets of those words, locked away, unseen by anyone! But I didn't want to tell Sirry. It might be hurtful to a man who had, even temporarily, lost his daughter, to know that her innermost secrets were to be trusted to me rather than to her father. Fortunately Sirry Pasha spared me any embarrassment by saying, 'She told me it was a secret between you two, so I don't expect you to tell me.'

'Just some books which we used to read and enjoy together,' I said. It seemed a convenient lie. 'I'll open them when I get home.'

I strolled back across the garden to Holt House and opened the parcel. They were just a few books, the slim diaries covering intimate entries over several years, and yet, now that I had them in my hands, I hesitated before starting to read. I was not afraid, yet hardly dared to search for entries over events which had changed the course of our lives. There was the night at Sakkara. What date was that? The evening would never be forgotten, but the actual date escaped me, the event was so much more important than the time. I placed it within the period, then glanced through the pages until I found it, a page in her excited handwriting, always as though she could hardly wait to get words on paper. It read:

Now I ask no more from life, for on this night I held Mark in my arms and when he was moving inside me and we were kissing each other I couldn't stop moving too until without warning I came, and as we lay together I felt so ashamed and started crying until Mark explained that there was nothing wrong in coming together, in fact it was the most beautiful thing in the world.

Why did this miracle never happen when Greg made love to me? He seemed to enjoy himself each time, but sometimes I was left frustrated. Oh dear, so complicated! Until this evening when Mark loved me I thought that was all there was to love. I did something else on this wonderful night; because I love Mark, I took none of the precautions which Greg had helped me to arrange when we became lovers. I knew what might happen when I pretended I was tired and we went to Sakkara – after all, I arranged it.

I remember how she had cried for a moment at Sakkara, but I had thought she had been crying with pleasure. It had been shame that prompted the tears – shame that she hadn't waited, like a good Egyptian, until her man had been satisfied. I had also wondered at the time whether she had taken any precautions, but I had asked no questions because I didn't want to spoil the beauty of the night. And of course later, when the baby was born prematurely, I had wondered again, but had never asked. Now though I riffled through the pages for the weeks ahead, searching for confirmation. As I did so my eye stopped on a short entry:

Went dancing with the others at the Gezira. Afterwards Greg and I went for a drive and made love in the back of his car. It was all over in a few moments. Am I wicked because I closed my eyes and pretended all the time that it was Mark? The illusion was so strong that after Greg had taken me home I rushed upstairs, lay naked on the bed, and pretended Mark was there until I replaced frustration with satisfaction of a sort.

There were many entries that didn't concern me: about the books she was reading, about her painting, details of clothes, but even then my name cropped up.

> Dress rehearsal for my first ball at the Abdin Palace. A low-cut neckline to my ball gown. I hope Mark likes it.

There were other entries about her preparations for marriage, the wedding, the honeymoon in America. But I was searching for one particular page, one entry that a girl would be sure to make in her diary. I found it at the foot of a page mainly concerned with painting in which she had written, 'I *won't* let Baptise force me to paint with a thick impasto. And though I know he doesn't like cerulean blue – "*Trop bleu!*" he says – I do. I love it.'

And there, at the end of the entry were the two lines which, in the circumstances, no woman could fail to note:

> Missed the curse. Should I be overjoyed at the thought of a lie which will give me a wonderful happiness, even though I will have to live with it for ever?

I looked for the date another month ahead, but by then she and Greg were well into their honeymoon in America. There I read an entry:

> A rabbit-test result proved positive. I am frightened and overjoyed. Must send a 'Hullo' postcard.

Idly I skimmed through some of the earlier passages, written even then in a good strong hand. There was the time when, as a child, she had been in hospital with typhoid, and I had returned from London. 'Uncle Mark arrived to see me and kissed the pain away.' And another, more mundane, 'Mama slapped me quite hard for biting my nails.' And there were many references to Nasrani throughout the pages. 'I saw a village wedding from the deck of the *Kismet*. If only I could be married like that. But Greg isn't the romantic sort. We'll probably have to leave the church under an archway of crossed polo sticks!'

There was much more, of course: the suffering she had endured when Greg was unable to make love with her, the discovery that he frequented the Sphinx. Greg's accident, his death. But on that first evening I skipped those pages. I wanted to read about us, and stayed on the veranda for a long time, reading.

Father and Chiffon were out for dinner – a rare occurrence for Father – and with several stiff whiskies as my only friend I hardly noticed the passing of dusk, the sunset over the Nile, the sudden, swift impact of night. It was as though my entire vocabulary was limited to one word: Jonothan. My Jonothan! *Our* Jonothan. Why oh why hadn't Serena shared this precious knowledge with me before? Why had she kept from me this one great secret which she could have revealed once Greg was dead – even if it had still to remain a secret between just the two of us? I was thinking back, becoming slightly maudlin, to the times I *had* spent with Jonothan, the way he picked up tiny toys and offered them to me, the odd little nod of pleasure he gave me when I accepted them, even the way he learned to reach up to kiss me.

Though Jonothan had been too young to talk I had once again become an 'uncle'. I seemed destined to play the role all my life! First for the girl who would become my lover, then the mother of my child. What would she call the boy in America? I wondered. Or would Serena tell him that his father was dead?

She couldn't do that, surely. It would raise too many complications when we lived together after the war, after she returned. And a big part of me secretly hoped that, given time, Parmi might one day relent and agree to a divorce. Then I could marry legally and become a father, legally. I don't know what I thought that evening on the balcony. About everything – and nothing. Random thoughts about the way it might have been, had we honestly stated at the very outset that we were in love. If only Serena hadn't been so 'Egyptian', hadn't believed so strongly in obedience to parental arrangements . . .

Perhaps I was to blame. I should have changed her mind for her. And yet, thinking back, it might well have ended in disaster. For I felt, from the things she had said, that her Egyptian character separated marriage from love very clearly, the lines between the two strictly demarcated.

Still, it was a terrible secret to keep from a man, especially by a woman who loved you passionately enough to betray a brother, to make love standing up under the cathedral tree in the garden, to 'set up house', so to speak, in our secret flat. What made a woman think in such a twisted way? I knew she felt it was for the best, but why?

It was ten days before I found out the answer. Jim Stevenson flew into Cairo from New York.

'With a letter for you,' he said. 'Marked "Official Business, Top Secret" so that it didn't have to go through a censor.'

How incredible, I reflected, that in the short space of time between a goodbye and a welcome letter Stevenson had been to New York and returned, he had seen Serena, helped her to arrange her new flat, taken her for dinner, and now had reappeared almost as though he had never been away.

'Here it is.' He handed it to me.

'Thanks.' I wanted to read it alone, but asked a banal question, 'How's she settled in?'

'Bearing up. It's been quite a jolt for her. But it isn't a jail term, she's got the baby, and I managed to find a coloured woman who seems trustworthy to look after her.'

'And her flat?'

'Small, but delightful. At the corner of Lexington and 55th Street. Two beds, two baths, a living room and dining room combined, but big enough for her to set up an easel in one corner. And of course it's in the heart of New York, three or four blocks from the St Regis, with Central Park just round the corner.'

'I'm very grateful to you for looking after her.' I meant it.

'The least I could do. The trouble is' – he spoke more seriously than usual – 'she'd better get adjusted, because we're in for a long war now that the Japs have got to be beaten as well as Hitler. And that means a long time till you can get over and see her. I flew to the Pentagon for an off-the-record briefing and, Mark, I can tell you that what I heard made my hair stand on end. We can see a chink of light in Europe, but Japan is going to be hell. It'll take years to wipe those bastards off the map, yet the only way we'll ever win *is* to wipe them off. They're fanatics. They'll fight to the last man because they don't mind dying.'

'There's no chance of Serena coming back to Cairo?'

He shook his head. 'Not in the foreseeable future. Of course Farouk might change his mind one day.'

I had the idea that he was trying to tell me, without actually admitting it, that he knew most of what the so-called scandal was about. Stevenson knew *everything*, I reflected ruefully once again. Except about Jonothan? Though Stevenson could count, especially in months up to nine.

The letter was very long, a sad letter from a lonely woman pouring out her heart to someone far away.

My very own Mark,

Even though we are separated by an ocean and I'm alone except for Jonothan occupied in his playpen, I feel that I am your very own and that you belong to me. Sometimes you seem so very close to me that I wait for you to come through the door, my tall, slim Mark with those steady brown eyes. Then I look at the door and the dreamed-up sight that I expected of you is blurred by tears and Jonothan looks up at me, stands up shaking the playpen, stretching out his arms towards me because he knows I am unhappy, that something is wrong, and then he bursts into tears. Isn't it sad, how easy it is to overcome problems like the ones we faced together, if only you can share them, sort them out as we used to?

One problem I could never share with anyone, not even you, my beloved, was Jonothan. From the moment I knew it was your son – before that, when I *prayed* that I would bear your child – my sense of happiness and fulfilment was doubled. I never felt the guilt I should have felt, perhaps because I was the only one who knew, though once or twice I wondered if you had guessed, because of the date.

I should have felt guilty, and perhaps it is a sin from which I shall never be absolved and that Farouk has taken over the mantle of the Prophet and meted out punishment! But no, I will not do a 'Parmi' on you. Again no, it was not a sin to bear your child; I had kept to my part of the honourable bargain between members of our families, and once Greg and I were married there was no way I could ever tell him the truth.

But when Greg died – ah! beloved, I can imagine what you are thinking: Why didn't she tell me about Jonothan then? But I intended to tell you at the proper time – at the time you expected us to live openly together. After all, I *have* told you now, when really there is no need to, because time and distance have blurred the need. I did not tell you after Greg's death because you told me with all your heart and love that you wanted to flaunt our love openly in front of everyone. And I wanted that, too. But I did not want the secret to be shared until you were about to take a step that, in Cairo anyway, might have damaged your career, your life. And for you to do that – and I was proud that you wanted to – you had to take this step for me and me alone.

I could never have borne it if later in life you had even *thought* that you had taken me as your unmarried wife because of Jonothan. So I decided to 'give' Jonothan to you as my supreme gift, conceived in the tenderest moment of my life, on our 'wedding night', the day I officially took up residence in Holt House and openly shared your bed.

When the Sadik crisis overwhelmed me I forgot everything, and when I knew that I had to leave you – leaving Egypt was unimportant compared to leaving you – I had to let you read the diaries. I was frightened to tell you about Jonothan at that time. I thought one shock for us both was enough; you deserved a breathing space. I had to let you know because now there was no way we could live together, get 'married' for years and years until the end of this fearful war, and by then Jonothan would be no longer a baby, but a little boy. And I knew that if you still loved me after these years have passed – beloved, how long will that be? – then it would be because of me. And I too am selfish, and now that I am alone and a little afraid I need you more than ever, the moral help of the man I love more than life itself.

I shall write to you often, my beloved Mark.

S

35

During the years after Serena was banished from Egypt her letters to me were a joy, and I only hope that I wrote to her as well as she wrote to me. Once the first weeks had passed I began to gain some picture of her life, of how Jonothan was, how she was, what she was doing, the new friends she had made. She was working hard at her painting, though missing Baptise. But she had, she said, found a friend who was prepared to back her in a one-woman show once she had finished enough canvases.

He's fabulously rich, about sixty, and called Bruce King [she wrote], with three divorces and two heart attacks behind him. But though he's a very sick man he's kind and he's introduced me to lots of nice people. He's the sort of generous person who always invites a dozen friends to a restaurant. He's a multi-millionaire – but don't worry and don't be jealous! Bruce is slowly dying. He always has to travel with his doctor, who says his next attack will be fatal. Anyway, all my love is devoted to my 'husband' and our son.

She mentioned much else besides, of course – the name of the gallery where she hoped to have her show, a newspaper clipping with a photo of herself taken at some charity gala. It was in the society section of the paper, and I felt a stab of jealousy because she was laughing so happily. Under the photo was a caption: 'Miss Serena Sirry, of Cairo, and Mr Bruce King, the thrice-married industrialist, enjoying a joke at the Armed Forces Ball in New York.'

King was tall, bald, with a gaunt face and sunken eyes, but though he looked ill he had the possessive air which rich men always seem to have when escorting beautiful women.

'Is Cairo still as beautiful?' she asked, ignoring the clipping, just enclosing it without comment. 'I miss it so much – and you.' 'Please tell me,' she pleaded in another letter, 'how is Papa? Really, I mean. His writing used to be so precise, but now it's becoming spidery – it *looks* frail.'

This letter arrived before a new blow descended on Sirry Pasha's shoulders, but even so it was sometimes hard to remember that all our parents and their friends were growing older. Only Father, with his usual streak of perversity, refused to change with the passing years. He was as sprightly as ever, though by 1942 he had reached the age of sixty-six. Chiffon didn't dance quite as energetically as before, but she still never missed a cocktail party, though I did notice that from time to time she looked around for a chair as a relief from standing for two hours balancing a glass of champagne in one hand and a canapé in the other. Nor was her tall figure quite so straight-backed as it used to be, though she was still a fine-looking woman. But she had become a little – what's the word I searched for when I wrote to Serena? – a little angular, and had developed the beginning of a slight stoop.

The Sirrys were different. I don't think any casual friends – even me, so concerned about the Sirrys because of my involvement with Serena – realised the deep sense of loss both of them suffered with the departure of their daughter. And though Sirry Pasha had put on a brave front when he first talked about our reunion party after the war, he was feeling his age; the more so because Nasrani had been the focus of his life.

'He's beginning to look older than he should,' I said to Father.

'It's natural,' said Father. 'The average Egyptian doesn't last as long as the average Anglo-Saxon.'

'You can't expect me to believe that!' I exclaimed.

'It's true. They're dashing and exuberant when they're young, but so often they seem to go all to pieces physically, as though they can't stand the pace. Don't you remember that doggerel they used to teach us at school?

> It's easy to be a starter
> But are you a sticker too?
> It's easy enough to begin a job,
> It's harder to see it through.

'It's true, you know. No stamina.'

I laughed and asked, 'Do you think Farouk will "see it through"?'

'Not a hope. Dr Phillips says he'll be dead before he's forty.'

'I hope so!' I said vindictively. 'And I wonder sometimes about Aly.'

'He's not a sticker either,' said Father. 'Now, Greg would have been,' he sighed. 'I know he burned the old candle quite a bit but, well' – more cheerfully – '*you're* all right, despite the mess you made of your marriage. Ever get any news from your wife?'

'Parmi sends occasional letters,' I said. 'Of course everything's censored, so she writes carefully – almost as though she's composed a rough draft first. They're very pleasant, and sometimes I have the feeling that once the war's over she might want to come back to me. It's only a hunch.'

'Would you want that?'

'God forbid! After buggering off and leaving me cold? Never! Besides,' I added with a grin, 'I'm too busy with my spying to think about marriage.'

'Spying – still?'

'Just that. I *am* a serving officer,' I pointed out, 'subject to military discipline. And I'm just about ready to end a year of frustration. I've spent twelve months trying to nail down a man who I know is a German, but I can't prove anything, even though I've got a contact sleeping with him. Very pretty girl.'

'You do lead an exotic life, my boy,' Father said, more than a trifle enviously.

Actually there was a great deal of drudgery attached to my job, especially through 1942, though the nature of my work during those first months of Serena's banishment kept me from thinking too much. Apart from anything else, I had to try to unravel the mystery of the German spy codenamed Cheops, who, I now knew, was (like Hatem, the Egyptian NCO) sleeping with Anna, a Polish informer posing as a sympathetic German, who was repeating every whispered confidence to Samia. The trouble was, the matter was becoming increasingly urgent, for our setbacks in the desert had been shattering. When Tobruk fell to the Germans in June 1942 we lost 15,000 Britons dead or wounded, and Rommel's men took 45,000 Allied prisoners. Not for months would Montgomery be ready to score his first major victory in North Africa.

'And now's the time we need to strike,' said Brigadier Monson. 'We know that Cheops is operating, but from where? He's sending radio messages to the Germans all the time. If we can only plug the leak – even better, use the transmitter to send false information – we could go right ahead.'

We were in his office, seated either side of a large oak desk.

'Can't you get something out of your girlfriend?' he continued. He always called Samia that. 'Go to bed with her or something?'

'Something, sir?' I asked with pretended innocence.

'Yes, do *something*, for God's sake. Now.'

I decided to see Samia, but when I phoned she immediately warned me, 'I'm beginning to join all the bits and pieces together, but it might be better if we met outside the Sphinx.' With a laugh she added, 'Would you be ashamed if we met at Groppi's?'

'Good God, no. But Groppi's is being watched day and night. Come to Holt House. Father would love to see you.'

'May I? The girls adored him.'

'No need to mention that!'

She arrived just forty minutes later, dark eyes in the perfectly oval face looking perhaps a little more tired, a little more lined than when I had first met her, but still every inch an enticing beauty.

'But I've had to go on a diet to stop gaining weight,' she said when I complimented her. 'I'm starving to death!' As we walked into the Long Gallery I looked at her closely. She had an almost unnatural vivacity, like an actress playing to an audience. She had all the signs of having just had a fix.

'I wish you'd give up dope,' I begged. 'We can't afford to lose beautiful women like you.'

'Especially as the real beauty has left,' she said. 'I heard that she's gone to live in America. Oh well, I always knew I didn't stand a chance. She's a real Egyptian, that girl. I could have seen her love for you in her eyes even if she'd worn a veil.'

Before Samia and I got down to business Father and Chiffon came downstairs dressed for dinner, Chiffon towering above Samia in a black taffeta dress and fluttering, 'Oh dear! I've lost my bag. Now, where did I put it?'

'Here, Mother dear.' It was on the hall stand, within six inches of her. 'You're just off?'

Father was on his best behaviour, with not even a conspiratorial wink, but when I told Chiffon that Samia was a friend of the king's and owned a bar in the Kasr el Nil she fluttered again.

'You said the Sphinx?' she asked. 'I *love* it! We have a bridge four every afternoon at a club not far from your bar, and sometimes two of us walk back to the house and pop in there.' At this *she* gave a conspiratorial giggle. 'For a drink to overcome the rigours of post-mortems. My congratulations, my dear. So unusual in Cairo to find a respectable lounge where people can sit and rest without being ogled.'

'It's very kind of you to say so, Lady Holt.' Samia looked suitably demure.

'Come along, my dear,' Father hurriedly interrupted the pair of them. 'Or we'll be late for dinner.'

★

Before Samia left I learned an enormous amount, which later that evening I put into the form of notes to offer to Brigadier Monson for immediate action.

Cheops was in fact the son of a German mother who had divorced her German husband and then married an Egyptian when her son was eleven. As a German the boy was called Hans Werner. As an Egyptian, by his mother's marriage, he took the name of his stepfather and called himself Hussein Abboud. According to Samia, he had retained dual nationality. He spoke fluent Arabic as well as German and also spoke English, which he had been taught as a German schoolboy. By now Abboud, who thrived on a life of big spending, heavy drinking and lots of women, seemed quite unsuitable material for a successful spy; until I discovered, via Samia and Anna, what motivated him: his stepfather had kicked Hussein Abboud out of the house. It was only a matter of time before hate for his Egyptian stepfather was transferred into admiration for Germany and memories of his real father and the 'master race'.

Werner was so besotted with Anna by now – and so convinced that she would make good 'spy material' – that on Samia's suggestion Anna told Werner that she was fed up with being taken upstairs at the Sphinx and then having to go back to work. She issued an ultimatum: from time to time she wanted to spend the night with him, to show Werner she really loved him. Otherwise, it was all over between them.

That way Anna finally discovered where he lived, and more visits followed. She learned, among other facts, that Werner's friend was also a German. His name was Malkomes. I myself had seen them several times but all trails previously had led to a dead end.

Now, during one of Werner's visits to the Sphinx, DSO men searched the German's flat, following a tip-off from Anna that a radio was hidden in the cellar. There we made an interesting discovery. There were *two* radio transmitters, but neither worked. We had been puzzled because transmissions to Rommel had ceased. Now we discovered why. One transmitter was broken, while the second was a new American set which had been acquired in Switzerland (the

Swiss acted for German interests in neutral Egypt) but which
Werner told Anna he couldn't use because there were no
instructions on hand to set it up. He was waiting for them to
come from Berne. Then a few days after the search we
returned for another look and the new set had suddenly
vanished from Werner's flat.

All this I learned from Samia. But at the same time curious
moves were afoot which other branches of Intelligence were
piecing together but which I didn't at first connect with
Werner. Most important was the fact that Nasser's Free
Officers' Movement had decided to contact Rommel and to
offer to organise an uprising against the British in Cairo if
Rommel in return would guarantee the independence of
Egypt after Germany won the war. The final draft of a
so-called treaty (which no one saw at the time) was to be
flown to the German headquarters behind the lines; and since
Rommel was barely fifty miles from Alex this seemed to pose
no problem. We were also warned that in order to show good
faith the Egyptian pilot defecting to Rommel would carry
with him aerial photos of British army positions.

My first reaction was that the Free Officers must be crazy
if they thought the Germans would honour such a treaty.

And then, how could they organise it? Nasser might be the
mastermind behind the plot, but some months previously he
had been posted to southern Egypt, hundreds of miles from
the fighting zone. How could they communicate if their radio
didn't operate? The fact that the American-made transmitter
had suddenly vanished indicated an urgent attempt by an
expert to explain how to make it work. But who? And where?
Suddenly I had a gut feeling who *was* hoping to make the
transmitter work. Nasser's second-in-command – Sadat. I
wouldn't have given the matter a second thought but for the
fact that I kept a routine check on all movements of Egyptian
officers who had given me cause for suspicion. And there
stood the answer – right in front of me: Captain Anwar el
Sadat has been posted to the Signals Corps of the Egyptian
army in Cairo. Had Sadat hidden the missing radio?

We were still puzzling this out when one night a British plane seconded to the Egyptian air force vanished. It was an old Gloucester Gladiator. It had been flown by an Egyptian pilot, Ahmed Saudi Hussein, on a routine flight when (according to later information) it suddenly changed course and flew straight into German airspace, where the Germans, knowing nothing of what was happening, shot it down. The pilot was killed as the plane exploded.

'That's our man,' said the 'Brig' at our kitchen cabinet conference. 'And you can bet that the bloody treaty has gone up in flames too. But its contents could be transmitted by radio – so we must find the transmitter.'

'Sadat, in signals?' I asked.

The 'Brig' nodded, then crisply issued the necessary orders. 'Arrest Werner, Malkomes and Sadat. No, *we* won't do it. Let the military police handle it for us, then some of us will organise the interrogation.'

The next day Werner and Sadat were duly arrested. But Malkomes had vanished. Both the other men professed total ignorance of the charges against them, but one article Werner could not explain away – the huge quantity of forged five-pound notes, which we knew had been printed in Germany. He began to realise for the first time, especially after the damning evidence by Anna, that he might face the death sentence as a spy, and though he admitted nothing he was sent to jail.

Sadat, however, posed a different problem. He displayed all the anger of a deeply insulted officer. How could a captain in the Egyptian army be a spy? Werner he had never met. And as to a radio transmitter, why not search his house? We did – and found nothing.

All of us, however, were convinced that Sadat was implicated in the plot, though for the moment he had to be freed 'under surveillance'. It was proved that Nasser was nowhere near the scene when the treaty was drafted, though none doubted that he knew all about it, for he *was* leader of the Free Officers. But someone high up had arranged for the plane to fly to Rommel. And someone had hidden the transmitter.

We might never have really solved the case had not Winston Churchill exercised his powerful sense of imagination. In the summer of 1942 Churchill had decided to meet Stalin in Moscow on 12 August. It was a long and hazardous air trip, and Churchill broke the journey in several places. On 5 August he landed in Cairo, where he held a series of briefings, including one with Brigadier Monson, who told him how Werner, codenamed Cheops, had been caught, how Malkomes had vanished, but how Werner had refused to implicate the leading Egyptians who were known to have been in touch with him in order to stage an uprising.

Churchill was nothing if not direct. 'Send Werner to me,' he grunted to the 'Brig'.

When confronted with the man Churchill bluntly offered him a choice: either be shot the next day as a German spy or confess full details of the Egyptian connection, in return for which Werner would be kept under comfortable house arrest with no harassment, and given his freedom the day the war ended.

Werner didn't hesitate. He not only named several German agents working in Cairo but gave details of codes and transmission times. He also told Churchill that Malkomes had been posted, though he didn't know where. Most important of all, he named Sadat, even where a copy of the secret treaty was, signed by Sadat.

Then, to my astonishment, Brigadier Monson sent for me and announced, 'Look your best! The PM wants to see you – 1100 hours at his headquarters, the Mena House Hotel.'

I drove out along the pyramid road, arriving at ten minutes to eleven, to find the great man swimming naked in the Mena House pool. He climbed out, put on a towelled robe and lit a cigar, beckoning me to a chair. His first words startled me.

Looking at me over the tops of his glasses, he grunted, 'I understand you are a bastard.'

'Sir?'

'That's what Mr Werner calls you. He's a prize fish we've landed and he knows – so does the brigadier – that you led the enquiries. But' – he mouthed his words, almost lisping – 'we must not rest on our laurels. Where's the other man? Can you identify him?'

'I don't know where Malkomes is, sir, but I will be able to

make a positive identification when we pick him up.'

'When I return after my visit to Stalin,' he said, 'I will arrange for others to hunt him down. And when we find him – and we will one day – I will see that you are sent to make sure we've got the right man. Good-day to you.'

Back at work we checked on the final remaining details. Most important: though we were now ready to arrest Sadat, where was the hidden radio transmitter? Werner had given the address of a small apartment in Zamalek. There, he said, Sadat had asked a friend to keep a vital package for a few days.

Sadat was picked up the following morning, court-martialled, stripped of his rank and sent to the Aliens' Jail in Upper Egypt for two years. The Aliens' Jail, used during the war for offences connected with espionage and sedition, was comfortable. Each cell had a bed, blankets, chair, small table and electric light, and prisoners were allowed to smoke, though a prison officer had to light Sadat's pipe because matches and lighters were forbidden. There was something else, which Sadat would remember gratefully in later life. From the moment Nasser heard of Sadat's fate he ordered that the Free Officers' funds should pay Sadat's family about ten pounds a week for the duration of his sentence.

While this was happening we mounted a raid on the unknown flat in Zamalek. I myself went on the operation. One glance round the room told me all I wanted to know: it was a one-roomed flat, a typical 'love nest' apartment with virtually no furniture except for a large bed, half a dozen mirrors, a bathroom, a tiny kitchen with a small fridge and a selection of bottles. It certainly wasn't used by anyone who lived there. But in the middle of the room was the transmitter, in a bulky packing-case, the top opened.

If only I had left ten minutes earlier! Three of us had entered the flat, and while we were examining the set – quietly, so as not to disturb the neighbours – I heard the sound of a key being turned in the lock. I rushed to press myself against the wall behind the point where the door would open inwards, my pistol drawn in case of trouble. One colleague was on the other side ready to grab the man; so of course I didn't see him first.

Unsuspecting, the man pushed open the door, laughing at the pretty Arab girl who came in with him.

One of my men dived for the intruder's legs. The girl who was following screamed and managed to escape. I banged the door as the intruder kicked himself free and faced him for the first time.

It was Aly Sirry.

'I might have known it,' I almost groaned.

'Judas!' he cried. 'British bastard! Sadat warned me about you.'

I turned to one of the men, suddenly feeling very tired – and thinking of the terrible shock, not only for the Sirrys but most of all for Serena when she heard. 'Take him to the cells,' I said.

Aly was formally charged with possessing a transmitter, which was strictly against the law. Because the set had obviously never been used – some of the seals were still intact – and because of my influence the question of espionage was never brought up. And I was able to offer proof that he had been holding the set for Sadat.

Aly was eventually sentenced to six months in jail and this time nothing could save him. The news almost destroyed what was left of Sirry Pasha, and turned Madame Sirry into a bitter old woman. It must have been the last straw, following the banishment of Serena – how one bad twist of fate seems always to follow another! As though Sirry Pasha didn't have enough troubles piled on his shoulders.

There was nothing anyone could do to help. Sadat was in a comfortable detention camp but Aly, I knew, had to share a cell with three other prisoners, who had one bucket for slops, no mattress on their bunks, and one blanket each. I wondered what effect it would have, not only on the Sirrys but on Aly himself. Would he emerge from prison a full-blooded revolutionary? Instinctively I felt that he would. But how sad, I thought, that in the good old days Greg and Aly and Serena all used to play in the royal palace, and now – Greg was dead, Aly was in jail, and Serena banished from her own country.

It took the best part of a year for others far away to get a lead on the last figure in the story: Malkomes, the spy who had vanished just before Churchill made his deal with Werner.

I had almost forgotten him, because by the summer of 1943 the entire picture of the war had changed. In Europe, British and American aircraft were pounding Germany day and night – including such daring feats as the 'dam busters' raid in the spring of 1943 when British aircraft flooded the Ruhr by breaching the Mohne and Eder dams with 'bouncing bombs'. The Russians had fought with incredible bravery, and the first signs indicated that they would soon launch a counter-offensive. In the Pacific the first islands were being regained. And from our point of view in Cairo victory was complete. Montgomery and the Eighth Army had electrified the world by clearing North Africa of the last German. By the end of May a quarter of a million Germans had surrendered in Tunisia, the last enemy toe-hold in Africa.

It was at this time that Brigadier Monson, almost with a broad grin, asked me, 'What did you say to Churchill when you met him in Cairo a year ago?'

'I said nothing, sir. *He* said he understood I was a bastard.'

'You seem to have made an impression on him. Perhaps this is his way of thanking you for the part you played in the Werner affair. Here, read this: it's been decoded. It's a message from Whitehall.' It read:

PERSONAL FROM PRIME MINISTER WHO WISHES COLONEL HOLT OF DSO MAKE POSITIVE IDENTIFICATION OF MALKOMES NOW BELIEVED WORKING GERMAN EMBASSY LISBON MESSAGE ENDS

I found it hard to believe. 'But it's almost a year ago,' I blurted.

'Churchill has a good memory,' chuckled Monson. 'Lucky dog.'

'You mean I'm to go?'

'Of course. Since when have you disobeyed the Prime

Minister? Top secret, though, and all you have to do is make your positive identification: other people will decide what to do with Malkomes. Once you get to Lisbon it'll only take you a couple of days to check your man out. Then come straight back.'

'Sounds wonderful.' I could hardly believe it. The prospect of spending a couple of days in a country with no troops around! And a *different* city – different cultures, different viewpoints, different coloured skins. But apart from and above all that, really neutral. Egypt in theory was neutral, but in reality it was an armed British camp in a country at war in all but name. It was true that in Cairo we wanted for nothing – we were probably better fed than the people in Lisbon. But *neutral!*

At that word, synonymous with peace, a sudden, wild thought struck me. Providing one's papers were in order there should be nothing to prevent one neutral from visiting another neutral country. A Swiss could visit Portugal, I supposed, providing he had a visa – and transport. Well, if that were possible, what was to stop a neutral Egyptian from visiting neutral Portugal? *And Serena was a neutral Egyptian.* Of course she would be bound hand and foot in red tape if she tried such a madcap adventure, but red tape was meant to be cut. It all depended on who was wielding the scissors.

Surely Jim Stevenson could arrange to find a spare seat in one of the scores of troop-carrying planes now crossing the Atlantic?

The 'Brig' interrupted my thoughts. 'You might have to wait ten days or so before you leave. After all, we can't go barging into neutral countries without getting the right bumf. But with Churchill giving the go-ahead there should be no problems.'

'In Lisbon – could I stay on for a few days – on leave, sir?'

He hesitated for only a few seconds.

'Ten days?'

'Thank you, sir.' I knew better than to exult. How I spent my leave would be my affair, but I didn't think the 'Brig' would look as favourably on my request had he known that I was going to try to mobilise the might of the

United States to arrange for me to meet my girlfriend.

Fortunately the 'Brig' immediately plunged into the technical details of the visit: codes, request for assistance in Lisbon, accommodation. He ended up, 'Carry on when you get there without informing me until you've made a positive identification. I'll arrange with Lisbon to report to me the details of your return flight to Cairo. After your leave.'

I could hardly control my excitement when I saw Stevenson two days later, the first moment both of us were free to meet.

'I need your help,' I cried. 'Now, more than ever before.'

'Hold your horses!' He beckoned to the barman at Shepheard's. 'Gimlet? You sound as though you've won the war single-handed.'

I sipped the ice-cold gin and lime, served as it should be in a champagne glass with crushed ice, and said, 'Jim, I've got to trust you. I wouldn't – except that I'm going abroad on a job, and the Americans will certainly have to fly me, so you're bound to see the manifest anyway.' I knew, of course, that there was a regular, almost daily direct flight from Cairo to Lisbon, now that there was no danger from the enemy.

'Lisbon?' he asked.

I nodded, finishing my drink.

'And then I've got ten days' leave,' I said. 'And I wondered – since Portugal is neutral, if – well, you can guess –'

'Serena?'

'Who else?'

'I must say' – he gave his slow wink and called for another round – 'you're a real glutton for punishment. You're sure she'd want to see you?'

'Absolutely certain.'

He thought for a moment. 'I expect it could be arranged,' he said finally.

For the best part of a week I waited. Suspense! The awful thing was that Serena and I couldn't discuss the preparations with each other. We couldn't phone, and we didn't dare cable anything to do with our plans: with my name on the DSO list, anything going through the censor would be reported right back to HQ. I didn't even dare phone Stevenson. I controlled my impatience and waited for him to contact me.

He did. Five days later.

'All laid on,' he said laconically, this time at Holt House. 'I see from the manifest that you're booked to leave a week on Monday. She'll arrive on the Thursday.'

'I'm told that Lisbon is jammed solid with civilians enjoying themselves. I wonder – I daren't book a double room through the embassy?'

'No need,' he said cheerfully. 'You've been fixed up with a regular love nest at Cascais, fifteen miles out of Lisbon.'

I had been to Cascais when we were young and I had vague memories of a tiny fishing village with very blue water.

'I must say, that sounds great.' I held up my glass in a silent toast. 'You *are* a good fixer.'

For once Stevenson was caught off-guard.

'Don't thank me,' he said. 'All the messages came through official channels working with us, but I gather that the – er – rendezvous was fixed by Serena. It's owned by a friend of hers – I've met the chap, a tycoon called Bruce King – he's the sort of guy who keeps a suite at the Ritz all year round, in case he pops in for the odd evening.'

'I know the name. Serena told me about him.'

'Well, he's lent you both his villa for a couple of weeks.'

'It's like a dream come true,' I almost whispered. 'I can hardly believe it.'

Though my mission was secret – and of course Stevenson had no idea about the nature of my job in Lisbon – I had to tell Sirry Pasha that I might be meeting Serena. By now I felt so utterly sorry for him that I couldn't deny him the pleasure of knowing that I was to see his beloved daughter.

The chance came when I saw him strolling round his garden. I walked across to join him, and together we made our way to the veranda, and sat down, looking across the Nile. How old and changed he had become! He had had such a well-filled figure, almost spruce when he used to travel on the *Kismet* to Nasrani. Now he looked dried up, the skin of his neck hung loosely, and even his clothes seemed too large for him.

'Sirry Pasha,' I said formally, 'as you know, the nature of my duties means that I have to work in complete secrecy.'

He smiled. 'Of course. I understand.'

'So please don't ask me any questions. I haven't even told Chiffon or my father. That's how secret it is. But you and I – well, I'm going to see Serena for a few days.'

He looked at me, unbelieving. The shock was so sudden that for a moment I thought he was going to cry.

'I'm so glad for you,' he said finally. 'And I'm going to see my daughter through your memory. Sometimes I have the feeling – stupid, I know – that I'll never see her again.'

'Nonsense,' I interrupted. 'What about the promised re-union when the war's over?'

'If I can make it. It's you two who matter. In a way you are the son I always wanted. And Serena is my love. The two of you – I'm so happy. Let me know how she looks when you return.'

'I will,' I promised and gave his arm a squeeze before going back to Holt House.

36

Serena arrived in Lisbon on a perfect summer's afternoon three days after I had made my positive identification of Malkomes and was a free man. I pressed my face to the window of the Portela Airport and picked her out immediately. She was dressed in a pale lemon jacket and skirt, her fair hair hanging over her shoulders. She stepped carefully down the metal steps from the grey and khaki camouflaged plane, long legs showing.

Looking around anxiously, she suddenly saw me, blew me a kiss, and twenty minutes later, formalities speeded by the Americans, she walked into the arrival hall, dropped her overnight bag and ran – literally ran – to throw her arms around me.

'It's been so long,' she whispered. 'So long, and I've been so lonely.' She kissed me, then gave the mischievous laugh that showed up her dimple. 'What will the porter think? Don't worry, I wiped my lipstick off before I left the plane.'

'I wouldn't have given a damn if you made me look like a Red Indian.' My voice was husky. 'I can't believe that I'm actually holding you.' I signalled for a porter to follow me to the self-drive car which had been provided for me. 'Actually holding your hand! I'd forgotten how long and slender your arms are – after all this wasted time.'

'We'll make up for it,' she said almost shyly, squeezing my arm, then holding me away from her. 'Let me look at you. You've lost weight. You look tired. But' – kissing me in front of everyone – 'you've still got your beautiful mop of hair. And tell me, darling, how are Mama and Papa?'

'Growing older,' I sighed. 'Aly's escapade didn't help to restore your father's faith in humanity.'

'Was it awful for Aly – in jail, I mean?'

'I don't know. It's always pretty rough in an Egyptian jail. He's out now, of course. But what about news for me – how's Jonothan?'

'Thriving. I tried everything I knew to get a place for him, but not a hope. After all, it was a US air force plane. There were only two other civilians on board. I did wonder what the air force would have said if I'd told them he was going to see his father. But I didn't dare.'

'I know. I asked Stevenson if it might have been possible for you to bring Jonothan along, but there was no way.'

'Never mind. We'll all meet soon. Now the Germans are out of North Africa, I'm sure it won't be long.'

I tipped the porter and took the wheel. 'We'll drive straight to Cascais,' I suggested. 'It's only a few miles and it's a wonderful place.'

'You know where it is?' she asked. 'Bruce gave me an address, and said there was a housekeeper there all year round. That's all I know.'

'It's heaven,' I answered. 'I've already been to see it, and

415

to check on the way to reach the villa. Mrs Lima, the house-keeper, is obviously a treasure. A sort of Portuguese Zola.'

'How far?' she asked. 'I want to soak in a bath – and then –'

'No time lag? It must be early morning in New York.'

'Not yet. After. First a bath' – again the slight touch of shyness, understandable perhaps after such a long absence – 'and then your arms, darling, and after that a long sleep. Unless' – her dimple showing as she laughed – 'you want to go dancing?'

'I'll settle for a sleep,' I replied gravely.

She had been looking at me as we drove along, studying me with those green eyes of hers. Suddenly she said, 'Yes, you've definitely lost weight. It suits you. Too much hard work?'

'Well, it wasn't much fun being present when Aly slipped up. And there have been some pretty hairy moments,' I admitted. 'But – sounds damned silly, I know – I really lost weight because I missed you. At first I felt so sick and miserable I couldn't eat. And when I lost the pounds they seemed to remain lost. I'll probably put it all back in the next ten days.'

We were driving leisurely, one of her hands resting on my knee, pressing it gently, as the road followed the Tagus, and I pointed out the string of yellow forts built in the seventeenth century to repulse an invasion by the Spaniards who, until then, regarded Portugal as their colony. Finally we rounded a bend and reached Cascais, the small village of colour-washed houses in the narrow main street, the tiny port and harbour, the blue sea on the left, and to our right as we drove in the hillsides sweeping to the sky, the forests of pine and eucalyptus dotted with villas tucked into the woods. I turned the car right and made for the hills and the forest. Finally I drew up before a wrought-iron gate opening on to some steps. I tooted the horn.

A comfortably built woman – Mrs Lima – came bustling down the steps to greet us and take our bags. We walked up the steps, a curious sensation because, as the villa was built on a levelled plateau sliced into the hillside, the view above emerged only piece by piece as with each step we climbed nearer the house and grounds.

Then it was all there. On the left stood a pink house in the shape of a double 'L', which formed a natural three-sided courtyard filled with summer furniture and umbrellas. In front the grounds consisted of an unusual form of landscape gardening. There were no flower-beds, only two acres of an exactly rectangular lush green lawn. The two longer sides were hidden from neighbours by big trees. The far end, facing the house, lay open to a distant view of sea fusing with sky until one walked there and could then look down the hillside to the houses of the village far below.

But what made the garden even more intriguing was that in the centre of the beautifully kept rectangle of grass was a pool in precisely the same proportions as the lawn. The effect was uncanny, because the pool and the surrounding marble tiles were painted the exact green of the lawn, instead of the almost traditional blue; and they so disguised the pool that at first I didn't realise it was there. Looking at the water was like looking at the lawn through the wrong end of a telescope.

The house inside was equally delightful. One big long room had a huge fireplace, two fat inviting sofas, a backgammon table – not one of my vices – and a small dining recess. In one of the two wings which formed the sides of the courtyards was a kitchen and a small room where Mrs Lima slept. The other had two bedrooms, each with a bathroom – one of them containing a large double bed, the other twin beds.

I couldn't speak a word of Portuguese while Mrs Lima couldn't speak a word of English, but she had spent several months working in Italy before the war and had acquired a smattering of Italian, so though I hardly knew the language it was easy to get the sense because so many words were similar to either English or French, and somehow we broke down the language barrier.

Her first Italian was a firm, '*La camera con il letto matrimoniale naturalmente, Signora?*'

'*Si, si, si, si,*' cried Serena with equal firmness, and then suddenly her first shyness seemed to vanish and, as Mrs Lima left the bags in the bedroom, she said, 'No bath for me.' She pointed to two towelling bathing wraps. 'And look. There's a shower by the edge of the pool. That'll do. Then a swim. Then bed.'

I was rummaging for my swimming trunks when she smiled, then said almost gently, 'No, not *those*. Put on the robe until we get to the pool – we don't want to shock Mrs Lima yet – and then we'll bathe in the nude.'

We did. We kissed and touched each other's bodies as we swam and splashed each other in the water, almost as though exploring one another after such a long absence. The water was crystal-clear, warm and caressing, and when Serena turned to float on her back she said, 'Just in case you can't remember what I look like.'

'I daren't show you what I look like,' I said.

'I'll feel you instead.' She groped for me under the water of the shallow end and then, as I moved towards her, feeling her, stroking her soft breasts, the wet hairs below, she said softly, 'No, not here. Don't let's waste it. Let's go to bed.'

Putting on our robes we ran back to the far end of the lawn and as we helped dry each other looked at the view where the ledge stopped.

'Better go inside,' I whispered, 'before Mrs Lima sees us.' I was worried lest Mrs Lima had already seen too much. I needn't have. When, wrapped, we reached the dark red stone floor of the living room and grabbed a couple of extra towels for our hair there was our housekeeper with a silver tray and two glasses saying with a smile, 'Now. A glass of iced white port will taste *really* good.'

Cold white port, though a popular apéritif in Portugal, was not my favourite tipple, but it did taste good.

'I still can't believe we're together.' We lay in each other's arms, pressed together, toes touching, faces and lips touching, her breasts squeezed against my chest, both of us savouring the delicious moments of anticipation, fighting not to make love too soon, making the anticipation last. I stroked her, kissed her all over, until finally neither of us could wait any longer and, no word spoken, she turned half over and opened her legs.

When it was all over she said sleepily, 'Stay inside me a bit longer.' It wasn't easy, lying there on top of her, hardly daring to move until, almost with a final sigh of happiness, she fell asleep. I had never seen anyone fall asleep like that, like an animal exhausted – after the time difference from New York, the movement of the plane, the exhaustion of playing in the pool, of holding back, the sense of happiness and joy.

Now I knew I could gently disentangle myself and sleep too, but by her side. That's what I thought, but then an extraordinary thing happened. As I prepared to move gently so as not to wake her, I looked at the half-smile on her lips, the beauty of her breasts, bare and firm on the pillow, and I suddenly felt myself growing firm again. Without realising what I was doing I began moving gently within her. She didn't respond, and I didn't want to wake her, yet I couldn't keep still. I moved so gently that she didn't know I was moving, and suddenly I was as strong as I had ever been, and I had to fight with all my will not to move faster, more impatiently. Still she slept on, occasionally moving her legs in her sleep as though dreaming, while I barely moved, just gently, until I thought I could no longer control my urge and would have to wake her. Only now it had become a point of excitement *not* to wake her. Suddenly it was all over, except that it wasn't only me. She had been dreaming – she still was – while fast asleep, but she moved once or twice again and without warning I felt a new moist heat inside her, and that was all I needed. When I turned gently away from her she was still smiling, the dimple showing as I, too, fell asleep.

It was eight o'clock when we woke, one of her arms thrown happily across my chest. I kissed her gently.

'I had such an erotic dream.' Sleepily she opened her big green eyes. 'You were making love to me. It was so real that I felt as though I had' – she hesitated – 'as though I'd come.'

'You did.' I kissed her again. 'You were dead to the world, and the last thing you asked me was to stay inside you for a few minutes. I tried, and then I grew excited, and I was determined not to wake you, and –'

'So you raped me!'

'Sort of. It was bliss. And you *did* come. I could actually feel it, all over me, hot. It was wonderful.'

★

We dined at the tiny harbour in Cascais, starting with grilled sardines, followed by wonderful lobsters broiled and served with a peppery sauce, and ice-cold local white wine.

After dark, bells started ringing. The patron, who spoke a little English, pointed out two of them, suspended under arches over the roof of a large building, perhaps the town hall, he didn't say. 'The bell is the signal that the evening's catch is arriving,' he explained. As he spoke half the village seemed to move towards the tiny harbour. 'You should go and watch the auction of the fish.'

We walked down to the beach, arm in arm. A score of lanterns on poles -- and others on the fishing boats being moored – flickered and danced, with dozens of moths banging ineffectually against the lights.

Barefoot fishwives arrived carrying what looked like empty stretchers. On these thousands of small wriggling silvery fish were piled, a stretcher for each catch, which was then carried to the man acting as auctioneer.

It was what is known in England as a 'Dutch auction'. He started by demanding a price that was obviously too high, for it was greeted with shouts of derision. He lowered the price until someone shouted, *'Tchai!'*

That was the Portuguese word for 'Sold'. The next stretcher of fish was soon sold off, and we walked back to the restaurant for strong coffee and the drive home.

'Back to bed,' she said.

'Not tonight, Josephine,' I laughed.

'Ah!' she taunted me. 'So you want me to go to sleep first. You've suddenly realised that you like me to behave like an Egyptian wife who just exists so that a man can pleasure himself without thinking of the woman.'

'You didn't do too badly!' I retorted.

We had so much to talk about, so much lost time to make up, that for the first three days we didn't even bother to drive into Lisbon. We stayed in bed late, and swam in the pool. Mrs Lima cooked us lunch, including one day a dish of local grilled fillets of fish with fried bananas; we dined in the village, often to the haunting music of a local fado singer and the beauty of flickering lanterns bobbing on the fishing boats far out to sea.

The photographs of Jonothan were a joy. Sitting on the chunky pink sofa we spread them out on the large coffee table in front of the empty fireplace – a long, oval Chinese table covered with plate-glass to protect the gold Chinese lacquer of an Oriental scene. The photos showed a sturdy boy who always seemed to be laughing and standing up straight, even when snapped offering an object to whoever took the picture. He had curly blond hair, and by now was four years old, dressed in shorts, with one of the T-shirts which had just become popular among the American GIs stationed in North Africa, and had suddenly become a craze among boys and girls across the United States. Serena said, 'Don't you think he looks exactly like you?'

He did. He had the same shaped face as mine, not as round as Greg's had been, though the little boy's features were obviously not yet fully formed.

She leaned forward and kissed Jonothan's face. 'Much more important, he has your character. He looks you straight in the eye when he answers you.'

'It's incredible to think that he's ours,' I said. 'Don't you think? I was wondering whether we shouldn't recognise legally who was his father, or at least to his friends in America.'

As throughout our lives, she knew exactly what I was thinking.

'Don't let's rush things,' she said. 'He has British nationality, he is called Jonothan Holt, so he bears your name, and I've told him that his father is away at the war. Let it rest at that. And when the war's over we'll see the simplest way to do it. Events have a habit of taking care of themselves if you wait long enough.'

'I wasn't thinking of that.' I hesitated. 'Of course I want him to be officially regarded as my son, but so long as everyone assumes that's the case –'

'Well, then?'

'I was being morbid. If anything happened to me? The title.'

'Don't ever think that, Mark.'

'People do get run over by buses,' I laughed.

'Well, you won't. Enough of that nonsense.' She added practically, 'Anyway, if anything did happen to us wouldn't young Jonothan be the rightful heir?'

Of course that was true. 'Let's forget the whole thing,' I said cheerfully, and went to look at the photos again. Several of them included Serena with Jonothan, and one or two were in groups. She told me about some of her friends, men and women, what they did, and one showed Jonothan offering a small toy to a thin, tall, balding man.

'He looks ill but prosperous – rich enough to be your friend King. I remember his face from the newspaper clipping you sent me.'

'Let me look. Yes, that's Bruce.'

'Why does he look so rich? It's not as though he's particularly well-dressed. Or –'

'I suppose it's the confidence that real wealth gives a man,' she said. 'Not being ostentatious, but regarding money as a normal sort of thing to have. You have a bit of that look about you. And your father even more.'

'You don't talk much about him. What's he like, your Mr King?'

'He's not *my* Mr King,' she said almost crossly. 'And if it comes to that I'm not his Mrs King. Got that clear?'

'Yes,' I smiled meekly.

'The most important thing about Bruce is that he's a rare man who's not only unbelievably rich but incredibly generous. In a quiet way. I don't mean endowing museums and art collections and that sort of thing.'

'In what way, then?'

'The other day he asked to see the salary list of his American holding company. Only a small staff. He discovered which five men were the lower paid – the going rate, but they hadn't yet made the grade; one of them was an office boy, for instance – and then sent the five of them with their families on a two-week holiday in California, everything paid. An extraordinary thing to do, when you think about it.'

'You sound very enthusiastic.' I was looking at the photo of Bruce King again.

'I am. It's thanks to him we've got this enchanting house.'

'I could have afforded a hotel,' I said.

'Of course you could, my beloved, but isn't this more wonderful?'

'I suppose so.' I was feeling vaguely jealous; not so much of the unknown Mr King, but of the circumstances that made him a close friend of Serena's. Of the life I knew nothing about, the friends, her entire lifestyle in America. In the past I had shared all Serena's life, even when she was married to Greg, even before we had fallen in love; everything since she had been one year old. Now I was looking at a group of obvious friends, laughing in the photos, a group to which war had posted a sign which might just as well have said, 'No Entry'.

I am sure that Serena knew what was passing through my mind, but she chose to ignore it, deliberately saying again, 'Wouldn't you be pleased if a friend offered you this house?'

I was thinking, Depends what rent he charges!

And this time she did read my thoughts and said, even more angrily, 'I told you, there's nothing between Bruce and me. Nothing at all. But he *is* very kind and he does help me in dozens of ways.'

'I'm sorry.' I kissed her. 'I didn't mean to be beastly, but I do get jealous of a life in which I can't share. And – oh! I don't know. Rich men have such an advantage.'

'Not always. I wouldn't call two almost fatal heart attacks much of a privilege, for all Bruce's fortunes. Money and happiness don't always go together.'

'I know.'

'On the other hand,' she added, unburdening herself, 'Papa wasn't exactly poor, but now he's no longer rich. I don't mean that he's going to be kicked out of our house or sack the servants, but – you understand. The war is changing all our values.'

'Of course. He told me as much. And does it affect you?'

'Only indirectly,' she explained. 'He still gives me the same allowance, but with inflation it doesn't go as far. And though

I did have a one-woman show earlier this year I only broke even after all the expenses. And this is where Bruce has helped – without asking anything in return.' She smiled. 'He owns dozens of apartments, including most of one block on Park Avenue, and so I changed the large one I first moved into for a smaller one which Bruce lets me have, through his lawyers, for a nominal rent. No, he's not saving anything. It seems that people living on Park Avenue expect to have a large apartment – the rent is unimportant to them – but they won't even look at a small place under their roof, like mine. It's been empty for years. It suits me fine. And in New York anyone who lives rent-free – well, that makes you a millionaire of a different kind.'

'I understand. And I'm not really jealous.'

'But I want to know about *you*,' she said. 'I want to know everything about everyone – all my friends, all that's happened –'

'Where shall we start?' I asked laughingly.

'What's Aly doing now?' she asked.

'I hardly see him. We're polite when we meet at Shepheard's, but of course he's not exactly popular. He's been kicked out of the Gezira. After all, he has a police record now. Samia has put him on a black list.'

'But why? Half the crooks in Cairo meet at the Sphinx.'

'Aly comes into a different category. He's got palace connections – and if there's any more scandal even touching your father, well, Samia feels it's better for him not to be seen there.'

'Very considerate of her,' she said sarcastically.

'Samia *is* considerate.'

'You see her often?'

'Very often.'

'Business or pleasure?'

'Business.'

'Then I forgive you – but I still remain suspicious. I've always known you have a soft spot for that singer. Ever since you slept with her.'

'Me?'

'I knew. For days you smirked like a cat who'd been licking

up cream.' Suddenly she asked, 'Once I'll forgive you, because that was before we fell in love. But since I left? Have you ever? In the course of duty, I mean?'

I shook my head. 'Scout's honour. But I have to keep on the right side of her. You can imagine what a source of information she is to someone she likes. And she does like me. *Like*.'

'Is she still on drugs?' asked Serena. 'You once told me she would grow fat and bloated. Has she?'

'No, she hasn't. She started taking the pills she refused to take before. She has her off-days when she looks a bit the worse for wear, but she's still an attractive woman. Kind of sultry, even though her face is a bit creased.'

'You seem to remember everything about her – almost as though you've made a study of her.'

'Always get to know everything you can about your contacts. That's a cardinal rule in our line of work!'

'By the way, how is that obstinate wife of yours?'

That was better; safer ground. 'As religious as ever,' I said cheerfully. 'Parmi writes occasionally. Keeps on saying that after the war she'd like to come and see me. After what she and her father have done to me – to us, to you – I'd run a thousand miles to miss her – unless she was serving divorce papers on me.'

The end of the perfect idyll came with brutal suddenness, all the more savage because we were both powerless to annihilate distance after tragedy had struck.

We had gone into Lisbon when the news came through. Despite the feverish war that surrounded this beautiful city the British doggedly pursued their traditions, and when we went to the Ajuda Sports Club for a pre-lunch drink we found a cricket match in full swing.

We planned to lunch at the Hotel Aviz. It was small, only thirty-one rooms, but with five staff to every guest, and we strolled up the Avenida Fontes Pereira de Malo, near the bull-ring. Inside, thick pile carpets deadened the sound of footsteps; there were mirrors everywhere, dark-coloured armchairs and a bar that looked like an English club. 'It's famous for its cuisine,' I found myself whispering.

'Glutton! But I suppose it's about time we had a change from fish and bananas,' laughed Serena as we sat down.

The dining room presented a strange, unreal scene, wonderful food, a delicious bottle of white wine, beautifully dressed women sipping champagne, but all this with one startling difference from the cosmopolitan equivalent in Cairo. The Aviz in Lisbon was crowded with army officers enjoying the delights of a neutral country; but the officers sitting at adjacent tables were ruthless antagonists on neutral territory – as many Germans clicking heels or adjusting monocles as there were easy-going British and American officers. This was a meeting-place for enemies, most of whom had exchanged their revolvers for hidden cameras or tape-recorders.

'It seems so sad,' I said, watching them. 'Here they are, sticking knives and forks into roast beef, but it's only by chance. If they'd been posted somewhere else they might be sticking their knives into each other.'

'There but for the grace of God goes my favourite spy – you,' she smiled.

We were toying with our coffee when I saw a young man in a grey flannel suit standing at the heavy plate-glass entrance doors to the restaurant as though looking for someone.

'Isn't that the American from the embassy?' I pointed him out to Serena. 'I suppose because you came under American auspices he looked after you when the plane landed and he got you through the customs.'

He had struck me during the few moments of meeting as a personable, easy-going man.

'I wonder who he's looking for?' she asked.

At that moment, as though catching sight of Serena's green eyes, he spotted us and gave a tentative wave of recognition.

'I'll go,' I said. 'He probably wants to check your flight time.' There were only three days to go before she was due to return.

I threaded my way past the tables. 'You remember me?' I shook his hand. 'I'm Colonel Holt.'

'Yes, sir. I'm so glad you came first. I drove to Cascais to catch you, and the housekeeper said you might go to the

Aviz.' He looked desperately ill at ease. 'I'm so glad I saw you first.'

I had a sudden premonition of disaster – and I knew that Serena almost always reacted as I did. 'What's the matter?' I could sense the urgency, almost bordering on panic in his tone, as though afraid.

'I don't know how to tell you, Colonel, but –'

'What the hell's the matter?' I almost shouted.

'It's Mrs Holt's son,' he started miserably. 'An accident.'

'How bad?'

'Very bad.' Something in his face must have communicated itself to Serena. I saw her jump up, upsetting the coffee cup on the snowy white linen cloth as she ran forward. I grabbed her arm, then her shoulders.

We stood by the doors for an eternity that lasted only seconds. A few people at the tables nearest us looked up, aware of the tension, of the sudden charge in the atmosphere, the presence of fear, of bad news.

'Is it Jonothan?' she cried. The man's silence was testimony enough.

'Tell me.' She almost shook the man as she grabbed his shoulders.

'It's your son, Mrs Holt, and I'm afraid' – his words tailed off as he mumbled – 'there's been an accident.' He was groping for words to try and minimise the shock. 'I've only received a short message. The little boy was – I'm sorry, Mrs Holt, but I had to tell you – he was apparently killed instantly.'

Though Serena was not the kind of woman to swoon at such a moment I held her up, steadying her, my own torment racking me as she uttered a wail of anguish. It had an almost unearthly ring, not a shriek, not an Anglo-Saxon sound at all, but an uncontrollable, tortured noise which I had heard in the past in Cairo.

Someone at a nearby table jumped up to help.

'Thank you.' I helped Serena out of the main dining room. 'She'll be all right in a minute.' Outside the dining room was a small circular annex, a few occasional tables and chairs covered with a peach-coloured velvet where one could wait for a guest who was late. But lunch was virtually over, and the room was empty.

I couldn't begin to analyse my own feelings of grief because I knew that at this moment in my life the most important single thing I could do was help Serena by trying to keep my own head.

'Sit down.' I helped her into a chair. She was dry-eyed still, but the expression of pain on her face was unbearable. I turned to the young American. 'Could you get some brandy – for all of us?' A waiter was hovering around.

Deathly pale, gripping the bleached wooden arms of the chair, she looked at the young American and, with an attempt at a smile, said, 'I'm sorry I made such a spectacle of myself.'

He smiled back, but I was thinking, confused by the shock of a son of mine whose death I couldn't explain to him, He must be eager to get away. And he'll be out for dinner tonight and have forgotten all about it. The man who bears bad tidings can forget them when the job is done.

'Not at all, ma'am,' he said politely. 'I'm only sorry –' The words tailed off.

The brandy arrived. The young man seemed to need it as much as we did. He downed his in one gulp.

Serena put the glass down on her small circular table. 'How did it happen?'

The first shock over – perhaps helped by the fact that it had been expressed so publicly in that one terrible wail – Serena now displayed all the character that made her such a wonderful woman. It was as though she physically forced herself to behave correctly. Certainly she behaved better than I did. I was stunned – and I am sure my face showed it. Yet I could say nothing – not until the American had left – except express my sorrow at the death of a nephew. There was no way – yet – in which I could display the agony at the loss of a son. I could not act like a father, and in a way it was as though she tried to help me, for she moved across to a sofa, patted the velvet-covering, and said quietly, 'Come and sit next to me' – so that the man thought she needed my help, though we knew that I needed hers.

Before the American left he told us briefly what had happened. Jonothan had been leaving Central Park with his nursemaid when he had run out into the busy street opposite the Pierre Hotel and had been knocked down. That was all. A lifetime ended before it had hardly begun. Trying to soften the blow for Serena, but not knowing of my involvement, he drew me aside and told me more details, thinking perhaps that I could absorb some of her shock.

'How did you get the news?' I asked finally.

'A Mr King – apparently he's a big industrialist – contacted the embassy, and arranged with them for your sister-in-law to fly home tomorrow. He got her a Category A priority. That's really big stuff. She's top of the flight list.'

He went on to explain details of the flight to Serena while I stood to one side, dumbly waiting. Then the American left. What a wicked irony it all was. Bruce King taking over – and I of course was grateful for the way he pulled strings – to attend to the funeral of *my* son. And there was no way I could be present. I could imagine the scornful refusal I would get from the top brass if I asked permission to fly to New York to attend the funeral of my nephew! So, in the morning, she would leave, fly west to shed her tears among her friends, and I – no need to use up more of my leave now – would fly east, tears unshed except in private.

Alone, we sat down again on the sofa, then got up, she pacing restlessly, but both of us unable to venture out into the busy street. The restaurant doors closed as the last lunchers left, and through the plate-glass I could see the staff move in with vacuum cleaners, brushes, clean tablecloths, napkins, silverware, ready to start all over again. I felt, sitting there in silence, that we were in a way acting as shock-absorbers to each other, but I was wrong. Her silence had not only been a sign of grief but of decision.

After what seemed like months of silence she turned to me and said, 'Mark, try to understand, please. But I don't want to go back to Cascais.'

'I do understand,' I said. 'We'll stay here.'

'No, not "We". I want to stay here alone till the plane goes tomorrow. I asked the embassy man to book a room for me;

they always keep a few for VIPs. Then he'll take me to the airport in the morning.'

'But we can't,' I said, adding selfishly, 'You can't leave me alone!'

'I must. Can't you see how terrible this is for me? How we've been punished, especially me, leaving our baby alone with some stupid, careless nanny. God has punished me.'

Like an echo from the past I thought of the words that Parmi had uttered when our daughter had died, and how she had refused ever to share my bed again, because God had punished her.

'Please,' I entreated her. 'I need help as much as you do. More. Even if we cry all night, at least let's share those tears in each other's arms. God knows how long it'll be before we meet again. Please.'

'I can't. It isn't that I don't love you, Mark, it's just that I can't. I'm beyond feeling at this moment. I'm numb – and I can't get it out of my head that in some way we've never realised until now, we're – we're *bad* for each other. Everything we do together turns sour and bitter. Greg. Aly – yes, though you weren't to blame – Nasrani, *everything*. And now, poor little Jonothan. Just starting out on life, and I left him. I left him just to spend a week making love to you. It's true! I'll never forgive myself for what I did. Never. If I hadn't been so anxious to jump into bed with you poor Jonothan would be alive today. You know it.'

'It's my fault as much as yours. Mine, yours – and the war.'

'It's too easy to blame everything on that.'

She was on the verge of tears when she asked, almost as a sudden thought, 'Do you think we made another baby at Cascais?' Laughing hysterically, she cried, 'One goes, a replacement arrives! What'll happen if we have made a baby? Shall I leave it alone one weekend when I dash off to go to bed with someone?'

I was horrified, reminded again of the ravings of Parmi. Reading my thoughts, she said, 'No, I'm not suffering from religious mania. One Parmi in the family is enough.'

'Listen, my beloved.'

I put my arms round her but she pushed them away.

'Please go. Please!' She raised her voice almost to a cry.
'Now?'
'Yes, now. It's better.'
'But your clothes?'
'Forget them! I never want to see anything from Cascais again. Never. Throw them all away. Go! Please. I implore you.'
'When we need each other more than ever –'
'For one more day?' she said bitterly.
I asked her for the last time. 'Please. Don't let me down when I need you most.'
Almost sadly, she said, 'I've always let you down.'
Without another word she all but ran to the reception desk at the end of the long marble corridor and demanded the keys. I caught a few words – 'No visitors, no phone calls except from the American Embassy.'
Then she clanged the grilled door of the wrought-iron lift and pressed the button. My last glimpse of her was of her long slim legs as the lift carried her upwards.

Deep inside me I knew what would happen when she was back in New York, and my fears were soon justified. Within six weeks she sent me a cable saying she had married Bruce King.

37

The letter was long and rambling and sad. I read it through with pain; but also in a curiously detached way that one experiences only when one slits open an envelope knowing full well the contents. It read:

Mark darling,
  By the time you read this I will have married Bruce King

and I want to try and explain why. But before that I want you to know that no one will replace you in my heart – never ever, even if we never meet again – and I want to make you understand why I behaved so badly on that last day in Lisbon. I was distraught with grief, but even worse I was filled up with anger for being so selfish as to leave little Jonothan alone and so far away.

Try to understand that to an Egyptian woman marriage is only one part of life. We can never marry now, I realise that. Your wife is adamant, and as bigoted as she was when we had the chance of marriage and her religion stood in the way. I have wrecked your life – all the Holt lives. And now the stupidity that allowed me to marry Greg instead of forgetting my 'duty' and marrying you is just made worse by this new and terrible tragedy. For it was my fault. I killed Jonothan by *my* selfishness and *my* carelessness. I am bad for you, and as a wife I would be worse still. But I cannot live alone with all these burdens any longer. I need some shoulder to lean on, even though I love you more than any man I've known. Marriage doesn't necessarily mean passionate love, as you know from most arranged marriages. It means respect and friendship (if a girl is lucky) but not love. Yet marriages such as this sometimes work better than a love like ours founded on passion.

All the traditions of my race and country instil in me the belief that the role of a wife is to be a help and a colleague, not necessarily an ardent lover, since 'ardency' (is there such a word, beloved?) is not regarded as 'proper' for a wife. So I am to marry a good, kind, generous man who won't beat me and pray that in the friendship of this marriage I will be a good wife to a man who will help rid me of the haunting memory of poor Jonothan. But maybe for you a new life for me will help you to break off bonds which have chained us. I hope this for you because I will always love you and I still hope that we meet, one day. I can't know how to put into words better than to say that I am not a 'bad' woman, but perhaps just a normal Egyptian wife. And even though we parted in anger, I won't say goodbye, only sign this letter in the way I did the first time I went to America.

Hullo.

What a sad letter! That was my first reaction. And the bit about breaking the bonds that had chained us. We had always been chained together. Yet that letter – and the marriage – undid the chain, and in a curious way it was as though a weight had been lifted off my back. Serena had made clear, in her special Egyptian way, the gulf that separates love and marriage. But did that mean that I was relegated to the role of occasional lover – if, that is, we ever did meet again?

And yet, who could be angry with Serena? I remember in Cascais telling her how envious I was because she could visualise everything that happened to me in Cairo, while I knew nothing of her life in New York. I realised, reading the letter again, that it worked the other way too. After all, we could not meet, and now her only anchor with the past – her baby – had died. She would be separated for years to come from all that had made life and love so wonderful – Egypt! She had been brought up with the culture and traditions of a great history and a way of life that could never be imitated in New York with its desperately hot summers and bitterly cold winters. Poor Serena! Utterly alone, she had clutched at a lifeline. I couldn't blame her.

The news of Serena's marriage astonished rather than shattered our two families.

'It's not as though she's run off with the pianist in a jazz band,' Sirry Pasha admitted when we all met, as though to discuss the news. 'But we don't *know* him – or anything about him.'

'We know he's rich.' Madame Sirry's philosophy of marriage was very French.

'I'm sure he's charming,' Chiffon chimed in. 'I do hope she'll be happy – like she was with Greg. First Greg, then Jonothan: it's too much for a woman to bear alone.'

And now me! I thought savagely. I don't quite know why,

for it was quite out of character, but I blurted out: 'It won't last long. I do know that much.'

'Mark!' Father looked puzzled, almost annoyed. 'What on earth makes you say a wicked thing like that?'

'It wasn't wicked,' I said almost truculently. 'He's a very sick man, that's why. Serena wrote to me before he married her.' I said 'wrote' because I had to be careful not to betray that we had met. 'She sent me some photos of him, and told me that he'd already had two bad heart attacks – and three divorces.'

'Three!' Father sounded almost disbelieving.

'So perhaps Serena just wants companionship,' I said.

To Father, of course, it was just another marriage to the widow of the son he had lost, but to Sirry Pasha, who knew of my meeting with Serena, it was more difficult to understand. I had to hope, too, that Sirry Pasha wouldn't tell of our Lisbon meeting. Although I needn't have worried – he would never have betrayed a confidence. 'I'm palace-trained,' he had once told me with a wry smile. 'Say the wrong thing at the wrong time in my line of work and your head rolls the next morning.' All he muttered now was, 'I don't understand it.'

'It's simple.' I tried to hide my bitterness and my self-pity. 'I'm sure she couldn't get over the death of her son, particularly the circumstances. And she has nowhere to turn for help, except to this man Bruce King.'

'She should never have left in the first place,' declared Chiffon.

Madame Sirry left early to attend some committee meeting for a charity concert she was organising, so I walked across the gardens with Sirry Pasha.

'I had hoped so much that you and Serena –' He sighed.

'So did I.'

'It must have been a great blow to you. Of course, you told me all about it when you returned – the row after the news about Jonothan. Even so, well, I hoped that time would heal everything, and that you'd get together again.'

'I did too. But what's happened is a natural consequence, if you think about it. The trouble with Serena and me is we're good for each other and we're bad for each other, just a couple of crazy people who marry the wrong partners.' I tried to smile.

'But if what you say is true, that King is a sick man –?'

'You mean wait – then step into his shoes? A bit of a morbid thought, isn't it?'

'After the war?' asked Sirry Pasha. 'He doesn't sound *that* stable – divorced three times. What's one more?'

'You forget I'm still married. Parmi's even making odd noises about coming back to Cairo.'

'If only I hadn't asked you to look after Miss Davidson that evening so long ago,' sighed Sirry Pasha. 'Tell me, do you think your wife will ever consent to a divorce? I'm – well, looking to the future. After the war.'

'I can see no signs of it.' Almost the contrary, in fact. Not that I was really worried. I had the feeling with Parmi that vague suggestions about returning to Cairo were not to be taken too seriously.

I read part of one of her letters to Chiffon, when we were having tea at Groppi's before I took her – as I did once every few weeks – to a cinema, in this case to see *In Which We Serve* at the Metro – not so much because of the film but because the Metro advertised that it was 'Cairo's only air-conditioned cinema'.

'Listen to this,' I read from Parmi's letter. ' "I have been trying to work in a mission run by Catholic nuns who look after orphans in foreign countries. I will let you know what happens." That doesn't sound as though she wants to return here, does it? You know, Chiffon, I think the girl's round the bend.'

'You shouldn't say that, it's unlucky,' she said, as we walked towards the cinema. I stopped, fascinated by an advertisement in the window of Dean Swift, a tailor in the Kasr el Nil which announced:

Garments are made with the taste that is associated with a well-dressed Englishman and all exaggeration is avoided.

I was pointing it out to Chiffon, when suddenly she cried,

'Oh, look! That Indian girl. I must say hullo to her.'

'Who?' I asked.

'The Indian girl from the embassy. I met her in the hospital before Greg died.'

It was Jasmine! She must have returned to the Sphinx.

Before I could stop her, Mother had touched the girl's sari, and as she turned round to see us both Chiffon said, 'You don't know me, my dear. I am Lady Holt and I saw you once in the Anglo–American Hospital. You had been visiting my son before he died.'

'I was so sorry.' Jasmine looked round wildly for help.

'You're at the embassy? You must call. I just wanted to say how grateful I am for all your kindness to my son when he was so depressed. He was a different man after your visits.'

I seemed to be running into everyone these days. One afternoon I met Aly just as he was climbing into a smart new American car.

'Nice model,' I said. 'Glad to see you're doing well. I hope,' I said, tripping over the words, 'that business, nothing to do with me really –'

'You can hardly expect anyone to jump for joy when an old friend slips the handcuffs on you.' His voice was as surly as before, but he did then give me a crooked smile. 'I know that you had a job to do, and that you didn't know I was involved. I don't bear any grudges. Heard anything from Mrs King lately?'

'Who?'

'Serena.'

'Oh!' I didn't appreciate the joke. 'Where are you living these days? At home?'

'No bloody fear. I see the old folks occasionally, but only out of a sense of duty. I'm in the same flat you raided in Zamalek. But no radio sets there, I promise you. I've got a steady job, so there are plenty of pretty girls around.'

'Good for you.' I waved as he let in the clutch and drove slowly away, wondering what his 'steady job' was, and how long it would last.

A few days later, having dinner with Jim Stevenson, I asked

him point-blank, 'What's happened to Aly Sirry? He runs a flashy car and says he's got a good job. Seems out of character.'

'It is. I don't have the answers.'

'That's unusual for you.'

'He's too small for us.' Stevenson smiled tolerantly. 'We don't normally keep tabs on small fry like Aly. But I'm sure he's up to no good. He never has been. He can say what he likes about his accidental involvement in the attempt on your father's life but he's still close to Nasser, and the Free Officers are using the Moslem Brotherhood hoodlums to do their dirty work. And Aly was a friend of one or two Brotherhood leaders.'

'But Aly's a Copt. He couldn't be a member of the Brotherhood.'

'Of course not. But he's the kind of man who's liaison officer to all sorts of crazy factions. I wouldn't trust him an inch.'

By 1943 the tide of war had definitely turned. We were still a long way from victory, but the Fifth and Eighth Armies were fighting in Italy, the Red Army was on the east bank of the River Dnieper, while in the Pacific MacArthur was on the point of retaking New Guinea.

Though there was little opportunity for espionage work, the life of a serving officer always seemed to be demanding, especially as Farouk was stirring up trouble in the Canal Zone – more vital to us than ever because of the tens of thousands of troops and guns we were pouring into the Far East to fight the Japanese.

I was partly involved in discovering that Farouk was fomenting unrest through his Italian 'kitchen cabinet', which included the four Italians led by Pulli, who had become right-hand man to Farouk after the death of Sadik. Pulli had become more and more powerful behind the royal scene.

Between us Brigadier Monson and I drafted a report which the 'Brig' sent to the ambassador. Lampson heaved his great bulk out of his chair and, nearly apoplectic with rage, cried, 'Why the hell are these Italians still not interned? They're enemy aliens. I'm going to have them shut up straight away.'

It took a few days for the internment orders to be executed and according to Sirry Pasha Farouk flew into a rage when he heard what was happening.

'Do something about it,' he shouted to Sirry. 'That man Lampson has no power to interfere with my friends. If I like Italians I shall have Italian friends. Tell him that.'

Sirry Pasha hesitated. 'I don't think I can do that, Your Majesty. They *are* enemy aliens.'

'They won't be much longer,' said Farouk loftily. 'I will not kowtow to this wretched Lampson. Prepare a decree right away.'

'A decree, sir?'

'Exactly. Give my four Italian friends Egyptian nationality and make them Moslems now — before dinner.'

And that is just what happened. The decree was rushed through, and when Lampson sent round an arresting officer to intern the Italians a few days later he discovered that they were now Egyptians — neutrals whom he could not touch.

It was Lampson's turn to be furious — only he was powerless. Farouk thought the whole episode a great joke, and could not resist a touch of morbid black humour at the expense of the ex-Italians. When the decree was promulgated Farouk confronted his four advisers and said, 'Since you are now good Moslems, you must be circumcised. I will send for the doctor tonight to prepare you. I can promise you that it's quite painless. A little discomfort for a couple of days, that's all.'

According to Sirry Pasha, Pulli and two of the others agreed more or less immediately. But the fourth member, Eduardo Cafazzi, was terrified. Farouk put an arm round the shoulders of Cafazzi and murmured, 'Don't worry. If you don't want to let's have a drink and forget it.'

The Italian gratefully accepted the drink, unaware that, with typical Farouk humour, it was spiked. The next thing Cafazzi knew was the next morning. He had passed out after the drink, been given a local anaesthetic, and the circumcision performed without his knowing a thing about it — until the next day.

Side by side with his private jokes there were Farouk's

438

continuing excesses in his public life: the way he was milking the coffers of Egypt's resources, his womanising, his gluttony.

The king's father and grandfather had shown how easy it was to make extra money by 'legitimate' means, as when Sirry Pasha had been forced to sell some of his land at a knock-down price. Before long Farouk thought of an idea of his own. He told Sirry Pasha to sell one of his yachts, the *Fakha-al-Behar*, for which his father had paid about £30,000 – a lot of money in those days. Ideally, Farouk went on, he should sell it to the Egyptian government as a VIP yacht. The price, he suggested, should be £100,000. Much against his will, Sirry Pasha arranged the purchase. The Egyptian government, having been lumbered with this yacht, decided that if they *did* want to use the yacht for visiting VIPs who wished to take a trip on the Nile it had to be reconditioned. That cost another £300,000.

As soon as it was ready Farouk requisitioned it for his personal use, on 'loan'.

'It's the easiest way I know,' said Sirry Pasha, 'of making a fortune.'

'And he's got a virtually new yacht as well!' laughed Father.

'This sort of thing isn't known to the general public, but what's really distressing is his escapades with women. You can't keep *them* private,' said Sirry Pasha. 'It's reached the stage where it's embarrassing, because nine times out of ten he can't do anything. And you can't keep that sort of thing secret. If nobody else talks the girls do. I heard of one girl who was invited, not unwillingly, to a sumptuous dinner at the palace, all leading up to the bedroom, and in the end the girl spent the night alone, and left the next day with a purse of gold.'

'But that's not enough to cause a scandal,' Father said to Sirry.

'It's the vicious circle that causes the problem,' said Sirry Pasha. 'His impotence may have no direct connection with his hormone disorder but the fatter the king gets the more lethargic he becomes, and the harder it is for him to get any sexual stimulation. The palace doctors tell me that he's reached the stage of obesity where even the act of love is difficult for him. Yet it seems that there's nothing anyone can do about either his fatness or his impotence – or his desire.'

Farouk's eating had become even more excessive. Sirry Pasha managed to see the details of one luncheon. He started with three dozen oysters, followed by lobster and two soles, then two chickens and mutton chops, with four different vegetables, six kinds of fruit – of which he ate six mangoes – and, to top off, his usual quart of ice-cream. With it he downed pint after pint of fizzy drinks.

Even Mrs Sadik was disgusted with Farouk's eating habits, though for different reasons. Chiffon said to me casually one day, 'I met Mrs Sadik last night at a charity bazaar. What a horrible woman. And she still goes on about that husband of hers and insists that he didn't die a natural death.'

38

The end of the war in Europe should have brought sighs of relief, signs of rejoicing. True, VE-day in 1945 was accompanied by fireworks, the pealing of bells, the prayers of thanks. But in Cairo the fireworks seemed damp, the bells cracked, the prayers sanctimonious and hypocritical.

It was not a real victory parade which we saw in Kasr el Nil or in the square at Abdin Palace when Farouk acknowledged the cheers of the crowds. It was more like the end of a preliminary match in an evening of boxing, with the main bout still to come: the title fight between Britain and Egypt.

Many factors contributed to the sour taste in the immediate post-war period; the hatred for the British matched only by the hatred for Farouk. But more important was the glaring evidence of the rich growing richer, the poor starving, all helping to foster the growing popularity of the young army officers plotting for the future. The existence of the Free

Officers was still a 'secret' in theory, but as Greg had once said to me the only fun of having a secret was to share it.

'And this "secret" is filled with the hope of a new era for Egypt,' said Father. 'The same kind of hope that Egypt had when Farouk ascended the throne. Now they want to kick him off it and find a new leader. Ironic, isn't it? The British as well,' he added thoughtfully. 'And of course the economic situation is playing into the hands of Nasser, Sadat and company.'

During the war the rich had increased their wealth beyond their wildest dreams. In 1940 there were fifty sterling million-aires in Egypt. Within three years the number had soared to a hundred and forty. During the same period bank deposits rose from £45 million to £120 million. Virtually every hotel tripled its dividends. As the assistant manager at Shepheard's told me, 'The money just keeps pouring in. We can't stop the flow.' Cotton firms, which had been doing badly until the war cut off other supplies, doubled their profits. So did the shippers of sugar. So did property. It was boom time.

There was so much money around, and gambling was so high at the Cairo Royal Automobile Club, that new members had to prove they were millionaires in order to be elected. Farouk was often there, sometimes sitting at the porter's lodge eating six dozen oysters, or on New Year's Eve after the war, partaking in a thirty-course dinner. He lost £850,000 in gambling that year.

All this was fine for the rich. For the fellahîn, as in most countries which had been involved in war, the outward appearance of prosperity masked a lie. It *seemed* all right – wages tried to keep up with soaring prices – but in wars there is always a delay. The prices rise before you get your salary increase, and by the time that comes prices have already risen again. For the rich it didn't matter whether a meal at Shepheard's cost one pound or two pounds. But the fellahîn was so badly hit that in 1942 the government had to give more than a million small farmers tax exemption.

To the Moslem Brotherhood in particular all this helped to spark off disorder. They were everywhere, holding their own meetings or infiltrating those of others. In fact one day, driving from my chambers, I saw opposite the Opera House a screaming crowd, and in the midst of it a face from the past.

You know how sometimes, for no apparent reason, you watch a sea of faces and out of it one jumps. That was what happened then. In the midst of the crowd I saw the face of Akif, the man I had years ago confronted at Nasrani and who had later tried to assassinate my father. Was it thought transference that made him look up and see my face at the instant I saw his? I stopped the car, ready to give chase, but he melted swiftly into the crowd and I drove on, wondering if I'd ever see him again.

There were other problems. The shops bulged, the bordellos were filled; yet products without which the fellahîn could not live simply vanished. Every country housewife in Egypt was lost without her Primus stove, but suddenly there was no paraffin. Another factor accentuated the bitterness: the drift from the country to the towns. For, while the war continued, there had always been work of some sort in every town. Before the war ended the British army in Egypt employed 200,000 civilians. Nearly half were skilled or semi-skilled. Soon the more sophisticated started to form trade unions. It was only a matter of time before they went on strike against long hours and low wages. Once the 'right' to strike had been demonstrated to the fellahîn all over the country they realised that if the British kept Farouk in power he would stamp out the hard-won reforms of the people. Thus men like Nasser and Sadat realised that the original idea of just ousting the British was not enough; they must get rid of Farouk too. So, in a curious way, all sections of civilian life were quietly advancing the cause of the Free Officers.

'The trouble is,' said Father, 'Farouk sees the red light all right – but only in the Clot Bey brothels. The man's a fool, and one day it'll cost him his throne. He's grown into a voluptuous vegetable.'

Father was now nearly seventy, and beginning to look his age. He was still regarded as the *éminence grise* of Anglo-Egyptian relations, and had lost nothing of his power. He loved the trappings of office; and he kept his old retainers like

Zola – how many years was it since Zola had tried to clutch the felucca as Serena and I drifted into the river? Zola was himself an old man now, but still the faithful servant, though he went to bed earlier each evening, and the 'late shift', as Father once described it, was in the hands of Zola's son, who had been brought up in the Nubian village where Zola's wife lived, and which Zola visited once a year. The son had entered the family as a matter of tradition, to be trained to take Zola's place.

With Father's wry sense of humour, he had – just as he had christened Zola – decided that the son of Zola should be called Emile, and Emile he was.

'Now if I need something I can shout "Emile Zola!" and know that one will come.'

Chiffon thought it a vulgar joke at other people's expense. 'It makes them sound like book-ends,' she said. Yet Emile insisted on announcing who he was to all new guests. Zola's father must have told his son that he should identify himself at the entrance hall, and more than once I heard him say to a visitor, 'Good morning, sir. Please come in. I am Emile, son of Zola.'

Relations between the king and his subjects were not improved when in 1948 Farouk divorced Queen Farida, for the people of Egypt loved her, and even the lowliest fellahîn knew how much Farouk had made this beautiful woman suffer. She and Farouk had hardly seen each other except on formal occasions. He brought his women back to the palace – sometimes two at the same time. Farida was powerless against even these insults. When the divorce papers were signed Farida reverted to her maiden name of Safinaz Zulficar, and moved into a villa she had built near the pyramids.

The king and queen might be divorced, but one other couple were married -- for the second time. Teddy, the reformed playboy, and Angela, almost as soon as Teddy was demobilised. True, they had had that secret ceremony in Beirut, but they decided it would be wisest to forget that, and they were married in full glory at the British cathedral, where I was best man.

They, of course, were the only people who knew of the idyllic interlude Serena and I had spent in Teddy's flat, and they begged Serena to come over for the wedding, asking me to write to her too. But I didn't dare. Apart from the fact that Serena was now Mrs Bruce King I was thinking of the words that Chiffon had uttered about Mrs Sadik. Though I didn't like to recall it, Serena had shot a man – and with the smell of revolution in the air she was wiser to stay away from Cairo.

'Our wedding marks the end of an era,' sighed Teddy with mock-resignation. 'I don't suppose I'll ever go on a desert ride to Sakkara again. And all that dancing! I never realised that dancing was only a play to get someone into bed. You don't need to waste all that energy dancing when you've settled for life in a double bed.'

'I'm not in your privileged position,' I said. 'So you must tell me all about it.'

'First of all, blow out the torch, old man,' Teddy suggested seriously. 'Great girl, Serena, but there's no hope. Find a surrogate.'

'Maybe you're right. I'll just have to find the next best thing and go on with my legal work.'

'Okay, fuddy-duddy,' Teddy laughed. 'It's up to you.'

In fact there was very little work in this post-war period, and Salem had many idle moments as my clerk. People didn't seem interested in litigation. My own feeling was that those who had made fortunes didn't need lawyers, and those who felt they had been cheated of their fortunes wouldn't relish standing up in court and being cross-examined about the details.

From time to time Serena and I exchanged letters. As the months turned into years hers would still contain an undercurrent of passion, not explicitly stated, yet – was it because I knew her better than anyone else? – a feeling apparently innocuous but clear enough for me to see. Not having met her Mr King I thought it better – legal training! – to write with more circumspection, though I was not afraid to tell her that I missed her. Perhaps she too could read between the lines.

I also felt that she was not really as happy as she appeared

444

to be. King was not only rich but liked to be seen at all the smart places; he was a socialite, as Serena wrote in one letter, and her life seemed more frenetic than it had been when we were together. She described a visit to Las Vegas, 'where I gambled so recklessly that even Bruce complained.'

And then there was her painting. It had changed, to become an echo of her frenetic existence. She sent me an illustrated catalogue of her latest one-woman show and she had forsaken the introspective, almost sad paintings like the one which still hung on the wall of my chambers. That painting had been like the walks we used to take – quiet and gentle, in search of peace or happiness. Now her colours were bolder, with an aggression that was alien to her nature.

I had toyed once or twice with the idea of going over to New York for a short break – in fact, she had suggested it. But something stopped me. If I had to meet her husband for the first time I wanted it to be on my home ground. I didn't relish the prospect of staying in a New York hotel and, in between meetings with her, going off alone to the top of the Empire State Building to see the view.

Our two families, of course, had planned a great reunion in New York after the war, but poor Sirry Pasha didn't feel up to it. The long flights were still arduous, with frequent delays, often involving nights in strange hotels until spare parts arrived. However, Madame Sirry was determined to make the journey, and after much preparation duly set off to see her daughter.

'Serena is very happy,' she reported on her return. 'Bruce is a generous, kind man but, *mon dieu*, what an uncivilised city is New York! You start every meal with salads and iced water, then stop for a smoke. *C'est affreux!*'

'And her husband's health?' I asked.

'He looked terribly ill,' said Madame Sirry.

And then in 1950 a triple bombshell arrived. Within a few days I received three letters. The first was from Bruce King who sent a polite, typed letter:

Dear Mark Holt,
    Though we have never met I feel I know you well

because my wife has talked so often about you, and I know that she is – to say the least of it – very fond of the man she sometimes laughingly calls her 'protector'.

However, that is by the way of introduction. This is essentially a business letter. I am planning a complete reorganisation of several large companies I control in various parts of Europe. I want to bring them under one umbrella, eventually to be centered in Switzerland. It will be a complex task involving company law, and if you are interested we could discuss possibilities of your handling the negotiations.

I shall be in Monte Carlo in early June with my wife, and my American attorneys will also be visiting. They will stay at the Hotel de Paris, but if you would care to please come and stay at our villa and enjoy a little swimming as well. If you do come, my secretary will make all the necessary arrangements. [Which was a polite way of emphasising that, as this was a business trip, all expenses would be paid.] I think you will find that the legal work involved may take up to a year, and of course your fees will be commensurate. Certainly I would not wish you to be out of pocket by any loss of business you might incur by not having the time to plead in the Cairo court.

Yours sincerely
Bruce King

The second letter was from Serena:

Mark darling,

Bruce wants to see you, but not as much as I do. He would like to judge whether you are the right man to handle a huge merger or whatever – I don't understand these things. He knows that you love me, and what we did in Cascais. He's very, very ill, he just wants a companion-wife and it is so long since I last saw you that please come for my sake if not for yours, and if only to say

Hullo.

Who could refuse such a letter, such temptation? Plus the fact that work at the bar seemed virtually non-existent, and King's offer looked like an exciting challenge. Not only did it sound like a very pleasant way of earning large fees, but the idea of meeting Mr King intrigued me.

It was ridiculous really, but the sight of Serena's strong handwriting, the memories, had an almost immediate effect on me. But then, I thought, toying with the letter, rereading it, forming pictures from memory of Serena lying naked on the bed at Sakkara; but then she was Serena, and perhaps that was why I had never really wanted to get involved with any other woman.

There had been the occasional stirrings, and attempts. Samia had more than once pointed out beautiful newcomers who had joined what she called 'my harem'. I had even tried one. It had been a disaster. The girl's body was beautiful, her simulated writhing enough to excite any man, but then, in the midst of everything, I had thought of Serena, and without warning everything went limp.

The girl looked at me with something close to horror – I suppose she regarded my failure as a slur on her professional dexterity. I declined her attempts to stimulate me in more erotic ways, and mumbled something about not feeling very well. I felt myself blush with the shame of it – and a sudden fear; I couldn't have become impotent so early in life, at the age of forty-one?

Of course it wasn't that, and I knew it now, reading Serena's letter again, moving uncomfortably in my chair. Well, as much as Serena attracted me I would have to behave correctly if I visited Monte Carlo. Especially as the guest of her husband. Or would I? After all, he couldn't make love. I wondered whether I would be strong enough to say No when she smiled in that special way of hers, even though I did know one thing: the laws governing misconduct between the wives of clients and barristers were strict.

And then came another letter – the most extraordinary one of all. It was from Parmi, containing news that I had never thought possible. I can't say I had read any of her earlier scrawled letters with any real interest, for a distant letter is supposed to conjure up a picture in the mind, and I had long since forgotten the funny little-girl-lost look of the dizzy blonde I had married, though at times I had wondered how this once-sexy wife coped with life. But when I opened *this* letter I had no idea of the momentous news it contained: she would agree 'passively' (whatever that meant) to an American-style 'quickie divorce'.

Chiffon was in the sitting room when I opened the letter, and I must have jumped out of my chair, the letter fluttering to the floor, for she said, 'My dear! You look as though you've seen a ghost. Is everything all right?'

'All right!' I whooped for joy. 'Parmi's agreed to a divorce!'

Chiffon's slightly dotty attitude to life was never shown to better advantage.

'Goodness me,' she cried. 'Whatever will that girl do next?'

But what had made Parmi forsake her deeply held convictions? Why after all these years of shackling me like a man in jail had she suddenly relented? It was the reason that was extraordinary. She had decided to become a nurse attached to a Catholic mission in China.

'I've been dreaming of the idea for a long time,' she wrote. 'I've even been taking classes studying the Chinese language – and nursing, of course. I won't be a qualified nurse really, but a lay helper where I believe my life can be most useful. Then everything crashed around me. The mission is in a very primitive area and no married women are allowed. It's just one of those laws that someone decided on, and there are no exceptions.'

According to Parmi's letter she had been to seek spiritual guidance from her church. 'Father MacCaskill is a very down-to-earth man,' she wrote, 'and he was very upset at the attitude of the nuns who pick volunteers like myself for lay work. He knows that I can never admit to a divorce, but he also believes that I should fulfil my destiny, which is mission work.'

So the clever Father MacCaskill decided that one minor sin could outweigh the good she would be able to do. True, he remained rigorously opposed to the idea of divorce but she would ('in order to fulfil my destiny') allow me in Cairo to divorce her on the grounds of desertion or incompatibility or whatever was easiest, and she would not contest it.

'Since I won't make an appearance at the proceedings I will in effect know nothing of what is happening, and the good Father says that in fact in the eyes of the Church I won't really be divorced and that if I married again God would regard me as guilty of bigamy. But whatever happens in the sight of the Lord it has nothing to do with what happens in the sight of the passport office. From their point of view I shall be able to describe myself as "unmarried". I hope this makes you happy.' In a PS she wrote, 'At least *you* will be divorced. Do you think you'll marry Serena?'

The divorce was merely a matter of signing the right forms. Under Egyptian law – based on French law handed down from the time of the Mixed Courts – marriage was regarded as a civil contract without any religious complications. Nor did the fact that Parmi was resident in America complicate the issue. A couple could obtain a civil divorce immediately (providing neither party objected) as long as they were domiciled in Egypt.

I had handled so many divorces of this type that I knew the details by heart: neither nationality nor place of residence had anything to do with country of domicile; this was the country I regarded as our permanent home. So a Frenchman living in China may be domiciled in Egypt, if he regards it as his permanent home. But no one may have two domiciles, and a wife's is normally regarded as being that of her husband.

In the meantime I cabled Bruce King accepting his offer to visit him in Monte Carlo.

39

Having decided on the date, I flew first from Cairo to Paris. For many years I had dealt with an old-fashioned firm of

solicitors near the British Embassy in the faubourg-St-
Honoré, and I owed them a courtesy visit. And, too, flights
from Cairo to Nice were infrequent. As if this were not
enough, there was a third reason: the Blue Train was the most
civilised way to travel from Paris to the South of France. One
set off from Paris in doubtful weather and arrived the next
morning after a good night's sleep to be greeted by the sun,
sea and flowers.

The Train Bleu left the Gare de Lyon at nine each evening,
and after the porter had taken my bag to the first-class berth
on the wagon-lit and the train, with its bumps and grinding
noises, had gathered speed and settled into the steady rhythm
of clacking wheels, I lurched to the dining car for the *premier
service*.

I had relished the prospect of the train journey. I spent so
much of my working life reading stuffy documents and
talking to clients that I found the prospect of an undisturbed
evening alone, without even a book, appealing. Yet, for some
reason it didn't turn out that way. I began to have doubts
about the trip to Monte Carlo – not serious, but a legal
balancing of pros and cons, tiny clouds flitting across a sky
which had at first promised to be a clear blue. I had never
met Serena's husband – I called him that in my mind rather
than Bruce King. I had no idea what he would be like. After
all, I had seen only photographs of a tall, bald man with the
easy smile which seemed to fit so many typical successful
Americans. And – all this passing through my mind as the
waiter brought baguettes to the table – he must have known
that Serena and I had been lovers, even at Cascais: Serena had
said as much. 'Kind, generous' . . . The casual, sophisticated
veneer of a millionaire must disguise a ruthlessness and, for
all I knew, unsuspected traits such as possessiveness and
jealousy. I wondered again if Serena were really happy.

The waiter came along, balancing skilfully against the sway
of the train. As I ate my solitary meal, I reflected whether
King might even be playing some double game, using me as
a pawn to make sure he didn't lose Serena. Was that too
fanciful? Perhaps King hoped that as I was 'safely' married,
and he knew that Serena loved me, he wouldn't ever have to

worry about my stealing Serena from him. Would he feel differently when I told him I was being divorced? Or, in view of what promised to be an enormous consultation fee, *should* I tell him? Did he really expect me to visit his villa and the girl I loved and behave like a sexless lawyer towards a woman who was married to a sexless man?

When I pulled up the blinds the next morning the sun streamed in. I know of few more beautiful moments than when the train which left Paris in the cold turns along the south coast of the French Riviera and, as it slides along, the hillsides are a riot of bougainvillaea, and one can see housewives in dressing-gowns appear on balconies and fling open the french windows to greet the warm air, the mountains, the villas, the flowers on one side, the blue sea on the other.

Once we reached the coastline we stopped at Cannes and Nice, and chugged slowly through smaller stations, each one evocative of sun and sea, until finally, around half past nine, the train squeaked to a halt at the spick-and-span station of Monte Carlo.

Leaning out of the window I immediately saw Serena, a vision in white, with blonde hair blowing in the breeze. She waved with frantic excitement and started blowing kisses. I moved along the corridor, tipped the attendant and the porters, then climbed down the steps. The next moment she was squeezing against me, kissing me, and whispering, 'How wonderful to see you. Am I forgiven? Oh! I've missed you so much.'

I held her at arm's length, almost as though inspecting her. She looked just the same. It was seven years since Cascais, seven years since the death of Jonothan, seven years since she had married a man who we all thought had only a few months to live. She had hardly changed: not a wrinkle anywhere at the age of thirty-one. Perhaps a little more maturity, the self-possession that comes with being a wife among a settled community of friends, with an attentive husband. Yet, looking at her beautiful white pleated skirt, the silk blouse, open-necked, the top button undone, the two gold bangles round her wrist, I smiled. 'Yes, you're still as beautiful as ever. And you still have the same dimple when you laugh! You even smell beautiful!' I laughed again.

'Put it down to my perfume – Shalimar.'

She led me out of the station to her car – she drove it herself, an Aston Martin convertible, sky blue and low slung. It seemed the perfect car for her, and she handled the gears with professional dexterity.

As we turned on to the main road, uphill with the beautiful Monte Carlo tennis club on the right, she said, 'Bruce is waiting at the villa to say hullo to you. You'll find him a bit – I ought to – well, not exactly warn you, but –'

I felt myself tense. A 'warning'? About what? Us? The past?

'What's wrong?' I asked lightly.

'Nothing's *wrong*. It's only that – well, remember Bruce did have two heart attacks, and he has to take things easily. Part of the cure that saved his life was to lose weight. Around thirty pounds. What do you call it in English – two stones?'

'I won't force him to take any exercise,' I laughed. 'I'm here on business – and to enjoy myself. Providing you behave respectably.'

Almost mockingly she laughed. 'You think you can guarantee that?'

'If you help.'

There was no time for more talk, except when she pointed to the hills and rocks flanking the land-side of the boulevard des Moulins.

'That's the Villa Fleuri.' It was closer to the road than I had expected, a big white square building with orange sun-blinds, and I caught a glimpse high above of a small, colourful garden as she swung the Aston Martin up a narrow lane which became even narrower as she turned right again.

'Dead-end,' she explained as we pulled up facing a tall wrought-iron gateway. She hooted twice and a man in shirt-sleeves came out. He pulled open the grill and waved her in.

My first thought was, How the hell can she ever turn the car round? Or do they back it down that awful lane? Then, as I followed her, I realised that the garage floor consisted of a turntable – the kind used to turn a railway engine round by hand.

'This way,' Serena explained. 'We take the elevator up.'

'Since when did you stop using the word "lift"?' I laughed.

'Since I married an American. But we'll call it a lift here. We need one because the hillside's so steep that the concierge and his wife, who acts as housekeeper, live on the ground floor, next to the garage, and the maids and laundry room and so on are on the next two floors, so you have to go upstairs to get to the living room, and even the garden.'

The lift was smooth and well-kept, with none of the usual creaks and groans of small French lifts, and when we arrived at the fourth floor a trim, middle-aged housekeeper who Serena introduced as Antoinette pulled open the door and we moved into a large sunny living room facing the sea.

'Bruce!' cried Serena. 'He's here!'

'Coming,' a voice shouted from the balcony that led off the living room. It sounded cheerful – and so, despite the 'warning', it gave me no real idea of what to expect when Serena's husband walked in from the sunlight. I had to fight not to gasp with surprise.

He looked like a skeleton, shrunk to a pitiful shadow of what he must have been years ago. Yet his handshake was firm as he cried, 'Good to see you. Let's have some coffee.' He had obviously bought an entirely new wardrobe, for his clothes hung well on his shoulders and round his waist despite the weight he had lost. Still, nothing could disguise his face, which was criss-crossed with wrinkles and pouched where the old flesh had refused to follow the contours of illness. It was the same with his neck, now stringy, the loose flesh turning into unsightly jowls.

The extraordinary thing was that he didn't seem to notice. I suppose that great wealth, combined with the aggressive personality that enables a man to amass a fortune, gives one a special outlook on life; not exactly imperious, but a way of seeing things which makes one indifferent to the reactions of other people.

On that first morning, during lunch, I caught Bruce watching me almost quizzically, as though studying me, sizing me up. Almost irritated, I looked up to face his intense inspection, and asked jokingly, 'What's the trouble, Bruce? Am I over-dressed for Monte Carlo?'

He laughed – the laugh robbing him of any malice.

'Good God, no. Was I staring? Forgive me. I didn't mean to. You'd blush if I told you what I was thinking.'

'Go on. Tell,' cried Serena.

'Frankly, darling' – he turned to smile at her – 'I was think-ing what a foolish girl you must have been.'

'Me?'

'Yes, you. Not to snap up a man like Mark and marry him before I came on the scene.'

And bought you, I thought, though all I mumbled was, 'I did ask. But Serena wouldn't have me.'

It was rather odd, that first day, almost as though the three of us was each playing a role, on our best behaviour. There was nothing amiss, but I had the feeling that, behind the good-natured jokes and talk, one thought dominated all others. I know that I was thinking, Shall we be able to go to bed together? I ached with longing, a physical pain. And I was sure that Serena felt the same. But Bruce? Was he watching, or was he wondering if I would ever do such a thing to his wife? And would he mind if he found out?

The tension was not apparent to us as a group. This was possibly because there was a fourth guest: Dr Severs, Bruce's personal physician. Serena had told me that he travelled everywhere with King. I liked him – quiet, solid and watch-ful. When, for a few moments, we found ourselves alone, he explained his patient's illness to me.

'Bruce should have died long ago,' he said. 'But he's been kept going all these years by a special new treatment. I won't go into technical details, but it's a cardiovascular preparation which increases the elasticity of the outer walls of the arteries, which otherwise tend to become less elastic as one grows older, and so hinder the free flow of blood regularly. But I'm afraid it's beginning to wear off. That's what gives us all great fears. The steady rhythm is no longer there, and that means a limited life.' He sighed. 'Such a brilliant man. But now, after all these years saved from the grave Bruce knows that it now *is* terminal. You wouldn't think so, would you? Just doesn't give a damn!'

Perhaps all this encouraged a sense of hidden tension; I don't know, though I did detect one change in Serena, a kind of brittleness in words and action, a frenetic quality I had never seen before – as though she was determined to cram in as much of life as she could before it was too late. Bruce was different. He was dying, and one could have understood it if he had wanted to be in a rush to enjoy life, especially with such an attractive wife to show off. But he, who should have been frenetic, was not in a rush. It was an unexpected contradiction.

On that first night all four of us went to the Salles Privées at the casino and almost immediately Serena started gambling with high stakes, plastering the roulette table with the rectangular plaques that denote high denominations.

'*Tout va!*' She gave the signal for 'no limit'.

'Why?' I asked, amused more than puzzled. 'It can't possibly make any difference to you whether you win or lose, can it?'

'Oh, but it does,' she retorted. 'It's a challenge. It's not the money. It's chalking up a victory against odds that are stacked against you.'

In fact she won a small fortune before Bruce said he was going home.

'Please don't think I'm being discourteous,' he explained. 'But I have a strict rule to retire at ten o'clock. Dr Severs is a martinet. Not much fun for Serena, I'm afraid.'

'Don't be silly, darling.' Serena smiled at him with genuine affection. 'I only stay out after you go to bed because you insist on my enjoying myself.'

'Well, you two go dancing this evening when you've run out of gambling money. And you, Mark – I don't mind you paying for her dinner if you want to, but don't stake her at the tables.'

'I wouldn't accept a penny of his money,' Serena laughed, putting a plaque for the equivalent of a hundred pounds on red, and losing.

'Come on, Bruce,' said Dr Severs firmly.

'Coming, Doc. You're the boss. Have fun, you two.' He kissed Serena gently, and she kissed him back.

Again I wondered what he was thinking and I felt an uneasy twinge of conscience. After all, Bruce King was not only a good and generous husband to Serena, he was a pleasant man in whose villa I was a guest.

For a moment I had a compulsion to leave the Salles Privées with the clatter of plaques, the cries of the croupier, the excited buzz of winners and simply escape – away from the casino, away from Monte Carlo, away from Serena. But of course that would be nonsense!

Yet, as King and the doctor walked slowly across the thick carpet to the exit where King knew his car would be waiting, I could sense that Serena was echoing my mood. The casino seemed suddenly silent – as though only the two of us counted in that awkward moment.

' "Having fun",' I said lightly, 'could mean a great deal to people like us.' I added, 'We can never kid each other – that is, if you still love me after all these years . . .' I let the sentence fade away.

'I'll always love you,' she smiled back. 'And as for the phrase Bruce used, he knows exactly what he says. His invitation to "have fun" is his way of giving us permission to do anything so long as it's discreet.' She looked towards the bar, suggested a drink, and then said, 'I know that you always have a conscience, but I think I should explain one thing. Bruce knows what to expect. He knows I will always love you, and I warned him – well, warn is an unpleasant word – I explained to him that if he insisted on inviting you, business or otherwise, he would have to realise that we would make love. You know what he said? "I can't keep you frustrated all your life, and I'd rather it was with someone you love than with some fly-by-night stud." '

'And he isn't jealous? You're sure? It seems an amazing attitude to take.'

'There's nothing he can do about it because Bruce knows that I love him – in the way that gratitude to a good man turns into a kind of love – and that I won't let him down.

When he rescued me – and he *did* rescue me, as much as if he'd thrown out a lifebelt into the sea – he told me he would never be able to make love physically, so he gave me absolute freedom, asking me only to be discreet, and I, in return, offered him a promise which I knew would give him peace of mind. I said that if I married him I'd never leave him. He's had a rough time with his previous wives – rich men in America always seem to have bad luck!'

'And were you discreet?' I asked almost harshly.

'There was nothing to be discreet about. Never has been,' she said, adding almost wryly, 'being in love with a man who can't marry you and looking after a semi-invalid – well, together that's a whole-time job.'

The Salles Privées, all faded red plush and gold, had a small bar in one corner, and she asked laughingly, 'How's your financial status these days? Can you run to Taittinger? Or can I offer to pay without insulting you?'

Marcel, the barman, coughed discreetly and said, 'Madame, Monsieur Bruce arranged for a bottle of champagne for you before he left.'

'Better still,' she cried. 'And how typical of Bruce.'

'Are you happy, Serena?' I asked suddenly.

'Who is?' she asked brightly, flippantly. 'Depends what you want out of life.'

'Money?' I asked.

'It helps.' There was a touch of bitterness in her voice. 'But it can't buy the things you want most.'

'I know.' It was a long time since Cascais, but I had to ask because it concerned us both. 'Like Jonothan.'

'Poor, darling little boy. I missed him terribly. I suppose that's one reason why I go on dancing all night in New York – because then I don't have any time to think.' She touched my hand, adding, 'Our link, our baby. I don't believe a mother ever really gets over a tragedy like that. And so, as we don't meet very often, my motto is live for today!' Raising her glass, she toasted us.

'For today,' I echoed. 'And tomorrow.'

'If tomorrow ever comes.'

'Tell me,' I asked more seriously. 'You said you were

happy with Bruce – but *are* you happy? Did you really promise you'd never leave him?'

'Yes, I did. It was the least I could do. Why do you ask?'

'Because if you aren't –' I began.

'I've always loved you, but you're unattainable. Bruce was
there and I married him because no one else could help
me – and funnily enough in spite of all his money he needed
help too. He knows he's living on borrowed time. That's one
reason why he wanted to see you – to put his European affairs
in order – for me. Meanwhile he asks nothing. Nothing but
discretion. He loves me in his own way – he loves having
me around as his hostess – he doesn't mind if I go dancing
all night. He never asks questions.' Twirling the stem of her
champagne glass, she said, 'So you see everything's
perfect – except that I can't have you.'

Very quietly, almost pausing for effect, I said, 'But you
might be able to if you want.'

'Meaning what? That Farouk has relented?'

'No. He'll never do that.'

'Well then?'

'I've got news, Serena. It looks as though I'll soon be free.
No longer free, white and twenty-one. A bit tattered at the
edges. But free, white and forty-one. Parmi finally agreed
to a divorce.'

The sound of her champagne glass hitting the brass rail of
the mahogany bar as it fell stopped the buzz of conversation
as though a gun had been fired. She jumped up, shaking away
the champagne which had spilt over her dress. Then she
squeezed my hand, digging in the nails until I thought they
would draw blood. Then, for the third time in my life, I saw
the almost animal look in her face. Overwhelmed with desire
brought about by the news, she ignored the shattered glass
on the carpet and just said huskily, 'Come on. I've got the
Aston Martin outside. Let's go.'

She grabbed her bag, not even bothering to change her
plaques. 'The beach!'

We left immediately. It was a very warm night, and neither
of us needed coats. Soon she was roaring up the 'fromage',
as the gardens in front of the casino were always called, along

the boulevard des Moulins, then right, past the tennis club, down the hill and towards the sea.

The Monte Carlo beach is divided into two sections. The beach proper, of pebbles, is lined with a row of extremely expensive tents, booked by the season for months, even years ahead. Where the pebbles of the beach end there's a sharp turn to form the bay and a headland, covered with pine-trees leading upwards to 'The Point'. Hidden in the trees are two dozen luxury chalets. It is the height of opulence, meant for the very rich who want to spend the day at the beach but not necessarily in the sun. During the day there is even room service from a restaurant, also discreetly hidden. There are tables for backgammon, lunches, chairs to put outside, even divans for those who want an afternoon nap. Only a few yards from 'The Point' iron steps are let into what has become a small cliff, or one can dive into deep water and swim out to a large raft, anchored fifty yards away.

'Almost there.' She switched off the engine, took a torch from the pocket by the dashboard and led the way to her particular chalet. 'It's always deserted at night.' She had opened the car door when she suddenly turned to me.

'Just now, seeing you again,' she whispered huskily, 'I just want to make love to you like we did at Sakkara. This way.' She held my hand and led me through the pines till we reached the chalet, where she opened the door. It was dark except for the moon shining right into the window facing the sea. I could hear rather than see her kick off her shoes impatiently and she said, 'It's warm tonight. Get undressed, Mark. Be quick, please, beloved. Be quick.'

She had undressed, was standing naked while I let my trousers fall to the ground and struggled to free myself of my dinner jacket and black tie.

'Come *on*!' she cried. Then she fell to her knees as I stood there and began kissing me gently. I could feel her breasts against my legs.

'Stop!' I cried. 'Please – *please* – stop before –'

She didn't say a word. She couldn't, and I stood there, so excited that I was powerless to stop her, just stood, almost trembling, reaching down with my arms so that I could stroke the top of her head, until finally I cried out, 'Oh God!'

Only then did she stand up and take me to the divan.

'Why did you?' I asked, trembling.

'Only this once I wanted to do it,' she whispered. 'To show my love for you. You can't do that unless you really love a man. Or else' – with a laugh – 'you're in an Egyptian harem.'

'You shouldn't have done that.'

'I loved it.' She lay next to me, wrapping her arms around me, as I kissed her, legs entwined, lips, tongues touching, bands of moonlight filtering into the room like strips of neon lighting.

'You shouldn't,' I repeated. 'Nobody ever did that to me before.'

'I've always wanted to. Only I've always been so excited I could never wait, but this time – you couldn't take off your tie – and I just suddenly seemed to be on my knees.' Then, with a laugh, she added, 'Did it please my lord and master?'

'Yes, slave!'

'And now, if it pleases my lord, I will start to encourage him to make love again in whatever fashion he pleases.'

'Normal,' I laughed.

'Peasant!' She laughed back and started to stroke me, rubbing herself against me, and I whispered, 'It won't be long, I promise you.'

When it was over for the second time and I had been able to wait until I satisfied her, she got up and walked over to a small fridge in the corner of the room, to return with a bottle of champagne. We sat on the side of the divan naked, while quietly, desire satisfied for the moment, I told her the details of Parmi's extraordinary conduct leading up to the decision to let me divorce her.

'It's the most wonderful news in the world. Let's celebrate with a midnight bathe.'

'A swim! I've got no costume – and no energy.'

'Honestly, Mark!' She almost giggled. 'You deliberately swam in the nude to show yourself off to Mrs Lima in Cascais. Remember? And now, in the dark, you're afraid a jellyfish will nip off your little thing.'

We did swim. We found an assortment of towelling robes in the cabin and some spare espadrilles. A guard, seeing the light, came to investigate politely, and gave us a *'Bonsoir, m'sieu et madame'*, regarding a midnight swim as perfectly normal. He walked back to his porter's cubby-hole.

'Race you to the raft,' she challenged me.

'If I can make it. But remember, I've been working harder than you,' I joked.

The lovemaking seemed to have liberated us in spirit, so that she ran ahead, crying, 'What a disgusting thing to say after all the help I gave you.'

'You loved it,' I shouted as she dived off the springboard jutting out of the headland, her naked body in a perfect swallow dive piercing the millpond calm of the water.

I dived after her, but couldn't catch her up.

She had already climbed on to the bobbing raft – anchored, of course, and big enough for a dozen people to lie on it and sunbathe during the day – by the time I pulled myself on to it. We lay there panting, tender love mixed with banter.

'You're tired out, poor old man,' she said.

'I'm not a poor old man!'

'I've never made love on a raft,' she said, stretched out on her back, body glinting in the moonlight. 'Have you?'

'No.'

'Now's your chance.'

'I don't think I could.'

'I warned you that you're getting old,' she teased.

'Remember I've already – well, twice this evening . . .'

She laughed – her own special, husky laugh – and said, 'That's true. So now you can do it to me.'

Almost instinctively she bent her knees as she opened her legs, and I put my head between them and she held my hair in her hands as I touched her with my lips in the one spot that caused her to shudder with joy.

'It won't be long,' she gasped with pleasure, and suddenly started to move with the same rhythm as a man makes, until as she grew more excited she cried out once and then almost roughly pushed my head away from her and lay almost breathless, moving slightly with after-love, until suddenly she arched her spine, then let go and lay flat on her back like a starfish, wordless.

After a few minutes of silence, she said very simply, 'My poor Egyptian sisters.'

'Why?'

'So many of them circumcised, never knowing the pleasure you have given me. And always the poor ones – who could at least know that pleasure even if they don't have enough money to have children. The supreme pleasure – and free.'

We swam back slowly, both exhausted, and once in the cabin towelled each other with the bathrobes, then dressed. It was three in the morning before we reached the Villa Fleuri; but everyone seemed to be asleep.

The following day after breakfast, Bruce said to me, 'I'd like to talk business with you – the preliminaries. It won't take long. I'll just tell you what I have in mind then leave you to work out the details after you've finished your vacation. Better take a scratch pad with you to make notes, though my attorney will confirm everything in writing.'

I found Bruce a very different man from the socialite who had played the tables and ordered champagne the night before. He was incisive, lucid, every relevant fact at his fingertips. Yet, though I tried hard, I found it difficult to concentrate. Images kept slipping in to disturb business. Serena on her knees, kissing me, and – an odd, fleeting memory that kept recurring – her breasts pushing against my legs.

How odd, I was thinking, as we sat on the sun-drenched terrace examining papers, making notes, the tiny garden edged with flowers, every single plant in bloom as though the entire garden had been filled with potted plants just the day before the Kings arrived. And on the other side of the villa, lining the boulevard des Moulins, the blue sea dancing in the sunlight as, a few hours ago, it had danced in the moonlight. What would people say if they knew my entire life story? An upstanding officer who had unmasked several spies, and an equally serious advocate who had even advised a king, without ever a word of gossip levelled against me. But all this masking a man who had got one girl into trouble, then another, went to bed with the madame of a whorehouse, where I even took my own father for a night's frolic! And to cap it all, specialised in seducing the wives of millionaires.

With some effort I concentrated on the subject on hand: King had been examining me quizzically. At first I had thought he was screwing up his eyes because of the strong sunlight backed by the Dufy-coloured blue sea; but I now realised it was a trick he had when he was secretly amused.

'We'll get down to details in a couple of days when my attorney and his staff arrive,' he said finally. 'At this stage I'd just say that our organisation – and that means me, as I'm the main stockholder – owns eleven factories in Europe, apart from our operations Stateside. A plastics factory over in Wales near Pontypridd. I have one hell of a job understanding the work force there. They all talk with an Indian lilt. We've one of the world's first computer factories near Cologne, Germany, a bottling plant in France. And so on. I make virtually everything except automobiles. The car industry is the kiss of death: nothing but labour problems. But I *do* own a motor-cycle factory turning out machines like Italian Vespas.'

'And all these properties?'

'At present they are loosely grouped as a division of my American operation. I want the eleven European factories re-formed under the umbrella of a trust based in Liechtenstein.'

'Have you spoken to your American attorneys about all these plans?'

He shook his head. 'Not yet. I thought I'd sound you out.'

'When you do talk with them I'm sure they'll confirm one problem.'

'Which is?'

'There's no double taxation clause between most countries and Liechtenstein. So that in some cases anyone exporting goods sold in, say, Britain or Germany may face withholding taxes taken off at source, if the money ends up in Liechtenstein. In Britain, for instance, it's forty per cent.'

'Christ! That's punitive.'

'There are ways round it. I'd advise – without having yet

463

given the matter much thought, but I had a similar problem recently – having the holding company in Zurich. There'd be no withholding taxes there from any European country. You'd pay Swiss taxes on net profits, but they're the lowest in the world.'

'And leave the money in Switzerland?'

I shook my head. 'Then we form a trust fund in Liechtenstein, but we have to overcome one snag. If the Swiss holding company pays money into Liechtenstein *they'd* face a problem over withholding tax. The way out of that one is to have the trust fund registered in Liechtenstein, but keep the money in an account, say in Geneva. I know several private banks where the money would be absolutely safe, and properly invested, and where the trust fund could make withdrawals or deal with any other problems at a moment's notice.'

'And in the event of my death?'

'The trust fund won't pay any taxes or death duties. It can be invested in any currency even if one country gets into trouble and starts freezing their money.'

'You've certainly done your homework.' King sounded pleased. 'I dream up plans, but I'm too busy – and at times too tired – to work them through. That's where men like you come in.'

'The trust fund you plan for Liechtenstein?' I asked. 'What's going to happen to the profits from investments? Sounds as though there'll be a fortune.'

'All for Serena. Every goddam penny. I'll handle the American side myself with my legal boys. The European operation – it's always been a kind of fun thing for me, building it up out of nothing, and I want Serena to have the lot when the time comes. Not a penny for any of those three bitches who walked out on me. And I want you to head the trust fund. I want it written into the articles that your fellow directors in Liechtenstein can't sack you except for misdemeanour.'

'That's very handsome of you.' I felt almost unworthy. The simple arithmetic of running a trust fund of that size told me that it would earn me lifetime fees worth a fortune. 'But you shouldn't decide immediately,' I said. 'Let me see how I can arrange matters to avoid unnecessary taxation, and if I succeed to your satisfaction, then –'

'Mark.' He held up the papers on the marble-topped table. 'I'm a very sick man. I hope to live another year or so – no, no sympathetic noises please, I've come to terms with the facts of life – and until then Doc Severs keeps me alive. But one sharp pain in the chest and it'll be the end. Best get things on paper quickly. I like quick decisions. Anyway, I want to be sure Serena is independent when' – he used a typical American phrase – 'when I pass on.'

'But why choose me to run the fund?'

'I trust you.'

'But you've only just met me! And Serena and I –'

'I know everything about you. I know you two love each other. I adore my Serena – but the real loving, the physical loving, that stopped after the second attack, long before I met Serena. All I want now is to have her thoughtfulness around me till I die. I couldn't stop her going to bed with a dozen men in New York if she wanted to. I'd never spy on her, I never have. But I've got my own way of stopping her from playing around.'

I must have looked puzzled.

'You!' He chuckled as Antoinette, the housekeeper, brought in coffee, Sanka for him. 'She's in love with you, always has been. She'll be faithful to you all her life.'

'But you can't trust *me*!'

'I trust you to love and cherish her. And I don't sleep very well now, so I heard you come in at 3 a.m. And I don't imagine you were sitting on a park bench admiring the view.'

I felt guilty, shocked even.

'Listen, Mark.' He stirred his coffee and said, 'God! This French milk tastes like piss.' Then he went on: 'Two things: first, I want you to be able to exercise some control over the fortune she's going to inherit. Right?'

I nodded agreement.

'Second – and this sounds quixotic – I don't want her to be entirely separated from you so that she forgets you and ends up marrying some jerk who's only interested in her dough. Sound reasonable? Right. So I asked you to come here to see if you both *do* still love each other. You know the cynical twist to the old saying? Absence makes the heart grow fonder – of somebody else. I wanted to see for myself how the hell your love story could last that long.'

'Well, we do love each other. But I've got a thriving law practice; I don't need to earn money of the kind my fees will be if I become head of your proposed trust fund. Only you're asking a hell of a lot to arrange for me to meet a girl I've been mad about all my life and behave like' – I ended lamely – 'like a gentleman.'

'Exactly. I wanted to make sure that you were, as you call it, a gentleman. You see, Serena made me a promise. Never to leave me, divorce me. I got fed up with wives walking out on me, and I want peace and quiet for the last years of my life. Now I know that she'll stay – because *you'll* insist that she honours her promise.'

What an extraordinary man! As he pushed the empty coffee cup away, he said, 'I think that's enough business for today. I guess you're a bit overwhelmed by Serena's arrival. Who wouldn't be? The day after tomorrow, when my legal boys arrive, we'll get round to the nitty-gritty.'

The holiday, interspersed with business, was wonderfully happy and relaxed, largely because Bruce had removed all my old-fashioned complexes. It *was* ironic that Serena should marry twice and always be in love with me, and that I would never love anyone but her. But Bruce's almost grateful acceptance of our love was like being granted an official visa; even so, neither of us felt easy about sneaking into each other's bedrooms at night.

That problem, however, was quickly solved. My father had an old friend who owned La Réserve at Beaulieu, possibly the finest hotel on the coast: a two-storey pink-washed hotel where I had stayed before the war on a family holiday. It was on the edge of the water, but with no beach, just rocks and a pool built into the sea, so that only hotel guests could swim there. It had just a few bedrooms, all extremely expensive. Each was furnished individually, with no two rooms alike. It also served wonderful Italian food.

We drove there the following morning in Serena's Aston Martin. 'You look out of this world,' I said. 'That yellow two-piece suit goes with your eyes and hair perfectly.'

'That's a lover speaking,' she smiled. 'You're exaggerating.'

I don't think I was, for the hotel owner stared at her for fully half a minute enraptured while I explained that I was one of Sir Geoffrey Holt's sons who had stayed at La Réserve, and now I had a problem.

'We're both married,' I told him frankly. Always be frank with a Frenchman when it comes to love, I had been told. 'And we're in love. But we are fond of our – er – spouses and don't want to hurt them.'

'*Pas de problème*. We are fully booked except for one small room overlooking the sea. I have to charge you normal rates, you understand, but here's the key. Come and go as you please.'

That was that. Sometimes we slipped in for an hour, sometimes – especially when Bruce was working on his American problems with his attorneys – we would go to La Réserve for a lunch of wafer-thin Parma ham and figs, or a cheese soufflé, with something light to follow, followed by a delicious hour or two in bed. But we took the greatest care not to give any offence to Bruce by staying away from the house too long. We arrived back home before he and Dr Severs returned after their meetings with his aides, which always took place at a suite in the Hotel de Paris.

'But isn't it ironic,' she said one afternoon, snuggling between La Réserve's expensive linen sheets, 'how our relationship has turned topsyturvy? After Greg's death all I wanted was to be your wife. But – apart from Farouk – we couldn't because you were married. Now *you're* soon to be free, and I'm married. We seem destined to have affairs like this for the rest of our lives.' She snuggled closer, breasts touching my chest. 'At least it makes for change.'

'It sounds ghoulish, but I wonder how long –?' I began, turning towards her.

'It's not ghoulish. That was part of the bargain and, you

know, I've brought great happiness to Bruce. Just by not letting him down after the way his other wives did. I really think he'd die if I left him, but Dr Severs says it's eighteen months at the most. When it happens I'll cry a few tears – no, it's *not* ghoulish – but then I'll rush off to the nearest register office. And then!' A sudden thought struck her. 'If I become a British citizen, will I be able to return to Egypt as your wife? Or will you have to practise at the bar in London, as you once said you might?'

'I don't know. Let's face that one when it arrives. Because there's something else.'

She looked up lazily, kissing me, touching the outside of my lips with the tip of her tongue as I fondled her breasts. 'Such as what?'

'I gave you a brief outline of the work I'd be involved in if I ran the trust for Bruce – apart, that is, from setting it up. It's a big task, co-ordinating the finances of eleven countries, and the fees will be more than I could earn in Cairo. Maybe we could go and live in Geneva, or Paris, and make running the trust a whole-time job. To hell with Cairo. It's changed so much, there's so much bitterness, I wonder if we wouldn't be happier living somewhere else.'

On the day before I was due to leave we held a business conference in Bruce's office – his attorney's suite – leaving Serena on the beach. On the way back to the villa Bruce said, 'I think you should visit the New York office once every couple of months to report progress while we're setting this deal up – at least for the next year. We have a company apartment there – the Delmonicos' Building on Park. I'll arrange for you to have the use of it. Better than a hotel. And I don't want my senior colleagues getting jealous – as they would – if they knew you always stayed with the boss each time you come to town.'

What a generous man! Not for offering me the use of the company flat – all my expenses would obviously be paid anyway – but for knowing the discreet uses to which an apartment could be put.

And when the time finally came for Serena to drive me to

the station to catch the Blue Train in the evening, Bruce held my hand in both of his and simply said, 'It's been a pleasure meeting you, Mark. And business-wise I'm very happy. I'll be seeing you in a couple of months. Now, Serena, see Mark off or he'll be missing his train.'

It was a brief farewell. She kissed me first, saying, 'It's not so hard, knowing I'll see you in a couple of months,' then blew kisses as I leaned out of the window and she stood, a little lost, alone on the Monte Carlo platform, which looked for all the world like a toy-town station for a model railway. Then with solemn puffs of smoke the train pulled out, leaving her waving, still blowing kisses.

40

Bruce died in July 1951, almost a year after our meeting in Monte Carlo, by which time the work of setting up the umbrella company had been finalised, the trust fund in Liechtenstein had been formed and the first funds were arriving via Switzerland.

During all that year Bruce had been growing steadily worse, yet he was determined that 'the deal', as he called it, should be completed before his death. It was this determination to ensure that Serena's future was secure that kept him alive.

During those twelve months I had given up all thoughts of private practice, though I kept on my clerk Salem as a liaison officer at 'headquarters', for I not only had to work fourteen hours a day, I had to travel all over Europe, engaging local tax consultants and lawyers and sorting out what Bruce, in another of his favourite phrases, always called 'the fine print'.

And of course I made regular trips to New York. So, for the first time for years, I was able to see Serena regularly; the

flat in Delmonicos' on Park Avenue was central, it had two
keys, no questions asked and unobtrusive maid service.

Poor Bruce! Though I couldn't help realising that both
Serena and I were for the first time in our lives both free to
marry, I did feel deeply saddened by his death. He might
have looked terrible with his skeletal frame and sunken eyes,
but that shambling, dying frame, kept alive by will power
and Dr Severs, contained a generous heart. It obviously
wasn't physical love for Serena that made him leave her a
fortune, but a kind of love born out of gratitude. 'She's the
only girl who's never let me down,' he said once. 'So I guess
I owe her.'

A month later Serena and I met in New York. We both knew
that the time had come to face up to a new life together,
which at first sight seemed simple, nothing more than a
question of waiting a respectable time before we married
quietly.

It wasn't as easy as that though.

'We may both be free,' I said, 'and yet for the moment
there's no question of our getting married.'

It was one of the few occasions when I saw Serena weep
openly. The irony of the situation was so desperate that she
couldn't hold back the tears, for she realised what we were
both thinking when I said, 'Imagine the gossip, the innuendo
if we married after just a short interval – say three months.
Think what people would say – or do.'

'But I've been married to Bruce for eight years. Nobody
could accuse me of being a gold-digger.'

'I know, but a year ago you and Bruce invited me – a
close friend of yours, related by marriage – to Monte Carlo.
Everyone must know that it was you who asked Bruce to
meet me.'

'But no one knows about us –'

'Don't be too sure. Gossip is a disease, especially in the
jealous boardrooms of Wall Street, with tycoons anxious
to keep their power when the boss dies. Imagine. I'm a
well-known legal figure. You introduce me to Bruce. Between the two of us we persuade a dying man to make a will

470

giving half his fortune to you. We then persuade him to give me the sole control of the trust fund set up to handle your estate, instead of letting his usual attorneys do it.'

'But that's not true. The whole thing was Bruce's idea.'

'Bruce is dead. He would never be able to prove that. And then, imagine what would happen with Dr Severs testifying that he'd told me Bruce had only eighteen months to live – as he *did* tell me. So we wrap everything up into a wonderful package, wait until Bruce dies, and then while the body is still warm pop off to get married and share the spoils.'

'You make it sound awful. And you know it's not true.'

'Yes, I know that. But it *does* sound terrible. And to cap it, imagine how a sharp lawyer would crucify me in any cross-examination if the will were contested. "And tell me, Mr Holt, you took over the financial arrangements of eleven large companies. Is it true that you had no experience of running a business?" They'd murder me.'

'And if we don't get married?' she asked in a small, toneless voice.

'Nothing will happen. Everybody admired you for the way you behaved when Bruce was alive, your consideration for him, how happy you made him. It was only natural that he should leave you a great deal of money. Otherwise' – I gave a wry smile – '*you'd* be going to lawyers to contest the will. But how different if we get married. The rich widow and her unscrupulous adviser. My God! It doesn't bear thinking about. Quite apart from us, the whole scandal would be spread across every front page in every Cairo newspaper. It would break your father's heart. And by linking our names together – well, Farouk would never relent and let you come home. More, it would give further ammunition to your enemy, Mrs Sadik.'

On the edge of more tears, she said, 'All I wanted from life was to be married to you. I loved you, I took you, but it wasn't enough.'

'Hey there!' I tried a feeble attempt at humour. 'Why the past tense? "I loved you", you said. What about the present tense, *to love*, and the future, *I will love*.' I kissed the back of her neck. This was no time for passion but for consolation.

'That's all I want from life as well. To be able to wake up in the morning next to you, legally. And I'm going to achieve it. It *will* come out all right, I promise you. Now, no more past tenses, please. The only thing is – we need time. Remember, if we do nothing, nothing will happen. Nobody's going to say a thing – unless, not thinking straight, you and I dash out and marry.'

Since we could not get married, why shouldn't Serena, who after all was Egyptian, say goodbye to America and settle nearer home? Cairo was out of the question, but what about Switzerland? For the time being anyway. She would excite no comment there, she would be unknown. She could even revert to her maiden name because, apart from anything else, Serena Sirry was her painter's name.

I could spend half my time in Geneva, even taking my holiday breaks there. Paris was less than a day's drive away, especially in her Aston Martin. I could fly directly to Cairo whenever I had to – two or three times a month – while Serena's mother and father could fly directly from Cairo to Geneva to see her.

When they came to Switzerland I could – for the sake of propriety – move into the flat I had bought in Geneva itself, in the old part of the city by the place du Cirque, at the far end of the rue de la Corraterie.

After a few weeks I found the perfect place for us – an old farmhouse at a village called Rolle, a twenty-minute car drive along the lake from Geneva. It was a sleepy little place, with one cinema, a tiny harbour, a good restaurant called Le Domino; and the house, which had the unusual name of Three Circles Farm, was low and long and white, and was to be sold as a going concern – in other words, completely furnished. Its previous owner, an Italian countess with impeccable taste, had spent much of the war there because she was in love with an American who, it seems from rumour, used to sneak across the frontier to meet his beloved. It was all very romantic, especially as in front of the courtyard was an ancient stone horse trough with water coming from a fountain playing an endless, quiet tune. And if Serena became bored all she had to do was move into my flat in Geneva itself for a few days.

In Egypt, history was being rewritten. The Free Officers were almost ready to seize power; it was just a question of how they did it, and when – and what Farouk would do.

The more I look back on those post-war years the more difficult it is to see, like episodes in a film serial, some of which I missed, the events leading up to the success of the Free Officers, and Nasser in particular, who did most of his planning in Cairo, either at the Egyptian Army Officers' Club or at his own home.

I still met Nasser and Sadat periodically – for they bore no grudge even after I had helped to arrest Sadat. Nasser actually enjoyed my company. But his dreams had been going on for so long that sometimes I felt it difficult to recognise the moments leading to his power. Since I was travelling a great deal it increased the sensation of seeing those intervening years as a series of flashbacks, even the evacuation of the British troops from Egypt, except in the Canal Zone. But I could see that there were almost daily strikes or riots against the British Canal forces, amounting almost to a kind of guerrilla war, and that the hoodlums of the Moslem Brotherhood were fomenting more and more agitation, more disruption, more riots against the British, while Farouk remained a hedonistic pawn, acting as though in a daze, struggling in vain to maintain some pretence of power.

Then, to make his throne more wobbly, Farouk decided to marry again. The girl, who was plump and rather bovine, wasn't presented to the king in the usual way. Farouk was tipped off by the court jeweller, Ahmed Naguib, who, in return for spending palace money at his establishment, regularly told Farouk if an attractive girl visited his shop.

'This one,' the jeweller told the king, 'is a rare beauty, just sixteen years old.' She had, he explained, a large bosom, which the king always enjoyed, voluptuous lips and a generous mouth. She was called Narriman and had made an appointment with Naguib for three o'clock that afternoon to choose an engagement ring. If the king cared to visit the shop just before three Farouk could hide in an adjoining room, peep through the window, and watch the girl without being seen.

It was the kind of challenge that Farouk could never resist. According to palace aides with whom the jeweller talked Farouk took one look at the girl then walked into the main shop and watched as she blushed with confusion as the king regarded the rings displayed in front of her.

'What's that cheap ring you're choosing?' asked Farouk.

'My engagement ring – from my fiancé, Majesty,' she stuttered.

'And who is he?'

'Zaki Hashim, in the diplomatic service, sire.'

'Give it back to him.' Farouk waved a hand, a gesture to take all the rings on display away.

Then he smiled expansively and said, 'Now. Let us examine a few rings worthy of your beauty. For you have just become engaged to your king.'

It was as simple as that. Narriman's unlucky fiancé was promptly transferred – the unkind might say deported – to a diplomatic post abroad, and on 6 May 1951 Farouk and Narriman were married in the Abdin Palace.

Before that Farouk, through Sirry Pasha, had arranged for hints to be dropped to the diplomatic corps throughout the world, and all other influential guests who would be invited, that the king would look with disfavour on any gifts that were not made of gold.

Most guests took the hint, and in a rare burst of confidence Farouk told Sirry Pasha almost gloomily, 'You never know what's going to happen these days.'

Farouk knew of the dissatisfaction among the people of Egypt, and took the necessary precautions. Within a few weeks of the wedding he had melted down every single ounce of wedding-gift gold into more easily disposable ingots.

Matters finally came to a head in January 1952. On the Friday – that must have been the 25th of January – I visited Sirry Pasha to bring him the customary box of Partagas cigars which I had given him every birthday. He was seventy-four.

'I'm too old to go gadding about,' he admitted. 'So all my closest friends are giving me a special birthday party in my honour in a private room at Shepheard's. I'm sorry your father's in bed with flu and can't come, and I'll miss Serena,' he added regretfully. 'But it's men only, anyway. A sad business, you two never getting married. But at least you see her in Switzerland. If only she could return to live in Cairo.'

I was sure Serena would have loved to return, but there was such a feeling of unease, of impending disaster, that I was frightened. Not only did people resent Farouk's cruelty over his second marriage, a resentment which for many was now an open hatred, but a new force had appeared to weaken his position still further. Lala Sadik, Osman Sadik's widow, had not been content to fade away into the background on the pension Farouk had arranged for her. Rather, an intelligent and intensely determined woman in her own right, she had skilfully worked her way up into the councils of the Free Officers, insisting fervently that her husband had been in favour of a peaceful revolution of the army, and hinting that his outspoken admiration of men like Nasser had resulted in his murder. Inevitably, some people began to wonder if there was any truth in her assertions.

The minds of many young army officers, men like the anti-British General el Masri, began to be invested with heroic legends out of all proportion to the truth, and the vituperation of Mrs Sadik towards the king played a large part in fostering them. Her own husband came to be regarded as a much-pitied victim of Farouk's wickedness. She also obliquely suggested that Serena had been involved in the 'scandal', hinting that she had been the king's mistress.

Mrs Sadik was a master in the art of veiled hints, the whispered intrigue. On his part Farouk knew all this talk amounted to nothing as long as Serena was not actually in Egypt to lend substance to rumour. I was sure in my own mind that if Serena *did* return to Cairo Farouk would stop at nothing to guard the secret which he thought no one but he and Serena shared.

'Have a good party tomorrow,' I said as I handed Sirry

Pasha the ritual box of Havanas. 'I hear there's some rioting, even open fighting, at Ismalia. And bloodshed can be very catching.'

Earlier in the day Jim Stevenson, who had recently been appointed special assistant to Jefferson Caffery, the US ambassador to Egypt, had warned me that fierce fighting in the Canal Zone had broken out between the British and eight hundred Egyptian auxiliary police, who had openly attacked British barracks at Tel el Kebir, the largest ammunition depot in the Middle East.

'The British gave the police an ultimatum to withdraw,' explained Stevenson. 'The local commander telephoned Cairo for instructions. He was told he mustn't surrender on any account.'

'They must be mad to resist,' I said.

'Not really,' said Stevenson. 'The Egyptian politicians saw immediately that if the police fought on they could force the British to take repressive measures, and for the price of a few Egyptians killed the Egyptians would be in a stronger position to reopen talks on the Canal bases.'

The bewildered police, armed only with rifles, did fight on. The British brought in tanks to guard their greatest military arsenal in the area. Before the end of the day seventy Egyptians lay dead.

'You can bet your bottom dollar there'll be hell to pay in Cairo before another day's out,' said Stevenson.

And, when I returned to Holt House, a quavering old Zola begged me, 'Stay in your home tomorrow, master. There is going to be big trouble.'

41

Early that morning I went to meet a foreign director of one of our European companies who was staying at Shepheard's.

I had suggested 'a working breakfast' – which meant a coffee for me.

I was waiting for him to come down to the veranda where we had arranged to meet when a large truck drew up and unloaded a group of men in dungarees, carrying implements which looked rather like vacuum cleaners.

Nothing unusual in that. I knew that all the big hotels welcomed (in their own interest) regular visits by a mobile squad who sprayed public rooms – especially the carpets and deep chairs – against mosquitoes and even vermin. They always came early in the day before most guests were about.

But I was surprised to see Aly arrive in his car, and start giving instructions to the men.

'Long time since I saw you,' I hailed him, sitting down on the veranda to await my guest.

He looked embarrassed.

'I'm a director of the firm,' he muttered. 'I make periodical checks to see they do their job properly.'

'Delighted,' I said and meant it.

'We've all got to work now,' he said almost briskly, 'trying to build a new Egypt.'

It seemed a little odd – not the kind of job a fervent nationalist like Aly would really enjoy – but on the other hand Sirry Pasha would probably be delighted that Aly was employed. It also passed through my mind that after his unfortunate lapse Aly might find it difficult to get a job – and though he probably didn't need the money it was a good thing for him to be *seen* to be working.

As Aly walked up the steps I framed the words to cry, Tell the boys to do a good job. Your father is being given a celebration birthday party today in Shepheard's. But at that moment the director I had arranged to meet, an Englishman called James Storey, walked down the steps, hand outstretched to greet me. A moment later we were sitting down on one of the rattan chairs on the veranda and had started to discuss business.

Storey was not only a director of our plastics firm; he had an import-export business of his own, and he wanted to open an office in Cairo. He had come to discuss possible safeguards he should have against the Egyptians seizing his assets in the event of a new government. What if there was a coup in Cairo?

There was no straight answer to that one, but he also wanted to know about customs tariffs and exemptions, and there I could help him.

'Will you be free all morning?' I asked. 'If I make an appointment for you?'

'I could be.'

I left to telephone James Ireland Craig, adviser to the Customs and Excise in Cairo.

'He's a first-rate chap,' I explained when I returned to the table. 'He'd be delighted to have a drink with you around half past eleven at the Turf Club. In Adly Pasha Street. I'll try and come along as well, and meet you there.'

'Most grateful. Can't be too careful these days. I'm really anxious to expand, and what's more I've got the cash. But – well, there's an odd feeling of nervousness in Cairo. I can sense it here, can you? A kind of suppressed anger.'

'You haven't read the vernacular newspapers?' I asked him. 'The headline's the same in every one: "Ismalia Massacre." It seems that seventy Egyptians were shot by the British after they tried to storm the British arsenal. There'll be trouble – bound to be. I heard on the seven o'clock news that the airport employees are already refusing to handle BOAC traffic.'

'Lucky I'm not returning this afternoon.' Storey didn't seem unduly worried.

'And they're gathering for huge protest marches,' I added.

'They're always having *them*,' he laughed.

'I agree. But this one is different. I watched some of them crossing the Kasr el Nil Bridge from Zamalek. Usually they dawdle – you know, carrying banners, chanting slogans, singing songs. But this morning they *marched*, almost like soldiers – briskly. And I saw why. Two significant things. The parade was not headed by the usual Communist or student firebrands but by half a dozen army officers who set the fast pace. Secondly, the Cairo police were openly fraternising with the protest marchers. In some sections the police and protesters and soldiers marched side by side, crying, "We want arms! We

478

demand the right to fight for the Canal!" '

I left Storey soon afterwards, promising to try to meet him at the Turf Club, and started to walk back to my chambers. Hundreds of people were gathering in different streams, some near the Opera, others milling around Ezbekieh Gardens. On the whole they seemed good-natured – protest marches usually included many hangers-on, determined to enjoy the day – and there was not yet any premonition of the real terror to come.

I followed the crowd. By the time it had converged on the pink and grey baroque cabinet offices – once the palace of a princess – there must have been thousands, all demanding that the Prime Minister should appear.

He didn't – that I could see in the distance – but the Minister for Social Affairs, Abdul Fattah Hassan, did step out on to the balcony facing the crowd, holding a microphone. I recognised him immediately, a swarthy, thick-set man, who always wore his fez at a jaunty angle. 'This is your day!' he cried. 'Today you will be avenged!'

Nobody took much notice. The dozens of soldiers who had joined the protesters had unbuttoned their tunics, put their caps back to front and draped their arms round the shoulders of students or policemen. One demonstrator had a microphone and shouted, 'We want a boycott of all British goods!' Another man seized the microphone and shouted, 'Let's ask the Russians to supply us with arms to fight the British.' There were cheers of approval, yet there were still no signs of violence.

I returned to my chambers just as Madame de Clozet, hand over the telephone receiver, cried, 'It's Madame Samia. She sounds terribly upset.'

'Thank God you're here,' Samia cried. 'Mark, they're trying to smash up the Sphinx.'

'The police?'

'They're standing by. Grinning. Please – help!'

'I'll be there right away.' I banged down the receiver. Thus I saw the first outrage in what later came to be called 'Black Saturday'.

The Ezbekieh Gardens were a good distance from the

Sphinx, but there was no question of driving a car through the crowds. It was much quicker to slip in and out on foot. So I started to run, cutting through Adly Pasha Street – still fairly quiet – then turning left along Emad el Dine Street until I reached the statue of Mustafa Kamal at the corner of the Kasr el Nil. From this major square it was a straight run down Kasr el Nil to the river and there, almost at the corner where Soliman Pasha Street crossed at Groppi's, I suddenly smelt burning, and saw the first spiral of smoke curl upwards to the sky.

At first I didn't connect the fire with the Sphinx. Near the nightclub was the Venus Photo Studio, and by the time I reached it the crowd, screaming abuse, had blocked any way through. Instead, I slipped down a narrow alley and reached the small terrace with its dozen or so tables in front of the Sphinx.

I could hardly believe what I saw. The terrace was in pandemonium – and burning. I saw Samia, more peasant than ladylike proprietress, screaming obscenities and beating people with her fists. I fought to get through to the terrace.

An Egyptian who seemed to be well-dressed was watching the scene.

'What happened?' I asked.

'Someone insulted an Egyptian police officer,' he answered and started to walk away.

I learned later what had touched off the spark that would soon engulf all Cairo in flames. The protesters were marching along the Kasr el Nil when one man saw a police officer sitting at the café outside the Sphinx drinking, joking and laughing with one of the Sphinx girls.

Someone shouted words to the effect, 'You swine. You ought to be ashamed of yourself, drinking and whoring while your brother police officers are being butchered in Ismalia.'

The police officer answered back, drawing his revolver. The woman with him laughed, sneered, then made an obscene gesture.

The infuriated crowd roared with anger. As the police officer and the girl ran from the terrace into the first bar, the enraged mob started smashing up all the tables and chairs, while Samia tried in vain to stop them. At first the crowd seemed content merely to break up the cane furniture and a few windows, but then – almost as I was running down the street – someone threw in a Molotov cocktail. In a split second, as the bottle of petrol burst, the furniture on the terrace roared like bonfire night, posing a serious threat to the main stone building of the club itself.

Samia phoned the fire brigade. For once it arrived promptly and forced a passage through the crowd, by now almost delirious with the taste of 'blood' – or rather, flames. It looked as though the main building would be saved from danger, and the terrace tables and chairs would not cost much to replace. But the furniture was well alight: nothing could save that. The firemen, however, were playing water from their hoses on to the walls behind until, without warning, the water seemed to hesitate, then abruptly stopped. The crowd cheered. The flames increased. Astonished firemen looked to see what had happened. They didn't have to look far: some men in the mob had slashed the hoses. I arrived just at that moment, as the hotheads escaped, crying, 'More fires! Burn down all British buildings!'

The first knot of people I appealed to was a group of policemen.

'After them!' I cried. 'Can't we stop the fire?'

Three of the men didn't answer, just looked at me scornfully and turned their backs. The last one looked me up and down and sneered two words, 'You British?'

I didn't need to make the instinctive nod because he immediately spat on my shoes.

I could have hit him. I knew that he hoped I would. 'Go on!' he taunted me.

It wasn't fear that stopped me – more a desire to get to Samia as the flames started to spread and greedily lick the outer walls. And one other thing, I suppose. I knew that if I had hit the policeman either he would have happily cracked open my skull or half a dozen men would have beaten the hell out of me and thrown me into jail without decent medical treatment – and then I would have been no use to anyone. No, this really was a time for discretion.

So, somewhat to the astonishment of the police officer, I ran across the burning terrace, and as he shouted 'Stop!' I dashed past the front door, already hot and singed, the paint bubbling blisters on the woodwork. He actually followed me in, shouting, 'You can't go in there, it's dangerous!'

As Samia threw welcoming arms round my neck she cried, 'Oh my God! Isn't this terrible?' Then, catching sight of the policeman entering, shouted at him, 'You pig. I saw what you did to this gentleman.' With the flames almost reaching the outer bar behind the terrace, she showered him with a string of oaths I couldn't understand, but which no doubt meant, 'We reserve the right to refuse admission to anyone.' Finally she shouted, 'Get out, pig!'

As he turned, stumbling and coughing with smoke, I tripped him up – deliberately. He fell headlong. I just had time to wipe the spit on my shoe off on to his uniform before he scrambled up and ran back across the terrace.

'Come on! Let's go,' I urged Samia. 'Another minute and we'll be held back by a wall of solid flame. All the girls are out?'

'All out.' She was not crying, but racked with dry sobs that seemed to wrench the heart out of her, tearing up the deeds of a dream. Because the building was of stone the flames had not reached far into the nightclub, but the heat was intense and the smoke swirled into our lungs. I still insisted, shaking her, trying to get some sense out of her, 'Come on, before it's too late. You're sure about the girls? I didn't see any come out.'

'Yes, yes, they're out,' she gasped, coughing. 'Through the back door.'

In the midst of all the fear, the heat, the sudden sound of crackling as the flames found a new easy part to devour, my brain shot out a question from the past. 'But you told me once there was no rear exit.'

'Of course there is. Under the stairs. The back door.'

'But when my brother was coming to the Sphinx and my father was inside, you said –'

Despite everything she spluttered between coughs, 'I lied! I didn't want to spoil your father's night out.'

'You devil!' But I said it with affection as we both bolted through the back door, round the alley and into the main street.

As we looked with a kind of dumb fascination I saw the first flames lick the roof. We never discovered what had happened, of course, but it seems probable that soon after we escaped the flames reached the curtains and soft furniture, and then it was only a matter of minutes before the wooden ceiling and the beds above were engulfed. With an abrupt crash the first-floor ceiling, with all its linen and beds, came crashing down and a cloud of dust seemed to spurt above the flames.

There was nothing to be done, nothing I could say.

Further up the street I saw more flames. 'Christ! That's Barclays Bank,' I cried. In a way sharing the agony helped to calm Samia, especially when another fire started – this time in Groppi's, on the other side of the street. Here the rioters emerged carrying trays of freshly baked pastries which they hurled into the street, trampling on them before setting the building alight.

A few hundred yards away another crowd, racing past us, across the square in front of the Opera House, was making for Ibrahim Pasha Street. For the first time I realised that there was some sort of vague organisation among the fire-raisers, for they were choosing carefully, almost all of their targets British. Outside the Rivoli Cinema I saw the leaders of a gang hurl petrol bombs into the foyer. And no sooner was the Rivoli well alight than the leaders of the fire-raisers issued orders about the next target. The Sphinx might have been burned by accident, but now the arson was being directed by experts. This was particularly noticeable when they set fire to comparatively small shops known to be British in Soliman Pasha, Kasr el Nil and Fuad Streets.

Special squads were determined that no British business houses should escape. Even small ones, most of which had pulled down and locked their metal grills, were not immune if they had British connections; the arsonists worked with men who forced open the iron curtains with picks or even acetylene burners. Then the arsonists squeezed through the narrow gap to set the fire.

Before long it was the turn of the big European and Jewish businesses and department stores. The TWA building, Ford's magnificent showrooms – all went up in flames.

Throughout the terror the police took no action. It wasn't that they couldn't have stopped the arsonists: they deliberately ignored every appeal for help. The only exception was at the approach roads to Garden City with its embassies. There, the few British troops manning machine-guns inside the embassy gardens (but who had deliberately kept out of sight) sent a message to the police guarding the entrance on the other side of the railings, warning them that if they didn't act decisively British troops would open fire. The Egyptian police took the hint and kept all the rioters out of the embassy area.

I had decided to leave Samia in my chambers, planning to let her spend the night at Holt House. The girls, she discovered before I left, were safe in the YWCA. I had to make my way now to keep my appointment with Storey – if he turned up, which I very much doubted. But he might, for among the British there was always a vague feeling, 'Don't let's exaggerate, old boy, they're only a bunch of disorganised wogs.'

These, though, were not disorganised. By now half the city – the European heart of Cairo – lay under a thick cloud of black, evil-smelling smoke, hanging over the burning buildings like a blanket.

I doubted if the mob would touch the Turf Club, any more than they would try to burn down the Abdin Palace, where on this very day Farouk was hosting a lunch for six hundred officer cadets. Adly Pasha Street wasn't far away, and the crowds seemed to be melting in another direction, more towards Abdin Palace. Even so I had to fight my way to reach the club. Half the buildings in Adly Pasha Street seemed to. be burning. Everyone I passed was retching, spitting, coughing the dirt out of smoke-filled lungs.

So it was that at first I could not see the fire ahead – and the horror that went with it. I was so frightened of the ghoulish mob that I hid in a doorway, watching. As I arrived at the Turf Club some kind of bomb – petrol, I suppose, but no one would ever know – burst inside the entrance, turning the club almost instantly into a sheet of flame. Then I saw three men screaming, their clothes partly on fire, running out of the building. They were Storey, Craig of the Customs, and another man whom I recognised, the Canadian chargé d'affaires. I knew immediately – from the speed with which they managed to get out – that they had been meeting in the small anteroom-cum-bar just on the right of the main entrance.

I remember I muttered, almost like a prayer, 'Thank God they're safe!'

Only they weren't.

As the three men stumbled to the ground, the small flames dying out on their clothes, the crazed crowd lurched forward with shrieks of fury as though robbed of their prey, and grabbed them. In a moment, still struggling and screaming with pain and terror, they were hurled back into the inferno. Only when the mob was sure the men were dead were the blackened bodies, bloated by heat, pulled back into the street, as though on public exhibition, amid cries of *'Allahbin Akbar'*, the trademark of the Moslem Brotherhood, 'There is none greater than God'.

As I cowered in the doorway, thinking of the sickening stupidity of it all, I felt a tug at my arm, and almost instinctively prepared to fight to the death. But it was two Britons, both with their faces covered, like mine, in smoke and filth. One was Dennis Birch, the Ford agent in Egypt, whom I knew slightly, the other a man called Wright.

'That was a close call.' Birch rubbed his eyes. 'Nobody was taking the riots seriously when suddenly my driver appeared in the bar and insisted on my leaving immediately. He literally pulled me by the arm out into my car. A couple of minutes more and I would have had it.'

Birch was fortunate. So was Wright, who worked for the Rivoli Cinema. 'It was actually too early for me to go to the cinema,' he said, 'but I went to have a look-see in case of trouble.' When the arsonists set fire to his cinema Wright ran to safety along one of the corridors, after a couple of thugs, with knives drawn, chased him. He only escaped by jumping from a second floor window.

Some of the most famous bars in Cairo received a slightly different treatment. As well as petrol they were doused in alcohol. The Cecil Bar, the St James, Kursaal's in Alfi Street, the Parisien, the Ritz café – all burned with a special brightness and a pungent smell as bottles of whisky, vodka and gin were added to the fires.

The streets were filled with the blackened, burned-out skeletons of cars which men of poverty had chosen to destroy in a country where a car was many a man's most treasured possession.

Miraculously, no one had yet touched Shepheard's. I was sure that, in any event, Sirry Pasha's celebration lunch would have been cancelled, but since the hotel was near my chambers, where Samia was waiting, I thought I would check. Indeed, that first sight was extraordinary, a capsule of time standing still. It was as though Shepheard's was 'Off Limits' to arsonists. The veranda was filled, the waiters in their clean white galabiyas moving from one table to another with unhurried calm. Wright of the Rivoli Cinema had told me outside the Turf Club that Shepheard's had been given 'protection' by the Moslem Brotherhood. And certainly everything appeared to be normal.

At the reception desk I asked whether the party given in honour of Sirry Pasha had been cancelled.

'Of course it hasn't been cancelled.' The assistant manager was indignant. 'This is Shepheard's, sir. We don't panic here, you know.'

'Still' – I rustled a note – 'I am the son of Sir Geoffrey Holt, and if I could have a word – it's on embassy business.'

'I don't think you can.' He was more polite now, but doubtful. 'This is a private reception. But I'll see what's happening.'

At that moment several things did happen. A phone shrilled on the reception desk, and the man spoke into it for barely half a minute. Then he picked up a hand microphone, probably part of a Tannoy system and, trying to keep the panic out of his voice, announced urgently, 'Ladies and gentlemen, please do not alarm yourselves, but will all guests proceed to their rooms for a short time. There is no need to worry. This is purely a precautionary measure.'

The startled guests moved quickly out of their chairs and made for the elevator corridors and the huge well-like lifts, with the great dome of Shepheard's above them. As some started to run, others tried to give the impression of unconcern. I begged the manager, 'Where's Sirry Pasha's room?'

'I don't know,' cried the man and ran off. The cavernous Arabesque lobby, with its elephant tusks, baroque or ivory inlaid tables, its huge fat sofas and thick curtains, emptied in record speed. Soon I was the only one left, and started to leave, for there was no way of finding which of the many conference rooms Sirry Pasha was using. At that moment the fire-raisers rushed in. I was standing on one side, face blackened – they probably never even saw me. Everyone had run away: the veranda was bare. After all this delay! Why had they razed hundreds of buildings in Cairo yet left Shepheard's to the last? Was it some kind of perverted desire to burn the brightest jewel in Britain's Egyptian presence? It seemed crazy.

I didn't think of them at first as fire-raisers, but now I was determined to find the conference rooms on the first floor and to warn Sirry Pasha. But then, as I ran back towards the lifts and staircase, I stopped for a moment, horror etched on my face. The men were tearing down curtains, rugs, making a huge pile in the central lobby, when I saw the head of the group. The leader of the 'detergent squad': Aly Sirry.

'Aly!' I shouted. 'What the hell –?'

'Get out,' he screamed. 'Get out before it's too late. All this stuff here' – he gave a sweeping gesture to include the curtains – 'it was sprayed with an inflammable substance this morning. Not detergent. Get out.'

As he spoke the men tore down the last of the curtains.

'What about your father?'

'What the hell's that got to do with it?'

'He's in there,' I cried. 'It's your father I'm going to look for.'

'No!' screamed Aly, running towards the pile of curtains.

'It's his birthday celebration,' I shouted and ran, just as I heard Aly cry to someone, 'Stop the fire!'

He was too late. One of the men had set light to the pile in the main lobby and all of them were racing to the veranda and the safety of the street. I ran one way, Aly the other. I didn't know what happened to him.

As I reached the back of the building it was as though a wall of flame in the high lounge shot up in a pillar of orange. That, I thought as I raced up the back stairs past the elevator bank, is what the atom bomb must have looked like. Because of the up-draught the A-bomb illusion was heightened. So it was that when the pillar of fire hit the dome a mushroom of smoke spread across the ceiling. Then the glass of the dome broke, falling in an uncountable shower of splinters.

I knew there were conference rooms on the first floor, but where? I burst open one room, to find a woman wearing only a pair of panties and a bra begging me, 'Tie these sheets to make a rope' – but I hadn't time. Back in the corridor I opened the next door. The flames had somehow come through the back way and were already devouring a large double bed. One woman's dress was on fire. I rolled her up in a blanket and told her to get to the window. I don't know if she escaped.

In a third bedroom I did help a woman who had knotted sheets into a rope. Together we dragged the bed to the window, tied one end of the sheet securely and, clutching her jewel case, she gently let herself down the twenty or so feet. She was starting to go down when some hooligans ran round the back, saw her, and set fire to the bottom of the sheets. She screamed and fell, scattering jewels on the ground as she died. Nobody bothered to grab a ring or a necklace; revenge was sweeter than riches.

I raced along the corridors searching for one of the private dining suites. Finally I found the right private room. Choking with smoke, I forced open the hot and blistered door which crashed to the floor as I banged it.

Inside, like grotesque caricatures of Dante's Inferno, were Sirry Pasha and his friends – or what was left of them. The men at the far end, who had obviously been overcome by fumes, still sat at the heavy wooden table, heads lying on the charred tablecloth. Most were dead of asphyxiation, others badly burned by the flames. Some, blackened and unrecognisable, were on the floor as though they had been crawling to freedom like giant black spiders.

There was no way in which I could recognise Sirry and at that moment the far wall crashed down, as though pushed out of the way to make room for more flames, which rushed in with terrific speed. Using my jacket, I picked up a chair, already crackling and burning, and hurled it through the biggest window. I had never been trapped in a fire before and what I found incredible was the way the flames ran along the side of any wall searching out any fragment of combustible material. In no time flames were blistering the wooden window-frames. I squeezed through on to an iron ledge outside where I found one of the fire escapes with steps leading down to within a few feet of the ground. From there I jumped, with nothing worse than a few bruises and a twisted arm, which I had held out to break my fall.

As soon as I reached Holt House I told Father and Chiffon some of the terrible things I had seen. The radio was on, and though Samia had been sent to bed suffering from delayed shock, we all listened as though mesmerised. Altogether four hundred buildings had been completely burned out. Nine Europeans had been burned alive at the Turf Club alone. No one was able to compute the number who had perished in Shepheard's because all the hotel records such as the guests' registry book and so on had gone up in flames.

'You'll have to phone soon to Serena in Switzerland,' Father said. 'Unless you'd like me to do it.' It was the moment I had been dreading.

'No, I'd rather.'

'Remember that with a fire like this it'll make page-one headlines in every edition of the *Journal de Genève*.'

I told her on the telephone late that afternoon, and after the first heartbroken shock she made the one decision that I knew in my heart she would make.

'I'm coming home,' she said through her tears. 'Quite apart

from me, I can't leave Mama alone in Cairo.'

'Don't cry, Serena.' There was no way I could help her, though I didn't of course tell her the part Aly had played. 'I understand. I knew you'd say that.' I paused, then asked, 'Farouk?'

'To hell with Farouk!' She almost shouted down the phone. The line was bad, but I heard her say, 'I'll catch the first available flight. I'll cable you.'

The next day she arrived, sad but composed. I was at Cairo Airport to meet the flight. As I waited, I was thinking of the day when I had waited to meet her in Lisbon. What a lot had happened to all of us since those happy moments. And now at last the banished Serena was coming home. I wondered, as I waved a greeting, what would happen to us now.

PART FOUR

1952–1953

42

Life would never be the same again in Cairo, not even after winter turned into summer, not even after the months which had been needed for Serena and her mother to come to terms with Sirry Pasha's death.

'The trouble with violent death of this kind,' said Serena, 'is that it provides you with a clear-cut picture which, however hard you try, you can't obliterate. If someone dies in their sleep you think of the picture with relief. But poor Papa! The picture of his death will haunt me for life.'

I had been able to do one thing: hide the truth about Aly. He had been directly responsible for burning his own father alive, not to mention the dozens of others who had perished. True, he hadn't known that his father would be there, but it had been Aly who had sprayed Shepheard's with so-called detergent, and *that* had been the cause of the heavy loss of life. Without that added hazard many of the hotel guests might easily have had time to be evacuated.

I was the only one who knew, yet I didn't say a word to Serena when finally Aly came to see his mother and sister. I wasn't there, of course, but I did see him leaving the house and sprinted across to speak to him, just as he was climbing into his car.

'I haven't said anything yet,' I started, 'though only because of Serena and your mother. But remember one thing: Nasser and Sadat would be horrified if they knew what you'd done.'

He started to interrupt, but I shouted, 'Just remember what they'd think – or do – if I told them. The Free Officers would probably arrange for you to disappear – conveniently. They don't want their hands stained with your blood. And if I ever need to I will tell.'

Fighting to control my anger, I went on, 'Your chums in

the Moslem Brotherhood tried to kill my father, and now you're involved with those bastards.'

The part played by the Brotherhood in the fires had become more and more apparent during the weeks that followed. I ended: 'Just don't get involved, that's all. Otherwise –' The threat was there, and I'm not quite sure why I made it. We lived in such a shifting world that it suddenly occurred to me, standing there, that one day I might need Nasser, and Aly might provide the way to see him.

I had waved the big stick at Aly not only because I despised him but also because of the vague forebodings about Serena's presence in Cairo. Farouk was now walking a tightrope. He probably didn't know of Serena's return, but any personal scandal was the last thing he wanted. At the same time the Free Officers – whom I was convinced had had nothing to do with the fires; they had used the Moslem Brotherhood from time to time, but not to burn down Cairo – were becoming more and more open in their defiance of Farouk. Nasser himself kept a low profile; his name was hardly known except to his most trusted lieutenants, though he was the organising genius behind the planning.

In early June, after months of grief which she could hardly hide, Madame Sirry suggested that she should go to stay with her sister in Paris. 'I'm not ill, but I want the best Paris doctors to check on my heart. Nothing serious, but it bumps too much.' In a blank, defeated voice, she asked Serena, 'You'll come along with me, won't you?'

I felt it would be a good idea – a *safe* idea – for Serena to go, but she wanted to stay, even though she was vaguely worried about her mother.

'Well, if you won't, I can't,' said Madame Sirry. 'I shan't leave you alone at a time like this.'

It was Chiffon who made the obvious suggestion just before I did – and in a way it came better from her.

'If you do feel you want a check-up you should go,' Chiffon told Madame Sirry. 'A change is just what you need, to get out of this awful house. And as for Serena – she'll stay with us, for as long as you both want. After all, I still think of her as my daughter-in-law. There, that's decided.' She rang the bell, crying 'Emile! Zola!' waiting for whoever came first. Then she told Emile, 'Prepare the blue bedroom for Mrs King. She'll be staying with us until further notice.'

I was delighted – for the blue room was next to mine; in fact it had originally been arranged as a suite, with a connecting door. I must have shown my excitement too obviously, for when Serena had returned home, planning to move later in the day, Chiffon almost laughed and said, 'Come with me to the flower room and we'll arrange a bouquet for Serena. Now, let's see, we should get blue flowers.' The gardener was hovering, and she told him, 'Pick some cornflowers from the bed at the far end.'

To me, she added, 'Perfect. And of course, to a woman who's half-French, very suggestive.'

'Suggestive?'

'In France,' she explained patiently, '*bluets*, as cornflowers are called, are supposed to be a signal from a man that he's – attracted to a girl, and that he's – er – willing; a sort of secret signal. There! Here's an extra one to pop in your buttonhole.'

I must have looked startled at her insight, for she smiled, gave me a kiss and said, 'You are a funny boy.'

'I am forty-two,' I said primly.

'Still, *my* boy. And I do wish you'd stop thinking that I'm so silly that I can't see what's happened. I do have eyes. Only don't do anything to upset your father. Behind that façade of his he's very straitlaced.'

'Yes, Chiffon,' I said meekly, thinking of Father's goodbye wave the evening he had walked up the stairs to spend the night in the Sphinx.

In fact it suited us all; even so, I wanted to keep Serena out of sight as much as possible. The government – even the secret police – were at sixes and sevens, and nobody knew what was happening or what line to take should they have to switch loyalties in a hurry; or perhaps no one was really giving a damn. As one civil servant said to me, 'We don't know who the hell we'll be working for next week.' But while I was certain that Farouk didn't know Serena was back in Egypt there was no point in taking chances.

'You know,' I said to her that first night in bed, after her return to Holt House, 'women really are extraordinary.'

'Not a very profound remark. Have you only just discovered it?' She cuddled up.

'No – but Chiffon knowing all about us. And all that time, pretending she knew nothing. Everyone seems to know.'

'Gossip does travel. Especially in Cairo. Do you mind? After all, you were the one who wanted to live openly with me. And since we're going to get married soon anyway . . .'

'Of course I don't care. I'm proud of the fact. But watch out. I can see the headline, "Middle-aged barrister grabs beautiful heiress." '

'I can see another headline,' she said, laughing. ' "Shop-soiled divorcee weds famous barrister." '

'The headline which really frightens me,' I confessed, 'is the one that Mrs Sadik would write if she could: "The mysterious visitor at the Villa Zelfa." '

'Don't.' She suddenly shivered. 'That woman frightens me.'

'You haven't seen her since you returned?'

Serena shook her head. 'I'm keeping out of the way. No parties, no – nothing.' She added softly, 'Except the love of a strong man to keep me from feeling sad.'

'Cairo's a village.' I squeezed her arm. 'I suppose you're bound to run across her sooner or later.'

It was sooner.

Mr and Mrs Teddy Pollock were celebrating their wedding anniversary. I didn't ask which one because, though I knew they had been married twice, others might not be aware of this. I had, however, said a firm 'No' to the anniversary party which had originally been planned as a dance on the roof-garden at Shepheard's. Alas, there was no longer a Shepheard's, so Teddy had booked the tables at the Gezira.

My 'No' had been based on the simple fact that I didn't want Serena to circulate too much. But I had agreed that we should meet for a pre-party drink at the Rendezvous, a bar with a balcony facing the street near the corner of the Egyptian

Museum in Mariette Pasha Street. It wasn't the greatest bar in town but it had a pleasant balcony and a cool breeze from the river in front. Also, because it was on the edge of Garden City, it had escaped the fires.

The Pollocks were to be joined by Jim Stevenson, and after drinks Serena and I would go home for a quiet dinner with the family. The others would carry on, just as we had carried on years ago, when Parmi had visited the club for the first time or when Farouk had invited himself to the Gezira and danced with Serena while Greg looked on.

'I'm glad we're not going,' I told Serena as we walked along the river-bank towards the bar. 'Too many memories.'

'The Rendezvous is just about the only place left,' she said. 'They've tried to get rid of all the other signs of British influence, but though you can burn down buildings you can't burn away memories.'

Teddy and Angie were already sitting on the veranda and waved as we approached.

'You look just as wonderful as ever,' said Teddy to Serena as we sat next to them round a large table and he ordered drinks. 'I'm only sorry you can't come along to our party.'

Angela was sitting next to Serena and asked jokingly, 'Tell me, what does it feel like to be an independent millionairess?'

'No different,' laughed Serena. 'Honestly, I mean it. You can't even do the things you want to with all the money in the world.'

'Such as?'

'I *was* hoping to do one thing. Buy back Nasrani, however much it cost. But I've been warned that the Free Officers are now so sure of themselves that they're drawing up plans for when they take power to limit the amount of land anyone can own. At least that's what Jim tells me.'

'Is it true?' Teddy asked, turning to me.

'It's on the cards,' I replied. 'Nasser's friends plan to limit one man's holding to about two hundred acres. And if it comes about it'll wipe out all the big absentee landlords with their exploitation of the fellahîn.'

'Anyway, that was my dream when I inherited all that money from Bruce,' said Serena. 'Nasrani was Papa's great love. I planned to buy it for him. I don't really think I'd want to have it back without him. Papa and Nasrani seemed to go with one another.'

Jim Stevenson had just had time to join us and sit down when I saw two people walking along Mariette Pasha Street, straight towards the Rendezvous bar. I gasped, then whispered urgently to Serena, 'Turn your back on the street. Quick! Mrs Sadik is arriving.'

What made me catch my breath was not only the appearance of Mrs Sadik. It was her escort – none other than Sadat. There was no way the two of them could avoid seeing me, though Serena was sitting with her back to the entry steps, so she was looking the other way, and with luck, Mrs Sadik wouldn't recognise her. They both strolled in and sat down at a nearby table. Mrs Sadik gave me an icy nod of recognition. Sadat smiled, lit up his pipe and then to my astonishment came to our table and said cheerfully, 'How are you, Stevenson? And you, Mr Holt? No more "Colonel", eh? That was your rank when you arrested me, wasn't it?'

'Duty.' I wasn't going to evade the question.

'Of course.' Sadat was expansive. 'Forget it. All future leaders have to spend a few months in jail – fortunes of war. Look at Nehru. Gandhi. It's all part of the training for leadership. One day in jail, the next day in power. No hard feelings.'

It was impossible to think badly of him, he was such a jovial character, so exuberant. Though this exchange had taken only a few moments Serena had kept her face averted while Mrs Sadik waited. As Sadat started to return to his table it was Stevenson who, looking puzzled, remarked, 'Somehow I didn't expect you and Mrs Sadik to meet socially.'

'Her late husband is one of the martyrs of the Free Officers,' Sadat explained. 'We know from what Lala Sadik has told us that all the time he was ADC to Farouk he was working secretly for us. Well, good-day to you all.'

'Bullshit!' I said after Sadat had left us. 'He was a crook and a pimp.'

'I know, but give Mrs Sadik her due,' said Stevenson.

'She's certainly made sure that people believe her version of events.'

It was at that moment that Serena turned round. As she was sitting on the right of Angie who was facing the street she couldn't see people like Mrs Sadik behind her, but when she shuffled the chair towards me Mrs Sadik must have seen her face for the first time for I heard – quite distinctly – the hiss of someone suddenly drawing in their breath with surprise, even fury. Serena heard it too. As she looked up she stared straight into the flaring, hate-filled eyes of Lala Sadik. In a loud voice Mrs Sadik said to Sadat, 'Please take me away, Colonel. I will not stay in the company of that woman.'

She motioned towards Serena, then rose and stalked down the three steps to the pavement. If she wished to carry on walking she had to pass where we were sitting. Sadat tried to hurry her along, but she pushed his arm away roughly and stopped directly in front of us. And as she spoke I again had the impression of hissing – as if she were a snake whose forked tongue was about to dart out.

Facing Serena she said, 'The king kicked you out of Egypt because you and he knew too much about my beloved husband. You wait. When we take over this country there'll be no room for people like you.'

As white as chalk Serena, never lacking in anger when roused, immediately started to reply, but I touched her arm to restrain her – I could feel the goose-pimples on her bare skin. As Mrs Sadik turned and walked on all Serena said was, 'The bitch! The bloody bitch!'

'She is indeed,' agreed Stevenson. He spoke in more serious tones than his usual laconic drawl. 'But she's a very powerful bitch. Watch out.'

With the prospect of Farouk abdicating – and even he now knew it was only a question of time – the secret police had become lax, censorship was more liberal and newspapers short of cash would print anything they dared, especially if paid. Thus many papers took cash for paid 'independent' articles, and Mrs Sadik seemed determined to spend every penny she had, launching a series of articles alleging that her husband had been murdered. She didn't mention Farouk personally, but in many of the reports she initiated Serena's name was brought into unwelcome prominence.

No one dared to print that Serena had been involved in murder, but even so the attacks were vitriolic. Questions were asked about the mysterious packages taken away at night; or the baffling disappearance of Mrs Sadik's husband. Had the king been at the Villa Zelfa that evening, and had General Sadik been there in his role as ADC? And why had his widow never been permitted to see his body? Other questions were asked to which there was no defence. How often had the king been invited privately to the Villa Zelfa? (The reports conveniently omitted the fact that Farouk always took his current girlfriend along to these dinners.) My name was mentioned as an occasional guest. And so the mystery of what happened that night at the Villa Zelfa was brought up time and time again.

Once or twice Serena wanted to sue, but I counselled her against it. 'Remember what happened to Oscar Wilde when he sued. He ended up in jail. Just preserve a dignified silence.' What I didn't say was the difficulty of fighting an action against a charge which contained more than a grain of truth.

There was another point which stopped Serena from taking any hasty action. 'If you did sue,' I said, 'it would probably take six months to reach the courts.' I shrugged. 'By that time anything could have happened. The coup might fail. You might have changed your name by then to Serena Holt. No, ignore everything. Don't even read the newspapers.'

'I don't,' she said angrily. 'Some sadist sends me all the clippings – with no letters. Delivered by hand. But you're right. After all,' she smiled, 'you are my legal adviser. I might as well take your advice.'

The coup that would change history was launched in July. Nasser had prepared the ground with all the attention to detail of a good staff officer. Though he was the officers' undisputed leader he felt instinctively that, if the army was to stage a coup, he needed a man of some prestige and rank as leader. 'Colonels aren't important enough to stage military uprisings,' he said to Stevenson. At first he thought of asking General Aziz el Masri, who had tried to help Rommel in the war, but he was too old. The choice finally fell on General Mohammed Naguib. Like Sadat he was a popular, pipe-smoking figure who had distinguished himself in the Palestine fiasco. Nasser made one stipulation in front of the other plotters: Naguib must have no delusions about wielding any real power. He would remain a figurehead. Nasser would rule, Nasser would decide. Naguib agreed in front of the other ringleaders, including Sadat. He was delighted, anyway, at the prospect of becoming the first 'President'.

By July, with the temperature in Cairo touching 117 degrees, Farouk had moved to his summer palace outside the city. So did the United States ambassador, Jefferson Caffery, who wanted to keep in constant touch with the king, while Stevenson, his special assistant, remained in Cairo to keep close to Nasser.

'I wouldn't say we know everything that Nasser is planning,' Stevenson told me. 'But we've a pretty good idea, simply because he's pragmatic, and he knows that he will need to be backed by the Americans, and that the US State Department wants Farouk out too. So one thing helps the other.'

'When do you think it's all going to start? It can't be long.'

'Nasser told me,' Stevenson said with a laugh, 'that the main reason they haven't staged the coup yet is so that the officers can collect their monthly pay packet at the end of July. So it's bound to be early August.'

In fact the Free Officers couldn't wait until August because Farouk, in a desperate last gamble, decided to arrest fourteen of the ringleaders. Nasser had to act quickly to avoid arrest himself. Even though he couldn't contact all the plotters, he put forward the date to 22 July.

The change was so unexpected that Sadat, who breathed more revolution that anyone else, couldn't be found early on the evening of the appointed day: he had taken his wife to the cinema. And when Nasser set off in his black Austin Ten to the house where for months arms had been secretly stored the Free Officer who guarded the cache had also gone out.

Undeterred, Nasser decided to join the other plotters, on the second floor of the Egyptian army GHQ at Kubbah, near the royal palace, and send someone for the arms later on. Then he ran into what was almost a disaster. As he drove towards GHQ a couple of motor-cycle police roared up, forced him to stop and demanded to see his papers.

'What's the trouble?' Nasser said as he leaned out of the front window.

'You're driving without lights,' snapped one of the police-man, adding sarcastically, 'Didn't you know it's illegal?'

Nasser had completely forgotten to switch on his lights. His only way out, he knew, was to wheedle and play the nervous driver. He acted the part for all he was worth. Finally the police told him to take more care in future, and drove off.

After that the operation went without a hitch. The arms were brought over, and Nasser and his volunteers stormed the Egyptian military GHQ on the floor below their meeting place, with Sadat rushing in to join them mid-coup. After a token resistance, Nasser took charge. Other members of the Free Officers occupied the state radio station, the airport, the huge military depot at Abbassiah. By 1.30 a.m. on 23 July the nerve centres of the Egyptian army had fallen: barely a couple of hours were needed to bring to a climax more than ten years of planning and hopes and dreams. Among the first things that the thirty-four-year-old Nasser did was to telephone Stevenson and ask him to tell the American am-bassador to warn Farouk. Caffery phoned Washington. From that moment events moved forward inexorably.

'With the Americans in charge of public relations,' said Father, when I told him, 'we can't do a damn thing.'

'We still have the Canal.'

'For how long? Anyway, I'm too old to play these games. I'm sick of the whole business of trying to get on with the Egyptians. Though I'll certainly be glad to see the back of Farouk. At least Naguib isn't a bad chap.'

Naguib was given the title of Commander-in-Chief of the Armed Forces of Egypt. With Nasser still keeping in the background, Naguib went on the radio and made all the announcements. But Nasser made all the decisions, including the very first, to Stevenson. At an interview before breakfast he told him, 'Better tell the US ambassador that Farouk must be out of the country within twenty-four hours, or forty-eight at the most.'

Many of the Free Officers hoped that Farouk would be executed for 'crimes against the state'; General el Masri, summoned at six the following morning, told Nasser, 'Execution is the only way. A head like Farouk's interests me only after it has fallen. You must kill and kill and kill. You may have to slay thousands in order to purge the country.'

Nasser would have none of it. 'This is supposed to be a *bloodless* coup,' he said. 'If we kill Farouk the mob will murder at least three hundred of his entourage the following day. There will be no way to stop the flow of blood once it's started.'

Nasser was also astute enough to realise that the sight of the bloated Farouk enjoying himself on the Riviera would do more to justify the revolution than any bloodshed. He went even further, insisting that Farouk should not be allowed to slip away, but had to sign the correct instrument of abdication and be *seen* to abdicate.

Sadat and Naguib flew to Alexandria to confront the king and arrange the details of the abdication.

Farouk had asked if he could leave on the royal yacht *Mahroussa*; Nasser had agreed to give him and the queen passage as far as Naples, after which the yacht would be returned to Alexandria.

When Sadat arrived Farouk and Narriman, all pretence of royal dignity forgotten, were engaged in a frenzied attempt to finish their last-minute packing. Every time they came across more personal belongings they found they didn't have enough suitcases. Officials made a dozen trips to the souk to buy tin trunks. Farouk had had the feeling that he might be made to abdicate, and so had taken everything he could lay his hands on to Alexandria – including, of course, the wedding gifts, now in the convenient form of gold ingots – which Nasser agreed he could take as they were his personal property.

All that last afternoon the luggage was stowed on board the royal yacht – 204 suitcases or trunks, together with several crates of champagne; presumably for entertaining, as Farouk was a teetotaller.

To the last Nasser was determined that Farouk's departure should be dignified. 'I don't want one of these squalid scenes, the way the Communist countries kick people out if they aren't wanted,' he admitted to a friend.

Just before six that evening Farouk, in the white uniform of an admiral of the fleet, boarded the *Mahroussa*. Jefferson Caffery saw him to the water's edge as the guns of Alexandria gave Farouk a twenty-one-gun salute and the *Mahroussa* slid from her moorings.

It was Jefferson Caffery who had the last word. Caffery, who would never have uttered an opinion flattering about the Free Officers without permission from the State Department, now said frankly, 'These young men can save Egypt from the red tide that Farouk's and the Pashas' abuses could not have failed to let loose over the country. They are going to carry out reforms – you can take my word for it – and raise the people's standard of living. We shall encourage them.'

'Balls,' I said to Stevenson when we read the transcript.

'Don't say that.' Stevenson pretended to look pained. 'I thought I phrased his statement rather well.'

'Congratulations,' I said, smiling. 'I remember the day when you told me that Roosevelt was determined Britain shouldn't remain too powerful in the Middle East after we'd won the war. Well, you had to mastermind a revolution to do it, but you've won through.'

The ink on Farouk's instrument of abdication was hardly dry before Lala Sadik struck – at a time when, in the euphoria of hard-won liberty from tyranny, over-zealous patriots were rooting out 'traitors', real or imagined.

Nasser had made it clear in no circumstances would he tolerate bloodshed; but a show trial was a different matter. Many were justified. Nasser was thinking particularly of the politicians or former army chiefs who had deliberately misled him in Palestine, sending his comrades to fight a war with guns that didn't fire, shells that didn't explode, rations that didn't exist, always to line their own pockets. Next the venal landlords were arraigned – in many case justly so. This made it easy to pounce on anyone of influence who nursed a private grudge. And though I had never really believed it possible that Mrs Sadik had any true influence, I did persuade Serena that she should leave for Switzerland. She agreed, but there was a snag. In an attempt to stop the guilty from fleeing, the government had decreed that no one could leave the country without an exit visa.

The delay wouldn't be long, and because Serena had American as well as Egyptian nationality Jim Stevenson was able to pull strings at the embassy, phoning back to me, 'Not to worry. Tell Serena I'll pick up her passport, stamped with her exit visa, tomorrow afternoon.' This was a Tuesday and he added, 'There's a flight to Geneva on Thursday morning and I've had the embassy book her on it. She can always cancel if she changes her mind – but she shouldn't.'

About eleven on the Wednesday morning Serena and Chiffon had gone shopping. Father was at the embassy. I was at home reading some documents which had just arrived from the Cologne office, planning to leave in half an hour for my chambers.

Vaguely I heard the old-fashioned bell peal at the entrance, the sound of argument, and as I reached the Long Gallery a pleading voice saying, 'Please, sir, your name. I am Emile, son of Zola.'

That meant a stranger. Then a voice in Arabic shouted the equivalent of 'Shut up!' and a wild-eyed Aly rushed along the hallway, grabbed me by the shoulders and cried hoarsely, 'Where's Serena?'

'Take your bloody hands off me!' Even the touch of him on my clothes made me feel physically sick, brought back a picture of that blackened figure on the floor at Shepheard's.

'Where's Serena?' he shouted. 'For God's sake!'

'What's the matter?' I asked roughly. 'You in trouble again?' Then, with real anger, I added, 'Your friend Sadat discovered what you did at Shepheard's?'

He ignored my words, whispering, 'It's not me. It's Serena.'

Even on that warm morning, I felt the chill of sudden fear.

'What do you mean?' It was my turn to grab *his* shoulders. I shook him, seeing the terror in his bloodshot eyes, suddenly realising that it was not for himself but for Serena. I all but screamed at him, 'What the hell are you talking about?'

'Where is she? Where can I find her? They're after her.'

'Who's after her?'

'The police.'

Aly seemed to hesitate, then his face crumpled and he cried, 'Can't you get her out of Egypt? Now?'

I shook my head. 'She's going tomorrow.'

'Switch planes, for God's sake!'

'No one can,' I said sharply. 'There's the small matter of an exit visa.'

'Then it's too late!'

'Too late for what?'

Suddenly he burst into tears and cried, 'There's a warrant out for her arrest.'

'What! It's not possible.'

'It's true. I promise you.'

Trying to hold back my worst fears, I said as calmly as I could, 'There must be some mistake. Damn it, apart from anything else she's an American citizen. Egyptians don't go around arresting wealthy American widows.'

'They're going to, this evening or tomorrow. I heard the news an hour ago and rushed round to see if I could get Serena to escape.'

'And the charge?' I found myself whispering, for I too was afraid – this time of the answer.

For the last time Aly hesitated, his normally brown face the colour of a bucket of dirty ashes. He still couldn't bring himself to look me in the eyes. Without warning, I slapped him across the face. He cried out, startled by the sudden violence, then spilled out the words in a rush.

'Murder!' he whispered, rubbing his cheek. 'She's going to be charged with the murder of General Osman Sadik.'

'Oh, my God!' It was my turn to feel my legs start to buckle. I beckoned Aly into the small sitting room, sat down heavily and motioned him to a chair.

Mind racing, I concentrated on two problems: I would have to get the finest barrister in Cairo to handle the case. Secondly, whatever else happened, even if Serena were remanded while we tried to stop the trial, she must on no account be held in jail: she would crack under the appalling prison conditions in Cairo. Yet, as I knew well, bail for anyone on a murder charge was virtually impossible.

There was only one action to take.

'Where's Nasser?' I asked. Aly seemed to be trying to disappear into the armchair. He looked as though he was shivering, and when I barked out the question asked, 'What? Nasser? I don't know.'

'Sadat then?'

'I do know where he is.'

'Then get round to him now – right away. He's been to your house – I remember he met Serena there. He'll understand this is all a pack of lies, but that's not the most important thing.'

'So – what then?'

'Sadat can pull rank. You can beg him – you'd better, Aly, on your bended knees if necessary – to stand surety for Serena's bail. I don't want her rotting in a prison cell. The word of someone like Sadat will be much more valuable than any money anyone could put up. If one of the leaders of the revolution personally guarantees that Serena won't leave the country that should be enough.'

43

There was a six-week delay before the case came to trial and Sadat – after prodding by Aly – was as good as his word. Serena was placed under 'house arrest', though her passport was taken away. One of Sadat's lieutenants even visited us in Holt House to apologise for the fact that the trial of such a distinguished lady had ever been permitted.

'But once the police start proceedings –' He shrugged, for Aly had been unable to prevent Serena's actual arrest.

'My dear Aly,' Sadat had told him, 'I wish I could stop this nonsense, but investigations must not only be made they must be seen to be made. In a progressive nation there must be no furtive cover-ups.'

Everybody rallied round Serena in those weeks of waiting, especially Jim Stevenson, who insisted that the whole trial was a farce.

'There is no way a judge can find you guilty,' he said. 'We're pulling all the strings we can at the State Department. After all, you're the widow of a highly important American citizen. And' – this with his usual sardonic touch – 'if you're an American millionaire you're considered to be above God, and the law.'

Poor Serena! At first she was so distraught that there was no way I could console her. I will never forget the moment when she returned from the shopping expedition with Chiffon and I broke the news to her. She didn't faint or drop into a chair, but just looked at me with her big green eyes, the tears springing out of each corner, and cried from the heart, 'Oh Mark. Help me. *Help me!*'

Later, more quietly, she said, 'There can't be any real proof, any real case to answer. It's not a verdict of guilty that I'm afraid of, it's standing up in court day after day with that woman digging out everything about my private life. Oh Mark! What a fool I was to come back to Cairo.'

I had never realised how hard it is to be tender and loving to someone who is afraid. When I held her hand as we walked in the garden, her fingers, which should have been warm and squeezing mine, were cold and limp.

Meanwhile I was wondering about something very different: why shouldn't Serena make a run for it? Escape? In theory all exits were blocked, but with all our money it would surely have been comparatively easy to avoid border crossings if we made for, say, the Sudan, or headed west to Tripoli. And the Americans would have given Serena a duplicate for her 'lost' passport.

'I don't know,' said Stevenson when I asked him. 'There's a great swell of pan-Arab feeling in the countries surrounding Egypt. All North Africa knows that Serena is wanted for murder. It's been in every newspaper in the world. She *might* escape – but then be sent back. That wouldn't look good, to say nothing of the position in which Sir Geoffrey would be placed.'

'Escape?' cried Serena in her turn. 'Never. It's unthinkable. The time to plan anything like that would be if I were found guilty. But that's unthinkable too.'

One evening I was talking alone with Stevenson when he said, 'You know that my outfit was involved to an extent in Sadik's goings-on. As a lead on Farouk. But everything that happened in those days was so hush-hush that we couldn't talk about it. The British would play hell if they ever found out what we did, even today. But I'm sure' – it wasn't like Stevenson to choose his words with such obvious care – 'that if the worst comes to the worst we might be able to dig up a little dirt for you.'

'Thanks,' I replied. 'I know you'll help all you can. She needs it – especially now that her mother can't come to Cairo.' For Madame Sirry's heart had started playing tricks, and though there was no immediate danger she was undergoing lengthy tests and there was no question of her flying back from Paris to see Serena.

'It's just as well she's not involved, it's too painful,' said Stevenson. 'What *is* a pity – in my opinion – is that you are.'

For I was, and in a way I hadn't anticipated. When I had first said to Serena that I must engage the finest counsel to defend her she had looked at me, eyes wide open with genuine astonishment.

'What's the matter?' I had asked.

'But *you*,' she blurted out, 'you're the finest barrister in Egypt. You're going to defend me.'

'Impossible,' I said. 'I couldn't do that. In view of our – well, love, and our shared secrets.'

'Shared secrets? Shared with who? No one in the world but us. And who else could you suggest?'

'But it's unethical.' Was it? It must be, I thought.

'To hell with your ethics!' She had the same look I remembered when she left the Hotel Aviz in Lisbon. She had made up her mind then, and had made it up now – only this time she wasn't going away.

'What about some of the American attorneys who worked for Bruce?' I said.

'Great,' she said sharply. 'You go and find a crack American lawyer who just happens to speak Arabic.'

That was a point. Donald Childs was the only English barrister I knew who spoke the language fluently, and I had to admit he wasn't as good a pleader as I was. The pitfalls of acting for Serena were obvious – especially if she was cross-examined about our relationship – but I would have two advantages: I could plead from the heart because I loved her; and, though it may sound odd, counsel for the defence often has a great advantage in a murder case if he knows the real truth.

All the same there were problems which I had to face. It was one thing for a 'neutral' advocate to defend a murder charge; it was very different with Serena and myself. Where would I stand if, in defending Serena, the prosecution started prying into my private life, a life which the prosecution must know about, if only from gossip? I had been a close friend of the Sirry family since Serena was born. I had been present when her husband was killed. I had been present at dinners at which she had entertained Farouk. A prosecutor might well ask why I was invited so frequently to the Villa Zelfa – and how it was possible for me to be impartial.

There was also the one question which I always shirked facing whenever possible. Even if the prosecution didn't know we were lovers the fact that we were put me ethically in the wrong. I didn't want to seem pompous, but the law is bound by a strong code of ethics and woe betide anyone who ignores it. Especially one who ignores it and is found out.

Of course I had insisted to Serena that this was a show trial, and that was partly true; but only partly, for there was another question from which we both shied away: that there *was* a case to answer. It was part of my job to reassure Serena in the weeks leading up to the trial; to give her confidence by regarding the whole business as a boring episode through which she had to suffer before (as I put it) 'the inevitable acquittal'.

But there were times when I did wonder whether it was wise of me to take the case. I even broached the subject with Stevenson.

'Of course you must take it,' he said firmly. 'There's no one else good enough to defend her in her own language.' Then he added a curious remark, 'Anyway, the unexpected chance twist often changes everything.'

'Chance!' I cried. 'You expect me to trust to chance in a murder case?'

'Yes, I do. Sometimes when you need it, and have friends, chance can be loaded in your favour.'

I took heart from this, and back home promised Serena that she had no cause for worry.

But could I make that promise come true? I had no idea who would be chosen as judge – nor could I approach him had I known – although I did know that Fatah Azzam would be leading for the prosecution. I was thinking back to the time Azzam and I had been giving a talk to the Law School and I had met young Nasser.

I had since opposed Azzam many times and respected his devious ways with argument. He was a hawk-like man with a large hooked nose and thin lips. Though he wore badly fitting clothes he had a dominating personality and a sharply sarcastic tongue. But I knew he was not a vindictive man, and would help me if he could.

I rang up Azzam and told him, 'I'm going to the Judicial Council to get a ruling that I am able to handle Mrs King's defence without being accused of any conflict of interests. I don't see any problem, but I'd appreciate a letter from you saying you have no objections.'

'So long as your hands are clean' – Azzam had a way of investing the most innocuous remarks with hidden meanings – 'I've no objection at all. But I can't help feeling you're backing a loser.'

'We'll see,' I said, laughing. 'Thanks for the clearance.'

I had no trouble with the Judicial Council. I knew many of

them well, old retired judges unchanged since the revolution; some had dined with my father, others with Sirry Pasha; but I wanted to be sure I faced no last-minute hitches.

'Thank you, gentlemen,' I said at the end of the meeting. 'I felt certain you would understand, but I also felt that as a matter of courtesy I should declare my interest officially to you.'

'Very proper,' mumbled the head of the panel of judges. 'There will be no problems.'

Those weeks of waiting for the trial – with Serena virtually a prisoner, however gilded the cage – were the longest of our lives.

There was nothing I could do to help. Too much expression of sympathy can become irritating. We slept together in our 'suite' of communicating rooms, but at times I would wake to hear her moan, perhaps dreaming; at others she couldn't sleep for hours on end and would lie at my side, tossing and turning.

During the day the house was wrapped in an atmosphere of gloom, almost as though the windows had been metaphorically shuttered. Everyone talked in whispers as if waiting for an invalid to die.

'I love you more than I've ever done,' I said, trying to console her. 'I just wish there was something *positive* I could do.'

'There is.' She gave a rare smile, rare for those days. 'Just having you around, that's enough. Without you I think I'd have gone mad.'

When the day of the trial arrived I went first to my chambers and from there decided to walk to the court in the Ministry of Justice Building in Kasr-el-Aini Street. The police had firmly told me that I could not escort Serena myself from our house to the court, though it was next-door in Garden City. Even though on bail she *was* under arrest, it was explained, and therefore had to be brought to the court by the proper authorities.

I could have left it to Salem to bring my papers, but I felt the need for all the fresh air I could breathe before being cooped up in a stuffy courtroom. So Salem trotted along beside me. His mahogany-coloured face, topped by its scarlet tarboosh, beamed up at me as he tried to match his stride with mine. Under each arm he carried bundles of folders tied with pink tape and in one chubby hand he clutched an array of pencils.

'You're prepared for a lot of writing,' I smiled.

'Always prepared, sir, always prepared.' His teeth gleamed reassuringly, testifying to his belief that enough pencils and ready references were all I needed to win. I couldn't help reflecting that in a cut-and-dried case that might be true; but this trial was little different from a military tribunal, except for the uniforms – to prove to the newly liberated citizens of Egypt that no one could escape justice by bribery or influence in the way Farouk and his cronies had done.

I had no doubt that the vicious tongue of Lala Sadik was spitting poison into the ears of as many people as possible. Her hints and half-hints about the mysterious death of her husband never stopped. People were not allowed to remember that the 'martyr' had once been the king's pimp. In Cairo people hardly bothered with reasoned lines of argument.

We reached the grey stone Justice Building. It was imposing in its way – it reminded me a little of Selfridges in London's Oxford Street – and the sun struck back from its face, giving a momentary effect of brilliant clarity.

The two Egyptian policemen standing sentry at the entrance made no acknowledgment as Salem and I entered. They were chewing gum, imitating the American cops they had seen in films, and their thumbs were hooked into belts that carried holstered revolvers. With a touch of melancholy I thought of the London police at the Law Courts when I had been reading for my Bar examinations – their gruff salutations graded according to the rank of judge, barrister or mere solicitor's clerk as they entered the building; 'sirs' and 'half-sirs' belonging to a system in which everything was in its ordered place.

Inside there were even greater contrasts. The Justice Building could once have been matched with the Law Courts of

London for orderliness; but now there was ugly evidence of the transition from one form of rule to another: paint peeled from bits of wall in the corridors, there were signs of scuffles on what had once been polished floors, fallen plaster had left laths exposed in some of the anteroom ceilings, unshaded bulbs cast a harsh light into corners filled with spent matches and cigarette ends. The shabbiness of the place depressed me.

Salem, who loved to demonstrate the efficiency of his clerical work, pointed out the anteroom adjoining the assize court. It contained a rough table and three chairs, one of which had a shaky leg, while another had a 'cushion' made out of a folded flag – the flag of pre-revolutionary Egypt, green with the white crescent embracing three stars in its centre – put there, I assumed, as an insult to Farouk. On one wall hung a photograph of General Naguib. Leaning against the wall below it was a discarded picture of Farouk with an obscene comment scrawled across it.

'Now, sir,' said Salem, opening one of his folders, 'our personnel are as follows –'

'Thank you,' I said quickly. 'I am fully aware of who they are.'

As indeed I was – only too well aware. Serena would be tried by a panel of three judges, a presiding judge and two assisting judges. There would be no jury.

The presiding judge I liked. Aziz Afifi was in his early sixties, a tall, saturnine man with considerable experience and as inscrutable as the Sphinx, but as impartial as was possible in the excited atmosphere of a 'progressive' regime. He had had a long and distinguished career, managing to escape several purges by Farouk, and I was delighted that he would preside because I had the feeling that though this *was* a show trial Nasser had deliberately picked a judge like Afifi to prove to the world press that it would at least be fairly run. I had the hunch that Nasser would be almost relieved if the judges brought in a 'Not Guilty' verdict.

It was hard to explain the reasons behind my conclusions, but they ran something like this: Nasser was known as 'El Rayis', the Boss – which he was, for Naguib was of course merely a cipher; but even so, Nasser had to allow the revolutionaries who had helped him to victory to demonstrate their powers. The great danger, as I saw it, was that Nasser, having done all he could by picking Afifi, would now have to let justice take its course, and the other two judges might think it in their best interests to side with the other officers, friends of Mrs Sadik.

The two assisting judges were certainly very different. I had come across both of them in legal battles and was not particularly impressed with either. Judge Mostapha Nessim seemed harmless enough – a man whose face was set in a perpetual smile, but I strongly suspected it was 'the smile of the tiger' rather than the smile of benevolence. Judge Tewfik Malimoud had a brooding, threatening presence, which he emphasised by his habit of sitting with his arms folded. I had heard vague rumours that he was friendly with several 'pro-Mrs Sadik' officers.

There was a wailing of sirens – it seemed that the police had adopted all the worst features of American films – and I wondered what Serena thought of such noisy vulgarity. But as she entered the anteroom her name could not have fitted her more aptly. She was serene and elegant. Fashions in 1952 had rebounded from the exaggerated 'New Look' of the post-war austerity period and she was dressed in a simple Chanel suit. Her two escorting policemen had posted themselves outside the door, and I held her at arm's length.

'I see you're determined to stun them.'

She smiled, though she grew less confident as she looked round the bare walls, the hard chairs, the deal table of the anteroom.

There were shouts. A bell rang, signalling the opening of the public entrance. The court was about to assemble. I opened the door leading from the anteroom and peered through. There were noisy scuffles and laughter as people poured on to the benches at the rear of the court. Somewhat incongruously two ushers were busy on stepladders fixing a line of national flags (the republican ones with the red, white and black horizontal stripes) across the court above the judges' table, as if some festival were being celebrated.

When Salem came through I asked him, 'Why the flags?'

He paused, contemplating for a moment the sheaf of pencils he still held in his hand.

'It is, I think, sir, to remind the people that they are the people, that no one has any privilege above them.'

'If they need reminding, it's because they must be uncertain,' I said mockingly; but I don't think Salem understood, for he beamed and changed the subject. 'All is ready, sir; your books and papers are on the table.'

A few minutes later we were summoned into court.

Shabbiness had invaded even the courtroom itself. Apart from the cassation court – the court of ultimate appeal – the assize was the highest court in the land, but the arrangement of flags could not disguise its plebeian atmosphere. Some of the oak panelling that had formed a background for the judges' tribune had been painted an uneven white; the tribune had been demolished and replaced with a deal dais no more than a foot high. On this was an army trestle-table covered with a grey blanket, and behind the table were three judges' chairs, as decrepit as those in the anteroom – though as a gesture towards comfort they had palm-leaf cushions. Counsel's accommodation was just as spartan: two army tables end to end, but with a space between them to indicate the breach between prosecution and defence. The books I had asked Salem to prepare were stacked in front of me, and he sat on my right. The arrangement was duplicated at the prosecutor's table to my left. Serena had been placed directly in front of my table, in a revolving office chair in padded leather so that she could face the judges or swivel round if she wanted to consult me. The witness box, draped with yet another republican flag, stood to our left.

The public benches behind us were filled with a rabble – all men – who seemed entirely concerned with bags of nuts or melon seeds and bottles of Coca-Cola. It was their day out. Trials in the civil courts were usually dull, but this was the 'trial of the century', and nobody was going to miss it.

There was no one I knew in the public gallery, nor in front of the noisy public, where two rows of hard chairs had been set out for VIPs. I thought I might spot a friendly face among them, but Serena had told all her friends not to attend, so only three strangers sat there. And of course there was no sign of Mrs Sadik. As a witness she was waiting in one of the anterooms.

Above our heads the harsh glow of unshaded light bulbs and the string of flags seemed to rob justice of all its dignity and turn it into a tawdry fairground spectacle.

I leaned across the table to Serena.

'Don't forget, you probably won't be called today, except to answer the charge. The prosecution has to build up a case from scraps of evidence about an event that happened over ten years ago. They've got their work cut out. The grapevine news is that Judge Afifi is tolerantly disposed towards both sides and will be quite happy to clinch the trial on a "No case to answer" note. So relax as much as you can.' I smiled encouragingly.

An usher wearing a soldierly suit of khaki tunic and drill shorts (far too wide for his stick-like legs) banged a staff on the floor and called in a thin voice: 'Stand!' The judges entered from a side door and made their way to their table. They too were in semi-military dress of khaki drill, but with slacks and tarbooshes. The presiding judge, Aziz Afifi, gave a brief nod of acknowledgment, the usher called squeakily, 'Court in session', and the buzz of excitement died down.

The prosecutor stood to open the case, pausing before glancing at the sheaf of papers in his hand. Azzam was a master of timing and gesture who deliberately did little about his appearance so that his opponent should be put off-guard.

'Mr President, this case is brought by the government of the Republic of Egypt on behalf of the People, against' – he paused and looked down at his papers, pretending to be confused – 'against Mrs Serena King, previously Mrs Serena Holt, previously Miss Serena Sirry –'

I jumped to my feet. 'Mr President, I object. My client's present name is all that concerns the court. It can scarcely be relevant that she has been twice tragically widowed.'

I thought I saw a shadow of a smile pass across Judge Afifi's face as he made a note. 'We will be satisfied with her present name,' he said. 'What is the charge?'

'The charge, Mr President, is that on or about 10 July, 1942 she, alone or in collaboration with others, caused the death of General Osman Sadik, aide-de-camp to ex-King Farouk' – he flourished a pair of horn-rimmed spectacles from his pocket – 'but a man truly of Egypt. In short, Mr President, a charge of murder.'

Again the pause before he added – his voice clear, his enunciation precise – 'Since my learned friend for the defence has seen fit to mention the state of widowhood I ask the court to consider the status of a lady who sits in this very building, awaiting her turn to testify, Mrs Lala Sadik, bereft of husband, support, home and family, all that could bring her happiness – a widow like Mrs King, but brought to that unhappy state, as I shall seek to prove, by the evil machinations of the accused.'

He had made up the lost ground; but I was not bothered at this stage. Assisting Judge Nessim smiled at Azzam, and then – out of a fairness? – carried his smile to Serena. Presiding Judge Afifi, his face impassive, leaned forward and asked, 'And the plea, Mrs King?'

I held my breath as Serena stood, her long blonde hair falling over the collar of her suit, catching the glint of the naked bulb above her. Her voice was firm and strong.

'I plead not guilty, Mr President.'

'Very well.' All three judges leaned forward and made notes. Then Malimoud refolded his arms, Nessim resumed his smile, and the President called on the prosecution to open his case.

Azzam's mood was one of supplication. I knew his tactics – to gain sympathy for a poor benighted soul now bereft, and so on; I had adopted the technique myself many times, and in the pre-republic days, when the court sat with a jury, the ploy could be effective. But now, with what amounted to a military-style tribunal, I felt it was to little effect. Even so I was suspicious. Azzam must have known that they would recognise his gambit for what it was. Had he something up his sleeve?

It was not long before he abandoned his histrionic approach and began to go into the background details. He deliberately kept his voice flat and unemotional as he sketched out Sadik's life and career, detailing his high qualities as a soldier, the fate that had directed him into the service of a king who was a traitor, the acumen he had shown as a political adviser, the recognition that had been bestowed upon him in the military funeral with full honours. 'After . . .' Azzam paused impressively, and in the silence I clearly heard the ludicrous sound of someone sucking Coca-Cola through a straw. There was a titter of laughter. To Azzam's credit he remained unruffled, simply extending the pause before reintroducing the cue line.

'. . . after, Mr President, his death from a heart attack had been announced while he was fulfilling a secret mission in some distant place.' Brushing the lapels of his suit – a habit of his – he picked up his sheaf of notes and flourished his spectacles. 'Somewhat oddly, the court may think, in a place of which neither the name nor location have ever been disclosed.' Deliberately lowering his voice he added: 'Too secret, perhaps?' He let the implication hang in the air for a moment, before going on, 'We shall see. I shall produce evidence that will, I think, convince the court that the victim of this heinous crime, far from being in some distant city at the time of the alleged heart attack, was very much – shall we say? – yes, let us say – *closer* to the accused than was good for him!'

After he had finished his opening address Azzam seemed in no hurry to back up his dramatic statement with any startling revelations. Instead he brought to the stand a string of unimportant witnesses, mostly officers testifying to Sadik's army career. There was very little I could do in the way of cross-examination; for though I could have deflated the evidence of some officers I wasn't sure it would be good tactics to discredit any of the near 'heroes' of the revolution.

All the same I couldn't resist a question when one officer went on and on about Sadik's bravery.

'May I ask if you could give me specific instances of this bravery?' I asked when the time came for me to cross-examine.

'I understand that –'

'You understand? You mean you weren't present? That your evidence is hearsay?'

'It's common knowledge,' said the man angrily.

'You may stand down,' I said, and as I turned to my brief I noticed a distinct look of annoyance on the face of Malimoud, the assisting judge; there was a boo from the public benches, quickly silenced by Judge Afifi.

It was much the same with the other witnesses. A military doctor told how he had served with Sadik for two years and had never seen a trace of any heart problem. It was pointless for me to try and wring out an admittance that people did die suddenly from totally unexpected heart attacks. Apart from antagonising one of the Free Officers I would soon get bogged down in medical jargon if I – no doctor – tried to take on a medical witness.

A couple of General Sadik's personal servants followed. His batman had obviously been skilfully rehearsed. He portrayed the dead man as bringing pride to any army. Sadik's military sergeant, who had attended to his army correspondence, said Sadik was punctilious, efficient and accurate. There was nothing I could do to discredit them. Each time Azzam turned to me and said, 'Your witness,' I could do nothing but reply, 'No questions.'

All this took up much of the first day and towards evening Judge Afifi asked the prosecutor, 'How many more witnesses do you propose to call, Mr Azzam?'

'My next witness will be Mrs Lala Sadik,' Azzam replied.

As the courtroom buzzed with excitement Judge Afifi conferred with his colleagues, then said, 'In that case, the court will adjourn and resume tomorrow at 10 a.m.'

I wasn't the only person in court who breathed a sigh of gratitude when the presiding judge decided to adjourn the case for the day. But I was totally unprepared for one more scene of drama. As I started to help Serena from her chair – her face the colour of my white notebook – towards the exit, Azzam rose and said, 'If I may crave the court's indulgence –'

'The court is adjourned,' said Afifi testily.

'I apologise, sir,' Azzam insisted, 'but I must ask for a ruling' – he looked towards Serena with a certain sympathy – 'on where the defendant should spend the night.'

The rabble in the public gallery stopped in their seats, suddenly riveted by this unexpected addition to the day's events.

'Spend the night?' asked Judge Afifi. 'Are you suggesting she should be taken into custody?'

Poor Azzam looked miserable, and I knew what was in his mind. This trial had political overtones and he had to be seen not to show any leniency towards the defendant.

'The case is of such a grave nature,' Azzam said, 'that it may be thought necessary for the defendant to remain in the cells until the court reconvenes in the morning. It is a ruling which I think you should give, sir.'

I felt suddenly sick. I couldn't see Serena's face, but I could see the white skin of her knuckles as she gripped the side of her chair.

'I object most strongly, Mr President,' I cried. 'This lady's appearance in court has been guaranteed by Sir Geoffrey Holt –'

'Your father!' shouted someone from the public benches, while another yelled, 'Lock her up. A night in the cells will do her good.'

'Clear the court – immediately!' roared Afifi. To the court ushers he cried, 'Get them out – everyone from the public gallery before I continue the arguments started by the prosecutor.'

'Sir, I have no wish to force this defendant –' began Azzam.

'I find that a little hard to believe.' Judge Nessim made one of his rare interruptions.

More tolerantly, Judge Afifi continued, 'I think I see your point, Mr Azzam. The publicity surrounding a trial involving the past of a deposed king and the start of a new future for Egypt is bound to attract worldwide publicity.' He added sarcastically, 'And since the readers of newspapers are rarely neutral you feel that she should be confined to the cells like anyone else accused of murder. Am I right in my assessment?'

It was a long speech and I had a curious feeling that not only was Judge Afifi on our side but so, in a different way, was Azzam.

'Thank you, sir,' he said. 'I have no wish to inflict further hardship on the defendant while the trial is in progress.'

'You have made your point,' said Afifi. 'But I think we can rely on the integrity of Sir Geoffrey Holt not to break his bond.' He discussed the matter for a few more moments while I waited, heart in mouth until Afifi said, 'The defendant will be permitted to remain in the custody of Sir Geoffrey at Holt House, but an extra police guard will patrol the grounds all night.'

'Thank God,' I breathed and tried to smile as we made our way to the door. There was one further moment of unexpected kindness on that dark day. As we brushed past Azzam, he muttered to me, 'I'm glad, Holt. I had to make the suggestion – there's an awful lot of political pressure on me, as you can imagine. But I hope I made it clear that I preferred your client to remain in your home.'

I muttered a genuine thank-you, and then we were in the crowded street making our way to the police cars. But this time the milling crowd, thwarted of their last few moments of courtroom drama, were determined to vent their feelings. 'There's still one law for the rich!' yelled one man. Another spat at the car. 'You murdered a hero!' screamed a third. Political feeling, as Azzam had said, was running high.

Somehow we managed to reach our car, and a couple of noisy minutes later we were in the peace of Holt House. An extra car-load of police followed. I told their sergeant that there would be food for anyone who was hungry in the kitchens.

Serena was fighting to hold back her tears.

'Go to your bedroom,' I whispered. 'I'll deal with my parents.'

Father was in the Chinese study, and I explained briefly what had happened.

'Can you leave the two of us alone?' I asked him. 'She's at the end of her tether.'

'Of course,' Father nodded. 'You two use the study. I'll tell Zola to serve your dinner there. And then go to bed – an early night is the finest medicine.'

'God knows what tomorrow will bring,' I said. 'But you're

right. A quiet dinner and bed. Thanks, Father.'

By the time Serena arrived in the study I was sitting behind Father's desk, drumming my fingers on the lacquer surface. Zola brought in the evening papers. Headlines like 'Murder Trial – Dramatic Turn' didn't improve my temper. The door-bell rang a dozen times, even though I had told Zola that I refused to see anyone, for reporters would try every trick for an interview.

'Azzam's thrown you, hasn't he?' asked a worried Serena. 'I couldn't have spent the night in the cell.'

'Of course not. Azzam's not a bad chap really; he's a good counsel and we're the best of friends outside court. But he has a job to do.' I paused. 'As I have.'

'I know. To get me off the hook. Are you regretting it? Taking the case, I mean?'

'Not for a minute,' I said. 'I have rough-and-tumbles with my ethical conscience, that's all.'

She was suddenly serious. 'Defending a woman you know to be lying? Wishing we were married so that you wouldn't be allowed to plead for me? Isn't that it?'

'Wishing we were married – God, yes! But thank God we're *not*. Because there would be no one – and I mean no one – I'd trust to defend you.'

'What do you think Mrs Sadik will say?'

'I honestly don't know. I only hope it's some worthless attempt to say how marvellous her husband was.'

But I didn't really believe that.

44

The court reassembled with surprising efficiency at ten o'clock prompt the following morning. Straggling latecomers were refused admission on the President's instructions and for a few moments, until they were driven off by gleeful police, we could hear their shouted protests because they knew that Mrs Sadik would be testifying. But Afifi wasn't going to stand any nonsense.

Before Azzam called for his first witness he made a more or less subtle plea for sympathy. 'Mr President, I scarcely need to remind the court of the distress Mrs Sadik has suffered since the fateful day when her husband met his end. Yet in the interests of justice she has nobly agreed to give evidence. I call Mrs Lala Sadik.'

There was a rustle of excitement and even Serena, who I had told always to face the judges, turned to watch the entrance of the star witness.

Lala Sadik made her way slowly to the stand, trying to create an image of tragic widowhood doubtless drilled into her by Azzam. Across at my table Serena had a sudden fit of coughing which I realised was suppressed laughter. No wonder. The Sadik woman looked ridiculous. She was dressed from top to toe in black – the widow's weeds of the Victorian era. Her earrings, necklace, rings, a bangle were all jet black. She held a black-edged handkerchief to her pale lips. I saw now that the stretched skin of her cheeks, usually coloured like a doll's, was almost white. The effect, far from being tragic, was grotesque.

Judge Afifi called for a chair to be brought and, when she was seated in the witness box, Azzam said with well-contrived concern, 'Now, Mrs Sadik, will you please tell the court something of the health of your late husband, the general?'

She looked at him with gratitude, and put both her hands in her lap. 'Oh, his health was excellent.'

'Can you perhaps elaborate on that statement?'

She proceeded to do so at length, embarking on a detailed account of Sadik's frequent visits to his doctor for check-ups, his diet, his exercise, the views of his many friends on his robust constitution. At last Judge Afifi interrupted her.

'Mrs Sadik, this court is concerned with facts, not hearsay. I must ask you to keep to the point.'

Azzam immediately made a deep bow towards the judges.

'I ask the court's indulgence, Mr President. My client is, as you see, considerably distressed.' He turned back to his witness. 'Mrs Sadik, what the court would like to hear is whether there was ever evidence of your husband suffering from any kind of heart condition?'

'None whatever.'

'Thank you.' Again Azzam addressed the judges. 'My purpose, Mr President, is to establish that the chance of General Sadik having died from natural causes is a remote one.'

Afifi did not attempt to hide his annoyance. 'So I gather, Mr Azzam. Please proceed. But I would remind you that we have already heard from a qualified doctor on the subject.'

Azzam ignored the rebuff and turned again to Mrs Sadik. 'Madame, will you tell the court precisely how you were notified of the death of your husband?'

Sniffing self-consciously Mrs Sadik said that one of Farouk's Rolls-Royces, complete with liveried chauffeur and footman, had been sent to collect her and take her to the Abdin Palace. There the king himself had broken the news to her.

I made a quick note. This was significant, something to be remembered when I came to my cross-examination. Farouk was not one to do any kind of dirty work himself unless it was strictly necessary. Normally some minion would have broken the news of an aide's death to his widow. Ergo, if Lala Sadik were telling the truth Farouk had considered a personal interview necessary – perhaps, to offer her the sort of pension that would satisfy her greed and quieten her suspicions.

Azzam was now in full flow. 'Madame, will you tell the court how you reacted to that shocking news?'

Mrs Sadik responded as if her puppet-master had pulled the wrong strings. She jerked into a sort of frenzy of emotion that would scarcely have convinced a child.

'Ah! I wept, I collapsed – before the very king I collapsed with grief. I could no longer hold myself with calm. Even the king could not but give me all his sympathy, but he was sharing my grief, for my husband had been like his brother!'

On and on she wailed, her performance as exaggerated as her clothes, but studied in its determination to gain the sympathy of the public gallery. And this I understood, for Egyptians are as easily moved to superficial grief as actors weeping glycerine tears.

Even Judge Nessim was grimacing. Malimoud had reacted to Lala's outburst to the extent of unfolding his arms and was leaning forward on his elbows as if to catch every nuance of misery that fell from Mrs Sadik's lips. Afifi was more controlled, but I could see that he too was shaken.

It seemed as though she would go on all day, and I had to admit that so far the balance of favour was on the prosecution's side. But I wasn't worried. In the normal course of events the President would soon call for the midday adjournment and Mrs Sadik had left herself wide open for some fairly harsh cross-examination when my turn came later in the day.

In the meantime, Azzam did all he could to protract the agony as Mrs Sadik grasped the glass of water on the ledge before her and went through the motions of recovering from what she hoped would be accepted as her telling of the great crisis of her life. I could feel the tension on the public benches. It was finally released by Judge Afifi for it was the time for *duhr*, the midday prayers.

'The court will adjourn for *duhr* and reassemble at 2 p.m.'

Like children switching their attention from the discipline of the classroom to the freedom of the playground the mob made an unruly rush towards the exit, above which was painted the legend — ironically, I thought, considering Lala Sadik's past and present performances — *'B'ism'llah, ma' sha' 'llah'*: a plea to God to keep evil from the house of justice.

I had decided that Serena and I should remain in the gloomy anteroom for the lunch recess because I wanted to go through the morning's evidence with her, undisturbed by any questions from Father or Chiffon. I arranged for Zola to bring us the Egyptian equivalent of a picnic lunch — some freshly baked bread, hummus, tahina and so on. No liquor was permitted on any government premises of course, but Zola brought in two bottles of mineral water; at least it looked like water. One, however, contained colourless arak from which I took a couple of grateful swigs. The other *was* water;

impossible to tell the difference unless you mixed them, for if you added water to arak it turned milky.

'How's it going? Honestly?' she asked. I could see that Serena was nervous. Sitting in a courtroom hour after hour, listening to endless repetitions can be terribly wearing, but at least there hadn't been any unexpected shocks.

'It's routine stuff,' I reassured her as I scooped up some hummus on a piece of fresh bread. 'She hasn't told us anything new. And you won't be called. Not unless it's —' I was about to say 'a matter of life and death' but managed to avoid the unfortunate phrase. 'Not unless I feel it will make it easier and quicker to stop the trial. I have the feeling that this afternoon will be crucial. I wouldn't be surprised if Azzam hasn't finished with Mrs Sadik for the moment. Then I'll cross-examine as soon as the *duhr* is over.'

That, in fact, is what happened. When the court re-assembled, and the presiding judge had made the usual demand for silence, Azzam rose, bowed to the judges and announced, 'I think I have caused enough distress to Mrs Sadik for one day, and am grateful for her patience during my examination.'

'I must say, Mr Azzam,' said Judge Afifi, 'that though I am sure your motives are well-intentioned we do not seem to have unearthed any new evidence to support the charge of murder against the defendant.' He added, almost unpleasantly, 'I will not tolerate any waste of any court's valuable time. I hope you will bear this in mind in the future.'

'My apologies, Mr President,' said Azzam almost meekly, then turned to me, 'Your witness, Lord Holt.'

It had always been useless to try and explain to Egyptians the hierarchy of the English peerage. A baronet becomes a lord. An heir becomes a lord because, being an heir, he is going to become a lord too! It makes for convenience, especially when all the drama of the courtroom is being spoken in Arabic, a passionate, gesticulating language with fiery phrases. It was all very different from the prosaic droning of an English court. Judge Afifi was the only man who realised I was plain 'Mr'.

I rose without haste. 'Mrs Sadik, your admiration for your

late husband is laudable,' I said. 'But as the President of the court has reminded us we are concerned with facts. So far we have heard an elaborate account of how you were summoned to the Abdin Palace, where the ex-king told you of your husband's death from a heart attack, plus your testimony, culled from his friends, that his constitution was robust, and that therefore he couldn't have died from a heart attack –'

Immediately Azzam was on his feet. 'I object, Mr President. Mrs Sadik clearly stated that General Sadik went regularly to his doctor for check-ups.'

'I think,' the President said, 'that we need not sail too deeply into technicalities. I take the point as being that the prosecution is trying to establish that General Sadik could not possibly have died of a heart attack, and the defence is equally concerned to establish that it was quite possible.'

The judge went on, 'Clearly it is not possible indisputably to establish the cause of death without exhuming the body, which I certainly have no intention of doing. Please continue.'

I understood his aversion. Good Moslems have a saying that nothing must be allowed to disturb the happiness of the departed. It is for this reason that gifts are buried with the dead. I proceeded with my cross-examination.

'Mrs Sadik, let us for the moment bypass the question of the cause of your husband's death and come to the accusations against my client.'

'She is a wicked woman. It is known to everyone,' cried Mrs Sadik.

'What is known to everyone,' I interrupted, 'even if true, is of no concern to the court. What *is* known – and I emphasise *known*, in the sense of being supported by factual evidence – by *you* is what we are after.'

She said nothing, but looked to Azzam for moral support.

'I have no wish to cause you any distress that can be avoided' – I tried to sound conciliatory – 'yet there are some questions I must put to you, madame. Were you and your husband a happily married couple?'

'Of course,' she replied.

'There is no "of course" about love between married couples,' I said mildly, 'and I hope to produce witnesses later who will testify, with dates and details, to your husband's regular infidelity.'

'Really!' Mrs Sadik almost shouted. 'You have no right to talk like that about a dead man who cannot defend himself. You are not a gentleman, sir.'

'I may not be a gentleman, madame,' I said sharply, 'but I am defending the honour of a lady, and I must ask you to confine your answers to my questions and not to indulge in personal remarks.'

'Please try to keep to the point, madame,' said Judge Afifi, and turning to me added, 'though I am not quite sure, Mr Holt, if I follow the line of your argument.'

'I am sorry, sir,' I replied. 'As I said, I have no wish to cause this witness distress, but I think it vital for the defence to see both sides of the character of a man who has so far been glowingly painted as one of the great heroes of the revolution. I only wish to establish the true facts.'

Judge Afifi consulted with the two assisting judges and I saw Malimoud glower as he whispered to Afifi.

'You may proceed, Mr Holt,' said the presiding judge finally, 'but I hope that it will not be necessary to indulge in any further personal abuse – from either side.'

'I understand, sir' – I bowed – 'though I must crave the court's indulgence when I have to put to the witness some questions that may seem rather direct and personal. Later I will call witnesses to prove whether Mrs Sadik's answers are true or false.'

'That seems reasonable.' Afifi consulted his colleagues who both nodded, though Malimoud still looked angry. 'You may proceed.'

I turned to Mrs Sadik and said, 'When I asked a previous witness for details of any military engagements in which your husband was involved he seemed to have forgotten. Can you refresh our memories, madame?'

'I don't understand.'

'Well,' I said smoothly, 'your husband was a much-decorated officer. No one seems to be able to tell us of the exploits of valour which earned him these decorations and led to his promotion to the rank of general.'

She looked round almost wildly, because of course both she and I knew there had been no such exploits on the battlefield. Finally she cried, 'I cannot say. I am the widow of a general. I am bound by oaths of secrecy.'

Nonsense, and I knew it, but I decided to drop the matter. The point had been made that Sadik was no hero.

'I quite understand, madame,' I said, and as I riffled through my brief saw Azzam breathe a sigh of relief. It was short-lived.

'Let us move on,' I began quietly. 'The personal relationships between your husband and His Majesty King Farouk. Your husband's duties as ADC – his hours must have been long, the work arduous?'

'He was a servant of his country. My husband never spared himself. He did everything the king asked him to do.'

'Everything?' I asked her. She nodded. 'Night work? Evening duties?' I suggested.

'If His Majesty wished his ADC to accompany him to any evening functions of course my husband went.'

'Functions, madame? Public functions – or private functions?'

'I don't know what you mean. A king has no private life – ever.'

'Not even in bed?'

'Of course he had to sleep,' she said scathingly.

'I meant in bed, but not asleep. I take it you won't disagree with what the public already knows – that King Farouk had an insatiable appetite for women – in bed.'

'I never listen to tittle-tattle,' she said haughtily.

'Come, madame. King Farouk's lechery was one of the reasons that led to his downfall and eventual abdication.'

'I cannot see what that has to do with me – or my late husband.'

I said quietly, 'Well, someone had to help provide the king with girls.'

'Are you daring to insinuate –' She was shouting now.

'I am asking you a question, madame, which just requires a "yes" or "no". Some of the duties of being equerry to a king might be distasteful, but one has to perform them nonetheless. There is no disgrace in doing one's duty.'

Mrs Sadik looked at Judge Afifi. 'Must I answer such questions?'

Afifi looked at Malimoud. Malimoud whispered, and Afifi nodded to him, at which Malimoud asked me, 'I think you are being unnecessarily offensive, Mr Holt, especially to a lady who has suffered, and whose husband had a highly distinguished record. We all know that an ADC to someone like King Farouk no doubt had many distasteful duties to perform –'

'Like pimping?' I interrupted.

At that the court erupted into boos, catcalls and even chanting from the public benches. For several minutes Afifi had to bang on his gavel before silence was restored and he warned, 'Any more disturbances and I will have the court cleared, not only for today but for the entire trial.'

At this moment Azzam came to Mrs Sadik's rescue. 'Mr President,' he said, as at last silence was restored, 'my client has had a gruelling time and I seek the clemency of the court to allow her to stand down and visit the anteroom, where her maid is in attendance and will no doubt minister to her distress.'

This time Afifi did not bother to consult with his fellow judges. 'It is quite irregular,' he said angrily. 'I certainly do not propose to waste the time of the court by calling an adjournment. Have you any other witness to call?'

I could see that Azzim had to think quickly. 'I have, Mr President.'

'Then I will grant a ten-minute recess. The court remains in session.'

The three judges withdrew and Lala Sadik was hastily conducted to the anteroom together with Azzam's clerk, who was presumably rushing to summon this new witness, whoever it might be. I leaned across to Serena.

'He's just playing for time, I'm sure. He'll either have to get the Sadik woman back on the stand or produce the proverbial rabbit from his hat. As it is, Afifi is getting fed-up with Mrs Sadik's antics. And as far as we're concerned that's all to the good.'

The two of us took advantage of the recess to spend the ten minutes in the anteroom, which luckily turned out to be empty. For a few moments I left Serena alone while I popped out to the toilet. As I walked out I saw Mrs Sadik at the far end of the corridor. She seemed to be arguing with Azzam's clerk. She was clutching a small packet and it seemed obvious in the few seconds I had to watch them both, that at first she didn't want to hand over the packet, but finally she gave it up to him.

When the court reconvened the new witness arrived, and Lala Sadik, of course, had to remain in the anteroom. The witness Assam brought into court turned out to be Lala Sadik's maid, whose name was Fatima. It had thrown Azzam when the President had begun to lose patience with Mrs Sadik and he had had to rely on what might be called 'running repairs' to his case. He began by telling the girl to look carefully at Serena and me.

'Now,' he said, repeating the parent-to-child attitude I had shown towards Mrs Sadik, 'have you seen the man sitting there at the table before today?'

The girl giggled. Nobody ever took notice of a servant girl, but here she was in a room full of people being asked for information that was apparently of interest to them. Also, she had the Egyptian's sense of loyalty. Dimly it seemed to her that she was being asked in some way to help her mistress. She looked pleadingly at Judge Malimoud.

'Come now,' Azzam said, 'you need have no fear. No one is going to punish you. And the question I ask you is a simple one.' He pointed dramatically at me. 'Have you seen that man before?'

'He is the Lord Holt.'

'Yes, yes, we know very well who he is. But by telling us you have answered the question. Had you not seen him before, you would not know who he is.'

'He is in the newspapers,' said the girl flatly. This was only too true. Every issue of the Cairo papers carried photographs of the cast in the drama.

I could imagine Azzam's irritation. He had cut a corner neatly, only to be blocked by his own witness. But he

controlled himself well, knowing that quick-fire questions
would only muddle the girl.

'Ah yes,' he said softly. 'We have all seen his picture, in
the newspapers; but that is not quite what I mean. Have you
seen *him*, the man himself, as you see him sitting there
now – have you seen him, in person, before?'

The girl looked at him in simple wonder. 'I see him, yes.
Allah be praised, my sight is good.'

It took Azzam a good five minutes to make the girl understand the question, and suddenly to answer brightly that, yes,
she had seen me many times before. And, yes, Mrs Serena
King too. At last the ground seemed to be firm.

But *was* it firm? I was puzzled by one thing. Had the servant
girl been to the Villa Zelfa? I knew that servants in Cairo
often 'lent' themselves to friendly neighbours when they were
hosting big parties. But surely Serena wouldn't borrow Mrs
Sadik's servant?

I leaned across and whispered to Serena, who turned in her
swivel chair and shook her head with an emphatic 'No!' It
was possible that the prosecution, in order to gain time, had
called a witness who had, in fact, never actually seen either
of us.

All this flashed through my mind before Azzam said,
'Thank you, Fatima.' He turned towards Afifi. 'I hope, Mr
President, the court will understand the reasons for the somewhat circuitous route by which I have established that the
witness has seen the accused and her defending counsel before?'

Afifi nodded, so Azzam turned to Fatima again.

'We know now that you are familiar – you have seen,
many times before, that man and that woman. Could you
tell us now in what circumstances you have seen them?'

This was at first beyond the girl's limited understanding – I
didn't envy Azzam – but at last she explained that she had
'borrowed the eyes' of a friend who worked at the Villa Zelfa,
and he or she had reported the numerous times when Serena
and I had been alone together there in what Azzam was clearly
going to imply were suspicious circumstances.

Now was the time to jump on that line of approach.

'Mr President, this witness's evidence is based on hearsay. It is in no sense reliable. May I plead that it be ignored?'

I reinforced my objection by pointing out that naturally I had visited the Villa Zelfa. Was I not Serena's brother-in-law, old friend of the Sirrys and the Holts?

'The court rules that hearsay evidence is unacceptable, so you make your point, Mr Holt.' The President leaned forward and made a note. 'Fatima's evidence up to now will be disregarded.'

It was not, however, quite so easy to disregard the implications of the evidence. Hearsay or not, and whether or not I was right legally, a doubt had been sown in the minds of the three judges. They could hardly ignore the fact that Mrs Sadik was making her point in a roundabout way: she was impugning Serena's character, if only by rumour. They might infer that I was biased in my handling of the case; and maybe – worse – that there had been some sort of collusion between us.

The next bit of evidence produced by the prosecution was far from circumstantial. It was, so far as I could see at the time, unshakeable.

Fatima stepped down from the witness box, her moment of glory over. As she was conducted by one of the court ushers into the anteroom, Serena indicated by a slight movement of her head that someone wanted to catch my eye. I turned and glimpsed Jim Stevenson in the row of VIP chairs. I was astonished to see him in such a place, until he gave me a discreet 'thumbs up' sign. When next I looked round he had vanished, having placed himself next to one of the court-room's several exits.

Serena whispered to me across the table, 'What –?'

'I don't know,' I replied. 'Though it can't be *bad* news. Perhaps –' But I didn't have time to complete the sentence, for Azzam was recalling Lala Sadik to the stand. She had changed her role once again: she was neither the sorrowful widow nor the wily opponent; this time she had a menacing air.

'Mr President,' Azzam said smoothly. 'I have persuaded

Madame Sadik that a document in her possession –'

All three judges sat forward with interest – I imagined because they were at last to see some concrete piece of evidence.

'– is so important to this case that though its revelation may cause her further distress it must be produced.'

From the folder in front of him Azzam took a letter typed on the heavy die-stamped paper of the Abdin Palace and handed it to the usher to take to the judges' table. Judge Afifi read it through quickly, his fellow judges glancing at it over his shoulder. After they had finished the letter was passed to me. It was terse and to the point.

'Sadik,' it read. 'Only in defence of my life or my honour will you use or display any violence or produce any firearm or other weapon. Any disregard of this order will bring you before the judges for treason to me. Farouk.' The letter was dated 14 September, 1941.

I failed for a moment to realise its significance. It seemed irrelevant to what the prosecution was seeking to prove.

'Mrs Sadik,' Azzam was saying, 'will you tell the court how you came into possession of this letter?'

'It was among my husband's papers, in the safe in which he kept all confidential documents connected with his tasks as the king's aide-de-camp.'

'To which you had the key?'

'No. Until – it must have been taken from my husband before he was – before his state funeral. The key was sent to me after the king's abdication, by the Italian Antonio Pulli.

'I didn't even know where the safe was and even had I known I would never have opened it. It was' – a dramatic pause – 'sacred to the memory of my husband. But recently, when having some renovations done, I came across the safe hidden behind a painting, and I thought, Ah! That is the missing safe. After much hesitation I opened it.'

Azzam allowed a pause and then asked: 'Will you tell the court, Mrs Sadik, your reason for being reluctant to produce that letter from the king to your husband?'

'It meant – oh, I knew it meant that the king must have had reasons for sending it. And I –' She was slipping into the pose of the distressed widow again. Azzam came to her rescue.

'Was not the reason that shortly before the date of the letter your husband had been involved in some violence to one of the king's – let us be blunt and direct, Mr President – one of the king's discarded mistresses?'

'I had heard so,' she whispered. 'My husband was a very – *virile* man.'

'So it would seem,' Judge Nessim interrupted.

'So. You had good reason for keeping the letter to yourself, for its disclosure would put a stain upon your husband's memory. Am I right?'

Again she nodded.

'And it would put a stain upon his memory because the inevitable inference from reading it is that the king had issued a warning which, to put it crudely – we are all men and women of the world, Mr President – meant "Keep your hands off my ex-girlfriends or it will be the worse for you." ' Azzam turned to me, his lips curled in a smile of triumph. 'Your witness, Lord Holt.'

Obviously Azzam's next step would be to show that Sadik had taken a liking to Serena – which she had resented. The production of the letter had shaken my confidence. Until then, Fatima's evidence had been laughable, and I had still hopes for a 'No case to answer' from the judges, with the proceedings fading into anticlimax. Now I was worried. If in a roundabout way, we were getting too close to the truth.

'Mr President,' I said, 'I find the production of this letter utterly irrelevant. What has it to do with the alleged murder or with the unjustified attack on my client's character?'

Azzam was on his feet again. 'If I may answer my learned friend, I think he is being a little impetuous. The letter the court has seen was not the *only* document in the safe. There was another.' He lowered his voice dramatically. 'Another – indisputably establishing that the late General Sadik was not away on any secret mission that night of 10 July, 1942, but was present, with the king, and the accused, in the Villa Zelfa.'

It was at this point, I think to everyone's relief, that Afifi decided there had been enough drama for one day, and called a halt to proceedings. This time there was no further drama as we made our way out of the court and into the waiting car.

Though it was only a short distance away the police insisted on driving Serena home with sirens and flashing lights, but they let me ride with her in the car, while a second car followed with the police who would guard the house. As we reached home the sirens stopped.

'I hope it wasn't too bad?' Father asked, while Zola poured us all drinks.

'It's all so terrifying,' Serena almost exploded. 'I had no idea – I wasn't frightened, but it was so sordid, so vulgar. The people in the public benches – it was like a Roman circus, throwing the Christians to the lions, or the Copts to the Moslems. And the horrible prosecutor with his shabby clothes and his awful hooked nose. Just like a vulture. Lala Sadik can't get away with it, can she?' She looked directly at me.

'Of course not.' I reassured her. 'But remember, she *is* the widow of a national hero.'

'Some hero,' snorted Chiffon. 'I wonder who did murder him. He was such a horrible man.'

'But he's still supposed to have died of a heart attack.' Serena looked up uneasily. 'Who would want to murder him?'

Chiffon looked surprised. 'Why, Farouk, of course.'

'What makes you say a thing like that?' asked Father.

'Well, the way I see it is that Farouk murdered Sadik, but since he's living abroad they can't try him, so this Sadik woman is trying to implicate Serena.'

'But Chiffon,' I protested. 'Nobody but Mrs Sadik believes he was murdered. You've been reading the gossip columns.'

'Oh, *please!*' cried Serena suddenly. 'Can't we forget this damnable case just for one evening? After all, I am on trial for murder.'

'Quite right!' said Father sternly. 'Unforgivable of us. No more of this nonsense unless you want advice, darling.'

'Thank you, *Papa*.' Serena used the French word from habit. She was quieter after the outburst.

Later, as we were going in to dinner, I said to her, 'The only thing that depresses me is to see the most beautiful woman in the world dragged through all this – just to satisfy a spiteful old widow.'

'Widow is the operative word,' Serena said bitterly. 'Someone made her a widow.'

After dinner I gave Serena a sleeping pill and sent her to bed early. I made no effort to see Father or Mother, for I wanted to sort out in my mind several alternative ways of handling the unknown evidence, working out what it might be.

At the back of my mind was the fact that I had at all costs to defend the case on the assumption that Sadik had never been murdered, that all this was the figment of a spiteful woman's imagination. Yet at the same time I was haunted by the fact that Sadik *had* been shot – and by Serena. If ever the real cause of death did come out – unlikely in a Moslem country which did not approve of disturbing graves – then I would have to think again. Then the plea would have to be self-defence.

Self-defence, I mused: a moment of panic, not a deliberate act of murder. Again my mind was wandering through a maze of possibilities, but outside these unlikely developments lay one picture engraved in my memory like a still from a film: the moment when Serena tore her dress *before* she shot Sadik. There was a kind of panic, true, but there was premeditation too, a deliberate tearing of her clothes to deceive Farouk. And there was no way anyone could escape a guilty verdict if a murder was premeditated.

Of course, I thought as I helped myself to a brandy, it would never come to that, for I was the only witness. But all that evening and later into the night, after I had tried in vain to sleep, that picture of Serena ripping off her clothes went whirling round my mind, and nothing I could do could banish it.

45

On the third day of the trial Serena and I were again allowed to drive to the court in the same car. Reporters lurked, almost comically, behind bushes, Rolleiflexes slung round necks, press cards pinned to shirts. They knew perfectly well that the rule of sub judice meant I couldn't say a word; but like all journalists they hoped that a carelessly dropped phrase would lead them to a big bylined story.

As we entered the court the buzz of conversation in the public seats fell to a whisper. There was something of a threat – a hope? – in that sudden hush. Like crowds everywhere they sensed a victim. Courtroom crowds are always eager to enjoy that most basic animal instinct – the detection of weakness in the prey.

The usher suddenly banged his staff and the judges entered. We were in session.

Azzam rose, his shabby suit in no way detracting from his new-found confidence. 'Mr President, with the court's permission I will recall Mrs Sadik to the stand.'

Afifi nodded curtly, Nessim smiled as if acknowledging the plaudits of a multitude, while Malimoud set his arms in their customary folded position.

Lala Sadik made her way slowly to the witness box. As soon as she was seated Azzam pushed back his creased coat, dusted his lapels and rested his fists on his hips.

'Mrs Sadik,' he began, 'the court will have every sympathy with the distress you must feel in the pursuit of justice and the establishment of the guilt of the accused' – here he glanced at Serena – 'but I am going to ask you to cast your mind back yet again to that day ten years ago when you attended the funeral of your late husband.'

He paused, allowing Mrs Sadik a moment to raise her

black-edged handkerchief to her lips. 'I am sure that that was a day you cannot easily forget?'

'I can never forget it. *Never*.'

'Naturally. The whole of Cairo remembers – the pomp and ceremony made in tribute to the memory of an officer who had served his country with dedication.'

Introducing an ominous note he added, 'We will leave for a moment the official story of the cause and location of his death – a story put about by the king who, as I intend to show, had every reason for shielding the accused.' Azzam continued with the tireless fluency of the Arab language. 'Now, Madame Sadik, the court will be particularly interested to hear how the day of the funeral began for you.'

She took a sip from the glass of water that stood on the shelf of the witness box, a woman overwrought, but one maintaining a dignified composure.

'The funeral was at ten in Abdin Square. My doctor had given me pills for the shock. When my maid woke me at eight she said that a man was waiting to see me on a confidential matter that was also urgent. I saw this man, a junior officer from the army section that deals with the ceremonial affairs, and he handed me a small package. He was very nervous, for he was bringing me the parcel containing my husband's personal effects. The rings from his fingers, his pocket diary, the gold pen which the king had given him. I put the package in my handbag.'

As her voice droned on two fragmentary recollections flickered into my mind. One was of that first meeting with Sadik in my chambers when he had come to discuss Samia's lease and I had noticed the four scarab rings glinting on his manicured hands; the other was a memory plucked from my meeting with Farouk at the Abdin Palace when he had told me of his decision to send Serena to America. Farouk had mentioned, as I recalled, that Sadik had kept a diary of his appointments. 'We made a search for it, all through Sadik's house, while she was at the funeral, but we never found it . . . she must have hidden it.'

Now, ten years later, Lala Sadik had supplied the answer. One could ignore her words about shock; I was sure she had probably opened the package at once, even scanned the diary on her way to the funeral. It was exactly the sort of property she would keep until an opportunity arose to use it to advantage. She could hardly act while Farouk was in power but, after Farouk's abdication, her chance had come.

Azzam had left the limelight to Lala Sadik but now, as her narrative tailed off, he unfolded his spectacles and took from his clerk a square book which he handed to the usher.

'Mrs Sadik, will you look at this document and tell the court what you know of it?'

She made a pretence of examining the book. 'That is . . . my husband's diary,' she said with a catch in her voice.

'You are certain?'

'I am.'

'Thank you. Will you now turn to the page for 10 July, 1942 and tell the court what is entered as his appointments for that day.'

She peered closely at the writing. 'It says "C BUS" in the morning section, "SP" in the afternoon, and there's another entry marked "Z/HM/SH2230".'

'Are those the only entries for that day?'

'Yes.'

'Thank you. Will you now, please, give the document to the usher to pass to the President as Exhibit B in this case.'

The diary was examined by all three judges, then brought over to me. I didn't have much time to study it in detail, though I knew I would be given every opportunity later. It had a blue vellum cover and it contained a page for every day. Most entries included what looked like coded messages or perhaps a kind of shorthand used by Sadik. Recalling the date when the king had sent the letter of reprimand to Sadik – 14 September, 1941 – I managed to see if Sadik had mentioned it. But what struck me at once was that there was no page for 13 September – the day *before* Farouk had written his note – only the frayed edges close to the spine. I was about to examine the diary more closely when I was asked to hand it back to the usher.

Azzam's face twisted into a smile. 'My learned friend can see that I was in earnest when I said yesterday that I had evidence of General Sadik's presence at the Villa Zelfa on the night of 10 July.'

I rose to my feet. 'With respect, Mr President, I would like to remind my learned friend that what he said was that he had a document *indisputably establishing* that General Sadik was present with the king and the accused that night. So far we have a diary with a few symbols.'

'We shall see.' Azzam turned back to Lala Sadik and asked, 'Madame, referring now to the diary, will you please tell the court what "C BUS" means?'

'It means court business. My husband had a little joke between us: whenever he was engaged with the king he said that such-and-such a time or such-and-such a day would be devoted to "C BUS". It was a little joke –'

'Yes, madame. I'm sure we all understand that devoted couples have their little intimate phrases. Could you tell us, please, what the "SP" allotted to the afternoon means?'

'It meant – it meant, I think . . .'

I caught Serena's glance. Lala Sadik attempting to be coy was not a pleasant sight.

'It meant . . . *special purposes* . . . when my husband had to accompany the king on his pleasures; you know, the king sought his pleasures in many places; and it was one of my husband's tasks as his aide-de-camp to attend and guard him during his –'

'Yes,' Azzam said. 'I think we know what you mean. Now, we come to the final entry for that day, the somewhat mysterious "Z/HM/SH2230". Let us not be too quick to jump to conclusions; but have you any suggestions as to what that code might mean?'

' "Z" can only mean Zelfa – the Villa Zelfa. "HM" would be His Majesty. And "SH" are the initials of *that woman*' – she spat out the words – 'who lured the king –'

Again I challenged. 'Objection, Mr President. The witness is running into the realms of fantasy again.'

Afifi nodded to Azzam. 'She had better keep to the facts.'

'As the court pleases. Madame, would you tell the court what you understand by the figures "2230"?'

Lala Sadik had regained some of her composure. 'Well, my

husband was a soldier. He always used the military method of time, the twenty-four-hour clock.'

'So may we infer, then, from that entry in the diary that General Sadik had been commanded to accompany the king to the Villa Zelfa at ten-thirty that night for a liaison with Mrs Serena Holt – as she then was?'

'That is so.'

Azzam looked triumphantly at me. 'Your witness.'

I adopted an attitude of cool confidence, invariably successful in disarming a witness on uncertain ground.

'Madame, we all know that King Farouk sent a stern letter to General Sadik on 14 September, 1941. Do you know why?'

'No, I don't.'

'Can you remember offhand if General Sadik recorded any impressions of that letter in the diary you have so zealously guarded – and no doubt read avidly?'

'Objection!' said Azzam sharply. 'The way in which a witness reads has nothing to do with the question.'

'Sustained,' said Presiding Judge Afifi. 'You should know better, Mr Holt.'

'I crave the court's indulgence.' I bowed meekly. 'Let me put it another way, Mrs Sadik. You have no recollection of the contents of the diary?'

'No, I haven't. I cannot be expected to remember everything my husband wrote down.'

'Quite so,' I murmured. 'Perhaps the usher would be kind enough to help you refresh your memory. May I ask the court if the witness be allowed to take the diary and read to us the notes that were made for 13 September – the day before the king wrote rebuking General Sadik.'

As the usher reached for the volume I could see Lala Sadik look at her counsel, frowning. Then, hand trembling, she took the diary and turned to the date. After a moment's pause she looked up and said – as I knew she would – 'It's not there. It's been torn out.'

'Precisely, madame.' Without a moment's hesitation, I asked innocently, 'Was it you who tore it out, Mrs Sadik?'

'Of course not!'

'You swear it?'

'I do.'

'So you have no idea what was on that page?'

'How could I? It must have been torn out by my husband.'

'Quite so. Of course. By your husband. Now, Mrs Sadik, I would like to turn to the entry in the diary for 10 July, 1942. Now you said – and I am looking at my clerk's note of your actual words – you said in response to my learned friend's request for suggestions that the "Z" in that little diary entry could only mean Zelfa, the Villa Zelfa.'

'Yes. What else could it mean?'

'It could mean any number of things. I'll suggest a few. It could mean Zagazig, Zeitun, Zifta or the Field of Zoan – all places within easy travelling distance of Cairo. It could mean the Zoo Garden near the pyramids.'

'Are you suggesting that my husband met the king at the zoo?' There was another titter from the crowd.

'I am suggesting, Mrs Sadik, that as neither you nor I know your late husband's intention when jotting down that reminder it would be as well for you to confine your assertions to what is indisputable.'

She took a sharp intake of breath. 'Well, I am sure in my own mind that he meant the Villa Zelfa.'

I put the diary gently down on the table. 'It has been pointed out to you before in this case, madame, that it is the minds of the eminent judges that have to be convinced, not your own. For all you or I know that entry might be a coded message that has nothing whatever to do with time, place or persons. As I said to my learned friend the symbols are not in dispute: it is their meaning we seek. I suggest to the court that it is the frailty of your evidence that is beyond dispute, not the existence of this diary.' I held the book up in a dramatic gesture. 'Or anything in it.'

I was on shaky ground and I knew it, but I was playing for time. I had in the back of my mind a vague association of ideas that I might be able to develop; only they needed investigation along lines I had not thought about before the diary was produced. All I could do was try to delay matters and cast doubts in the judges' minds about the value of the diary. Azzam grasped my intention only too clearly. He was quite composed as he rose to challenge me.

'Mr President, unless my learned friend is determined to split hairs *ad infinitum* Mrs Sadik's interpretation of the diary entry is a perfectly reasonable one. The court may safely assume that the presence of the accused and the king and the late General Sadik in the Villa Zelfa on the night in question is beyond doubt.'

Judge Afifi, who had been consulting with his fellow judges, raised his head at this and said with heavy sarcasm, 'Thank you, Mr Azzam, for your lecture on legal matters.' Much to my relief, he added that in the court's view nothing yet *had* been established beyond reasonable doubt.

At that moment there was an interruption. A sergeant in uniform walked into the courtroom, pointed to the judges' bench and showed that he was carrying a large envelope. Judge Afifi looked angry, but an usher, looking nervous himself, approached the judges' bench, followed by the sergeant who was still clutching the envelope.

I heard the usher say to Afifi, 'A message for you, sir, from General Naguib.'

I could see as well as sense the change in Afifi's attitude.

'Hand it to me,' he said to the sergeant. He tore open the envelope, dismissed the sergeant and the usher, and read the letter slowly before conferring with his two assisting judges.

I had no idea what was in it, of course. Neither had anyone else in court, until Afifi announced abruptly, 'I have been summoned to the presence of General Naguib to give my views on certain questions of constitutional law. In view of this,' he said, 'the court will adjourn until 10 a.m. tomorrow morning.'

Afifi's sudden summons sent a shiver of apprehension through me. Constitutional law? In the midst of a murder trial? I *might* be entirely wrong. Afifi *might* have to discuss something with Naguib that had nothing to do with the trial. But I didn't like it at all.

This was a *cause célèbre*, and it could mean that pressure was to be put on Afifi to ensure that any 'defamation' of a national hero such as Sadik would not be tolerated. A Guilty verdict would be a simple way to make sure. Afifi was incorruptible, but he was also an Egyptian; and military governments that suddenly seize power do not always employ subtle methods.

46

In all my legal career I had never been quite so glad of a breathing space.

'Thank God for Naguib and his need for advice on constitutional law,' I said as Serena and I sat down together in the Chinese Room. 'I need time to plan a campaign.' I decided to keep my fears to myself.

'But I thought the Sadik woman made a complete fool of herself,' said Serena, looking at me anxiously.

'In a way,' I said. 'But there are two pluses on her side, and Azzam won't hesitate to push them. He's no fool.'

'You'll have to explain for me.'

'Well, it's true that superficially I've made her interpretation of the diary entry no more than that – just her interpretation. The trouble is, that entry could well mean what she says it means. And . . .' I let my words tail away.

'Of course.' She looked worried. The strain was already showing; there was no need for her to say more.

'Also,' I went on, 'a lot of the theory of evidence is based on psychology. If you can, by implication, plant ideas in a court's mind you're halfway to making them believe you. What Lala Sadik's done is to use smears to blacken your character, to hint at evidence that can't be totally proved – how could it be? – but can't be totally disproved either.'

I poured a couple of drinks. For a moment I was thinking – I don't know why – of Father with his self-heating plate of scrambled eggs and his breakfast tipple.

'There's another point,' I said. 'The way Sadik's been turned into a military hero.'

'But we know Sadik was never that,' said Serena bitterly. 'Instead of trying to discredit Lala, why don't you attack Sadik directly?'

'The trouble is,' I said almost moodily, 'we're up against a tough new regime. Who'd dare to say anything about one of their national heroes in open court?'

'But there must be someone who's not afraid of Sadik – or his widow,' cried Serena, as frustrated as I was. 'Someone who has nothing to fear from the new regime.'

'I wonder.' I was thinking aloud. 'Instead of letting Lala Sadik pretend that her husband's only fault was his virility – which Egyptians admire anyway – if I could introduce direct evidence to show that Sadik was a monster, what then?' I went on: 'Instead of defending you I'll make the prosecution defend Sadik. But I need at least one cast-iron case from an independent witness. It'll be a dirty business, but the dirtier the better.'

I knew where to start, the only hope. It had to be Samia. She would know every speck of dirt swept under every carpet in Cairo.

The Sphinx was just then being rebuilt, and during the meantime Samia had rented a small nightclub in Adly Pasha Street. However, when I phoned I was told she wasn't there but was at her flat. Luckily I had always kept her home phone number, so I rang her and asked if I could go round to see her right away.

'There'll be a drink waiting for you.' I could sense her smile on the telephone.

I must hand it to Samia. She had taken the fire that ruined the Sphinx in her stride, never complaining. 'It's the way you're brought up as a peasant.' She shrugged her shoulders. 'When your livelihood is at the mercy of storms and floods or droughts you can take a small fire without noticing it. Well, hardly.'

She had changed little. A touch more haggard perhaps – the drugs and drink – but she had learned how to take pills so she hadn't put on any weight. She was still a slinky, beautiful woman, whose slightly weary face gave her an odd added allure.

I noticed that she was smoking 'neat'.

'Where's your Gertrude Lawrence cigarette holder?' I asked.

'I lost it in the fire. I'm delighted! Smoking through a holder destroyed the joy of inhaling strong cigarettes. It was part of the décor of the Sphinx. Once that went I didn't bother to replace the holder.'

I was sitting before her on the white sofa covered with a kind of fine-grained canvas and piped with blue edges, where I had sat so long ago. As briefly as I could I explained my problem.

'I want any dirt we can find, so long as it's solid evidence,' I explained. 'But we've got to be able to produce the victims – for want of a better word – in the witness box. I'm especially intrigued by the fact that several pages of Sadik's diaries are missing.'

'At least none of *my* diary pages are missing,' she laughed.

'You keep a diary!' I must have looked amazed. The idea of a woman who ran a bordello keeping details of her life seemed surprising, even unwise. 'I'd have thought you'd want to make sure there was no written record of your activities.'

She shook her head. 'It's not a diary really. It's a daily list of the girls, how much they're owed, when they leave, when new ones come in. You'd be surprised how often a girl goes missing – maybe leaves us, vanishes – and the police come round, asking awkward questions. I'm able to give the exact date when every girl arrived or left the Sphinx. Fair enough?'

'Very sensible. But not really what I wanted.'

'Well, if something serious happens I do make a note of it.'

'How long back, Samia?' I poured another drink after she nodded in the direction of the bar.

'Since we started. What had you in mind?'

'As a matter of fact, 13 September, 1941.'

It was her turn to look at me with astonishment. Finally, as though she could hardly believe it, she said, 'You *have* chosen your date, haven't you? I don't need a diary to remember what happened on that night. How did you know about it?'

Puzzled, I said, 'But I don't know what happened.' I explained the significance of the missing page in Sadik's diary. 'I just thought, in view of the letter from Farouk which you've read about in the papers, a page torn out might be important.'

'It certainly was. Prepare yourself for a shock. On that night one girl was killed and another badly beaten up – by Sadik. At the Sphinx.'

'Killed?'

Since I didn't know the poor girl's name, I found it impossible to hide the thrill of excitement in my voice.

'You needn't sound so pleased.' Samia sounded almost annoyed. 'Dolores was a lovely girl and she died a terrible death.'

'I'm sorry.' I explained why I had been so excited, and Samia nodded.

'Tell me what happened,' I said.

Samia did – at length and with full details and names. It was a story that had everything, though I could see one possible problem: it was one thing for her to tell me the details, but with most people afraid of becoming involved with the new regime would the participants be willing to testify in court? Hearsay was not enough.

'I don't see why not,' said Samia. 'I'm willing. I hate Sadik, even his memory. Dolores is dead, of course, but the girl who saw everything – she's called Zeineb and works as a belly-dancer – I know she'd help.'

'And how was the cause of death established?'

'Dr Khittab. He was in the Sphinx at the time. He's the best pox doctor in Egypt, inspects all our girls and gets paid in kind.'

'But are you sure he'd be willing to testify?' I asked. 'You've got to realise that Serena really is in trouble. I hope we *can* get her off – but that doctor's evidence might be vital. Supposing –'

'He'd have to come or,' said Samia, 'you could subpoena him.'

That was how we discovered the vital evidence necessary to turn defence into attack. Six of the twenty hours had passed before the court was due to rise.

'Don't worry,' said Samia. 'You'll have all the witnesses you want, nicely scrubbed and dressed and ready for you tomorrow morning.'

'I don't know how I can ever thank you.' I gave her a hug.

'I'll send in my account when you've won your case,' she said softly. 'Maybe I should do what my pox doctor does – take my fees in person.'

I made a mental note to be sure that Serena and I left for Geneva before Samia presented her bill!

I had one other chore before going back to Holt House. I had been certain in my own mind that it was Lala Sadik who had torn out the missing pages of the diary. I was even more convinced now, after learning more about that terrible evening. But suspecting was one thing; proving another. It would strengthen my case immensely if I could show that Lala Sadik had lied when she swore that it was her husband who had torn out those pages ten years previously. What I needed was an expert witness. The evidence of such witnesses is always accepted if there is no other expert to challenge. And for what I had in mind there would be no challenger. I knew just the man: Professor Walter Prettyman of the Imperial Chemical Industries, with premises on Shampolion Street.

I had acted for ICI in two cases of alleged patent infringement and knew Prettyman (whose name was a joke which he himself made much of) enough to exchange drinks when we met, and he had invited me round to his flat for a drink. It was dark when I drove through the city with its clanking trams, its itinerant sherbet and melon sellers, its sinister soldiery and its dark alleyways, down the Old Cairo Road, and explained what I had in mind.

For the third time we assembled beneath the shabby flags and the fly-blown light bulbs to face the three judges behind their army table. Salem, sleek and shiny in respectable black and clutching his forest of pencils, slid into place beside me as the ushers went through their opening preamble.

'Mr President,' I said, 'if it please the court I should like to call as my first witness Professor Walter Prettyman.'

A titter ran through the English-speaking reporters and members of the public as he took the stand.

Walter Prettyman was virtually spherical in shape. He had dark, curling hair, a button nose between two apple-red cheeks, and a tiny mouth that might have come from a Tintoretto cherub. The effect was ludicrous even if you didn't know his name. To make it worse he had the treble voice of a choirboy.

Yet that same high-pitched voice carried a note of authority, and his whole presence was surprisingly impressive. He had once told me that for anyone to emerge unscathed from the Billy Bunter ridicule of Harrow, Oxford and Heidelberg 'the vestiges of authority must rub off on you somewhere'.

'Professor Prettyman,' I opened, 'will you please tell the court your profession?'

'I am an industrial chemist.'

Judge Malimoud unfolded his arms and apparently requested Afifi's permission to ask a question. Afifi nodded.

'Professor,' Malimoud said, 'is this the profession that lives in little shops and sells us pills and potions for our headaches?'

If he had any thought of discrediting my witness, he must have been shocked by the put-down that greeted him.

With the utmost urbanity, Prettyman said, 'No, sir. I am employed by Imperial Chemical Industries as an authority on the chemistry of paper. It has no connection with the noble but very different calling of the pharmacist.'

Afifi asked with unruffled politeness, 'Can you enlighten us, Professor, about what your own calling involves?'

'I can indeed, sir. I can tell you everything about the chemistry of paper – and indeed of papyrus, vellum, silk, wood, and a score of other materials on which scribes have throughout the ages recorded the goings-on around them. But you would not thank me, sir. Indeed you would justly reprove me for wasting the court's time. For to tell the whole of what I know of the chemistry of paper would take several hours. I simply seek to convince the court that I know what I'm talking about.'

Afifi, I fancy, suppressed a smile. 'Thank you, Professor. The court is convinced.' He nodded to me to proceed.

I asked the judge if the usher could let me see General Sadik's diary, and when I held it up I said, 'Professor, I will pass to you this diary for the year 1941. You will see that it has a number of pages torn from it, including the page for 13 September. Is it possible to tell the court with any degree of accuracy when that page was torn from the book?'

The usher handed the diary to Prettyman.

'That will depend on the kind and quality of the paper and on various technical details connected with its manufacture. If a large period of time is involved a laboratory test may be necessary.'

With a folding magnifying glass similar to one I had seen Sirry Pasha use to inspect the weft and warp of a length of cotton, Prettyman opened the diary and examined one of the pages which he held delicately between thumb and forefinger. Then he held it up to the light. 'A fine rag paper by Smythson of London,' he announced. Then he leaned forward with the diary open. 'No laboratory test will be necessary, for no time element *is* involved. The page for 13 September was torn from the book within the last seven days.'

Despite a roar of 'Silence!' from Afifi, the buzz of excitement couldn't be immediately suppressed. People leaned forward, some in the back rows stood up, there was a mutter mingled with the noise of the inevitable coke cans. I waited for quiet to return.

'Thank you, Professor.' I turned slightly and bowed to Azzam. 'Your witness.'

I had to hand it to him. Though the professor's evidence must have pulled several rugs from under his feet, nevertheless Azzam was on them in a flash.

'Professor, I am a simple man. I ask you a simple question. How can you be so certain?'

'I can be certain because for thirty years I have concentrated on attaining that certainty. But if the court would bear with me for a few moments I will explain that, as I have said, this is a fine paper made from cotton rags. It is tub-sized – that is, it is dipped by hand into a tub containing a liquid mixture called "size" compounded of resin, alum and gelatine. The size penetrates the fibres of the cotton pulp and gives it a surface on which you can write with ink – unlike blotting paper, which is simply unsized paper. When torn, the fibres of the paper "bleed" for varying periods according to the quality of the paper. This particular paper bleeds for five to seven days. I can see under my glass that the ends of the fibres are within twelve or so hours of self-healing their ends. Therefore I say with every degree of certainty that the page was torn from the diary within the last seven days.'

Azzam tried to bluff his way out. 'Well, of course, we know from experience that expert witnesses are frequently at odds with one another. Perhaps –'

Prettyman was unshaken. 'There is no need for me to be falsely modest, sir. There are two experts of an equivalent status to myself in the world. One of them works for the IG Farben company in Germany, the other for Dupont in the United States.'

Unperturbed though he may previously have been, Azzam was now floored. 'Thank you, Professor,' he said flatly. 'I have no further questions.'

I had no further questions either. Nor did I recall Lala Sadik to the stand. There was no need: she had been proved a liar beyond question. No further purpose could have been served by recalling her, other than to rub in her humiliation.

Azzam apparently came to the same conclusion. He stood up, begged the judge leave to speak, and said smoothly, 'I do not wish to dispute the discourse of our learned witness, but may I respectfully point out, Mr President, that the object of this trial is to prove that Mrs King is guilty, and it does not in the least concern us whether or not Mrs Sadik has forgotten that a certain page in a diary has been torn out.'

Malimoud looked at Afifi for permission then said to me coldly, 'Mr Azzam has a point, Mr Holt. I do not see where this evidence will lead you.'

'I will be as brief as possible, sir. But if you will bear with me –'

'I will try, Mr Holt,' said Malimoud sarcastically.

I had to continue with my plan to blacken the character of both Sadiks, but I realised that it might be a double-edged weapon if I did it too openly. On the other hand, I needed Samia, and I wasted no time with my next move.

'I would like to call to the stand Madame Samia,' I said.

47

A buzz of excitement seemed to echo round the court at her name. She was still a national figure, for while she no longer sang in public her records sold by the million. And as she stepped towards the stand it was clear that her charm was as spell-binding as ever. The men in the public benches did everything but clap her entrance.

She was wearing a decorous dark blue dress which yet somehow accentuated her exciting figure. I addressed her confidently.

'Madame Samia, will you please tell the court your occupation?'

'I own a nightclub.'

Azzam jumped up. 'I object, Mr President,' he said. 'This is an over-simplification. What is her present and complete occupation?'

'I think the objection must be overruled,' said Afifi. 'A man or woman may have several occupations. A nightclub owner seems a fairly substantial description.'

'There are other aspects, Mr President,' muttered Azzam.

'I am sure there are, as I am that you will make the most of them when you cross-examine. But for the moment –' He gave a nod of dismissal.

Heartened, I started by asking, 'I suggest that the court will need no further proof that you are a public figure – a singer whose cabaret performances were a star attraction and whose records have sold in hundreds of thousands. Am I right?'

Samia bowed. 'That is true, sir. I think it is as widely known that when I was forced to stop singing – through illness – His Majesty King Farouk gave me a nightclub.'

'May I suggest –' began Azzam angrily, jumping to his feet.

'I think not, Mr Azzam,' said the President. 'I can appreciate that there may be more to Madame Samia than meets the eye, but let us hear her evidence first.'

'Thank you, sir,' I said. 'Now, Madame Samia, will you tell the court in your own words about the events of the night of 13 September, 1941?'

'Yes, of course. I remember it well.'

I could sense the tension mounting as Samia began her narrative, her voice husky with emotion, and admitting, by the nature of her evidence, that she *did* run a bordello.

'On that night General Sadik was at the Sphinx. He was a frequent visitor, and he knew where to come for what he called his "specialities".'

' "Specialities" is a curious word. Did General Sadik always refer to them with that term?'

'Yes, sir. He told me once that he sometimes referred to them by the initials "SP". He kept a diary, you see.' With an innocent look at the judges she added, 'I too keep a diary, Mr President. But mine don't have any pages torn out.'

'I object most strongly,' cried Azzam.

'Objection sustained,' said Afifi. 'That most improper re-mark will be stricken from the record.' Turning to Samia he said firmly, 'I must ask you not to make such statements. Just confine your answers to the questions asked.'

'I apologise, sir,' said Samia demurely.

'Mr Holt, please proceed. And do not try to lead the witness.'

'My learned friend has tried to enlarge on the occupation you described as "nightclub owner". So I must put it to you, madame, especially in view of the evidence which the court is about to hear, that you were not averse to allowing men to visit your premises for the purposes of obtaining sexual gratification for payment.'

'That is so.'

'Thank you. May I ask what you mean by General Sadik's "peculiarities"?'

'Well, he was a very *virile* man.'

I gave a sideways glance and saw Lala Sadik blanch.

'Virile?' I asked. 'Meaning exactly what?'

'His virility meant that he could easily achieve three or sometimes four' – she paused – 'orgasms within a few hours. But he was bored with the normal way of making love. He not only preferred two or three girls at a time; he was always offering me handsome rewards if I would procure children for him. I always refused.'

'Children? How old were they?'

'He liked them under age – some twelve or so.'

'And why did you refuse?'

'Because I believed that the Sphinx was a perfectly respectable place, providing the women concerned followed their trade of their own free will; but I did not approve of the innocent being corrupted.'

'Thank you. Please continue. You were explaining about your client's "specialities".'

'Yes, sir. Flagellation, of course – many older men enjoy this, and we had supplies of whips, bonds and other devices for those who wished to use them. For those who, like General Sadik, paid generously, two or three girls were always available for simultaneous normal, oral and' – another hesitation, as though embarrassed – 'masturbatory satisfaction.'

'I think we get the picture. A highly sexed man willing to pay for any form of satisfaction you were able to provide?'

'I would not provide everything,' said Samia.

'No. I understand. You drew the line at children.'

'Not only that. I always told the girls they could refuse buggery if they wished. The choice was entirely theirs so long as they made it clear in advance if they wanted to refuse.'

'And General Sadik was one of those who insisted on anal congress?'

'Yes, sir. On this particular night he took two girls, Zeineb and Dolores, upstairs. I was down in the bar, talking with several visitors, including Dr Khittab, who looked after the girls and who will bear me out. I heard a scream, but I wasn't worried at first. The girls often screamed a little as part of their act. But when I heard a second scream I went up-stairs.'

'But can you tell us why you did that?'

'This was different – unusual.'

'How – "unusual"?' I asked gently.

'I can't tell you exactly. But it was like a scream of death. And it wasn't a woman shrieking once and then going on to make more noises. There was no second scream. I had a premonition, I almost didn't dare to go.'

She paused, recalling the moment, until quietly I asked, 'And then –?'

'The scream had come from the blue room. All our rooms are named after colours. I did go up. I could hear my heart pounding, I remember. And when I crossed the landing I pushed open the door of the room and, sir, I almost fainted. The chair near the bed had been upturned and there was Zeineb, on the floor, without a stitch on, in a faint. Her face was covered with blood. I went in, screaming for help and nearly tripped over a whip which Zeineb told me later Sadik had used to slash her across the face when she tried to help Dolores.'

'And Dolores?'

'She was on the bed, in the centre of the room. Sadik was on top of her trying to make love to her. I tried to pull him off, but he pushed me so hard that I fell to the ground. Two other girls came to help, but they waited at the door. They were scared.'

'And Dolores?' I repeated. 'What sort of condition was she in?'

'She was naked, of course, and her head was half hanging over the edge of the bed. Only it was twisted – or her neck was, I couldn't be sure. But the most awful thing was that as Sadik struggled on top of her her eyes were wide open – yet she didn't move or make any sound. Those eyes – and that silence. I knew in my heart she was dead.'

'Can you tell me how Dolores died?'

'Zeineb told me that Sadik hit her very hard when she refused him.'

'Objection. Hearsay,' interrupted Azzam.

'Sustained,' agreed Afifi. 'The remark will be struck from the record.'

'A medical witness will later testify to the cause of death, Mr President,' I said. 'But first I would like to put to Miss Samia one or two more questions.' Turning to her I asked, 'What did you do when you believed that the girl was dead? Were there no men to help restrain General Sadik?'

'No, sir. The Sphinx is a club of great discretion. Most of the men left in a hurry.'

'But what did you do?'

'I rushed down to find Dr Khittab. He told me –'

'Objection,' repeated Azzam. 'Hearsay again.'

'Sustained.' Afifi turned to Samia and explained gently, 'You must try not to tell the court what you heard. I know it's sometimes difficult, but you must understand.'

'Yes, sir,' said Samia meekly.

To Samia I asked, 'Just let me put it to you at this stage, that you left this hero of the Egyptian army in a state of copulation with the corpse of a girl. Is that correct?'

'That is correct.'

'But didn't you call the police? After all, a girl had been murdered.'

'I called the police immediately. I told them a girl had been killed. They promised to come right away. But there was another difficulty – a complication.'

'Complication?' I asked. 'In what way?'

'Sir, at that time General Sadik was ADC to King Farouk. And Sadik had warned me earlier that His Majesty planned to visit the club.'

'I see. And did His Majesty honour you with a visit? Just tell the court in your own words what happened next. You called the police, and then?'

'The police promised to come quietly. I was determined to have Sadik arrested. I hated him. But before they arrived His Majesty himself walked in. It was terrible. A dead girl upstairs with the king's aide-de-camp; the few clients left were bowing themselves out in case they were arrested for displeasing the king in some way.'

'What did you do?'

'I was so angry, I bowed to the king and said, "Your Majesty, there's a friend of yours upstairs and he's just murdered a girl – one of Your Majesty's favourites, Dolores." '

'And he went and saw?'

'Yes, sir. He was furious with Sadik. But he chose to hush everything up. When the police arrived I heard the king tell their chief that he'd lose his job and pension if one word of the affair ever got out.'

'Thank you, Madame Samia,' I said and bowed to Azzam. 'Your witness.'

Azzam, who had been listening intently, stood up, almost indolently, then, like a pistol shot, he asked Samia, 'Were you the king's mistress?'

Above the stir in the public gallery, despite the feeling of tension and expectancy, Samia retorted, equally swiftly, 'Yes and no.'

'That is no answer, madame,' said Azzam furiously. 'The presiding judge has already warned you to answer my questions properly.'

Samia, looking pleadingly at Afifi, said, 'Sir, I was doing just what you told me to do.'

'Perhaps you could explain,' said Afifi.

Samia thought before replying. The sense of excitement in the courtroom grew until it was almost overpowering.

'The king took a liking to me, Mr President, and after many refusals I agreed to visit him at the palace – at night, and knowing what to expect. He was waiting for me in his bedroom. He wore only a loose gown which he left open, showing his – sir, his genitals.'

'And then?' asked Azzam.

'He asked me to undress and I did so and went into his bed.'

'So you *did* –' Azzam left the sentence unfinished.

'No, sir,' cried Samia. 'He tried, but he couldn't.'

There was almost an uproar in court, as Samia continued, I tried to stimulate him, but he could not get an erection.'

Afifi banged with his gavel on the wooden table and cried, 'One more interruption of this sort and I will clear the court. Proceed, Miss Samia.'

'And so, sir, it was a failure.'

'I see,' said Afifi, and turned to the prosecution. 'I think, Mr Azzam, we may leave this part of the cross-examination and regard the answer as the non-consummation of the sexual act. Whether or not this makes the witness the ex-king's mistress is hardly relevant.'

Azzam replied with heavy irony – and some justification – 'I wonder, Mr President, having heard the lady's vivid description of a night in her – brothel – I am beginning to wonder whether it is Mrs Serena King who is on trial here for murder or whether the defence is more concerned with the sexual proclivities of the late General Sadik?'

'The same idea has crossed my mind,' Afifi said. 'Do you wish to add to your cross-examination?'

Azzam adjusted his glasses and peered at Samia. 'One remark of yours I noted, Madame Samia.' He glanced down at a slip of paper in his hand. 'You said, and I quote, "I was determined to have Sadik arrested. I hated him." I suggest that your entire evidence to this court has been based on a malicious desire to blacken the name of the late General Sadik.'

Samia gripped the front of the witness box. 'That is not true. I hated him, yes, but I was called as a witness to tell the truth and I have done so.'

'Perhaps,' Azzam said. The innuendo could not have been more obvious; and he evidently thought it sufficient to leave it at that. 'No more questions.'

The three judges looked at me expectantly and Afifi spoke for them: 'Have you any more witnesses, Mr Holt?'

'Indeed I have, sir. I would like to call Dr Amal Khittab.'

Khittab was a compact man, neatly bearded and balding. He looked very respectable, and I immediately established his credentials without giving Azzam a chance to challenge them.

'You are Dr Amal Khittab,' I said, 'a graduate of London University Medical School, a Member of the Royal College

560

of Surgeons. You are a Gold Medallist in the specialised subject of venereology.'

'That is correct.'

'Thank you, Doctor. You have with you, I believe, the medical record of Dolores Blasco, a prostitute once employed by the previous witness.'

'I have. I also have a copy of the death certificate, dated 14 September, 1941.'

The usher passed the papers to the judges, who examined them closely. 'I understand from this record,' Afifi said, 'that you had been treating the girl for something called chancroid. What is that, Doctor?'

'It's a minor form of venereal disease, caused by a tiny bacillus called *Haemophilus ducrevi* which gets into the lining of the vagina through any minute abrasion and sets up a painful irritation.'

'Chancroid, then, isn't a fatal disease?'

'By no means. It's a matter of a few days' treatment.'

'I ask,' Afifi said, 'because you say on your certificate, which you have signed – I take it that is your signature?'

'It is indeed.'

Suddenly Judge Afifi motioned to the doctor to wait a moment and called out, 'Usher!'

The usher, in pseudo-khaki uniform, jumped up from his seat in the VIP chairs, approached the table and asked, 'Sir?'

'Usher, I think the assisting judges should have another look at this certificate, and then please show it to the prosecuting and defence counsel.'

It would have been quite easy – in fact normal – for Afifi to show the death certificate to the other judges in private, but it was clear that he wanted to make a special point. After Azzam had studied it the paper was returned to the President.

I of course had already seen it, but I knew why Afifi had been anxious to show the paper round.

'I asked everyone to examine the document carefully,' said Afifi, turning to the doctor, 'because you say in the certificate that this young woman died of natural causes. What, then, was the nature of her terminal illness?'

'The nature of her terminal illness, sir, was a fracture of

the spinal cord caused by a blow to the head which broke her neck.'

'Hardly a natural cause, Doctor.'

'It was not. May I explain?'

'I think,' Afifi interrupted, 'that you had better.'

'I happened to be on the premises, which I visit frequently, on the evening of 13 September,' went on Khittab, 'and was called to attend to a girl who was dead. I examined the body carefully and was about to sign the certificate of death when King Farouk walked into the room. Sadik was half-dressed, no uniform jacket on, and was slumped in a chair, his head in his hands. The king, who was angry, shouted to Sadik to wait in his car. When I was alone with him the king seemed to change, his anger gone. He smiled and said, "How sad that such a young and pretty girl should die of an incurable disease. Isn't it, Dr Khittab?" '

'So you were in effect forced to sign so that General Sadik would not be charged?' asked Afifi.

Khittab bowed his head.

'Thank you, Dr Khittab. Unless you have any questions to this witness, Mr Azzam, he may stand down.'

'No questions,' Azzam said.

With Azzam not cross-examining Khittab, I was beginning to feel a niggling worry that my calculated risk was not proving a success. Maybe my strategy in attempting to blacken the name of Sadik was wrong? The President's next words bore this out.

'Are you sure, Mr Holt,' asked Afifi, 'that you are pursuing the right line in questioning?'

'Mr President?'

'It would seem that you are concentrating on painting a horrible picture of a man who is dead when you should be concentrating on the defence of your client.'

'I was only trying, sir, to –'

'I know perfectly well what you are trying to do,' said the judge. 'But you should remember that many men who have achieved prominence in their public field may still have their – shall we say – peculiar habits in private.'

'I appreciate that, Mr President. I have no wish to speak ill of the dead.'

'You surprise me.' Afifi could be as sarcastic as Azzam, but he looked up angrily when the public tittered. 'As far as this court is concerned, General Sadik rose to the rank of general, occupied a prominent position in the circles of King Farouk during his reign, and really –' He all but shrugged his shoulders.

Crowd psychology is curious. In a long legal career I had never failed to react to it. Afifi's threatened anger had subdued the salacious laughter; but the following silence was discomforting: a change of mood, a brooding unrest such as I had detected in the attitude of the police escort, in heads turning as reporters whispered to each other – in the words of tomorrow's headlines. Or was I imagining things? I hoped so. But in any case the trial was not going as I had hoped. I had been convinced that Serena would be acquitted, for nobody had *proof* of anything, and yet, in what was tantamount to a military court, did one have to prove anything? In theory, any element of doubt should result in an acquittal. But this was a 'show trial', rich versus poor, old regime versus new, privileged royalty versus newly privileged proletariat. Afifi was becoming restive and slightly irritated.

When, after listening to the sordid evidence of Samia and Dr Khittab, I proposed calling Zeineb, the belly-dancer, Afifi asked, 'May I ask for what purpose, Mr Holt?'

'She was at the Sphinx and saw what happened, Mr President. I wish to ask her to corroborate her evidence.'

'I should have thought that the evidence of Miss Samia and' – with a gesture of distaste – 'Dr Khittab would be corroboration enough. I don't like wasting time on useless questioning.'

At that moment someone entered the court and waved to an usher. With some trepidation he approached Salem. Salem whispered to me, got up and walked to the back of the court. I hadn't the faintest idea what was happening, but I remember thinking, Oh God! Not more bad news.

The man at the door brandished an envelope. Azzam stopped talking and Afifi looked up sharply. Salem brought the envelope to me, and I almost gasped as I opened it. The contents were so startling that at first I didn't hear the judge's curt, 'Well, Mr Holt?'

'My apologies, Mr President. I have just received news which suggests the possibility of producing fresh evidence which might –' I hesitated, not for effect or to appease the President of the court, but because I just couldn't believe it. 'Which might allow us to reach an acquittal more quickly than if we have to delve into the dozen or more witnesses I propose to call.'

I didn't have a 'dozen or more witnesses', but the note I was reading did demand a ruling from the judge, and I knew he was frustrated by the slowness of the proceedings.

'If you can do that I would be the first to express my approval,' he said. 'What is the nature of this new evidence?'

It was now or never. I had no time to consult Serena, no time to improvise, only time to put my trust in Jim Stevenson, for in front of me was a note from him which read:

I didn't want to do this unless necessary because I am betraying a trust and shouldn't do it, but I have to, because hotheads in the army are pressing for a verdict of guilty. You can prove Serena's innocence easily if you do as I say. Ask no questions, trust me.

Ask the judge to order an exhumation of Sadik's coffin.

Was he mad? The one thing that Sadik's body would show was that he had been shot. You can't disguise that, even in a decomposed body, even in a body ten years old. And yet . . .

'Well, Mr Holt,' said Judge Malimoud irritably. 'Do we have to waste more of the court's time?'

I took a deep breath, looked straight in front of me with eyes that saw nothing, and said in a stony voice, 'I beg leave, Mr President, to request that the coffin of the late General Sadik be exhumed.'

There was a moment of silence, followed by a general gasp of astonishment. Out of the corner of my eyes I saw two reporters dash from the makeshift press gallery. Mrs Sadik, sitting behind Azzam, leaned forward, her face and hands transfixed as though she were about to clap. Azzam regarded me as though I had gone mad, the slow smile of disbelief at my stupidity broadening into a grin of triumph. I must say I felt like that myself, and when a terrified Serena turned round in her chair, tears of fear in the corners of her eyes, I said with a confidence I *had* to feel, 'Don't worry. Ask no questions. Just trust me.' I had time for nothing more than a quick squeeze of her shoulder as the three judges conferred, obviously astonished by my request.

'Are you quite sure you wish to take this – er – unusual course, Mr Holt? As you know, an exhumation is most distasteful to all good Moslems.'

'Quite sure, Mr President,' I said, and, risking all, added, 'apart from anything else, sir, the prosecution's case rests entirely on the belief that General Sadik was shot. I think – I hope – an exhumation will prove that he was not.'

After deliberating with his colleagues Afifi agreed that the coffin would be exhumed the following morning at 6 a.m. 'I choose this early hour,' he said, 'because I have no wish to disrupt the funerals already arranged for that day. And I will instruct the police to admit no members of the press or public. I do not wish them to indulge in sensation. You and Mr Azzam will of course be present, together with a doctor appointed by the court.'

Azzam was on his feet. 'If it may please the court, may Mrs Sadik be permitted to attend for the purpose of identification?'

'No, she may not, Mr Azzam,' said Afifi firmly. 'Exhumation of a decomposed body is unpleasant and sad. Should identification be necessary Mrs Sadik will be given every opportunity to visit the mortuary. Court adjourned. We meet here at 5.30 tomorrow morning and will proceed in police cars to the National Military Cemetery at Abbasiyah.'

I knew the cemetery well. It was near the one-time British military barracks on the way to Heliopolis, where the British had established their first garrison in 1882. But before that, immediately after the court adjourned, I had some questions to ask Stevenson. And I intended to demand some answers.

I might have known that Stevenson would remain as elusive as ever. When I reached home with Serena, who was almost trembling with panic, there was a one-line message awaiting me. It read, 'Gone to Alex for the night. Worry not. Jim.'

48

It was cold. I had walked round from my house, leaving Serena, who had spent a night fraught with doubts and worries, sleeping fitfully. The convoy of cars waited outside the Justice Building and I got into my allotted vehicle as quickly as possible. The judges occupied the first car, with Afifi sitting in front next to the driver. The usher and a doctor sat in the second, while Azzam and I shared the third. It was followed by an ambulance. One police car preceded us, another followed.

Azzam and I exchanged only a few words on the short drive to Heliopolis and the military cemetery at Abbasiyah. The streets were empty at that time of the day as the area contained no productive farmland and there were few of the carts and donkeys that cluttered the roads leading from Giza.

All cemeteries are miserable, but this one was worse than most, for as well as the ever-present sense of death this had the soulless, impersonal stamp of the military. You came to be buried here, not to be mourned. Smart sentries opened the iron gates and we drove through the trim roads towards the corner reserved for officers of high rank.

'They always have exhumations at the crack of dawn, don't they?' I asked Azzam.

'Yes, not only to avoid publicity, but because the bodies smell less when it's cold.' He gave a sour smile. 'Damned farce, this one. What do you expect to find?'

'Ah!' I said, wishing I knew.

Fortunately someone had attended to the preliminaries: under the watchful eyes of two court officials who had travelled to the cemetery an hour before us gravediggers had already cut out the sods surrounding the grave, taken off the marble surrounds, and had started digging out the top layer of earth.

Tradition – and legal caution – dictated that the earth over the grave had to be removed in the presence of the judges responsible for ordering the exhumation, and so the two gravediggers, their heads wrapped around in dirty scarves, waited with their spades by the ornate marble headstone, looking expectantly at the group and wondering who was the leader.

'You may proceed,' said Judge Afifi. The two men started shovelling, grunting and panting with the early morning exertion.

It took some time for the two men, who used a short ladder as they dug deeper, to reach a depth of five or six feet. I had an almost overpowering desire to peer over the edge of the grave to see what progress they were making but stopped, thinking such curiosity indecent.

As we waited the three judges talked quietly among themselves. The doctor – obviously a police surgeon – stood next to the usher with whom he had travelled, and I suddenly heard him half-stifle a burst of laughter. For a second I was shocked. It seemed obscene, but then I thought to myself, What the hell. Nothing could be more obscene than the body we were going to examine. And to a doctor, used to this sort of thing, a little light relief was understandable.

There was a sudden silence, a quickening of interest as the gravediggers climbed out of the grave, straightened their backs and dug their spades into the sandy soil. I heard one say to the court usher, 'We're nearly there, sir. But we'll need the other three men.'

A moment later one of the police cars sped off to summon three helpers who had not been necessary during the actual digging.

'To haul up the coffin,' explained Azzam.

The men had left the ladder in the grave, and so I seized the opportunity to peer over the edge.

Only a thin coating of sandy soil covered the coffin, and I could see its outline clearly. All round the edges the earth was packed in close, yet somehow they would have to get ropes under the coffin in order to haul it to the surface. But they were experts at this kind of operation, and I realised that as soon as they half-pulled up one end of the coffin the earth round the sides would fall in and make it simple to slide ropes underneath.

Within minutes the three additional gravediggers arrived in the police car and descended the short ladder. However apprehensive I was it didn't stop me from being fascinated by their technique and by the professional manner with which they went about their grim business. It was light now, a little warmer too, with the sun slanting across the cemetery, turning some of the marble headstones a faint pink.

The first two men climbed down and scrabbled with their hands until they found two of the handles near the top end of the coffin. Even when they had done this they still couldn't place the ropes under the coffin. They first threaded a couple of ropes round each coffin handle, climbed on to the steps, pulled the steps and the ropes up, then heaved the top end of the coffin with a strange scraping noise until it stood at an angle at the bottom of the grave. As four men kept their weight on the end that was slightly lifted the fifth man managed to slide another rope under the top end of the coffin. It was not easy. He looped the rope under, then pulled first one way, then another, until finally he had one rope firmly underneath. I couldn't help contrasting the exhumation with the gentle, reverent way the coffin would have been lowered into the ground ten years before.

Soon it was nearly over. The process was repeated at the other end, and then, with two men at each corner, they hauled up the coffin containing the mortal remains of the man I hated.

In the first dawn light the whole scene seemed even more eerie than before, for now I could hear the bustle of the outside world as only a few yards away car horns screeched and tyres squealed. I waited in an agony of suspense. I didn't think that once in the mortuary a cursory examination of a ten-year-old corpse would necessarily reveal that he had been shot, but it might — especially if half the head had been blown several visitors, including Dr Khittab, who looked after the girls and who will bear me out. I heard a scream, but I wasn't worried at first. The girls often screamed a little as part of their act. But when I heard a second scream I went upstairs.'

'But can you tell us why you did that?'

'This was different – unusual.'

'How – "unusual"?' I asked gently.

'I can't tell you exactly. But it was like a scream of death. And it wasn't a woman shrieking once and then going on to make more noises. There was no second scream. I had a premonition, I almost didn't dare to go.'

She paused, recalling the moment, until quietly I asked, 'And then –?'

'The scream had come from the blue room. All our rooms are named after colours. I did go up. I could hear my heart pounding, I remember. And when I crossed the landing I pushed open the door of the room and, sir, I almost fainted. The chair near the bed had been upturned and there was Zeineb, on the floor, without a stitch on, in a faint. Her face was covered with blood. I went in, screaming for help and nearly tripped over a whip which Zeineb told me later Sadik had used to slash her across the face when she tried to help Dolores.'

'And Dolores?'

'She was on the bed, in the centre of the room. Sadik was on top of her trying to make love to her. I tried to pull him off, but he pushed me so hard that I fell to the ground. Two other girls came to help, but they waited at the door. They were scared.'

'And Dolores?' I repeated. 'What sort of condition was she in?'

'She was naked, of course, and her head was half hanging over the edge of the bed. Only it was twisted – or her neck was, I couldn't be sure. But the most awful thing was that as Sadik struggled on top of her her eyes were wide open – yet she didn't move or make any sound. Those eyes – and that silence. I knew in my heart she was dead.'

'Can you tell me how Dolores died?'

'Zeineb told me that Sadik hit her very hard when she refused him.'

'Objection. Hearsay,' interrupted Azzam.

'Sustained,' agreed Afifi. 'The remark will be struck from the record.'

'A medical witness will later testify to the cause of death, Mr President,' I said. 'But first I would like to put to Miss Samia one or two more questions.' Turning to her I asked, 'What did you do when you believed that the girl was dead? Were there no men to help restrain General Sadik?'

'No, sir. The Sphinx is a club of great discretion. Most of the men left in a hurry.'

'But what did you do?'

'I rushed down to find Dr Khittab. He told me –'

'Objection,' repeated Azzam. 'Hearsay again.'

'Sustained.' Afifi turned to Samia and explained gently, 'You must try not to tell the court what you heard. I know it's sometimes difficult, but you must understand.'

'Yes, sir,' said Samia meekly.

To Samia I asked, 'Just let me put it to you at this stage, that you left this hero of the Egyptian army in a state of copulation with the corpse of a girl. Is that correct?'

'That is correct.'

'But didn't you call the police? After all, a girl had been murdered.'

'I called the police immediately. I told them a girl had been killed. They promised to come right away. But there was another difficulty – a complication.'

'Complication?' I asked. 'In what way?'

'Sir, at that time General Sadik was ADC to King Farouk. And Sadik had warned me earlier that His Majesty planned to visit the club.'

'I see. And did His Majesty honour you with a visit? Just tell the court in your own words what happened next. You called the police, and then?'

'The police promised to come quietly. I was determined to have Sadik arrested. I hated him. But before they arrived His Majesty himself walked in. It was terrible. A dead girl upstairs with the king's aide-de-camp; the few clients left were bowing away. I tried to recall what Sadik had looked like when I had last seen him, and felt the sweat running into my eyes – thinking, suddenly terrified, *This is what I am afraid to see.*

The gravediggers acted as 'ushers' and carried the coffin by the handles into the ambulance and closed the door behind them. Then we set off for the mortuary, which was sited in the police station adjoining the Justice Building.

The mortuary itself was a refrigerated room below ground, like a depository of outsized filing-cabinets, but the body of Sadik was not at first placed in one of these compartments, as it had to be opened in the presence of one or more of the judges, the usher, the doctor, and of course Azzam and myself if we wished.

Two workmen unscrewed the coffin lid, placing the large screws carefully to one side. I felt again the sweat running into my eyes, and wiped them with my handkerchief. As the lid was taken off I saw a shroud still covered Sadik's body, but it was no longer laid out decorously straight according to funeral rites, but was nothing more than a bunched-up white bundle.

It looked so tiny, so pathetic, it hardly looked like a body at all. Judge Afifi formally announced, 'Now that we have legally witnessed the exhumation, and the lid of the coffin has been removed in your presence, it will be necessary for the body to be prepared for identification and examination with a view to being used in evidence.

'You may take the body out of the coffin,' Afifi then instructed the workmen, 'and place it in one of the drawers. The door of the locker will remain locked until the doctor has had an opportunity to examine the body and arrange for identification.'

As gently as possible the men started to lift the bundle out of the coffin, preparing to slide it into the locker. Then, before the stupefied eyes of everyone – already suffering from nausea at the prolonged proceedings – half the 'body' fell off and slipped back into the coffin.

The mortuary attendants screamed with terror, and without a second's hesitation bolted from the room as though they had seen a ghost. And indeed that was my first terrified thought. Judge Afifi went as white as the shroud – whiter, if possible – and then the court usher, who had witnessed many exhumations, cried:

'Mr President, sir, that – that isn't a body!'

'What on earth do you mean?' asked Afifi, anger restoring his dignity.

I looked. The shroud was still in one piece. It was the contents that had divided in two, as though the body had been sliced in half. But the court usher was right. At first I couldn't believe it, but as I peered closer I saw the ragged, brownish edges of a sack, and out of it a trickle of sand where it had fallen into the coffin.

I didn't dare to utter a word. My entire defence depended on letting other people talk. Azzam looked stupefied. Afifi cried, sternly, 'What does this mean?'

The remaining attendants didn't dare approach the coffin, but the court usher did. I recognised him from his appearances in court, but now, because of his dramatic participation in an exhumation he had changed his khaki 'uniform' for a suit. He even wore a tie. And as though to make the most of this historic moment, he paused while we all waited then, without any inhibitions he put his hand into the box, pulled away the shroud and showed us.

'Three sacks of sand, that's all, Mr President,' he said. 'That's General Sadik's grave, no doubt about it. But there's no body inside; never has been.' Then he added the words which all of us were thinking, 'The whole military funeral must have been a royal hoax.'

'I will thank you, Mr Usher, not to make comments in front of counsel,' said Afifi. 'If anyone wishes to comment it will be me.'

'I'm sorry, sir,' said the usher, but we all knew one thing – without a body, without any proof that Sadik had been shot, it would be virtually impossible to convict Serena of murder. Azzam knew it. Exultantly (and, mystified, thanking Stevenson) I knew it.

It might in some cases be possible to convict a defendant

without producing the body of a murdered person, but this was no ordinary murder trial. It not only smacked of royal deceit years previously but effectually demolished the prosecution's case. Even the presiding judge realised this immediately, for he said to Azzam and myself, 'Obviously, gentlemen, the case has collapsed. Tomorrow, Friday, being a day of rest, we will reconvene at ten o'clock on Saturday morning. The result may be a foregone conclusion, but no doubt you, Mr Holt, will wish to discuss the question of costs and so on. In the meantime, I think you can tell your client she can sleep easily.'

49

Thursday lunch took on the air of a celebration. With the case as good as over, Serena telephoned Paris and spoke to her mother in hospital. My father had returned earlier than expected and opened two bottles of his most treasured champagne, a Dom Perignon '43.

'Well, thank goodness that's over.' Chiffon sounded practical. 'Now you'll be able to go to the annual Gezira Ball.'

I didn't think this the moment to explain that the post-revolution Gezira bore little resemblance to the club where we had danced our youth away. To Father, she said surprisingly, 'Yes, dear, I *will* have a glass of champagne to celebrate. Not only your success, my dears, but to the downfall of that horrible woman.'

'I wonder what did happen to the body?' asked Father. 'Damned gruesome, even for the widow – learning about an empty coffin like that.'

'I even felt sorry for her – for a moment,' I admitted.

'Well, it's all over now.' Serena raised her glass to me. 'It is, isn't it?'

'Of course.'

'There's only one thing I couldn't understand,' she said when we were alone. 'Presiding Judge Afifi seemed really angry at what he called wasting the judges' time. Why didn't he just announce the verdict as soon as he returned to the court from the cemetery?'

'Two reasons,' I explained. 'The first was to give him time to talk with the assisting judges, and decide whether or not to take action against Mrs Sadik for having lied in her testimony to the court. She may still have powerful friends but I'd be surprised if he lets her go free.'

'And the second reason?'

'Something we didn't have time to discuss before the court rose. Costs. I shall demand that my costs be met by the government or the police. I don't see why you should pay. Afifi will agree with me, I'm sure, that the charge against you was activated by malice.'

'I'd pay a million dollars just to have your advice. Don't worry about the costs.'

'I do – for one reason. Soon we'll be married. And then you're going to live on my money. No, I mean it. I'm a successful barrister. With my private income and the fees from the Trust I earn enough to keep us both, and I'm not going to be labelled as "The man who married a millionaire widow." '

'But all that money! I'm not extravagant – what shall I do with it all?'

'If there's a crisis and you need a large sum, that's different. But otherwise – well, I'll let you pay for the four children through school, if you like.'

'Four?'

'Any objection?'

'No, not if you want four. And the rest?'

'Leave it in the trust fund where it'll double or treble by the time we're old. Then we'll decide what to do with it. And,' I said, teasing, 'if I want to borrow a few piastres now and again –'

After lunch that Thursday afternoon Serena and I were walking through the garden, in the direction of the cathedral tree, when I heard the distant jangle of the old bell. A few moments later Zola came out, walking slowly across the path and announced, 'Sir, Mr Salem, your clerk, asks leave to speak to you urgently.'

'Salem?' I looked at Serena. 'What can he want? What a bore. Still, I'll have to give him a couple of minutes. No, you stay here. All right, Zola, ask Salem to come into the garden.'

Because Salem was 'off-duty' he no longer clutched his bundle of pencils, nor was he dressed in sedate black. Incongruously, as though he hadn't had time to change, he wore a pair of dove-grey flannels and a blue blazer, its breast pocket showing a golden line of fountain pens and propelling pencils in place of the usual ones he clutched. On the pocket was a crest. I knew it at once.

'Yes, sir,' he said proudly. 'That's the badge of Oriel College.'

'My college!' I was not sure whether to be annoyed or not.

'I felt that as the clerk to your chambers, sir, it would perhaps be appropriate, so I acquired it. Of course, I only wear it when I'm not at court.'

'It suits you, Salem,' said Serena.

'Thank you, madame,' he replied, but still solemnly. 'May I offer my congratulations, though of course the issue was never in doubt.'

It was not a particularly hot afternoon, but Salem took off his tarboosh and wiped his forehead with a large coloured handkerchief. I had a sudden premonition, an impression that he was uneasy, then realised that it was a long time since I had seen Salem without his showing those bright teeth in a smile. They didn't show now.

'Well, what's the trouble?' I asked.

'It is a private matter, sir.' He looked at the ground. 'If I could have a moment of your time alone?' His black eyes were now darting from one of us to the other, as though begging for help.

'Does it concern the case, the state v king?' Without thinking I had dropped into legal jargon.

He nodded.

'If that's so,' I said briskly, 'there's no need to leave this garden. Mrs King knows all that's happened in this case. If you have something to add I'm sure she'll be interested to hear. And' – with a chuckle – 'it'll save me from having to repeat it all to her later, eh?'

Lowering his voice to a whisper he said nervously, 'The matter is *extremely* private, sir. Please do not think I'm impertinent.' He wiped his forehead again, and looked beseechingly at Serena. 'But I have given my word –'

Serena came to the poor man's rescue, saying with a laugh, 'I'll leave you two conspirators to plot behind my back. And by the way, Mr Salem, my sincere thanks for all the help you gave me in this case.'

'It was an honour, madame.' He gave a slight bow. 'I hope I can be of help to you again if ever –'

'I'd rather the occasion didn't arise,' she said humorously.

'Who knows?' said Salem gloomily as Serena walked towards the house.

'What the hell's got into you?' I asked him angrily. 'You're like some prophet of doom. What's the trouble? It'd better be important.'

'Yes, sir.' Looking in my direction, but with downcast eyes, he said in his pedantic voice, 'I am the bearer of very bad tidings. I am what in England you would call the go-between.'

'What *is* all this about?'

'Certain allegations have been made to me by another party' – he spoke carefully as though he had rehearsed every inflection of his voice, let alone every word – 'and sir, these allegations are so serious – I hardly dare to inform you – the allegations, if proven, would ruin your career. It would mean disbarment, sir, automatically.'

'I'm listening,' I said flatly, and the very resignation in my voice helped to give poor Salem courage.

'The gist of the matter, sir, is that a man on behalf of Mrs Sadik, and with her knowledge, alleges that Mrs King' – he had now taken off his tarboosh and was fingering it nervously – 'and your good self, sir, have been lovers since before Mrs King's marriage to your brother, now no longer with us, alas. And that the liaison has proceeded at intervals for many years.'

'Bloody rubbish!' I cried. 'She's mad – I knew it. She's a mental case.'

'I hope so, sir,' Salem said carefully, though he knew that I knew it was true. Even so, he lowered his voice, despite the fact that we were alone. We walked again, approaching the cathedral tree. As we stopped beneath it he coughed gently and added, 'I *do* hope so, sir. But there is another allegation, sir. It is one I hardly dare to mention.'

'More?'

'I regret, sir, that this evil woman, through the intermediary with whom I am acting, is alleging that your good self is the father of Mrs King's late son, and that he was conceived at Sakkara.'

'But these are just lies put about by a mad woman,' I said.

'Alas, sir, it is not so. There is proof existing.' He fished in the inside pocket of his blazer and silently handed me two sheets of paper. The words were typed and I read,

Now I ask no more from life, for on this night I held Mark in my arms and when he was moving inside me and we were kissing each other, I couldn't stop moving until without warning I came.

I felt myself blushing as I read on the second sheet,

I did something else on this wonderful night; because I love Mark I took none of the precautions which Greg had helped me to arrange when we became lovers.

'These are typed forgeries,' I shouted.

'They are copies, sir. I understand they are extracts from a diary which Mrs King kept earlier in her life.'

'But I have the diaries!' I blurted out.

'It is admitted by the other side, sir, that the most vital and incriminating diary was purloined without your knowledge, and is now resting in the hands of Mrs Sadik. If we could proceed to the room where you usually keep the diaries, sir, we could see for ourselves.'

I couldn't believe it. All the work to make sure of Serena's freedom, and now both our worlds were about to crash around us. I was so short of breath – almost as though my heart was constricted – that I had to rest for a few moments. Under the cathedral tree I was thinking as I looked at the impenetrable, evil branches, how much had happened since the day when I had carried baby Serena to safety, all those twisting branches like the bars of a cage from which we could never escape from each other.

I walked into the house. I had kept the diaries in a locked bookshelf in my study, a glass-fronted old-fashioned mahogany bookshelf with a key.

'Come on, let's go and find out,' I said to Salem.

Of course the vital volume of Serena's diaries was missing The lock of the door was so old and rudimentary that it must have been easy either to pick it or carry a dozen simple keys that would fit it. No panes of glass were broken, and there was no reason why I should ever have noticed the diaries, let alone read them again after all these years. Ten years or so had passed since Sirry Pasha had handed them to me. I looked carefully at the other books. I had the impression that the thief, whoever he was, hadn't really known what he was looking for. Yet I felt certain that the thief knew the inside of Holt House, at least the small room where I kept my books and papers when I worked at home on a case. But who? And what had he been searching for? Nothing in particular, I felt; only something incriminating.

'Do you know who the thief is?'

'No, sir.' For once I wondered if Salem might be lying. 'They were delivered by messenger,' he explained uneasily.

As I pondered what to do next Salem's voice broke into my thoughts. 'Of course, sir' – he coughed discreetly – 'there is a way of getting the diary back.'

'How?'

'The man with whom I have been dealing as the intermediary informs me that the original diary is for sale.'

I had fought and beaten a dozen or more blackmailers in court, but every case had been more wretched than the last. Blackmail! The very word sent a shudder through me. And even a man who won a case – even if unnamed in court, as

Mr X – somehow felt humiliated, even in victory. It was one of the most despicable of crimes.

And now the wretched Lala Sadik was blackmailing us. And if I fought her, if I didn't do a deal with her, she would take her revenge when the court reconvened on Saturday. She would produce new evidence, Azzam for the prosecution would pounce on it, and Serena would be branded as what the Victorians called 'a scarlet woman'.

Even so, I thought, we had nothing to make us panic. The prospect of being blackmailed as lovers was hateful, but our relationship was fairly common knowledge among our friends. And even the problem of my legal career wasn't really important when placed against my huge interests in the Trust. Except for one thing.

What worried me was this: unless Serena paid up, Mrs Sadik would surely reveal that I was Jonothan's father, and that would be a staggering shock to a great many people, not least Madame Sirry and my family. A few sceptics might have wondered about Jonothan, but a world of difference separates speculation from confirmation. For our families to be told all the lurid details about Jonothan in the Cairo gutter press didn't bear thinking about. That was the real problem we faced: that all the world – including our own private family world – would then know that Serena had secretly hoped I would father her child, and then let my brother believe that Jonothan was his son. That was something that we *had* to hide.

'Have you any instructions for me, sir?' asked Salem, still nervously fingering the rim of his tarboosh.

'I have to think,' I muttered. 'I'll go to my chambers in two hours. Do you mind meeting me there so late, Salem? Say six o'clock?'

'Of course not, sir.' He clamped on his tarboosh. 'Shall I make any contact with –'

'No,' I said sharply. 'Nothing till I come.'

'Sorry, sir.' He almost ran from the room in his relief.

Pacing the bookshelves, backwards and forwards, raging like a wild beast suddenly deprived of liberty, I tried to sort out my thoughts. First, should I tell Serena? Or could I handle this quietly? Second, should I break every instinctive rule and pay up? Above everything else, I couldn't subject Serena to the scandal.

There was a knock at the door, and I shouted irritably, 'Who is it?'

'Only me.' I heard the unusually meek voice of Serena as she half-opened the door. I should have known that neither of us could ever worry without the other being aware of it. 'What is it, Mark? You look as though you've seen a ghost.'

I never hesitated, and told her everything I had learned from Salem. For a moment I thought that she was going to faint. She gripped the nearest chair, knuckles showing white with the effort of holding on, and guided herself by touch, almost as though suddenly blind, until she found the security of a seat.

'*She knows that?*' she whispered, half-covering her face. 'It's impossible.'

'She knows about Jonothan, that he was our son.'

'Oh no!' Not since Cascais had I heard that Egyptian wail of mixed sorrow and futility. 'It's wicked! Is this what Salem came to tell you?'

I too sat down, nodding, wordless.

'I can't believe it. We've never told a soul. Even Papa or Mama. It's not possible.'

For a few moments we sat, each afraid to speak, and then, as though bracing herself to face up to reality, she asked me, 'But how did she find out? Nobody could have talked –'

'Not talked.' I looked up at the glass-cased bookshelf. 'Someone read. They stole one of your diaries.'

'Oh no!' Her first reaction, like mine, was one of disgust. 'The thought that this filthy woman has actually shared our secrets, gloating over my confessions of love for you.' She stood up. 'Of course it's obvious that the Sadik woman is trying to blackmail you.' She was making a statement rather than asking a question.

'Yes.'

'Then pay up,' cried Serena. 'The most important thing, darling, is that to us the money doesn't matter a damn. And once you actually *have* the diary in your possession, there's no way she can blackmail you! All I'd have to do is swear that I've never kept a diary in my life – so long as I have the original.'

She couldn't copy the entire diary out by hand, I explained – try to forge it. That would be a criminal act. Nor could she use a copying machine. The early models that existed in Cairo then didn't have any facilities for copying more than one page at a time: there was no way one could insert an entire book, however slim, into the copier.

The only way Mrs Sadik could keep a true copy of a page or two of Serena's diary – perhaps with a thought to future blackmail – would be to tear out the pages. And I wasn't too worried about that. Mrs Sadik had already been branded as a woman who had lied after tearing out a vital page from one diary. She would never dare to try the same trick again.

'What I think we must do,' I said, thinking aloud, 'is to ask Jim Stevenson for help. I can't be the go-between. Not that I'm afraid, but just in case there's any legal backlash on me that would make you suffer. I'll ring him up and ask him to meet me at my chambers.'

Serena had sat down again, and was looking smaller than I had ever remembered her, as though she wanted to squeeze into the chair and disappear.

'Don't worry, it'll be all right,' I promised her, trying to inject into my voice a little of the conviction I didn't feel.

She wore a puzzled frown – not one of fear, nor one of fury at this unexpected disaster, but one of perplexity.

'There's something that worries me.' She was speaking slowly from the depths of the chair, thinking aloud. 'The theft of the diary.' Then suddenly she sat up, the glaze in her dulled eyes replaced by a sudden brightness.

'It won't help us to beat the Sadik woman,' she said, 'but I'm sure I know who stole the diary.'

'You do?' I must have looked incredulous, for she actually smiled.

'It's the father of Hekmet's daughter.'

'The man who tried to kill my father? What makes you so sure it was Akif?'

'That's the man! I couldn't remember his name after all

these years. You remember, you first forced him to pay some money to Hekmet at Nasrani when he got the girl into trouble.'

'But why Akif?'

Briefly she explained. Hekmet had remained as nanny to baby Jonothan during the Villa Zelfa period, and when Serena left for America Hekmet had joined the Sirry household. It was the typical Egyptian way of keeping families of servants intact. One mouth more or less, one wage more or less was of no account. When Madame Sirry left for Paris Hekmet had moved over to Holt House as Serena's personal maid, and generally helped in the house.

'I asked Chiffon, who was delighted,' said Serena.

'And Akif has reappeared?' I asked the question, knowing the answer.

'Vaguely,' she replied. 'I'm not likely to forget his face.'

'Neither am I. If we hadn't been lucky he'd have killed my father. But like a bloody fool, I let him escape when Parmi fell off the stage.'

The scene in the study came flooding back to me – me peeping through the crack in the garden door, Akif forcing my father to walk through the study door into the Long Gallery, and at that very moment, when Akif was pointing the gun at my father's back, charging in and hurling myself at him, diverting his attention for a second so that he shot wide . . .

'Tell me why you think it's Akif?' I asked.

She had found Hekmet in tears one day and had dragged the truth out of her.

'She's not in the family way again?'

'No, no. Akif just demands money from her from time to time.'

The matter had come out after her tears when Hekmet had asked for an advance on her wages. Such a thing was unheard of, except for a wedding – or a funeral. But it appeared Akif had demanded money with the threat, backed by law, 'If you don't pay I will take away my daughter.' In Egypt, the father had sole rights over his child.

'I remembered that he'd seduced Hekmet but at first I didn't connect him with the murder charge,' confessed Serena. 'I never saw him, you see. But of course Akif had been in your house just before the attempt on your father. You remember Parmi, who was alone, telling you how Akif forced Zola to let him in.'

I could see now what must have happened. Akif had a vague knowledge of our house. Obviously he was working with Lala Sadik, looking for any evidence he could find. This immediate reaction was borne out when I questioned the servants. A tearful Hekmet admitted that Akif had visited her in the Sirry house before she moved across to us. Yes, she had noticed that bookshelves and desks in the Sirry house had been disturbed. She thought someone was looking for Madame Sirry's correspondence.

'Akif probably thought that if you had any love letters you'd have taken them with you to Holt House,' I said to Serena. 'He probably watched your movements when you were at court so there would be no police guard, then waited till Father left for the embassy or Mother went shopping, and slipped in the back way.'

'I wonder where Akif is?'

'One man will find out,' I said grimly and asked for the telephone number of a flat in Zamalek.

'Aly,' I said when he replied. 'Get round here this evening. About ten o'clock. Yes, of course it's urgent. It's a chance to help your sister. Okay?' Without giving him a chance to reply I banged down the receiver.

Stevenson was already there when I parked my car and walked across from Ezbekieh Gardens. Salem was waiting in the outer office.

'We have a visitor, sir,' he began. 'It's Mr Stevenson. I didn't know how to get rid of him.'

'Don't worry. I asked Mr Stevenson to come. I want to talk to him.'

'Not about –'

'Yes, about that. Wait outside a few moments, Salem, while I brief Mr Stevenson. Then perhaps you'd be kind enough to join us when I ring.'

'Congratulations on the outcome of the trial.' Stevenson

shook hands as I walked round my desk. 'The verdict is a formality, of course?'

'Congratulations to you, Jim,' I replied with real feeling.

'A pleasure,' he said, adding sardonically, 'All part of the new Anglo-American special relationship. Though why it's not called American-Anglo, I don't know.'

Normally I would have responded in kind, but I wasn't in the mood for joking; and the tiredness, perhaps the way I sat down heavily on the other side of the desk, warned him that I was worried.

'What's the matter?' he asked.

I told him as briefly as I could.

'You keep right out of this,' he advised firmly when I'd finished. 'Let me handle it. I'll tell you one thing, though – a provisional judgment based on what you've told me. You'll have to pay. I wouldn't say you should except for one thing: you're not being blackmailed over, say, an indecent photograph where the blackmailer could return a year later with another copy after promising the original photo had been destroyed. There's only one copy of the diary. So you'll pay now, but once you've got the diary you won't have any fears for the future.'

I rang for Salem and invited him to sit down. He did so, perched uneasily on the edge of his chair – the very chair, I suddenly remembered, used by Sadik years ago.

'You must realise, Salem, that I can't act for Mrs King in this matter. Not while I'm her advocate. After all, the trial hasn't ended. We have to wait for the formal verdict. So Mr Stevenson will discuss the whole matter with you.'

He looked a little blank, started to mutter, 'The other intermediary –'

'Mr Stevenson and you can take care of that. I'll ask only one question.' Then I shot it out: 'How much is Akif's cut going to be?'

He looked horrified. 'You know about Akif?'

'Of course.'

'But, sir, he's not the middleman. He was asked by Mrs Sadik – that is my understanding, sir – to provide the evidence. The middleman is a Lebanese lawyer.'

'And how much is this gentleman – or Mrs Sadik – asking for the return of the "evidence"?'

'I understand, sir, that the sum in question is a quarter of a million dollars.'

'Preposterous!' I lost my temper.

'Mark!' cried Stevenson sharply. 'Why don't you go home and look after Serena? I'll find out all there is to know, the practical details and so on, then come back to your house – if you don't mind my staying here now and using your chambers.'

'You're right. I don't make sense any longer.'

Thank God for Stevenson! Sorting this out would be child's play to him. At least I hoped so.

'There's only one more thing I want to know,' I said. 'The exhumation? How did you know?'

'Tomorrow,' he smiled. 'One thing at a time. Tomorrow.'

Stevenson returned around ten o'clock.

'Because you're so rich and won't miss quarter of a million dollars,' he began, 'I think all of us will sleep better tonight if we take it as agreed that we have no option but to pay up. If you don't pay the diary will be presented to the court on Saturday morning. And then – well.'

'We'll pay,' I said for both of us. 'We'd already decided that before you returned from my chambers.'

'The only thing,' said Serena, 'is to get it over with, and never think of it again.'

'How?' I asked Stevenson. 'Obviously I can't get hold of a sum like that tomorrow – the Moslem Sabbath anyway – and if we *are* threatened with blackmail I must have the diary back before the court rises.'

Stevenson explained the way it would operate. It was ingenious and apparently foolproof – as one might expect since it had been devised by a Lebanese lawyer. Serena's trust fund in Liechtenstein (or me as her trustee) would make an irrevocable deed of gift to 'The General Sadik Memorial Fund'. Stevenson's agents would open an account in Switzerland to receive the money. Mrs Sadik would have complete control of the account. The deed would be dated the day following the acquittal, so there could be no question of any collusion or tampering with justice. Mrs Sadik's lawyer would also be given a covering 'notwithstanding' letter bearing the current date, outlining details of the deed of gift. This would be her insurance against anyone tearing up the deed because it was post-dated. Mrs Sadik's lawyer would keep the covering letter. Once the fund was officially started and the money deposited the covering letter would be returned by the Lebanese lawyer to Stevenson, who would destroy it.

'I'll have all the legal work done through my chaps at the office,' said Stevenson. 'The fact that the agreement is being handled by a US government agency is an added bonus for Mrs Sadik, for her lawyers know that we'll not double-cross her unless she tries any tricks with us.' And to me he added, 'You should really keep right out of this, Mark. It's a dirty business, no place' – with a mock bow – 'for an English gentleman and the girl he intends to marry.'

'The Americans? Some of them will have to know?'

'I see no reason why,' said Stevenson. 'They'll know nothing about the blackmail angle. There'll be no mention of conditions, of the diary. The deed of gift will be handed over at the exact moment we receive the diary. The Americans in Cairo, who of course know all about Serena, will put it down as a typical American gesture by a typical American nutcase. In fact' – Stevenson couldn't resist his usual sardonic grin – 'I wouldn't be surprised if Serena's shares shoot up on the market. She might even make a profit on the deal.'

'And when will this transfer take place?' I asked. I still didn't feel in the mood for humour.

'We'll have the documents ready by tomorrow at three. Thank God the Americans don't try and use the Moslem Sabbath as a pretence for having two Sundays a week, like the British. You'll have to keep in touch, Mark, because as executor to the trust fund your signature will probably be necessary.'

'I'll never be able to thank you enough,' said Serena.

Suddenly Stevenson grew silent, as though wondering how to tell us something. He paused while I refilled our glasses before saying slowly, 'Mrs Sadik's lawyer will come to our office at three tomorrow to make a final check with our legal department that the documents are foolproof.'

'Well, that's fine then,' I said. 'You can hand over the documents if the lawyer is satisfied and he can give you the diary.'

'He won't have the diary with him,' said Stevenson slowly. 'The actual exchange will take place at six tomorrow evening. And Mrs Sadik insists on one condition.' Stevenson hesitated. 'And she's absolutely adamant about it.'

'*She* demands conditions!' I stood up angrily. 'When she's getting a fortune!'

'What is the condition?' Serena's voice was brittle and angry.

Stevenson took a deep breath. 'She expects you to go to her flat in Zamalek at six o'clock and hand over the documents yourself.'

'Never!' cried Serena.

'You'll have to.' Stevenson passed a hand across tired eyes. We forgot he had really had a hard night's work. 'I'll come with you.'

'I can't,' cried Serena. 'I can't demean myself.'

'That's the whole idea,' said Stevenson wearily. 'That you *do* demean yourself.'

'Must I?' Serena appealed to me. 'Mark, can't you think of a way we can get out of this? Can't you go instead of me?'

'Of course I can.'

Even as I spoke, Stevenson shook his head. 'Impossible,' he said. 'Mrs Sadik knows the money really means nothing to you. To her, the final insult is going to be worth more than all the money. That's the *real* price you have to pay.'

Serena took a swift gulp of whisky, downing it.

'All right, damn her eyes, I'll do it.' She put down the glass with a bang. Then without warning she put her arms around me, kissed me, and said, 'You saved *me*, Mark. Now it's my turn. I'm not going to have *your* career ruined just because I haven't got the guts to face that woman.'

50

It was a bad day, that final Friday. Serena looked drawn, angry and pale, and it was obvious that she was dreading the confrontation even more than the final moment when the verdict would be announced.

I was nervous too, for everything had now been taken out of my hands and I felt the special kind of tension that lives with inaction, with waiting, powerless to use any influence.

The previous night, just after Stevenson left, Aly arrived, and I told him what Akif had done. 'You might pass the word along to some of your pals in the Moslem Brotherhood,' I said bitterly. 'Tell them that Akif not only tried to kill my father, but is a thief who has landed your sister in deep trouble.'

He left without another word.

During the morning I received a phone call from Stevenson. My signature was needed as the trustee. I went round to his 'office' – he still operated from the old Anglo–American Information Office Building where he had worked with Greg. He hadn't even changed the name of the firm, for that was his cover. Not that there was much information to exchange; but then that wasn't its purpose.

I signed before a notary in the presence of the Lebanese lawyer, a nondescript man whose name I didn't catch, and it was after he had gone that Stevenson revealed to me one puzzle I had never been able to solve: why Sadik's coffin was empty. It was quite simple – once you knew. With the war at its height and Rommel on the run it was becoming clear, even to Farouk, that Germany could never win, and high-ranking American diplomats and the US Intelligence Service (by which, though Stevenson didn't name names, I knew he meant himself) tried to give Farouk all the undercover help he needed in case he had to make a quick run for it. The plan was long-term – nobody expected him to have to make a quick getaway – but the Americans were anxious for Farouk to leave after the Allies finally beat Germany, because they knew that with Farouk remaining in Egypt the British would use him as a useful prop to remain in the area. They could stay, promising to 'protect' the wayward king, and the Americans didn't want that. They wanted British power to be lessened in the area, and the surest way to do that was to get rid of Farouk – or rather, encourage Egyptians to get rid of him with American help – and produce a new revolutionary Egypt in which there would be no place for the British.

'But what's all that got to do with an empty coffin?' I asked.

'All the plans depended on an absolutely truthful exchange of confidential information,' explained Stevenson. 'Among the hundreds of questions to which the American Intelligence Service demanded specific answers were the disappearance of several girls, the role of Pulli and so on. All of these Farouk answered to the best of his ability, and among them was the mystery of Sadik's death. Farouk told all – or nearly all: how Sadik had been shot in error, how Farouk hadn't dared to tell the truth, how Pulli's men had dumped the body in the Nile and how the military funeral had been held with an empty coffin.

'Which was why, of course,' explained Stevenson, 'Mrs Sadik was never allowed to see the body. Nothing could have disguised the fact that the supposed heart attack was untrue. Sadik had been shot. That's all.'

I wondered if that *was* all; how much, if any more, Stevenson knew? But he would never tell me that he knew more. Or anyone.

I wasn't present the following evening after all the preliminary arrangements had been made, and Stevenson took Serena along to Mrs Sadik, who lived in Zamalek, in a flat overlooking the northern side of the Gezira Club.

When they returned to Holt House, about seven o'clock, Serena was in tears, white as chalk, and sobbed, 'It's over, it's over! Now I'm going to burn every stitch of clothes I'm wearing, even the shoes, every damn thing. I'm all right, darling, but I won't kiss you, I won't touch you till I've had a bath and scrubbed every inch of myself with carbolic soap. I feel so dirty.'

Without another word she rushed upstairs.

It was from Stevenson – with later additions from Serena – that I learned what had happened at the confrontation.

The two of them arrived at Mrs Sadik's flat and were ushered into a vulgar, ultra-modern living room – 'all white and chromium,' Stevenson remembered. Mrs Sadik kept them waiting for ten minutes, deliberately no doubt.

Finally she arrived with her lawyer. She was dressed in a long, flowing dark blue housecoat, almost like a galabiya. The stretched skin of her face was accentuated by black hair brushed tightly back, showing tell-tale scars behind the ears – the sign of skin grafts.

She had walked into the room completely ignoring Serena.

'You are Mr Stevenson?' She held out a hand to Jim.

Stevenson deliberately ignored the outstretched hand and asked, 'You have the diary?'

Trying hard to conceal her anger at Stevenson's snub, she retorted, 'You have the deed of gift?'

'It is here. And the diary?'

'My lawyer has it.' At this the Lebanese held up the precious diary.

All this time Mrs Sadik had never once looked at Serena.

'Then perhaps we can conclude our business,' Stevenson said.

Without a word, Mrs Sadik clicked her fingers at the lawyer and took the diary in her hand. Then she said to Stevenson, in the voice of one giving an order that had to be obeyed, 'Give this woman your documents.'

Stevenson handed the package to Serena. Holding back tears of mortification, Serena held out her hand, not saying a word, to offer the papers to Mrs Sadik who held out the slim diary.

But as she took the documents from Serena, Mrs Sadik

threw the diary on the floor at Serena's feet. Stevenson bent to pick it up.

'No!' shouted Mrs Sadik. 'It's *her* diary. Let her pick it up.'

Serena did so.

Then, with Serena upright again, Mrs Sadik uttered her only words to Serena.

'Whore and murderess!' she shouted, and spitting on Serena's dress, stalked out of the room.

The acquittal, as everyone expected, was a formality. Judge Afifi even said, 'The accused leaves the court without a stain on her character, and in my opinion there is no doubt that the entire action was brought wrongfully, even maliciously.'

We had always decided that when the fuss died down we would return quietly to Switzerland, get married and resume our old life there, for Geneva was now important to my business affairs. After all, Cairo had changed. The heady days of the war, with all its excitement, had gone for ever, and the city in which we had grown up and loved so much had altered beyond recognition.

Yet though we had a house waiting ready for us in Rolle, on Lake Geneva, we found many things to do, many reasons to delay our departure. There seemed so many loose ends to tie up, so many people to see. I never realised how many friends we had until Serena asked with mock-innocence, 'How many friends do we have in Geneva?'

'Four bankers,' I grinned.

Serena had started painting again, and though dear Baptise had died, Monsieur Laffont still ran his gallery in Cairo and was begging her to have a new one-woman show.

'If we stay on a month or two,' Serena suggested, 'I could produce enough material for a show. I love the light here: it seems to suit my work. I've gone back to the gentle tones.'

We faced other problems. What was going to happen to my parents? Father was seventy-seven now, and his job as Egyptian adviser had been made redundant. I visualised poor Father and Mother, bereft of all the trappings of their long life in Cairo, settling down to a flat in Cheltenham or a cottage in the Cotswolds. I even offered them my flat in Geneva.

'I'm going to stay in Cairo,' Father finally decided. 'I've been to see the government. Nasser knows us – and you too, it seems – and we're being allowed to stay at Holt House for a nominal rent until I kick the bucket. The money's no problem. We're going to miss you, but on the other hand Cairo and Geneva are next-door to each other in this air age. Of course, when you live in Geneva' – his voice dropped to a conspiratorial whisper – 'we're going to miss you at the Sphinx. It's almost rebuilt, ready to open in a couple of months.'

Two other persons had left – one in a hurry. Lala Sadik, rich beyond her dreams, had been laughed and jeered out of Cairo and as soon as she was able to, emigrated to a new life in Rome.

'To pester Farouk?' asked Stevenson ironically.

The other person didn't exactly 'leave' Cairo, and certainly his absence was not voluntary. A few days after the trial Akif's body, which had been knifed in the back, was found floating in the Nile. Nobody ever discovered who had killed him, but as Stevenson said wryly, 'I guess Aly finally paid his debts.'

We were still debating the date of our final departure when Teddy and Angie Pollock invited us to a 'special celebration party'. I was puzzled: it couldn't be another wedding anniversary.

'No, it's not that,' Teddy confessed. 'Angie's going to have a baby. We've just *got* to celebrate!'

'Where?' I asked, knowing how the Gezira Club had changed.

'At Sakkara,' he exclaimed. 'To see if we can recapture the spirit of the good old days. All the gang. Jim Stevenson's coming along, the old fishing fleet – and their husbands, most are married now – we're going to live it up for one night. I've ordered a huge *sewan*.' It seemed years since we had held a party in one of those magnificent tents erected for desert picnics.

'The only difference,' Teddy added, 'is that riding across the desert is out. We don't want any miscarriages. Besides,

590

cars are more comfortable – and they've got more space to carry the drinks.'

It was strange, that night, but somehow we *did* all recapture the spirit of our youth. Did Sakkara have some special magic for us that allowed us to shrug off the years?

We ate a huge meal by moonlight, mopping up the gravy with *baladi*, the fresh village bread, and drank a great deal. The scene reminded me of our first magical time there. It was unchanged, the dyke roads criss-crossing the flooded low-lying land, the dark outlines of the monuments to men and women dead five thousand years ago. And in clusters around them stood the groves of date-palms, in straight lines, their tufted tops like upturned mops.

After dinner, with plans for a swim later at Mena House when dawn broke, most people prepared for a snooze in the big, communal tent. Instead, Serena whispered to me and we crept out of the tent. She carried a carrier and a cashmere rug. We both knew that we were making for the old Rest House in front of the Step Pyramid itself.

'Nobody'll miss us for half an hour,' she said, putting her arm through mine. 'I love you, I love you, I love you.'

Both thinking of the night we had spent there so long ago, I asked, 'I suppose there's champagne in that bag?'

'Yes. And this time I've brought a couple of glasses. Remember those dirty mugs?'

'Champagne never tasted better.'

And when we were naked together, lying on the clean cashmere rug, she said, 'I'm so glad we came. And tonight, my love, we'll make the first of the four babies you want. Remember the legend: "Those who consummate their love at Sakkara will be assured of eternal happiness." '

Afterwards we walked back to the tent, hand in hand like young lovers. Through the lines of palms the moon shone on the still waters of the Nile. Both of us, words unspoken, were occupied with exactly similar thoughts.

How *dared* we be so presumptuous as to look at the great stone monument, the flat steps symbolising history, and disdainfully declare that 'Cairo had changed'! We were treading in a land crowded with visible history, its stones, its temples, its graves, its great water of the Nile slicing through the most fertile land on earth, reminding us at every turn that one could not in a couple of decades change a history which had lain around us for five thousand years.

As we walked past Sakkara itself, that awesome pyramid to a long dead king, I saw, at a point where the water almost met the land, the silhouette of a flat boat with a bullock tied to its stern, the owner leading his animal through the flooded land to the oasis of his modest plot on higher ground.

'It's beautiful.' We stopped and I kissed her, knowing, as with all our joint life, we still had no need for words: we never had needed words at moments of decision.

'Shall I tell them, or will you?' I asked as we pulled back the flap of the tent and the others, awake now, were laughing and drinking.

'Where have you two been?' asked Teddy. He must have known full well, for he immediately added, 'At your age, Mark!'

'Silence, please!' cried Serena. 'As you already know, Mark and I are getting married soon, but he has another announcement to make.'

There was a pause, everyone expectant.

'Ladies and gentlemen,' I began. 'Serena and I have both come to the same conclusion. We have decided not to go and live in Geneva, or anywhere else. We are Cairenes, and we are going to stay and live in Cairo.'

There was an outburst of cheering, even some clapping, and one or two of the servants, borrowed for the night, smiled at the compliment to their country. I was explaining the details, how I could commute two days a week to Geneva and so on, when Stevenson tapped the edge of his glass with a spoon for silence and cried, 'A toast! After all, I'm going to be the best man at the wedding. So I give you: Serena and Mark. Coupled with the magic of Cairo.'

We drank. Then I tapped *my* glass for silence, and said the last words before we all tumbled into our cars to drive to the Mena House for a swim, as the sun rose over the Nile.

'And a special toast – to the magic of Sakkara.'

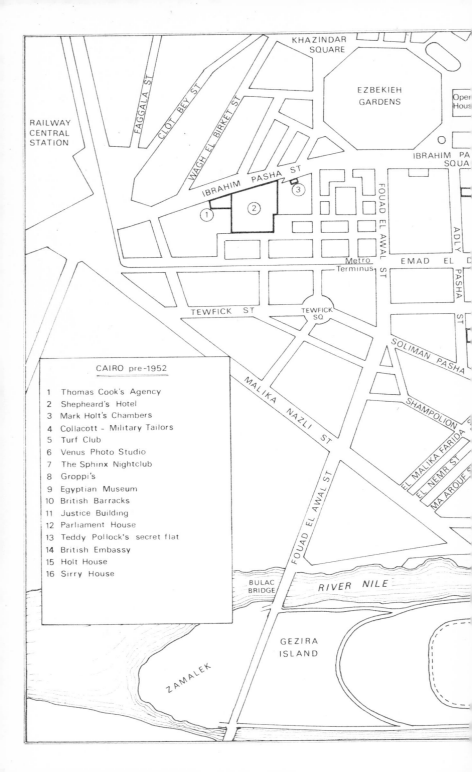